TABLE OF CON

ACKNOWLEDGMENTS ....
ALSO BY ANDRÉ VAN WYCK 4
FOREWORD 6
PART I 7
   PROLOGUE 8
      CHAPTER 1 – THE CHASE 16
      CHAPTER 2 – MAHARKOO 36
      CHAPTER 3 – ECLIPSE 67
      CHAPTER 4 – NEW DAY 109
      CHAPTER 5 – SPRING 119
      CHAPTER 6 – ONE JOURNEY ENDS 142
PART II 169
      CHAPTER 7 – PEBBLES 174
      CHAPTER 8 – HAWKS AND GEESE 201
      CHAPTER 9 – A DARK RIPPLE 228
      CHAPTER 10 – A DAY OFF 265
      CHAPTER 11 – CAMOUFLAGE 300
PART III 328
      CHAPTER 12 – A NEW DIRECTION 332
      CHAPTER 13 – OUT OF SIGHT 373
      CHAPTER 14 – BLUE OR GREEN 405
      CHAPTER 15 – UNMASKED 460
      CHAPTER 16 – DEEP 503
PART IV 516
      CHAPTER 17 – UNBOUND 522
      CHAPTER 18 – RESCUE 570
      CHAPTER 19 – AN END TO DREAMING 587
   EPILOGUE 613
– END OF BOOK I – 616
About the Author 617

FOREWORD

Welcome, dear reader, to The Waking Worlds series. A couple of things you should know:

When *A Clatter of Chains* was first published, it was a monster work by a debut novelist. I decided to return to it, a couple of books later, to pluck out some of the literary parsley and croutons and add some salad dressing. Like Theseus's salad, it remains unchanged.

However, this second edition of *A Clatter of Chains* is a much leaner, meaner meal than its predecessor.

Enterprising readers, who would like a map of the Empire, or perhaps a glossary, are welcome to write their local Inquisitori chapter and lodge an application.

See you again in Book II!

PART I

Prologue

The final days of the Age of Magic
The day of the Fall
The Iron Ocean, Some Hundred Leagues off the coast of Thell

ON THIS DAY, there was no solace to be had at sea. The sway of the deck didn't soothe and salt failed to drown the stink of defeat.

The view from beneath his admiral's hat showed a covey of priests, clustered amidships.

They were not doing anything, save getting underfoot.

And still – watching them – he sensed a squall brewing.

His shoulders itched. His sire's strop, which the old drunkard had named 'the ocean', had left him some indelible lessons.

'See what happens when ye turn yer back on the ocean?'

Yet, he happily ignored the waves in favor of keeping a weather eye on the priests. His thoughts gathered darkly.

How had it come to this? The Priesthood used to be a non-entity at court – something taken out and dusted off for special occasions.

Now, the sum total of Imperial might pivoted on their say-so.

It had begun small, as such things did. The mad rantings of street corner prophets – proponents of unpopular gods – repeated with surety from atop Helia's own pulpits.

The end of the world.

Overnight, it went from being a minor annoyance – deterred by a few loose coppers or a kick – to a divine promise.

The citizenry had turned first, as sheep were wont to do. Quiet faith, turning into loud fervor, turning into bleating fanaticism.

Within a year, all other faiths were anathema. The old gods were banished – their erstwhile followers forced to stay.

The merchants had gone over next, placating a workforce unwilling to labor beneath unbelievers.

The nobility, of course, had simply tacked into the wind. Some had been wealthy, stubborn or stupid enough to stand on principle. But principle could not protect against an enemy who lived under your stairs. Served your food. Turned down your bed. Even the stupid had learned to pay lip service to the new regime.

By the end, the throne's steps had been greased in blood and gold. The new emperor's first decree had heralded a theocracy.

From there, to this.

He let his gaze wander, lest a priest glimpse his scowl.

His ship, *Helia's Pride*, led a fleet. Six hundred and twelve of the best, most brutal warships ever built. They were products of a forced labor drive that had spared no carpenter or cripple. Even in their infancy – ribs rising slowly from the shipyards – these leviathans had been a forbidding sight.

The end of the world. *Perdition*, the priests called it.

They had made the oldest scriptures – that told of the dark places – come to life with their dire promises. They'd peopled the minds of the populace with every manner of nightmare and had then pointed their collective finger:

Thell. A desolate continent. Mostly uninhabited. Largely uninhabitable.

There, the priests had said, would the dark places tear open to spew forth Perdition. Only there, and only then, could it be fought.

And only Helia's chosen stood a hope of stemming it.

Tasting bile, he studied the surrounding warships' waterlines. They rode high, absent the vast majority of Helia's chosen, now fodder for the monsters that had claimed Thell.

The monsters, at least, the priests had gotten right.

Following the rout, his deck had turned into a triage. He hoped never to see such wounds again. Men, broken and burst. Some with bites taken from their steel armor, others melting within it. Women too – the priests had broken with tradition to broaden conscription.

Though the bloodstains had been scoured, the scent lingered.

He shook his head.

An army, defeated, was a terrible thing. An unpredictable thing. Anger, resentment and the impulse to strike back at *something* was a combustible brew. He swore he could see it in the tarnish of the hulls and the half-hearted billow of the pennants.

His storm-sense swung his gaze back to the priests.

Helia's *chosen* had fared badly. Her *choosers* had fared worse.

Malaise was not a big enough word for what maligned the priests. Their maladies were varied. Some had gibbered, pulling their hair from the root and clawing their own faces. A bare handful had gone berserk. Madness had mercifully stolen their battle magicks. They'd been easy to put down.

Most had turned totally despondent, refusing to either rise or eat. One man's muttered litany had stuck with him.

'Gone... gone... gone...'

The Priesthood's failure was the worst kind of betrayal. They had shoved themselves down the empire's throat, becoming its steel spine. Now, they were proving rotten and rusted through.

Was redemption possible, when one had failed one's god?

The group beneath his gaze began to break apart purposefully.

These were the odd ones – those who had suffered the same sickness but had come through haggard and somehow *hardened*.

Watching them set his teeth on edge.

A humorless clomping announced his second's arrival. The wan woman snapped a salute. Deep purple bruises marred her eyes.

"Any sign of the rearguard?" he forestalled.

The *Lady's Tears* had been the last ship to leave Thell. Her fate was unknown and her cargo precious, though few knew it.

"No, admiral," his second backtracked. "I… regret to report…"

More bad news.

"Spit it out, lieutenant."

She gathered herself. "It's Chaplain Moorstone, sir…"

He felt a dull ache in his chest.

"…he came up on deck, carrying a ballast stone. I saw him set it on the rail and climb up after it. Then I saw the rope-"

He stopped listening, his pulse pounding in his ears.

Moorstone had been chaplain to the First Legion. A man with a barkeep's belly-laugh and a mason's merciless touch. Hands that could bring a gentle end to a friend or a grievous one to a foe.

The priest and he had cultivated a cautious friendship over the course of their voyage. That Moorstone, of all people, would ride a ballast stone into the deep...

"We are ready."

He throttled grief's impulse to lash out. The clergy, he saw, were drifting toward the prow. Their spokesman had approached unnoticed. The priest was scarecrow thin and could have been the twin of his lieutenant.

"What was that? Father?" he added at a warning glance from his second. She was of the new generation, too young to have known the old empire or its freedoms. Her prudence was, perhaps, not misplaced.

He took a tighter rein on his temper. The leading cause of death in the empire was immolation by priest. It was a sentence reserved for unbelievers. Supposedly, faith provided an absolute defense.

If you believed that kind of twaddle.

"We are ready," the spokesman repeated.

When his expectant look went unaddressed, he pressed, "For?"

"Ready to *leave*," the man added unhelpfully.

He caught the hope that flashed across his second's face.

"That will be all, lieutenant."

Conditioned to blind obedience, she left, though her feet dragged. He turned back to the soon-to-be concussed priest. Immolation would spare him the shame of reporting his defeat to the emperor.

"Leave?" he scoffed. "We're months from the nearest landmass, not counting Thell. But I'd be happy to lend you a rowboat...?"

A ballast stone might be quicker. He grimaced.

The priest seemed not to notice the impropriety. "We must *all* away, as many as we can take. Order the other vessels closer, lest they be left behind."

He stared, his blood heating.

Was there no end to the Priesthood's ill-thought schemes? Could they not stop issuing orders? Even when they'd run out of semi-sensible orders to give?

He cast a desperate plea for patience to the sky... and stiffened.

True, they traveled uncharted waters, watched over by a host of unfamiliar constellations. But he surely would have noticed a daytime star before now...?

As though he'd met the eye of an inimical god, weight pressed down on him. He shook off the silly notion. A call for the ship's cartographer rose in his throat – and he stalled once more.

Was it his imagination, or was the star *moving*?

"We have little time," the priest judged, following his gaze.

As his questions warred for precedence, more priests arrived. Two of their number led a third by the elbows. The ancient's eyes were milky with cataracts, the dull centers of sunburst tattoos. Alone among their number, the elder's face was serene.

The old one's minders began disrobing him.

The admiral caught his breath.

The ancient's flesh was freshly branded. Holy script traced curlicues on every bit of exposed skin, beading pink with blood.

"What," he grated at the spokesman, "have you done?"

"What was necessary. What was commanded."

His hand shot out, tangling in the priest's collar.

"What," he demanded, nose-to-nose, "have you done?!"

All motion ceased. Heads turned in disbelief.

It was said one could see the purifying flame, fomenting in the priests' eyes. He looked – really looked.

His hand sprang open.

Gone... gone... gone...

"The other vessels," the spokesman insisted. "Now."

His retort was drowned by thunder. The sea fell from beneath the Pride's keel. For one, horrible heartbeat, he was weightless. Then the deck clubbed the back of his head. Sputtering, he saw a flash of light – the star, sleeting past at impossible speed.

Rolling to his stomach, he was just in time to see its fiery trail disappear over the taffrail. Toward Thell.

Sounds of chaos slowly started to penetrate his ringing ears.

"Man overboard!" he bellowed, pushing up. "Lines out!"

"It is too late for them."

The priest had stood firm, as though he had barnacles for feet. Over the man's shoulder, holy light bathed the prow. The venerable ancient shone with its blessing.

As he stared, the stooped one's back straightened, arms rising in supplication. The branded script came to life, its seams running with molten gold. The hallowed ancient slowly rose from the deck.

"Quickly now."

He met the priest's empty gaze.

"Belay my last!"

Crewmen flinched from the snap in his voice. Those in the water wailed as they sensed hope's hand withdraw.

"Signal the fleet! Close ranks!"

Around him, the ship quickened, thrumming with the thump of bare feet. Semaphore flags churned, relaying his orders.

"Fog formation! One line's cast between vessels!"

Despite the noon sun, his crew cast long shadows. The ancient had become a conflagration. He saw similar sunbursts, leading the ships alongside them.

"Batten the hatches! Tie down whatever isn't nailed down!"

A chorus of uncertain *ayes* sounded in response.

And pray these priests aren't as insane as they sound...

He glanced at the burning ancient. The light burgeoned, forcing him to look away. Purple afterimages scored his vision.

The Stalwart swam slowly into focus, her sails listless as a lame gull. As he watched, her canvas gave a fitful twitch... and flopped, flaccid. Atop her main mast, the long pennant writhed a moment more and then drooped, dead.

Port and starboard showed the same. All around, he heard the rigging still. His soles felt the squeal of fled momentum. They were becalmed, on an ocean gone smooth as glass. Panicked breathing, near to hand, said others had noticed too.

The sword he'd unwittingly drawn clanged to the deck.

He ran, scattering crew.

Vaulting to the poop deck, he careened into the aft rail. His spyglass made a bid for escape. He snatched it back by his fingertips and rammed the eyepiece home.

The horizon jumped into grainy proximity.

If he were the kind of man to tremble, he might have thought a skyline in flux a symptom of palsy. But he knew better.

What he saw was an ocean, given will and direction – a wave like a mountain, roaring towards them.

He sensed its approach across his shoulders and in his water.

His water wanted very much to flee down his leg.

"Great Dariel," he addressed his bastard father's abandoned god, "turn your merciless gaze away..."

At least I'll get my burial at sea.

Behind him, the air split loudly. He whirled.

The ancient, buoyed by light, bled golden energy. Similar streams siphoned from the lead ships. The power quenched itself in the sea, birthing a massive fogbank that coiled and crackled as darkly as a nascent typhoon.

It yawned at them, stretching a maw fit to swallow every ship in sight. At the back of its throat, he spied a night-darkened ocean, reflecting stars and a sliver of moon.

Escape.

For a moment, he feared his dry throat would defeat him.

"Pile on sail!" he roared. "Every scrap you can! Rig sheets to the yardarm! Spread your damned shirts to the wind!"

"But, admiral," a tremulous voice said, "there *is* no wind...?"

He made a grab. The crewman went limp in his grip, arms thrown wide in pre-emptive surrender. He met the man's eyes, rolling like those of a horse being winched into the hold.

"Then you fucking get off and push!" he screamed, adding word to deed. The crewman clunked to the deck, even as the first promissory gust plucked his admiral's hat from his head.

"Forward!" he bellowed, pointing toward the sorcerous gate.

Chapter 1 – The Chase

No history of the Empire can be complete without a thorough understanding of its underlying theological structure. The ever-ascending Heli peak has its foundation in the Mother Temple, which is in turn supported by the old scriptures, as if by pillars. These pillars are inviolable. Incandescent. Beware, foolish moths and historians alike, who would peer too close…
~ *Pella Monop, Foreword to 'A Treatise on Empire', unpublished.*

Present day
Foothills Outside Tellar
The Heli Empire

FALSE DAWN LIT the fog and muddled the landscape into muted grays and dappled shadow. Trampled frost pointed to the party atop the knoll. Morning mist curdled about their ponies' hooves.

Hillmen. In rawhide, thick furs and cold iron.

Their canted eyes and curved noses were trained ahead. Their tracker straightened from his study, giving the Huntmaster a nod.

They were closing on their quarry.

The warrior sniffed, the familiar flavors of snow and spruce mingled with the unwanted scents of turned earth and city smoke.

Their most taxing Hunt yet – to take them so far from home.

He spurred his mount. The shaggy beast trotted downhill.

The mist would soon burn off, he reflected, in the lowlands' unwelcome heat. But, for now…

…it hid the Hunt.

THE IMPERIAL CAPITAL of Tellar was in full festival swing. Solstice cheer raced through it like a living thing, sweeping up the devout and the lax alike. The streets were awash with color, a thousand instruments ringing in the new season. Feastday chants and stomping feet marched alongside the great parade. Solid excitement did nearly as much to hold the puppets aloft as did the poles of their handlers. Paper ribbons rained down from crowded balconies as homeowners tried to entice the parade their way.

The official opening ceremony, as always, had been a dull and stately affair. Justin had stood in Sun Square, at dawn – smothering yawns – as the proper prayers and blessing were performed. Decrepit priests in costly garb, swinging perfumed censers.

Bah!

Justin had slipped from the Temple's main procession as soon as he was able. The troupes at the back-end of the parade had all the fun, away from the austere regard of the archons. And the jostling crowds had had more time to… marinate. Though he hated to admit it, the slightly softer – more sodden – edge to the crowd was easier on his *other* sense.

Registering the approach before he saw it, he sidestepped.

A bunch of boisterous boys breached their way past.

More nimble, but not forewarned, some handlers fumbled their poles. Above them, history was rewritten. The likeness of a long-dead chieftain turned its capitulation into a head-butt.

"…sorry!" came the boys' belated apology.

Mild swearing turned to mirthful play. The puppet archon – so assaulted – turned, wielding its crook of office like a club.

Justin gave voice to the laugh that also marked his mask. Hoping to coax some cooler air, he flapped the front of his robes. The sweat did little to dampen his mood, but he was no longer a young man. It was high time for him to excuse himself and go-

Something dark skittered across his consciousness.

It was sharp, to have cut through the clangor of the parade, and he flinched from the contact. Curiosity piqued, he reached out…

There! Too slight to trace. Too fast…

His steps slowed as he honed his focus. When the whisper of awareness breathed by again, he seized it, hissing as it sliced him.

Merciful Goddess, such distress!

Mentally rocking on his heels, he worked to firm his grip.

Gentle hands steered him from the press as his steps faltered. Two of his students – empaths, like him. Neither possessed his level of sensitivity, but they were attuned to him nonetheless.

"Father Justin? Are you alright?"

The strand of consciousness he held vibrated with tension.

"Come," he commanded, plunging into the crowd.

Alone, it would have been impossible – in a press like this – to winkle free a lone thread of feeling. But with his students, perhaps unconsciously echoing his fierce concentration, it became easier.

The three of them fell into lockstep.

Working as fast as he dared, he peeled back the obscuring clutter. As if to defy his efforts, the link he held grew fainter. Such a poor connection would peter out with distance. Concentrating desperately, he divined its direction.

Like a flight of geese, his party turned down an intersection, leaving the parade behind. The crowd stepped swiftly from the path of three priests, moving purposefully and in haste.

They were closer now, the details clearer. The mind he sensed was wild with fear and wretched with fatigue, its owner close to collapse. Unconsciousness would sever their connection.

He increased his pace

Unseen, the festival flashed by to either side.

Proximity was affording a clearer picture. Turning sharply, he led his party down an alley. They were in a seedier section of the city now. But, even here, their priestly robes would protect them.

The link was failing, lurching like a heartbeat.

He ran down a side street, only faintly aware – and caring not at all – that the fear he felt was not his own.

The weak pulse faded from his awareness.

Staggering to a stop, he bowed his head, bending all of his considerable faculties upon his extra sense…

Sensation. Little more than smoke from a snuffed candle.

He spun toward it.

At a broken pace, a small figure hobbled from a dark alley and collapsed. He caught the unfortunate, cradling them against him.

"Merciful Mother…" one of the stunned students breathed.

"Dread of the Dark Places!" Cyrus exclaimed, entering the draped cubicle. They were in one of the Temple's infirmaries. The elderly priest's outcry was for the emaciated form on the pallet. Even under a sheet, the boy's bones stuck up at hips and shoulders. Painfully thin limbs framed a stomach swollen by malnutrition. Dirt and other unidentifiables brindled the boy's sallow skin.

"Thank you for coming so quickly," he said from the corner.

"Justin," Cyrus identified, "if I had known it was this bad, I would have run. What happened?"

He let the comment pass. At his friend's age, the only thing Cyrus could still run was a fever.

"I don't know. He was weaving through Cadre's Warren."

Cyrus slowed in the act of unslinging his healer's satchel.

"Rough neighborhood. A good thing you found him, then."

Sleeves pinned back, the healer pressed a liver-spotted hand to the boy's forehead, then an ear to his chest.

"Has he said anything?"

"No. Fright chased him headlong into a faint."

His laden tone caught the healer's attention.

"I've never felt fear like that, Cyrus," he explained. "Ever."

His friend stared. "I'll take your word for it. In any event, he's safe here. Now, let's see about getting him back on his feet."

The elder priest produced a palm-sided crystal, mouthing a prayer over it. Justin joined in. His sense of his friend diffused as the man slipped deftly into the streaming trance.

Cyrus was no empath. But the old man easily outstripped every other streamer when it came to the healing arts. The luminary disc, being passed over the boy's prone body, glowed with the violet light of at least three separate sigils.

"Well?"

"Quiet. I'm concentrating."

The curt tone pricked a smile from Justin.

A healer was the sole captain of their patient's survivorship. The lowliest green-sash could countermand the High Archon himself, in theory. But few could push the bounds of propriety like Cyrus. The man would have had a seat on the Assembly already, if not for his abrasive manner. As it was, respect for his singular talents regularly saved him from reprimand.

With no room to pace, Justin tightly furled his fingers.

"What will you do with him?" Cyrus wondered aloud.

He shrugged. "Wait for the morrow then find the boy's kin."

"Ha! If *they* were in the city, there'd be an uproar."

Seeing that he didn't follow, the healer scolded him.

"Use your eyes, too, on occasion, Master Empath."

He complied. "I see a lost boy."

"I applaud your racial blindness," Cyrus scoffed. "But blindness is no boon to a would-be investigator. Look again."

Again, he noted the boy's blue-black hair – straight, despite the caked filth. Broad cheekbones, canted eyes, custard skin...

"Half the peninsula is of Kender descent, Cyrus."

"Kender...?" the healer smirked. "With that nose? Those eyebrows? Or, rather, eye*brow*?"

Seeing where the healer was headed, he laughed aloud.

"A Hillman? You're not serious?"

"*Then*," the old priest insisted, "there's the green spruce, stuck in his hair. This time of year, everything below the snowline is red. See those rusty smears? Iron ore, from near the northern mines."

"You're not suggesting that this boy – this *little* boy – ran the Barrier Ranges, naked?"

"An amazing feat," Cyrus mused, becoming distracted.

"What?"

"Unsure. Help me turn him over..."

Together, they gently pitched the boy onto his stomach.

Cyrus resumed his crystal scrying, wizened ears perked.

"Ah. Interesting. See what you make of this..."

The reef of vertebrae stretched the boy's skin thin, so he more closely resembling a splayed fish than a slumbering child.

"What am I looking for?" he Justin asked, leaning in.

"Wait. Watch..."

The old healer's face grew slack with the effort of manifesting a fourth sigil – Bartolom's Brand, if Justin wasn't mistaken. The crystal shone brighter. Shadows retreated into the gullies between the boy's ribs. The sigil's power peaked, forcing the light over the threshold from violet into pure white. Under the force of its incandescence, ghostly marks emerged.

Justin caught his breath. "Are those...?"

"Arrow wounds?" Cyrus supplied. "No."

Unconsciously, Justin smoothed his robe over his hamstring.

"I have an identical scar that says you're wrong."

Testily, Cyrus let the crystal's light wink out.

"I *know* they're not arrow wounds because the boy isn't dead. Also, there's no trace of trauma in the deep tissue. Whatever did this, it didn't scratch more than the skin."

Justin shuddered. Apart from their penchant for savagery, little was known about the Hillmen. Their mountain home was desolate, devoid of resources and – hence – of no interest to the Empire.

"I'm envisioning a toddler in armor," he said, feeling sick.

Cyrus shrugged. "Water would also rob an arrow of power."

"He's not a carp, Cyrus. Nor a soldier. He's what? Five?"

"*Blessed*, is what he is. If this *was* an arrow wound, the Hillmen possess healers more skilled than I…"

His friend paused in the act of putting the crystal away.

"…they don't, do they?"

He shook his head. He didn't know.

"Huh," Cyrus grumbled, the moment of self-doubt passing. "The savages probably just practice ritual scarification."

Justin didn't point out that there *were* no scars – the blemishes had faded, along with the Brand's light.

He had known, in a roundabout way, that children were resilient. But this was uncanny.

"Will the boy live?" was the important question.

"I'm not sure how he's alive right now," Cyrus admitted gravely. "He's been pushed past his breaking point. His body has begun to consume itself. I've balanced it out as best I can."

"But will he survive?"

Exasperated, the healer turner on him.

"Justin, I've done all that is humanly possible. If you're looking for more – take it up with Helia."

He flushed. "Forgive me. I spoke out of turn."

As an empath, he should know better than to take his friend's professionalism at face value. He could *feel* the man's concern.

"Help me turn him back over," Cyrus grumped. "He'll get a crick in his neck, sleeping like that."

Together they righted the little figure.

"The sisters who serve here will send word if the boy wakes."

"Thank you, old friend."

"Don't thank me yet," the elder priest growled, turning away.

There came a time when a gentle hand shook Justin awake, though he could remember neither sitting down nor falling asleep.

"You should go, father," a kindly nun whispered. "If you worry yourself sick, you'll steal a bed from a deserving soul."

Muzzily, he noted the lit lanterns and darkened windows.

She followed his gaze. "The boy has not woken, though we've wiped him down and spooned some broth into him."

"Will he be alright?" he asked, rubbing sleep from his eyes.

"That is not for me to say."

On unsteady feet, he found his way from the infirmary.

He was, he reflected, too old to be falling asleep in chairs. Aches hounded him through the atrium and up the many stairs. He shouldered open his cell door. The stone floor was piled high with books and scrolls. By feel, he hunted up his lamp.

His unmade bed looked no better by its yellow glow. Sheets of parchment outnumbered their linen counterparts.

Time to requisition another bookcase, he reflected, gazing about his crowded cell. *And more walls, to lean them against.*

He should stop resisting his promotion to Keeper. If nothing else, access to proper glow globes would save him from blindly striking a spark amidst all this tinder.

Applying the flint-and-striker tongs to his ceramic stove, he set about brewing some strong tea. Work still waited on his desk: a half-written report on the trading customs of the Neril tribesmen.

Some well-meaning soul had mentioned him as an expert.

Worst luck.

Dipping his quill, he set about scuttling the Chapter of Beasts' proposal – diplomatically, of course. The Neril would more easily trade their lives than their ponies – a history lesson that seemed to have been lost on the mercers chapter.

That he had to explain the difference between the Neril and the Nemil showed the depth of the money grubbers' ignorance.

He understood the impulse to circumvent the Purlian stranglehold on the horse trade. Those imports invariably went to the Imperial stables. The far-off Skordian front had promised spoils of horse flesh. But that war had unexpectedly stalled.

War, war, war.

Historian though he was, he could point to no single period in the Empire's long history when they'd been at peace.

If they could but put the stale conflict with the Renali to bed, they'd be counting horses in no time. Perhaps he'd publish a paper. A carefully worded, politically correct, non-seditious paper.

He shoved a partially translated Jade Islands scroll aside.

His own projects would have to wait, he knew.

However, the little boy in the infirmary refused to vacate his thoughts. His war wounds ached, as though the weather was turning. It brought home bad memories.

He'd been a newly promised priest, green as a spring twig and thrilled at being dispatched to the Renali front.

An idiot in other words.

As he'd learned, patriotism was the first casualty of triage.

He'd promised to carry dying words to countless kith and kin. The sound of maimed soldiers, crying out for their mothers, could still wake him at night. The clinging ash, from the great funeral pyres, had scrubbed out easily by comparison.

Even today, he could still speak last rites by rote.

He'd found death to be a master of ambush. One that possessed, for lack of a better word, a morbid sense of humor:

An arrow had come, bowing over the fortifications. His leg had buckled beneath it. The next shaft, instead of finding his back, had speared the soldier on the litter he'd dropped – a hero, who'd carried his felled commander from the field. They had just spent frantic bells, cutting a bolt from the brave soldier's chest.

Only to have death summarily replace it.

On bad nights, his nightmares dumped him back beside that litter. Unable to rise, listening to the enemy rams upon the gates.

…thud…

…thud…

He woke to the sound of pounding upon his door.

"Father Justin! Father Justin, wake up!"

He started up from his desk, parchment papered to his cheek.

Upsetting his chair, he reached the door in three long strides.

"It's open-"

The acolyte half-fell into his arms and almost brained him.

"Father! Come quick!" She set off at a dead run.

It took his sleep-dulled mind a moment to note her green sash.

The boy…

He dashed after her, haring down the steps. He spent no breath on questions, throwing himself hard around corners. Ahead, she judged his speed and wrenched the infirmary door out of his way.

He ran headlong into pandemonium.

Priests and patients skidded among tumbled furniture. A single voice rose, screaming, above the general panic. And a wave of animal terror rolled off the boy, almost bowling Justin over.

He forced his way through a knot of healers to the bedside.

"Pin that leg!"

"I've got his arm!"

"Someone help me hold this!"

"Ow! My nose!"

The boy put up a terrific fight, clawing, kicking and biting.

A small hand slammed into Justin's midriff in passing. Winded, he pinned it to the mattress. Fever sweat slicked the boy's skin.

A burly masha'na, head trailing bandages, shouldered easily through the press. The warrior monk bore down on the boy's breast and opposite arm, pressing him flat.

The child screeched, straining so hard his toes curled.

At this rate, administering a sedative would cost someone a finger. Weighing the risk of discovery, he manifested his self-made streaming sigil and strained his empathic sense through it.

The sense of calm shredded apart as it came near the boy.

"Somebody fetch Father Cyrus!" he wheezed.

In the chaos, he wasn't sure anyone heard.

"I'm here," the healer announced in a distracted monotone.

A crystal's violet glow bathed them. There was a brilliant flash.

He rocked back alongside the rest, the spell's backlash making his head spin. He fought to retain his hold. But there was no need.

The boy was out cold.

Of the poignant terror, only a faint aftertaste lingered.

He let go, watching guiltily as his fingermarks faded.

"Helia's mercy," someone offered in thanks.

Tangible relief ran through the room, shambles though it was. Moving stiffly, people drifted off to begin straightening up.

An initiate bent by a prone priestess. "Are you alright, mother?"

"I fink de shild bloke my gnose…"

An elderly priest offered up a neat bite mark to be bandaged.

"I told'em all this gruel could drive a body to cannibalism…"

The joke seemed to steady the pale initiate helping him.

Two youthful acolytes passed by.

"I refuse to tell people a toddler gave me this black eye."

"If you'll say *you* gave me this split lip, I'll say I hit you."

"Deal! What should we say we fought about?"

"Doctrine, obviously."

"Ah. And I won."

"No. I did."

"Did not."

"You want another black eye?"

Their bickering faded as they moved off.

Most of the injuries, it seemed, were blessedly minor.

"You alright, Cyrus?"

The eldering healer was being helped to a seat by the masha'na.

"Fine," the old one huffed. "That little display of mine… and all those stairs… Helia! How I hate stairs…!"

If he was complaining, he'd be alright.

"Speaking of…" he cast a furtive look at the masha'na but could sense that the man's attention was elsewhere, "…what exactly *was* that little display?"

He might not be a healer but he'd have heard tell of such a potent sigil. It most certainly had not come from the Lexicon.

"Douse your torch, witch hunter," Cyrus said. "That was the Calming Wreathe. Or, at least, a minor reinterpretation. I confess, I can't claim credit as its inventor, I was merely its first victim."

"Victim?"

The healer nodded. "One of my master classes. Never did get along with that instructor. Can't remember her name. Scary woman. Legs like logs. She was demonstrating the sigil – on me – and her crystal was primed with a jumble of teaching aids. Anyway, a spider rappelled, right past my ear." Cyrus rubbed his head at the memory of a blow. "I was comatose for days."

"Days?!"

"Don't fret. I've refined its structure a lot since then."

Justin studied the boy. "How long will he sleep?"

Cyrus seesawed a hand uncertainly. "Until tomorrow evening?"

"Then we've got time," he muttered, turning to the burly monk.

"Apologies, brother, I don't know your name…?" They gripped hands over introductions. "Can you tell me what went on here?"

The warrior seemed unfazed by the incident.

"Most everyone'd gone to sleep. 'cept me. I'm use to patrolin' the parapets at night. So, I'm lyin' here, starin' at the ceilin', when your lad starts stirrin'. That got the healers pretty excited. But he takes one look at the smilin' lot o' them – an' he's off like a hare."

He felt the monk's grudging respect.

"He'd have made it out, too, if not for that levelheaded lass."

He followed the man's finger to the initiate who'd fetched him.

"Slammed the door in his face, she did. Lad's fast, I'll give 'im that. Dodged these healers like they was tax collectors. Luckily, that there chamber pot tripped him up. The rest, you saw."

He thanked the masha'na, feeling no more enlightened.

Why would the boy have such a strong reaction to the healers?

A familiar face drew his eye. Empathy was rare, and weak unto uselessness nine times out of ten. Ismus – he recalled the student's name – would never be required to take the oaths.

Still…

"Ismus," he greeted, drifting over.

"Father Justin," the young man winced while a priestess tried to poultice his chin. "Sad business this, isn't it?"

"So it seems. Tell me, were you here when the boy woke?"

"I was. We were relieved. We hadn't held out much hope."

He nodded his understanding. "Did you get a Sense of him?"

The priestess hissed a warning as Ismus tried to duck his head.

"I'm no Sensitive, father," the acolyte said, embarrassed.

Most latent empaths were naturally adept at reading a room. Ismus was as latent as they came. But even an untrained empath might remark upon a sudden, strong shift in emotion.

"Try," he prompted.

Biting a lip, Ismus did. "He woke really, really scared…"

"That much I gathered."

The young man's shaken head earned him an exasperated look.

"Sorry, mother. No. I mean he *woke up* scared. Like his terror surfaced before he did. It's like… fear has worn a groove so deep, his mind can't escape it."

"Monstrous…" the priestess echoed Justin's thought.

JUSTIN PACED RESTLESSLY while Cyrus looked on. The healer had unearthed the kettle from a stack of scrolls and made tea.

"Stand still, will you? You're going to strain my eyes."

"What are we going to do, Cyrus?" he demanded once more.

"You're sure you can't just… *slide* into his head?"

He grimaced at the older priest's explicit gesture.

"No. I am not a squid and the boy's head is not a bottle."

That uncorked terror had torn his strongest sending to pieces.

"Can we reason with him in the conventional way, then?"

They were arguing in circles. "No. His fear is mindless, Cyrus, and always in the forefront. There's nothing to reason *with*."

"I could drug him?" the healer offered.

"For the rest of his life?"

"If not, we need to reconsider-"

"*Don't* suggest the sanitarium! That place is little better than a prison... You're sure you found nothing physically amiss?"

At Cyrus's sour look, he heard the accusation in his own voice. "Sorry."

The healer waved him off. "You can't fix him and *I* can't find a fault with him. We won't leave him suspended in a fugue or strapped to a bed or ensconced in an asylum..."

"Yes?" he prompted.

"I'm thinking."

He slumped. "Dammit."

Cyrus rubbed at tired eyes, looking defeated. Slogging through severed limbs, the man was in his element. This ailment of the mind must have caught him out of his depth.

"I'm sorry I yelled."

"Forget it," the old priest huffed, cradling a lined face in a liver-spotted hand. "I don't know, Justin. I hate to say it – because it smacks of surrender. But, I think, it might be time to consider... sending the boy on his way. Peacefully, as it were. There would be no panic or pain – my word on it. And we might yet save his soul."

When the expected explosion did not occur, Cyrus glanced up.

"Justin? Did you hear me? Are you alright? Look, I just-"

"Say that again?" he interrupted, reeling.

"Death would be a mercy-"

"No! Before that," he waved irritably. "I said I was sorry I yelled at you, and *you* said...?" he paused expectantly.

"'Forget it'?"

"That's it!" he slapped his palms together. "Cyrus, that's *it*!"

"Eh?" the priest was nonplussed. "Now, see here, Justin. We *made* this our problem. We can't just pass it off-"

He interrupted excitedly, "Whatever experience has so unbalanced the boy, it lives in the forefront of his mind, obscuring all else. If we can tie off that memory, we can work around it."

Cyrus eyed him blankly. Then, "Is this madness catching…?"

"It's not mad, Cyrus, its *medicine*."

"It most assuredly is not," the old priest protested. "What you're talking about is a memory block. It exist nowhere in the Lexicon-"

"Yes, it does! Torpor's Push-"

"Don't lecture me about healing sigils, son. Torpor's Push is meant to treat *shock*. It is an amalgamation of Lull and Balance and half a dozen other Life sigils you've probably never heard off. Its grip on traumatic memories is tenuous at best and it begins to unravel the moment you stop powering it."

Sensing his victory, Justin leaned across the desk.

"So does the Calming Wreath."

The old healer's eyes shot wide.

IT WAS, OF COURSE, NOT THAT SIMPLE.

Justin spent long bells arguing with his learned friend. Together, they dissected sigil components, disputed ways to transpose them, debated the merits of obscure manuals and disagreed over the synergy of certain pairings and hybrids.

As Justin saw it, they had three problems.

"Even if we succeed," Cyrus had said, "the block will be impermanent. I shall have to coax the boy's own spirit into sustaining it – like a tick. It may cripple the child's streaming potential. Or even shorten his lifespan."

"You suggested a mercy killing not a bell ago, Cyrus."

The healer had scowled. "I'd hoped you hadn't heard that…"

The second problem was not so easily overcome. Once they'd tallied the list of promising sigils, it became clear that they could not hope to power all of them themselves. They needed help.

Which brought them to their third problem: forsaking the Lexicon of approved sigils was – in point of fact – illegal. Anyone who helped them risked more than mere excommunication.

The fourth – unspoken – hurdle was a matter of conscience.

Magic that warped the mind was witchery. Many thought Torpor's Push belonged on that pyre as well. For what Justin and his compatriots planned to do, they would answer to Helia – if the Inquisitori didn't uncover them first.

"Are they even healers?" Cyrus sneered of his two students.

They were all in Justin's cell, ranged around the patient's pallet.

"They were there when I found the boy. They want to help. Besides, you'll be the only one performing actual healing. The rest of us are simply accessories."

The healer glowered at him. "You realize we are simply walling off the madness? It will out, eventually. Your little boy singlehandedly demolished an infirmary. He will only grow bigger and stronger. He will need constant supervision."

"We'll keep him here, where we can watch him."

"For the rest of his life? You don't think that's cruel?"

"*We* don't complain."

"*We* are priests!"

"He can be one too."

His friend had wanted to argue further but the fact was that the Temple routinely took in charges far younger than the boy.

It was well past noon before everything was ready.

Justin's books had been stacked aside, giving the pallet pride of place. Cyrus stood, referencing a thick grimoire and making some last-moment notations. The two students, from his Advanced Acuity class, quit their quiet discussion and drifted over.

Having spent the night splicing together new sigils, Cyrus looked wan. But the healer's bloodshot eyes were resolute.

"Now, pay attention. This interplay of constructs is delicate and draws heavily on the major sigil of Spirit. The balance of power must be precise. A miscalculation could knock us all into last week, mentally speaking – not to mention killing the patient."

They all nodded, expressions somber.

"Then let us begin."

Cyrus knelt by the bedside, crystal framed in a splay-fingered grip. They joined in the healer's droning prayer, its familiar cadences easing their way into the streaming trance.

"Unity through faith," they chorused.

The crystal lit as Cyrus primed it with the first construct.

Though the sigils were – in effect – nameless, Justin had instructed his empaths to conceptualize them. He thought of the one the healer was building right now as Sieve. That one would be his to power. Next came Burrow and Bulwark, for his students. Then Mortar, which he would also take. That left Mimic and Sooth to Cyrus – who insisted these could be entrusted to no one else.

With its seven gantries six-parts-filled, the crystal shone bright.

Feeling his friend's demand, he poured power into Sieve while the healer added splashes of Mimic and Sooth. Justin tapered off as the students were tapped for touches of Burrow and Bulwark.

Such smooth choreography normally required years of practice and streaming hymns. The kind the *senso'norus* was famed for. With three empaths, they shared perfect synchronicity. What they *lacked* was energy equal to that of the vaunted battle choirs.

Even inside the trance, Justin winced as Cyrus wrung every drop of power first from Burrow, then from Bulwark.

Gritting his teeth, he shored them up with Mortar.

The violet light grew blinding. Saturated with power, the air sizzled. A persistent ringing ground at Justin skull. Hidden in the glare, Cyrus crooned a madcap calibration at the crystal.

The healer began applying Mimic and Sooth in an intricate rhythm, so nimbly Justin couldn't parse it. All he could do was add dollops of Mortar whenever Cyrus directed.

The unruly energies whirled around them, winkling free loose papers that could be heard fluttering by in the whiteout.

To his shock, Justin felt his friend start construction on a seventh sigil. A Life-aspected one – Recovery.

They were losing the boy.

He felt the healer falter but could do nothing to help. Sigils were not like sentences – you couldn't finish someone else's.

Then Cyrus's reedy voice rose above the cacophony. A chant, in an Old Temple dialect. Working by rote, guided by the mantra's cadences, the healer completed the sigil.

Scraping the bottom of the barrel, Justin streamed everything he had left into Recovery.

Pace bordering on breakneck speed, Cyrus beat furiously between Mimic and Sooth.

Somewhere, amidst the miniature hurricane, the healer's song reached a crescendo.

Unbound power blasted Justin from his feet.

He came to, buried in the wreckage of a bookcase. Ears ringing, he fought his way free. It seemed he'd lost only moments.

His students were similarly staggering upright, their hair stuck on end by residual energy. Cyrus sprawled across the cot. Still.

"Oh, Guardian Mother," he prayed, stumbling over. His probing fingers found a weak neck pulse.

"'m not dead yet," his friend fended him off.

"Are you alright? How do you feel?"

"Like the Dark Places pinched me off, midway," the healer cursed, sitting up. "How's the child?"

The boy seemed no different. The crystal lay, smoking, atop his breastbone. It came away with a dry crackle, revealing a circular burn that would most certainly scar.

"Help me up…"

Side by side they took in the blasted room.

"Did it work?" one of the students wondered dazedly.

Justin cocked his head at Cyrus, who shrugged. "Time will tell."

They found the tin kettle in a far corner, flattened beyond use. Which was fine. They all needed something stronger, anyway.

"Another?" he asked, once he'd shepherded his students out.

"Holy hymns, *yes*." The healer had coughed miserably through his first brandy but gamely held his glass for a second.

"So, what happens now?"

"Now?" Justin considered. "Now I drum up some dead relations and sponsor my orphaned kin for a novitiate."

"'Drum up' dead relations? Whew! Witchcraft *and* necromancy. Slow down, son. Save some heresy for tomorrow."

"Be serious," he chided.

Cyrus's expression turned wooden with worry.

"What if the boy doesn't remember how to hold a spoon?"

"I'll deal with it."

"Have you thought of a name?"

He hadn't. But one came, unbidden, to his mind.

"*Maharkoo*," he pronounced in the Old Temple dialect.

"'Foundling'," the healer translated, tone teasing. "Or 'rediscovery', depending on context. Trite. But apt. Huh. Look at you – waxing poetic."

"Oh, shut up," he muttered, refilling both their glasses.

Chapter 2 – Maharkoo

It is a marked phenomenon that the simplicity – or, conversely, the complexity – of one's mind molds one's reality. The simple goatherd exists in elegant dichotomy. A pious life will lead him unto Grace. If not, Perdition awaits. To the goatherd, these places are as real as the rock upon which his feet rest. In contrast, scholars and priests paint the world in shades of grey, using metaphor and parable. Yet, if the scriptures are absolute, who is to say that it is not the goatherd who is right?

In time, this question may engender its own treatise.

~ *Pella Monop, Introduction to 'A Treatise on Empire', unpublished.*

"Marco!"

He skidded to a stop. A storm of pebbles showered the priest.

"Father?" he replied between heaving breaths.

"You-" the priest was bowled over as three more boys arrived.

From within the tangle a youthful voice crowed, "You're it!"

"No fair!" Marco denied.

"Thanks, father," another said. "He's near impossible to tag!"

Many hands pulled the priest up and set to dusting his robes.

"What the-" the man objected. "Line up over there!"

The four novices obediently stood at arm's length. Elbowed recriminations were exchanged as they awaited sentencing.

"Like running, do you?" the priest growled. "Mayhap you'd like all of next week's fetch-and-carry duty?"

They blanched. With Festival not far-off, that duty was murder.

Satisfied, the priest stuck his hands up his sleeves.

"Now then. I believe *three* of you have chores waiting?"

The three so addressed mulled on this, distrustful of mercy.

"Go," the priest brooked no argument.

With a last commiserating glance, his compatriots pelted away.

"As for *you*," the priest reclaimed his attention. "I believe Keeper Justin has been expecting you for the better part of a bell?"

His eyes went wide.

"I suggest-" The priest stammered to a stop, suddenly alone.

The gardens sleeted past on either side as Marco exploited every shortcut he knew. He couldn't *believe* he'd forgotten about the keeper's lesson!

He'd happily skip Scriptures in favor of tag. Or swimming. Or tree-climbing. But Keeper Justin's lessons were *sacred-*

Jumping a hedge, he upset an acolyte's wheelbarrow by landing on it. The older boy shouted imprecations at his back.

-he didn't know *what* he'd done to endear himself to the keeper. But he was desperate to retain that goodwill-

A librarian, blinded by an armload of books, started as he sheared past her. The sound of thick spines, cascading to the tiles, spurred him.

-it wasn't that he and the keeper were related. At least, he didn't think that was it. Between them, his tag-friends had two uncles and a grandmother at Temple whom they hardly knew-

A handful of donors, bearing the weight of a wardrobe down the stairs, cringed as he bounded past on the banister.

-it had all been leading up to this. All the boring breathing and the tedious trances. All the meditation and prayer. Today, the keeper would introduce him... to *magic*!

Streaming, he corrected conscientiously. Helia's gift. Distinct from the wild, unholy arts of pagan practitioners-

"Where's the fire, lad?" a passing masha'na called after him.

-the *danger*, of course, was why these introductory lessons were conducted one-on-one. Supervised by streaming experts.

He slid to a halt before the keeper's door, hand upraised.

The portal swung open before his knock could land – showcasing Keeper Justin's knack for knowing when he was near.

"Finally made it, I see."

Hugging the stitch in his side, he nodded.

"Should we postpone Streaming while you master Astronomy and Numbers? Maybe then you'll be able to tell time...?"

Panting, he shook his head.

"You're sure?"

He nodded emphatically.

"Well, I suppose you'd better come in then. Tea?"

Glad to have the day's heat as an excuse, he declined.

"You're my last lesson today. So we need not rush. Sit."

He sank gratefully onto a cushion, the keeper across from him.

"How fare your studies?" the priest enquired, rattling cups.

"Fine," he started guiltily, aware his results weren't stellar.

"Oh? Your Numbers master seems to think you're lagging...?"

"'By a goodly percentage,'" he quoted, remembering.

The keeper suppressed a smile. "History is going well?"

He wondered how the priest knew that.

"I like the stories," he nodded.

"And Calligraphy? The master says you have a neat hand..."

He blinked. The master had never told *him* any such thing.

"I like the quiet," he said, "and the smell of ink and parchment."

No magic, heathen or otherwise, could have driven him to admit he felt safe surrounded by those smells. It smelled like the keeper.

Well, he corrected, watching the man dump some rancid yak's butter in the tea, *near enough like the keeper*.

"And are you excited to learn streaming?"

His fringe flopped as he nodded.

"Well, then! Lesson two..." The keeper produced a stubby candle, set in a wooden saucer, and placed it between them.

"Um," he put his hand in the air, confused.

"Yes," the keeper forestalled. "We'll get to lesson *one*, later."

Frowning, he decided the keeper must know what he was about.

"Streaming," the priest began, "is the art of harnessing one's lifeforce, one's spirit. You siphon from the energy within-" the keeper's eyes went half-mast, "-to affect the world without…"

The stub of candle sputtered to life.

Marco snatched his hands into his lap to keep from clapping.

The keeper bowed as though he'd heard the applause anyway.

"Now. Streaming is like Numbers. It has strict rules. It allows no shortcuts. And it punishes miscalculation with catastrophe…"

The flame hissed, tossing like it might tear free of its wick.

Marco pressed warily back in his seat.

"Then again," the keeper continued, "streaming is like Calligraphy. It is fluid, comes from a place of serenity and will reward artful innovation…"

The tamed flame beat itself flat, spreading patterned wings.

Rapt, he watched the bright butterfly flap once, twice, and fade.

The keeper chuckled. "Ostentatious, isn't it? It is a minor sigil – a streaming construct – called Rafik's Filigree."

Reaching behind him, the priest hefted an open tome. Cramped writing ran over two pages and showed an illustration of the vanished butterfly. Justin tapped at the large, decorative design that headed the chapter – a collection of nonsensical angles and whorls.

"This is the sigil Father Rafik spent a decade developing."

Marco eyed it askance.

"A decade? It doesn't look so complicated to me…"

Given half a bell, and his calligraphy brush, he was certain he could do just as well.

Justin smiled. "This is merely a cross-section. It does not embody the true construct, any more than an architect's drawing does a building. To function, the sigil must be made mentally manifest by the streamer – in its entirety – and then powered."

Justin began turning pages. Each one contained more and more complex diagrams, annotations and instructions. They all seemed to make up some small, hidden part of the larger design.

"The Lexicon organizes all approved streaming constructs by tier and sigil. Father Rafik had to tirelessly study – and seamlessly integrate – the existing sigils for *fire*, *mirror*, *mimicry* and *synergy* to achieve this effect. It was a masterwork – a demonstration of skill. And still, it is only a minor sigil."

"Minor?" Marco dismayed. This didn't look 'minor' anymore.

"Minor sigils are more specific in their purpose, simpler to construct and less strenuous to power than the major sigils from which they derive. Major sigils, in turn, are mere aspect of the infinitely more potent and vastly more complex *arc sigils* – which we call Constants.

"Constants are the fundamental driving forces of the world. They are not for mortal men to meddle with or, in most cases, even perceive. By Helia's hand and her infinite grace, *we* were gifted access to two of them – Light and Life. All sigils in the Lexicon stem from these two primal sources."

Transfixed, Marco leaned toward the book.

"All the sigils are in here?" he breathed in wonder.

Justin blinked. "Have you ever been to the Low Library?"

He shook his head. Novices weren't allowed.

"Well, *all* the sigils are in there. *This* is just Rafik's Filigree."

Jaw dropping in chagrin, he stared at the thick grimoire.

Eyes crinkling at the corners, Justin set it aside.

"Pace yourself, Marco. We're nowhere near studying sigils yet. Doing so would be meaningless before we knew whether or not you could power one. Not to mention it would be dangerous."

"Dangerous?"

Nodding, the priest raised the burning candle between them.

"Sigils are manifestations of nature and nature follows its own course. Fire is a minor sigil but, like all fire, its inclination is to spread – to consume the available fuel. Right now, this tiny flame is devouring wick and wax for nourishment. But while its sigil is active, the *streamer* is the fuel. An incautious practitioner can end up fighting for their lives against their own construct."

Marco stared, aghast. "Lighting a candle could kill you?"

"Me? No. You…?" Giving him a bland look, the priest puffed once. The candle guttered out.

Gulping, Marco leaned away from the wisp of smoke.

"Are you properly scared?"

He nodded vehemently.

"Good. Then we can begin.

"Lesson one. To learn how to harness your own lifeforce, first you must learn to perceive it. Here, give me your hand…"

The keeper's palms were warm and dry, the bones prominent.

"Excellent. How did you do that?"

"Do what?"

"You gave me you hand. How?"

"It's my hand," he posited. "It does what I tell it."

"Oh? If you owned a leg of lamb, would *it* do what you told it?"

He snorted. "Probably not?"

"And a good thing, too," the priest muttered archly. "Now, tell me, what sets your arm apart from a hock of ham?"

He knew this one, from scripture. "The spirit of Helia. It is what lends us life and, afterwards, leads us to her in Grace."

"So, you possess this spirit. Good. Can you point it out?"

"Um…"

He must have been climbing trees, or catching frogs, when they'd covered this in class. His fingers twitched toward his heart, where hung his circle pendant. Then, uncertainly, toward his head.

"Um…"

"Want some help?" the keeper offered.

He nodded.

"Ow…!" he snatched his hand back, staring. A delicate needle protruded from the flesh between his thumb and forefinger.

"Father, you-? You-?!"

"Stuck a pin in you?" the priest offered. "Relax. This is an age-old Jade Islands discipline. Though it is not a streaming technique, it recognizes that lifeforce wells up and flows through each of us, like a current. By entirely mundane means, the Jade Islanders have puzzled out how to redirect these eddies to promote certain effects. Tell me, are you alarmed at all?"

"I…" he gaped, the pin occluding all else, "…don't think so?"

"This particular flow counteracts tension and promotes calm."

He would sooner credit Justin's presence than the pin's for that.

"Mind, body and spirit working in concert. What affects the one affects the others – as well as the other way around. Once you have touched on the streaming trance – the required equilibrium of body and mind – your spirit shall be revealed to you."

Fearing that he already knew the answer, he asked, "How?"

"Study, prayer, meditation… and practice. Lots of it."

Of course.

"So, are you ready to try?"

Squaring his shoulders, he settled his speared hand on his knee. The keeper nodded. "Then breathe as I do…"

※ ※ ※

THE TRANSITION TO the new plane was jarring.

The creature arrived in agony, its screech of pain carrying only on the ether. The animals – mere smears to its lidless eyes – reacted, stampeding to the far corners of their pens. Their human minders bellowed in surprise, blind to the threat.

Shivering, bleeding substance, the specter gathered itself. Something had gone awry with its crossing. The aperture had been unstable. Only this slaughter yard, steeped in death, had saved it from shredding apart on arrival. Even so, it did not have long.

What it *did* have, was a purpose.

Digging claws into the dead earth, it dragged itself toward the nearby lantern light. In fits and spurts, it forced its way under the door. The aura of death was stronger here, where carcasses hung from the ceiling. The blood-laden air buoyed it.

Hooks and handsaws and cleavers and mallets lined the workstations it wafted by. Aproned men toiled steadily, bloody to their elbows. It coiled about several, staring into their eyes and tasting their spirits, though they could not see or hear it.

What it needed was a mind that was open to the ether but unguarded. One that would allow it entry…

Ah, yes. This one.

A natural sensitive, the butcher had shunted his self aside in order to endure his work, leaving the seat of his mind vacant.

No longer.

* * *

MARCO SAT, STARING glumly at the inert glow globe. He'd seen their like many times, in the libraries, where lanterns were a fire hazard. Also, lighting the Lily's higher corridors, where the senior priests lived. He'd never seen one dark and lusterless until he'd started studying streaming with the keeper.

"I think this one's defective," he complained.

The keeper huffed disagreeably, which was as close as the man ever came to critique. "It is perfect – the ideal training tool for an untested streamer. A sigil is incorporated into its very construction, so you need neither study nor manifest one. All you must do is provide it raw, unshaped power and it will stir its own alchemical contents to life – an instant, inarguable result."

The keeper considered a moment. "Glow globes are no longer manufactured. The surviving ones are quite... irreplaceable. If we broke this one, we'd be shipped off to the Purlian salt mines."

Marco frowned uncertainly at the keeper.

"It's not broken," the man reassured. "I checked."

This did not cheer him in the least.

"Now, again, please."

Sighing, Marco closed his eyes and concentrated on his breathing, relaxing tense muscles.

It had been weeks since he'd had to resort to sticking a pin in his hand to achieve the proper meditative state.

He let the bellow of his lungs be the loudest thing in the world, drowning out his worries. He descended into a place of peace and, there, was enveloped by the streaming trance.

In his mind's eye, the silver currents of his spirit woke, shimmering with his lifeforce. He strained and they split off into dimmer deltas, overflowing their banks and his body. Fighting against their swirl of resistance, he forced them toward the globe.

In his mind's eye, he saw them sink into the relic. It brightened. From an ember to a brand, drinking energy until it blazed-

He risked a peek.

His mind's eye was a liar. The glow globe sat, exactly as it always did, dark and lifeless. He'd done nothing.

Sagging on his cushion, he puffed in frustration.

"Perhaps we could get me a crystal," he suggested hopefully. "They make streaming easier, right?"

"Quit the opposite," Justin objected. "A well-made crystal makes streaming that much harder."

He stared, aghast. "Why would anyone use them, then?"

Justin's dark eyes sparkled with suppressed humor.

"Let us say you are a talented but inexperienced streamer who must mend a broken bone. The healing requires two minor sigils to be used simultaneously. Grasp, from the major sigil, Root. And its intersect with the major sigil of Growth, called Recovery.

"Talented streamer though you are, it is nearly impossible to manifest two sigil structures at once. A healer might know the hybrid sigil, Hamato's Bridge – which was developed specifically for this situation – but you do not. So, what do you do?"

He bit his lip. "I carry the injured person to Keeper Justin?"

The priest looked him wryly up and down.

Though Marco was nearly twelve, his Kender blood would keep him short and he was, as yet, sinewy and devoid of shoulders.

He sighed. "I use a crystal?"

"You use a crystal," the keeper confirmed, drawing one from his sleeve. Marco duly accepted the violet gem.

"Several materials can accept and conduct energy. Purified metals are very useful for wardsmithing, once engraved with the proper sigils. Infused gems can be used to power other, static constructs. Hold that crystal up to the light. What do you see?"

He turned the faceted disc toward the open window.

"It's filled with filaments. Like a glittery ball of yarn."

"Nodes," the keeper explained. "The crystals are custom grown by the Temple *Factori*. By manifesting a sigil *through* the crystal, the streamer connects the nodes with energy and primes the crystal with that structure or 'memory'. As long as it is fed sufficient power, the sigil remains manifest. This allows the streamer access to multiple sigils at once – at a commensurate cost in lifeforce."

Marco stared at the gem in wonder.

"High quality crystals have layers, or gantries, each capable of retaining one sigil. Single gantry crystals take a handful of years to grow. What you're holding is a *six* gantry crystal."

Eyes wide, Marco gentled his hold immediately.

"Not to worry," the keeper laughed, pinching it from his slack grip, "they're quite hardy. Just don't hammer any nails with one."

So much for his crystal idea.

"Don't pout," the keeper chided. "Now, try again."

Feeling rebellious, he nevertheless closed his eyes.

Corralling his errant thoughts and chasing off his frustrations took longer this time. Eventually, he settled into a brittle trance.

His discontented spirit churned and he drew off its spume, struggling to stand his ground as it gushed outward.

Father Justin had said that this should be difficult, so he imagined it difficult. But he could visualize it all just as well without the gritting and straining. Which probably meant he wasn't doing much of anything except deluding himself.

The moment of doubt threatened to upset the trance. He shook it off as his lifeforce approached the glow globe.

Long moments passed while he shoved power into it.

A warm light spilled over his closed eyelids.

Gasping, he snapped out of the trance.

The glow globe sat, dull and unpowered. Outside, the half-mast sun had sunk past the window frame to fall across his face.

"Forgot to draw the drapes," the keeper muttered, getting up.

Dejection crashed over Marco. He collapsed off his cushion and unto his back. The over-bright daylight had teared up his eyes and he hid them beneath his sleeve.

The empath spoke softly from across the room.

"I have never seen anyone work so hard at mastering the streaming disciplines. But I think it is past time we took a break."

Marco's breath hitched and he felt his traitorous bottom lip curl at this. He did not trust his voice not to betray him if he spoke.

"Your peers have all moved on to other fields of study and you fall further and further behind by the day. You are a talented student, Marco, and I delight in teaching you. But I cannot continue to do so at the expense of your broader education."

His streaming aspirations wilted and crumbled.

"We shall continue these classes, if you so choose, but at a more sedate pace. *While* you pursue one of the set curriculums."

He was shocked into sitting up, not hiding his streaked cheeks.

The priest met his surprise with a slight smile. "Sound good?"

He gave a tearful nod.

The priest rubbed his palms together briskly.

"Excellent. Then, since your day just opened up tomorrow…"

MORNING FOUND MARCO beside the narrow arch of the Arbor Gate, damp grasses finding the chinks in his sandals. Juggling his scribe's board, he blew on his hands. Two masha'na gate guards, resplendent in orange and umber, ignored him and the cold both.

"Good, you're on time."

He turned.

Modest gray robes hid the priestly purple ones and the plain walking staff betrayed no hint of gilt. The wandering prophets of old were depicted so, in the sacred texts, but for one detail.

"You like my hat?" the keeper noticed him staring.

The straw monstrosity had a fraying brim and a bobbled crown.

One of the masha'na rescued him from having to reply.

"Off to conquer the unrighteous, father?"

"Alas," the keeper sighed, "my smiting stick has run off."

"Just as well," the gate guard snorted, producing her key.

"Mm," her companion added. "If the keeper took up smiting…"

"…we'd soon run out of the unrighteous," she agreed.

Shocked by the irreverence – and the keeper's easy acceptance of it – he kept his head down and trailed after the priest. His sandals slapped loudly inside the passage undercutting the wall.

"Why not use the main gate, father?"

"I can't stomach all that flash and fanfare, so early in the morning. Today, I'd like to walk small."

Not really understanding, he let it lie.

"Holler when you want back in," the masha'na advised.

A narrow belt of greenery rimmed the outer walls. Beyond it, the streets heaved. He was no stranger to crowds. He queued alongside hundreds, for prayer and meals, daily. Yet, as he plunged into the throng, he experienced tumult. Like that time he'd surfaced beneath the lily pond's water spout, he felt turned around and tumbled about. Noise gushed and everyone moved at cross-purposes. He took three steps and bumped into as many people.

Panicked, he grabbed ahold of the keeper's cloak.

The straw hat turned. "Mm. A quieter thoroughfare, yes?"

Fearful of the jostle, hugging his scribe's board, he held tight as the priest towed him along. They broke into abrupt calm.

A less crowded street, he saw. Lined by houses, not hawkers.

"There, now. That wasn't so bad, was it?" the keeper soothed.

"Like being inside a waterfall," he admitted.

The keeper laughed. "You're doing fine. Come on…"

Embarrassed, he left an arm's length between them.

"Where are we going?" he finally dared.

"The harbor. An old acquaintance of mine is a ship's captain of renown. He is widely traveled and has a fine eye for rare and collectible texts. For a premium, he reserves me first pick."

Premium. He knew the word... "Like a goodwill offering?"

"I should say not! Rasibeal is, first and foremost, a mercer."

Coin was an abstract to him. Novices paid their way in devotion and elbow grease. He'd never handled so much as a copper.

"Where does the money come from?" he wondered.

"As a Keeper of the Faith, I have a sizable discretionary fund."

"The Temple has money?"

The keeper's tone spoke volumes, "Oh, yes."

"A lot of money?" he guessed.

"As much again as the Empire itself." The keeper eyed him wryly. "But gold never slaked a parched soul. Remember that."

He nodded dutifully, hoping there wouldn't be a test.

Foot traffic was picking up again.

"The harbor isn't far. We're coming up on the fish market." The priest considered him. "Do we need to go around?"

Trying to radiate certainty, he shook his head.

"Alright. Stay close..."

He weathered the thickening throng better this time. Though he was all but walking on the priest's heels, he kept his hands to himself. His lack of height meant he couldn't see much, but he noticed when the air became redolent with raw and rotten fish.

"Hail, priest!" a vendor called, waving a heavy cleaver.

"And good morning to you!" the keeper returned.

"A blessing, priest!" entreated a passerby, carrying a keg.

"Goddess go with you!" the keeper complied, hand upraised.

"What news, father?" a woman huffed, flipping griddle cakes.

"Another beautiful day in the goddess's country!"
"How 'bout a prayer for fair weather?" enquired a fisherman.
"Have pity on the farmers, my son," the keeper admonished.
"Here you go, dearie…" an apple was pressed on him.
He stared after the old lady and her basket.
"Thank you!" he called belatedly.
He met the keeper's smiling eyes.
"Do all these people know you, father?"
"They recognize me as a servant of Helia, Marco."
He pointed. "That fishmonger there just called you by name."

The keeper modestly adjusted his hat. "*Unity through faith* works both ways, Marco. Now come on. We're close."

Stuffing the apple inside his inner robe, he followed.

As they neared the harbor, he caught glimpses of masts and rigging rising above the rooftops. The great stone piers wended slowly into view. From his lessons, he knew the harbor to be one of the engineering feats of the Old Empire – after the Lily Tower and the Imperial Palace. But it paled before the dark green sea. Mesmerized, he watched the waves – usually still from atop the Temple walls – surge and swell. Abruptly, it dawned on him how little he'd seen of the world, content inside his novice's cell.

"There," the keeper pointed. "That's where we're going."

He gawped.

Many ships bobbed beside the dock. Some were sleek, exuding a sense of speed. Others were great, wallowing tubs. He didn't know enough to tell which were local but some were obviously outlandish. One had ribbed sails, lavishly painted: A Jade Islands vessel, judging by the jaguar so depicted. Another boasted not one or two but three hulls, bridged by spars and netting.

The vessel the keeper approached was the largest. No, wait…

"What are *those*?" he breathed. A seawall secluded a section of harbor. The ships moored there were enormous. And menacing.

"A squadron of the Imperial fleet, probably on shore leave."

"What are those things, stuck to their fronts?"

"Rams."

He frowned. "As in, 'male sheep'?"

"As in, a scuttled ship," the keeper answered gravely.

"Oh..." He'd look it up, later.

"Here we are!"

Distracted by the distant warships, he hadn't noticed the nearing gangplank. He counted three rows of portholes and twice as many masts. The vessel's name was painted in bold, Ribald script.

"'The Isus Spear,'" he translated.

"Well done," the keeper complimented. Turning from him, the priest cupped hands to his mouth. "Ahoy the Spear!"

A sun browned sailor in knee breeks peered over the rail.

"Ho, ye se'f," the man returned in an unknown language.

"Permission to come aboard?"

"Wit chor berd'nis 'ere, dan?" the man enquired.

"I'm Keeper Justin, here at your captain's invitation."

"O, ay? Bedr'n git ye se'f op 'ere, dan."

The keeper motioned for him to follow. The wooden ramp wobbled alarmingly beneath them, though the priest didn't seem to notice. Marco risked extending his scribe's board for balance.

"Wol' wit' mah," said the sailor. "Tak' ye ta'e cap'n ah wheel."

"Very kind of you," the keeper acknowledged. They trailed the bowlegged man to the rear of the ship, down shallow stairs and a cramped corridor, to an artfully carved door.

"Wet ye 'ere," the sailor commanded and disappeared inside.

"What language was he speaking, father?"

The keeper turned to him in surprise. "Why, Common."

He blinked. "That didn't sound like Common."

"He does have a harsh accent," the keeper conceded.

He marveled. In just a half bell, he'd learned three entirely new things: Tellar's streets buzzed as busily as the Temple bee-cotes; the ocean was caught in constant flux; and sailors spoke as though they wished to leave their words behind. Not a bad day's study.

The door opened. "Cap'n 'al see ye. Irf yeh'l f'low mah?"

Marco stared at the man's lips, concentrating on every syllable.

"Lead on," the keeper agreed.

Eyeing Marco askance, the sailor led them inside and left.

"Ah, Keeper Justin," a rich baritone greeted, straining the owner's silk shirt. Oiled ringlets and a fanciful mustachio framed a sharp smile. Buckled boots clomped nearer.

"An' who be this?"

"Captain Puttin, meet Marco, my ward."

His chest swelled at being publicly named so.

"Ah," the captain drawled. "An' were ye thinkin' o' sellin' 'im tae me, perchance? I could use me a new cabin boy..."

The seafarer's hand rasped speculatively over stubble.

Meeting the man's dark eyes, Marco quailed.

The keeper chortled good-naturedly, "Buying him would bankrupt you, Rasibeal. No, he's merely here to examine the new merchandise. Young eyes, if you will, to spare my tired ones."

He blinked at that. No ailment of the eye could stop someone armed with Heli-made lenses. And the keeper had access to some of the best artificers of the Temple *Factori*.

"Squintin' by candlelight'll spoil your eyes, priest," the captain said, hefting a heavy chest. "Try getting' out tae sea some."

The footlocker was duly carried over to a bolted-down desk.

"'Ere ye go, swabby," the man invited. "Have at it."

The keeper pulled a rolled scroll from his sleeve.

"Marco, this is a list of texts I own and subjects that intrigue me. Go through the captain's chest and set aside anything you find that is either similar or interesting."

"Yes, father," he stammered, overawed by the responsibility.

"Interim-wise," the captain continued, "there's somethin' down in me hold I'd like yer expert opinion on, priest…"

"Find me on deck when you're done, Marco…"

And then, quite suddenly, he was alone. Without the captain in it, the cabin didn't seem as cramped. Littered charts, abandoned instruments and scattered coins chased chunks of chalk across the desk. Brine wafted from the open window.

The gently pitching planks weren't helping his nerves.

Steadying himself, he set up his scribe's board. The keeper's catalogue proved lengthy. A list of subjects the scholar *wasn't* interested in might have been shorter.

He persevered.

The captain's chest was a trove. But the treasures were packed around by dross. He shook his head over the time and expense that had produced a leather-bound and engraved text entitled, *The Migratory Birds of the Greater Ren.*

He recognized a scroll of wooden lathes, seared with runic letters, as Hidchi. But he couldn't decipher the list of ingredients and instructions. If not for the gruesome depictions, it might have been a fish stew recipe. Feeling his soul imperiled, he set it aside.

A collection of Renali fables followed suite. So did a dog-eared account dedicated to the diseases of sheep.

He grinned as he regarded a Rasrini title, *A Treatise on the Neglect of Technology.* The keeper would want to see that. *The Re-emergence of Magic by P. Lorant*, a Renali volume, and *A Philosopher's View of Religion*, also joined that illustrious pile. He hesitated briefly before adding a Purli scroll labeled *Properties of*

Poisonous Blue-Vein Cacti. Whether or not blue-veined cacti existed beyond the Purlian wastes, two other texts on harmful plants existed on the keeper's list. He added it.

The remainder of the footlocker proved less fruitful. He turned over a Renali volume, *The Recollected Adventures of Eris Bolk – Master Swordsman,* twice before putting it in the discard pile.

He meticulously copied down those titles, in case the keeper wanted to see them. Having neatly stacked their purchases, he stoppered his ink bottle and collapsed his scribe's board.

Then he stepped out to the deck and into some commotion.

The sailor from before was bodily blocking access to the deck, shouting angrily at the pier. Two figures in official gray cloaks and helms were shouting back. As he watched, one marched determinedly up the gangplank. More crewmen clustered together. The uniformed man drew up, baring a hand's breadth steel.

The sailors jumped, setting their feet and suddenly brandishing knives and belaying pins.

His heart raced. Unless someone did something right *now*-

"Hold there!"

The bellow stilled everyone.

Captain Puttin rose from the cargo hold, earrings aglint.

He sighed in relief when he saw Keeper Justin following.

"Cap'n...!" was as much as he understood of the sailor's garbled explanation, though it seemed thick with accusation.

"I see," the captain drawled, stepping up to the rail. "An' what brings the city watch tae me berth? The docks're the jurisdiction o' the port authority an' me dues are paid up."

Watchmen?

He'd never seen one. They didn't operate on Temple grounds.

"Apologies, captain," the watchwoman on the pier shouted up. "We were told Keeper Wisenpraal might be found here."

It took him a moment to place the keeper's family name.

Brows quirked in question, the priest stepped up to the rail.

"You heard correctly, lieutenant. What can I do for you?"

"Sir!" the watchwoman's relief was palpable. "Commander Greystone asks to see you, sir. At your first possible convenience."

There was no mistaking the meaning of 'first possible convenience'. Marco frowned. He'd never heard anyone called 'sir' before. The correct address for a hierarch was 'your holiness'.

"It would seem," the keeper mused to the captain, holding out a hand, "I am needed elsewhere. Until next time?"

"Hmm." The seafarer eyed the watchmen suspiciously. "Look after yourself, priest. I'll see your purchases get delivered."

The keeper turned to the gangplank. "Gentlemen?"

Sailors parted reluctantly to let them pass.

Eyeing the watchmen, one spat pointedly over the side.

"Sheathe that sword, constable!" the lieutenant warned.

Her comrade turned stiffly to precede the priest down the plank. Trying to look small, Marco scrambled after.

"What is this all about, lieutenant?" the keeper asked.

The woman was expressionless. "Commander didn't say, sir."

"Didn't say? Or didn't *need* to say?"

The blockish woman chewed her lip. "A reading, sir."

Bemused, the priest glanced at the upset sailors.

"And the Temple had no empaths to spare?"

"Commander said to bring *you*, sir, or no one at all."

The keeper's expression closed. He gave Marco a quick glance.

"Alright. Lead on, lieutenant."

"Sir!"

The watchmen's shouts cleared them a path through the press. Marco blundered along, wondering what was going on.

A *reading*, the lieutenant had said. And she wasn't after a homily. Being an empath was a mandatory endorsement to the Tempe. It gathered all empaths to itself, ensuring their gifts were used in accordance with the oaths and Helia's will. The keeper was said to be one of the most talented empaths of their generation…

He frowned. Did the watch want to use the keeper's extra faculty for ferreting out lies? Was that even allowed?

Empaths weren't mind-readers – the keeper would scoff at the very suggestion. The extra sense simply allowed perception of emotions. It could no more plumb a lie's particulars than taste could determine which tree had produced a particular pear.

These thoughts busied him all the way to the Watch House – a drab building identified by big, rusting letters that wept down the once-grand exterior. Guards flanked the entrance.

"Brace yourself, father," one muttered as they passed.

The inside was a flurry of activity. Gray-uniformed men and women scuttled through the chaos. Boots stomped, chairs scraped, parchment crumpled, chains clanked, and – everywhere – voices were raised in enquiry. It was worse than the fish market.

It took effort to see past the grime, to the carved columns and elegant banisters: remnants of some previous purpose.

Their escort sidled through the crowded desks and up a grand staircase. The racket looked no better from above. Marco mentally added a prayer, for those who toiled here, to his evening quota.

Their guide knocked at an unmarked office.

"Come!"

She held the door for them but spoke to the occupant.

"Keeper's here, sir."

The commander stood to greet them. "Thank you for coming."

Marco unobtrusively took up a runner's station by the door, albeit, on the wrong side of it. He shouldn't, but he was curious. And the keeper seemed disinclined to chase him out.

The commander was a trim but tired looking man, his stiff back at odds with the bags beneath his eyes. The space was sparse, paperwork stacked in neat piles on a battered desk. A gaudy letter opener – its intricate gift-ribbon dusty – lay in a box of bent quills. The foot of the washing stand, in the far corner, was spotted around with wet. It bore a folding razor and a damp towel.

The men exchanged perfunctory greetings. The keeper sat.

"Your officers seem to think there is something extraordinary about this reading? I'm flattered you would think of me."

"Don't be flattered, keeper. Be frightened. Helia knows, I am."

"Tell me," the priest said in all seriousness.

"Two of my constables were called to the Warren to investigate a domestic disturbance. A rare occurrence in and of itself. Housing there is informal. The inhabitants are not in the habit of involving the authorities. But this was a putrid smell in one of the tenements. My men were expecting to find a body. An addict who had overdosed on banal, perhaps. Or some forgotten war widow or veteran, left to ripen. What they found instead-"

Abruptly, the commander glanced at Marco, standing by the door. The officer cleared his throat, skipping ahead.

"Suffice to say, we don't know what to make of it. We arrested a suspect on the scene, but he's not spoken a word."

"The law," the keeper said, at length, "will not allow the results of a reading to aid in a conviction."

The commander was shaking his head.

"I'm not worried about a conviction, keeper. I want to know where to deliver our prisoner. To the place where the wardens wear helmets? Or to the one where they wear habits?"

Habits? Marco wondered. *Like the penitent priestesses wear?*

"You suspect he is mentally disturbed?"

"Oh, I *know* he's disturbed. After seeing what he did, *I'm* disturbed. I want you to tell me whether he's *possessed*."

Marco suppressed a gasp. The keeper leaned back.

"There hasn't been a verified case of possession in centuries."

The set of the commander's jaw didn't change.

At long last, the keeper agreed, "Alright."

The commander stood. "This way…"

They were led down dank spiral stairs.

"You're not holding him in the general lock-up?" wondered the keeper, who was obviously familiar with the Watch House layout.

"Word of what he's done has spread," the commander said, lighting their way with a lantern. "Not even the most callous of cellmates would hesitate to pulp this man's pate."

"I see."

"I've had to carefully pick the guards I post down here, too…"

A single watchman hove into view, outlined by the light of a lone lamp. A thick, barred door was etched into the shadows. The inset grill was cautiously inspected before any keys jangled.

The portal swung inward.

Marco gulped in apprehension.

Eyeing him, the keeper hesitated. "Is it safe?"

The commander nodded distractedly. "He's fully restrained and not the talkative type. There should be little danger."

So he followed the two men into the cell, his eyes darting.

The stench hit him first. The first-year Mending students had once been required to wash maggots in class. This was like that, only stronger. Strangling a cough, he covered his nose and mouth with his sleeve and jumped as the door clanged shut behind him.

"This is how we found him. He has said nothing. He has not moved. Not even to resist or run when we arrested him."

A burly watchman stood attendance over a bedraggled figure.

It was scrawny, seated bound by the wrists to a heavy table. Hunched shoulders poked through grime encrusted rags. Greasy hair overhung dull eyes. Sallow skin, a weak chin and a coin-sized bald spot made the shackles seem oversized.

"If you would, father," the commander invited.

"Marco?"

He jumped, again, as the keeper recalled his attention. He plastered himself into to the corner where the priest pointed.

Sweeping up gray over-robes, his mentor sat.

"My name is Justin. Can you tell me your name?"

The man betrayed no sign of having heard.

With a look, the priest lofted the question at the commander.

"Neighbors identified him as Perner Meum."

"Perner?" the keeper tried. "Do you know where you are?"

Stillness.

"Can you tell me where you were last night?"

Silence.

"What is the last thing you remember, Perner?"

When the man still failed to stir, the keeper grimaced.

Assessing the room, his mentor's gaze lingered on him, perhaps considering sending him away.

"From here on," the priest warned them all, "no noise, please."

The cleric folded his hands and bowed his head.

In his corner, Marco copied his mentor, mouthing a prayer.

The keeper's breathing was the loudest thing in the room. Slowing. Slowing... The priest sunk in upon himself, face and shoulders slack, questing toward Perner Meum.

The moment dragged on.

Not even the buzz of the main hall penetrated the dark stone.

Spots swam before Marco's eyes, his galloping heart outstripping the slow breath he was emulating. A droplet of icy sweat startled him by rattling down his ribcage.

There was a suggestion of motion.

A rope of the prisoner's tangled hair swung almost imperceptibly. The man's head rose at a torturously slow rate. From amid the greasy coils, empty eyes played over the keeper.

Meeting them, Marco felt like a mouse overtaken by an owl-shaped shadow. The watchman beside him stiffened. The commander surreptitiously reached for an absent sword.

Father Justin placidly returned that horrible stare.

Marco ached to pull the priest away but could not move.

The silence built whilst his heart battered away at his ribs.

At last, Father Justin broke the spell, sitting back with a sigh. As though released, Meum's muscles slackened, his head sinking to hide his eyes. Stupor reclaimed him. Tension fled the room.

Stiffly, the keeper stood, his expression severe.

"Show me," the priest commanded, "where this happened."

COMMANDER GREYSTONE LED them to the crime scene himself.

Marco strained his gait, keeping up with the two taller men. The watchwoman-lieutenant brought up the rear, her expression grave.

He didn't dare ask about the reading, but he wished the commander would. The man marched, brow crinkled and hands clasped at his back. Possibly he didn't have the nerve, either.

Concentrating on his feet, Marco noticed when they exchanged cobbles for packed dirt. The sun abandoned his back and he looked up in surprise. They'd come a long way. The stone buildings here were pocked and poor, their upper stories no more than nests of ramshackle timbers. Laden washing lines conspired against the light, their loads hanging drab and desolate.

A nearby alley brimmed with refuse. A fugue of flies fanned the stink into the street. He averted his gaze, eyes hunting for a clean surface to rest on. He resolved to breathe through his mouth.

Obviously there were no ready hands here to sweep and polish.

He knew the scriptures as well as any novice. He paid attention to the sermons, mostly. Words he'd heard many times – but never understood – were offering themselves up for re-evaluation.

Here, he sensed, lay the difference between the Temple's self-imposed, *simple* life – and a desperately *poor* one.

"Here," the commander brought them to a halt.

The first two stories were crumbling brick and rotten mortar. Two more, of timber, sat askew and bulged like cankers. The building was little different from those around it.

Save for the watchman standing guard at its entry.

The air inside had been breathed many times and then baked into the brick. Despite this, there was no evidence of life in the close confines. The swaybacked stairs were silent. The surrounding rooms felt hollowed, like they'd been abandoned in a hurry.

They reached the first of the wooden landings and the commander turned them down the short passage. What they'd come to see hid behind one of these two doors...

"Sirs?" the watchwoman said uncertainly, her eyes on him.

"Yes," the keeper recalled. "Marco, kindly wait there."

It stung. The keeper had never been... *brusque* with him before.

He retreated quickly to the gloomy corner atop the stairs.

The commander led the procession through the first door and out of sight, leaving Marco out in the hall.

He leaned in his corner, listening to their muffled footsteps and murmuring. Holding his breath, he strained his ears.

Beneath him, the wooden floor exuded heat.

Cooking in his novice's robes, he wiped his clammy brow. Dust motes broiled lazily in spars of light. The air was turgid and hard to breathe. Abruptly lightheaded, he leaned against the creaking wall. Wool stuffed his ears. Purple spots cavorted across his vision.

As though he were back on the ship, the planks tilted beneath his feet, heaving nearer. He realized he was on his knees. Mortar dust and urine-stink assaulted him. He stared at the woodgrain, trying to right his breathing. Among the purple blotches, one bloomed a brilliant red.

Stunned, he watched two more drops of blood join the first. He fumbled at his nostrils, his fingers coming away crimson.

A creak sounded.

Blearily, he raised his head.

The door rocked again, on its stiff leather hinges.

Its hot breath rolled over him and his eyes teared.

Gripped by a terrible urgency, he coughed his way upright.

There was danger there, where the keeper was.

His sight swayed and he swallowed back a rush of nausea.

Gritting his teeth, he forced himself to step forward. The passage stretched, drawing the doorway to an impossible distance.

A second wretched gust buffeted him, stealing his breath.

He weathered it. The ringing in his ears splintered, mimicking the clunk of coins down many steps.

Another sepulchral breath scoured him, sharpening the metallic noise into a screech. His front knee buckled and his fingernails dug splinters from the wood.

He fetched up against the opposite wall, glaring at the door across from him. With a growl he pushed off…

And half-fell through the frame.

"Marco, kindly wait there."

Instantly, Justin cursed his lack of tact. He gentled his tone but had no more to say. He would apologize later. Right now, he needed all of his faculties. If not for the quick-witted watchwoman, he'd have walked through that door with the boy in tow.

He'd have done better to have his ward escorted back to the Temple. Outside of its walls, the old habit – of having the boy always within eyesight – had unexpectedly resurged.

Greystone motioned him ahead. Barely breathing, he complied.

The tenement trapped the day's heat. Inside the apartment, oven-baked air plastered his robes to his skin. On it rose a stink that pricked sweat across his back.

The interior was just two rooms. A paneless window dimly lit a living area. The way the frame had been shored up said it hadn't been installed thoughtlessly. He twitched the faded curtain off its nail. A thin bar of sunlight stirred angry motes.

The low table was cobbled together from an old crate. Upset bowls and a congealed dinner stained it. A crock of wildflowers, miraculously left standing, cried wilted petals onto the tabletop.

Scattered cushions had provided seating and, by their layout, bedding. A stuffed toy lay, forlorn, on a stack of blankets.

He turned.

A battered oil stove. A balding broom. A tin washing-up bucket.

Only the blood gave the lie to the domestic surrounds.

The parched wood had lapped it up. Black spatters and sprays licked the walls. A solid streak – drag marks – lolled from beneath the bedroom curtain.

Steeling himself, he trailed after it.

The second room had become a slaughterhouse.

He clenched his teeth against the bile burning his throat.

"We left it as it lay," the commander offered from behind him.

He nodded mutely, seeing why.

"Neighbors said Meum works as a butcher, down by the dockside stockyards and cattle pens."

Ah, yes. Butcher's tools – knives, hooks, mallets – could be spied, gummed to the floor by gristle.

"A quiet man, they said. Kind. Well-liked."

The straw mattress had soaked up a good deal of blood. Else they might have stood ankle deep. The remainder had drained through the cracks in the warped boards.

"He had a wife. Three children. Two small girls…"

For a moment, the commander's calm cracked. There was no visible hint, other than that small hitch. But Justin felt the man – a kiln of fear and fury – before professionalism closed up once more.

"…and a newborn. A boy."

Finally, he raised his gaze to the carcasses, slowly swiveling on their hooks: *A wife. Two small girls.*

The mutilations were made more grotesque by the gray and bloating flesh. It was hard to imagine that the scattered pieces added up to three whole people. But the hardest to look at was the little figure. Whole. Nailed to the bedstead.

A newborn. Merciful goddess…

He pushed the prayer aside. There would be time for that later.

"And these?" he indicated the symbols. They were scrawled across every bit of exposed wood and scored into the victims' skins – goddess grant they'd been dead at the time.

"I was hoping *you*'d answer that," the commander growled. "By all accounts, Meum is illiterate. And this certainly looks like no writing I've ever seen. You don't recognize any of it?"

He shook his head. "They remind me of Hidchi runes. But these are closer to pictographs…"

He trailed off.

"What?" the commander prompted.

"Nothing," he lied, unwilling to explain.

Part of being an empath was mastering your *own* emotions. And his were stirring with primal panic at the sight of these scribbles.

They didn't belong. And neither did whoever had drawn them.

"Order your men to touch nothing and let no one near. This scene is being ceded to the Temple's jurisdiction."

"Murder is a watch matter," the commander objected mildly.

"Yes, it is," he allowed. *But heresy is not.*

The word hung between them. Unspoken. Adding to the stink.

Resentment pricked the commander's thoughts – but made it nowhere near the man's face. Instead, long-held resignation surfaced. The man had expected this. Was that why they'd insisted on Justin? He'd always gone out of his way to aid the watch…

"I'll do my best to keep you informed of our investigation."

The commander cautiously inclined his head. "And Meum?"

"Is not possessed," Justin hedged.

After all, possession implied some sort of occupancy. Perner Meum had been hollowed out. Emptied. What remained was a husk of flesh, absent either will or soul.

There had been an echo, though, in the darkness. The disquiet it had woken in him was what had driven him to see this place.

He eyed the unfamiliar script.

If wild witchcraft were taking root in Tellar, the Temple needed to know. But he could not voice such suspicions before a layman.

A commotion caught his ear.

An unwelcome sensation washed up against his extra sense. One he'd not felt in many long years. It was leaner now. Less vicious. But still much too much. It registered a moment before Marco tumbled through the door, tear-streaked and confused.

"Father?" his ward gurgled, casting about.

Too late, he grabbed at the door hanging. The boy's gaze moved past him. Found the bedroom and the bloodbath within.

The boy's terror rose like an ocean. He found himself choking in it, drowning. He knew what came next.

"Grab him!" he gasped, tottering.

The lieutenant was nearest. She'd already started toward Marco. But, at his command, her concerned hands turned serious. Even so, she was not nearly fast enough.

There was a dull thud as his ward bounced from the hallway wall. A mad scrabbling sounded toward the stairs.

"Marco! *Stop!*" his laden command bounced off the boy's panic. Its backlash made the lieutenant stagger.

He pelted for the door, the commander on his heels. Gathering his accursed robes, he pounded down the stairs at an unsafe speed.

"Constable," the commander bellowed ahead, "stop the boy!"

They burst out into relative brightness to find the watchman picking himself out of the dust. There was no sign of Marco.

"He went right over top of me," the baffled man gaped.

"Which way?" the commander snapped.

"Dunno, sir," the man cringed. "I was on my nose for that part."

He turned a deaf ear, his sense of the boy dwindling. One thread among millions. Fading… fading…

Gone.

"I don't suppose he'll be able to find his own way home?"

He shook his head. How could he explain that, even had Marco known the first thing about Tellar, the boy might be incapable of forming any desire to return to the Temple.

Awkwardly, the commander consoled him. "We'll find him."

Yes, he worried. *But will he still be himself when we do…?*

Chapter 3 – Eclipse

If Grace and Perdition are not simple intellectual constructs but – as the scriptures suggest – also real planes of existence, how many other planes might not exist? Further, is death the only passage to these otherworldly realms? Examples can be cited from scripture – see footnotes – of historical personages making the transition whilst alive. And, further, if such travel is possible, why are there no recent records of attempts to breach the veil between worlds?

~ *Pella Monop, 'Musings on the Material Worlds'. Draft, incomplete.*

There was running… And then there was not.

Marco wasn't certain what had happened to the time in between. He slowed, straining to stay conscious. His lungs burned and his throat was raw. His heart filled his ears and his spleen had set its teeth in his side. On jellied legs, he sank against a wall.

He threw up.

And then he passed out.

Reality reared as a hazy tunnel, a view of his feet at its end.

He'd lost a sandal, he saw. He reached for his gnawed foot and noticing the heels of his hands were scuffed. Had he fallen?

His shin throbbed and his knee was stiff. He hiked up his robes to see he'd lost skin on both and they were already scabbing.

His fingers were a mess of splinters. He vaguely recalled getting those. In the Warren. With the keeper…

Next thing, he was face-down and dry-heaving. His ribs creaked with the effort of expelling the horrible image.

Oh, Helia, those poor people…

It couldn't be true. He'd seen wrong.

People just didn't *do* that to people.

He needed to find the keeper. With a few wise words, Justin would defang the nightmare and make it all make sense.

Spitting miserably, he rose. He was in a rubbish-littered alley. People-sounds drifted from the street on a slightly fresher breeze. He moved toward its twilight glow.

It would have been too much to ask, to step out within sight of the Lily Tower.

Unfamiliar roads curved to his left and right. The buildings matched the cobbles in their state of disrepair. Second-hand sunlight painted everything a rusty red. He turned slowly, hoping for a glimpse of the Spire, rising above the crusted roofs.

Nothing.

Haggard figures pattered past, their heads held low. A few strode purposefully, wearing indiscriminate scowls.

He hastily dropped his gaze.

He'd never shied from speaking to anyone in his life. Yet the prospect of asking for directions – here – filled him with dread.

Brine wafted on the wind. Perhaps, if he found the pier, he could retrace the way he'd come with the keeper.

There seemed a general flow to the foot traffic. Tugging off his lone sandal, he joined it. He needed to find someone in uniform. Or, better yet, a local Temple. But, for a city that practically tolled at midday, Tellar seemed suddenly devoid of houses of worship.

He limped along, feeling unfriendly eyes on him.

A mutt, patchy with mange, limped from a nearby alley. He extended a hand toward it and it snapped at him with gray-flecked gums. An old woman, seated on a low step, cackled at his fright.

He hurried on, finding more people and even a few stalls.

These bore little resemblance to the morning's fish market. And, without the keeper, it was not nearly as forgiving.

"Watch it!" a man spat, though their contact could not possibly have hurt him as much as it had Marco.

His apology was plowed under by whatever hit his hip.

"Oi! Careful, you!"

"Sorry," he got out, before a laden barrow rammed his ankle.

"Out of the way, brat!" an urchin, not much older than himself, cussed and almost rolled over him.

He staggered.

"One side, boy!" Someone wrenched him around by his ear.

"Move, you!" a burly voice shoved him between the shoulders.

For a horrifying moment, he feared he would sprawl and be flattened by indifferent feet. He clutched at people in his panic. Curses rained down and someone slapped his head, hard.

"Sorry, sorry, sorry…" he chanted, pressing his way through.

He broke into relative calm. Peering from between his elbows, he saw he'd wedged himself in a gap between two stalls.

The vendor in his eye-line plunged her arm into a cask of water, coming up with a striped eel. The fish gaped as she impaled it, its ribbon-like length resisting as she threaded it onto a skewer. It was added to a dozen others, slowly browning on a grill.

Despite the cruelty, his twice-emptied stomach craved it.

His averted eyes fell on the fruit vendor next-door. The spotted bananas, wilting cabbages and wooden carrots seemed poor fare. But the wrinkled apples recalled to him his own apple, still bulging his inner robe. Hastily, he dug it out.

The glossy globe crunched crisply as he bit down.

"Thief!" the fat vendor shrieked, neck veins bulging.

He saw the misunderstanding immediately.

"Mmpf!" he explained, his mouth full.

"Thief!" the man lunged across the table, spittle flying.

He staggered out of reach of a stout cosh.

The crowd began to congeal around them. He saw a man, brandishing a length of wood, wade purposely toward him. Other eager faces were converging from the press.

Abandoning his apple, he bolted.

Sharp fingers hooked his hair but he tore free, bouncing from person to person in his haste. Startled oaths tracked his progress but he could feel his pursuers gaining. They had superior shoving power. If he stayed in the crowd, they'd catch up.

An alley beckoned.

Given a clear path, he rose onto his toes and *ran*. But, even with fright dimming his hurts, he hobbled. A backward glance showed two long-legged vigilantes gaining on him. On a good day, he might have outrun them. But this was the worst day of his life.

He careened around a corner.

"Pssst!"

The urgent hiss broke his stride. Something hauled back on his collar. He glimpsed the inside of a wooden crate. Then a tarp rustled and he was alone in the dark, save for his haggard breathing and the sharp weight, pinning him down.

"Shhh!" it said, a hand clamping across his mouth.

Loud footsteps rounded the corner.

"Where'd he go? Did y'see 'im?"

"'e came 'round 'ere, din' he?"

"Must've shot over that there fence!"

"C'm on! We can catch 'im on the other side!"

Their rushed footfalls faded.

"Wow," the darkness whispered. "*That* was close."

The tarp was torn aside; light flooded in. A wealth of frazzled hair stuck up around a freckled face. She flashed him a missing front tooth.

"Mpff!" he objected.

"Huh?" she freed his jaw.

"*Your knee...*" he wheezed desperately.

"Oh," she said. "Sorry."

* * *

THE JAGGED ROCKS were salt slick and burned his bruised feet. Out in the surf, waves dashed themselves on the seawall, geysers spuming. They bore no relation to the docile waters Marco had seen, lapping beneath the docks that morning. The tide, she'd said. He'd learned of it, of course. But no one had bothered to describe the violent majesty of it.

"Hey!" Icy seawater splashed his face.

She scowled at him, up to her knees and elbows in the tide pool.

"Stop dawdling," she lisped, "or you'll bed-down hungry."

She'd introduced herself as Sunny, citing hair that might have been red once, under all that muck and grime.

"Sunny," he tried again, "please-"

"I'm not takin' you to the Temple."

"But *why* not?"

"'cause."

"That's not a proper reason!"

"Says who?" she challenged.

She was immune to his Temple-taught logic. "Everyone!"

"Everyone who?"

"What...? Everyone!"

"I haven't met everyone."

He gaped, dumbfounded. "But-"

"No. Now, get busy."

At a loss, he hefted the stick she'd given him. His robes stirred up a storm on the pool's bottom. Its rocky sides were festooned with mollusks in black-green half-shells. He reached down.

She didn't look up. "Not that one. Only the ones near the bottom. The ones that've breathed air will make you sick."

Sighing, he plunged deeper. Try as he might, he could pry not a single one of the little creatures from their perches.

"You 'ave to surprise 'em," she coached. "Don't wriggle 'round so much, elsewise they hold on tighter. Just see where's the best place..." she took careful aim, "an' go all at once..."

Beneath her ministrations, an armored creature came unstuck.

"Easy," she gave him her holed smile. "See?"

Despite her insistence, he could spy no 'best place' on any of the shells. He suspected she'd given him a bad stick.

Glaring, he took careful aim, and lunged. Seawater fountained.

She collapsed into hopeless giggles, watching the water drip from him. "You're the worst at this!"

Sand crunched as he ground his teeth. Through stinging eyes, he spotted something dark settle to the bottom.

"Aha!" he flourished the black limpet.

"Good," she begrudged. "Now, like this..." She speared the little creature, scraping it from its home. It was a lot harder than it looked. And the featureless lump writhed in tandem with his guilt.

"And now," she prompted, slurping the slimy invertebrate from its plate. Tossing the husk, she turned an expectant stare on him.

The beige blob sat heavily in his hand and on his conscience.

He couldn't eat *this*...

His stomach rumbled.

Easy for you to say, he thought, *you don't have eyes.*

Squeezing his own shut, he wrestled the morsel down his throat. It tasted of the sea. And salt. But, mostly, it tasted of snot. The tiny creature tried to cleave to his insides, like he was a new tidal pool.

He swallowed again. Gasped. Swallowed. Coughed.

"The trick," she chortled, "is to not chew."

He glared. She might have told him that *up front*.

"You eat this all the time?" He shuddered at the thought.

"Only when other pickin's are slim," she said, up to her elbows again. She made quick work of another shell. "This is better than nothin' but you can only eat a handful. Else you get the runs."

"The runs?"

She made a rude noise and an explosive gesture.

"Oh!" he ducked his head, embarrassed.

"I still can't believe," she said, with equal amounts admiration and scorn, "you ate that apple right in front of him."

"For the last time, I didn't steal that apple!"

She eyed him. "I'm gonna have to teach you to lie better."

"I swear, I didn't!"

"Now see – *that* was better."

"I'm not lying!"

"That was worse again."

He threw down his stick in frustration.

"We'd better get going," she warned. "Tide's almost here."

The sea had crept up on them while they'd been arguing.

His robe remained waterlogged despite strenuous efforts to wring it dry. Its bottom hem crusted white, sanding at his skin as he hurried after Sunny.

"Where are we going?"

"Home."

"The Temple?" he asked hopefully.

"No. *Home*. Why would I take you to the Temple?"

"It's where I live."

"It's where *priests* live," she scoffed. "Are you a priest?"

"Well..." Lying was a sin. "No. But..."

"Then you don't," she concluded. "Everyone knows that."

"'Everyone who?'" he pounced, usurping her own argument.

"Everyone who's worth listening to."

He frowned. *He* should have thought to say that.

"Please?" He resorted to begging.

She whirled. "D'you wanna stay here?! Alone?!"

She stood a hand taller than he and had an impressive glare.

Gulping, he gazed at the deserted beach. The bleak dunes, the darkening waves, the stinging wind... "No?"

"Then shut up about it, alright? And follow me."

She stomped off. After a moment, he trailed her.

"So," he tried, awkwardly, "where *do* you live?"

"Wherever I want," she proclaimed.

It finally dawned on him. "Sunny, do you not have a home?"

"Sure I do. Lots."

He slowed. "Where are your parents?"

An orphan himself, he was not entirely sure what parents actually *did* – beyond bustle about and be necessary.

"I got a dad out there somewhere," she mused. "*Probably*."

She gave him a hand up a steep slope.

"But it was only ever mama and me. It was nice. Food every day. Some friendly uncles. Not much shouting. A lot of the time I had to keep quiet and out of sight. But I'm good at that. We moved lots. The last place had a leaky roof. Mama got sick..."

Though her tone was casual, he saw her shoulders go taut.

"Mama stopped eating. The day she stopped breathing, I left."

He gaped at her back. "What about your uncles?"

She gave him a quizzical glance.

"They weren't *really* my uncles, silly. And, before she went, mama warned me to stay away from them. So I did."

He was silent as she led them among the ramshackle buildings.

"*I'm* an orphan," he admitted, at last.

"Oh, I tried the orphanage," she dismissed. "Didn't like it. The other kids were bigger'n me an' the nuns were mean. Want me to scrub floors for gruel? Ha! Now, *I* take care of me."

So saying, she clambered up onto a crate.

"What are you doing?"

"Sun's setting," she explained. "S'not safe on the ground after dark. Come on…"

He watched her shimmy up onto a roof. Hesitantly, he followed.

The crumbly tiles and sharp-edged gutter pipes proved less accommodating than the boughs of the Temple orchards. But, despite his sorry state, he was not about to be outdone by a girl.

By the time he flopped onto the roof, he was breathing hard.

"No time to nap," she prodded him with a toe. "Come on."

Groaning, he dragged himself after her. The salt had cured his feet, and the icy water had helped his knee. He managed a half-jog.

"Catch me if you can!" She pulled ahead.

He sped in pursuit, afraid he might lose her in the gloom. She combed confidently between chimneys, sidestepping smokestacks. In her wake, he ducked garroting wash lines and high-stepped over rusted nails and broken bottles. She skipped across the close-packed roofs and, after a moment's pause, so did he.

He drew lever with her. He was, he marveled, having fun.

They hurdled the roofs in tandem and she laughed aloud.

Cheating, she turned a sharp right and left him, scrambling to catch up. He tore after her, only to have her break abruptly in a different direction again. Grinning, he gained on her once more…

Without warning, she was flying.

Unable to halt his headlong sprint, he grit his teeth and followed. Beneath him, his shadow dropped six stories – *Holy hymns, that's high!* – and raced up the opposite wall to meet him. He didn't so much land as collapse.

Above the heaving of his chest, he heard her helpless laughter.

"Not funny!" he objected, his voice a bit thin.

Tears of mirth cut runnels through her grime. Well beyond words, she mimed his jump at him, pulling fish-eyed faces.

Scrambling up, he crossed sullen arms.

Against all convention, she *in*haled when she laughed. It was graceless. And infectious. An unwelcome smile spoiled his scowl.

For a moment, he forgot the horrors of the day. Up high, he let the last sliver of sunlight – the goddess's gift – lave him.

A sonorous note rolled across the rooftops. He spun toward it.

Taking their cue from Old Greencall, Tellar's countless other bells and gongs woke, voicing the city's evensong. But not before that deep, bronze throat-clearing had drawn his gaze.

The Temple!

The Lily Tower reared like a lighthouse, its summit still ablaze with the last touch of sun. The sprawling city hid its base. But, somewhere there, Keeper Justin waited.

"Sunny…" he pointed.

Her laughter had faded. He met her plaintive expression.

"What d'you want to go there for?!"

"You weren't planning for me to see it," he realized.

She didn't deny it, her jaw jutting at him.

"They'll worry about me," he explained. "They'll look for me."

"They'll stop," she assured him. "Eventually."

He shook his head. "Not Keeper Justin."

"Oh? Where is he, then?" her frown raked across the rooftops, as though the priest should pop up from a chimney. "Did he save you from that lynching? Did he teach you how to eat limpets? Will he show you a safe place to sleep? No! That's all *me*!"

She thumbed her thin chest, taking an angry step toward him.

"Sunny..." he argued, but had no idea what to say.

"It's not so bad out here," she promised. "Better, when you're alone. But you're alright-ish. I can show you-"

"It's where I belong," he forestalled.

She wiped her tear-streaked cheeks, no longer laughing.

Her fists bunched. "Then go."

"Sunny..."

"Go!" she raged, shoving him roughly.

"You can come with me-"

She kicked at the roof, showering him with debris. "Go!"

Her flushed glare dared him to speak again.

Under threat of further violence, he turned away.

The white spire stood out, starkly, in the darkness.

He paused after a few paces. "I'll come back for you."

She spat.

He loped away on leaden feet, angling towards the distant tower. After a score paces, he turned – but she had gone.

True night hid his surrounds, the spire a pale smear across the stars. The lantern-lit heart of the city was still far off.

Without Sunny to lead the way, clotheslines turned into tripwires and every plummet became a pitfall. Chimneys cast deep shadows that could conceal... a pair of glowing eyes – tracking him. The cat yowled, embarrassed at being seen, and sped off.

Unnerved, he quickened his pace, his ears perked.

Nighttime, in the Temple compound, was restful. But the city...

Coarse laughter gushed here and there, clinking with glass and sawing with music. The night was peppered with babies' cries and barking dogs. Loud crashes and screams drifted from afar.

Shoulders hunched against the unknown, he forged ahead.

The spire didn't seem to be getting any closer. Would the gate guards remember him? Would the keeper be waiting-

"No!"

The desperate sound breached, seemingly from right beneath his feet. He stilled in fright.

"I swear I– ugh!"

"Quiet you," a rough voice commanded.

There were men, in the alley below him.

"If not you," a third, reedy voice said, "how'd he find out, eh?"

"Please," the first voice sounded pained, "I just followed up on an error in the ledgers! I didn't mean to get anyone into trouble-"

There was a muted splat. Like someone patting porridge with a spoon. A very *big* spoon.

"Oh," the rough voice interjected. "Didn't mean to get no one in trouble, eh? We'll show you *mean*, Master Bookkeeper…"

"No!" the bookkeeper, entreated. "I can fix this! Let me go back! I can muddle the figures, get him to rehire you-"

There was another splat. Someone fell, gasping for breath.

"Too late, Master Bookkeeper," Reedy said. "You should've found out who ruled the stockyard *afore* you started pokin' about."

Scuffs and kicks sounded, interspersed with whimpering.

The other voice – Rough – laughed, "Look 't 'im cringe!"

Up on the roof, shock held Marco still.

The need to flee asserted itself. The nearest jump was right across the fraught alley. An abandoned workmen's scaffold, abutting the opposite eave, made the distance feasible.

He wouldn't backtrack. He couldn't risk losing sight of the spire for a moment. For all its monument size, it disappeared too easily.

As he prepared to abandon the poor bookkeeper to his beating, he felt shame. But he was no watchman. No Keeper Justin. He was small and scared and lost – and *home* was right there…

Blocking out the horrible noises, he retreated into a run-up, eyeing the scaffold and screwing up his courage.

His landing might cause a racket. He'd have to be gone before they looked up.

His heart rate redoubled. Desperation lent him speed and panic gave him wings. He soared across the gap.

Merciful Mother, he prayed, *please don't let them look up…*

There was a deafening crack. The scaffold splintered under him. He dropped and the boards beneath also gave way. He plummeted through blinding dust, pummeled by planks. Something hard spun him around and he glimpsed the next beam a moment before it brained him. He hardly felt the ground. The world spun. Insistent pain nipped faintly at the edges of his awareness.

Through the swirl of dust came a callused hand, to clamp about his jaw. It hauled him up before a scarred and scowling face.

"What's this then, eh?" Rough wondered.

Another pair of eyes appeared, plucking at his robes.

"Priest-in-training, maybe? He looks like a run-away."

"Not runnin' no more, is he…?"

A man-sized fist drove into his stomach. He had no thought to breaking his fall. His head bounced off the cobbles. The world wobbled on its axis. He wondered if he might sick-up again.

"Where's the bookkeeper?"

"Legged it, looks like."

Run… yes…

"Too bad. I kinda liked 'im. Think he'll go to the watch?"

"Nah, 'e knows we can find 'im again."

The watch… where?

"An' this one?"

"Mm," Reedy mused. "There's a ship in port as'll pay sil'er for 'im. Or I knows a man down Delve-side as'll trade in kind."

"Yeah?" Rough didn't seem to be listening.

"'e won't be worth much, broken," Reedy warned.

He blocked them out. He just wanted to wake up, now, and find out that this had all been a horrible dream.

"*Coin* won't cheer me like *this* will," Rough argued.

The blow seesawed Marco's vision. Strangely, it hurt little.

"Will 't, soft skin?"

Raise your hand to answer a question, he thought muzzily. He tried his best. What had he wanted to say? Oh, yes:

"Please…"

"'Please'? Oh, that's good. I like 'please'. Say it again…"

His collar dug into his nape. He heard his roughspuns rip.

"Please…" he struggled to squeeze the words out. The darkness, at the edge of his vision, drew closer with his every heartbeat.

He was past processing more pain. Neither slap nor rough handling really registered. His rope belt surrendered with a snap.

None of it had to do with him. A narrow strip of sky peeked from between the roofs. Stars floated like lily pads. So peaceful…

As he watched, a red petal broke from the night's ceiling.

Sunny landed on the scarred man's back, clawing for his eyes. Rough grunted in surprise as uneven teeth sank into his shoulder. He snagged a handful of wild hair and heaved. Sunny careened across the cobbles, rolling half a dozen times. She shot to her feet, clutching a length of scaffold like a club. She hissed.

"Need some help there?" Reedy sniggered.

"Shut up."

Straining against its immense weight, Marco managed to raise his head. *Sunny…*

She charged.

No!

Rough caught her blow in one fist. The other arced upward.

No!

It caught her under the chin, catapulting her off her feet. Her stick-limbs flailed and she hit the wall. The sound – of skull on brick – was the loudest thing he'd ever heard. She slid into a heap and sat like a ragdoll, her eyes blank in her startled face.

Despair rolled him under and he let it steal his sight.

"… over did … no coin… careless…"

"… still warm … matters … shut …"

"… fine … quick … go…"

Somewhere in the distance, metal clanged furiously.

Watch bells, maybe, he thought. *Too late now…*

* * *

THEY'D FOUND MACRO.

A watchman led the way, and Justin had little patience for the man's moderate pace. Not caring that it skirted his oaths, he manifested Empath's Echo and broadcast a bit of his own urgency.

Prodded, the watchman quickened his step.

"You're sure he's alive?" he demanded once more.

"Far as I know, sir." The man had studiously avoided giving any straight answers. "Commander said to fetch you to the scene."

The scene.

Dread coiled in his stomach.

There were many things – worse than death – that could befall a child on these city streets. He tried not to read into the watchman's practiced apathy. It was not true callousness. Merely a cure-all many of the city's peacekeepers cultivated.

His haste cared little for this rationale.

He tried to assuage it, absorbing some of the slumbering city's restfulness. Lamp men drifted past, patiently dousing lanterns with their long poles. First light was little more than a bell off.

Already, he could sense the mishmash of human cogs, gearing up to lock teeth and drive the great mill of industry once more.

Most bakeries already stirred. And, nearer the dark city outskirts, some alehouses were only now closing.

The constable unshuttered his watch lantern and they became one more light, moving among the early-morning oxcarts. In a bell, these narrow streets would be too choked up to manage deliveries.

"Get on home, you two," the constable cautioned a couple of singing drunkards. The pair jeered disagreeably.

Unwilling to brook any delay, he stepped forward.

"Alcohol is an evil, my sons."

At sight of him, they sobered, paling visibly. Ducking their heads and drawing wrong-handed circles over their hearts, they hurried off. Their racket started up again, on the next road over.

His worry worsened with each step the constable led them deeper along these unsavory streets. This area was all adjunct dockyard, a hodgepodge of warehouses and worn mercer's offices. At night, it catered to the rougher tastes of dockers and yardmen.

And it was a favored haunt of criminals.

His heart beat faster as the watchman slowed.

Two more lounged, on either side of an alley mouth, warning onlookers away with their gaze. Several insomniacs and passersby had gathered, hoping for a peek beyond the improvised barrier.

As they neared, the nailed-up canvas parted. Greystone appeared, wiping his hands on his tunic. Above the man's head, long silhouettes stalked the lurid lamp light on the alley walls.

As Justin made to brush past, the commander caught his elbow.

"A word, keeper, before you continue…"

The man's concern merely set him further on edge. "Why?"

"It's carnage in there," the man reasoned, "and I don't want you coming to the wrong conclusion. Your boy's alive – and liable to remain so, though he has yet to regain consciousness."

He frowned. "Then why so cautious, commander?"

The man let go his arm.

"Because we found him naked and not alone. Understand?"

Oh, holy Helia, guardian mother…

He steeled himself. Anything less than death, he could fix.

The commander stood aside.

The many lanterns merely swept the shadows into the corners. Watchmen ghosted about, giving the covered bodies a wide berth.

Ignoring them, he hurried straight to Marco.

A blanket wrapped his ward from the shoulders down. He set a hand on the boy's brow, outwardly feeling for fever.

He streamed Illian's Augur, tallying a laundry list of hurts. Scuffs and sprains, mostly, injuries that might as easily have been sustained in a tumble. He would need Cyrus, to delve deeper – to gauge the state of the memory block.

"Sorry?" he said, surfacing from his assessment.

"I said, the lad's been like that since we found him."

It was the watchwoman lieutenant from before. He hadn't noticed her, hovering near the boy. Guarding him.

"Good thing, too," she commented, casting a grim eye about.

For the first time, he studied his surroundings.

The alley looked to have been hit by a hurricane. The remnants of a scaffold lay, scattered like so much flotsam. And, everywhere, there was blood. The tarped corpses sprawled in pools of it.

"Sad, that."

He followed the lieutenant's gaze. To a tiny, draped figure.

"Female adolescent," another watchman said, bustling by. "Someone stove the back of her head in. Probably bashed against those bricks there. You can just make out the splatter, see…?"

The raised lantern also lit the speaker. Though the man wore watch grays, he was spectacled and stoop shouldered. Bookish. By his medical bag, he appeared to be a mender.

"Cause of death," the man concluded, "'wall'. *This* one, however, has me stumped-"

"Blort…" the lieutenant warned, as the excited mender went to one knee beside another of the bodies.

The man didn't seem to hear. The canvas was twitched aside.

Justin caught his breath.

"I want to say… 'jaguar'?" Blort mused. "Or 'wolf'? The bite pattern is too small for bear, I suppose. But what do I know? If a bear picked up a broken bottle or half-brick – *that* wound I'd recognize. This? I haven't even *found* the rest of the throat yet-"

"Blort-" the lieutenant growled.

"And this one!" The man frog-stepped over to the other tarp. "Hamstrung! Look at the way the back has been shredded – like something tried to dig right through the ribs-"

"Blort!"

The man blinked up at them. "Eh?"

Greystone had returned. "Mender, this is *Keeper* Wisenpraal."

"Ah?" the man extended a hand. "Pleased to meet you…"

Justin regarded the bloodied appendage.

The lieutenant pinched the bridge of her nose.

"You must excuse Blort," Greystone said, giving the mender a severe, sidelong glance. "He is a nincompoop when it comes to the living. But I can vouch that he is no necromance."

Finally catching on, Blort shook his head in vehement denial.

"And," the commander continued, for the mender's benefit, "last time I checked, there are no bears in Tellar."

"Technically untrue," the man raised a gory finger. "There is the Imperial menagerie. Something could have escaped. Or, perhaps it was something more exotic, smuggled into port?"

The mender met his commander's steely glare.

"Or it could've been a dog?" the man muttered, downcast.

"That killed two grown dockers?"

"A feral *pack*, then. They've been known to roam around."

"That's a myth," the lieutenant disagreed.

"Did you *find* any dog tracks?" the commander pressed.

"I wouldn't, would I? What, with everyone traipsing through? I keep telling them: cordon off the scene, *then* call me-"

"So, no tracks," Greystone concluded. "As you were, mender."

Grateful at being dismissed, the man scuttled off.

"I'd like to take Marco home, now," he told the watchmen, in no uncertain terms. While he crouched by the boy, the commander sent his subordinate off to organize a litter and transportation.

He became aware of the officer's brimming disquiet.

"What?" he asked.

Squatting beside him, Greystone whispered, "I don't like coincidences, keeper. When last I saw your boy, it was amid dismembered bodies. It's just a few bells later, and look..."

The man's eyes encompassed the grisly scene.

"You're not suggesting Marco somehow caused this?"

The watchman did not flinch. "My mender tells me I'm looking for something with fangs and claws. Your boy has neither."

"So, what are you saying?"

"What I'm *saying* is that the palace bean counters – who read my reports – don't want to hear about killer *circus bears*. I even breathe a word of that story, I'll be booted out of office so fast my bottom won't scuff the polish."

The man gave him an earnest look.

"What would *you* say happened here, keeper?"

Abruptly, he understood. If a hierarch – like himself – co-authored the report, it would become instantly credible. Looking in Greystone's eyes, he wasn't fooled. Whatever official story they concocted, he Imperial Menagerie could expect a visit.

"Like your mender said – feral dogs. Probably starving and attracted by the smell." He carefully didn't look at the dead urchin. "The dockers ran afoul of the pack. Somewhere, during the fray, the old scaffold came down and scared the beasts off."

He chose his words carefully.

"My ward was probably superfluous to the whole event."

Despite broiling emotions, the commander kept a blank face.

"As you say, keeper."

They didn't speak again until Marco was settled in the bed of a commandeered wagon. The boards smelled strongly of beeswax. A chandler, somewhere, was about to have a bad start to his day.

As they made to depart, Greystone set an arresting hand on the sideboard. The man pitched his words for the priest's ears alone.

"I've just been told that a civilian reported a crime in this area. Apparently, a trellis almost collapsed atop him, allowing him to escape two attackers. He mentioned no children. Or animals."

Justin stared. He didn't get the sense this was new information. The watchman's mind was a mire of suspicion. But, since this was always the case, it offered no clue as to the man's motivation.

Greystone offered the answer himself, glancing at Marco.

"I'd be interested to know what he remembers."

"And if, as I hope, he remembers nothing?"

The man's mien hardened – if that were possible.

"Then kindly keep him off my streets and in your Temple."

It was not quite a threat. Not quite an order. Greystone didn't have the authority. And, though Justin rarely saw the need to don his own mantle, he did so now. For Marco's sake.

He met the man's level gaze. "*Your* Temple too, commander."

Castigated, Greystone looked away first.

"As you say, keeper."

* * *

CONVENTIONAL WISDOM held that all things looked better by morning's light. Having watched his ward's flesh purple and puff, Justin disagreed.

Cyrus had just left.

The bruises were fading discolorations, one eye still swollen.

Uncomfortable in his favorite chair, Justin waited for the boy to wake. Cyrus's words milled through his head.

"It's damaged," the healer had said of the memory block.

"Can't you fix it?" he'd demanded.

Cyrus had shaken a grizzled head.

"I'm not going to *touch* it. It's holding together – haphazard as a house of sticks. Tweak a single support and the whole thing could come down. The shock of that would surely kill the boy."

Alarmed, he'd asked, "Does the spell still function?"

"No way of knowing. We'll see when he wakes, I suppose. You're sure you don't want me to stick around for that? He's not a toddler anymore, if you hadn't noticed."

"I'll take my chances."

Grunting sourly, the old man had shown himself out.

Justin sighed. Forging blindly ahead *was* foolhardy. But, if a priest could not have faith in Helia's mercy, what was the point?

He voiced his umpteenth prayer.

A bell later, he sensed the boy's awareness resurfacing.

He gripped his chair's armrests to still his trembling hands.

Streamers of his caliber – if not his skill – were rare. Empaths as strong as he were rarer still. And the chances of these two traits converging in the same person were next to nil. Which was, perhaps, why the codices were silent on using the two in tandem.

Should his self-taught technique ever be discovered – he was certain – a new entry would be penned under 'heresy'.

Right now, he didn't care. Streaming Empath's Echo, he saturated the space with strains of calm.

Long moments passed.

Slowly, his sense of Marco sharpened.

Eyelids fluttered. Opened. Found him in his chair.

He held his breath.

He watched the first inkling of a smile run headlong into recollection. The languid reawakening blew apart like autumn leaves. The boy's breath quickened and his gaze grew wide. Muscles tensed beneath memory's abuse.

Justin weathered the emotional explosion – bereft of facts to give it shape: Panic. Pain. Shock. Disbelief. Despair.

Shame.

His cage of insulating calm shuddered beneath the assault.

Guilt.

It fell like a hammer blow, buckling the fragile latticework.

A slow tear leaked from the stricken boy.

"She's dead, isn't she?"

It took him a moment. *Ah. The nameless little girl…*
"I'm afraid she is."
The storm of emotion gathered. Shrieked in a single direction. *Grief.*
The gale swept his efforts aside.
Marco broke down, voicing sobs and wails of such inconsolable hurt his own throat closed in response.
Merciful Goddess, how do I stitch such a wound?
With aching hands, he kept himself in his seat.
Because he sensed the undirected anger, roiling within that storm, waiting to ground itself on the first hint of sympathy. If it were allowed to sear shut this outlet, these unshed tears might fester in the boy's soul.
I can't watch this and do nothing, he railed.
Somehow, he held himself still while the boy cried himself hoarse. Until, at long last, raw eyes held steadily on the ceiling.
"Where is she?" Marco rasped quietly.
"A local Temple, waiting on family to come collect her."
"There was no one."
"Unclaimed… remains… are cremated and scattered at sea."
Twice buried. A pauper's funeral.
"She deserves better."
He nodded. "I'll arrange for her to be interred here."
He would manage it, too. Somehow.
But the boy shook his head. "She did not want to be here."
"Then I'll see to purchasing a plot at a nearby cemetery."
Anyone who questioned the expense could take it up with him.
The boy nodded, exhausted by grief's unrelenting grip.
"I'll go see to it. Will you be alright on your own for a while?"
The boy nodded again, brow furrowed and lip trembling.
He paused at the door. "I'll need a name. For the grave marker."

Amid many false starts and much pained swallowing, Marco finally managed to choke out a word: "Sunny."

He nodded. "I'll have some food sent up. I know you don't feel like it, but try to eat something. Your body has seen an ordeal – streamed Recovery included – and needs to replenish its stores."

The boy turned his back, looking haggard and heartsick.

He closed the door between them... and promptly collapsed against it. His shaking hands fisted in his robes, as though he could physically stifle the pain he'd soaked up.

It would take days to rid himself of it. But it had been worth it.

Sane, he rejoiced.

Damaged, yes. Grief stricken. But sane.

He steadied himself with a deep breath.

Holy Helia, he praised. *Guardian Mother. For your attentive regard on your servant, Marco... I give thanks.*

INQUISITOR TORVAN MATTANUY stepped down from his black lacquered carriage. The quarter's squalor and stink curled his lip and he had to concentrate to smell *potential* rather than piss.

Behind him, his assistants rushed to ready his equipment.

Before him rose the tenement from the preliminary report.

Finding out about these 'butcher murders' had been mere coincidence. If his random daily review hadn't trawled in the request-for-transfer-of-jurisdiction-form, the matter would not have gone to his branch but to the *Experimenti*.

Where it would not have advanced *anyone*'s career.

He made a mental note to reprimand the original applicant.

He could tell that his injunction against entering the building had been disobeyed – the two masha'na, guarding the door, hid disgust beneath their stoicism.

It was exactly that independence of action that had driven the *Inquisitori* to dispense with masha'na. They had armed and maintained their own loyal, lower ranks instead.

Passing the holy warriors, he added their reprimands to his list.

A gray uniform stepped forward and tried to introduce itself as the city watch intermediary. His assistants headed it off before it could try something pedestrian, like shaking his hand.

Blort? Is that a name?

He swept up the stairs, his assistants in tow, the watchman huffing unnecessary directions from the rear.

Another masha'na marked the correct door and did not attempt to open it for him. One of his assistants rushed to do so.

A step beyond the threshold, he halted, allowing himself to absorb the scene. He tilted his head in annoyance and his assistants forcefully shushed the noisy watchman.

In silence, he turned a full circle.

A rustic scene came alive before his eyes. He heard the laughter of children, the happy clank of utensils and the ditty someone used to whistle while sweeping up.

Then came the violence.

He mapped out the macabre dance of death as it had spread from this room to the next. The phantoms of his mind re-enacted their brutal trek to the bedroom, him on their heels.

He panned around dispassionately.

The humid heat was playing havoc with the remains. He'd have them moved to the Temple ice houses with all haste. But first…

An assistant settled a charcoal stylus between his waiting fingers. The other couched a sketch board in the crook of his arm.

He drew, capturing the slain, the glyphs and all the other sordid details with sure lines.

Inwardly, he grinned.

The last sanctioned witch burning had been before his birth. The last purge, even longer still. The Inquisitori had become a stale bureaucracy, leaving little room for advancement.

His career had been stagnant long enough.

It was a small service. Justin did the address himself. He and Marco, in their formal robes, standing over a child-sized coffin. And the grave digger, cap doffed, keeping solemn vigil.

His ward had insisted they detour to the beach before the ceremony. He could not guess at the significance of the limpet shell the boy had placed so reverently. And he'd not asked.

'*Sunny*', the grave marker had read. '*A friend.*'

Destitute indeed, to merit only such simple descriptors.

He'd chosen a more obscure passage for his homily, opting for simple words and striking imagery. It had been hard, bearing up under Marco's silent tears and strident grief.

"Would you like to say something…?" he'd invited at the end.

Shoulders drawn around his ears, the boy had stepped forward.

"I'm sorry I didn't do more…"

Feeling the boy drawn across the gulf of guilt, he'd reached out a gentle hand. Sudden anger had sparked beneath it, giving the illusion of energy. The boy had raged.

"She saved me! She saved me and I killed her…"

Words had snared in the snarl of emotions. "*I couldn't…*"

Unable to stand it any longer, he'd pulled the boy into a one-armed hug. For a moment, resistance had held.

And then Marco had slumped, hanging from him.

In fits and starts, coughing over tear-choked words and grief induced hiccups, the boy had told the story.

He'd received it in silence, making no move to wipe his eyes.

His analytical self had noted the absence of dogs in the tale.

When it was done, he'd nodded discreetly to the grave digger.

Then and there, he'd had to be strong for the boy.

Now, sitting in Cyrus's apartments, he was himself a wreck.

Emotionally speaking, he possessed a thick skin – a product of living with the daily deluge of others' impulses. But Marco's pain had found a chink in his armor. A Renali lance – pinning back a lifetime of carefully cultivated distance.

"You're telling me you believe in *boggles* now?" Cyrus scoffed.

"Fairytale monsters did not murder those men."

"Neither did your boy. And, if Helia wants to send wild hounds to his defense, my advice to you is – take the miracle and run."

"You might be right," he mused.

"Of course I'm right. Now, bugger off. I'm busy."

Which was his friend's way of saying he should get some rest.

One of the reasons why he – an empath – got on so well with Cyrus, was that the man's blunt words unabashedly mirrored his emotions. His friend was as subtle as a battering ram.

"What are you working on?" he pressed instead, not ready to be alone with his thoughts just yet.

"How's your tea?" the healer asked, changing the subject.

He regarded his cup. "Fine. Why?"

"The milk's a week old."

He sniffed it politely. Even by Temple cold cellar standards, that was a feat. Personally, he *preferred* tea with a bit more bite. But this brew was toothless. "Nothing wrong with the milk."

Cyrus smiled as if at a secret. "*And* it hasn't left my office."

This gave him pause. Subjected to the healer's sour demeanor, even fresh cream should have curdled by second bell.

"You didn't try reducing it to powder again, did you?"

He scraped his tongue over his teeth at the distasteful memory.

Preening, the healer plonked a pitcher down before him. True to the man's word, the Temple-grade glass held no lingering chill.

"A week? In this? In *here*? How?"

The healer handed him a bundle of twine, beaded with beeswax. It was the pull-string that had held the milk jug's cork. Completely ordinary but for the ends – braided into a complicated knot.

He chortled. "A yarn charm?"

Cyrus stared at him, a pillar of seriousness.

"Oh, surely not," he refuted. "They are not magical. Their only power lies in keeping children busy for bells on end. You might as well credit flower arrangement or calligraphy."

The silence stretched, eroding his certainty.

Finally, Cyrus stood, gathering his staff. "Come see this…"

The old priest's private laboratory looked like little more than the manse of a deranged cartographer. Scrolls, maps and diagrams unfurled across every surface including the ceiling. They charted no recognizable landmass or firmament and were festooned with nonsensical symbols and scribbles. One whole wall was given over to a labyrinthine assemblage of glass piping, their multicolored beakers inert above cold burners.

"Where are your assistants?" he wondered, hoping the unfortunates weren't decomposing beneath the layered chaos.

"Those lickspittles the Assembly set to spy on me? I sent them off after ore samples. I think. Huh. They should be fine."

"And what is it, exactly, you didn't want the Assembly to see?"

"Ever meet Brother Obeiam? From the Low Library?"

All Cyrus's abrupt about-turns were leaving him dizzy.

"I don't think so," he admitted.

"I'm not surprised. Even for a devoted book-botherer, the man rarely comes above ground. I actually think he was suffering mild altitude sickness when I ran into him in the Low Library. He works in the basement, you see."

A response seemed called for. "Rewarding work, I'm sure."

"*Dull*, is what it is. Brother Obeiam spends most of his day – every day – charging the glow globes that light the Low Library."

"That sounds…" he tried to be diplomatic, "uneventful."

"So was our conversation. The man is a bore. But he was complaining – in a roundabout sort of way – about some prankster acolytes. Apparently, they've been sneaking in, under cover of night – and *charging* the glow globes in his stead."

Justin tried to contain his smile. "The vandals."

"Mm. Out of character for our *hardworking* future hierophants."

"Please tell me you're not trying to devise a better *monk*-trap?"

"No need. The steel trap of my mind immediately deduced that no acolytes were involved." His friend unlocked a shallow cabinet. "*These* spontaneously charged themselves just a few days ago."

The cupboard was stocked with glow globes. One or two burned bright. Of the rest, about a third were faint and the remainder flat.

"Alright," he allowed at last, "I'm ready for the punch-line."

"No jokes," Cyrus growled. "I asked Obeiam for his records – the man is unparalleled in his drudgery. By my reckoning, this phenomenon has been observable, at odd intervals, for years. And it's speeding. Becoming more pronounced."

He was intrigued despite himself. "You've confirmed this?"

"You think I keep glow globes in my closet for the ambience?"

He considered the rows of spheres.

"How does your yarn charm tie into this?"

"Our brethren in the *Factori* have been trying to rediscover the secrets of glow globe-manufacture for centuries. But it is *old magic*, little suited to our modern methodologies. To corroborate my findings, my best recourse was equally old magic…"

The healer hefted a dog-eared manual. The faded pages were filled with illustrations on the finer points of braiding yarn charms.

He eyed it skeptically. "You're saying, whatever lit your cabinet, it also enervated this snarl of string?"

Seeing his doubt, Cyrus snatched a sheet off a nearby rack. A row of sealed milk jugs sat on it. Some were decidedly green.

"The potency waxes and wanes. But the basement records allowed me to predict the event's apex. Behold," the healer pointed to a pristine jar. "You just drank its twin."

"Color me convinced," he said. "May I?"

At Cyrus's nod, he hefted the specimen. The milk inside sloshed but did not seem inclined to attack the glass. Only a little reassured, he manifested Illian's Augur. Under the eye of the Perception sigil, a skein of power wrapped the jug, gossamer as a silkworm's web and almost as weak. Structured energy seeped from the waxed twine as though it were a charged crystal. But that was patently impossible. Something so flimsy could not hold magic for more than a moment – not to mention a week.

"Any theories," he mused, "on what's causing it?"

Cyrus shrugged, seemingly delighted. "Some naturally occurring surge and ebb in the ambient magic of the world?"

"My streaming seems no more potent than usual," he refuted.

"It wouldn't. Streaming is dependent on your internal energy. Whatever source powers this, its external. Remote. Unseen."

He gave Cyrus a sharp look. "Like an entity, perhaps?"

The healer shrugged. "Is the natural order an entity?"

That sounds like the seed of a heretical thought.

"Exciting, isn't it?" Cyrus enthused, throwing scarecrow arms wide. "Magic is returning to the world!"

He smiled wryly. "I wasn't aware it had gone anywhere."

"Of course you were!" his old mentor gave him a *look* that said he was being obtuse. "Think about it. The bridge at Orkto Ganalwi? The Lldar canyon caves? The Rasrini channel? Even our own Lily Tower – magic-made edifices one and all.

"Even should you yoke every streamer in the Empire, you could not hope to match the kind of power that made these structures. Our own scriptures say whole *islands* could once be banished to the sea bottom, or raised from its bed. If a *tenth* of those tales are a *tenth*-part true, magic used to be a force in the world to rival the heavens."

The pronouncement hung heavily between them.

Justin spoke seriously, "In the scriptures, rivaling the heavens is normally the bit that precedes all the smiting. Mayhap that is what happened to elder magic?"

Cyrus shrugged, unwilling to concede the point.

"Or perhaps it went into hibernation? Who knows? This could be a cyclic occurrence, like… cosmic tides. It certainly seems the magical waterline is on the rise. Pray it will lift our boat as well."

"Or," he built on the old priest's hibernation metaphor, "it will come from its cave, ravenous and raring to consume us all."

With unquenchable good humor, his friend gripped his shoulders. "In either event – our *world* is awakening."

It was impossible to completely escape Cyrus's excitement. But one of them had to be the voice of caution.

"Who else knows about this?"

They couldn't afford common citizens fiddling with the arcana. No one wanted to see the return of rampant witch burnings.

Shared cynicism finally sobered his friend.

"Perhaps Brother Obeiam. But he doesn't talk to anyone who isn't a glow globe. So. Effectively? You and me."

"Let's keep it that way. For now, at least?"

Cyrus patted his arm companionably.

"Come back any time you need more cheering up."

* * *

Junior inquisitors all but genuflected as Mattanuy marched past, his sharp footfalls ringing off the marble. He barely saw.

He'd just come from the Black Library, the repository of all Inquisitori knowledge on pagan practices. And he'd yet to find a single parallel for the runes left at the butcher murders' scene.

There seemed little doubt that the butcher himself, Meum, had done the deed. Mattanuy had moved the wreck of a man to an Inquisitori 'sanitarium' and even *they* had been unable to wring so much as a scream from the wretch.

Though he'd held high hopes of uncovering a ring of cultists – whose pyre could have shone brightly on his career – his investigation had stalled.

He'd been born too late. *Centuries* too late.

Instead of pagan practitioners, he rooted out erroneous paperwork and craftsmen with expired writs. He didn't pound down back alleys after blasphemers.

For him, there was merely the plod of deduction.

Of course, he was appallingly *good* at it. That wasn't the point.

Getting noticed was difficult when you rode a desk.

Quietly seething, he entered his office.

Its atmosphere was awry – he was not alone.

Rather than cast around like a fool, he made his way to the sideboard. He did not indulge in alcohol himself and he could just barely conjure the Fire sigil. But, together, the two could turn a decanter of distilled spirits into a thrown fireball.

"Can I offer you something?" he asked, holding up a glass. In its reflection, he found his infiltrator, seated behind his desk.

"You can put that down, inquisitor. *I* don't drink either."

Ah.

The voice was rich, cultured and recognizable.

Invading his office, usurping his desk, exhibiting knowledge of his habits and intent – this was a play for power, not for his life.

"Archon Hallet," he identified, though they'd never spoken. "To what do I owe this unexpected pleasure, your anointedness?"

Emion Hallet – the Emperor's spiritual advisor and first on the Imperial Council – smiled leisurely. The man's ease belied his importance. Everyone knew Hallet had the Emperor's ear. Mattanuy suspected he had the mouth, spine and sundries too.

"I need a matter investigated," the archon said. "Quietly."

He carefully controlled his expression. Hallet operated one of the most accomplished spy networks at court. So successful, in fact, that Mattanuy had failed to infiltrate it on several occasions.

He kept his voice diffident. "Why come to me?"

"You have a reputation for stellar results. Also, you are uniquely positioned to pursue this enquiry."

Ah. So the man was after someone in the Temple, not the court.

"The Inquisitori do not investigate in-house," he reminded.

Not that the prohibition had ever stopped him. But Hallet had yet to speak of recompense.

"Yes. An antiquated rule the *High Inquisitor* might change…?"

Ruthlessly, the throttled his excitement. High Inquisitor Crozius was old. Mattanuy was at least a decade away from being considered an acceptable replacement. But, with the Emperor's advisor sponsoring him for the position…

"What critical matter might justify such a change…?"

Hallet regarded him weighingly, measuring his words.

"What do you know of the modernist movement?"

Mattanuy tamped his surprise. Modernists in the Temple? Last he'd checked, that particular malady was the province of fat mercers, sitting atop their fortunes and tossing aphorisms at the 'downtrodden masses' like morsels of food.

It was this season's fashionable thing to do.

He had dossiers on each of those mercers. On what they said in their cups as well as into their pillows. He knew fashion could not stand up to self-interest. Lifting the Imperial yoke off the colonies, as the modernists advocated, would see the Empire's finances – those mercers' finances – flag.

None of their morally bankrupt lot would risk it.

But if modernism was also taking ahold inside the Temple…

Hallet was still waiting for his answer.

"'Movement' implies progress," he said. "What the modernists are chasing is a recession. Without Imperial governance, protection or trade, the colonies would revert to fiefs and yurts inside a year."

"And their faith," Hallet added darkly, "would falter."

He did not buy the advisor's pious concern.

The Empire was at war. The Empire was *always* at war. Conquered territory provided converts and conscripts to conquer yet *more* territory. What was good for the faith was good for the economy. Hallet was trying to protect someone's purse.

Or, more likely, ruin someone else's.

An inquisitorial inquest, even just the whisper of one, was a powerful political force. He would be Hallet's tool.

Tools could be discarded. He would have to proceed carefully.

"I see you understand," Hallet said, misinterpreting his sudden introspection. The man rose. "May I count on your support, then?"

He drew himself up. "As I shall, in turn, rely on yours."

"Unity through faith," Hallet said, over a shoulder.

"Unity through faith," he echoed, deep in thought, but the man had already gone.

What if Hallet was not merely maneuvering? What if there *was* a modernist conspiracy at Temple? It would mean the dissidents had evaded his detection for years. He thrilled at the challenge.

Who are you, my little modernist mastermind?

* * *

"Justin-?"

"It's been a month, Cyrus! A *month*!"

Quill suspended, the bemused healer watched him pace.

"He doesn't eat. He doesn't sleep. He doesn't speak unless prodded, and then, only in single syllables. His instructors are at their wits' end. His friends have given up. He's slowly wasting away before my eyes and I just can't get *through* to him!"

"This is young Marco we're talking about?"

"Who else would I be talking about?!"

"Don't get snippy with me. *I* didn't just barge into *your* office."

Reining himself in, he breathed through his nose. "I'm sorry."

"I should think so," Cyrus huffed. "Now. What's wrong?"

"I literally just told you."

"That was a rant, not a diagnosis. Try again."

He shook his head helplessly.

"This is unlike you." Cyrus laid the quill aside. "You usually slide into people's heads like a bad habit. What's keeping you?"

"This is a unique case," he defended, ignoring the jibe.

"Codswallop," the healer drawled.

"What?"

"It's *not* a unique case. At all. It's a unique *relationship* and that's got you scared. Stop mollycoddling the boy and *help* him."

"I don't know how!" he admitted.

"Yes, you do! The boy's been through a violent trauma. It's blown a hill-sized hole in his self-worth. In layman's terms, he's had his power stolen. However much you might try, you cannot *give* it back to him. He must take it. And he must *want* to take it-"

"You don't think I know? I've been trying, Cyrus! I set him the most challenging papers and tasks. But my praise means nothing-"

"You're implementing half-measures," the healer condemned. "I understand your reluctance. I know how close this boy is to you. But sometimes, to save a life, you have to lop off a limb."

He stared. "I don't know what that means."

"Well," the healer shooed, "come back when you do."

Having a social battering ram for a friend, he reflected – as he slammed the door – was sometimes a hard blow.

His need to pace not yet alleviated, he picked a random corridor. He briefly considered the crisp air and violent winds of the High Vantage, at the Spire's summit. But his pent up energy had no patience for the long ride up in the old iron casket today.

How dare Cyrus?

True, the man was rarely kind – but he was generally well-meaning... Justin slowed. An extra sense was of little use if you didn't pay attention to it. Thinking back, he'd sensed nothing but determined concern from his old friend.

Lopping off a limb, he realized. *Being cruel to be kind.*

His one-time mentor was setting an example.

He *was*, perhaps, overcautious of Marco's fragile sensibilities.

Under the guise of streaming instruction, he had set his ward a strict regimen of mental strengthening exercises. When the memory dam finally broke and the floodwaters came down – he'd reasoned – the boy would have a parapet to set his feet on.

He had not stopped to ponder what emotional resilience his efforts might produce – though the evidence was before him.

Fine, then. He needed something that would force the boy's attention and keep him too busy to indulge his grief. Something structured and strenuous, that delivered tangible rewards-

His pacing had hastened while he planned. Had he been paying attention, he would have avoided the collision altogether.

A large hand caught his arm, saving him from a sprawl.

"Your pardon, hierarch," the owner rumbled. "My fault – for walking around with my head in the clouds."

The rearing masha'na was of the Inith. One of the rare throwbacks born to that race once or twice a generation. A giant.

He put that together with the man's insignia of rank.

"Master Sergeant Groon," he realized, shaking the hand that still held him. "Please, don't apologize. I was slow in sensing your approach and it was *your* quick reflexes that spared me."

Which was no small thing. This man had once broken a Renali cavalry charge, all by himself. The story was, Groon had felled the lead horse with a fist and then shouldered on through the rest, slamming knights from their saddles as he went.

That the Temple warrior had managed to gentle their chance contact, despite a stormy mood, was even more miraculous.

Justin squinted upwards. "Though, if you don't mind me saying, your 'clouds' appear to be thunderheads?"

"Ah. That makes *you* Keeper Justin." The heavy-lidded man smiled at his surprise. "The masha'na hear stories too. Well met."

Tribal braids swinging, the warrior indicated the passage beyond his shoulder. "As to my, uh, climate – I've just come from my quarrel- Ahem! *Quarterly*, report with Exarch Sule."

Ah, yes. Sule.

The incurable bureaucrat was a latent elitist, who took pains – and a curling iron – to present a purebred Imperial front.

Facing this savage crusader was bound to upset Sule.

"I trust the exarch judged your report fairly?" he probed.

"It is the recruitment issue," the giant sighed, "and the poor retention rate. Clatter Court has not produced a full complement of masha'na in years. Oh, we have no shortage of students. Our sword schooling has become *fashionable* among the nobility. They take our instruction but not our oaths. And many of the unscrupulous slink off, preferring the army's pay over our vows of poverty."

Groon trailed off. "I did not mean to bore you, keeper."

"Pardon my distraction," he said, smiling broadly, "I was pondering a mutually beneficial proposal…"

MARCO TRUDGED BLEARILY behind the keeper.

He'd not asked where they were headed and could not muster the will to care. Had it not been Justin, shaking his shoulder, he'd have resisted the attempt to even rouse him from bed.

Little roused him anymore.

His classes passed in a blur, his instructors spouting nonsense syllables he didn't bother to parse. Those who would have pounced on his wandering attention before now failed to oblige him, perhaps sensing how he longed for their rebuke.

His dorm mates had made a last effort to rile him. But neither their concern, nor their carefully crafted insults, had had the power to move him. They had drifted too far apart.

Even his efforts with the keeper were empty. He'd submitted a subpar Skordian transcription and the keeper's praise had done nothing but underscore the sham of it all.

He no longer cared for streaming and had let his exercises lapse.

Though his days had become torturous, his sleep was worse. He fled the terrible nightmares at a walk, clinging with hollow-eyed desperation to wakefulness. But, eventually, fatigue would force him to stop, to sit, to sag. He would nod off...

And the scaffolding would give way beneath him again.

If he was lucky, the shock of impact slammed him awake.

If not, if the dreams managed to drag him under...

The feel of blunt fingers. The sound of ripping roughspuns. Sunny's slow, graceless arc through the air.

The crack – of her skull – catapulted him from bed, time and again. But, always, the look in her eyes stayed with him.

Recrimination. Accusation. Disgust.

He had let her die. He hadn't even *tried* to help.

And those were just the nightmares he remembered.

The rest left him snarled in sweat-soaked sheets, scrabbling out of reach of the faceless horrors that hounded him.

And now, at last, the carefully closed expressions all around him also hung on the keeper's face. Once, he may have felt the priest's surrender keenly. Now, he suffered only a perverse satisfaction – at having proven that pain trumped altruism.

Distracted and wallowing, he almost walked into the keeper.

He had not noticed the rising racket. Around him stood Clatter Court, the masha'na training grounds. Wooden swords clacked and students crowed from within paper-screened practice halls.

He stood at the bottom step of one such building, below two masha'na in orange and umber. One was a giant, his armor richly embossed. The other was a severe man in simple, gathered robes.

"Scrawny," the latter observed shortly, as though the act of speaking were distasteful. Hand resting on a wooden sword, stuck through his sash, the man exuded an air of imminent motion.

"It is late in the semester," the giant smiled. "He will soon eat enough dust to fatten him up." The hulking man turned to the priest. "Rest easy, keeper. Crysopher here is our best. He could make a holy warrior out of a cured ham, given time."

The severe man – Crysopher – huffed without moving.

A hard hand turned him to face the keeper.

"Marco, as of today, Master Crysopher is in charge of your curriculum. I look forward to hearing of your progress."

With no more than that, his erstwhile mentor turned away.

For a long moment, the hollow in his chest held sway, holding him mum. By the time he thought to protest, the keeper was gone.

He'd been abandoned.

Crysopher and he silently assessed one another. It was hard to tell which of them was the least impressed.

"Come," the man barked, not waiting to see if he followed.

He had to skip to catch up. Crysopher moved in the same manner he spoke – without frills.

"You are now part of my class. You will either suffer and succeed, or fail – and suffer some more. The only release is through graduation. Joining late buys you no leeway."

Stairs that squealed under Marco seemed too scared to squeak at Crysopher. Sliding doors hissed apart at the man's touch.

Inside the hall, practice dummies and padded posts punctuated one wall. Wooden swords and staves marched down the other. Climbing rings and rope ladders peppered the ceiling. A double row of students, in pure umber, dominated the floor. Hidden behind faceguards, the pairs moved in perfect time, weighted wood rising and falling in waves.

Step, *clack*, *clack*, shuffle, *clack*, lunge, *clack!*

Over and over.

The master led him inside. "Here, discipline is everything. You will do as you are told. You will speak when spoken to. You will give your all. If you flag, or fail, discipline will reform you."

The master turned on him, the movement just slightly too fast.

He couldn't help but flinch from those hard eyes.

"Do not tempt me to tutor you personally. You do *not* want that much of my attention."

Even in the depths of his despondence, he felt a lick of fear.

"Break!" the man shouted, making him jump. All around them, motion ceased. "Circle up! Djenja, center!"

The touch on his shoulder was firm. It gave the impression of having been greatly gentled. He suspected it could as easily have crushed him as propelled him toward the fast-forming ring.

A student stepped forward, offering a wooden sword as though it were live steel. He fumbled the weapon Master Crysopher thrust at him, and shied as a practice helm was rammed atop his head.

A shove sent him stumbling into the circle.

His opponent overtopped him by at least a head. Though helmed, her freckled hands and feet betrayed a Betopian or perhaps even a Hinterlander heritage. She *flowed* – there was no better word – into a ready stance.

Ignorant as Marco was of swordplay, he could tell by the cant of her head that she was serious. His apathy was about to come under attack – by a girl with a stick.

This is ridiculous, he thought. *I didn't agree to this…*

He made to drop the stupid weapon.

"Begin!"

Only his violent start – at her sudden movement – kept him from being stabbed clean through the face. He watched the weighted wood flash by in astonishment. She did something with her wrists and the helm was ripped right from his head.

He staggered, searing words rising like bile. A length of wood, leaping for his chest, forestalled him. He jerked his stick up between them. A resounding *clack!* traveled up his arm. For a moment, he thought he'd warded her blow. Then her weapon windmilled with his, springing it from his stung grip.

Something bit at the back of his knee, a moment before the floorboards slammed into it. For the span of an instant, physical pain eclipsed all other hurts. The fake sword fell toward his neck, cutting the relief short. He threw himself from his crouch, rolling.

A blunt tip bounced from the boards in his wake. Thumping feet pursued and foiled his next roll, stomping down on his trailing robes. From his back, he glared up as her downward stroke-

"Break!"

-stalled, under perfect control, against his brow.

"Thank you, Djenja."

Dismissing Marco, the girl stepped clear, bowing to the master before turning her back. Autumn colored curls, dark with sweat, tumbled as she dragged her helm free...

Scything through the air, the sound of skull on brick-

It was not Sunny. But, still, he couldn't breathe.

Master Crysopher's impassive face hovered above him.

"We shall spend today on how to properly *hold* a sword."

Chapter 4 – New Day

Further support for the multiple realms thesis. Doctrine states that Perdition is home to a host of denizens, oft described as terrifying beasts or monsters. Whilst a saw snout, bulkbear or sea serpent might earn this appellation, these species have been studied. They live, hunt and breed in known locales. Now, take the fire breathing gorghoul of scripture – a creature seemingly singular in its existence. Yet exist it did, for its remains are on display in the Primus Sanctori. No beast, fitting its unique description, has been recorded before or since. Such an otherworldly specimen must stem from a similarly otherworldly locale, not so?

~ *Pella Monop, 'Musings on the Material Worlds'. Draft, incomplete.*

"Cyrus!?!" Justin cried.

The healer stumbled, mid-release. The thrown axe shattered a glass beaker. Viscous fluid bore stacked scrolls to the floor.

"Pity," Cyrus remarked. "That had almost done fermenting."

"What...?" he breathed, at a complete loss for words.

The old priest, perhaps the most unlikely person to ever do so, hefted another throwing axe and took careful aim.

He goggled. "Is that a Hinterland axe board?"

"Maybe."

He gaped, "And is that a Neril *death fetish* nailed to it?"

"Could be..."

He stared at the snarl of hair, teeth and twigs – stapled to the bull's eye. He shuddered to think how Cyrus had sourced that. Neril shamans used to fashion such wards, against ill-luck in battle. As the charms incorporated human remains – from the bearer's family – the Temple had cried witchcraft. Cooler heads had nipped genocide in the bud, but it had been a near thing.

Now scattered, modern Neril still wore wrist- and anklets, sporting beads that did not bear too close an examination.

"Dare I ask what you're doing?" he managed.

"Experiment," Cyrus affirmed, sighting with one watery eye. "To see if ambient magic enervates the fetish. The next swell is tomorrow, near noon. If I can't hit the damned thing then, I'll know it's working…"

"Mm," he mused.

A murder of flightless axes were strewn about. The target itself showed not a single nick, though the wall surrounding it was scarred . "You may want to rethink your methodology…"

His eyes shot wide as another thought occurred.

"You weren't doing *this* when Speaker Willionson was here?"

He'd glimpsed the assembly member, leaving the laboratory.

His friend's silence was telling.

"Cyrus!" he wailed in disapproval.

"At least he didn't peek in that drawer…" the healer pointed.

"Why?" He reached out. "What have you got in-"

He blanched.

Swaddled in silk, the dun sphere was smooth as glass, just slightly too big to fit comfortably in one's palm. A casual glance might mistake it for a glow globe. But he knew better.

"*Meno Gorgis*," he groaned. "Cyrus, you didn't!"

"It was just sitting there," the healer reasoned.

"In the Primus Sanctori? Behind unbreakable crystal?"

"What *'break'*?" Cyrus scoffed. "I used a key. Besides, it's an *eye* – I'm sure it's glad of the change in scenery."

"It's *the* eye," he argued, "of a mythical, fire-breathing gorghoul, slain by a holy saint!"

"And I found it a very handsome drawer."

He hid his face, at this newest blasphemy.

"Relax," Cyrus bid. "I replaced it with a most excellent fake."
"Oh, good," he said, his sarcasm lost on his incorrigible friend.
"I can't wait to see what it does during the surge!"
He shook his head. "Get us both excommunicated, is what."
"No reward without risk…" With a grunt, Cyrus let fly another axe. It struck the board – haft first – and kicked off into a lazy tumble. The old priest dodged with unexpected alacrity.
Another crash sounded, somewhere in the crowded laboratory.
He couldn't help laughing. "You're due a lot of reward then."
"I'm busy," Cyrus griped, finally catching on to his mockery. "What do you want?"
He handed over the hide bound book he'd brought. "To help. I recently purchased this. I'd quite forgotten I had it."
The healer fished some spectacles from his robes' front.
"'*The Re-emergence of Magic by P. Lorant*'," Cyrus read. "Who in perdition is 'P. Lorant'?"
"No idea."
Cyrus glared at the offending manual, "Well *my* research is obviously going swimmingly. How's your little project doing?"

"HAH!" MARCO CHORUSED, slamming into a lunge – his *seirin* steady, his shoulders level. They all stilled as the master spoke.
"Balance. Between speed and accuracy. Between reach and power. The full lunge overextends you. Use it only if your opponent has lost footing and, for preference, consciousness."
No one laughed. Master Crysopher didn't make jokes.
"Again!"
They moved in unison, sliding back into guard stances.
"Nine!" the master counted.
"Hah!" the class answered, *seirins* snapping forward.

"Balance," the man emphasized, moving among them, righting misalignments and – occasionally – kicking at an ankle to send someone sprawling. "A warrior teeters, constantly, on the edge between life and death. Loss of footing or focus lets you down on one side only. Again!"

"Hah!"

"Are you tired?" Master Crysopher demanded.

"No, master!" they chorused.

His hair was matted and his brows dripped with sweat. Every student was ringed by damp planks.

"Would you like a rest?"

"No, master!" he wheezed. His arms were leaden and his thighs on fire. He'd kill for a taste of water – but was more likely to die, if he had to battle one of his peers to get it.

"Think I'm pushing you hard?" the master posed. "Masha'na war for days – days! – wearing four stone of armor!"

No one batted an eye at the idea of two dozen children, fitted with lamellar plate and chain. Here, they weren't children.

"Once more! One!"

"Hah!"

"Two!"

He lost himself to the slash and slide of movement, the burn of muscle and the red hot breath in his chest.

"Hah!"

"Hah!"

Concentration consumed him from corner to cranny, crowding out all but the grip in his hands and the voice in his ear.

"Hah!"

The hole in his soul had stopped seeping and started scarring. Jaggedly – it was true – but steadily. It pained him still. Distractingly so at times. He accepted any bruise or punishment this earned him during practice. He would keep Sunny's memory close to his heart, he'd resolved, no matter how it hurt.

"Hah!"

He attacked his pain, determined to whittle it down.

"Hah!"

His *seirin* had started trembling before the master called a halt.

"Laps at first light," the man reminded them. "Don't be late."

Tension traipsed out on the master's heels. Several people collapsed in relief. Some took to stretching, trying to forestall tomorrow's stiff muscles. The very fit struck up conversation. Most drifted door-wards.

He was among those still standing, staring down at his sword hand. So much had changed in a few short months. Monster blisters had broken and reformed and broken again. His pads were now covered in calluses. He'd grown. Not just taller but tougher. Almost, he thought, tough enough to bear up under his sins without buckling… But not quite yet.

A familiar, hoarse laugh reached his ears, drawing his eye.

Djenja stood, swapping words with her two friends. Or, perhaps, *one* friend and a mirror: the Kender twins were the daughters of some noble house and alike as peas in a pod. Canted eyes were set in identical faces and framed by severe fringes. He was not the only one mesmerized. But, for him, their tangerine skin was merely a backdrop to Djenja's snowy swirl. His preoccupation with the taller girl was not at all romantic, he reminded himself.

She stood among the three most skilled students in the class. And, by besting him that first day, she'd set herself in his mind as the golden standard. He'd not be satisfied until he'd surpassed her. Since he presently languished near the bottom rung, that happy day was still far off. He shook his head in vexation.

"Better give up on that idea," someone whispered in his ear.

"Lokus!" he jumped. "Make some noise when you walk!"

Chortling unabashedly, his friend swiveled them around.

"See what happened to the last pesky suiter?"

His friend pointed out a pimply boy, one of their peers, with a bandage bisecting his face.

Noting their attention, two deeply bruised eyes glared from above a badly broken nose.

"He busted that tussling with the training dummies," Marco repeated the story he'd heard uncertainly.

"How?" Lokus scoffed. "It's not like they hit back, is it? Plus, notice how he no longer tries to sidle into their conversation?"

He looked again. The boy's angry gaze did seem to wince away from Djenja's very proximity. But still…

"He used to talk to her?"

How hadn't he noticed that?

"*Tried* to, I said," Lokus corrected with mock moroseness. "He finally got past Snicker and Giggle – poor bastard. Now, none of them can keep a straight face. 'cept her highness, of course…"

Lured by Lokus's words, he tossed another surreptitious glance at Djenja – only to have it deflected by her sharp stare.

Snicker and Giggle – who were, in actuality, the ladies Serenity and Generosity Kuwon – flashed him identical, anticipatory grins.

He hastily turned his back on their titters – or, in one's case, a snicker – towing his friend along.

"Ouch," Lokus commiserated. Still draped across his shoulders like a sloth, the taller boy's toes dragged the boards. "You want I should punch you in the nose, now, and spare you the suspense?"

"It's not like that…" He slapped irritably at his friend's limply questing fist, finally managing to shrug free.

Lokus swayed upright, somehow seeming to sashay while standing still, and absently tossed his sheaf of sweat-darkened hair. Several girls glanced enviously at the blonde cascade.

"So you say," his friend, scoffed, "but try telling *her* that…"

The hair rose on the back of his neck at Lokus's thoughtful tone. His friend floated through life like a leaf on the breeze and only ever gave serious thought to mischief. Sure enough, those seafoam eyes sparkled with sudden inspiration.

"No!" he prayed, his desperate grab missing the lanky boy, who promptly billowed toward the trio of girls, arm upraised.

"Hey, Djen-!"

Abandoning his seirin to the boards, he leapt after Lokus, modifying a headlock so he could ram a hand over that rampant mouth. He felt a broad smile break against his palm.

Lokus, for all his lack of seriousness and lackadaisical sword skill, was a savant when it came to grappling.

It was like trying to grip a greased eel.

He knew, if Lokus hadn't allowed him, he'd never have wrestled their writhing pile of limbs past the staring girls.

Finally, he had the fiend pinned to the boards outside, straddling the lighter boy's chest and both hands pressed to his mouth.

"Are you going to behave?" he panted.

"Mmmpff!" Lokus's overlong lashes waved in surrender.

He relaxed his grip.

In a blink, he was on his face, Lokus's knee in the small of his back and the boy's laughter in his ears.

"Snake!" he squeezed past squashed lips, thumping the boards.

"Hey," his friend's grip slackened curiously. "Who's the guy in the purple pajamas?"

He struggled to raise his head.

A familiar figure waited at the bottom of the stairs.

"Keeper...?" he breathed.

At his sudden stillness, Lokus scrambled off him.

Barely aware of doing so, he rose. His heart took the steps a dozen at a time while his feet lagged behind.

It really was Justin, kindly face unaccountably tense and eyeing him uncertainly.

As memory of his abandonment resurged, his pace petered. He halted on the last step, putting him at eye level with the priest.

"You look well," Justin ventured tentatively, the statement curling with the hint of a question.

Marco's fists balled.

*No thanks to you...*he wanted to say.

"Why are you here?" he demanded instead. He did not care that the priest could see his anger, not to mention sense it.

It was a good thing Master Crysopher was not present to witness this disrespect, or else there'd be no end to the laps.

Far from seeming affronted, the priest's eyes softened.

"Your instructor informed me that you were ready to receive visitors. He has been judiciously guarding your time."

"My time?" he frowned. "Wait, *you* talk to Master Crysopher?"

The keeper gave him a puzzled look. "Of course. Once a week, every week, without fail. It was one of my conditions when I enrolled you – in turn for my promise that I would keep my distance until such time as Master Crysopher allowed otherwise."

Master Crysopher had closed the court to the keeper?

"Why?" he blurted.

"I imagine it was to help you immerse and acclimate to your new role and surroundings. To settle, as it were, away from painful reminders." Mouth twisting, the priest toyed with his chain of office. "It was hard – not being able to look in on you. But, seeing you now, I admit that the masha'na knew best. You have made enormous strides. And, if I'm not mistaken, a friend?"

The keeper glanced to where Lokus still leaned on the rail above, making no effort to disguise his rapt attention.

"That's not what I meant," Marco scowled, stoking hard at his flagging anger. "*Why* were you trying to see me?"

The priest's brow furrowed. "Because I- Ahem, so *we* could resume your studies, of course. Unless…?"

The priest's eyes lit with understanding. "I apologize if I have presumed. You would be a credit to the ranks of the masha'na. Only… I had hoped you would wish to resume your scholarship?"

Marco's breath sped.

He had taken it as a given that he had lost the keeper's endorsement, along with the man's favor. He'd made peace with it.

So he was surprised by the surge of sudden yearning he felt.

But…

He glanced back at Lokus's uncharacteristically somber face. He took in the raised court that hid Djenja and where Master Crysopher would work them all to the bone again tomorrow.

"I…" he stammered. "I'm not finished here."

"And you won't be," Justin agreed, somewhat sourly, "until you are raised to the red. I swear, I could strike sparks off your Master Crysopher's stubbornness. But he has *graciously* agreed to release you to me, for several evenings a week-"

The disbelief loud in his ears, Marco sat unsteadily on the steps.

"-curriculum will have to be curtailed, of course," the keeper was explaining. "We would focus on your strengths. History, language, cultural studies and so forth. Even so, yours will be an exceedingly full schedule. If, that is, you're feeling up to it?"

The tide of relief carried his gaze to meet that of the keeper.

The mentor he'd thought had abandoned him had been shadowing him, looking out for him this entire time.

He reconsidered his unspoken words.

"I am. Thanks to you."

The keeper smiled beatifically.

"It's settled then."

Chapter 5 – Spring

> Time is the enemy of knowledge. All our certainties, painstakingly penned on the skin of history, fade over the span of a single generation. Until what was once visceral truth is reduced to a scrawl, faded and unclear. How then, is a scholar to trace the birth of an empire that spans untold generations? Moreover, given how tightly the current generation grasps their visceral truths, why would such a scholar waste the ink?
>
> ~ *Pella Monop, Introduction to 'A Treatise on Empire', unpublished.*

WITH A DEFT PINCH, the colonel turned the dragoon upside down.

Calm, sure strokes painted the tiny steed's plaster belly.

It had taken to the mold perfectly, with no blemishes or bubbles. Setting his miniscule brush aside, the colonel peered through the Temple-made magnifying lens, blowing lightly on the figurine.

He heaved himself from his chair.

On the massive map table, turfed in felt, sprawled Maller's Field. Several leagues to the north of this fort, the real Maller's Field hadn't seen battle in a generation. But he had faithfully recreated that seminal victory here, in his office.

He stretched on his tiptoes to place the newly minted cavalryman – shown galloping behind a blind hill to flank the Renali forces. Pleased, he stood away, studiously righting the company of skirmishers his gut had flattened.

He wandered back to his desk and re-dipped his brush. A hurried knock at his door almost sent his next stroke awry.

"Come!"

"Colonel, sir!" his aide burst in, face flushed a decidedly non-military shade.

The colonel's fingers twitched toward a pot labeled *flesh tone*.

"What is it, major?" he growled his displeasure.

"Renali elements, sir!" the man wheezed.

Suppressing a sigh, he returned to his miniature endeavor. The major was new to this border posting and had not yet caught on to the fact that the Renali war was tepid as yesterday's tea. The most action this forgotten fort ever saw was giving distant patrols dirty looks. And, occasionally, giving chase – for appearances' sake.

The real front line – the Skordian campaign – wasn't even on this continent.

Keeps the men occupied, I suppose, he reflected.

"Did we pursue?"

"No, sir!"

He frowned severely at this failure. "Why ever not, major?"

"They came to meet us, sir."

Battle? Now that was more like it! Smiling, he slapped at his desk. Some of the old military bluster crept back into his voice.

"Ha! Gave 'em a good what-for, did you?"

"No– You misunderstand, sir," the major persevered, beneath his superior's intensifying glare. "They came to *meet* us, sir. Under a banner of truce. They're here, sir. At the gate."

"What!?"

Wincing, the major rushed to reassure. "Minimal military escort, sir, for some kind of diplomat. Says he's carrying a sealed missive for the Emperor. Showed me the scroll, sir. It's all official. He's downstairs, in the waiting room, insisting we provide him safe conduct to the capital."

Renali? Inside *the fort...?*

Powdery pieces of dragoon pattered onto his desk.

"Sir?"

* * *

"Your greatest enemy is always on the hilt-ward side of your sword."

Eyes closed, Marco felt Master Crysopher breathe past.

Where he knelt, hands relaxed atop his thighs, he barely heard his classmates' breathing. Two years had reduced their number from two dozen to just sixteen. Like him, they hung on the master's every word.

"Your meanest foe," the man continued, padding between the rows, "rests right behind your eyes. Fear, pain, fatigue, and confusion. These are the voices that tell you, you cannot fight on. That you cannot win. If you heed them – even for a moment – you will have lost."

He sat, mute, as the master ghosted among them.

"I have trained your bodies to give voice to the sword. If you can manage to also quiet your minds, your song will be the sharper for it."

The voice reversed direction. "Any fool with a sword can be lethal. To be *masha'na*, you must be able to divorce thought from action. Let your blade lead and your body follow, leaving your mind behind. This, we call the *fighting focus*."

Despite himself, his breath sped.

"When it is kill-or-be-killed, it is often the less skilled – but more focused – who leaves the field alive."

Uncertainty niggled at him. As it had, more and more often, every day their red graduation drew near. The masha'na were *holy* warriors, defending the faith and the faithful from a host of foreign evils and their false gods.

That was proper. It was Helia's will being done.

The scriptures he held dear were filled with examples of virtuous men doing vile deeds. The prophet, Prelion, had smothered a slumbering traitor in cold blood. The possessed Yorimund had been tossed from a sea cliff by his disciples.

But, when his own hands were on the sword's hilt, he could not help but be reminded that *taking a life* was a cardinal sin.

He'd have been happier if he were struggling to reconcile these contradictions within himself. Instead, he'd discovered something... disquieting. With a hilt in hand, and anger in his heart, he conjured images of two dockers in a back alley. When his will flagged, or his energy petered, he envisioned a scarred face before him. He imagined the crunch of throat cartilage or the crack of blunt fingers under his blows... and, each time, he found the drive to press on.

He'd avoided broaching the subject with the keeper, fearing the priest would sense what lay in his secret heart.

That would be unbearable.

"Start with a breathing exercise," the master's voice intruded.

Glad of the opportunity, he strove to calm his thoughts.

"In through your nose... Out through your mouth..."

The hall sighed steadily – a bellows, being operated by Master Crysopher's expert hand. He felt it fan a hot flame in his gut and he fed all his errant thoughts, all his doubts, to it.

Until everything was ashes.

"Find your feet."

He rose, distantly aware of the rustle of others around him.

"First form, first movement..." the master commanded.

He shifted into the first pose, seirin at the ready.

"One..." the master prompted.

He stepped forward, sweeping a slow arc.

"Two."

Pivot. Slide.

"Three."

Parry. Riposte.

"Four…"

Even dancing blind, they did not bump one another, every seirin describing a bubble of calm. Mesmerized, he lost himself in the familiarity of the dance, a passenger inside his own body.

"Twenty one," the master finished.

He returned to a ready stance.

"Raise your hand," the master maintained, "if you feel you can sustain this focus into a sparring match."

He raised his hand. It had been a fruitful two years.

"I will come and guide you to your circle – concentrate on keeping your focus. Everyone else, clear a space. Quietly."

A profusion of bare feet whispered away.

The hand that settled on his shoulder overlay strength with control. He found it a comforting mixture. In silence, he allowed it to steer him.

"Alright," the master announced at last. "Open."

Clatter Court held no official rankings. Rooms were assigned randomly and chores divvied up equally. That didn't mean everyone didn't know where they stood in relation to everybody else. He was eighth of sixteen. Lokus was at ten. There was some argument as to whether the twins were four and five or four and four. Djenja was number one.

And the boy across from him, with the aquiline nose and the noble brow of a High House, held number three. Lokus said they'd left the silver spoon too long in Jeral Stalia's mouth. Hence the permanent sneer.

He resisted the urge to see if the other pairings were similarly unequal. Under Jeral's eager eyes, his focus wobbled.

Calm, he reminded himself, accepting the faceguard someone handed him.

His opponent had the longer reach. He'd have to close, fast.

"Begin!"

He caught Jeral off guard, springing into a lunge.

The highborn was lightning, flashing out from under his attack, leaving wisps of hair to trail as an afterimage.

Thwack! Thwack!

Two stinging blows, to his elbow and upper arm. Numbness was but a beat behind. Gritting his teeth, he shifted his grip and spun into a guarded crouch. But the expected barrage did not fall.

Instead of pressing the advantage, Jeral had pulled back. The noble stood on the starting line – not his own – as if the bout were yet to begin.

Confused, he sought a glimpse of his opponent's shaded eyes…

And came to an unwelcome epiphany.

The lightning jabs had been a jibe. The lackluster defense an insult. And taking his starting line – like candy from a baby – was a taunt. That disdainful gaze plainly said so.

Whatever focus he'd managed to finagle flew apart. Why didn't Master Crysopher take Jeral to task for–

What, exactly? Striking and moving in a sparring circle? The noble had done nothing illegal.

Catching his glance in the master's direction – and correctly guessing the cant of his thoughts – white teeth flashed behind Jeral's helm. The noble knuckled at his faceguard's cheek, as though at some hindrance. There was none.

Baby gonna cry?

Temper flaring at the injustice, his grip tightened on his seirin–

No, he thought. *That's what he wants. To undermine my focus.*

But focus was long gone. Without it, he didn't have a prayer.

Prayer? he thought.

His opponent's sneer hitched higher at seeing his seirin droop. He ignored it as he slid into well-worn mental grooves. He might be new to this *fighting focus*... But he'd spent veritable months mastering the streaming trance. Despite seasons of neglect, it embraced him at his merest prod.

The world contracted until it held only himself. And Jeral.

Rolling his numb shoulder, he stepped forward.

The sneering boy made to casually punch past his guard. The technique perfectly polished. A deafening *clack!* punctuated its failure. The stunned silence slowly filled with Jeral's outrage.

And then the blows came down like hail.

The trance shuddered, threatening instant collapse. He realized his mistake: He'd only ever practiced it while blind and motionless, with plenty of opportunity to control his breathing.

He weathered the deluge. But defense required footwork.

The two seirins rang a rapid tattoo.

Frustration rolled off the noble, along with the furious assault.

Puffing, Marco's tried to maintain his tranced breath but fumbled his next parry. A riposte drove into his side and sent him staggering. His physical and mental balance teetered but he snatched them back, exhaling forcefully.

He had to finish this quickly, before he lost the trance-

The treble of tortured wood filled the hall. The watching students were statues on the periphery, still but for their eyes.

Stick found flesh with a meaty retort. A hilt dropped from nerveless fingers. A set of knees banged into the boards.

A seirin skittered away.

He stared, stunned, as the tiered ceiling swam above him. The planks were a cool compress at his back. Taking the offered hand by rote, he caught his breath as he was jerked up. In that moment of closeness, pitched for his ears alone, a voice whispered:

"You belong behind a spade, not a sword."

Cold contempt met his gaze. "Go back to the farm."

A parting slap, meant to look comradely, stung his sore shoulder. And then the nobleman's son had swept past.

"Alright," the master announced. "Enough for today."

"If you tilt your head and squint, it looks like a butterfly..." Lokus opined, poking him in his side. He hissed in pain.

"Like that, yes!"

They sat atop the court steps, his robes parted down his front.

"You'll live," his friend diagnosed. "It didn't break the skin."

"It still hurts!" he slapped the probing finger away.

"You'd be dead if it didn't."

"He almost *was* dead," someone observed.

The twins strolled up. He hastily rearranged his robes.

"Taking Jeral head-on?" said Sera – or maybe Gena?

They shook their heads in perfect unison. "Insane."

Uncowed, Lokus arched an impudent eyebrow at them.

"You think he should have let Jeral herd him from the circle?"

"Or just run out," one supplied, summoning her sister's smirk.

"That doesn't sound like much fun," Lokus argued.

"That doesn't *look* like much fun," the agreeable twin pointed.

"Are you joking? He had the time of his life!"

Lokus made the mistake of clapping him on the shoulder. He sucked in a pained breath.

The sisters gave voice to their signature laughter.

"Help me up," Marco growled, wanting to be away from the giggling. But Lokus seemed eager to talk to the twins.

"Could *you* have beaten Jeral?" the blond boy wondered aloud.

"Of course," the girls chorused.

Lokus's eyes narrowed. "Separately? Fighting one-on-one?

The sisters shared a considering glance.

"No," one declared.

"Probably not," the other agreed.

Far from being put out by the admission, they smiled brilliantly.

"You didn't do badly, though," one turned to console him.

"We might have to watch our backs," the other finished.

Djenja had stepped from the hall, drawing his eyes.

"We're off," one sister announced, spotting her too.

"See you later," the other echoed.

"Gena, Sera," Lokus nodded goodbyes to them in turn.

They paused.

"*I'm* Gena," one said severely. "*She's* Sera."

But Lokus merely gave them his mischievous grin.

"No," he stated with certainty, "you're not."

Caught in a lie, the sister who'd objected scowled. The other beamed and waved shyly at Lokus before she followed her sibling.

Marco barely noticed.

Djenja watched on, mirroring Master Crysopher's unamused expression. Meeting it made him feel small but he refused to look away. He only began breathing again when she had descended the stairs and the twins' pratting had dwindled into the distance.

"They're right, you know," Lokus said, pulling him from his preoccupation and to his feet. Pain returned with a vengeance.

"About?" he wheezed, glad of the distraction.

"You damned near landed a blow on his highness in there."

"It's a streaming trick," he huffed. "I'll show you."

Lokus dropped his voice conspiratorially. "You were using magic?" Far from sounding horrified at this illegal use of the arcane arts, his friend seemed impressed.

"No. Can't."

Strangely, the admission did not sting as much as his side did.

Lokus shrugged easily. "Well, then I guess you'll just have to settle for being a wizard with the sword."

"YOU'VE HEARD?" Justin asked.

"Along with half the city, it seems," Cyrus said. "The Assembly is abuzz. You can damn-near feel the hot air from here."

Passing amid the press, an acolyte paused, jaw dropping at even so mild a swearword coming from a venerable sitter.

Ignoring her, the older priest fell into step beside him, using a staff of office as a gilded walking stick and setting a brisk pace.

"What's the Emperor's reaction?"

"No word, yet," Cyrus critiqued, clomping along the vaulted passage. "Not that we'd be able to hear his imperial majesty over the howling of his generals."

"That bad?" he winced.

Cyrus scoffed. "Half expect to invade tomorrow. The other half are confused at the delay."

"No doubt the chapter houses have added their voices?"

"Little better than a murder of crows are the mercers," Cyrus nodded, "each angling for their own pound of flesh."

It said something – about the Empire's near constant state of war – that the suggestion of *peace* could cause such disarray.

"Interesting times," he opined. Cyrus snorted humorlessly.

The great doors to the Heart stood open but choked with priests – who fell back from Cyrus's wildly wielded staff.

"Vultures...!" his friend huffed, as the masha'na door guards – noting their regalia – nodded the two senior priests through.

They made their way down among the tiered seats, which were only half full. In contrast, the balconies were jam packed, as had been the halls outside. Cyrus picked a back row to sidle into.

"Not joining your fellow sitters?" Justin asked, eyeing the plush chairs ringing the broad dais.

"I can procrastinate well enough from here. Stupid thing…!"

Justin ducked the staff as it was maneuvered beneath their seats.

Below, the master of ceremony waited upon the mirrored brass floor, watching the senior priests file in. Behind the man loomed the raised alcoves of the archons, empty as yet.

Justin glanced again at the galleries. Every soul who didn't rate a seat at the Assembly seemed to be there, jockeying for position. Even to a non-empath, the tension was palpable.

"What a spectacle," Cyrus tutted disapprovingly.

"It's the biggest news since the Tamorian capitulation."

His friend huffed. "How fares your boy?"

He took the change of subject in stride.

"Better than I have any right to expect," he bowed his head reverently. "His studies progress apace. With his unorthodox schedule, it will take him a year or two longer than most to earn his satchel and sash. But I have little doubt he will succeed."

Cyrus cast a jaded eye over him, waiting patiently for more.

Justin chewed his lip.

"He has nightmares," he admitted in an undertone.

"After what he's seen, it would be stranger if he did not."

Justin nodded. An ignorant man might fret that he had steered the boy onto a path to violence. But it took a mere evening's tutoring – with his gentle and forthright charge – to allay his fears. What Marco took away from the masha'na regimen was their discipline and diligence. *That* was something he could build on.

Still, it would not do to relax his vigil. The boy was prone to bad luck – Helia's penchant for sending errant priests, goodhearted urchins and even wild dogs to his ward's defense notwithstanding.

"And," he lowered his voice, "your own... experiment?"

Cyrus squirmed, like a confession was being wrung from him on the rack. "Your book has been of some help."

He hid his smile. While otherwise pragmatic, the fact that some upstart scholar had beaten him to a discovery irked Cyrus no end.

"Glad to hear it," he needled.

"O, hush," his friend grumped, "it's starting..."

The master of ceremony's staff rung off the brass floor.

"Help me up," Cyrus wheezed into the silence.

"Rise for the High Archon," the master of ceremony intoned.

The Temple's ruling body appeared atop their high seats. One, in particular, drew the eye.

"It's serious then..." Cyrus judged, noticing.

Emion Hallet stood, in his usually vacant space, beside the High Archon. It was rare to see the Emperor's spiritual advisor away from his charge. The situation at court must be tumultuous, indeed, for Hallet to come take the Temple's pulse in person.

High Archon Prelace appeared, bowed beneath the pauldrons of his office, his bronze mitre threatening to unseat his weary head.

"Join me in prayer," Helia's mortal voice commanded, cracked with age but heady with authority. A sea of heads bowed.

"Holy Helia, guardian mother," the high archon entreated, in the Old Temple tongue, "look upon us this day, your faithful children. Grant us your strength, to see us through the perilous times ahead-"

That does not bode well, Justin thought.

"-bless us with your wisdom, so we may better serve your will. Instill us with calm, so we may perceive the tasks you set us. And gift us your mercy, for we know ourselves to be undeserving. Unity through faith."

"Unity through faith," echoed the chamber, sounding a susurrus as hands drew circles over hearts. The high archon sat first. The master of ceremony rapped his staff, needlessly, for quiet.

"We are now in session," the man boomed, symbolically ceding the floor. "The Assembly recognizes Archon Emion Hallet."

The Emperor's advisor stood, mouth set in a severe line.

"Is it true?" someone from the galleries called out, in breach of all protocol. "Have the Renali sent an emissary?"

Unperturbed by the interruption, Hallet nodded. "It is true."

The hall erupted.

Justin clenched his jaw against the mental racket. Rampant fright, fury and bewilderment ran along the balconies.

The master's insistent bellows and wild bashing finally quelled the noise, letting Hallet proceed.

"An ambassador has applied at Fort Bearox, seeking an imperial audience. They travel at speed and will arrive within a fortnight."

"Is it a new declaration of war?" someone dared.

Noise burgeoned. Fuming, the master of ceremony swung in search of the culprit who'd spoken out of turn.

"Please, brothers and sisters," Archon Hallet entreated, rather than answer, "let us respect the traditions of the Assembly."

The cacophony dwindled to an acceptable rumble. A flurry of hands shot up among the front seats. The master pointed.

"The Assembly recognizes Speaker Zusia Sillen."

The elderly speaker did not deign to rise to her feet.

"Whence comes this information?" she quavered.

"The chaplain at Fort Bearox sent a bird," Hallet allowed.

"The assembly recognizes Sitter Animosi."

"Thank you," Animosi said. "Tell us please, what has the Emperor's council proposed to do?"

Which was to say, what had Hallet proposed to the Emperor's council? Speculative whispers awaited the man's response.

"The court prepares to meet the foreign ambassador with all the courtesy and gravity the situation calls for," the archon hedged.

There was a muttering of dissatisfaction at this answer.

"You are the Emperor's closest counsel, Emion," the learned sitter pressed. "Surely you can tell us how this news sits at court?"

Half-voiced agreements rounded the hall, raining on the archon.

"With the Renali purpose as yet uncertain, any planning would – at this point – be premature."

Skillfully cutting across the upsurge of voices, the archon picked the next questioner himself. "Speaker Tel Loosia?"

"Archon," the younger woman addressed, "is there any reliable intelligence as to this diplomat's purpose?"

The master looked peeved at being bypassed, especially since the Heart then quieted without his interference.

The speaker remained standing, signaling another question.

"Other than that his mandate comes from the Renali king, no."

"Is it fair," Tel Loosia continued, "to speculate as to peace?"

The hall went dead silent. Tensions took an updraft. At the center of attention, the archon pursed thin lips, considering.

"It seems likely-"

A growing clamor drowned out the end of the archon's speech.

"*Peace!?*" someone scorned loudly. "They should *surrender*!"

The Assembly began to devolve, the master hammering nails.

"Interesting times indeed," he reaffirmed.

Uncharacteristically, Cyrus said nothing.

Inquisitor Torvan Mattanuy stood in a screened alcove. Ahead, the private doors to the archons' high seats opened as the elders left. Disagreement rang from the Assembly at their backs.

The Temple's six most senior priests and priestesses shuffled into the passage, wrapped in quiet discussion and spangly robes.

Imperial Advisor Emion Hallet was conspicuous in their company by reason of youth – the man was scarcely fifty. He towered above the stooped shoulders and bent backs of his peers.

Mattanuy moved – by the minutest, deliberate degree – and saw that Hallet marked him immediately.

So. You watch the shadows, even here, in the Temple's heart...

Whether due to paranoia or prudence, Mattanuy approved.

Hallet led the elders a safe distance beyond the dark alcove, then made an excuse to double back.

Shoulders stiff with displeasure, the advisor swept the drapes aside. "I do not appreciate these informational ambushes, Mattanuy. If you have something to communicate, use my agent."

Hallet's idea of a spy was a sausage of a priestess, named Anochria. Her paralytic manner defied his closest scrutiny.

And he found her presence unsettling.

"This rated a face-to-face," he assured the archon.

Hallet's gaze sharpened. "You've found something at last?"

In fact, once he'd begun to look in earnest, he'd found lots. But nothing he could peg as patently seditious. The modernist influence was nebulous unto nothingness.

"No. And it seems increasingly unlikely that I will."

The archon's lips thinned. "Is not sniffing out sin your specialty? Or does your expertise end at coercing confessions?"

He bared his teeth at the jibe and pressed on.

"My efforts at finding the modernist web have failed because its strands are spun too subtly. If we wish to *see* its master move, we must first stir something within its demesne. To that end, I need to borrow your influence. To drop a fly in the ointment, as it were."

Calculation lit the man's face. To his credit, he figured it out quite quickly. "The Renali peace offer?"

Ah, so it *was* a peace offer. The information he'd been able to gather had made that only nine-tenths certain.

Hallet was musing on some inner, political landscape.

"So," the man said at last, "we set the board – and see whose game pieces move to block ours?"

Inwardly, Mattanuy grimaced at having his metaphor undermined. Outwardly, he grinned.

"Exactly."

LURID RED LIGHT bathed Marco's upturned palms. All else was black. His thoughts were soft-edged and slow, his attention skittish...

Where...?

Drip...

The small sound echoed hugely, carving space from the nothingness-

Drip...

A slim opening skewed into view, a slightly brighter smudge against the dark. He neared, giving no thought to the lack of sensation in his feet. At the sight of raw rock, he came to understand that he was inside a cavern of some sort.

Beyond the rocky crag, shallow stairs wound down, into the gloom. In the prescient way of dreams, he knew terror lurked somewhere below. Also in the way of dreams, he was powerless to resist his uncooperative feet, drawing him downward.

At his first footfall, the cavern tolled a deep, tortuous note. Rock shook, strained, cracked and bled.

Something sped up the winding stairway. A sound.

Clawed air scythed him from his feet, tumbling him along as it flayed his flesh. He felt the cavern wall, speeding to meet him-

Smack!

He shot up with a yell, toppling Lokus from the bed. Between hastily raised forearms and frantic breaths, Marco recognized his cell, lit by moonlight.

No horrors lurked in its corners or hid in its murk. The door was firmly shut and his roommate's bed was... empty?

Someone groaned from the floor by his cot.

"Lokus?" he gasped. "Lokus, is that you?"

A tousled mane reared up in the semi-dark. "Might be. Though I just hit my head pretty hard, so, you tell me?"

Fright slowly gave way to suspicion. "What were you doing?"

"What else?" his friend waggled expressive eyebrows. "Waking you from your magical sleep with a kiss, of course, princess."

He became aware of his cheek, hot and stinging.

Lokus made a show of shaking feeling back into a numb hand.

"Bastard," Marco cussed. The swearword had adopted him, since his coming to Clatter Court. You could not properly express your dismay – at being whacked with a stick – with words such as 'darn' or 'drat'. A lifetime ago he'd not have said those either.

Rising, unrepentant, Lokus gave him a one-shouldered shrug.

Marco chafed at his cheek, trying to spread the pain a little thinner. "You could have just shaken me awake."

His friend dove back into bed. Blankets billowed in the gloom.

"Tried that," Lokus assured. "But you were under deep."

Grumbling, he punched his pillow harder than necessary.

"So," Lokus asked, as silence settled, "were you chasing carts?"

He raised his hands for inspection. A ghost-memory winked.

"I... can't remember," he admitted.

"Just as well. I don't need your nightmares, following me to sleep."

"At least then," he sighed wistfully, "I'd get to slap *you* awake."

"Me, asleep, is about the only time you *could* land a blow."

"Oh, yeah?"

He sent his pillow toward his half-seen friend's head.

A heartbeat later, Lokus's pillow knocked him flat.

"You've got eyes like an owl!" he accused, between mouthfuls of linen. "And what's in this thing? Rocks?"

"Those would be my weighty thoughts and solid good nature."

"Hmm," he observed. "So this is where you hide them..."

The rustle of sheets gave a moment's warning. He fended off his homeward-bound pillow and ripped the other from beneath his head. He heard Lokus snag it from mid-flight.

"Now go to sleep," he reprimanded his friend.

"You are not the boss of me!" Lokus hissed a whisper.

"Oh, I am too the boss of you!"

"Pfft!" Lokus grumbled to himself. "Somebody gives him a bright new belt and he thinks he's a Prime returned..."

A Prime? No, he did not aspire to the status of warrior-saint.

He stretched out a blind hand, feeling at the red graduation belt, hanging on its peg. It had been an austere ceremony, with a half-dozen masha'na standing attendance, as per Temple Law. Civilians weren't, strictly speaking, allowed in Clatter Court. Several of the students' parents were high-placed people though. So they'd all crowded into the south garden chapel instead.

The presiding priest, Exarch Sule, had seemed more interested in the parents than the protocols. Even so, perfunctorily smiles and speedy congratulations had done little to spoil the true achievement – receiving Master Crysopher's grudging nod.

The master had disappeared directly after the ceremony, whereas Exarch Sule had come alive, making animated conversation with the attending nobles.

The reunion between parents and progeny had been… a little bitter to watch. He'd stayed out of the way, sitting beside Lokus – whose family was dirt poor and from a far-off prefecture besides.

Orphans, of a sort, together.

The full force of their boundless energy unbridled, the twins had literally leapt into the arms of a thickset man in dark silks.

"*Patri! Patri!*" they'd chorused, as the Kender noble swept them up and around, forcing others to duck out of the way.

"Looks just like his mother…" Lokus had commented, nodding.

Across the crowded hall, Jeral had been in staid conversation with his parents, hands sedately clasped behind his back. The approaching Exarch Sule had been rebuffed by the lord's bluff demeanor. A few words through the lady's razor sneer – so like her son's – had set the priest scurrying.

Curious, Marco had been casting around for Djenja's relations.

Lokus had elbowed him. "Say, ain't that your sponsor?"

Through a gap in the crowd, out the open door and across the kempt grass, a priestly figure had been visible, glinting with a keeper's regalia. He'd already been half a dozen paces away before he'd remembered Lokus.

"Go, idiot!" his friend had spurred him.

He'd needed no more encouragement to bound out the door.

"Congratulations," had been the keeper's first words.

"You're here!" he'd exclaimed.

"Of course."

"Why not come inside?"

The priest had eyed the lit chapel – and, perhaps, Exarch Sule – with mild distaste. "You know how I dislike crowds…"

He'd snorted at that.

"You asleep?" Lokus interrupted his reverie.

He sighed, sinking deeper into his pillow. "Yes."

"Oh. Well. Goodnight, then."

"You too."

The silence stretched. "Lokus?"

"I thought you were asleep?"

He ignored that. "Where do you think we stand?"

He didn't need to explain. Their dwindling numbers had forced a dozen red-ribboned classes together. They were more than a half-hundred students now, studying various forms under a succession of trainers daily. While top students – like Djenja and Jeral – had been knocked down in the rankings a short step only, he and Lokus had as-good-as been shoved down the stairs.

"Still somewhere in the middle," Lokus guessed. "Master Crysopher's students are a cut above the rest – pun intended."

Unbidden, he recalled his fraught first day of enrollment.

"I once heard someone call him Clatter Court's best trainer."

"Obviously, his excellence has rubbed off," Lokus preened.

Maybe, he thought. But Djenja was further away than ever...

That thought followed him to sleep.

Less than a bell later, he began to quietly thrash and moan, drawing Lokus to his bedside once more. He did not see his friend wind up for another slap.

And he would not remember receiving it, come morning.

"It's open!" Cyrus called, in response to his knock.

Justin pushed at the door.

"I didn't realize you already had company," he apologized.

The old priest's missive had made no mention. Still, he recognized the big, bearded man, taking tea across from Cyrus.

"Shall I come back later?"

"Nonsense," his friend beckoned. "Join us."

Sensing an ambush, he shut the door with care.

"Justin, you know Sitter Willion Willionson?"

"Of course," he offered the man his hand. "Sitter, I've read your proposal on colonial reform. It was inspired."

"Thank you," the man's beard bobbed diffidently. "Though I fear I shall not see those goals realized in my lifetime."

"'Even the most daunting journey...'" he quoted.

"'...starts with a single step.'" The sitter completed. "From the gospel of Geamon – one of the rare war prophets who successfully married conquest to compromise."

"Ahem," Cyrus interrupted impatiently. "In addition to being a sitter on the Assembly, Will also heads the foreign affairs sub-committee."

The bearded priest's mood darkened. "The Renali diplomat has appeared before court and delivered a formal address to the Emperor."

"I heard." He'd have liked to gauge that gathering in person, but Marco's graduation had taken priority. "The offer of peace has been officially presented?"

Willionson, and his beard, nodded.

Even without his extra sense, the sitter was easy to read.

"I take it you're not best pleased?"

"It's a fine offer," the man allowed, his ire spiking. "A shame we're going to piss– I mean, *squander* it."

"Squander?" He looked from one sitter to the other in shock. "But I thought the Emperor was dispatching one of his own bloodline to act as ambassador and see to negotiations?"

Though the honor of such a thing might be lost on the Renali.

"It is not the *courtly* delegation that is the problem."

Ah. He might have suspected the chapter houses. Those mercers were apt to stumble over their own greed. But a simple proclamation could as easily seize their assets as tax them into oblivion. They had reason to tread lightly.

That left only the Temple delegation.

"Who?" he breathed, abruptly understanding.

"Melando is the current favorite," Cyrus supplied.

Melando?

The man was certainly qualified. Devout. Dour.

As a young chaplain on the Tamorian front, Melando had assumed command, after the general's untimely fall. Under Melando's unsubtle – and, frankly, unfeeling – lash, the Empire's territory had been expanded by bloody swathes.

The political uproar, at this blatant disregard for the division of powers, had almost cost an intercession by the Emperor.

Melando's style was that of the war prophets of old. His idea of diplomacy no doubt involved the heathens running for the hills. He was exactly the wrong kind of person for delicate negotiations.

The word 'fanatic' came to mind.

Willionson read the horror on his face. "I see you understand."

"Can't something be done?" he enquired breathlessly.

"I'm here, exploring that very question," the sitter promised.

"Will is of the opinion," Cyrus elaborated, "that he can lobby for Melando's replacement, given a compelling enough argument."

Willionson nodded. "Melando might not be popular but he is respected. And he comes at the Imperial Advisor's recommendation. My proposal would require a replacement of equal rank and renown."

Cyrus expanded, "And someone versed in foreign cultures, with experience of the Renali in particular. A proven diplomat."

"But even that would not be enough," Willionson worried. "This person would have to possess a decided advantage – not only over Melando – but at any trade negotiations to follow."

Sensing Cyrus's anticipation, he scowled. Ambush indeed.

"Anyone spring to mind?" asked the old healer, unrepentantly.

Temple politics, he reflected, were no less involved or divided than that of any other small country. With an added complication – the Temple led a much larger, more powerful country. Often by the nose. And without regard for little details like logistics, resources or political ramifications.

Right-thinking people, like Cyrus and Willion, kept their feet to the floor and their fingers to the breeze. Through their nudging, the dictatorship was steered clear of the sharp reefs.

He'd be a poor priest if he let their efforts flounder.

"Excellent," the sitter said, seeing the grudging agreement on his face. "I'll set things in motion."

Justin walked the man to the door in Cyrus's stead. He would have some harsh words for his friend, once they were alone.

"One more thing," the sitter forestalled. "There will be factions, both at home and abroad, who will want this treaty to fail. You are a student of history, Justin. You know public opinion is a sea with powerful tides. The citizenry live close to the Temple. The shortest route to another war is for you to get yourself killed over there.

"You'll have a small contingent of masha'na, of course," the sitter continued, "but they're not exactly unobtrusive. You will need someone to guard you at close quarters, someone you have an excuse to keep on hand."

Cyrus met his surreptitious glare with an innocent shrug.

Oh, poor Marco…

"It shouldn't be a problem," he grated.

Chapter 6 – One Journey Ends

In the history of every *civilized* society – for lack of a better word – there are dark chapters. Chapters its descendants would rather skim over. It is the sacred duty of the scholar and the historian to wade into these bloody and often shameful bogs. Though their efforts will, invariably, set them apart. This outcome is to be desired. Alienation only aids objectivity.

~ *Pella Monop, Introduction to 'A Treatise on Empire', unpublished.*

THE TALL WINDOW in Inquisitor Torvan Mattanuy's office afforded a fine view of the Granary Gate. From this distance, he could appreciate the orderly paths, clipped lawns and shaped shrubs without dealing with the affronting reek of compost.

His steepled fingers and air of serenity were misleading. He was listening intently. To his left, a single, dark pane had been polished to a mirror sheen. In its reflection, his office door stood open.

He would be damned if he let Hallet's agent – that slug, Anochria – sneak up on him once more. Such petty grandstanding was, of course, beneath him. But so was the pestilent priestess, and she needed to learn her place-

"Pretty view," she commented, from beside his elbow.

Only supreme self-control kept him from jumping. Grinding his teeth, he sneered at her sidelong.

She was a short lump of suet, cheeks drooping into her neck and dragging lazy eyelids after them. Oddly elegant hands perched on the round of her belly.

"You think so?" he prodded, examining her dead eyes.

She gave the view due consideration. Such a vista might easily inspire a homily, concerning toil and reward. An artist might remark on how the lines drew the eye to the magnificent gate. A cleaner might have wondered why one pane had been singled out, above the rest, for polishing.

What Anochria said, after a lazy blink, was, "Yes."

He suspected she wouldn't know 'pretty' if it tried nesting in her neck folds. Likely, she'd been the kind of child who had learned to smile with the aid of diagrams.

In the distance, a sturdy carriage had trundled into view, complete with a shingled roof and narrow chimney. It was flanked by a dozen mounted masha'na in orange and umber – a rare sight.

"Our snare has snagged something," he observed pointedly.

"Keeper Justin Wisenpraal," she nodded, displacing jowl fat.

"Not my first suspect," Mattanuy admitted, "but he fits the bill. Clever, influential and a friend to the faceless masses."

They watched the convoy trundle toward the gate.

"The keeper will soon pass beyond my reach," he lied. "An interrogation – now – might save us a lot of needless effort."

She shook her head without considering it.

"His premature disappearance would draw all the wrong kinds of attention. Seeing who he reaches out to, when he thinks himself safe, may be more informative than thumbscrews. In the meantime, Sitter Willionson went to great lengths to manage this reassignment. Refocus your investigation there. Quietly."

Inwardly, he bridled. If she thought she could simply jerk on his chain, and bring him to heel, she was sorely mistaken. Tightly tamping his anger, he turned to her. "I will not-"

But she was gone.

Damn the woman!

He stalked stiffly to his desk-side cabinet. Unlocking it, he ran his fingers along the hard spines of the folders within.

"'Refocus' indeed…" he growled, finding the volume he sought. It shed nearly two years' worth of dust, smacking onto the desktop. Untwining its ties, he cracked it open. Across the topmost page, in his own hand, was printed, 'The Butcher Murders'.

"'Keeper Justin Wisenpraal'," he mused.

He knew he'd read that name before.

* * *

THE HORSE TOSSED its head, causing Marco to snatch at the saddle horn – needlessly – to stay in his seat.

"Still not getting along, eh, Bumble?" a wagon driver behind him chortled, sitting secure despite the rutted road.

His ears heating, Marco kept his gaze on the passing countryside. The mare they'd found for him was as docile as the day was long. But he'd not yet had the horsemanship part of his masha'na training, nor any other training to prepare him for traveling with a convoy like this.

He'd changed a lot over the past two years. He was tougher now. Surer. He'd earned his red sash; he could dance fourteen forms – blindfolded; and he could do a hundred press-ups without slowing. Yet, somehow, none of it mattered. It had only taken being treated like a know-nothing novice – by the distracted soldiers and staff – for him to fall back into that role.

Full of wounded Clatter Court pride, he'd spent that whole first day in the saddle, ignoring all advice, convinced that sheer force of will would eventually conquer the beast beneath him.

So intent had he been, on matching minds with the mare, he'd forgotten his trepidation at facing Tellar's crowded streets again. It had taken the convoy half a day to win free of the bustling city, and he'd spent that time, facing a horse inside the fighting focus.

Evening had found them riding into their first coach in. Only then had he let go his death grip. His legs had seized during his graceless dismount, dumping him in the dust. One foot stuck in the stirrup, he'd groaned helplessly while the mare had slowly towed him toward the water trough.

The head hostler had laughed so hard, the man's assistant had had to help him over to a mounting block to sit down.

By the second day, *everyone* knew about the keeper's bumbling assistant.

"Everything alright up there, Bumble?"

Grimacing, he nodded mutely, eyeing the scenery through his fringe. Beneath his breath, he counted to ten. In Renali.

He missed Clatter Court. He missed Lokus.

Worst of all, he was missing training. Every plodding pace, toward the Renali Kingdom, was another step Djenja was pulling further and further ahead of him.

They'd been on the road over a month. They must be nearing-

"That should be Twohaven, up there," the driver mused.

As if responding to the man's words, Marco's mare raised its head toward the distant town.

He snatched at the reins.

It wasn't that he was ungrateful for the fortune in horseflesh they'd been supplied. He just couldn't help but wonder whether he might not be better off with a simple mule. Or, perhaps, an ox.

When it seemed reasonably certain the mare intended no murder, he eased back in the saddle for a look.

Though dew yet clung to the grasses near to hand, Twohaven's steeple sat in a spot of sunlight amid velvet fields. Beyond it reared Mount Meltwater – and their route through the Barrier Range.

The Renali delegation had crossed further to the south, where spring had already shaken loose the mountains' snowy shawls. The Heli ambassador, however, would not hear of a detour.

As second cousin to the Emperor, Lord Harvain Malconte – First seat of high house Malconte, erstwhile Minister of the Interior and one-time Chief Imperial Treasurer – could afford to reject any advice he wished.

The man's carriage – a monstrous, eight-wheeled mansion, drawn by as many horses – trundled at the forefront of the train. Much to the chagrin of Strike-Captain Iolus, who was charged with the ambassador's safety.

The man's platoon of Imperial Elites, imposing in their gold-trimmed ebony plate, rode in formation around it.

In contrast, the strike-captain got on swimmingly with Chapter Master Adrio Bulgaron.

The pre-eminent mercer, with the steely beard and unbending demeanor, could pass for a retired officer himself. Certainly, the man seemed comfortable with both sword and saddle.

Every evening, with military precision, Bulgaron's armored retainers raised a command tent inside a cordon of smaller tents. Like they were an army of twelve marching to battle.

Of the masha'na, of course, were was no sign. Lightly armored and astride swift mounts, the dozen Temple warriors ranged far afield of the convoy, acting as scouts.

Marco tensed as his horse whuffed once more.

He should let the keeper know Twohaven was close.

Swallowing, he tapped tentative heels to the mare's flanks… and overshot the keeper's carriage before he could convince her to slow again. He weathered the passing wagoners' smirks.

Eventually, the keeper's conveyance caught up.

Though it looked like a mobile farmstead from the outside, inside it was mostly bookshelf. Even the keeper's bed folded away to make space for more tomes and scrolls.

He thumped at its side. "We're nearing Twohaven, Father!"

"Ah, good!" came the muffled reply.

Drawers rattled and books thumped as his mentor prepared to disembark. Today would be an early halt – to rest up and resupply. Twohaven was the last Imperial settlement this side of the range. Tomorrow would see them traversing the pass.

Twohaven's palisades were adorned with festival bunting. A man with a mayoral sheen of sweat was trying to keep the gate clear of geese. Imperial logisticians had preceded the convoy by weeks, preparing their path. Many a small town had taken its arrival as an excuse for festivities and feasting.

Marco felt a pang for the hapless pillar of the community, who would soon be whittled down by Lord Malconte's critique.

The unsuspecting man was flanked by the commander of the local garrison, who offered Strike-Captain Iolus a salute.

The caravan rolled into Twohaven without incident.

There was some self-conscious applause and even an overloud whistle – Twohaven was not a big place. The village children kept pace, their energy far outstripping that of their elders. Bulgaron's bearish mount snapped its teeth at one, instantly elevating the urchin to celebrity status among his peers.

The buildings were narrow, steeply peaked and slate-roofed, so as to shed snow and flung torches both. Dark timbers stood out starkly against the whitewashed clay walls. Imperial advancement provided thick, honey-colored windows for the Betopian-style buildings. This far east, the winters were long and gray and even the illusion of summer-tinted light was a relief.

The village green had been cleared for the convoy's use.

Gingerly, he worked his feet free of the stirrups and eased himself to the ground. The mare eyed him askance. Ignoring her, and the knowing chuckles, he handed the horse off to a groom.

Slinking off to the keeper's carriage, he wrestled the rear-facing steps down just as its hatch yawned.

"There you are," the priest said, spotting him. "Perfect timing!"

He hid his smile among the bags being handed down.

"Mm. Did you notice the Betopian architecture?"

He nodded dutifully as he helped the keeper down.

Vertebrae popped as the priest stretched and promptly headed for the inn. "My old back could really do with a solid bed tonight."

The innkeeper became flustered at the sight of a hierarch's robes. The poor man probably could not distinguish between a keeper's regalia and that of a sitter or speaker. And he kept addressing the priest as 'excellency' instead of 'holiness' as he stammered through the menu. Marco shook his head sadly.

Justin, of course, took no offense. But the innkeeper was unlikely to survive a conversation with the ambassador.

"Can I build you a fire, father?" he offered, eyeing the stacked hearth and stocked wood bin in their room. This close to the iced peaks the cold really pounced once one stepped out of the sun.

Sensing his impatience, the keeper arched an eyebrow at him.

"I see you straining at the bit. Go."

He grinned, appreciating the sentiment as much as the Renali idiom. They had both been practicing, talking around the keeper's god-given gifts. The Kingdom had no love of sorcery and would doubtless tar empaths with the same brush.

Nodding, he snatched his seirin and bolted for the door.

Both stable yard and village green would be bustling for some time yet. So he made his way behind the inn, to the small garden where even the rampant weeds had been arrested by winter.

Shrugging off his over robe, he shivered as he hefted his seirin. He resolved to suffer his shoes, rather than frozen toes.

It had been Lokus, who had pressed the practice sword on him, despite the strictures over court property.

"Master Crysopher insisted," his friend had assured him.

He'd chosen to believe it.

The unkempt garden made for unsure footing and the chill delayed his warm-up cadence but eventually he flowed into the first form. He settled into a strained trance as stiff muscles stirred to life. He'd moved to the third form before he felt the first prick of sweat and to the fourth before he felt the prick of eyes.

His swing finally found a fellow seirin with a familiar *clack!*

It was Finch this time. Closest to him in size, the blue-jawed masha'na was at least two decades his senior, but still spry.

Lightning attacks probed at his defense, wood clacking sharply. The masha'na was still only limbering up but already Marco felt his streaming trance under assault.

The trance was unlike the fighting focus. It had been created as a technique for harnessing lifeforce. It demanded meditative stillness and a strict breathing pattern. It was not designed for leaping about or ducking blows. A fact Finch brought home by forcing him back, crunching over mossy gravel.

Goddess's grace the man was fast!

Fielding blows close to his body, he feinted hard left and darted right. Pebbles sprayed as he drew up, a breath short of the masha'na's waiting blade. He eyed the hard wood barring the path of his nose. The trance snorted apart.

"He's getting better," someone called.

The rest of the masha'na had annexed the inner porch, dragging a table and chairs outside. Steam wafted from their tankards and smoke curled from Bear's spindly pipe, looking small in the huge man's hands.

"Hmm," Finch agreed, sauntering over to the table to collect a drink. "Another season and he'll be some trouble."

Marco hid his blush by bowing his thanks.

The short masha'na toasted him in turn, then pulled a face.

"Blegh. All that has put me in the mood for something chilled."

"Good luck enlisting the innkeeper," Jossram grumbled. "The ambassador was still shouting when I passed by earlier."

Bear huffed an agreement, raising blue smoke.

Shrugging, Finch took another swig and sat.

"Chilled?" Longjaw objected, only his dark eyes showing between the ruff of his cloak and his cowl. "It's glacial out here!"

"Islander," scoffed Parish, pale in his shirtsleeves.

Reclaiming his robe, Marco settled down within earshot.

In his experience, masha'na had been either silent sentinels or stern instructors. He'd never seen them in a social setting. The holy warriors were not at all what he'd imagined. Not least because they didn't seem to mind a snot-nosed, red-sashed student hanging about. But, also, because they drank and joked and smoked and swore. He didn't know to whom the chipped seirin belonged, but they parceled it – and his education – out among them.

He said a quiet prayer of thanks.

"Should have known I'd find you all drinking somewhere…" Kryskin said, rounding the corner.

The leonine man was young to be their leader. Since the masha'na was a strict meritocracy, this spoke volumes for his skill.

Ryhorn, whose mace-kissed face bore a permanent scowl, and Bear, who was every bit as imposing as his namesake, moved over.

Leffley poured their captain a dram. "So? We up at first light?"

"*You* will be," the man mock-growled, "running off all this alcohol."

"S'long as my poor ass is spared a saddle," Longjaw groaned.

"Hah! Fish foot," Parish scorned.

"Snow mole," Longjaw glared over the rim of his collar.

"Saltlick!"

Bear did nothing. But his chair creaked warningly. The arguing pair gave over, staring innocently in opposite directions.

The conversation turned toward the next few days.

Working some wax into his seirin's scuffed wood, he sat back to listen, reflecting that he was – all things considered – quite content.

✳ ✳ ✳

"SOMEONE ORDER THE mussel soup for lunch…?"

An inquisitorial carriage had drawn up, lacquered a forbidding black and promising gastric distress for *someone*.

The Tellar watchmen on door duty exchanged wary glances.

"Think we can send it back?" one whispered.

These two had once stood a riot-line, in the Warren, without backing down. Now, they retreated behind blank expressions as Torvan Mattanuy marched up the Watch House steps. A leather folder rode the crook of the man's arm, like a headsman's axe.

A heavy silence preceded the inquisitor, spilling over the duty officer and forcing the man to surface from a bog of paperwork.

"Can I help-?" the officer paled at sight of the black sash.

"Commander Greystone," Mattanuy demanded – as though the watch commander might be produced from the nearest desk drawer. Instantly. Or else.

The officer rallied. "The commander is indispo-"

Mattanuy's eyes narrowed.

"-in his office. Upstairs."

Under the inquisitor's sharp stare, the man rose. "This way…"

He hounded the officer's heels up the steps and down the passage. Impressively, the man retained the presence of mind to knock before cracking open his commander's door.

"What are you doing away from your post, sergeant?"

Not waiting to be announced, Mattanuy strolled in.

"Ah." The commander's face blanked. "Dismissed, watchman."

Mattanuy took the unoffered seat, across from the City Watch commander. His speculative gaze had been known to make grown men gibber but Greystone suffered it without ill effect.

Thrilling at the challenge, he set the file on the desk before him.

"I have questions," he began.

The commander glanced at the folder. "If I recall, you declined Watch aid. The words 'interference' and 'tolerate' were used. For better or worse inquisitor, the butcher murders are your baby. Unless," the man gave him a measuring look, "you're here to abandon it on our doorstep?"

"This actually concerns another case of yours. A dockside slaying that occurred at around the same time."

The proximity of the two events had hinted at more than mere coincidence. Now, his suspicions required proof.

The commander sat back. "You want access to our records?"

Grinning maliciously, Mattanuy tapped his folder. "I *have* access to your records. I'm here for access to *your* recollection."

The watchman frowned. "Even two years ago, I rarely investigated cases personally. And a dockside slaying? We have, on average, one of those every week."

"You would remember this one," Mattanuy promised.

Cracking the file, he read from memory, keeping his eyes on Greyston's expression, "'...*investigating officer concluded that feral dogs were responsible....*'"

How much of that conclusion had come from the 'Temple consultant', listed in the file, he wondered? "Care to comment?"

"Animal attacks are accidents, inquisitor," the man shrugged. "Not murders. Therefore, not watch business."

"I agree," he said. "Let's talk about whose business it is. In fact, I'd like to know everyone who was present. And, why."

Off course, the first rule of inquisition was to never ask a question to which you did not already have the answer. He'd secretly interviewed several watchmen concerning that night – and it was a testament to their fear of him that none had tipped off their commander. Still, he'd wanted to confront the man himself. To see whether he could spot a shadow of guilt in the man's complexion.

And to judge how far the modernist conspiracy had spread.

Half a bell later, he left the cacophony of the watch house, his thoughts racing. He had already been halfway convinced that this Justin Wisenpraal was a seditionist. The hierarch had built his own cabal of loyal students. He routinely funneled large sums of Temple funds to foreign vessels. And he seemed to have the local constabulary in his pocket.

Yet, never once had Mattanuy thought to give closer scrutiny to the man's ward. Well, he would remedy that, presently.

※ ※ ※

MARCO MADE HIS bleary way to bed, thankful his feet weren't crunching through an icy crust. The tame snow, that had come to Tellar one cold winter, had lent itself to snowball fights and snowmen. In contrast, the knee-deep drifts of the pass had threatened to gnaw his feet to nubs. Despite this, the wagoners declared their convoy had weathered the passing well.

He drew his over robe tighter about himself, not looking forward to his cold tent after the warmth of the keeper's carriage.

With what lay ahead of them, he and his mentor had more reason than ever to discuss political history and court intrigue. The masha'na, also, had shared a wealth of stories and some had raised questions for him. Mentioning these to the keeper had uncorked a fount of Imperial history he'd never have suspected: Yon Kama, one of the Empire's greatest generals, had been a drunk who'd drowned in a decorative fishpond. Lillin Darkheart, the vilest of dissidents, had been the then-Emperor's sister...

He'd soaked it all up. Until-

"Helia's mercy!" the priest had cut their discussion short. "It's nearly daybreak! Off to bed! Quick, while you have a couple of bells worth of sleep yet!"

He'd made to argue but his mentor had been adamant.

"*My* bed is on wheels, young one. Whereas you..."

He had envisioned himself, falling asleep in the saddle – and then falling *out of* the saddle – and had taken his reluctant leave.

The keeper's carriage was one of the few remaining sources of light. The cook fires had collapsed to cinders and the infrequent braziers were burning low. Beyond these reared the dark boles of a Renali forest, filled with foreign smells and discomfiting sounds. Breath pluming, he hunched his shoulders against the local crickets' and frogs' unfamiliar tune.

The caravan's trek was two-thirds done. And, despite all the hardships – the teasing, the trudging and the horse-troubles – he was having a grand old adventure. One he wasn't sure he wanted to see end. The easy community he'd found, with the masha'na, was precious. And he had as much of the keeper's attention as he could stand. Neither thing would survive their arrival at Keystone.

Also, he had no idea how to scribe for an important diplomat, despite all of the priest's preparation. The lessons on highborn manners served only to illustrate how far out of his depth he was.

"What if I can't get it right in time?" he'd worried one evening.

"Then," the keeper had assured, "we introduce you as my bodyguard and all you'll have to do is stand there and scowl."

As they had the first time, the words woke a smile.

Him! A bodyguard! *Ha!*

As he hurried back to his tent, he found himself wishing the caravan would be slowed by another treefall or difficult fjord… and berated himself severely for the selfish thought. He didn't need any more penitent prayers, added between him and sleep-

He missed a step as a scream tore the night in two.

In fright, he gulped frigid air as a wagon hatch beside him slammed open. Their night-shirted chef peeked out.

"What was that, Bumble?" the man said, spotting him.

He mutely shook his head while the cook clambered down, barefoot. A plump woman, her nightcap askew, stuck her head out after him.

"What's wrong, Edgin?"

"I don't know, wife. Best you stay inside until I-"

A squealing horse burst from the black at a full gallop. Astride it reared a stark figure, swinging a mace. There was a sound – like a bag of flour striking the floor. And then the charger was shouldering Edgin's limp corpse aside.

A widow's wail in his ears, Marco stared as the dark horse and rider bore down on him, the mace's sharp flanges shredding air.

Shock crowded out every single thing he'd ever learned at Clatter Court. He stupidly threw up his arms. Something snagged his heel and he fell, the speeding flange tore a furrow from his forearm. The ground slammed the breath from him. The horse passed over top of him and a hind hoof clipped his brow.

Vision collapsed and he didn't know whether the sickly beat he heard was his heart – or the behemoth, passing into camp.

Screams seemed to tip down the sides of a well toward him.

For a terrifying moment, he was lying at the bottom of an alley amid a scaffold's wreckage. Purple stars cavorted above him.

The vision scared him upright and he canted, groggily, to his feet. Cradling his bleeding arm, he cast about, striving for sense. Edgin was being shaken by his widow, as though he might wake. She was mewling softly.

Then who is screaming?

Thoughts sluggish, he stumbled off, heeding an urge to flee. A cluster of tents were afire, herding a low mist to coil about his knees. Colors bled into it, shrouding everything in gray and swallowing far-off shouts. Shadow puppets, little more than ashen smudges to his eyes, raced across its surface.

A nightmare rider reared, twice life-size, against the flames.

He blinked. His head was clearing. One of many armored horseman rode down a row of tents, he saw, torch outstretched. A bow thwacked and the attacker toppled. A rough hand dragged Marco from the path of the galloping horse as it raced past.

A masha'na – Finch – screamed in his ear.

"Gather as many of ours as you can and get under cover!"

Nocking another shaft, the slight warrior dashed into the mist.

Only now did Marco register the running feet, all around, and feel their infectious panic. People screeched and scattered as a mercer's guard drove one of the attackers across their path, furiously hacking and slashing.

It was unlike any of the sparring matches or demonstration duels Marco had ever seen. There was no finesse, only the desperate frenzy that sought to cling to life and deliver death.

It was terrifying.

Gather as many as you can, the masha'na had ordered.

Would they be any safer in the forest, he wondered?

A score of mounted figures blazed about, through the mist.

At the very least, they'd be harder to see among the dark boles.

"This way!" he yelled, angling toward the tree line. "Come on!"

The elbow he grabbed turned on him, bloodying his teeth. He staggered back as the person skittered away in fright.

A shrill scream spun him around.

She pelted from the mist – fleet as a deer, her face made unfamiliar by terror. A rider pursued from the flames behind her. The tangle of tent lines, to either side of her, would have tripped up the horse. Down the straight, with two hands full of hoisted nightgown, her speed counted for nothing.

A sword licked out, wetting the side of her neck. Her braid whipped wide, her fleet-footedness vanished.

She bowled him over as the rider blew past.

He'd caught her by reflex and they hit the ground hard, skidding to a stop. She was alive, her wide eyes filled with terrible prescience. He clapped a hand to the ruin that was her neck. Blood welled thickly, heedless of his efforts. Her gaze held him as she tried to draw one more breath, one more breath…

"Somebody, help!" he appealed, unable to look away.

Her throat bobbed, her swallows cut short. Red bubbled.

"You're going to be alright," he sobbed. "You're going-"

Life fell away from her face.

He lay in the dirt, her blood pooling around him.

Her eyes were dull olive, not apple. Her hair auburn, not autumn. Not a freckle to be seen. And still, he saw Sunny.

It happened slowly – the iron tang on his tongue sank roots to his stomach, kindling something fierce and fevered.

Absurdly calm, he found his feet.

His tent was nearby, collapsed. He reached inside, fingers finding his *seirin*. The weighted wood felt balanced in his grip.

He left the canvas to the flames, following the sound of screaming. The prayer for the dead rolled from him in one, unbroken undulation – he wasn't sure for whom.

Sounds of fighting spurred him to a jog.

He navigated around a dozen small fires, evidence of some concerted razing. An orange roar suggested that at least one wagon was ablaze. Smoke coiled through the mists as he loped along, leaping trampled tents and avoiding riderless horses.

A burning two-wheeled cart held the white at bay. Through its haze, he made out a dark rider, raining blows on someone in sooty orange and umber.

He did not fumble for the fighting trance as he sped. Rage filled him from corner to cranny and left no space for calm.

Flames reached for him as he raced up the cart's canted bed. Ignoring the crackle of singed hair, he skimmed the backboard. Buoyed by heat and fire, he sprung at the rider's back.

He cleared the horse's rump, his seirin keening around with all his might. Weighted wood shattered off a helm, juddering his shoulders as he sailed past.

The invader pitched from the saddle and to the ground in a clank of armor, pawing at a helmet that suddenly sat askew. Between strap and mail, the man's unprotected throat showed.

Marco's seirin had broken off in a jagged point. He hefted the makeshift stake as he stepped forward-

He started as gleaming steel punched down.

"Whew!" Kryskin breathed, leaning on the impaling weirin.

He'd forgotten the rider's masha'na opponent. His rage guttered like a candle, letting confusion rush in.

The holy warrior motioned at him. "You look like some war-painted pagan."

The nameless girl's blood... he realized in horror.

"Leave it," the captain forestalled. "If it scares the next man half as much as it did me, you won't even need this..."

Kryskin scooped up the fallen rider's sword.

An unfamiliar pommel was pressed into his palm.

"Now, stay close and stay sharp," the warrior bid.

Ignoring the beginnings of terror, he trotted at Kryskin's heels.

The masha'na led them through the demolished camp, straight into the thick of things. Two attackers, afoot, were moments from overpowering a mercer's guard and the head farrier. The latter's stubby claw hammer swept in powerful but short arcs, barely keeping a longsword at bay. The former was conducting a clumsy, wrong-handed defense against a feinting spear.

Kryskin rushed ahead.

Were the man anything but masha'na, the answering stop thrust would have spitted him. Instead, the warrior slid around it, leaving off sheering through the spear's neck in favor of shearing through the spearman's.

That was as much as Marco saw before he blew past the farrier. Through terror, as much as tactics, he let his feet go out from under him. Gravel gouged through his robes, grating away skin. The longsword licked out overhead, missing him. A yell overflowed his lungs as he brought his own blade up to his cheek, sliding past to open his opponent's inner thigh.

It was a good hit, an arterial strike that would sap the man's strength in moments. Marco's timing was off and his form was atrocious but it would have won him any sparring bout. Except that this wasn't Clatter Court and his opponent wasn't about to meekly slink off to the starting square.

In his mind, Master Crysopher's voice castigated him severely.

'Given a moment, a mortally wounded enemy will still kill you.'

The longsword chopped toward his eyes.

He frantically raised his sword but he'd sacrificed his footing for a killing stroke and could not fully field the blow.

Master Crysopher would have tutted in disgust.

He blunted the attack's edge but his own blade's flat hammered his face. A moment later, his attacker joined him on the ground, pate crushed by a claw hammer.

"You alive, novice?"

He was pulled into a sitting position.

"How many fingers?" Kryskin queried, not holding any up.

"Too soon," huffed the farrier, who had lost several and was hastily wrapping his spurting stumps.

Marco was hoisted to his feet, probing at a nose bridge that felt cloven in two. He hoped the wetness was blood, not snot or tears.

"Well, you're no prettier," the masha'na diagnosed, "but perhaps you're a little wiser now, yes?"

"I'll get this one out of here," the farrier informed them, bearing up under the weight of the mercer's guard. "Before he bleeds out."

"Can you make the tree line?" Kryskin asked.

"Watch us…" the man shuffled off, hammer raised in salute.

"We should get going too," Kryskin said. "It's not over yet."

His heart labored but he tumbled after the masha'na, as though he were a kite and the holy warrior held his string.

They raced headlong into conflagration and chaos. A dozen men danced a melee, backlit by a blazing wagon. Kryskin flew into the fray, laying about with such skill and speed it seemed men fell to his gaze rather than his steel.

Marco made a crude attempt at copying the masha'na and fended the first two blows by luck alone. The foreign sword sat, awkward and unbalanced, in his grip. The unaccustomed weight dragged at his arm. Blind panic dulled any skill he may have possessed. An ill-thought block nearly bucked the rider's sword from his hold. His legs churned to stay beneath him and he slammed into a wagon wheel. Its iron rim rapped the back of the head and he sagged.

Acrid copper filled his croup and he feared he would pass out…

A figure advanced, weapon upraised, features smeared by smoke and slaughter. His nightmares sketched in the details – the scars, the crooked teeth, the rough laughter…

The ember, smoldering in the pit of his stomach, roared to life. At his back, the wagon surrendered to the char. Its traces and chains tumbled taut, tilting him onto his feet.

He plunged ahead, the foreign sword a feather in his hands. It clanged beautifully, its straight edges biting sparks from its fellows. He concentrated on hanging on to the weapon as it leapt from place to place.

He hacked a crimson swathe through their foes-

And could not land a single killing blow.

It was Kryskin.

The holy warrior was everywhere, slipping into openings, sliding around strikes… *stealing* his kills. Unaccountably enraged, he sought to break away from the masha'na's shadow.

The keening hunger in his gut grew. He bellowed with the pain of it but, however he pressed, he could not match the masha'na.

Frustration foamed from his lips and occluded his view.

Faster, he pushed. *Faster!*

The effort stole his sense of time.

A new opponent reared from the red. His rush stalled as the defender deftly locked their weapons together. He freed one hand to punch past the deadlock, aiming for the throat...

Another fist enveloped his in a firm hold.

"Marco!" someone shouted, right in his face.

He staggered back, blinking at the masha'na.

"Kryskin? What...?" It didn't matter. "We've got to-"

The holy warrior shook him roughly, "It's *over*, Marco. It's *done.*"

"We've got to- What? *Over-?*"

"They're all dead or fled," the man insisted, holding his eyes.

The haze was retreating from around his vision, leaving him dazed. The camp's timbre had changed. Mournful wails and the crackling of flames continued. But the note of panic had died down. No clash of steel sounded. People were staggering purposely about, toting buckets and shouting instruction to one another. He stood, bathed in the light of a burning wagon, ringed by wary defenders. Felled riders were scattered about.

"We've won," the masha'na assured him. "They're gone."

With gentle pressure, Kryskin got him to lower his weapon.

Abruptly, his arms were leaden. They surrendered the sword. Folding, he followed it down, catching himself on hands and knees. The blade was soiled from point to pommel. Strands of hair and sinew were snagged in the notches and streaks of marrow gummed the fullers. It reeked of ravaged flesh and spilled bowel-

Whatever spell had held him fled. He added his stomach contents to the gruesome display. Bile burned his broken nose.

A comforting hand patted his convulsing back.

"First-fight jitters," Kryskin soothed. "They will pass."

"'s not right," he managed at last, spitting foam-flecked vomit.

He wasn't sure whether he meant the killing, or how he'd been overcome by it, or how right-minded people couldn't possibly-

"No," the holy warrior agreed, eyeing the carnage. "But would you rather be us? Or them?"

As homilies went, it was too cutthroat for comfort.

WITH A CLANK, the corpse was toed over, morning dew cascading off its armor. Marco forced himself to meet its vacant gaze. His muddled memory of the night's fight notwithstanding, he might be standing over one of his victims. The least he could do was look.

Guilt squirmed in his gut and he longed to say a prayer. Bear did not seem to share his sentiment, kneeling with a short bladed knife in-hand. Blackened plates were peeled off to reveal a stained gambeson beneath. The masha'na started working his way through pockets and pouches.

"This is the gravest of insults!" Ambassador Malconte gushed, voice climbing toward incoherence. The round little man, in the rich silks, bounced on the balls of his feet. "An assault on the personage of the Imperial Ambassador is tantamount to an assault on the Emperor himself! *Someone* will *sink* for this and I don't particularly care whom!"

A sweaty glare slanted in the direction of Strike-Captain Iolus – who pretended not to notice. When the battle had broken out, the Imperial Elites had locked the ambassador in his carriage and established a cordon around it, firing arrows from its roof. This, however, was not why the man was so miffed. Apparently, he had not taken kindly to having bloody or soot-smeared stragglers herded inside with him and his expensive possessions.

"I doubt *insult* was the intent, ambassador," Chapter Master Bulgaron pointed out, standing at parade rest. "More likely – our valuables. We must look a tantalizing sight. No doubt these brigands had hoped to catch us all asleep."

So said the man who had rushed into battle, armed in nothing but boots, a bobbled night cap and a broadsword.

"They'd have done better to wait until just before daybreak," Kryskin commented, "when the sentries were exhausted."

Marco was alone in seeing the keeper's brow crease at this.

"You think these were simple brigands?" the ambassador scorned. "Astride *horses*? Pah! These were patently assassins!"

"Horseflesh is common currency here," the mercer argued knowledgeably, "and this would be prime hunting ground for bandits. Trade across the border is unsanctioned and, therefore, void of official escort. This lone artery probably supports some robber-baron's fiefdom."

"Helia send the baron is one of these bodies, then," Iolus said.

The attackers had largely carried off their dead, denying the convoy an accurate headcount.

As the sun had risen over the charred ruins of their camp, they'd taken stock. They'd lost a score of tents and three wagons – currently being cannibalized for parts. Some horses had bolted and the hostlers were off collecting the ones they could find.

Despite the fact that the raiders had been caught wrong-footed by the caravan's swift response, the death toll was high. Besides the chef, Edgin, and his wife – who'd been found trampled, atop his body – they'd lost seven souls. Including the nameless girl.

The chapter master's command tent had been converted into a triage. The keeper and he had just come from there. Though the priest was adamant he was no healer, there was an Imperial lancer – with his arm in a sling, instead of a satchel – who would beg to differ. Streaming could do nothing for the farrier's lost fingers but had worked wonders with the disfiguring burns of others.

The caravan's mender had sent them off at first light.

He kept a wary eye on the keeper. Streaming was draining work and the priest had bruises beneath his eyes that rivaled Marco's own. And *he* had a broken nose, now expertly set.

'*You should've seen 'im,*' an injured hostler had insisted, while Marco wrapped the man's ribs. '*That rider was fixin' to roll over the preacher like a barrel 'o bricks. I thought 'e was a goner! Then 'is holiness looks at 'im – just looks – and the 'orse spooks like it's hock-deep in snakes! Rider must've broke every bone in 'is body, comin' down. And that 'orse is prob'ly still runnin'...*'

Sensing his regard, the priest gave him a cautious smile.

He dropped his eyes, ashamed of what the keeper might see in them – some speck of the night's bloodlust. Doubtless the hierarch already knew all. Even if the evidence had not been as plain as the nose on his face, there'd been the way Kryskin had delivered the dead rider's sword to the triage. Apparently, it was now his.

At the keeper's warning cough, he left off probing his itchy stitches. He'd refused to have the keeper fix it.

"We could try to track the survivors to their camp," the mercer mused. "Stamp out the threat for good...?"

"Ah, dutiful general," the ambassador said, his quicksilver mood on the upswing, "let us not invite further delay. We have an appointment with a ruler, albeit the ruler of this backwater kingdom. And we do not wish to track dirt into our host's house."

No one had anything to say to that.

Bear shook his head at Kryskin, his search proving fruitless.

The masha'na leader's lips thinned irritably.

Marco was aware of the ambassador's continued exposition, but his attention was for the keeper. The priest had turned his head toward the forest, a frown slowly forming.

Kryskin noticed too.

A masha'na was sprinting from the trees, robes stark against the winter bark, a flatbow in-hand. Bear straightened, cutting short the conversation. Tensions rose as the scout skipped toward them.

"Or, perhaps the robber-baron will find *us*..." the chapter master mused, not sounding too perturbed by the idea.

The masha'na skidded to a halt before Kryskin to make his urgent report – to the ambassador's obvious annoyance.

"Riders," the scout gasped. "Dozens. In formation. In colors."

"More bandits?" the ambassador said, as if at an inconvenience.

"Not wearing uniform, surely?" the chapter master observed, earning a sharp glance from the high lord. "Could you make out their livery?"

The scout shook his head.

"How long?" Kryskin asked the pertinent question.

"Not long," the masha'na, on foot, apologized.

"I'll get my men organized," the chapter master bustled off.

"We'll guard the flanks," Kryskin told the strike-captain.

"And we will hold the center," the man agreed, trotting off.

"Split the troupe," Kryskin told his two masha'na. "Take to the trees. Stay your arrows, unless we're attacked first."

Nodding, the two men raced away, loosing shrill whistles. Within a blink, they'd disappeared, far more completely than men wearing orange should be able to.

"I doubt these cautions are necessary, captain," the keeper said, earning a sidelong glance.

"Something I ought to know, hoilness?" the masha'na demanded. The troupe, of course, were well aware of the keeper's capabilities.

"Not in the way you mean, my son. Just an old man's hunch."

"Then, if it's all the same to you, holiness, I'd just as soon be ready to repel an attack."

"I bow to your expertise."

With a last, searching glance, the commander hurried off.

"I had best go change," the ambassador announced.

Change? Marco stared after the man. The high lord was the only one of them not scorched or soot-stained. He wouldn't look out of place at a state dinner. What could he want to change into?

"Shall we go have a look as well?" the priest finally invited.

They made their way down to the narrow stream, where two burnt out wagons were being wedged into a crude barricade.

Walking jostled the bristles on Marco face and drummed his sinuses. It itched abominably.

"Don't," the keeper commanded, not turning, "or it'll scar."

He snatched his hands down.

Eschewing their mounts, the Imperial Elites had formed a shield wall, bristling with billhooks. Strike-Captain Iolus's back-borne crest fluttered in the morning breeze.

The mercer's guards stood at their backs, armed with spears.

Of the holy warriors, there was no sign.

"Here we go," the keeper whispered.

A single masha'na had appeared atop the rise to give warning.

Marco didn't need the keeper's gift to feel the apprehension in the air. All eyes were trained on the tree line, straining for a sign.

There!

Movement between the trees resolved into a pair of mounts. The riders sat high in the saddle, polished helms topping oiled great coats. Another pair appeared behind them. And another. And *another…*

Swallowing hard, he watched the double file of cavalry fan slowly from the forest. More than two score, all told, almost twice the convoy's number. The foremost had reached the stream before the tail end of the column cleared the forest. The lead rider came on alone, outflung arms exposing a bright tabard and its motif.

A rampant stork on a lake of blue.

"I am Commander Fermont, of His Majesty's Royal Guard," the rider boomed. "By courtesy of the king, I offer you escort to the capital."

Beside him, the keeper gave a gratified grunt.

"Oh, good," someone else muttered. "We're saved."

By André van Wyck

PART II

The final days of the Age of Magic
The day of the Fall
The coast of Thell

"WE MUST CAST off *now*!"

The captain remained silent, letting his panicked first mate see his contempt. But fear made the man blind to nuance.

"We wait," he repeated.

He'd much preferred his old first mate. But a freak accident had stolen the man away. And the chain of command had shackled him with this... yellow streak of brine. Scent of the man's fear had grown progressively more pungent as the day, and the exodus, wore on. Endless soldiers, limping down the gorge, to wing away on transports. Those sails had long since dwindled, carrying the remnants of the Holy Legion away.

His was the last ship at anchor.

And *The Lady's Tears* wasn't going anywhere.

"Captain-!" the first mate's eyes bulged bigger now than when the earth had shifted and stones had tumbled from the cliffs above, setting the *Lady* bobbing like a cork in a tub.

His lip curled in disgust. So many stalwart men and women, dead, on foreign soil. And this coward would get to go home.

"We risk being beached by the low tide!" the first mate whimpered at the prospect. "And the fire moat is *failing*!"

He turned his back, lest he say something regrettable. His eyes climbed the steep, snaking trail to the cliff's lip, far above the bay. From here, he could only just make out the crest of the fiery wall.

It was, indeed, looking wan. Its smoke had palled from angry black to spent gray. Its furious flames now writhed weakly. There might already be breaks in that magical barrier. He could not begin to fathom the force of will that had kept it burning for bells on end. But he could well guess at the cost it had exacted.

And he would not dishonor it by cutting anchor before time.

His first mate harangued his composure. His fingers twitched toward the dockers' knife, tucked behind his naval sabre. The pips on his collar were a fine thing. But they didn't add up to a thimble of piss on the open water. You needed to be a sailor, first. And he *was* a sailor, through and through.

"Captain, we dare not tarry longer! None could have survived beyond the wall! We are awaiting a rearguard that won't *ugh-!*"

He hadn't realized he'd moved. Not until his first mate was gurgling in his face. He had the fool's throat in his fist and could hear heels, scuffing the planks. Oh, well. His career was likely over anyway. He hoisted the soiled flag of a man up the aft mast.

The crew watched resolutely. They'd seen their captain face off against typhoons, wearing this same expression.

The first mate's struggles became feeble, eyes rolling white.

"Hands, ahoy!" came the cry from the crow's nest. Others picked it up, pointing up the cliff face.

At last!

He let the retching, wretched man collapse to the deck.

"Weigh anchor!" he bellowed, fanning his ship into a frenzy. "All hands to stations! Ship the oars! Sails at the ready!"

"The longboats, captain? They can't swim out to us in armor!?"

He shaded his eyes. Far up the precipice, a handful of figures were pelting down the trail. Even as he watched, they forsook the zigzagging path, to leap from promontory to outcrop. In great arcs, they descended the bluff, moving with inhuman speed and grace.

"Nay!" he determined, stilling the hands at the longboats' lines.

"But… captain…?"

"Nay, I said!" he thundered, gauging the approaching figures' pace. Monstrous silhouettes were boiling over the lip in pursuit.

"Ramming speed!" he swore at the rowers, making them start.

"Helmsman!" he pointed. "Bring us under that outcrop!"

"Aye, sir!" a chorus answered him.

Oarlocks and men strained to comply. The Lady shot forward.

"Heave!" The ship strained beneath him. "Heave…! Heave!"

His would-be passengers had guessed his intent and were headed for the overhang too. He began to pick out details. Four disparate figures, sheathed in blood and propelled by tireless legs.

But the monstrous horde was also heaving into focus, gaining, with teeth and claws and chaos. Unfamiliar, long-limbed creatures loped ahead, galloping across the cliff face as if over level ground.

"Archers to the stern!" he spurred. Other voices took up his call. Leather-clad soldiers rushed to the rear, setting shafts to strings.

"Draw!" he ordered, answered by the rattle and groan of wood.

"Loose!"

The volley arched high, falling viciously into the teeth of the enemy front. Many nameless creatures sprawled… merely to get back up. Others continued, unfazed, with shafts sticking from them. Too few stayed down, to be trampled by their fellows.

"Draw! Loose!" Another volley shot skyward, peppering the horde – and the rocks – with as little effect. "Draw! Loose!"

A shadow passed overhead. The stone outcrop, twice again as high above them as the main mast. He squinted as the fleeing figures reached it, running surefooted as mountain goats.

"Clear the poop deck!" he screamed. Confused sailors scrambled to obey, leaving the highest level free. Save for the wide-eyed helmsman, who was white-knuckling the wheel.

The fleeing figures had reached the end of the spar.

Gasps sounded as they launched themselves, unhesitatingly, into thin air. Torn cloaks flapped and blood-slick hair whipped, as they arrowed down.

Separate impacts rocked *The Lady's Tears*, the last with a splintering crash. Four figures knelt atop the poop deck, reeking of offal and painted in the gore of war and every manner of ichor.

The outcrop's shadow passed. The oarsmen cut a wide groove, finding their stroke. Some enterprising monsters splashed down in their wake, already out of range. Others roared their frustration from atop the promontory. A smattering of enemy arrows found the deck, most falling short. They drew out onto the open ocean.

The kneeling figures rose.

"Captain," the foremost rumbled, "permission to come aboard?"

He bowed. "*The Lady's Tears* is pleased to host the Primes."

Somewhere behind him, the first mate was loudly sick.

CHAPTER 7 – PEBBLES

On the subject of alternate planes of existence. It is tempting to speculate that such realms are solely spiritual and, therefore, forever intangible. But might they not encompass their own profusion of material elements, similar to ours? Case in point – despite ceaseless study and experimentation by the greatest alchemists, metallurgists and arcanists of this and every previous generation, the ancient alloy called 'eversteel' has never been satisfactorily reproduced. Might this not be because a mineral or catalyst critical to the construction of those holy relics – those weapons borne by the Primes – simply does not exist on our plane? This raises questions as to the origins of the Primes themselves...
~ *Pella Monop, 'Musings on the Material Worlds'. Draft, incomplete.*

Present day
Southern Cantella
The Renali Kingdom

IT WAS A magnificent mansion for a rural lord. The Cantella fief owed its riches to the innocuous haired yam. Of which it was the sole producer. The disgusting plant was wholly inedible and smelled of rot, when raw, and of loosed bowels when boiled.

With the correct alchemical recipe, though, it could be refined – into a virulent drug, lending the illusion of boundless energy.

But its main thrust, as it were, was as an aphrodisiac.

In the desert cities, where demand was greatest, it was called *hisang ar banak*. Song of the Sandcat.

A sandcat, in season, would couple with anything it could run down – which was basically everything. And its mating sessions were notoriously long-lived and loud.

Lord Cantella himself had grown fat and influential on desert gold. And his appetites were legendary. Overuse had rendered him rampantly paranoid – an unsung side effect of the drug.

He'd not left his walls in years. Said walls were patrolled by a small army. Added to which, the lord's alchemists – and, if rumor told it true, *wizards* – added their own brand of protection.

None of which ever seemed to satisfy the lord.

Sometimes, of course, paranoia was well-earned.

Cantella overflowed his favorite throne. Gold leaf over reinforced oak creaked under the man's weight. Fat fingers flitted among proffered delicacies, competing with scantily clad dancers for the lord's attention. Sweat beaded the man's brow, dripping from his three chins as he chewed.

The dusky performers – gift of some grateful desert prince – twirled beneath his fevered gaze.

He motioned absently to his fan girl, turning in annoyance when no breeze stirred at his command.

The loin-clothed adolescent was staring in disbelief, fan forgotten, as a dagger dropped into existence above the lord.

A gauntleted hand held it, the disembodied arm disappearing into a rent that bled jagged shadows. The weapon writhed, its inlay trailing molten afterimages as it stabbed down.

Magical protections flared but failed to halt its descent. Wards blew apart, pouring forge-fired breath over the fan girl. Enchanted jewels popped audibly, like ticks on a hot rock.

Cantella gasped as his imbibed potions boiled in protest.

The sorcerous blade sheared easily between vertebrae.

The armored arm withdrew, leaving the weapon to work its dying magic – melting itself and the corpse to slag.

The darkness drew in upon itself. Shadows rushed to retreat as the rent stitched itself shut, leaving no trace.

A moment later the fire, and the screaming, started in earnest.

UNSEEN, THE ASSASSIN stepped off Castle Cantella's parapet.

Leaving the panic-stricken manse behind, she plummeted toward the treed canopy. Yinra y'bin Toh strolled out a moment later, her fisherwoman's drab dress beneath notice or suspicion.

She was not a violent person by nature but by vocation. Pleasure was a perilous emotion. Those who enjoyed killing, she reasoned, were simply not taking their jobs seriously. She had met such killers, of course. She'd sometimes been the last person *they'd* met. Those who reveled in the pursuit, and in their victims' desperate pleas. The ones who sought the soul's last spark in the eyes. For her, there was no satisfaction to be had in such things.

Killing was a cold business. And so, she contented herself with knowledge of a task – and a target – meticulously executed.

She had one last appointment tonight.

She preferred to keep her clients at arms' length. But, as her intermediary had mysteriously vanished, the errand was unavoidable. She would get it done, get paid and get gone, quickly. Before the manor's alarm spilled over into the sleepy village.

She felt ill at ease, eyeing the appointed tavern. She disliked the living, preferring the dead and the soon-to-be-dead.

It wasn't that she was *bad* with people. She could play a role to perfection. She could *be* a prostitute, a princess or anything in between. If accosted, she could share directions with a traveler or gossip with a villager, all in the local dialect. Her disguise even knew where the fish had been biting today. But, stripped of it, she'd as soon sever someone's throat as suffer a conversation.

She slunk around the back, counting windows. The cat-hooks she strapped to her palms made short work of the sheer climb.

Soon, she crouched on the sill of the open window. Her client had lit no lamps, lounging in a dark corner that faced the door.

Cautious, she approved.

Her muttered cantrip tasted of dust and desiccation. Her eyes drank the dim light in response, bringing the room into pale focus.

A hooded head turned, its face hidden in even deeper shadow.

And thorough, she nodded mildly.

"Is it done?" the woman demanded in elegant diction.

She nodded.

"And it cannot be traced to you?"

She shook her head. The high arcanist himself would be at a loss to unravel her spellwork.

"Good," the client commended. "Castle Cantella was said to be impregnable. If you can repeat such feats, I have another assignment available. At triple your current fee."

She blinked. Her current fee would have bankrupted a middling noble. Who paid that for an audition? Whose death could be worth that, three times over? And who could afford to pay such sums?

She stared hard at her client's cowl.

Yinra's vices included neither greed, nor curiosity. Caution was her currency. As a rule, she didn't perform back to back jobs for the same patron. It invited dependency, or worse, propriety. And killing clients was bad for business. Better to maintain a healthy distance – engaged but not retained.

"No," she quietly determined.

"No?" The cowl cocked to one side. "The fee *is* negotiable…?"

Not, she thought, unless it is being offered by the bankers guild or the royal mint. Or someone who didn't expect to have to pay.

"Thank you," she nodded courteously, "but, no."

"You are positive I cannot convince you to reconsider?"

She shook her head. The client sighed, too easily.

"In that case," the figure motioned, "the remainder of your fee."

She slid from the sill, padding over to the lone table. On it sat a simple wooden box with no latch. She circled it, wary of coiling serpents, spring-loaded quarrels and poisonous puffs of gas. Holding her breath, she tilted the lid toward her... or tried to.

The moment her fingers alighted, her night sight failed and her muscles seized. The spell sank its teeth deeply, like the little varnished box was a bear trap. Pain speared her as her layered wards collapsed under the pressure of its bite.

Tutting in disappointment, the client rose, dawdling over rearranging her rich dress.

"A pity, to waste someone of your talents. But a weapon I do not hold might be wielded against me, someday."

There was a whisper of steel. "I'm sure you understand..."

A delicate blade glinted in the gloom.

Unable to either move or speak, she stood dispassionately as the razor's edge parted the skin beneath her eye. The poison made itself felt immediately. A hot numbness coiled from the cut.

Feather snake, she identified. *Expensive stuff.*

She collapsed as the ensorcelled box was collected. Paralyzed, lungs slowly filling with foam, she glimpsed her killer.

And then she was alone, dying amidst betrayal.

It was fit death for an assassin, she reflected.

If only she could have given the honor to one more worthy.

A SHORT LEAGUE away, on the shore of the lake, candlelight still spilled from the seams of a wooden shack. Inside, a straw effigy – clothed in assassin's black – collapsed, connection fading along with life.

A bowed head gave up its vigil and a single, bitter tear anointed the fallen puppet.

City of Oaragh
Purlia

JIMINY'S LEGS BURNED and his breath was all but gone.

This was ridiculous! The city's redbacks were supposed to give up the chase after just a few blocks. *These* ones were proving as persistent as their lousy namesakes.

He risked another glance over his shoulder. The pedestrians he'd merely jostled went sprawling as someone bigger bulled by.

Salt and silver!

He leapt a haphazard stack of crates and turned a corner. A half-dozen heartbeats later, wood splintered in his wake.

They were actually gaining on him.

Impossible! To a man, the city guards sported bellies rounder than those of their scimitars. They couldn't possibly outrun *him*.

A familiar dead-end alley beckoned. He raced up the wall, riding his momentum halfway up and kicking off hard. A twist and his outflung arms latched onto a low balcony forested with potted plants. He swung over the rail and scrambled off across the roof.

Below, heavy boots banged off a sheer wall. Pottery splintered.

Crap!

He hadn't even done anything!

Today.

Sure, he'd stolen stuff – for survival's sake. How was one supposed to live without the little luxuries? Or the slightly larger ones, come to that?

He took the jump to the neighboring roof in stride. At its far end, another out-of-uniform redback clambered into view.

Dammit! He veered toward the adjacent building, aware of boots pounding in pursuit... wait, boots?

Redbacks didn't wear *boots*. And why were these ones out of uniform? And where were the customary cries? He'd yet to hear a single *Stop, thief!* or *Hey, you!*

And that was another thing. How hadn't he spotted them sooner? Usually, he could tell from the nervous shifting on *this* street whether there was a patrol in the *next* street. Yet, he'd barely slipped his ratty *gadi* as it was snatched off his back.

The platters of powdered spice he'd been pretending to peruse had provided a precious head start. He'd shot from the choking clouds of mustard-yellow and peppery-red, already at full speed.

And now this. A pursuit spanning ten blocks. It was unheard of.

The next building was too far to jump.

Quietly thanking the larcenous fraternity's foresight, he tight-roped across a cat line, camouflaged among the many washing lines. Speed warred with balance as he shuffled along the silken cord. He resumed his run with less urgency.

Let's see those lead-footed mules follow me now-

The crash of booted feet startled a hiccup from him.

Bastard actually jumped it! he thought, leaning into a sprint.

What had he done to deserve this? All his recent knifings had been in accordance with alley law. He'd not stabbed or screwed anyone who had this kind of pull. Except... His head pounded.

Last night's sins were lost in a hungover haze.

He'd remember if he'd killed someone. Sure he would.

Shit.

He dropped to a lower ledge a heartbeat before something silvery brushed by. The throwing knife bit sparks and mortar from the brick up ahead. He watched, in amazement, as his earring trekked a bloody arc across his vision. Clapping a hand to his head, he glowered behind him just as another knife winged his way.

He ducked, watching it skitter across the roof tiles.

Nameless dead of the dunes!

They were trying to kill him. The realization lent him new strength and he surged away across the rooftop.

That cinched it. These weren't redbacks. Blackeyes, maybe? Some princeling's private army, out for his blood? He'd expected to be unmasked, one day. But not today. Not like this.

The city's merchant-marauders played a complicated game of one-upmanship. It was a game that had birthed a particularly cut-throat market of professional thieves-for-hire.

And he may have, occasionally, neglected the *being hired*-part.

Perhaps a prince had finally gotten wise to his scheme? They were infamous for their tempers and inventive in their vengeance.

They were also shit at city planning, which was how Jiminy almost tumbled into closed-in courtyard. A cat line beckoned.

Bad idea.

He would be vulnerable while he traversed it. Better to circle around or find a handy window or balcony to-

Boots reverberated on the roof behind him.

Swearing, he shuffled out onto the wobbly cord. So focused was he, he almost missed the telltale glint on his periphery – a blackeye, on an opposite roof, sighting carefully along the stock of a crossbow.

Oh, shivering sands...

He dropped to all fours, grabbing at the cord as a bolt ripped the air above him. The line tried to buck him off, throwing clear his crossed ankles. Four stories up, he found himself treading air. With a sharp retort, the silk snapped. The line went limp. He dropped. The jerk, as the slack ran out, slid through his grip by an arm's length, scorching his palms. He held so tight his knuckles cracked.

He swung and couldn't raise his legs in time. Instead of his soles, the rushing wall met his shoulder. His hands threatened to spring open but he hung on, wrestling through pain for breath. Beneath him waited a two story drop and no more rope. He would have to climb, he realized. And he'd have to reach the top before his pursuers. And before the crossbowman could reload.

Luckily, the contraptions were notoriously difficult to-

His heart skipped a beat as he spotted the crossbowman, already sighting on him again, just waiting for a lull in his swing. For the first time, he noted the dual ribs of the double crossbow.

Well, skewer me sideways and spice me sweetly...

He kicked off the wall. The shooter must have tracked his fall because the next bolt whizzed by beneath him. If he weren't so terrified, he might have been impressed. Except that the old pottery kiln he dropped towards filled his vision. And – he realized as he neared – the rotted boards hid no crumbling kiln.

He crashed through the wooden sewer cover and down the dank shaft. Because gods forbid he should fall only two stories. Potsherds and debris bounced off the pit's sides, pummeling him.

Knee deep sludge – not enough to break his fall – fountained in all directions. Splintered planks and broken bricks came down atop him, driving his head beneath the muck. Every enemy who'd ever told him to eat shit was instantly vindicated. Spitting, sputtering, he clawed his way weakly from beneath the heap.

Sunlight speared down from above, seeming impossibly distant. He would still be visible from up there, he reflected. Gagging, he dragged himself clear of the wreckage and out of sight.

The stench was debilitating, the swirl of noxious fumes dizzying. But he managed to wedge himself in a shallow niche.

The slime-slick walls had begun to dribble down his neck before he registered the unhealthy throb below his ribs. A bloody splinter, as thick around as his thumb, stuck from his side.

Groaning, he sagged against the semi-soft brick, imagining the amount of gold it would take to set such a wound aright.

He would rest here awhile, he decided, and gather his strength. However zealous these bastards were, they weren't about to follo-

Splash!

His eyes stretched wide in the gloom. Who *were* these people?

He went perfectly still. Above the turgid gurgle-and-drip of sewer-snot, his own heart's hammering deafened him. He quested quietly for his knife… and found its sheath empty. Swearing, he switched to his backup, and then to his backup-backup, and came up empty. He'd lost them in the fall. His eyes squeezed shut.

Misbegotten get of a dockside whore…

He shuffled deeper into his niche. Was that the scuff of a boot? The rasp of leather on brick? How hard were they likely to look f-

A hand closed around his throat. He jumped, aiding the upward momentum as his captor dragged him free. He clawed at the brawny forearm that pinned him to the wall. Toes dangling, he was aware of a rough hand, patting him down.

"Where is it?" his captor queried, accent unfamiliar.

Apparently, he was too slow to answer. The man bounced his head off the brick. "Where?"

He ignored the dazzling stars and the demand both, concentrating fiercely on his ring-finger.

Come on… come on… he begged.

"I said," the man growled, teeth a bright grimace, "where is it?"

Head threatening to split, he bent all his attention on one finger.

Come on, you good-for-nothing bauble! Come on!

"We don't want to hurt you, boy," his captor said, sounding insufferably reasonable. Jiminy read the lie in the man's eye. "But you *are* going to tell us what we want to know. One way…"

A hand drifted down to the splinter in his side.

"Or another…"

The stub of wood was twisted slowly.

His heels drummed the slick bricks, churning piss. He strained against the man's grip, to no avail. What he patently did *not* do, was scream. Hissing through his teeth, he glared at his captor.

Come on, dammit! Come on!

"Yeah, you've got guts, kid. But that ain't gonna save you. How long this takes…" the stake was driver deeper, "…is up to you."

He groaned through gritted jaws, writhing in the man's grip.

Come on! I'm dying *here!*

A shrill whistle sounded, echoing down into the dank sewer. His captor turned slightly aside, lips pursed to return the signal.

Static tingled Jiminy's palm as the lazy magic stirred at last.

Yes!

He punched the knife through his captor's jugular and up under that bristled jaw. A jerk carved out the windpipe and any whistle.

Gaping twice over, the dead man grabbed at a ruined throat.

Freed, Jiminy slid down the wall into waste, suppressing a coughing fit. The gurgling corpse splashed down beside him.

From atop the shaft, that expectant whistle sounded again.

Did he dare respond? Would they come down if he did? Or if he *didn't*? He quickly took stock. He wasn't running anywhere. Not with a log in his side and a twiggy ankle. He'd be worse than helpless in a fight. If they came down, the best he could do was-

Splash!

-hide.

Holding tight to his miraculous knife, he lay back in the filth and drew the dead body atop him. He would have to trust in the murk to mask him. As a plan, it rankled. But no more so than his surrounds. Taking a deep breath, trying not to think about what he was doing, he ducked his head beneath the surface and lay still.

The muck pressed down, drowning all sound. He imagined he could detect the swish of feet through the surrounding swirl. Something, the toe of a boot perhaps, brushed his knee. It took all his wherewithal not to flinch. Or worse, inhale. Even so, he couldn't stop his eyes from springing open. Through the stinging film and floating filth, he spied his dead captor's face, suspended above him. Two fingers withdrew from the man's throat, where they'd been feeling for a pulse. A moment later, he sensed his unseen hunter trudging on.

Above him, the corpse slowly lost its buoyancy.

He held his breath as long as he could. Until his head ached and his lungs threatened to suck shit through the spigot in his side. He surfaced. Not gasping for air was an exercise in self-control. But he managed. He peered above the dead man's shoulder, squinting up and down the empty tunnel. He tried to hear through the gunk caking his ears, but was greeted only by dank dripping noises.

Risking it, he rose and had to wrestle the settling corpse off him. He bit his lip at the pain in his side, then wished he hadn't at the taste. Finally, he managed to shimmy up the wall and stand.

He was so tired, he could have gone to sleep right there, collapsing in crap with a corpse for company. But he had to move, before these guys came back to collect their dead comrade.

The dagger his captor hadn't found, the one that had saved his life, was hot in his grip. Even ill lit and covered in grime, the silver shone, showing off geometric whorls. It was a thing of beauty.

"Took your fucking time," he swore at it.

Letting it go was a struggle. He had to relax each finger individually. Eventually, he let it fall. It disintegrated into a gentle, silver swirl. The metallic motes snaked up and around his finger, condensing into a simple, silver band. He'd brass it up again later, with wood stain or glue or something.

After he'd gotten out of here. After he'd had his side patched. And *definitely* after a bath. Possibly several. In turpentine.

Then – then! – he'd find out whose these thugs were. And why they had such a hard-on for him.

* * *

SEEING HIS QUARRY pass, Mattanuy pounced.

"Ismus!" he said, with a broad smile.

At the unexpected hail, the healer acolyte turned.

It took the idiot a moment. Then he blanched in recognition.

"Inquisitor…?"

"Mattanuy. Indeed! How kind of you to remember me."

They had, in fact, met once. As a novice, Ismus had accompanied a senior healer to the Inquisitori infirmary. The inquisition did, of course, boast their own menders – ones who were skilled at wringing words from the recalcitrant.

The mortally wounded spy Mattanuy had foisted on them had been willing, merely delirious. With the healer's help, the man had clung to life long enough to whisper his missive. Had it been louder than a whisper, Ismus and his mentor may well have followed their patient into Grace.

Facing him, Ismus swallowed hard. "Off course I remember."

Ah. It seemed the young man's file was correct in claiming he was a latent empath. That he'd been trained by Justin himself called into question *how* latent he actually was. No matter. Empaths were easy to lie to. Provided one spoke only the truth.

"I'm glad to have run into you," he grinned, meaning it.

"You are?"

"Indeed! I was just on my way to the healing hall."

True, since he had purposely looked up Ismus's shift schedule.

Not waiting for an invitation, he put a comradely arm around the man's shoulders, steering him away. "Have you a moment?"

"Actually," the healer-in-training stammered stiffly, "I've just come off a double shift and I'm terribly-"

"I have a healing-related question."

"Oh! I, uh... I suppose-"

"I fear I have overused my voice."

True, since he'd rather not be speaking to the moron.

Ismus relaxed slightly. "Um. Any difficulty swallowing?"

I'm having trouble swallowing my pride, right now...

"Some," he downplayed.

"Any irritation?"

He bared his teeth. "Like you wouldn't believe!"

The acolyte bobbed. "Then I'd prescribe a soothing infusion of honey, lemon and shaved ginger, with just a touch of brandy. That should take care of any incipient infection, too."

"Ah," he squeezed the man's arm, "such keen insight, I can see now why Keeper Justin assessed you so highly."

He would have praised the dolt's healing skills too, if it meant shifting him to a different learning track.

Ismus had the bad grace to look believing. "Keeper Justin?"

He nodded. "I believe you were also instrumental in aiding him with his unruly ward, once. Quite a ruckus in the infirmary, I'd heard...?"

Of course, he'd already uncovered the fake family relation forms the keeper had filed. Bar the bare fact that there *had* been a tenement fire and that people *had* died in far-off Genla, nothing suggested that the boy was a blood relation of the keeper's.

A dozen children went missing at Solstice every year, during the chaos of the parade, never to return. The timing suggested that the hierarch had snatched this particular one up off the street.

He was determined to find out why.

"A miraculous recovery." Ismus brightened with reflected glory. "But I cannot claim any of the credit. Keeper Justin was the one who worked wonders with that boy."

"Oh, you are much too modest. Please," Mattanuy insisted, "I want to hear *all about it*..."

* * *

'Keystone Keep' was a misnomer, Marco thought. It brought to mind gray rock and dreary battlements. And, certainly, there were plenty of those. On the outside. *Inside* was a riot of color.

Right now, he stood on a landing of plush stairs.

Below, a ballroom languished, tiled in glittering marble.

A ballroom, he marveled. He'd discovered several so far. As a rule, priests didn't dance. So he found the whole idea outlandish.

Since coming to the Renali capital, and being granted rooms in the keep, he'd spent some part of every free day exploring.

Despite Ambassador Malconte's cutting scorn, he was sure the Imperial Palace in Tellar must pale by comparison.

The last time he'd felt so overawed had been on his first visit to the Primus Sanctori, in the Mother Temple.

But, he hurriedly amended to himself, one was a collection of holy artifacts and armor, once wielded by the four warrior-saints who had founded the Empire.

The other was something dancers trod on.

His eyes were drawn to the dais at the far end, where a quartet of empty thrones waited. Only the royals set foot there. Two princesses – one of an age with him, the other older – and a sickly prince, still on his nurse's apron strings.

And the king.

The scriptures always depicted rulers as either wise, white-haired old men or as fiery warriors. King Stentoric was neither.

Or rather, both.

The monarch possessed imposing shoulders and wore steel on his brow and at his side. Yet, his voice carried soft assurance and his eyes were unveiled and open.

At the delegation's welcome dinner, Stentoric had impressed everyone by delivering his closing address – his high hopes for the summit – in only lightly accented Heli.

Marco had felt himself distinctly out of place at that dinner. None of the other diplomats' aids or servants had attended. Nevertheless, there had been a place setting for him.

The word 'ward' didn't translate well into Renali. The closest analogues were either 'honored hostage' or 'borrowed servant'. The organizers had apparently decided to split the difference and had seated Marco among the minor nobility.

The wispy bearded man beside him had beckoned a servant, no doubt to enquire as to whom he was seated next to – and had thereafter studiously ignored Marco. In contrast, the old lady at his opposite elbow had chatted at him gamely. But, with her so hard of hearing, it had been little better than a monologue.

Despite his coaching, the cutlery had been confusing.

He was more at home with a quill in his hand.

From his distant seat, he'd just been able to spot Keeper Justin, sharing supper and convivial conversation at the high table.

Scribing for the priest had turned out to be quite taxing. Even armed with shorthand, his wrist threatened a sprain twice daily. He must have scrawled sufficient pages to bury the keep by now.

And the *politics*! He comprehended less than half of what he recorded. And, despite the king's courtesy, the air around the conference table regularly echoed a sparring circle.

As the youngest person present, he was mostly just grateful to hide behind his fringe and scribble quietly. No one lobbed logistical queries at him – like Chapter Master Bulgaron sometimes did at his own aid. Nor did anyone ask him innocent, rhetorical questions – like Ambassador Malconte did his attendant, I lieu of insulting one of the dignitaries directly.

King Stentoric's presence kept a lid on the incivility. The monarch did an admirable job of playing referee at his own table. But – Marco had noticed – the summit did not proceed at the same fevered pace without the ambassador's tantrums to add impetus.

So, perhaps it was good for the talks that the king's other commitments kept him away as often as not. Certainly, it wasn't because Marco found the man's august presence intimidating.

"This meeting," the king had declared, at their first session, "would have been unthinkable in my great-grandsire's time. I consider it an honor to wear the crown during this pivotal age. I only wish my lord father could have lived to see us all, seated together in his hall. May our efforts here usher in a lasting peace."

He remembered meeting the keeper's pleased smile and mirroring it with a more pronounced one. The king had taken note.

"Splendid! I see my enthusiasm is shared...?"

The keeper had rescued him from introducing himself.

"Apologies for the oversight, majesty. My ward and personal assistant – Marco dei Toriam, novice of the Holy Temple."

Remembering his lessons, he'd shot to his feet and bowed low.

"Well met, young Marco. What think you of our kingdom?"

He'd feared he might vomit his heart onto the varnished tabletop. But he'd managed a squeaky reply.

"It is an honor, your majesty," he'd responded formally, before answering. "It is very beautiful, your majesty."

"Sit, sit, young one," the king had released him, offering a conspiratorial wink. "Let us get to work!"

The ruler had pushed up his ermine sleeves.

The meetings had since fallen into a predictable pattern, starting soon after breakfast, breaking briefly for lunch and pushing on until an early supper. Endless bells of policy debate, trade negotiation and political maneuvering.

And then there were Marco's lessons with the keeper.

By the time he fell into bed each night, he could barely summon the energy to kick off his shoes.

These free days were as near to bliss as he could get.

He ran a hand curiously along the stairs' alabaster banister. The material was too warm to be stone, too dense to be timber…

"Beautiful, isn't it?" a voice echoed his thought.

A girl – no, a young woman – shared the rail with him. She was dressed as though to join the non-existent ball below. Her skin's luster put the balustrade to shame as she turned a smile on him.

He stared. He'd only ever seen her from a distance, but…

"Your highness!"

Bowing, he narrowly missed banging his head on the banister.

Through his shock of hair, he caught her look of mild dismay.

"Oh, dear," she sighed. "I'd hoped you wouldn't recognize me."

Wondering how she thought anyone might mistake her, he half-straightened before he could halt himself. "Highness?"

"Please, don't bow," she pleaded.

He over-corrected in his haste to comply. His spine popped.

Hearing the crack of his back, her eyes rounded in alarm.

"Oh, I'm sorry!" she trilled, raising a hand. "Are you alright?"

Teetering, he eyed her perfectly manicured nails as though they were poisonous. Touching a royal was taboo, his etiquette lessons said. He took a hurried step out of reach but could think of no way to strip the act of offence other than to bob at her again.

Brought up short by his retreat, the princess snatched her hand back as though warned by the heat of a kettle's handle. Resigned, she let it drop, an apology evident in the set of her shoulders.

"I'm hale, highness!" he rushed to reassure. "I simply spend too much time hunched over my scribing and-"

Fool! She's not interested in your tedious goings-on!

Courtesy flashed a belated card.

"It is most gracious of her highness to concern herself."

But, in its headlong flight, his fluent Renali failed him.

"Your accent is... hardly noticeable," she opined politely, giving the lie by switching to Common.

He winced but had no choice but to follow her lead.

He needed to extricate himself – diplomatically – before his awkwardness caused an international incident.

"Her highness is too kind," he persevered, thinking hard. "I did not mean to intrude on her highness's privacy. Please, allow me…"

He was already reviewing the proper procedure – *bow, retreat three steps, bow again and turn* – when she sighed softly.

Something about the plaintive sound caused him to forget his etiquette and meet her eye.

She had retreated behind a courteous smile. But he saw the tail-end of dejection, slinking off behind her eyes.

"You are excused," she murmured, turning back to the rail.

Though he was hard-pressed to explain why, he halted.

Helia's mercy, he realized, recognizing the signs. *She's lonely…*

More likely, another part of him argued, she was bored. Either way, it was nothing to do with him. Nothing good – literally, *nothing* – could come of his talking to her. And yet…

"Would her highness know," he wondered, hoping to blame any missteps on his 'bad' Renali, "what this is made of?"

He rapped at the balustrade.

She glanced over hopefully, searching his face.

"Um. Or I could leave…?"

"No!" she said, too quickly. Recovering herself, she delicately cleared her throat. "I mean, your company does not offend us."

Which was not exactly an invitation. He hesitated.

"Stay," she commanded, then ruined it with, "please?"

Hoping it was his best foot, he put it forward. "The railing?"

"Like I said," she remarked, "beautiful, yes?"

His heart beat like a bosun's drum. "I've never seen its like."

"It is a tusk," she mourned, hands playing over the ivory plane.

This was not an answer he had expected. "Like a boar's tusk?"

"Not boar, no," she confirmed. "Wyrm."

"Worm?" Perhaps his Renali really *did* need work.

"W*y*rm," she enunciated. "What the North-Sea Mariners call great serpents – aquatic creatures that nest under the ice floes."

"This is a sea-serpent tusk?" he gaped. Several such creatures could be found – in the illuminated margins of the more decorative scriptures. He'd always thought them mere flights of fancy.

"Not just one, though you'd be hard pressed to find the joins. This banister looted several of the leviathans at least."

That, or the whole Barrier Range's supply of boars.

He considered. "You sound as though that saddens you?"

She smiled sorrowfully. "The wyrms reach maturity over several human lifetimes. The Mariners butcher whatever they manage to lure from the water. What you see here represents at least two generations of wyrm. There will be no next generation."

"I don't understand," he was forced to admit.

"Father once gave winter lodging to a minstrel, who had traveled among the Mariners. The man sang of serpents as great as the ships that hunted them. Ancient wyrms that, once angered, could coil their bodies about such vessels and drag them down. There are ballads of bold Mariners, who would bait the beasts from the black and slay them, in something resembling combat. The latest such song is three hundred years old, marking the last time a serpent was seen. The Mariners hunted them into extinction."

He regarded the railing with newfound chagrin.

"We are *lucky*," she emphasized, "to have so much of it."

The change in intonation gave her away. "Your words?"

"My sister's," she grimaced. "Always the pragmatist."

She turned to him, apparently deciding on *some* formality.

"I am Dailill Avrintir Stentoric," she needlessly introduced, offering a hand. "You may call me Dailill, when we are alone."

Ah. The keeper had skimmed over the kingdom's custom of kissing a lady's hand. Cheeks heating, he stepped forward-

And jumped, as someone loudly cleared their throat.

"Or," the princess sighed, "as alone as I ever am…"

The man, leaning casually in the archway, was whipcord thin. Tight leathers – rather than plate – nevertheless bore the Royal Guard insignia. The man's stare was too frank to be polite.

"Play nice, Luvid," the princess reprimanded.

To Marco, she added a rueful explanation. "My minder."

He nodded, retreating a respectful step.

"I am Marco dei Toriam," he said.

"Marco," she mispronounced, testing the foreign sound. "You show promise as a conversationalist. I may call on you again."

With a swish of skirts and lace, she was gone, gliding by Luvid.

The bodyguard remained a moment, eyeing him and casually caressing the hunting knife that balanced a heavy sword. Violence permeated the man's person deeply enough to stain.

Swallowing, Marco squared his shoulders.

The leather-clad bodyguard shrugged upright with alarming speed, stretched leisurely, then sauntered after his mistress.

Watching the odd pair go, he let out a nervous breath.

* * *

IT WAS WELL known, Jiminy reflected, that the port city of Oaragh never slept. But it frequently dozed – limbs twitching and lips curling to show yellowed fangs.

He snuck along under just such a threatening moon, the day's heat still cloying in the cramped alleys. Around him, clay tenements gave way to brick warehouses. Rightminded people went out of their way to avoid these streets, even by daylight.

Somewhere ahead, the desert dunes were being raked flat by the incoming tide. He took a deep breath of the salt stink, testing the healed puncture in his side.

He hated magic. And its practitioners. A sandcat on a leash was more predictable. *And* less likely to try and screw you.

True, yesterday his damnable ring – which sometimes made pretend it was a dagger – had saved him. But it might as easily not have. In fact, its recalcitrance had almost seen him killed. It rarely responded to desperate need and never to a whim. It was utterly unreliable and he feared it would one day let him down. Fatally.

He took another experimental breath but it seemed Old Cobb's magical patch would hold. Unlike the half-mended pots and pans the tinker hawked. What good was a money-back guarantee if a chance defect left you dead, anyway?

It had pained him to part with two wheels of silver. But it was a small price if it spared him the brown death. Suffering even a shallow puncture in a sewer could spell catastrophe.

And he needed to be fast on his feet *right now*.

He still didn't know who had sent those thugs after him. And, after a little thought, he'd ultimately decided that he didn't care. Oaragh wouldn't be the first city he'd quit. The time was ripe.

A caravan could carry him east, toward the Greenwall, making a circuit of Oaragh's sister cities. A well-worn route and one that he'd traveled before. But caravans were slow and easily overtaken by men ahorse. Any *karwan*, worth his salt, would sell a wanted man in a heartbeat. To *whoever* wanted him.

Quite apart from being waylaid, a north-bound caravan could only end in a loss of livelihood and limb, on the Barbarian Plains.

South wasn't an option. Even if he somehow survived the deadly Diamond Fields and their salt traps, there was nothing out there. He'd either have to traverse the towering snowcaps, that separated the desert from the morass of empire, or turn back.

No, the only direction that held any appeal for him was west, across the ocean. Let the tides decide his next port of call.

There was a whole wide world out there he'd yet to rob.

He twitched at the hood of his stolen *gadi*.

These slums held no surprises for him. You'd have to be sun-addled stupid to expect anything but an ambush at the bottleneck ahead. He signaled with one hand and his would-be muggers settled back into their shadows, satisfied that he belonged.

The hand-signs changed with the fullness of the moon. The same gesture, given the next night, would get someone's throat slit.

He wended his way among the sprawl of alleys until he found a massive figure, mending nets by feel as much as by candlelight.

"Flint," he greeted the fisherman-by-day with the deft fingers.

"Jiminy.".

He eyed the brass-bound cudgel, lying within reach of those salt-split hands. "Crawly inside?"

"Go on in," Flint nodded, concentrating on a snarl of string.

Jiminy continued on into the gloom.

Crawly had set up his usual office, where several alley mouths locked jaws. The space was stacked high with pallets and loose planks, creating the illusion of a cramped room, roofed by stars.

Holding court in the middle, his throne a packing crate and his desk an upturned barrel, was Crawly himself.

Stick thin, hunched inside an oversized cloak, the man's leathery ears brought to mind a bat. Dry skin flaked from around sickly pink eyes as the albino smiled.

"Ah," the lender enthused, "now *this* is a Surprise."

"For one of us," he sighed, having suffered the joke before.

There were but a handful of people in the whole world who knew that Jiminy, the pickpocket, was also the master sneak-thief, Surprise. The fact that Crawly was one of them really rankled.

"What are you doing back in the gutter? I heard you'd moved on up – gotten in good with the princes. And a couple of the concubines too, eh? Eh?"

"Glad to be back, Crawly," he lied. "How's business?"

"Good, good. I'm close to completing my kneecap collection."

"Right," he drawled. It paid to remember that the lender had lots of pull. Debtors came from all walks of life and would routinely commit murder, in return for a reprieve from their loans.

Also, Crawley was mad as a sun-addled asp.

"You're holding my backup stash for me," he said.

"Yes, yes, yes. Of course. Seventy two suns, eleven crescents and a double fistful of coppers. Let's see now..." Crawly's brow crinkled needlessly. Just like the people in his pocket, the figures in the albino's head never dared step out of line.

"With interest, that comes to sixty three suns and a silver."

"That's less than I gave you," he pointed out.

"Well, you know. The economy! Inflation, taxes, currency devaluation, state corruption... It all adds up. Then there's the holding fee, of course, and a small administration fee. The drawing fee, assuming you want it all made liquid?"

"I brought a satchel, not a wineskin. I want it in coin," he said, not wanting to waste time haggling. "And I need you to book me passage with one of your smuggler friends. A sea captain. One setting sail on the morrow."

"A sabbatical, is it? Wild oats to sow?" A leer cracked Crawly's face. "Or has the desert climate become bad for your health?"

Warily meeting that knowing gaze, he kept silent.

"The *Green Kelp*," Crawly continued, "ships out for Quincaan with the next tide. The *Merry Maid* is making a run to the Jade Isles in two days' time. And the *Fortuner* is setting sail north, up the coast of Yutan, at the end of the week..."

"Can you get me on the *Kelp*?"

"Certainly I *can*. It would take waking her captain – dreadful inconvenience on all accounts. Especially yours."

"How much?"

"Oh," Crawly's broad grin shed skin the way his eyes did avarice. "Not to worry. The negotiations are in capable hands..."

Burly arms dropped across Jiminy's chest, hoisting him from his feet. For such a big man, he reflected, Flint could move very quietly. He strained against the fisherman's grip, his arms pinned.

"What is this?!" he demanded as Crawly cackled.

"Simple supply and demand," the albino assured him, rising. "And, right now, you're a hot commodity!"

He stared in disbelief. The bastard was after a bounty?

"Handing me over to the blackeyes goes against Alley Law," he growled. "You'll answer to Hammerham Nan."

To his shock, threat of the Mule Street matriarch failed to faze the lender.

"Who said anything about the authorities?" the albino pointed out the loophole.

He gaped. "Who then?"

"I dare say, you'll find out sooner than I..."

At Crawly's gesture, the arms around him constricted. His ribs creaked. Breath fled. Consciousness would soon follow. Already, blood pounded behind his eyes.

He kicked his legs up as high as he could and swung his heels down hard. Flint's knee gave with a crack. The fisherman pitched drunkenly and Jiminy snapped his head back. From the feel of it, he missed the oft-maligned nose but found the front teeth.

He tumbled free and lodged his objection – and a flat throwing knife – in Flint's foot. A bellow sounded above him and he burst from his sprinter's start, straight at Crawly.

The lender staggered and fell across the crate chair.

With supreme satisfaction, he trod on the man's crotch and launched himself at the nearest eave.

Splinters bit his fingers but he clawed his way up and over.

And then he was racing away across the rooftops.

This, he thought, was worse than he'd feared. If it was neither the peacekeepers nor the princes who were after him, he'd be fair game for every named clan and back alley gang in Oaragh.

It seemed it *did* matter who was looking for him.

If the bounty they offered was big enough to turn the albino's head, Jiminy wouldn't have a friend left in the city, come morning.

Bar, perhaps, one.

His feet angled toward Mule Street.

Now that his planned escape by sea was discovered, the docks would doubtless be watched. But not well enough. He was a sneak thief, after all. Still, he'd give the vessels Crawly had mentioned a wide berth, just to be on the safe side.

He settled into a light-footed lope.

There was still the question of coin. He'd been counting on his main stash. He had emergency caches, secreted around the city, but none as convenient as that held by the lousy lender.

He sighed. It was going to be a busy night.

Chapter 8 – Hawks and Geese

> Lost records make the exact age of the Empire difficult to determine. Recourse may be had to comparative histories in this regard. Imperial scholars are privileged to possess works and records drawn from myriad exotic troves. In many cases, these histories are all that remain of a conquered culture. A cursory study shows that a great many, despite being separated by oceans and continents, share particular story elements. Specifically, record of a great upheaval, characterized by earthquakes, tidal waves, volcanic eruptions and sundry natural disasters. This catastrophe is, strangely, absent from the Heli origin myth. Unless one credits the account of Helia, the goddess herself, descending to earth to slam shut Perdition's mouth.
>
> ~ *Pella Monop, Introduction to 'A Treatise on Empire', unpublished.*

MARCO WRIGGLED UNCOMFORTABLY in his nest of carpets and cushions, papered about with scrolls. He was finding his reading assignment, on the Chirrin Dynasty, trying.

He'd braved the crowds this morning, on his free day, to visit the masha'na compound for a bit of a spar. King Stentoric, despite being an accommodating host, hadn't seen fit let a foreign force take up residence in his very fortress.

Bear had mercifully pulled his blows but Marco feared *he'd* pulled something too. Most likely a muscle or a tendon.

"Just let me look at it," the keeper offered in an aside, absorbed in a thick communication they'd received from home that morning.

"No need," he pasted on a bright smile. "I'm perfectly fine."

He would spare the keeper the drain of streaming, if he could.

The priest glanced up and over his head. A moment later, there came a knock at their door.

He jumped to his feet, biting his lip against the pain and refusing to meet the keeper's pointed regard.

The page, waiting in the hallway beyond, forsook any formal greeting at the sight of him. Rooming in the servant's quarters, off the keeper's suite, had cemented his status in the minds of the staff.

A missive was shoved, wordlessly, into his hands.

"Thank you," he called after the sullen man in the peacock hose.

He placed the roll of parchment on the pile by the keeper's elbow and torturously retook his seat.

"This is not for me..." the priest mused a moment later.

He glanced up to find Father Justin scrutinizing the new scroll.

The priest offered it to him. "It's addressed to you."

For a moment, he sat stunned. Who would be writing him?

"It must be a mistake," he supposed, struggling to his feet.

The keeper seemed to be straining against a smile. "I doubt it."

Mystified, he accepted the missive. It bore his full name – that he never used – in flowing script. The sender's sigil, pressed into the wax seal, showed a swan on a field of lilies.

"Princesses," the keeper spurred, "are not to be kept waiting."

His ears heating, he whirled away. His fingers wasted no time unfurling the scroll and his eyes flew down the elegant lines.

"She's invited me to go hawking!" he exclaimed, as meaning emerged. Mouth dry, he turned to the keeper. "What do I do?!"

"What everyone does, when receiving a royal summons, I'd imagine," the keeper said, scrawling a lazy note. "You go."

"But-" he sputtered. "It's not my place! She is... And *I* am-"

"-going to be fine," the keeper interrupted. "*Breathe*, Marco."

Struggling to obey, he was only half-aware of the priest brushing past. He heard the little silver bell echoing down the hallway, summoning a servant.

"But," he implored, "what if I say the wrong thing? What if I embarrass myself – or the *Empire*? I could *ruin* our relationship. Our countries' relationship, I mean!"

"More so than a thousand years of war?" the keeper chortled, closing the door behind a departing page.

"Yes!" he gushed, the keeper's gentle bemusement lost on him.

"Then I suppose," the priest opined, "we'd best revise your royal etiquette. Do you have something presentable to wear?"

So saying, the keeper crossed into the adjoining quarters. There was the distinctive sound of Marco's travel chest opening.

"These riding boots will do – after a good polish. And where is that doublet you wore to the welcome dinner? It will want brushing..."

The racket, of Father Justin rooting through his wardrobe, served only heighten his hysteria. "I can't possibly *go*!"

"You can't very well refuse," came the muffled reply.

Inspiration struck. "We can say I'm sick! Or hurt!"

"You told me just a moment ago that you were perfectly fine," the priest pointed out judiciously.

His eyes fell on a sturdy footstool. He could say he tripped.

"Abandon that thought right there!" the keeper countermanded, without even having him in line of sight.

Still, he hesitated... before sagging onto the seat instead.

"When is this proposed outing?"

"Tomorrow," he dreaded, his head in his hands.

"Then," the priest reappeared, arms heaped high, "we'd best work fast. Boil up some water and we'll see about this stain-"

"Father," he made a last, heartfelt appeal, willing his mentor to understand. "I *can't* go."

The priest stilled, spilling errant garments.

"You've already *accepted*," the man pointed out.

Accepted?

He followed the keeper's quizzical gaze to the door. And the departed page. Bearing the lazily scribbled note.

Understanding crashed down, and he slid with it, to the floor.

"You didn't…?!" he gasped. "On my behalf…?!"

"Of course I did. Building bridges between nations is fine. But the connection between *people* is what will see peace prosper.

"Plus, you need to be spending more time with those your own age. Now, can we get started? Or have you any more questions?"

Defeated, he whispered through the cage of his fingers.

"Just one – what in Helia's name is 'hawking'?"

MORNING FOUND MARCO riding across the grassy morass the castellans called 'the moor' and which the princess called 'the back garden'. The sprawling expanse of hills, woods – and, of course, lakes – was of such size as to make the far-off fortress seem small.

After their previous encounter, he'd half expected that he and the princess might be alone. That hope had been dashed.

She had brought two ladies-in-waiting – chaperones – who had brought two servants each. Besides their birds, the three falconers had brought one assistant apiece. A dozen royal guardsmen brought up the rear and as many servants trailed them, toting brightly beribboned baskets.

They looked like an invading army, rather than a picnic.

He was not happy about being back in the saddle, despite the heavy dew that clung to the high grasses. Everyone, not astride a horse, was soaked to mid-thigh and shivering.

He glanced ahead at the princess.

She'd greeted him with a formality bordering on boredom, before retreating between her chaperones. Of the vulnerable young woman he'd met on the stairs, he'd seen no sign at all. The three bantered back and forth, voices pitched just below hearing. From time to time, one or all of them would glance sidelong at him and the trio would giggle together.

He'd spent some time trying to spur his mount in their direction. But they were accomplished riders and he never managed to close the distance. Besides, the terrain had changed to steep sloping hills that challenged his ability to stay in the saddle.

The last thing he needed was to take an undiplomatic spill.

The bright chestnut they'd given him looked terribly sleek and muscled. At every toss of its head, he feared he'd be launched like a stone from a catapult. It had not cheered him in the least to learn the stallion's name was Firebrand.

'E's a good 'orse,' the groom had promised.

Grooms. What did they know?

As the morning progressed, Firebrand succeeded in lulling him into a false sense of confidence. At length, he sat a little straighter.

Why had the princess invited him at all?

Watching her from beneath his fringe, he wished he had Father Justin's ability to gauge a person's feelings. His own emotions were a muddle. Excitement had ebbed, making way for bitterness at being ignored. Which did nothing to diminish the jealousy he felt for the ladies-in-waiting. There was frustration, at his inability to turn the social tables, and shame at feeling any of this at all.

And, through it all, he retained the desperate desire to converse with the princess. It was pathetic. *He* was pathetic.

He racked his brain, raking through everything he knew of history, theology, philosophy and rhetoric – looking for some interesting tinder to start a conversation.

He was still ruminating when their party pulled up. He tugged unnecessary at his halted horse's reins.

Below them spread a grassy basin, a breeze combing the stalks.

The lead falconer declared it adequate.

Servants rushed to fit the ladies with protective gloves and the falconers coaxed their feathery charges onto the ready gauntlets.

"Highness," the foremost said, tugging at his forelock. The raptor, perched on the princess's arm, was unhooded.

It shook out its feathers, golden eyes glaring about ferociously.

With a bright smile and a deft flick, the princess sent it skyward. It seemed to quadruple in size as its wings unfurled.

It climbed effortlessly into the blue, to the very rim of the sky, where it looped a lazy circuit. Marco was not alone in shading his eyes to track it. The excerpt he'd read had claimed this was a *hunting* sport. So far, it was little different from flying a paper kite.

He risked a peek at the princess. The ride had flushed her porcelain cheeks. Her creamy neck craned-

Gasps sounded around him and he snapped his guilty gaze back to the sky. The raptor plummeted from on high, like plumed lightning. It plunged among the grasses and, for a moment, he was certain it had either brained- or buried itself. Then it broke cover, wings fighting for height and weighted down by a ball of fluff. It skimmed the stalks toward them, relinquishing its prize to retake its perch on the princess's wrist.

An assistant stepped up to offer the bird a morsel of meat.

Scattered cheers sounded from the servants as the falconers gathered around the downed prey.

"A clean kill, highness," the lead falconer pronounced, beaming as though he'd brought down the hare himself. "Back-broken!"

"Breathtaking, yes?"

He started. He hadn't heard the princess sidle her horse over to his. Her color was up and her eyes were bright with excitement.

"Very," he affirmed, hoping she thought he meant the spectacle.

"If I had my way," she cooed, "I'd have them just *fly*. But they are, first and foremost, predators... Would you like to pet her?"

"Pet?" he gaped, nonplussed.

The princess turned her horse expertly, extending her arm.

He leaned away from the proffered bird, its avian eyes burning coldly and its cruel beak and talons streaked with blood.

It was even bigger up close.

The princess gave him an encouraging nod.

Swallowing hard, he extended a hand, consoling himself with the fact that it was his left. He needed his right for scribing.

The raptor eyed his approaching digits, deciding whether these were also morsels to be gulped.

He gently trailed his knuckles down the dun feathers, feeling both the heat and hollow hardness of the hunter's frame.

The third falconer was ready with the bird's hood.

Marco breathed a sigh as its mad eyes were mercifully hidden.

"Isn't she magnificent?"

He started to smile his agreement. Wait... "She?"

He'd assumed, from its size, that the raptor was male.

"Princess Clariona is a woad hawk. The red-tailed males are more flashy but she's the better hunter."

"'*Princess*...?'" he became aware he was stroking Princess – the bird's – breast and snatched his hand back.

The falconer saved him from further embarrassment, shuffling between them, to relieve the royal of both raptor and glove.

Servants rushed up. One held a silver bowl of lilac tinged water, the other used a soft cloth to gently clean the princess's hand.

"Father says my sister and I should be as hawks," she mused as they worked. "Proud. Proficient. Prepared to perch on a worthy man's wrist... or go for his eyes, if he isn't."

Which reminded him... "Where are your chaperones?"

She struggled against an impish grin, making sure the servants were out of earshot before leaning conspiratorially toward him.

Harsh lilac and soft lily reached his nose.

"You mean my sister's eyes and ears?" she whispered.

She backed her horse so he could see past her.

One of the ladies slumped in the saddle, being frantically fanned by the other. The woman's pallor had gone decidedly gray.

"Janelle has a delicate constitution and cannot abide the sight of blood. A condition she constantly discounts." Raising her voice, the princess commanded the company at large. "Someone dampen her wrists. She's come over faint. Poor thing."

As servants rushed to obey, she confided in him. "Sometimes, during embroidery, I prick my finger just to see her swoon…"

This, he realized in wonder, was the girl he'd met on the stairs.

The princess graciously decreed an early end to the expedition. And, while the others fussed over the overcome lady-in-waiting, the two of them rode, side by side, at the head of the procession.

Freed from scrutiny, she plagued him with constant questions, all the way to the keep. They spoke of too many things to recall, touching on customs and culture, books read, music heard and even favorite teas. She described a complex-sounding, twelve-stringed instrument and promised to show him how to play. He told her of the Temple, from its subterranean libraries to its rearing orchards. They swapped stories with such ease, he even found himself forgetting he was astride a horse.

"And then," she related mischievously, "when I was six, I had to choose a bird – to front my personal crest."

"The swan?" he said, recalling the day before's invitation.

She chortled delightedly. "Father was beside himself! The Stentoric line has had birds of prey since before the Greenwall. But he had promised. So, after that, I was his little 'persuading swan'."

He laughed, imagining her as a little girl in a lace frock, a bow in the hair, matching glares with the king.

"I pity your lord father!"

But she was no longer laughing. They'd reached the stable yard and she'd stiffened in the saddle. He followed her gaze. A figure stood, carefully beyond the sun's reach. The severe stance and expression identified the elder princess, Villet.

"Dailill?" he queried, uncertain.

"Best you call me by my title again," she advised, and he heard the dispassion she'd greeted him with that morning, creeping back.

Something about the elder princess's gaze unnerved him.

"Highness, your sister's crest," he recalled, "it's-"

"The hangman's hawk," she grimly confirmed. "The only hawk known to hunt its own kind."

She cleared her throat, exuding royal formality once more.

"Master Dei Toriam, our thanks, for your company today."

Unsure what to say, he bowed deeply from the saddle.

She heeled her horse away, without a backward glance.

He couldn't help but feel he was somehow abandoning her in her time of need. That was when he happened to meet the elder princess's eye. Her flat regard snared him, setting his heart agallop.

Fortunately, Firebrand sidestepped, interrupting their stare.

Relieved, he clambered down, making sure to keep the horse between him and the royal as he headed inside.

* * *

SHIPS. SAND-SPAWNED, wind-wasted ships!

If Jiminy had known stowing away would be this bad, he'd have taken his chances back home.

The hidey hole he'd cleared in the cargo hold had just enough space for him, and his bucket, to sit upright in. He eyed the wretched pail, ignoring the dull ache of his tailbone and the more insistent burbling of his belly.

He was not seasick, obviously. You couldn't walk a wire, or do a dozen tumbles, on a weak stomach. It was simply that a steady diet of salted pork and pickles didn't agree with him.

There was better fare to be had, in the ship's galley. But, excellent sneak thief though he was, braving the ship's bustling centers would be unnecessarily stupid.

Also, the cook slept there, cuddling an enormous cleaver.

He whittled idly, whiling away the day. Rats were being blamed for the barrels he'd breached and he was getting good at carving a 'gnawed' pattern.

It was a horrible waste of his lone candle but the dark was oppressive today. He'd not seen the sun in a week and his – and his bucket's – nightly sojourns did little to relieve his restlessness.

As he sat, shaving wood, he pondered his predicament.

The thugs, who had tried to run him down, had not been redbacks. He'd had enough dealings with the city constabulary to spot that, straight off.

Despite the absence of any identifying kohl, he'd thought they must be blackeyes. Night sky knew, there were a dozen princes who would pay handsomely to have Jiminy's head prised off.

But paying should not have worked.

The upper crust had many tricks to circumvent Alley Law. One was to hire a secret intermediary – some seedy street gang who could, by rights, offer a bounty. Crawly had denied that this was the case, of course. If it came out that the lender had knowingly sold someone to the princes, his peers would carve him to pieces.

Crawly had evidently considered the risk minimal.

And then there was what the thug had said.

'Where is it?'

They did not simply want Jiminy. They wanted something he *had*. Or *thought* he had. That gave him leverage, of a sort. He could offer the… whatever it was, to have his bounty overturned. That plan would likely involve him stealing the goods back from whoever had bought it – or whoever had commissioned the theft in the first place – but that would be half the fun.

A shame the strong-arm in the sewer had not been more specific. If Jiminy only knew what it was he was supposed to have taken, he'd know which prince to approach.

One might think the answer simple – that it had to be the most valuable thing he'd ever swiped – but that wasn't the way a prince's mind worked. To the petty potentates, coin was dross. What mattered was reputation. His patrons spent fortunes on saving face, or – better yet – embarrassing their enemies.

Jiminy had once been commissioned to steal the ashes of one prince's ancestor, just so another could have them turned into a chamber pot. His patron had wanted to brag that he literally pissed on his rival's family each day.

He'd once been paid to carry a clandestine message – a parcel containing a pair of human testicles – and leave it in an impregnable mansion, on an unfaithful lover's pillow.

He sincerely hoped, whoever was after him, they weren't seeking their lost scrotum. He was *not* stealing that back.

He had, of course, also pilfered more traditional prizes – gold and gems and jewelry. Rare art and artifacts. Other stuff.

The princes, who thought this kind of turn-and-turnabout was great fun, quickly lost their sense of humor when common thieves – commoner than they, at least – tried to join their game.

One wronged prince had tried to get him killed outright, hiring him for an impossible job – and also forewarning his mark.

That's where Jiminy had earned his unfortunate nickname. In retrospect, he should have shouted something else – anything else – when he had heeled away on that prince's prize horse, leaving the man in the middle of the desert at a fake handoff.

'Surprise!'

He shook his head at his younger self's folly.

There was still another way he might identify his pursuer. If he could flush out the intermediaries, the ones who had offered coin for his capture, he might follow them to their irate principal.

He'd needed an information broker. With that in mind, he'd made his way to the Mule Street Orphanage.

The fate of its parentless progeny was not exactly a priority for Oaragh's rulers. They cared more for currying favor with the princes. And so, yearly, countless children fell through the cracks.

Right into the arms of Hammerham Nan and those like her.

The Mule Street Orphanage gathered in the city's waifs and runaways, churning out some of the best thieves, swindlers, pickpockets and prostitutes in Purlia.

It's where Jiminy had gotten his formal education. Seeing the old place always brought on a warm, fuzzy feeling. Like mold.

He'd gone in quietly, swinging through Nan's office window.

"That was *almost* decently done," she'd harrumphed, her broad back to him, pouring brandy at the sideboard.

"You're a marvel, Nan."

She'd turned her bulk toward him, treating him to her flat gaze. "Flattery will get you fuck-all."

"Not even a drink?"

Nan had a *look* with knuckles in it. He'd smiled to see it. No one drank Nan's green fig brandy but Nan. As a child, he'd stolen a dram – and drunk it – just to prove he could. He'd been so sick, afterward, he hadn't even run when she'd taken the strop to him.

"I see you've heard," she'd remarked, eyeing his pared ear.

Old Cobb's quackery had not been up to re-growing the lost lobe. So Jiminy had seen no point in paying for more than stitches.

"Har-har."

But Nan wasn't done. "I remember promising you I'd peel those off, unless you used them. Did you listen to nothing I taught you? Have you been about your business with your face bare, boy?"

That tone, unforgiving as a quince switch, had reached across the years and stood him up straight.

"No, Nan! Properly masked at all times, promise!"

"Then how," she'd pounced, "did the son-of-a-sow who left *this*, know to come sniffing at my door?"

A purse had landed between them, raising a golden clangor.

He'd been dismayed by its size. "That bad?"

"Worse. The kind of coin on offer would turn even one of my kids' heads. I couldn't risk running a warning to you."

He hadn't bothered to ask whether she'd been tempted herself, nor to wonder who had let slip his true identity. "Crawly…"

It seemed there was little the lender wouldn't sell.

"I need help, Nan. One of the princes-"

"It's not them," she'd cut him off.

"What? Of course it's them-"

"Oh," she'd scathed. "Apologies, Master Burglar. Did you come here to *tell* me who it is? Or to *ask* me who it is?"

Chastised, he'd shut him up. There was no doubting Nan.

His thoughts racing, he'd turned the problem over in his head. New possibilities had opened up. If the princes were *not* involved… then he didn't have to tiptoe.

He could meet the problem, and his pursuers, edge-on.

"Alright, where can I find-"

"No."

That had brought him up short. "I haven't asked a question yet."

"Then let me skip ahead. *No*, I don't know who they are. *No*, I'm not telling you where they are. *No*, you can't handle them and, *no*, you can't change my mind."

Obedience to Nan was a strong reflex to squash. It struggled against his natural inclination – defiance in the face of authority.

"Why?" he'd compromised.

She had looked at him a long time, weighing, before answering.

"Prince Raman sent your new fans an underling, to extort the usual dues. The jackal limped home. Naturally, the prince sent a pack of blackeyes next, to educate the foreigners. Raman's best returned – stapled to the palace gates, screaming and on fire."

Shock had held him. No one challenged the princes. Not directly, anyway. But, if the interlopers were foreign – and he would trust Nan's assessment, since she'd apparently spoken with one of them – they might simply be ignorant.

Either way, he didn't want to tangle with an outfit that could broil a band of blackeyes and who thumbed their noses at a prince.

His first plan had begun to look more attractive by the moment.

"I should probably leave," he'd mused, meaning the country. It would be a tragedy to deprive Purlia of its top sneak-thief – especially seeing as how he'd just started earning that reputation.

If he were lucky, Raman would solve his problem for him.

Nan had kicked idly at the discarded purse, scattering golden coins – of a currency he hadn't recognized – across the carpet.

"Need any money?" she'd offered gruffly.

He'd left the riches where they lay. The orphanage would put it to better use than he would. He'd turned for the window.

"See you, Nan."

In the pane's reflection, he'd seen her toast him.

Now, hidden in the cargo hold of a ship, his senses came awake. *Something was wrong.*

He pinched out his candle, cocking an ear to the darkness.

Some of the crew came down here periodically. But that wasn't what he was feeling. He'd spent days with nothing to do but learn the creak and cant of the ship. Both were askew. A storm? Wouldn't that be just what he needed...

He'd chosen this boat because it was the biggest one in port. There were two whole decks between him and the sky. Still, he could make out faint yelling and the rushed thumping of feet. Something about the sounds spoke of panic.

If this tub sinks, he thought, *it'll trap me down here.*

He wouldn't call drowning a *fear* of his, exactly. But, if he had to face death, he could hope for a fairer contest than swimming.

He had a sudden vision, of all the skiffs gone and the ship abandoned, except for him.

He eased from hiding.

The fact that his feet were still dry was a good omen.

Slinking toward the stairs, he spotted a faint corona of daylight.

The banging and shouting intensified as he tracked it upward. Belowdecks seemed deserted, all the action concentrated above.

Skittish as a buzzard confronted by a blinking corpse, he approached the last landing and its closed hatch. The sounds resolved into screams and bellows, underpinned by the unmistakable clash of weapons.

Trust him to pick a ship of mutineers.

It was nothing to do with him, he judged. He would do well to wait it out, quietly, in the hold. He bit his lip.

Just a quick peek, he decided, hand settling on the latch-

The door before him was wrenched wide, snagging his wrist.

He spilled bodily out into blinding light and loud chaos.

Sprawling, he scrambled to sit up.

A bullish figure reared above him, raising something that blocked out the sun – an axe of pitted iron.

Instinct took over. Jiminy kicked out hard, skidding on his behind. That did not quite win him an axe handle's worth of grace, so he spayed his legs wide – praying to anyone who would listen.

The axe head gouged wood, a finger short of his crotch.

The hunk of whoresteel was wrenched upward. He followed, as though the axeman were an angler who'd hooked something horrible. The 'something horrible' went in under the man's short ribs, reaching for the liver.

"I! Might! Want! Kids!" he shrilled as he worked his knife.

Stab! Stab! Stab! Stab!

Outdone, the axe keeled over and took its wielder with it.

Jiminy stood, a little wild-eyed, pawing at the front of his pantaloons. He found everything in its proper place. "Phew!"

Only then did the greater melee merit his attention.

Everywhere he looked, rough men were hacking away at each other. He did a double take – another ships' sails poked above the rail to his right. Sharp grapnels had scored the wood and, even as he watched, more boarders clambered into view.

He glanced at the slain axeman. The brands of half a dozen portside gaols puckered the corpse's skin.

Pirate, he identified.

Desert-born he might be, but even *he* knew pirates stuck to the Summer archipelago, where Heli patrols were scattered and thin.

A band of lost buccaneers, he grimaced. *Great.*

Said buccaneers boiled toward him, forcing him away from the hatch and the relative safety of the hold.

He'd have preferred to wait and see who won before picking a side. But that possibility lay dead at his feet, its blood on his knife.

And, he realized immediately, he was at a disadvantage. The crew would take him for a pirate; the pirates would assume he was crew. And he was stuck in the middle, not knowing who was who.

Crap.

Except… there was a captain's tricorn hat, bobbing atop the rear deck. Where the fighting was thickest, of course.

Now, he thought, absently slipping under a cutlass, *if I can just get there without getting skewered-*

He hastily sidestepped a screaming midget with a morningstar, ducked beneath a hurled harpoon, and missed getting hit with a mallet as he made his way through the fray.

Tussling bodies blocked the stairs, so he leapt for the handrail. A hatchet swung for his heel, and a spiked club for his shin, but neither came close as he skipped ahead. At the top, he sprang for the closest pirate's back. He landed blades-first.

A man with a knife hooked under either shoulder blade is, basically, a slab of beef. He swung his meat shield around, fending blows with pirate flesh as he backed toward the defenders.

"What in blazes?"

That bellow made the thickly muscled man the first mate – none too happy at finding an unfamiliar face on his flank.

By way of explanation, Jiminy shoved his skewered pirate beneath the feet of a fresh onslaught. A silvery rapier reached over his shoulder, the captain's face hard behind it. That expression promised that the questions to follow would be at least as pointed.

A spurting swashbuckler fell. Then the rest arrived.

Jiminy's close-work knives could hold their own against the assembled swords and cutty things. But the heavier hatchets and hammers posed a problem. He couldn't very well dodge blows that would then brain his allies. Left with little choice, he forsook his normal fighting style and met these haymakers head-on.

A particularly hard hit almost lost him his grip and he fumbled his riposte. A rough hand jerked him from harm's way, a rapier covering his retreat. As though he were no more than an off-hand dagger, the captain thrust him forward. He went willingly, sliding low to open an artery. The attacker fell to the deck, howl cut short by the first mate's fanged club.

Though Jiminy had no experience fighting in a group, he'd run his share of shell-games as a child. This was similar.

He was the shill – the easy win – too tantalizing to pass up. The captain was the shell man, using speed and guile to befuddle. And while the silver tongue of the rapier held the audience's attention, Jiminy slit their pouches, all unseen. The first mate was the muscle, making sure the fuss was kept down. Permanently.

Once he realized this, he fell into a ragged rhythm.

Which was not to say it was easy.

Despite his best efforts, his fingers quickly became a shredded mess. A club had glanced off his ribs and a pirate – who hadn't been quite dead enough – had sunk teeth into his calf.

Too soon, his cache of knives was spent, studding throats and thighs all around. He held the last pair in aching hands.

The first mate kicked out. A broken buccaneer bowled over the reinforcements rushing up the stairs. In the lull, Jiminy tried to gauge the tide of the battle. Fighting had spilled onto the pirate ship, where black smoke rose. As he watched, the last of the lines lashing the ships together were severed. They groaned apart.

Panicked pirates raced for the side, pitching themselves over the rail. The lucky ones hit water.

Jiminy recognized the ship's cook – a kitchen knife clenched between bared teeth – lobbing a rag-stopped bottle. It trailed smoke over the rail and burst below with a whoosh of flame.

Pirates yowled.

Quite suddenly, a semblance of silence descended, bar the harsh breathing of the survivors. The pirate ship listed into view, limping for the horizon. It was over. He let his knives droop and sagged to his knees as a cheer went up.

The captain let it run for a moment, then began barking orders. The first mate belted these out for all to hear.

He paid them no mind. Weak and sparsely watered, he was on the verge of spitting up and passing out.

Irrelevant details warred for his attention.

He stared at a dead pirate's meticulous manicure.

A pair of boots interrupted his sightline. Blearily he glanced up at the captain, who still held a bloody rapier in a loose grip.

"Are you a merman?" the man asked, in passable Purli.

"No, sir," he wheezed, in Common.

"Be ye a frost ghost, then?" The accent was even more pronounced in the trader's tongue. "Or a wave hopper? I've ne'er heard tell o' a male siren. Be ye a fire-mist sprite?"

He shook his head, trying to look harmless. "I am as I seem."

The captain chewed on his curled moustaches. "Just a lad who ought no' be on me ship?"

At the unsubtle accusation, he nodded anyway.

"Alright then." The captain straightened, gesturing curtly.

He'd forgotten about the first mate.

The blow landed neatly, pitching him to the deck.

MATTANUY SAT, BROODING over a stack of books in the Black Library. Since his investigation into the butcher murders had begun, he'd become a regular feature here, in the vaults.

Tonight, though, he was not bent over ever more obscure accounts of necromantic rites and rituals. Tonight, he was researching something far closer to home.

Over the centuries, the Inquisitori had suppressed hundreds of sigil development experiments, both sanctioned and not. The confiscated materials were ensconced here.

Their sheer volume could make anyone wonder whether the venerable Auctorati had a lick of sense between them.

There was no official filing system. But it was staggering how many treatises – sometimes separated by decades and centuries – skirted the same seditious pitfalls.

He'd already come across three separate accounts, seeking to remedy the loss of a limb. At least one of them had openly proposed incorporating dead matter.

He shook his head.

It was like the fools had never even heard of necromancy!

Even so, it encouraged him. If the incautious Auctorati had come *that* close to crossing the line, by accident, he was sure some past empath had come at least as close to-

His back stiffened. *Here...*

Feverish, skimming the page with a finger, he read and re-read the account again. A grim smile crinkled his lips.

It was an old entry, incomplete and barely legible – a sigil, by which an empath could invade the sanctity of another's mind. Force them to fear, fool them to trust or even enflame them to rage.

That was witchery. *That* was heresy.

His suspicion confirmed, he sat back to tally the facts:

Meum – a ritual murderer, emptied of every animal whim.

Marco – a random urchin, instilled with savage survival skills.

And, straddling the cases?

Justin – a streamer and empath of unusual power, now seconded to a pagan kingdom, where magic went unsupervised.

A conspiracy, far larger than colonial reform, was taking shape.

Whatever the man had done to his ward, it seemed slapdash – a rehearsal. If so, should the Renali expect their own spate of grisly murders soon? To what end? What would the keeper do, once he'd perfected his way of weaponizing children?

And, more to the point, what could Mattanuy do with it?

Now, more than ever, he needed this priest under his thumb.

WAKING AT ALL was a surprise. Though not, Jiminy reflected, necessarily a pleasant one. His head ached and his hands throbbed.

Bars hemmed him. Fetid murk surrounded him. For a moment, he was back in Oaragh's sewers. But the reek of pitch and brine disabused him. Ankle deep water sloshed with the roll of the ship.

He was in the bilges. More specifically, the brig – a space little more than an afterthought, squeezed between the ribs of the ship.

His own ribs complained as he sat up, lowering his feet into the swell. Chains held his narrow cot to the ship's belly, the bars so close there was hardly any room for his knees. Space was reserved for cargo, obviously, not prisoners.

He gained a new appreciation for the term '*pitch* black'.

He could barely make out his hands – two useless snarls of bandage, smelling of camphor.

That boded well. You didn't waste medicine on someone you were going to murder, surely?

He grimaced. He put little stock in the reason of others.

Hampered by his swaddled fingers and sundry aches, he felt around his cell's confines. The clunks from beneath his bench turned out to be a waste bucket. In the cramped space, its use would require spectacular bodily contortions. Shuddering, he made note of the cooper's hoop, holding it together. It was something that might be fashioned into a tool, or a weapon, with some effort.

His actual toolkit might as well be an ocean away, still stashed in a dry corner of the cargo hold. He had some emergency coin, wound into his sash, but he wasn't picking any locks with that.

He sagged against the damp planks, consigned to suffering the sting of captivity. And of stupidity. He should have stayed hidden.

He listened to the incontinent drips, the creak of the timbers and the thump of feet, far overhead.

His bone deep bruises, especially his ribs, made a mockery of his stoicism. He shifted continually, searching for a semi-comfortable position but couldn't find one.

Eventually, the wallowing ship soothed him to a fitful doze…

A metallic clang, in his ear, yanked him from sleep and halfway upright before his splintered side could object.

"Ow," he wheezed, slumping back under pain's weight.

He rolled his eyes toward the bars. Burnished by lantern light, the burly first mate looked even more muscled, with club in hand. A new scar scabbed the man's scalp. It fitted right in with the rest.

"'said," the man repeated, "cap'n wants t' see ye."

A key rattled and rusty hinges screeched wide.

Biting down on his pain, he swung his legs off the cot. He'd be hard pressed to hurt a fly if he fell on it. But that was no reason to look pathetic. A ship was just a floating gang and he knew how to handle those. He stood as straight as he dared, which was still only midway to the first mate's chest.

It wasn't the first time he'd been caught on another group's turf.

"I'll not keep the captain waiting, then," he offered.

The man grunted, unimpressed, and motioned him ahead.

The light on deck was dazzling. It hid the gallows crowd he could sense, watching him from all sides.

The burly mate bellowed. "Get on, you lot! Back tae work!"

Before the sullen figures could come into focus, he was herded down a short passage and to a narrow door.

"Knock," the first mate commanded.

He gritted his teeth and raised his swathed fist.

"Come," came the curt reply.

The first mate pressed in behind him, making the small room even smaller, and shut the door. Having the man at his back woke the old itch between his shoulders – just one more discomfort.

The captain's desk was bolted to the floor and overflowing with books, maps and brass instruments that – at first glance – smacked of torture devices. The man himself was making an annotation, seemingly absorbed by something that looked to be the bastard offspring of a jeweler's tongs and a dinner fork, a piece of chalk held in its mandibles.

From flowing locks to downturned boots, the captain was so signally a swashbuckler Jiminy found himself scanning the stateroom for evidence of a parrot.

"So," the ship's boss drawled, setting his measures aside, "this bodes tae be a' intrestin' tale. We'll start, methinks, with yer name, if ye please…?"

A gold-capped incisor flashed at him. There was real humor there, but the man's eyes remained both fathomless and fickle. Plainly, this was going to be Jiminy's one chance to talk himself out of a swim that would last the rest of his life.

The damp between his toes, he found, was no longer all brine.

But he'd faced down desert princes as mad as sun-addled asps before. He'd survived some of the shrewdest swindlers, fleecers and horse-mongers Purlia had ever produced.

"Davin, sir," he supplied, face open and honest and fearful.

"'Davin', is it tae be?" the captain smirked brightly. "Care tae make up a family name, *Davin*?"

"Don't have one, sir," he said, seeing the captain register the ring of truth – he'd have to play this carefully. "Orphan, sir."

The man chewed his curled moustaches a moment. "I be Rasibeal Puttin, captain o' the Isus Spear. Ye've met me first mate," muscles flexed audibly nearby, "Master Uriban Lenk."

"Pleased to make your acquaintance, sir," he said, humble as a one-camel *karwan*, and cursing the necessity.

"Ha!" the captain gushed. "Tha' remains tae be seen."

The man leaned forward, tone inviting confidence and not so much as a hint of murder in his eyes. Jiminy was not fooled.

"Tell me true – be ye a *pirate*, Davin No Name?"

"Wha-? Master-! No!"

Sincerity was the key. Once you learned to fake that, you were golden. Also, it helped when what you were saying was true.

"Then how came ye tae be aboard me ship, Davin?"

The question fell like a whip. He bowed his back beneath it.

"Stowaway, sir," he supplied, in as small a voice as possible.

The savvy captain sat back, letting silence make its weight felt. When Jiminy judged he'd squirmed enough, he rushed to fill it.

"I snuck aboard in Oaragh, master. Been hiding in the cargo hold, master. I didn't mean nobody no harm, honest!"

All this humility was leaving a sour taste in his mouth.

"An' whereaboots in me cargo hav' ye b'n hidin', Davin?"

The question was casually asked, like one might strop a razor. This was where a pirate's story would fall apart. He didn't hesitate.

"Second level, master. Way in the back. Between the bolts of silk and the crates marked with what looks like a hummingbird."

At the captain's glance, Master Lenk put his head out the door. There was a muffled exchange, followed by some fading footsteps.

"I didn't break nothing," he rushed to reassure. "I swear."

Now, more than ever, he was glad he'd hidden his picks away from his hidey-hole. He would not care to gamble on this Puttin seeing the distinction between a pirate and a professional pilferer.

He severely disliked throwing himself on the man's mercy like this; he sensed it was a small, migratory target. There was no telling to what extent his aid against the pirates had plumped it.

If his kit turned up…

"Normally," the captain mused, "I'd no' bother. But these be no' pirate waters, ye see. Yet, there they were. Black sails on the rise. The Spear be faster 'n she looks but the ol' gel be a trader a' heart an' she be a bit tubby." A beringed hand caressed the desk in absentminded apology. "Madness it seemed – one schooner takin' on the Spear? I feared more'd be waitin' in Reacher's Bluff – an' those keel-guttin' shoals be damned. Turns out they were even brasher than tha', takin' us on alone, the cocky bastards…"

Jiminy felt the pirates had inconvenienced *him* more so than they had the vessel or crew but he doubted he'd get any sympathy.

"I carry only the best merchandise," the captain continued. "Ye don't keep a girl like the Spear afloat by sailin' stupid. Me men be well paid an' well do they know it. I'll no' take just any riffraff fer crew neither. Ye'll find no' more experienced bunch betwixt Quincaan an' Rasrin. So, believe me when I tell ye, Davin No Name, tha' the hands w' lost will be mighty hard tae replace."

The moustaches coiled angrily. "*Mighty* hard."

He felt his chances of survival slimming.

"Look askance a' tha' sort o' thing, does the crew. I'll nae lie tae ye – they be fixin' tae hang themselves a pirate. And I be of a mind tae hand ye over."

Those golden canines flashed grimly.

"Please, master! No! I'm no pirate, I swear!" He'd be disgusted by this unseemly begging, later – if he were lucky. "I only-"

The door, opening, interrupted him. Master Lenk received a whispered report and gave the captain a grudging nod.

"Well, now!" The captain didn't sound surprised. "Stowaway ye be indeed! I fear me I've misjudged ye, Davin No Name."

Real relief threatened to topple him from his feet.

"But stowaway *ye be*," the captain observed. "By ships' law, I should hav' ye tossed o'erboard an' hav' done w' ye."

The captain dusted his hands in demonstration, eyeing him as if inviting a rebuttal. He knew better.

"But," the man drawled, when it became clear he wouldn't poke his nose after the bait, "I find m'self several hands short, far fra' port, on a pirate-infested sea where no pirates should be."

He allowed himself a glimmer of hope and didn't bother to keep it off his face.

"No sailor ye be, tha' much be plain. But fight ye can," came the considered admission, "and fight ye hav'. In need I am o' a capable pair o' hands. Hav' ye such hands, Davin No Name?"

He blinked. Was the captain asking him to help crew the ship? And him wearing more bandages than clothes? Was the man blind?

"Yes, captain!" He didn't have to scrounge hard for some enthusiasm and came disgustingly close to an outright salute.

A sharp silence fell. The captain's grin turned predatory.

"Ye boarded me ship fer yer own convenience, Davin No Name. It be only fair ye now stay fer mine. This then, be our accord. Ye'll crew fer me, at my convenience, until such time as I choose tae replace ye."

He gaped. "That sounds like..."

Indentured servitude. He was going to be a ship's slave.

"The best deal of yer life?" the captain guessed.

A hand was proffered. What else could he do? He clasped it.

"Excellent! Master Lenk will see ye settled. Welcome aboard, Master Noname."

The swashbuckler seemed to put him instantly out of mind.

Lightheaded, he was left to follow the first mate from the cabin.

Still alive, he steeled himself. This tub would have to put in to port at some point. When it did, he was gone.

He resolved to walk a little taller.

His sense of secret victory lasted until he went back for his picks, a few nights later.

And found their hiding place under the stairs empty.

CHAPTER 9 – A DARK RIPPLE

Pella Monop, Journal entry #64

Finally! My academic rigor has found reward. I've been offered the position of visiting professor at the Imperial Institute of Learning. What's more, I've been asked to complete the project of my absconded peer and predecessor, Dayna Bruen. Peer! Ha! I knew that pig's bladder would one day put on enough airs to foist herself right out of academia. I'm only sad I wasn't here to see her spiral. Once I'm done writing the seminal Heli history, I may yet thank her in the foreword. Or, perhaps, in a footnote. A small one.

Amazing...

Marco very much wanted to linger over the outlandish artworks, but the hard gazes of the Royal Guard discouraged dawdling. The curve of the corridor conspired to put him in view of at least one of their number at all times. He'd not been aware of their attention earlier, when one the princess's ladies-in-waiting had escorted him. Now, returning alone, their disapproval was palpable.

His only thought, upon trudging from the dining hall this eve, had been of bed. He'd overeaten and had intended to sleep like a bear. A light touch on his elbow had forestalled him.

"Sir Scribe, my lady has invited you to after-dinner tea."

He'd blinked up at her unfamiliar face. "What lady?"

"A certain swan," she had clarified, amused.

Only then had he recognized her from the hawking expedition – the stalwart lady who had not fainted.

The princess's confidant had led him along a maze of darkened back passages and servants' stairs.

Arriving abruptly in the well-lit, vaulted corridors, he'd caught his breath. "These are the royal apartments!"

"Did you think I was leading you to the stables?" she'd asked, sounding both scandalized and scornful.

He'd frowned. "Why would we have tea in the stables?"

Her sharp look had turned searching and she'd shaken her head.

There was so much about Renali culture he still did not grasp.

He *did* understand the irrefusable honor of being served pastries by the princess's own hand. In the princess's own sitting rooms.

Tongue-tied, he'd stuffed his mouth with lemon sponges, staving off speaking until he was sure he wouldn't stammer.

"You can relax," she'd said at last, misapprehending the source of his anxiety. "My sister finds herself beset by the masons guild this night. She is much too busy to check up on me."

"Masons guild?" he'd mumbled around a mouthful.

"Hmm. Something about a minor detail I *accidentally* overlooked in their annual contract. Villet never could pass up an opportunity to be seen correcting my mistakes."

Contritely sipping tea, her eyes had laughed nevertheless.

Their exchange had flowed easily from there, as fellow conspirators, and had ended far too soon.

Not even his overfull stomach had been able to spoil it.

Now, however, the rich sweets sat askew atop his savory supper. A confused mélange seared from his croup and between his teeth.

Aniseed, he groaningly identified. *Or poppy seed?*

Out of nowhere, another flavor shouldered past, turning his stomach. His gorge rose at the hint of rotten soil and bitter sap, like he'd eaten a month-old mud pie and leaf mulch.

He staggered to a halt, clutching his stomach. It took a moment to realize the sense had come from somewhere else. He looked up.

It came, coiling down the corridor, clinging to the cornices.

Smoke? Fire!

As he drew breath to give the alarm, the entire apparition heaved into view – a tattered shade, roiling fitfully as it decanted itself from vault to vault, whispering like dead leaves on the bough.

Witchery! He could feel the wrongness of it. It grated, like a false note in a choir. Eyes watering, he blinked hard, dragging his gaze to meet that of the nearest Royal Guard.

The man's pedestrian glare made clear he could not see what passed overhead. And Marco hadn't the Renali words to tell him.

He spun. For a moment, he thought his imagination had played a cruel joke. The ceiling was clear. But as he strained, breathless and unblinking, the evil stain bled back into sight.

It was headed the way he'd come – to the Royal Apartments.

Dailill!

"No!"

The guard, who'd taken an uncertain step toward him, jumped. He dodged the man's sudden grab and tore up the corridor after the apparition. An alarm finally rose. He barely noticed.

At a loss for how to stop the shade, he snatched a ceramic pot from a niche. The little urn passed near the heart of the mass and shattered against the vault. Potsherds and ash pattered down.

The shade churned angrily and, though it had no eyes, he felt it fix its attention to him. Cringing he refused to retreat…

And the apparition quickened, speeding ahead.

Oh, no.

A hand snagged his over robe and he shrugged out of the garment, galloping after the shade. Angry guards converged. He weaved around them and their unwieldy halberds, refusing to fail.

Again. He refused to fail *again*.

He left curses and the clatter of armor in his wake, gaining on the manifestation. If its smoke-like appearance matched its consistency, it could slip under the princess's door. A door that would surely stay barred to him. He would have to fight the men charged with Dailill's safety while, a dozen paces away, she died.

The next guard who lunged at him met his training head on.

Faint. Reverse.

He split his scalp on the helm's bridge guard but the man stumbled from the unexpected blow, knee folding to a kick.

Pivot. Throw.

More men went down as their colleague crashed into them.

Halberd now in hand, he mustered every bit of his strength for a toss. The heavy polearm punched through the outer edge of the shadow and somehow stuck in the plaster.

The shade sped on.

Out of ideas, he found himself ahead of it, back pedaling.

This couldn't be happening. After all that training, all that sweat and pain, how could he still be this helpless? This *useless*?

Boots pounded deafeningly all around. Hands grabbed at his wrists and robes, yanking him off balance.

Master Crysopher's sure voice rose in his mind, cutting through his panic.

Elbow, palm, knee...

His body reacted as it had been drilled to.

He spun into the air, hips twisting and legs scything. Hands fell away. One sturdy guardsman, teeth bloodied, retained a blind grip. He found handholds in the man's half-plate and climbed, lashing out with a knee as he went. Stepping on a solid shoulder he launched himself at the ceiling. And at the shade, as it passed.

Time slowed.

Helia-!

The one-word prayer sounded small and desperate, even to him.

His splayed fingers sank straight through the shade.

A graveyard stench clogged his nose. The buzzing of a million flies sawed, laughingly, at his ears.

And then he was falling. Failing.

Dailill, I'm so sor-

Something solid skimmed his fingertips and they spasmed shut.

There was a beat of resistance and then the shade surrendered with a ripping sound. He plummeted, holding tight.

It was a bad landing, fouled by armored figures. At least one landed on him in a dogpile. The pressure threatened to pop his full belly. But the weight rolled off in an instant – a wiry figure, masked and wrapped entirely in black, shot away up the corridor.

"Fortune's fetlocks!"

"Assassin!"

"After him!"

With something solid in sight to pursue, he was the first to his feet, bruised though they were. Knowing how and where to strike at an armored man did not make it hurt any less. He was still faster than the encumbered guards, though, and he flew ahead.

An assassin! And one whose pagan arts had slipped past who knew how many layers of the keep's protections?

One who might try again, if not stopped tonight.

Gritting his teeth, he fought his cramping stomach for speed.

The assassin was *fast*.

Rounding a bend, he caught a bare glimpse of black down the next intersection. Guards appeared at the far end, racing toward him. He turned the corner just ahead of them.

The assassin had disappeared. But a door halfway down the hall hung ajar. Sprinting, he shouldered it aside. Behind him the guards swore as they overshot, skidding on the slick tiles.

The room was disused, dusty and deserted.

Half-formed worries – of an assassin, waiting behind the portal – proved baseless. The would-be killer was prioritizing escape.

A lone window stood open. A dirty footprint marred the drop cloth, covering the sill and side table. He rushed over.

The sun had long since set. City lights shone in the distance. Below him, the tower's sheer side was bare, lit by sporadic slits of lamplight. No rappelling assassin. No flattened corpses, far below. Not even so much as a rope-

Fine flakes, loosened from above, fell past his ear.

Gasping, he craned around. There, impossibly scaling the vertical expanse, was the assassin.

What in Helia's name…?

As he watched, the figure slipped among the merlons.

Even if he could find the stairs, a keep full of confused guards stood between him and the roof. Any delay would see the assassin escape. He slapped at the gray stone in frustration, finding it overwhelmingly smooth and solid. The blocks were tightly fitted, allowing less than a finger's width between them.

Only a madman would try-

Behind him, the door banged off the wall as guards boiled in.

He found himself on the window ledge, fingers forced into a likely seam. He strained upward, not daring to linger over this ill-conceived course. If he did, it was even odds whether his grip or his nerve would give out first.

Shouted imprecations hounded him up the wall.

This was a mistake, he thought, halting after several arm spans. His digits were agony, his heels shaking with palsy as he scrabbled to retain a toehold. A gust of wind tried to pry him from his perch.

Helia have mercy!

At his downward glance, the ground seemed to drag at him.

Climbing down would be impossible and, when his strength failed – soon – he would fall anyway. Wheezing terror through his teeth, he pressed on. His fingertips went wooded with the pressure. His calves bucked with uncertainty. He spared little thought for the assassin anymore, concentrating only on surviving the climb.

Finally, he looped a limp arm over a crenellation. In acute relief, he rolled onto the roof. His hands were a vague burn beyond his wrists, his every tendon overdrawn.

He surprised himself by struggling to his feet.

There was no sign of the assassin. But there was only one possible path from here. He stumbled along the narrow walkway, navigating the round tower. At the back, a flying buttress joined it to the peak of the palace proper, far below.

Running along the spine of the lower ridge was the assassin.

Without meaning to, he found himself skidding down the stone chute, wind tossing his hair. The roof rushed up to meet him and he hit awkwardly, tumbling across the slick plating. He arrested his slide on raw hands and skinned knees. The assassin was a fading smudge against the dark.

Not yet, he thought, scrabbling in pursuit.

Just as he gained the roof's peak, the assassin stepped off it, disappearing down the slope. Without weighing the wisdom of it, he ran to do the same. Frayed robes and frayed nerves alike flapping, he skated toward the arched back of a walkway. Fast. He slapped ineffectually at the lead tiles, trying to shed some speed-

The roof dropped away beneath him.

He might have screamed, if his jaws weren't locked in a terrified rictus. He snagged a gutter as he went over. The half-pipe took his weight with a squeal. Feet dangling above the walkway, he judged he could make it if he timed his swing-

A metallic screech as the guttering gave way. The walkway knocked the feeling from his legs. Somewhere, far below, the piece of pipe clunked off hard cobbles.

Stomach pressing on his straining lungs, he hobbled on.

There! The assassin was somehow ascending the next roof's slope at a dead run. Marco scrambled after, using both hands and feet to gain the peak.

Its spine ran straight and narrow. No walkways, no windows, no buttresses in sight. And a sheer drop at the end. Ha! He had the assassin cornered. Crowing inside, he closed the distance.

Got you!

The black clad figure reached the end of the run… and turned.

Marco skidded to a halt, his optimism evaporating as he got his first good look. Clad in soft cloth and supple leathers, the slender figure was breathing easily. The glint of eyes, in the cleft between mask and cowl, showed no signs of fear or defeat.

He was abruptly aware of his bloody face and ragged robes, his scuffed skin and bruised bones. He was in no shape for a fight. He'd foolishly thought he was cornering the assassin. Clearly, it was the other way around. But, perhaps, he could delay…

Over the sound of his ragged panting, he could hear the distant shouts of the guards he'd outpaced.

Helia keep me in her sight, he prayed, raising his fists.

The assassin cocked a hooded head at him quizzically.

Readiness took its toll and he began to tremble.

Finally, the black clad figure moved. It took a deliberate step back. Then another, heels dangling over the roof's lip. One darkly glittering eye winked at him. And then the assassin pushed off, plummeting into the darkness.

For a moment, there was only Marco and the breeze.

Stunned, he stumbled to the edge and peered down.

The earth fell away from the keep – itself built atop a promontory – to a canopy of conifers far below.

He'd be surprised if the suicidal assassin wasn't still falling…

Intense relief buckled his legs and he sat down. Fear sweat soaked him and the lead tiles were pleasantly cool against him. Through them, he could feel the approach of many pounding boots.

He'd done it. It was over-

Lemon sponges came, spewing out his mouth and nose.

* * *

"Secure that sail, Master Noname!"

"Aye-aye!" Jiminy responded.

A watcher might think it was the whip of command that set him wincing. In truth, it was the effort to appear obedient that galled. It was a slight distinction, to be sure, but an important one. Without it, he really would be just another one of the crew.

Superficially, at least.

Suspicions remained. Despite their skipper endorsing him as a stowaway, he was the subject of many suspicious glances.

Dangling easily from a spar, high above the deck, he left his hands to the knot work while his eyes roved among his shipmates.

One of them, he knew, had found his thieving tools. Whoever it was, they were sitting on the secret. A secret that could, quite literally, sink him. He could only surmise that they intended to somehow blackmail him with it, when the opportunity arose. Or simply sabotage him, when the mood struck.

He was determined to strike first. Unless they'd thrown his kit overboard – which he doubted – he would find it. And them.

So far, though, his search had proven fruitless.

Canvas safely stowed, he leapt from the crosstree to the shroud.

Compared to cat burglary, ratlines were easy. He was learning a wealth of new words. He was even adding to his trove of known knots – and having fun, figuring out how to get free of them.

His hands were mostly healed, thanks to Squint's camphor concoction, and he'd added mace- and hatchet marks to his knife scars. With any luck, his pinky nail would eventually grow back.

Feet thumping onto the deck, he felt eyes marking his passage.

First Mate Lenk was no nursemaid. Tour aside, the man had basically dumped him in the ship's kitchen. The 'galley' was the territory of Squint – the cleaver-wielding, firebomb-flinging cook.

'Ev'ryone calls me Cookie, though. I 'spect ye will too...'

Victim of an unwanted moniker himself, he'd resolved not to.

Squint was a stooped stick figure, tough as tarred rope. The soft-spoken seafarer with the sun-bleached eyes had been teaching him the rudiments of sailing.

Other survival skills, he'd already had.

He walked as though openly trespassing on a neutral gang's turf – swaggering on the knife's edge between confidence and confrontation. He'd gotten a nick or two, for his trouble, and could feel the whetted regard of Master Meris from across the deck.

One of his first shipboard duties had been ladling out the morning gruel. The plateful of porridge had made an incontinent splat as it was shoved back against his chest.

"Hey!" he'd shouted angrily, craning up for his first glance at Master Meris – a massive man, with all the social charm and hygiene of a lump of lard left out in the sun.

"Watch yer'self, cabin booy!"

He'd known what was coming next.

"Did ye see tha'?" the lump had appealed to everyone within earshot. "Knocked me breakfas' righ' oot o' me hand, he did. Don't like us much, methinks. *Stowaway,* is he*?* Codswallop!"

Outlying body parts had bulged as the man leant in to glower, concluding in a stage whisper, "Meris says ye smell like a *pirate!*"

It was a poor pickpocket who couldn't read a crowd. Meris wasn't popular. He might have a toady or two, but no real proponents. The trick lay in keeping it that way.

He'd picked the man's most obvious personal flaw.

"I'm surprised you can smell anything," he'd said, pawing at the air before his nose. He knew he'd hit the mark when a chuckle or two sounded among the spectators.

Meris's piggy eyes had bulged, broad face purpling.

Jiminy had made no protest as he was pulled up by his collar. Taking a beating, he knew, could be as instructive as giving one. Unarmed, he was unlikely to triumph over Meris. But he *could* win his shipmates' respect and improve his standing. He'd hung still, letting them see his lack of fear in his faint smile.

"Wh*aaa*t did ye say?!" Meris had screamed apoplectically, shaking him. "Did ye hear what 'e said t' me?!"

A pause, then…

"Nae need tae shout, we c'n all smell ye!" someone in the back had dared, to a general run of guffaws.

"What?!" Meris had sprayed at the onlookers. "Who said tha'?"

"Could you lower your arms?" he'd wondered aloud, winning Meris's attention again. "Your pits are attracting flies…"

Though he'd seen the backhanded blow coming a league off, it still hurt. Spots had danced before his eyes and only long practice had let him roll onto all fours instead of onto his face.

Seeing his ready crouch, someone had offered two-to-one odds on the 'cabin boy' and the crew had exploded in a flurry of betting.

Outraged, Meris had drawn back for a kick.

"What's goin' on here?"

The familiar roar had uprooted the excitement. Sudden silence had descended, along with Master Lenk, from the middeck.

"Master Meris?" the first mate had inquired.

"Just helpin' oor new cabin booy up, 'swain!"

Fat fingers had yanked him to his feet.

"'E took a nasty spill on this 'ere mess of porridge, see?"

The first mate had pointedly eyed his split lip. "That so…?"

The crew had drawn a collective breath.

"Aye, 'swain," he'd confirmed. "Master Merris is dead handy."

Unamused, the first mate had treated them both to a long stare.

"As ye were!" the man had finally barked, dispersing the crowd.

"Nex' time, cabin booy," Meris had whispered, surreptitiously digging into his shoulder, before strolling away.

Dabbing at his lip, he'd scraped up the mess and wrestled the pot and plates back to the galley, where Squint had been elbow deep in sudsy water.

"Thank you," he'd told the man's bent back. Because, despite the cook's best efforts, he'd recognized that voice in the crowd.

He'd received a noncommittal grunt in reply.

That was some time ago.

Grinning at the memory, he leaned his elbows on the ship's rail, looking out over the ocean. A bit of land bobbed in the distance. It was little more than a rock – a Heli resupply post, he was told. The captain did a brisk trade, selling luxury items to the officers unlucky enough to be posted there. And it was better than having to *buy* fresh water, in Oaragh, to replenish the Spear's stores.

He watched the gray fort loom closer against an iron sky.

To him, it looked like salvation.

If he couldn't recover his kit – before it dragged him over the side by his shorthairs – his only option was to jump ship. And, while the bleak rock didn't look very inviting, it was bound to be better than the axe hovering over his head.

"Drop anchor! Ready the longboats!"

And there was the hitch. Only naval vessels were allowed to dock. He eyed the churning green waves uncertainly. He'd have to swim it. And he *could* swim – after a fashion. A concubine from the Jade Islands had delighted in teaching him. But these waters were nothing like her cuckolded prince's pleasure pool.

"You're out of uniform, Master Noname," the first mate said.

He looked down at himself.

He'd traded his ruined pantaloons for a pair of canvas breeks Squint had sewn and he wore his hip jacket shirtless. His appearance was every bit as motley as the rest of the crew's.

"What uniform?"

Showing a rare smile, Master Lenk brought a heavy length of chain from behind his back. The blackened links giggled together.

"Your girdle," the man grinned. "Captain's orders."

Understanding, he glanced at the fort, more distant than ever.

Well, crap…

* * *

MARCO SAT, SHIVERING amid the filthy straw of his cell. The throbbing in his head had eased, even as his cooling muscles had clenched tight. The last of his nausea had passed – taking the shortcut up his throat. His self-recrimination remained, though.

What had he been thinking? Chasing headlong after an assassin in the dark? And a pagan practitioner at that!? He'd come *this close* to joining in the killer's spectacular suicide. That he yet lived was a testament to Helia's love of fools and madmen.

He huddled in a corner, as far as possible from the pool of his own embarrassment. His robes were ripe with fear-sweat and he'd stooped to using the lone, urine-smelling blanket. As pathetic a mess as he must look, he felt worse.

He cursed himself again for mutely accepting the guards' escort. He'd expected they were taking him back to his quarters. Or to see someone official, at least. The sound of the cell door swinging shut behind him had come as a surprise.

He'd given up yelling at the bars. His pleas and entreaties were lost on the empty corridor. Even his lone window did not look out but up a narrow shaft. Faint light had begun to filter down.

A rusty wail intruded on his reverie and he raised his head from the cradle of his knees. The distant door clanged shut again and two sets of footfalls resumed their approach.

He was at the bars in an instant, throat too tight to call out.

He could not see up the corridor but an eddy of air brought a whiff of crumbly parchment, sharp ink and rancid butter. He drank it in, his legs threatening to give way in relief – *Father Justin*.

If the keeper was here, everything would be alright. His mentor would straighten out this misunderstanding.

He waited forever for the footsteps to halt outside his cell.

"Are you hurt?"

Did they hurt you? He read the real question in the way Justin's fingers curled around the bars.

"Scrapes and bruises is all," he allowed, feeling braver already.

"Can we get this open?"

"I don't see why not," the keeper's companion acquiesced.

Keys rattled and the heavy door squealed aside.

Justin swept in, settling a gentle hand on his shoulder and his anxiety fled. A watcher might see only a priest, offering a prayer. But Marco also felt a faint tickling that raised his fine hairs.

"Scrapes and bruises?" the keeper demanded, disbelieving.

He shrugged uncomfortably – then winced at the pain.

"I'm fine," he rushed to reassure. "I just took a tumble or two, chasing after the assassin-"

"*Alleged* assassin."

For the first time, he focused beyond the keeper and on a high-level Renali functionary. Rich robes hung from the man's scarecrow shoulders and short, strangely colorless hair stood on end from a taut scalp.

Father Justin huffed in exasperation and the functionary grinned, unaccountably delighted.

With a start, Marco realized he'd seen a leer like that before – on the stuffed man-eating-lizard that had dangled from the rafters of his cultural studies class. The Terror of the Summer Isles.

"Marco," the keeper introduced, "this is Invigilator Nestor Reed, the king's… chief investigator."

"*Alleged* assassin?" Marco blurted, nonplussed.

It was true that he was not very worldly. And he could not reliably pick a chestnut horse from a roan. But a man, dressed from tip to toes in black and dropping into the royal apartments from a pocket of unholy magic, was unlikely to be a lost chimney sweep.

"I'm certain it was an assassin," he assured. "One of the guards even yelled 'assassin!'"

The invigilator grinned. "*That* hue and cry was for *you*."

Marco blinked stupidly at the man. "I don't understand…"

"No? What else would you call a foreign agent, who infiltrates the royal sanctum, assaults the guards and presses toward the princess' rooms?"

The blood drained from Marco's face as the man gestured languidly, indicating him. He *had* done all of that.

"No! I was trying to *stop* the smoke- I mean, the real assassin-"

"Oh? I find it highly unlikely that the royal guard would oppose you in such an honorable endeavor, hmm?"

He jumped at the dangled lifeline, his words petering as he heard them, spoken aloud. "That's because they couldn't see the assassin. Because he was… invisible."

The invigilator's eyes danced hungrily.

"An imaginary assassin. Imagine that."

Marco shook his head in denial. He had accepted that the guards had not seen the roiling shadow – as he had. But he was certain that the pagan practitioner, once torn from the sorcerous screen, had been perceived by all.

What if he'd been wrong? What if the guards had stayed blind to the interloper and had been chasing Marco all along?

But no. He'd seen them react. Had he not been the fleeter of foot, *they* would have led the chase. He was sure.

"The assassin was real," he insisted. "After his magic failed and he fell, the guards could see him too. Ask them."

"I have interrogated the guards at length," the invigilator promised, giving Marco an arch look. "However, after suffering severe blows to the head, their testimony is unreliable."

Keeper Justin glanced up sharply. Marco hung his head. He'd fought without restraint, lashing out in desperation.

However, it was Reed who had snared the empath's attention.

Marco ran over the invigilator's words himself and frowned at the dual meaning. Was the man really suggesting that the royal guards had been beaten until they had recanted?

"Out of curiosity," the invigilator continued, "is it common for Heli scribes to be so well versed in unarmed combat? Are you even more dangerous with a quill in hand?"

The scope of Marco's blunder broadened at once. His martial training had been meant to remain a secret, along with the keeper's empathic and streaming abilities. His cheeks burned.

"Here are the facts," the invigilator presented, counting them off on thin fingers. "You were trespassing in the royal apartments. You fled when the guards tried to detain you. You resisted arrest. You assaulted several of their number. You failed to surrender and were only apprehended when you ran out of roof."

Marco wanted to object, to say the princess had invited him.

As he drew a hurried breath, the keeper caught his eye.

The priest's fists pressed together at stomach height in what might look like a casual posture. But Marco recognized the meditative form. Obediently, he tried to tamp his desperation.

"And," Reed added, as though in afterthought, "you vandalized palace property. That vase you broke contained the ashes of Ludowise the Librarian, of the king's line. I am tempted to charge you with desecration of royal remains."

Marco blanched, feeling sick. He'd *inhaled* that librarian.

Reed's leer leaned closer. Marco cringed back.

"If you were a citizen," the invigilator confided, "the headsman would be shaving your nape right about now."

"Nestor!" the keeper jumped in, his tone scandalized.

Marco barely heard. He was having trouble swallowing.

Unrepentant, Reed stood away, speaking casually.

"Unfortunately, things are not so simple. I am forced to respect your diplomatic immunity – for the moment. Your status is being taken under review. Until a resolution is reached, you are hereby remanded into the custody of your immediate superior."

Lizard eyes flicked towards the keeper.

Marco didn't dare to hope. "I'm free to go?"

"Conditionally: You will speak to no one of last night's events. You have never seen nor heard of any 'assassin'. You have never been to the royal apartments. And, as a courtesy, you will confine yourself to your quarters until after our deliberations.

"I trust that is acceptable?" the man asked of the keeper.

Justin nodded.

This rapid turn of events left him dizzy. Despite his schooling, he couldn't begin to guess at the politics at play. Disoriented, he clutched at what he knew to be true. "There *was* an assass-"

The keeper squeezed his shoulder. "Enough, Marco."

He wilted under the rebuke.

"This way, then…"

A quartet of stone-faced guards fell into step around them.

"Out of curiosity," the invigilator said, turning down a corridor, "how did you manage the climb to the battlements? I inspected that wall myself. A fit man would have needed rope and light both."

Safe beside the keeper, sullen rebellion stirred.

"*Alleged* climb," he told the invigilator.

That delighted leer spread across Reed's face. "Quite so."

"Let's go, Marco," Justin said, shepherding him away.

The trek back to their apartments was an awkward affair. Few, except for servants, were about at the crack of dawn. And those few stood, agog, until the royal guards' glares sent them scurrying.

The longer their march, the more he reflected on the terrible position he'd forced the keeper into. If the priest were required to take responsibility for his junior's actions, the Temple might be pried from the negotiating table. Somehow, he doubted either the ambassador or the chapter master would bemoan the loss – the keeper's efforts to curb greed were too egalitarian for their tastes.

Finally he could stand the silence no longer, "Father, I-"

"Hush, Marco."

Stung, he ducked his head, trudging in silence until he recognized their corridor's carpeting.

A guard took up station outside their rooms and, with a pang, he realized he'd effectively placed the keeper under guard as well.

He had a lot to answer for.

Miserable tears threatened. He shut his eyes, and the door, to the passage. Alone, he hunched in the doorway, listening to the keeper spark the fire tongs. Glass cups rattled.

For a change, the odor of steeping tea failed to soothe. He waited for the keeper's disapproval.

"Well," his mentor said at last, clinking over to the thick rug, "that could have gone worse."

He was startled into opening his eyes.

With an easy wave, the keeper bade him sit.

"Father... you're not mad?"

The keeper's brows rose. "I am many things: Relieved. A little proud. If I am angry, it is born of worry. What were you thinking, Marco? Setting off after an assassin? Once you've safeguarded the flock, you don't chase into the woods after the wolf."

Tension left his legs and he folded onto the indicated cushion.

"You believe me?"

"Of course I believe you. So does the invigilator and, I daresay, the king. Else we'd not be having this conversation – diplomatic immunity or no. Now, help me understand what happened?"

He fiddled with the cups, avoiding the priest's eyes.

In fits and starts, he told the entire tale, starting with the invitation to tea and ending in his miserable cell.

Afterward, Justin sat in contemplative silence.

"I apologize," the priest said at last, surprising him. "I assumed you gave in to the base urge to give chase. I should have known better. Even in the midst of panic, you were thinking ahead – to the continued threat to your friend and how best to counteract it."

Marco blushed, not sure he had been thinking any such thing.

"More mature men than you have failed the test of selflessness. You are an instrument of Helia, Marco. Do not doubt it."

Embarrassed by the undeserved praise, he changed the subject.

"If the invigilator knew I was telling the truth, then why…?"

"To scare you into silence," Justin said. "Like many brilliant and calculating people, Nestor has trouble trusting those he cannot control or predict. To him, a promise is only as weighty as the threat that counterbalances it. Put his words from your mind."

Remembering, Marco rubbed at the base of his neck.

"I meant," he pressed on, "why keep it secret at all?"

"To avoid upheaval," the keeper answered. "Keystone Keep is the royal seat and singular among Renali strongholds – protected by spells as well as steel. If it were known that an assassin had set foot outside the royal bedchambers…?

"It would shake confidence in the crown and undermine national stability. The Renali are not as solidaric as they seem. The king's position, on peace, is unpopular. Were his supporters to turn into detractors, he could be deposed. The civil war to follow would be sure to put paid to any peaceful relations between our nations."

Marco stared. He'd not realized the scope…

"A good thing the assassin committed suicide, then," he blurted, before hastily adding, "Helia have mercy on his soul."

The keeper made a noncommittal noise.

"What is it, father?"

"A swathe of guards has been scouring the Low Garden creek – where the assassin fell – since last night. They've not returned. In my experience, a *successful* search ends earlier, rather than later."

He suppressed a nervous laugh. "Father, you're not suggesting the assassin survived such a fall? And then *escaped...?*"

His mentor's expression was grim.

"Perhaps. But I fear our problems may be more immediate and, ah, *involved.* You, um, visited the princess's private quarters...?"

He waited expectantly for the rest of the question. "Yes?"

The keeper sighed, seeming chagrined. "You can't see how it looks? A lowborn suiter – an Imperial at that – making midnight calls on the crown's youngest daughter? Not to be uncouth, but the king is already being accused of being in bed with the Heli..."

Realization dawned slowly. Heat climbed from his collar.

"I didn't..." he stammered. "We're not-"

"Oh, I know," the priest assured. "But rumor is a powerful political force in itself. I'd advise you to restrict your activities to the public eye. Though I doubt you'll have the opportunity again."

Yes. After this debacle, he'd be lucky to get within a league of the princess. But she'd be alive – that's what mattered.

"What now?" he wondered aloud.

"That depends, in great part, on our hosts. *You,*" Justin pronounced, "need a wash and a lie-down. *I* need to go head-off our ambassador. News travels fast, it seems, and *secret* news is even speedier. Lord Malconte is in a particularly... *loud* mood."

Only then did he notice the priest's attention – turning to track something in the passages beyond.

"Now?" he gasped.

"Unless you'd prefer to speak to him yourself?"

He bolted for his room and barred himself inside.

A pounding started up almost immediately.

"Priest! Open this door! I require an explanation!"

Gingerly, Marco leaned his ear against the wood.

"Ah, ambassador," came the keeper's muffled greeting. "I see you've heard of this morning's misunderstanding?"

"Misunderstanding? My manservant laying out ermine, when I wanted mink, is a *misunderstanding*. *This* is a catastrophe!"

The carpet buzzed angrily beneath someone's soles.

"One of *our* junior delegates!" the ambassador moaned, sputtering in his rage. "I hold you personally responsible, priest! If this kills the summit, Helia help me, you won't be far behind!"

Marco bristled at hearing Keeper Justin addressed so.

"How," Malconte continued, "do you intend to rectify this?"

"I don't believe I will have to. Tea?"

"No, dammit, I don't want any tea! I want deniability! If the Temple intended a regicide, they could have done me the courtesy of providing me an alibi! Your incompetence is ruining my summit and my reputation!"

The man's tone left no doubt as to which was the greater crime.

"You are misinformed, Lord Malconte. Though, given your history, I can see how you could come to the wrong conclusion."

"My history? *What*? Have a care where you tread, priest-"

"A moment, ambassador. Come in, Adrio," the keeper called.

An abortive knock announced the chapter master's arrival.

"A fine mess, this," were the man's first words. "I hear your dogrobber has been arrested in connection with an assassination?"

"Momentarily detained, is all," the keeper said, ignoring Malconte's angry huff. "They are mindful of his immunity."

"Oh? Then they must be trying to salvage the summit. Good. We should reciprocate. Turn the boy over to them."

Hidden behind his door, Marco caught his breath.

"A peace offering, yes!" the ambassador enthused. "Better still to silence the boy ourselves and deliver his head. Show our commitment without risking our secrets."

Marco found himself leaning on the doorframe for support.

"Gentlemen," Justin interjected in a calming voice. "While I appreciate your political acumen, as well as your... candor, such action would be precipitous. The Renali prize loyalty. What message would it send if we so easily sell out one of our own?

"I would also remind you that we're talking about a *failed* assassination and haven't yet discussed *why* it failed. You are planning to sell for a pittance an asset that may prove invaluable."

Marco joined in the pregnant pause that followed.

"Fine," the ambassador growled. "Pray tell, priest."

"I'm in a position to know that the royal apartments are warded – with high art – against intrusion. Yet, those magical alarms were blind to the threat, as was the naked eye. If not for the happy accident of Marco's presence, the killer may have slipped past."

"Most impressive," Malconte snorted. "But how is it pertinent?"

"Ah, I see," the master mercer breathed. "The assassin survived? Yes. Then the Renali have a need..."

"...that only we can meet," Justin finished.

There was a brief pause.

"Excellent," said the ambassador, sounding mightily pleased.

What need? Marco wondered. *What are they talking about?*

"Still," the chapter master grumped. "Scribe, scrapper, streamer... How many more mantles does your boy wear, keeper? You're sure he's not a Temple-trained infiltrator?"

"Marco is no spy, nor even a streamer. Your logical assumption aside, that's not how he saw through the assassin."

"He is an empath then, like yourself?"

"He is not burdened by that particular blessing. But his senses – both spiritual and mundane – have been well developed.

"I also surmise that the assassin relied on arts that draw from aspects of death or darkness. Witchery. As one of Helia's anointed, Marco would be especially sensitive to such influences."

Marco was finding all of this hard to follow. *Anointed?* He was an unordained novice. And what *spiritual sense?* Prayer and meditation aside, the closest he got to streaming was the toothless trance he struggled to hold onto while sword training.

"It seems we have much more to discuss," the ambassador admitted, proper respect creeping into his voice at last. "I think I shall take that tea now, keeper. And then, I should like to speak to your wide-eyed ward myself."

"I, as well," the chapter master agreed gruffly.

The prospect should have scared Marco spitless. Strangely, it didn't.

"I will make us a fresh pot," Justin acceded. "Alas, this one is tepid and contains a strong sedative besides – I thought it best to have the poor boy rest after his ordeal. I will make him available to you, once he recovers…"

The words took too long to register.

Sedative? Wha…?

A taste, even more foul than usual, lingered on his tongue. With an effort, he recalled the keeper's cold cup, sitting… sitting…

When had he slid down to the floor?

Blearily, he crawled toward his cot.

Marco's confinement lasted two more days.

The talks were temporarily halted. The king was cloistered with his advisors. The keeper seemed determined to scrawl on every last scrap of parchment in the Kingdom. The veritable covey of letters, winging toward Tellar, could have blotted out the sun.

Marco had survived his interrogation by the chapter master. That the man had looked as though longing for a pair of white hot pincers, throughout, hadn't helped. In contrast, the ambassador had been uncharacteristically cordial, if intense. The man's questions had been off topic though, completely skirting the assassin issue.

But that had been the last bit of excitement. By day two, Marco began imagining bars on the windows and dirty straw on the floor.

Far from running errands, the guard's glares discouraged his even answering the door. His attention kept slipping from the scrolls the keeper had bid him study. And he'd given up practicing sword forms after the third time Justin had glanced over mildly.

Now despondent, he went around lighting lamps against the gathering dusk. The smell of citronella slowly filled their suite. The Kingdom of Lakes, predictably, bred abundant mosquitoes. He suspected the large 'lime lancers', as the locals named them, got inside each night by boring through the walls.

He drew the shutters anyway, lest three or more of the bloodsuckers band together to carry off either the keeper or himself.

Insects were the least of what kept him from sleep. His nightly terrors now included a headlong flight, from an invisible foe, over treacherous roofs. The twisted visions saw *him* falling from that precipice, only to slam awake at the moment of impact.

He worried that he was developing a fear of heights.

Even so, those dreams were preferable to the *other* kind.

Those, he would spring awake from, covered in sweat and completely convinced he wasn't alone. Breath and heart racing, he would scramble away from the shadowed corners of the room.

To his shame, he'd taken to sleeping with a lit taper.

Amid these dark thoughts, the knocking at the door startled him.

"Enter!" the keeper called, his creased brow clearing.

Invigilator Nestor Reed let himself in. "Evening, Justin. Busy?"

"I'm never too busy for good news."

"Oh? Most people, seeing me, do not assume *good* news."

"There's no headsman at your back," the priest explained.

Reed shrugged. "It's a heavy axe and there are a lot of stairs."

The lamp Marco held rattled audibly in its glass.

"Nestor," the keeper disapproved, "he does not know you jest."

"But *you* always do," the invigilator sighed. "I don't know why I still bother. You are no fun, Justin."

"You enjoy the challenge," the priest disagreed.

A wide smile broke across Reed's face. "I suppose I do. Now, grab your best robes you two, you're late for a royal audience."

A little later, properly accoutered and coifed, Reed led them through the keep. Marco took his cue from the keeper, affecting stately silence. He wasn't sure he fooled anybody.

Servants ghosted through the keep, lighting lanterns, lugging brooms and buckets and casting surreptitious glances.

Seeing the royal apartments again set Marco's teeth on edge.

"Here we are," Reed announced at last.

The great double doors were doubly guarded.

Heli sensibilities ran to light, lamellar armor and serpentine swords. Something a soldier could march in, or crew a ship in.

The Renali's faceless juggernauts, in full plate, seemed alien to his eyes. Their bare swords, standing as tall as their armored chins, looked too heavy to heft.

By rote, he began cataloguing their weak points, as Master Crysopher had taught. The insides of the elbows; the backs of the knees; in the groin; up under the arms; through the visor slit-

Appalled, he shook such thoughts from his head. These people were to be their allies.

"We usually have extra hands to do this," Reed apologized, heaving at the doors, "but we don't need the extra ears tonight."

Scores of mirrored lanterns, and a handful of gargantuan chandeliers, still failed to pierce the high vault of the throne room. Banners drooped from the dark, matching the azure of the dais.

A military officer, festooned with medals, flanked the monarch. Beside the throne stooped a robed figure, leaning on a cane.

Simple steel circlet glinting, the king brooded on his gilded seat, elbows resting on his knees. "Welcome, honored guests."

The invigilator bowed low and they followed suit.

"Majesty," Nestor Reed intoned, "as commanded, I present Keeper Wisenpraal and Master Dei Toriam of the Heli Temple."

Announcement accomplished, the invigilator abandoned them.

"It is good to see you both again," the king greeted gravely.

"You honor us, majesty," the keeper executed another bow – which Marco hastily copied. "How may we be of service?"

"First," the king forestalled, "permit me to introduce High Arcanist Peril Lorant, the royal archmage."

The wrinkled man in the colorless robes smiled amiable.

"And," the king continued, "Lancer-General Elil Raide, commander of my Royal Guard and chief of palace security."

Fire had taken the general's eye but smoldered still in its twin.

"My lords," Justin greeted, giving each a half-bow.

"You know why you are here, keeper?"

"I imagine, majesty, to explore the events of three nights past?"

"Just so," the monarch nodded. "Allow me, before we begin, to apologize for any upset you or your scribe may have suffered during this emergency. I trust you can forgive me my caution."

The keeper gave a noncommittal smile and did not speak.

"Master Dei Toriam-"

He jumped. The monarch's mien had turned stern.

"-I have spoken at length to my daughter…"

Swallowing was suddenly beyond him. How had he not noticed before that the king was almost as big a man as Bear?

"She assures me you trespassed in the royal apartments at her insistence and that your presence in her chambers was invited."

He felt his neck heating.

"As for what followed, I would like to hear your account, in your words." The king turned. "With your permission, keeper."

The priest waved him on. "Go ahead, Marco."

He shuffled uncomfortably and took a deliberate step forward. Despite its many retellings, the tale did not unfold smoothly. The king received it all in stony silence. The general caressed his sword hilt at every mention of the assassin. The arcanist seemed to doze.

"And you do not know," the king questioned when he was done, "why you alone were able to pierce the assassin's spell?"

At his shaken head, the king glanced at the arcanist.

The wizened man came to himself and caned carefully down the dais steps. His voice, when he spoke, was reedy with age but clear and sure. "How do you call yourself, young one?"

He cleared his throat nervously. "Marco."

"A pleasure, Marco." The man pronounced it perfectly. "I'm Peril. I would like to examine you, if that's alright?"

"Examine?" His tongue cleaved to the roof of his mouth.

"Nothing onerous, I assure you. A touch upon your brow is all."

He rolled fearful eyes at the keeper. In the normal course, a priest would bridle at having pagan arts performed anywhere near him. But Justin just gave him an encouraging nod.

"Alright…" he wheezed.

"Excellent." The arcanist shuffled nearer. "Simply hold still."

From the folds of his robe, the wrinkled pagan produced a peculiar device. All of one piece, it resembled nothing so much as a two-tine dinner fork, albeit a strange one. The arcanist rapped it on the head of his cane – and the metal woke in song. One pure, sustained note-

Was all he had time to register, before the butt of the fork was pressed to his forehead and its tune shivered through his skull. The reverberations rang down his spine, along his arms and legs, tickling his nail beds. He gritted his teeth against the sensation but that somehow made it worse. He thought the arcanist had added his own voice to the harmony but couldn't be sure.

The sound built and built until it squeezed at his heart and pressed on his ears, hovering on the threshold of pain.

-that was abruptly gone.

He gasped as his hearing returned.

"There now." The arcanist said. "All done."

Turning, the royal archmage met his king's regard with a wry shrug and began crutching back up the dais.

The king said nothing for a long moment. Then, "General?"

"Sire." The military man came to attention but spoke to the room at large. "Our best efforts have failed to find how the intruder gained entry to the keep. A thorough search of the Low Garden and environs has also proven fruitless. At present," the man concluded through clenched teeth, eye blazing, "we must assume the assassin has escaped and may yet return."

If it had been Raide on that roof, Marco felt certain, the general would have leapt after the assassin in pursuit.

"I," the high arcanist commiserated, "have also been unable to identify the resonances left in the intruder's wake. Your Empire has much more experience with outlandish arcana, keeper. Might you have some inkling as to what threatens us?"

The keeper grimaced an apology. "I'm afraid the Temple's edict has always been to expunge pagan arts, not study them. That said, our *Inquisitori* keep extensive records of their encounters. Based on Marco's description, I could order an inquest. But any useful information, if it exists, would be a long time in reaching us here."

"As I feared," the arcanist said sadly.

"Where does that leave us?" the invigilator piped up.

Marco jumped, having failed to see the man, lurking by the door. Nestor Reed treated him to a sly smile.

"Young Marco."

All eyes turned to the king.

"You owe me no fealty. And you've done me a great service already. But I fear I must ask a further boon of you."

"Sire!" The general objected and was quelled with a gesture.

The king rose from his throne. Everyone dropped to a bow. Everyone except him. He was transfixed by the king's regard, craning incredulously as the man descended to stand before him.

"I am not your sovereign. I cannot command you. Instead, I ask you, one man to another – will you help me safeguard my family?"

He looked into the king's earnest eyes and saw a wisp of fear.

Tongue tied, overawed, he did the only thing he could.

He nodded.

A great hand gripped his arm. "You have an old man's thanks."

Fear winked out. In a flurry of robes, the king retook his throne.

"Now," the man boomed, "receive a king's thanks..."

"CONSCRIPTED?!" THE AMBASSADOR cried, aghast.

Exercising iron self-control, Justin didn't scowl. Malconte's moods were taxing him more than usual. Eventually, the man would tire himself into tractability. But waiting was a chore.

He explained once more. "It is a rather more unprecedented duty – bodyguard to the throne. On loan, if you will."

"On loan-!" the ambassador scoffed.

Bulgaron was his practical self. "This may work in our favor. If the talks don't go our way, we would head home – assassin-detector and all. Is this the outcome you foresaw, keeper?"

"It is quite a bit better than I'd hoped," he hedged, not speaking to the man's mercenary mentality. "Instead of being embedded with the royal guard, Marco has been assigned to Princess Dailill's personal protection. It is an unprecedented honor. For an Imperial."

"Honor?!" Malconte shrilled. "It is an unconscionable risk! If the assassin's next attempt succeeds, it will be all our necks!"

A stubby finger stabbed at Justin. "Instruct your ward, keeper. If *any* ill befalls the royal spawn, he is to ensure he dies trying to protect her! Valiantly, for preference, but *visibly* above all!"

Justin stared, waiting for common decency to catch up to the man. But Malconte had apparently outpaced it long ago.

"Marco will acquit himself well. He knows no other way."

Not at all placated, the ambassador resumed pacing. "At least we'll have an ear close to the princess. Better had it been the king. You're sure we can't manage that?"

"If his own general failed to convince him, I doubt I would. The king concluded – rightly, I think – that he was not the target. Besides," he added, "did you not last disapprove of espionage?"

"Only when it does not benefit me."

"*I* am intrigued by this gift the king bestowed," Bulgaron interceded. "You've seen it up close, keeper. Is it authentic?"

Even the ambassador slowed his pacing to listen.

"*Hiss'orda*," he confirmed. "Eversteel. I believe so."

"How is that possible?" Malconte sniped. "Those holy artifacts are all accounted for, locked in the *Primus Sanctori*, not so?"

The accusation was fair. The Temple's sanctum was supposedly inviolable. He wished he still believed it so. But he had first-hand knowledge of Cyrus 'borrowing' the Eye – a holy artifact itself – and replacing it with a replica. He couldn't let that slip, though.

"I haven't the foggiest," he admitted. "For any relic to go missing, without uproar, is rare. For an eversteel blade to do so beggars belief. I can only speculate it was issued to a holy warrior, and lost to the Kingdom in a skirmish – along with any record."

And praise Helia for that, he reflected, else the Empire would have launched a war of reclamation against the Renali long since.

Having handled the orin himself, he understood its draw, pacifist though he was. With Marco's help, he'd drawn a detailed sketch of the shortsword, to send home. Its rediscovery was bound to cause consternation among the scholarly ranks.

"And now," the ambassador mused into the silence, "that priceless blade hangs on the belt of your quill wrangler…"

"The Mercers Chapter lays claim to it," Bulgaron preempted, shifting unconsciously for ease of access to an absent sword. "Under article seven of the salvage accords-"

"Nonsense!" Malconte snapped. "It is a gift of esteem between nations. As such, it is the rightful due of the Emperor-"

Justin stopped listening. He also refrained from pointing out that, as a holy artifact, the orin fell under the exclusive purview of the Temple. He quite understood the infighting. With the secrets of smelting eversteel lost to the ages, acquiring a sample – not already ensconced in the Temple – would be a coup for either camp.

For that matter, the Renali were famed metalworkers. Why should their king give up such a treasure? Watching the two Imperials politely tear into each other, he feared he might see why – King Stentoric was shrewd indeed.

He just hoped poor Marco wouldn't get caught in the cross-fire. The boy had been so outrageously pleased at receiving the relic…

A timely knock distracted him and, for a moment, he expected to see his ward skip over to answer the door. But the boy was gone.

"My lords," he excused himself, unnoticed by either party.

The page, waiting in the corridor, disappeared the moment she'd delivered her missive. Odd. They usually awaited a reply.

Stranger still, he saw, the scrap of scroll was unsealed. The palace servants made a brisk trade, selling the aristocracy's secrets. Neglecting to safeguard one's letters was a good way to-

Oh, he thought, unrolling it.

Temple script, dating from the Turing Dynasty, confronted him. Good as any cipher. But who, save himself, could have penned it?

A mystery.

It was unsigned. But it appointed a meeting place and time.

"I must step out awhile," he mused, unheard by the bickerers.

While Keystone Keep wasn't a tithe on the Emperor's Palace in Tellar, it sprawled sufficiently. And its innards had been designed to confuse invaders. A bare year ago, that would have included him. Suppressing a smile, he found his way to the indicated atrium.

Architects of later ages had endeavored to marry what was essentially a fort, to aesthetics. They'd met with mixed success. Even close to midday, the lush planters and trellises of the courtyard hung heavy with the morning's dew. A dank, limestone smell competed with that of rich loam and greenery.

Seeing no one, he set out toward the unseen sun's emerald promise. He began to suspect, as he pressed among the fronds, that he'd gotten lost after all – his empathic sense said he was alone.

Pretending interest in a trumpet flower, he cast his awareness wide, wary of some kind of ambush or-

"Beautiful, aren't they?"

He nearly crushed the little bloom between his fingers.

"Apologies," the high arcanist chuckled good naturedly, seeing him jump. "I didn't mean to startle you."

Justin stared. The aged scholar sat improbably close to hand, enjoying a patch of bright heat. A cane nestled on upturned palms, wrinkles and robes both affably arranged.

To his senses, the man slowly filled out into a solid presence.

"My fault," Justin marveled, "I was distracted."

He'd been no such thing. He'd never met anyone capable of slipping under his perception. Though he should probably be disturbed by the discovery, he was intrigued. "You were so still!"

"My mind was far afield," the old man huffed.

He grasped the offered hand, pulling the arcanist to his feet amid an orchestra of popping joints.

"Ugh! Treacherous limbs," the man cursed, knuckling a bent back. "Never get old, Justin. May I call you Justin?"

"Of course, high arcanist."

"Then, please. Call me Peril."

"An... unusual name," he reflected, not for the first time.

"My mother claimed a touch of Fortune's foresight. Though her later predictions mostly involved me and a switch, as I recall."

The ancient's hold lingered on his elbow, ostensibly for support, as the man steered them along the garden path.

"I was very surprised to receive your note," he admitted. "Wherever did you acquire such anachronistic learning?"

"Oh," the man murmured, "I have consumed a great many books – and even written some. After so many decades, it all tends to run together. I'm no longer certain where I purloined what."

A belated thought shuffled into place.

"You're *that* P. Lorant!" Justin realized. How had he not put it together before? "Author of 'The Re-emergence of Magic'?

"Hmm," the Kingdom's court mage agreed, turning morose. "And a dear price I paid for that particular knowledge."

Regret, and remembered pain, pricked between them. The scholar twitched at a sleeve, an old burn scar peeking beneath it.

"What happened?" Justin asked. "If it's not a rude question?"

The arcanist answered readily. "A lifetime ago, in my brash youth, I identified a most peculiar phenomenon – a marked oscillation around the median of ambient energy. Believing that anything that could be observed and predicted could be controlled, I set to taming that power. In my arrogance, I fitted it with a bridle, of my own devising, and settled it with a saddle.

"Needless to say, it bucked me off."

Justin gaped. "You tried to conduct its potential at the point of coalescence? What kind of construct could withstand such a load?"

The arcanist chuckled wryly.

"This kind…" the man tapped at his own chest – and, presumably, more horrific scarring. "Hubris. Even siphoning the merest sliver of power, I could contain it only a moment. I escaped by the skin of my teeth. Or rather, without it."

Justin shook his head. What the old scholar described was a masterwork. He couldn't begin to fathom the arcane permutations to be accounted for, nor conceive of the necessary aides and safeguards required. It would take a greater mind – and one far more heretical – than his to attempt.

"My friend, Cyrus," he laughed, "would love to meet you. He, also, is a master thaumaturge and has studied this anomaly thoroughly. Helped, in no small part, by your treatise."

He bit his lip before he could blurt all of Cyrus's breakthroughs.

"Mm," the arcanist mused. "Your Heli crystals are well suited to taking advantage of the surges. That is why I based the palace protections on your brand of wardsmithing. Worst luck."

At his quizzical expression, the arcanist explained.

"We do not suffer the same strict regulation your Empire does. But the Kingdom is home to strong superstition. Here, the arcane arts are distrusted. Shunned, even. I am old. I have no *choirs* to augment my magic. I make do with a single, middling apprentice."

"Your wards," Justin guessed, "are powered by the ambient anomaly? But then..." he realized, "...the lulls between charges?"

Like sentries, who flag just before the dawn, the wards would be at their weakest in the days leading up to a new surge.

"A vulnerability our visitor exploited," the arcanist confirmed.

Sensing the man's self-reproof, he tried to soothe it. "I doubt even Cyrus could have engineered a more elegant system."

"Cyrus..." the high arcanist mulled over the name. "You hold him in high esteem. Is he the one who spelled your boy?"

Justin stumbled.

Suspicions confirmed, the old scholar grunted. "It is, perhaps, the most subtle working I've ever seen. And so dense as to boggle the mind. I suspect that is partly its purpose? The boy's mind?"

Mouth gone dry, he regretted the political turn that had allowed the Kingdom's pre-eminent mage to examine Marco.

"You've divined much," he dismayed.

"An educated guess, is all." The man made an off-hand gesture with his cane. "The healing arts were never my interest. Even so, I am not without insight. I surmise it is some great preventative measure? It is benign, as such things go. Integral, even. It is also why I wanted to speak with you, away from inopportune ears."

"You've not told anyone?" he hoped.

"Whose business is it, but the boy's and yours? Besides, given the circumstance, sharing would be... indelicate."

"What circumstances?"

"This reservoir – for that is the shape I perceive – this *dam*, your Cyrus built," the high arcanist said, "is failing. I cannot tell what seeps from inside, only that it is erosive. And it is speeding."

He had a horrific vision, of Marco's madness boiling over for all to see. He'd gone to great lengths, under the guise of streaming instruction, to prepare the boy. Exercises designed to entrench a sense of self. Mental resilience instilled for firm footing amid the flood. Masha'na discipline had built upon these foundations. But whether their ramparts could survive the deluge…?

He felt hollow, his heart faint in his chest.

"How long?" he begged, feet halting.

"Like I said, the healing arts aren't my area."

They'd come within sight of the circuit's end. The high arcanist gave him a consoling pat, pulling away. A tapping cane carried the man beyond the sunlight and into the shade of the passage.

"But," Peril spoke parting words over his shoulder, "if I've inherited any of my mother's gift… a season? Perhaps two."

And then Justin stood alone, stranded in this little moment of brightness, surrounded by the cold dark. For the first time in a very long time, he could not find the words for a prayer.

Chapter 10 – A Day Off

Pella Monop, Journal entry #79

I had hoped Dayna Bruen's research would provide me some modest direction – if only so I could avoid her plodding approach. I had known she was a poor excuse for a person. But her work had always been… adequate. Up to now. Her notes, though copious, are a chaotic mess lacking even a unifying language. Nothing is in order and she meanders through her findings like a stunned cow through a stony field. Of the actual history she was commissioned to write, I've found scant pages. If I didn't know any better, I would think she had purposely made her work impenetrable.

Dennik fidgeted nervously. His royal guardsman's sword – grip and scabbard as yet unscuffed – pulled at his hip. It was heavier, the hilt longer, than his previous issue and still got in his way occasionally. None of which dulled his pride at wearing it.

Though his helm's underpadding helped, nervous sweat fled down his jaw. He resisted the urge to reach up, remaining at attention. Rigid discipline was unlikely to save him, in the coming confrontation, but it was all he had.

He refused to look to his right.

Only a handful of names retained the antiquated appellation of 'swordmaster'. And he was sharing a room with one of them.

Bandell, Quon, Mercon, Verrilk…

Unable to help himself, he glanced aside.

…Enderam Lelouch.

The elder princess Villet's personal bodyguard.

The man shifted, somehow aware of his attention. He hurriedly averted his gaze. That just brought home, again, where he was.

They did not look like a princess's apartments. They were spare and unfrilled and he didn't know what he was doing in them. The bodyguard had not deigned to explain, merely crooked a finger for him to follow. Upon arrival, a patch of floor had been pointed out, and he occupied it still.

It had been a while, and wrestling his nerves had exhausted him.

Without fanfare, Lelouch straightened.

Villet Ibernis Stentoric swept into the room, her face as smooth as her step and her gaze as cold as the ashen hearth. Her lone concession to the hour was her hair, loosed from its perennial bun.

He bowed reflexively but did not trust himself to speak.

The elder royal made her unhurried way to the only chair and took her time arranging her skirts. All the while, he became more and more mindful of his exposed nape. Bodyguards were exempt from bowing and the speed of Lelouch's draw was legendary.

That would, at least, be a quick and painless end. As opposed to whatever the elder princess had planned. It was whispered that her displeasure was keener and quicker than any blade's bite.

"So," she said at last. "You know how to remain silent. That bodes well. Stand up straight, guardsman."

He snapped back to attention, careful to direct his gaze to the middle distance, rather than risking her gaze. "Highness!"

Under her piercing regard, he began to perspire in earnest.

"Tell me," she commanded at length, "what happened in the hallway of the royal apartments."

Fortune's fetlocks! It had to be that!

"Highness," he objected, "Invigilator Reed-"

Had been very clear – and very graphic – as to what would happen to him if he uttered a single word of what he'd witnessed.

"Is not here," she cut in sharply. A scent, like spilled blood and sword oil, saturated the room. "More importantly, he was not *there*. You were. Now, tell me what you saw. I will not ask again."

A heavy hush descended. His mouth was terribly dry.

For the first time, he fervently wished he'd followed in his father's footsteps and became a potter. But he'd wanted palace life and politics. Now, here he was – at a full gallop with no girth strap.

The invigilator wielded the king's authority. But the princess was of royal blood. Disappointing either would be a dreadful – and short lived – mistake. Desperately, he tried to reason it out. Reed might never learn of this betrayal. Whereas, the princess was sure to snuff his career, should he refuse her. He made his choice.

"It was well past last wick," he began, "headed for midnight…"

He'd disapproved of the Imperial brat, roaming around the corridors. He might have bitten his tongue, had the lout not chosen to linger near his post. He'd about decided to hurry things along – invitation be damned – when he'd noticed the dolt's distress.

At first, he'd thought the foreigner had been spooked by a down spider. When rain threatened, the creepy crawlies tended to crowd the ceilings. Though alarming, they weren't normally aggressive.

But when he'd tried to lay hands on the interloper, the boy had bucked as though trapped in a burning barn. He'd given chase.

It both irked and awed him, to recall the ease with which the whelp had outmaneuvered them all. He'd seen the boy rise from the crush, as though astride a rearing stallion.

He trembled, with remembered terror, as he recounted the assassin's sudden appearance – a flare of shadow, a whiff of rot...

Magic! Luck's lopsided balls! I came this *close to magic!*

By the end, he was breathing hard, as though he'd run the rooftops himself.

The princess sat, impassive and introspective.

Despite her diluted attention, he didn't dare relax.

"Here," she pronounced at last, "is what you will do…"

His sweat froze to him as he received his new instructions. Then he saluted, turned on his heel, and made a hurried escape.

With no girth strap, he cringed, *and galloping cliffward*.

✳ ✳ ✳

"The last time I sought you out," Inquisitor Mattanuy said, "you gave me an earful about secrecy." Breath pluming, he eyed the tracks they'd carved in the frost. "This is hardly private."

Imperial Advisor Emion Hallet's bloodless lips quirked, looking comfortable in his fox fur stole.

"The dead are dab hands at keeping secrets," the man gestured.

Around them, a dozen chilled slabs held corpses. The Temple's cold house was pressed into service in special cases only.

He held his gaze carefully averted from the Butcher Murder victims, kept here on his order, under false names. Occasionally, he'd come down to stare at them, in hopes of insight.

But Hallet couldn't possibly know that.

"What news?" the Emperor's counsel inquired.

"The evidence is encouraging," he grated. Apparently, he'd been summoned to make a report. While he resented the necessity, he still needed Hallet's resources. "Circumstances suggest a pre-existing relationship between Justin Wisenpraal and the current Renali spymaster, Nestor Reed. I've already confirmed that they were posted on the front at around the same time, a lifetime ago. If they kept in contact, that would constitute treason."

The archon tsked, unimpressed. "That embargo is about as sound as a wicker-bottomed boat. I'd have to arrest half the council for treason. What else have you uncovered?"

"The keeper continues to rise in eminence," he said, hiding his annoyance. "And has managed to ingratiate himself with the royal family, in rather unprecedented fashion."

"Performing streaming tricks at court, is he?" Hallet scoffed.

"Nothing so crude, no. He's managed to pair his scribe with one of the princesses. Apparently, the boy foiled an assassination."

That brought Hallet up short. "I've heard of no such attempt."

Gloating, he watched the man mull over the implications.

"Did the keeper stage this so-called assassination?"

"It seems too fortuitous to be otherwise," he allowed.

"Find out. If there's another player in the game, I need to know. If not, this modernist is far more resourceful than we imagined." The archon frowned. "What of the scribe? Is he anything special?"

Oh, you have no idea...

"Marco dei Toriam," he promptly provided. "Parents died in a tenement fire. Initiated into the Temple on the keeper's insistence."

Hand-picked, he amended to himself, *and purposely mind-broken by the most talented empath of our age. Fragments of personality crushed into fertile soil that lay fallow.*

"The usual education, save for the keeper's direct involvement."

The dark fruit of ritual, carefully ripened on a poor butcher's soul. The seeds plucked from that husk and transplanted to the boy. Those first crimson shoots, breaking momentarily from the keeper's control, had claimed three lives before dawn.

"Transferred to the martial track, more than two years ago. But continued a custom curriculum of language, literature and history."

He subsided, happy for the politician to furnish his own, uninformed theory. The man didn't disappoint.

"So," the Emperor's advisor tapped at his front teeth with a fingernail, "the keeper raised himself a spy…"

At length, Hallet nodded into his fox fur. "I fear we've let this go on too long. Co-operation with the Renali can't be seen to work. It undermines the model of Empire. This troublesome priest, and his pesky progeny, must be addressed."

"That," Mattanuy pounced, "may prove easier than anticipated. I've uncovered a stakeholder, at the heart of the Renali succession, who shares our short-term goals."

"A sympathizer?" the archon's eyes narrowed.

"Not quite. But they would work with us to… remove the keeper from court – provided the blame falls on a particular royal."

"Ha! And your mystery malcontent imagines there will still *be* a throne, after the Holy Heli Empire retaliates?"

"War is full of opportunity. In repelling the Purli hordes, the Renali built the Greenwall and birthed an enduring monarchy. I suspect someone wishes to repeat that success."

"More fool them. I suppose having a local noble in our pocket would be convenient, should we need a puppet ruler for our new prefecture." The man considered. "Well enough."

Mattanuy hid his glee. "I will see to the arrangements-"

"No," Hallet cut him off. "I will send Anochria."

"Your anointedness! I hardly think-"

"It is bad enough," the man overrode, "that I must trust *you*. Now you ask me to put my faith in some scheming infidel? No. I will have my own agent seeing to my interests. End of discussion."

Mattanuy bowed to hide his hot gaze. "As you say, archon."

"Now, leave me. I enjoy the cold."

Turning on his heel, Mattanuy forged a third trail through the frost. Already, he was planning how best to work around Anochria.

"One last thing," Hallet forestalled, forcing him to turn.

The archon's hands rested lightly on the linen hiding the butcher's wife. "Have these burned, will you? They're unsightly."

He grit his teeth. So, not only was the Emperor's advisor having him watched, but the man also deigned to punish him – for his purportedly poor performance – by denying him his distractions.

He nodded stiffly and resumed walking.

Blind bastard, he thought. *Once I have Justin Wisenpraal's confession – and his secrets – I will have no need of your support.*

The keeper's ward, of course, would have to be put down. But not before the man had told him how to make more. Because catching a heretic was one thing. Saving the Empire from a sudden and inexplicable spate of child possessions – that was the kind of thing that made an inquisitor's career.

He smiled in anticipation.

* * *

JIMINY WATCHED the Heli city of Genla bob closer – a bright pearl, nestled in a natural peninsula and shadowed by a balding peak.

They had not yet weighted him with his chains. But he now knew better than to read into that. Once before, looking out over the moonlit inlet of Meno-maji, he'd thought to make a swim for it.

"I would'nae," Squint had said, as he'd excused himself on some invented errand. "'Meno-maji' means 'hungry water'. There're prob'ly a hun'red saw-snouts between ye an' shore."

The Summer Island inlet had looked tranquil enough to him. "Saw-snouts?"

"Large, saltwater lizards. Lots and lots o' teeth."

He shook himself free of the memory. As he would shake himself free of the chains, next time they were cinched around his waist. Though he'd yet to find his kit, he'd finally managed to salvage serviceable picks from loose odds and ends aboard ship.

Genla, he swore, would be his last indentured stop.

He found himself echoing the crew's excitement. Their last port of call, more than a moon hence, had been Rasrin. If the massive, man-made sea gate hadn't been a clue, the ballistae-bristling galleys would have been – Rasrin did not welcome visitors.

Unsurprisingly, they'd been denied entry.

"Jus' as well," Squint had confided as they bobbed in its bay. "Half'n the crew ne'er return from carousin' in Rasrin."

"Is it that dangerous?" he'd wondered, with renewed interest.

"Nay. But the laws be labyrinthine an' easy as breathin' tae break. Even minor fines leave men workin' off debt fer decades."

No stranger to slave labor by then, he'd grimaced and let it pass.

Now, with Genla's musk on the breeze, the crew was all but kicking down the stable doors. For weeks, the only talk aboard ship had been of the city's whorehouses and gambling dens.

"But," he'd objected, "isn't Genla an Imperial city? Does their sun goddess even allow that sort of thing?"

A crewman had winked at him. "Genla is the ass-end of the Empire, as far from Tellar as you can get. You want to look up the Imperial skirt? Genla is what you'll see, smiling back at you."

What a hairy proposition, he'd thought.

A familiar jingling intruded on his thoughts.

"Brought me my 'corset'?" he guessed, without turning.

An unexpected voice answered. "Brought ye yer purse."

Surprised, he looked into Squint's gap-toothed grin.

"Cap'n says ye've paid yer dues." The cook offered a clinking pouch, balanced on one palm. There was no chain in sight.

It took a moment to grasp the significance. "I can leave?"

"If'n ye like," the man bounced the little bag toward him. He snatched it reflexively. Through the canvas, he felt coins.

"And what's this?"

"What's it look like?"

"It looks," he hazarded, "like the wages you pay the crew."

"Well?"

"Well?" he echoed. "Why?"

Squint shrugged self-consciously. "I may have mentioned tae the cap'n that, the way tae entice a valuable crewman to return, is tae give 'im a taste o' the Spear's generosity."

"You're offering me a job?" he deadpanned, struggling against the insult. Honest work? *Him?* "And the captain is on board with this cock-and-bull idea of yours?"

Squint turned serious. "It so happ'ns I've crewed fer the cap'n a *looong* time – as I crewed fer 'is father afore 'im. It may be, m' voice carries some weight. And *I* says ye've the makin's o' as fine a sailor as I e'er seen... Be a shame tae lose ye tae saw-snouts."

"I don't know what to say," he lied. He'd have to say 'no'. If they were addled enough to set him free, he wasn't walking back into the debacle his kit was sure to cause. Whenever it turned up.

"Say ye'll consider it, a' least."

He throttled his relief – he wasn't off the ship yet. With an unexpected pang, he grasped Squint's arm. This was likely the last time he'd see the irascible cook.

Abruptly, the man pulled him close, hissing in his ear.

"I don't know what's chasin' ye," Squint said. "But I know a man, at sea, be damn near impossible tae catch."

Startling, deep-sea-green eyes washed to their usual pale blue as Squint stepped from the shade of their embrace. "Consider it, eh?"

Staring at the man's back, he looked to see what had been thrust into his arms. He clutched his brace of knives.

And his roll of picks.

"It was *you*...?" But Squint had gone.

And, he realized, it was high time he had, too.

CAPTAIN PUTTIN LISTENED to light feet pad up to the poop deck. His long-time cook became a comforting presence by his side.

"If'n ye were serious aboot keepin' 'im, Master Squint," he ventured, "ye should 'o let me tie 'im tae the mast."

"Hmm," the old one rumbled. "Then ye'd have been short a mast, once 'e'd manage to gnaw through. I recognize 'is type. If'n 'e don't choose tae stay, ain't no power will 'old 'im."

The captain grinned lopsidedly. "Not even yours?"

But Squint wasn't listening. "Sum'n dark swims in 'is wake. Sum'n I ain't scented in a long time. 'E's liable tae keep runnin'."

"Pity," Puttin sighed. "We could 'o used a decent burglar."

JIMINY FOUND THE transition from deck to dock jarring. After so long at sea, dry ground didn't seem to move right. He didn't let that distract him from the sights and sounds of Genla City though.

Once he pushed past the pitch and brine stink of the port, he came to the tumult of the fish market. He heard Common, the language of commerce, being murdered by a dozen different accents. Midnight skinned Summer Islanders mingled with almond eyed Kenders. Flame freckled Hintlanders rubbed shoulders with top-knotted tribesmen. He saw peoples from every nation he knew and many he did not.

He eyed it all askance. Nothing he'd heard, of the fanatical Heli, had hinted at forbearance for foreign peoples. Pretending interest in an assortment of abalone, he watched a guard patrol stroll past. Not redbacks. Greycapes? They were a mismatched pair. An olive skinned Imperial and a tattooed Jade Islander. Unless he missed his guess, the diminutive Islander was in charge. What?

Stranger still, no one flinched from the greycapes' path or cast guarded glances after them. They passed, for the most part, unremarked. If the Genlani were a subjugated people – as was all of the empire – they had a strange way of showing subservience.

"Been at sea a long time, eh?" the stall owner said, eyebrows waggling across her table of anatomically suggestive abalone.

Giving her a guffaw, he moved on.

Genla appeared prosperous. The streets were cobbled, the wooden shops brightly daubed and the stone residences slate-roofed. Money obviously rolled uphill here, with palatial residences riding up the mountain slopes. He might sojourn there after sundown, professionally, should he decide to stay.

But first things first.

He found a tavern, in a busy street, with tables outside. The serving girl gave his sailors' garb a dirty look but didn't seem up to actually chasing him away. He took a seat and settled in to watch.

People wearing wool, not silk, trod worn cobbles on ordinary errands. Baskets and barrels bobbed by, bearers exchanging shouts and greetings. Shops did a brisk trade and gossip ran rampant. Carts trundled, beggars begged and dogs barked.

He drank it all in, absorbing the look and feel of Genlani life.

"You gonna order something?" said the server, flouncing over.

"A full plate and a tall beer," he gave her a coin and his best grin – to no discernable effect. "Nothing pickled or weevilled."

Glaring, she pocketed his money and pranced off. He shook his head. Perhaps he was trespassing on some local custom?

The service was fast, if not friendly. He reduced half a honey-and-lemon basted bird to bare bones and devoured a heel of dark bread in record time. After weeks of salt pork, pickles and black eggs, it was a feast. He didn't even miss the sharp spices of home. Much. The beer wasn't half bad, even watered as it was.

Picking his teeth with a bone, he belched to show he was done.

He'd spotted several pickpockets already, through lidded eyes. Common might be the tongue of choice here, but it was not nearly as accommodating as body language. In Oaragh, most of these amateurs would have been headless or handless by dusk.

Draining his tankard, he stood. Outwardly straightening his hip jacket, he confirmed the comforting weight of his hidden knives.

The server, who'd hovered hawkishly, swooped to collect his plate and pitcher. Perhaps she was afraid he might steal them.

"Do you live in Helia's light?" she demanded reprovingly, crockery in one hand and her circle pendant clutched in the other.

"Sure," he winked. "At least until sundown."

Huffing indignantly, she stomped off.

Laughing, he moved on and promptly lost himself in the crowd.

He made a point of moving slower than the foot traffic, gawking at the shops and spectacles. Whenever he accidentally-on-purpose bumped into people, he apologized profusely. In Purli. All the while, his purse dangled an open invitation, not even properly tied to his sash. In short, he seemed the perfect mark.

The cutpurse, approaching from the front, certainly thought so. Blind lifters, they were called: 'Oof, watch where you're going!' With fist upraised, to hold your attention, while quick fingers pilfered your purse.

But that wasn't what he needed.

Careful not to interrupt his charade, he met the man's eyes. Whether at the flash of steel across his face, or across his fingers, the would-be thief reversed direction in a dead panic.

"Careful, fool!" someone exclaimed.

More abuse marked the man's stumbling retreat.

Jiminy shook his head in scorn. A lifter worth the name would have gotten at least one purse from such a convincing tangle.

He wandered on.

A block later, a boy in rags abandoned a begging bowl and began to follow him at a discreet distance.

He slowed as the urchin crept gradually closer. When a grubby hand finally darted under his hip jacket, he seized it.

Skinny arm twisted up behind his back, the boy squealed. A deluge of dockside curses – in a dozen languages – followed. Weathering the tirade, he steered the boy into the nearest alley.

They garnered curious glances. Some passersby even looked sympathetic – but in that enlightened way that lent no actual aid. It was a bitter thought that, even in the Holy Heli Empire – moral center of the civilized world – a child's cries brought no help.

Street noise faded. A dozen steps deep, he unspooled the arm.

Grip tight against his captive's tugs, he grabbed a handful of greasy hair, saving his wrist from a vicious bite. Reading the boy's desperate intent, he trod on the foot contemplating his crotch.

"Hey!" he shook the thief by the roots. "You speak Common?"

Straining stick-limbs stilled. "Yeah, what's it to you?"

"I could use some directions."

"So?!" the boy griped, giving another jerk. "Ask somebody!"

"You're somebody. I'm asking you. And I'm paying..."

With a look, he warned the suddenly attentive urchin to stillness. Letting go the greasy scalp, he employed a little sleight of hand. A coin appeared, pinched between his fingers.

The little thief frowned at it. "That was in my hair?"

"What? No! Seriously kid, you've never seen a magic trick?"

"Magic is illegal. You'd better have a writ."

"I had it in my- Never mind. You want it or not?"

"What've I got to do?" Dirty cheeks pulled in distaste. Good things didn't happen to children, in back alleys, for money. "You could get directions from anybody, for free."

"Not to the places I want to go," he assured. "I want the houses of ill-repute – held in high esteem, understand? I don't want the dives where they hustle you going in, fleece you going out, and roll you in the gutter minus your teeth."

His captive appraised him anew, noting his knife scars, taking in his stained sash and careful stance. Street recognized street.

"Whatchoo lookin' for, master?" the urchin asked.

Gingerly, he eased off the little thief's toes. "Somewhere the girls are clean, the bouncers are bored and the wine isn't watered."

Alright, so maybe he *had* been a long time at sea.

For one so young, the boy possessed a truly spectacular leer. "You want Madam Thorpe's. For another coin, I'll take you. But I can't promise they'll let you in, looking the way you do."

With a flourish, he let the money between his fingers multiply.

"Half now," he flicked one over, "the rest when we get there."

Grinning, the boy motioned him to follow. "I'm Gav, by the way. You don't need to tell me your name. You're sure you're not a streamer? I know a place in the Furrow that'll forge you a writ if you need. You look like a sailor. Do you have a cutlass? I want a sword. One of them with the frilly bits on the handle…"

Gav singlehandedly kept up the conversation all the way to their destination – an unassuming, six tier building on the end of a row of silent shops. No sign hung out front. But the man who slipped out furtively, face hidden under a fancy hood, was as good as an advertisement. It seemed his guide had led him aright.

"This is as far as I go," Gav announced, cupping an expectant palm. "Madam Thorpe has *views* and I'm not allowed."

He paid the promised coin. The boy made it disappear with speed, if not aplomb. "For another, I'll wait here till you're done."

"I'll find my way," he said, but threw in a third coin on a whim.

Grinning hugely, Gav scarpered. "Tell 'em I sent choo. An' ask for Merly – she's real big on short guys!"

"*Bye*, Gav," he gritted.

He waited, until the little bastard had gone, to rap on the door. It opened into an antechamber where rose-tinted lamps maintained eternal twilight. It lent the wood paneling luster and turned the copper fittings to gold. Most men were probably distracted by the perky blonde with the high smile and low bodice. But he kept a wary eye on the enormous man who closed the portal behind him.

"Welcome to Madam Thorpe's Misty Meadows," the girl chirped. "A cover charge of one gold is payable by entrants. Please feel free to leave your cloak and weapons with me."

He didn't have a cloak. But then, he must also not look like he had a gold. Luckily, the row of Purli suns – stitched into his pick kit's seams – had stayed undisturbed. They now swelled his purse.

He paid up and disarmed.

"Ahem," the blonde coughed when he made to step away.

So not just a pretty face, he thought, surrendering his last knife.

"Enjoy your stay!" she trilled.

He pressed through some heavy drapes and into a fugue of sweet-smelling perfume and curling hookah smoke. The half-gloom hid shapely forms, lounging mostly clad, on low couches and cushions. Husky conversation and the click of playing tiles underpinned the sultry music of some stringed instrument.

He would reconnoiter first, he decided, heading for the bar.

"Who," a sharp voice forestalled, "let this wharf rat in?"

An older, silver haired woman stepped from the dark, sharp ribs and shoulders wrapped in silk. The madam's severe mouth was turned down, her delicate pipe steaming with disapproval.

Silence fell, save for the music, which picked its way across a foreboding bridge to a more desperate tune.

Ah, crap.

He hated feigning respect.

"I assure you, mistress, I wiped my feet at your threshold. And I've brought friends." A light touch set his purse chiming. "Say you won't turn us away, mistress?"

All heads swung back to the madam.

Unimpressed, she strolled over to inspect him properly. He hid his annoyance at finding she was taller than he.

"I don't know you, sailor," she said, staring down her nose.

"I was referred," he assured, "by a knowledgeable young man I happened to meet today."

"Named?"

Damn... "Gav."

Her lip pulled in distaste. Apparently her views were stronger than even Gav realized. He played the only card he had left.

"I was told to ask for Merly."

The madam's expression cleared. The atmosphere in the room lightened at once. He thought he heard a snicker.

"Is that so?" Amusement crinkled the corner of the madam's eye. "Merly, come and have a look at this one, would you?"

The music cut off, mid-strum, and the musician approached.

He'd meant to look her in the eye but missed. It was incredibly hard to drag his gaze further up, to find her face. He'd seen tall women before. More, since leaving home. But this Merly could tuck the tallest man he'd even seen under her arm.

It was as if some hedonistic deity had molded the perfect female specimen, guaranteed to set any man's pulse racing, and had then said, 'Let her be *more…*'

She's real big on short guys, he recalled, staring.

The giantess grinned. "I'll take him…"

A steel grip fastened on his wrist and he found himself being towed bodily up the stairs. More than one person laughed.

If he survived this, he vowed, he was going to *kill* Gav!

IF HE SURVIVED this, Jiminy vowed, he was going to *kiss* Gav.

Sated, collapsed among the tangled sheets, he struggled for breath. He'd never been smothered, smooshed or set-upon in a more salacious manner. And he had the bites and bruises to prove it. He took great pride in the haggard breathing at his back.

Either Merly was a very gifted actress – difficult to believe of her forthright manner – or he'd outperformed himself. He'd choose to believe the latter, even if it was a sweet fiction.

A shapely leg emerged from the blankets to hook around his waist. Delicious muscle bunched. To his horror, he found himself sliding across the bedding and back into her embrace.

The woman possessed not a thimble of fat – else he'd have found it. What she *did* have was an appetite six times his size.

"Again?" he fretted. "You'd cripple me."

She moaned her displeasure in his ear.

Despite all reason, his blood reversed direction to his groin.

"I'd bankrupt you first," she promised, nuzzling his ear. "Do you have the coin to pay for another bell?"

He glanced at his purse, lying dilapidated on her dresser.

"You'd be the happiest pauper in Genla…?" she persuaded.

He would be, too. But the light through the shutters had acquired a twilight hue. "I should get going."

"Aww," she groaned breathily. Her full lips trailed down his side where she nipped at one of his ribs.

Spurred, he sprang from the bed before she could convince him further. For a moment, his legs buckled beneath him. His joints felt loosened in their sockets. *He*'d never been the one pinned during love-making. It had been a... novel experience.

"Do all desert men taste of fig leaves?" she wondered aloud.

"I wouldn't know," he admitted, hunting for his clothes.

Chortling, she shifted onto her elbows to eye him.

"These are ruined," he mourned, holding his tattered garments up to the light. Merly was nothing if not direct.

"Look in that chest of drawers," she told him.

He did. "Why do you have so many men's clothes?"

These must be the ones who hadn't survived, he thought, sifting through the odds and ends for something less foppish.

"You'd look good in that," she opined.

He eyed the maroon silk askance. "Not on your life."

Some rummaging offered up a shirt that would do – once he sheared off the lace – and dun knee breeks missing their stockings.

She stayed comfortably naked, seeming to enjoy watching him dress. The sight of her back's supple curve and her slowly scything calves made lacing up his leggings a hard task.

"Here," he surprised himself by tossing his last golden piece onto the sheets. "Thanks for the adventure."

It was an extravagant price for a whore and absolutely unheard of as a gratuity. But he couldn't bring himself to regret it. Many ladies of the night had taught at Nan's. And he'd seen everything from the wide eyed waif to the foul mouthed groper. This Merly would have been the shining prize in any prince's harem.

Leaving the coin where it lay, she rolled onto her back, breasts bouncing and mane spilling off the bed.

"You missed," she husked, giving him such a smile...

Salt and silver!

He spun to face the window while he finished dressing, doing his best to ignore her knowing rumble.

The view over the rooftops was sublime, the sunset picking out peach and passionfruit tones on the tiles. This sight, and the heavy scent of sex, would forever supplant Genla in his memory.

He wanted more of this. A miserable sailor's wage? Ha! He was going to steal himself rich before he'd begun graying. With the leftovers of euphoria burning in his blood, the childhood dream seemed less dim. He'd be the prince of pickpockets; the cream of cat burglars; the greatest sneak thief the world had *never* seen.

A dead friend's words, those.

A flash of light, from beyond the pane, pricked his sudden melancholy apart. It was but a chance reflection off a bit of glass or, perhaps, an errant nail. But for a moment it recalled a crossbowman on an Oaragh rooftop, taking aim at him.

As though cinched to memory's quarrel, another image slammed into him – a dead pirate, lying prone on the Spear's deck.

One man's features he'd glimpsed as he'd fallen. The other's he'd barely parsed before passing out. But, quite suddenly, he was certain – they'd been the same man.

Spirits of the sand!

Shock held him still. He'd offended his share of princes but never any pirates. That he knew of. Had those buccaneers been after the Spear's booty? Or after its cabin boy? Were his pursuers even stymied by oceans at all? Shivering sands, he'd never met a problem he couldn't cure by moving to a neighboring city. Now here he was, having nearly circumnavigated the Pearl Sea – and he suddenly felt unsafe.

That ship could be barreling in the Spear's wake, right now...

He hadn't heard Merly pad off the bed. He only felt her overpowering body heat press close to his back.

"You alright? You're pale as a ghost. I didn't pop your pancreas or something, did I?"

Pulling himself together, he reached around to cup her bare buttock... and settled for patting the back of her thigh instead.

"Not to belittle your efforts," he reassured, deep in thought, "but I think I might be differently screwed."

"Thank you for your business, please come again!"

The cheerful blonde's voice followed Jiminy outside. He made sure it was the only thing following him as he slunk down the street. He'd snuck out of Madam Thorpe's, careful as a fat cat in a famine. If a pirate ship could be bought, bullied or browbeaten, a whorehouse certainly could.

If only the brain, dangling between his legs, had had the sense to pull out earlier. Now, late in the day, long shadows barred his way and bided in dark corners. The first stars weren't far off and his boast of finding his own way rang abruptly hollow.

His original idea – finding an inn – now seemed folly. He wouldn't trust the local thieves' den to offer asylum, even if he could track them down. He *could* return to the Spear. But it didn't set sail for another week. Until then, it was just a floating platter. Another ship, then? Overland? Perhaps he was being paranoid-

"Pssst!"

He spun, knives fanned between his fingers for a side-armed throw. He was not above skewering a feral stray in his caution.

"Mother's minge!" A little figure fell over itself, ducking.

"Gav?"

"Who did you think?!" the urchin hissed urgently. "Get off the street before someone sees you!"

Hesitating only a moment, he sprinted for the alley.

"What are you trying to do? Kill me?" the cutpurse complained.

"Crossed my mind," he admitted.

"And after I just saved your life? How's that for gratitude?"

"What," he demanded, eyes narrowing, "are you supposed to have saved my life *from*?"

Gav huffed importantly. "The armed knockers camped all around your ship. The word is out. There's gold to be had for word of where you are. And a fat purse for whoever nabs you."

Cat scat on a skewer! They were already here.

"So, why aren't *you* collecting? You could have led them right to me. They'd have caught me with my pants down. Literally."

Gav shrugged, looking sour. "Maybe I like you…?"

"Or," he drew from experience, "maybe you didn't think they'd pay up to a snot-nosed kid?"

A fierce scowl and jutting bottom lip said he'd guessed right. The little urchin looked positively apoplectic.

"Fine," he sighed, yanking his purse from its string. "Here. It's not gold. But it's everything I've got on me."

"There's nearly nothing in here!" Gav scathed.

"And whose fault is that? 'Ask for Merly,' indeed."

The boy grinned broadly. "Was it good? Will you tell me?"

He slapped the back of the little bastard's greasy head, to the sound of unabashed giggling.

"Shut it, you. Now," he growled, "point me to the docks…"

It was high time, he thought, that he got a look at these goons.

JIMINY TOOK TO the rooftops, for the high ground-advantage. These foreign tiles, so pleasing to the eye, were both spit-slick and bone-brittle underfoot. But he persevered.

Full night had fallen, hiding him from prying eyes as he wended his way toward the wharf. Gav hadn't known where to find the swashbucklers themselves, but had been able to point out a likely choke point. After backtracking a time or two, he approached the potential ambush site from above.

He spotted the lookout almost immediately, hiding in an alleyway. No one had taught the idiot to stand still while trying to blend into the background.

Now, Jiminy perched on the eave, directly above the man. Low voices and the faint crackle of a fire drifted from the deeper recesses of the passage – the rest of the man's party.

The smart thing to do, he thought, would be to snatch the sentinel, bleed him for information, and disappear.

He thumbed at his absent earlobe.

Screw that idea...

He unlimbered his heaviest knife, pinching the pommel between thumb and forefinger. He couldn't see himself sneaking close enough to slit the man's throat but...

Centering it carefully, he let go the dangling knife.

It dropped straight, punching through lookout's pate with a wooden retort. The man straightened in alarm at the sound.

Head wounds, he reflected wryly, could be odd.

The sentinel slowly reached up, questing fingers finding first blood, then blade, then protruding haft.

"Oh, no..." the man said, slurring, and promptly sagged.

Jiminy listened carefully but it didn't seem the man's compatriots had heard his collapse. Good.

Clambering down quietly, he retrieved his knife.

Blegh... brains, he thought, wiping it on the man's pant leg.

He felt a strange satisfaction, crouching over the corpse. He hadn't killed anyone – in cold blood – in years. It took a moment to realize he was angry. Hound him from his home, would they?

Bristling, he padded down the narrow alley.

He peered into a small stockyard. Two bruisers stood, warming their hands over the rusty glow of a bucket-turned-brazier, conversing in grunts. Behind them, almost hidden in the shadows, sat a figure swaddled in a cloak. Three. He could handle three, with surprise on his side. So long as the cross-legged man didn't turn out to be a swordmaster or some such.

Unsheathing another knife, he rounded the corner at a dead run.

The docker, facing him, startled at the whisper of footfalls. But, night-blinded by the fire, the fool saw only a glint of flying steel. The blade buried itself in a hastily raised forearm.

Jiminy swore at the miss as he plowed into the nearer one's back. Rocked back on his heels, he snagged a handful of shirt and pulled himself close to plant his knife again. And again.

Heart. Lung. Kidney.

When killing someone thrice your size, he reasoned, best to kill them three times over. Only as the man collapsed, already coughing pink foam, did he recognize Master Meris. The rank sailor had probably leapt at the chance to rat him out.

What do I smell like now, you fly-blown bastard?

Deep in shock, the knife-studded docker took a wild swing but used his wounded arm. As the limb passed, Jiminy plucked his blade from it – and traced a jagged path through the man's jugular.

Brushing past the gurgling corpse, he turned his attention to their cloaked compatriot who'd leapt upright.

The man's cape fell open around a clunky breastplate. The wrought iron was etched with a scowling face: pursed lips bound around by great spools of copper wire.

Idiot, he thought, watching the awkward man stumble.

Heat bit at his ring finger even as the chanting began.

A dune-damned sorcerer!

He let fly with both daggers.

The magicker slapped at the arcane armor. Energy spat. The speeding knives bent from their paths, as though blown off course.

Crap!

The key to spell casting, he knew, was concentration…

Skipping a step, he kicked out hard. The bucket bounced and spun away, vomiting coals and cinders over the man.

Crying out, the caster abandoned his spell to shield his eyes.

Three long leaps closed the distance. Jiminy gathered the man's hands and slammed them to the wall above their heads. The mage drew breath – and choked on the blade depressing his tongue.

Eyes wide, the sorcerer screeched wordless supplication.

A coward, then. Good. That would make this easy.

"Twitch," he growled, "and you'll be whistling out your ear."

The Jade Islander blanched beneath his tattoos.

"One word," he warned, "just one – in a tongue I don't know – and I split yours down the middle. Understand me, you snake?"

The sorcerer blinked a furious affirmative.

"Tell me who you are."

He removed his knife from the man's mouth, to threaten a nostril instead. A runnel of bloody spit rolled down the man's chin.

"Rulis Cuvvis," the mage coughed, "I own a copper goods shop on Stile Street. Please, my writ doesn't include conduit use-"

"Who," he cut in, "is paying you? Who's looking for me?"

"I swear I don't know him!" the man sobbed. "I'd never seen him before today. His kind don't set up shop in the Empire. He just walked into my store, smelling of death. Him, and a small army of mercenaries. Merciful goddess, he just *walked right in*! He burnt out every one of my wards just being there!"

He felt the hair on the back of his neck rise. "A mage?"

"Mage?!" Rulis laughed, a hysterical glint to his eye. "*I'm* a mage. And my head nearly split just looking at that... that *thing*!"

Salt and silver! An army of mercenaries and a mage who had other mages pissing their pants?

Rulis was still blubbering incoherently.

"Focus." He rapped at the man's nose. "Why do they want me?"

"I don't know-"

He hoisted the man's nostril on the point of his knife.

"Aagh! I swear I don't know! The way he kept calling you 'thief' I thought, maybe, you'd stolen something from him!"

"Stolen *what*?" he demanded.

"On my life, I don't know! But I... I heard him talking to one of his sellswords. He said something about a- a key...?"

A key? *Now* they were getting somewhere! As it happened, he'd had occasion to steal several keys, both for himself and others. Most notably, the one to a certain *falahdin*'s chastity belt, that her father had held hostage. That one, she'd ostensibly wanted for herself. But, having been paid in kind, he considered he'd benefitted equally. Then, there'd been the skeleton key to Prince Dhamin's bizarre dungeon of-

He'd let his attention wander from Rulis.

His ring gave a moment's warning. The mage's angry breastplate bridled with stinging force. Jiminy staggered back-

And a crossbow bolt, as thick around as his thumb, missed him by a hair to thump into Rulis. Whatever magic or metal comprised that armor apparently couldn't stand up to a quarrel.

He whipped around to see more mercenaries stream into the stockyard, raising crossbows.

Sorry, Rulis, he thought, pulling the man in front of him.

Iron screeched as broad-head bodkins breached Rulis's back plate. Peeking over the man's shoulder, he saw a cloaked and cowled figure in command of the mercenaries. Air, and the will to move, was crushed from him as he met those unseen eyes.

Here, it appeared, was Rulis's dread mage. In the flesh–

No, wait. He could spy brickwork *through* the robed form, between the murky folds. The magicker wasn't here in truth!

But his henchmen are, he thought, as the sellswords dropped their spent crossbows in favor of blades.

He dropped his spent Rulis in favor of running as fast as he could. He felt the mage's ghostly gaze, hungry, on his back. Almost – almost! – it was enough lame his legs. But not quite.

The question, he revised as he took to his heels, was no longer which way to run. It was whether he could run *far enough*.

※ ※ ※

How, Marco wondered, did the Royal Guard stand it – 'stand' being the operative word – with no knowledge of waking trances? Shifts lasting eight bells? The boredom would have broken him if not for his Clatter Court training and his long practice at prayer.

At least when the guardsmen had stood their two tapers, as the Renali reckoned time, they could retire to the barracks. But not him. *He* was irreplaceable. Which sounded grand, when said aloud – and was anything but, when stood in silence.

'Don't fidget. And keep your fingers clear of your face and your gigglestick...' had been the extent of his orientation.

He'd not even been issued a 'gigglestick' – whatever that was. Some kind of baton? He did not lack for a weapon, though.

He settled a hand on the hilt at his side, imagining he could sense the orin's rich history. The umber colored blade was single edged and slightly curved, the honeycomb pattern of eversteel unmistakable. That it was a mere shortsword didn't faze him. Yet, he frequently wondered what could have become of its companion longsword – its weirin. Oh, to have both…

Reluctantly, he let go his grip before someone mistook it for a threat. Not that he garnered many curious glances anymore – Dailill was an expert at commanding attention.

"That is not the issue," the princess was saying, to the po-faced man seated opposite her. She was meeting with several serious-looking people of the mercantile persuasion. "Of course we must plan for the future. But our port is not free of the Heli blockade *yet*. Worrying about the influx of foreign ores won't…"

He stifled a yawn.

Being a one-of-a-kind bodyguard meant pulling double – sometimes triple – duty. He suspected the master of his schedule, the disagreeable Muro Heiss, had a hand in that. The lieutenant seemed less taken with keeping up a random rotation and more in depriving Marco of sleep. The man took some perverted pleasure in wake-up calls, delivered at boot point.

The rest of the Royal Guard had not been too welcoming either. He did not bunk in their barracks nor wear their uniform. And, when he'd tried taking his meal in the guards' commissary…

As he'd made his way to a seat, a hard nudge had upset his tray. Finding himself the focus of a spreading pool of disapproval, he'd knelt to scrape up the mess. Eager to avoid hard eyes, he'd wedged himself at the nearest table. Only to have the other occupants immediately desert it. Burning with embarrassment, he'd glued his gaze to the woodgrain.

The normal hubbub had returned by painful increments.

The fresh bowl of stew and bread, sliding to a halt before him, had come as a surprise.

"Don't mind them," a young guardsman, lean of face and frame, had taken the seat beside him. "It's a bitter tonic they've been told to swallow and they're a bit upset."

"I don't understand," he'd whispered, grateful for a halfway civil word from someone. "What bitter tonic?"

The man had given him a disbelieving look. Then, "Do you know what it takes to become a Royal Guardsman? Years, sometimes decades, of service. Recommendations of excellence. And that's just to get you in the door. After that, the competition turns truly fierce. Aspirants are beaten away with a stick. Literally. The trials break scores more than they raise. The Guard is as high as a lowborn man might aspire to climb in this kingdom.

"And then along comes you. Not even a fighter, and worse yet – a foreigner. And you beat your way past the lot of us to save the princess from under our noses. And now we're being told to heed you, should you go haring off again."

Stunned, he'd stammered, "I didn't know... I didn't mean-"

"Relax. We can hold our noses long enough to stomach you."

Marco had glanced at his ruined plate.

"Ah," the guardsman had said, following his gaze. "That was Fenroth. You knocked out his front teeth – and his chances with a certain chambermaid. I'd not hold out for his approval."

He'd ducked his head in abject apology.

"Chin up," the guardsman had chided. "The clear eyed among us recognize what you did. See?"

Another royal guardsman had taken up a seat, opposite the table from them. Although the man had said no word and hadn't looked friendly, he'd glanced up from his meal to give a grim nod.

"Thank you for explaining," he'd said, "um...?"

"We've actually met before," the man had said. "Though you were in too much of a hurry for introductions. I'm Dennik."

He'd clasped the offered hand, "I'm-"

"Oh, don't worry. I know who you are."

The man's other comment had penetrated. "You were there?"

Tearing a loaf in half, Dennik had given him a wry nod.

"I didn't...?" he worried.

"Knock anything of mine out? No."

They'd spent some time in silence, eating.

"Can I ask something, Dennik?" He'd gotten an encouraging nod. "Who do I see about my gigglestick?"

Dennik had sprayed crumbs all over the table.

Even now, his ears flamed at the remembered explanation.

"...with all due respect, highness," the po-faced mercer was saying, "if we do not establish sanctions ahead of time..."

Aware that he'd been daydreaming, he dutifully eyed the vaults and cornices, the dark corners and drapes. He even cocked an ear for the telltale crackle that accompanied the shade...

Nothing.

The only threat the princess had faced so far was from belligerent politicians and petitioners. And she needed no help handling those.

"Your concern," she said, "for the Kingdom's economy is commendable. And, I'm sure, unconnected to you maintaining your mining monopoly. Tell me, how would you fare, were the crown forced to annex the mines in support of the war effort?"

The man smiled uncertainly. "Pardon, highness... What war?"

"The one your proposed sanctions are sure to spark, of course."

Purpling, the man pursed angry lips, but said nothing further.

"Moving on," Dailill declared, pulling the next piece of parchment toward her. The big table looked like a whirlwind had been locked in a library. The mercers resumed batting facts and figures back and forth, shoving twice as many page scraps and scribbles at the princess as at each other.

Would he comprehend more if he were forced to take notes? These meetings were similar to the summit gatherings, except for everyone speaking Renali. *Guildsmen!* He recalled the word. The Kingdom organized their merchants into guilds, not chapters.

"Are we all agreed?" the princess concluded. "Four across the board, for the first term. Down to three-and-three-quarters thereafter. With a guaranteed three-and-a-third for the last two?"

"And," an older guildswoman, with startlingly red lips, insisted, "exclusive import rights for two years."

"Under the condition," the princess agreed, "of accurate tally, by royal auditor, and inflation capped at one quarter. Yes."

"Then we are agreed." Nods rounded the table.

"Well then," the princess stood, drawing the assembled mercers to their feet, "this has been profitable. I shall have the proper agreements drafted. May fortune follow in your footsteps."

They bowed, gathering papers and making their goodbyes.

"A privilege, as always, highness," the last one said, leaving.

Only once the door had closed did Dailill collapse in her chair.

"Ugh!" she sighed, daintily rubbing her eyes. "Who's next?"

The attending scribe shuffled a thick sheaf of pages.

"I believe that was the last one for the day, highness," the man tolled in a graveyard voice. "Or, for the evening, I should say."

"Fortune's fetlocks!" the princess sat bolt upright, eyeing the lit lamps. "It's night?"

"It's well into fourth wick, your highness."

Groaning, she hid her eyes in the crook of her elbow. "You may go, Ghelis. My apologies, to Maud and the girls, for keeping you."

If the dry-toned stick figure was taken aback by the breadth of the princess's knowledge, there was no sign. But the scribe bowed deeply, quills clutched to a pigeon chest, before bobbing off.

The heavy portal sighed closed, leaving the two of them alone.

Dailill peered at him. "You look dead on your feet."

He made an effort to stand taller. He'd caught about three bells' worth of precious sleep before Lieutenant Heiss's boot had ousted him from bed. But he knew himself to be presentable.

"It is an honor to guard you, your highness," he bowed.

Her crooked grin said he was about to pay, for being so formal, when they were alone. "So that is honor swelling the bags under your eyes? A curious place to keep it. Was your purse full?"

"I don't have a purse, highness," he admitted.

"And yet," she observed, "you're being run ragged as a serf."

"You forget, highness, I watch you work almost every day. While I twiddle my toes you wrestle, wrangle and whip a kingdom into wellbeing. It is, by far, the more perilous undertaking."

Her sister, the princess Villet, got first pick of the tasks their lord father delegated. Somehow, Dailill managed to wring success from the difficult dregs and tiresome twaddle she was handed.

She waved him off. "You concern yourself over me needlessly."

"If that were true, highness," he countered, "I'd not be spending most nights outside your door."

At her severe frown, he knew he'd made a misstep.

She was ill at ease with the arrangement her father had foisted upon her. In a rare show of solidarity, the sisters had argued for Marco's protection to go to the king. But the combined might of the persuading swan and the hangman's hawk had proven insufficient. They'd compromised by moving Dailill's sleeping quarters closer to those of her lord father.

"Does your newfound responsibility chafe?" she asked quietly.

He could sense her willingness to petition the king for his freedom again. And he couldn't have that. Royal bargain aside, the thought of *not* spending the day near her twisted his stomach.

He tamped his instinctive panic. He knew her well enough by now to know she'd be more receptive to a reasoned argument, rather than a sincere denial.

"'To leave undone that which only we can do is to defy divine will,'" he quoted, channeling his inner Justin. With any luck, he sounded fulfilled, and not half as pretentious as he felt. Coming from an Imperial, most people would take scripture as gospel truth – even in its crass, Renali translation. But she didn't seem swayed.

He added his own conviction. "I am where I need to be."

She studied him a moment more. He'd been witness to her incredible leaps of insight. If she weren't Renali, he'd have suspected her of being an empath. He weathered her weighing regard. But whatever she saw seemed to satisfy her.

"Does not you goddess," she queried, "also mandate a day off?"

"She does," he agreed. "But the threat is constant, highness. And so must I be. There is nothing either of us can do about that."

A mischievous grin overtook her.

"You doubt my ability to arrange a respite for you?"

"No-" he caught himself in time. "Her highness is certainly very capable. I'm simply saying that I am in no need of-"

"Then it's settled!" she shot from her seat, like a toddler from a swing. In a billow of skirts, she turned, at once a princess again.

"We believe," she said archly, "we are due a day off…"

Swallowing hard, he scampered to open the door she marched toward. Somehow, he doubted she'd meant the royal 'we'.

"A DAY OFF," Dennik scoffed, watching the gruel gloop from his spoon without enthusiasm. "That's a good one."

Marco paused, a bit of bread halfway to his lips. "How so?"

"Well, she's a princess isn't she? Apart from looking beautiful, dancing at balls and making royal babies, she can pretty much follow whatever fancy fortune throws her way, can't she?"

"She's not like that," he scowled at the guardsman.

"And don't I know it. My point is, if she decides to take a day to go… let's say horse riding, where are you going to be?"

Taking his thoughtful silence as a cue, Dennik continued.

"On the horse right beside her, is where. See?"

His spoon dropped from nerveless fingers. "More like *under* the horse right beside her," he feared, the image so clear he could taste the mud. "What do I do?" he appealed.

"What else can you do?" his friend chortled. "Accept with good grace. Try not to make too big a fool of yourself. And whatever you do," Dennik warned with a finger, "*don't* make a fool of her."

"I guess," he sighed, defeated.

His friend continued in a serious vein. "And take my advice. Don't repeat what you've told me to anyone."

"Huh? Why?"

Dennik seemed to consider carefully before answering.

"The princesses are good at keeping noble suitors at arm's length. The only men they regularly see are their guards. And we police our own. Any man, who gets above his station, gets put down hard. This lot," Dennik raked his gaze over the half-full commissary, "haven't gotten over your last bout of popularity yet."

When he finally grasped what was being hinted at, he ducked his head to hide his blush.

"Thanks for looking out for me, Dennik. You're a good friend."

The young guardsman winced, clearly uncomfortable.

They ate in silence for a while.

"So," the man said eventually, "you excited for the festival?"

"What festival?"

The guardsman gawped. "Marco, we're a week shy of *Marliev*! The palace has been abuzz with nothing else for near on a month!"

It has?

He'd seen servants, bustling about at all bells. But he'd hardly noticed. Sleep, however fraught, had become far more important.

Dennik read the confusion on his face, expression turning droll.

"I supposed the fact has escaped you. Along with your brush."

Hurriedly smoothing his hair, Marco thought hard.

"Marliev... Marliev..."

He snapped his fingers. "Of course! The completion of the Greenwall. Interestingly, the laying of the last stone actually occurred several months later. Marliev more closely coincides with the final pitched battle with the Purli, at Hanging Cleft, in the Year of the Rising Moon, Renali calendar. King Ullusik-"

Dennik leaned away, as though Marco was speaking in tongues.

Coloring, he stoppered his mouth with another spoonful. It was too easy to forget that the education he flaunted was not at all that common. Half the Guard couldn't even read.

"You're such a dolt," Dennik sighed, unoffended, "it's hard to remember you've had learning. Well, eat up, scholar."

"Scribe," he corrected. "And priest-in-training."

"Whatever."

He decided to change the subject, before Dennik could do the same mental arithmetic as the invigilator and ask why a novice should be able to immobilize royal guardsman two at a time.

"So, Marliev. Is it a *big* parade?"

"Parade?" his friend scoffed. "Hah! The entire Acreage is transformed into one big market. There'll be minstrels and mummers and acrobats, food from all over... But none of it," the young guardsman's eyes brightened, "holds a candle to the lists!"

"Lists of what?"

"The lists!" Dennik insisted. "You know? Jousting?"

Jousting? he thought, recalling his notes on Renali culture.

"'A knightly sport, played from horseback'," he recited.

"That's the one!" his friend beamed. "The nobles have been streaming to Keystone for weeks. You'd have seen them, at the high table, if you weren't supping with us grunts every day.

"Ah..." Dennik reminisced, "I wish you could've seen the bout between Duke Scholos of Etchmund and the Raif of Rayborn..."

His friend's chest puffed, excited eyes fixed on the past.

"I don't think you're a grunt, Dennik," he said softly.

That earned him a strange look. "Finish your breakfast."

He obeyed musingly. Marliev. It sounded fantastic. For everyone else. But he knew where he'd be, come the day – ten paces or less from the princess.

Perhaps, he consoled himself, he'd get to see this 'joust'.

CHAPTER 11 – CAMOUFLAGE

Pella Monop, Journal entry #94

Electing to work backwards was undoubtedly the correct strategy. The history of the Empire is as murky as a mineral hot springs and only gradual immersion has saved my mental skin. Now, I fear, I've hit bottom. The very oldest surviving records are holy texts, written in High Heli – the original Temple dialect. Added to which, the Mother Temple is adamant that only the ordained be allowed access to their elder archives. However, they have accepted the proctor of my institute's compromise – I am to take up Helia's torch. An honorary title, I am assured. As if speaking the oaths will blunt the nib of my quill. Ha! I do not expect I'll stumble over their tests. I have read so much scripture this past season, I could deliver a dissertation, never mind a sermon.

THIS, JIMINY THOUGHT, was not going to end well.

His eyes roved over the band of approaching youths. He recognized the type. Their village, a hamlet named Hedrik, was a collection of lights across the dark field. It, no doubt, offered little outlet for those of a malignant or casually malicious persuasion.

Jiminy's small band of lepers was an easy target. The malformed figures, huddled around their meagre fire, flinched at the approaching footsteps.

The villagers swaggered into sight, adult-sized incarnations of childhood bullies. He fostered a simmering hatred for their kind. Growing up small and slight, in a street-run orphanage, did that.

"Looky looky what we got 'ere!" the expedition's leader laughed, drawing up short.

Your average bully, Jiminy knew, is little more than fear bundled in bluster. But even pond scum has better sense than to come within a switch's swing of a leper.

The Imperial disgust, at leprosy, left him wrong-footed. Sure, the unfortunates looked decrepit and 'unclean' in their dirty yellow wraps. But so would *any* outcast, living rough. And the lepers had it rougher than most. They survived only as nomads, settling on the outskirts – until civilization encouraged their migration by way of food, blankets and other necessities.

It was an artful system of extortion Jiminy could appreciate.

Of course, 'civilization' was a relative term. Sometimes villagers took a more direct approach to discourage dawdling.

"Come to bother good, god fearin' folk, have ya?" one spat.

If abuse was the only thing hurled tonight, Jiminy thought, the lepers would consider themselves lucky.

His fellows made themselves small, hoping to escape notice. It was worth a try. Many Imperials wouldn't even *look* at a leper. As if the disease was communicable by sight.

It made their company perfect camouflage for a thief on the run.

More so, since no one had even pried after his name, so far.

He wished their spokesperson, Amn, were here. But the man was off helping another of their number, somewhere in the dark woods. If not for his yellow dress and ruined face, the leader of their rag-tag band could still pass for the priest he'd once been.

Jiminy had come across Amn while hunting for an unseen route out of Genla – which sealed its gates at night. Nestled among the belfries, in the pre-dawn dark, he'd been startled by voices.

"…will you have any trouble, getting past the gate guards?"

Hidden among the overlapping eaves, his ears had perked.

"None," a sanguine voice had assured. "While we are rarely welcomed, we are always welcome to leave."

"I pray for the goddess's regard on your pilgrimage, my son."

"Thank you again, exarch, for your Temple's generosity."

Peeking from concealment, Jiminy had spotted the moth-eaten man, cloaked in ragged ends of yellow. Staff in hand, the shepherd had led his deformed flock toward the distant gate. The occasional torch or brazier had backlit a menagerie of marching horrors.

From a side alley a furtive man had appeared in their path, clutching an armload of yellow cloth. Amn had settled a consoling arm around those downtrodden shoulders and taken quiet sobs in stride. And the lepers' party had grown by one.

Before they'd reached the city gate, they'd grown by one more. Jiminy had filched a discolored bedsheet, billowing from a line. Quick knife-work and long practice had left only his eyes bare.

He'd been welcomed without a word.

He'd never have guessed he could pass unseen by daylight. But the early morning crowd had recoiled, covering noses and mouths, and the gate guards had wafted them through with averted eyes.

The lepers mostly moved at a crawl, many missing one or both feet. Before the crenelated walls of Genla had been properly out of sight, a mounted man had overtaken them.

"You there!" the rider had scowled, horse prancing.

A mercenary attitude. An unfamiliar accent. A uniform lacking all insignia. The distinctive double crossbow had cinched it.

Jiminy had resisted the urge to draw his wraps tighter.

Amn had stepped up. "How may we be of service, master?"

"Keep your damn distance, for one! Tell me, have you seen anyone else travel this road? Or heard any horses pass by?"

"Saving your honored self? No, master. And we've been at it since sunup. Granted, some of us are missing eyes and ears…"

Spitting at Amn's feet, the rider had put spurs to his horse.

A rough voice pulled Jiminy back to his immediate problem.

"'said, 'Come to bother good, godfearin' folk, have ya?'"

"It ain't *god* they need to fear right now, is it?"

These villagers weren't about to let them off with a bit of spit.

"This one ain't even 'folk'. Look 'ere! It's in a wain!"

Laughing, the louts clustered around Mad Bergha, who glared from beneath her mop of wild gray hair. The leper had no legs. She got around on a small box cart, with four uneven wheels. When none of her companions could be browbeaten into towing her, she rowed herself down the dusty roads by means of poles, buckled to her forearms. Sometimes, at night, she left her seat and waddled around camp on her callused palms, cackling manically.

"It's an ox cart," one idiot gushed. "And an ox!"

Bergha swatted ineffectually at their poking sticks.

Jiminy saw the decision come into her crazed eyes.

"Yeah? Come closer!" she challenged, snapping mismatched teeth at the nearest crotch. "I'll show *you* an ox!"

A club swung. Bergha's short trunk struck the dirt, rolling beneath blows and raucous laughter.

He looked away, as did the other lepers – honoring Bergha's sacrifice. She would not want for someone to pull her cart, come morning. But the sounds of struggle were not so easily ignored.

Gritting his teeth, he gripped his legs, forcing them to stillness.

It was the second time he'd had to sit through such a scene. In another fly-speck village, a skulk of cowardly jackals – immunized against illness by drink – had worried at Pant. The large mute had been harmless long before leprosy had stolen his hands.

He'd stood in defense of his brother, refusing to be shooed.

The siblings depended on each other. The lamed Hersh rode his brother's back by day and fed the helpless Pant by hand.

Hersh, mired in his sibling's shadow, had raged uselessly.

"Leave off 'im ya godless bastards! Come 'ere, I'll murder ya!"

The man's impotent tears had wicked Jiminy's temper like lamp oil.

But, like the desert caravans traveling from oasis to oasis, the lepers depended on the charity of the villages. If just the *rumor* of violence clung to them, that charity would dry up. They'd starve.

They had lived like this, long before Jiminy had arrived. And they needed to be able to go on, long after he left.

That night, ignoring his red hot and screaming knives, he'd grabbed Hersh's frayed shirt collar instead.

"What're you doin'? I need to help me brother! Lemme go!"

Dragging Hersh, Pant retreating in their wake, they'd escaped.

That had taken everything he had. And it had taken Amn to cover their retreat, placating their abusers with promises.

"Who's an ox, now, eh?!"

Bergha's defiant lows were waning. She'd given up fending blows with her bloodied forearms. Her face was buried in the dirt, her arms heaped atop her head. And still the sticks swung.

Sun sear his soul – he wasn't strong enough to just *sit* here! He wasn't the equal of these stalwart cripples. He couldn't match the depths of their restraint – to ensure everyone ate again tomorrow.

Hands itching for his hilts, he squeezed his eyes shut and tried to distract himself.

Hammerham had once sent him to put down an upstart gang.

"The *Dog Piss* Clan?" he remembered scoffing.

"The Moorah brothers. Cousins of Black Droguul," Nan had said, swirling a snifter of fig brandy. "We can't afford to offend Droguul. So this can't be no bar-side stabbing. If we want to avoid blood reprisal, it's got to go strictly by Alley Law."

He'd started at the implication. "You want me to challenge for clan leadership? I don't want to have to compete with you, Nan."

"I'm not saying you should. Once you've got control, disband the clan. And besides – what competition? I'm no clan leader."

"Seems like the Moorah brothers heard that too."

"More fool them. Now get going."

"Yes, *khashjit*," he'd bowed formally to his clan head. Then, laughing, he'd ducked a ballistic tumbler of fig brandy.

He'd sauntered into the Dog Piss den, bold as brass, and issued his challenge. The Moorah brothers could have refused him – he had no standing. But they were bullies. And Jiminy was so *small*.

They'd come at him together.

The looks on their faces, dripping with first blood, could still warm his heart at night. He'd won.

But snubbed bullies were *so* predictable.

Bucking for his death, they'd bulled back in.

And he'd cut them to ribbons.

Dancing, he'd split ears, lips and eyelids; he'd skinned noses, knuckles and knees; he'd carved chests, backs and buttocks.

He'd blunted his knife on them.

Into the shocked silence, as their erstwhile leaders bled out in the dirt, he'd declared the clan disbanded and spun on his heel.

His bloody reverie was ripped from him by coarse laughter.

Wood whacked into Bergha's flesh.

Jiminy's rage roiled like an adder in a bag.

He broke, gathering his legs beneath him.

A sudden hand pressed him back in his seat.

"Stop!" Amn passed him by, striding toward their tormentors.

Something in the ex-priest's voice backed the yokels up by half a step. But as the firelight revealed the sickly yellow of the leper's robes, they recovered. Somewhat.

The foremost brought his stick to hover under Amn's nose.

"Your kind ain't welcome here. Take your sickness and go!"

Jiminy's jaw ached. In his experience, strength of conviction rarely stood up to a stout stick. But stand up to them the preacher did, cowing them with his presence alone.

"Leave!" the ringleader tried, one last time. Then, "Let's go!"

With much glaring and spitting, and more idle threats, the bumpkins slunk off. Back to their warm village hearths, to report to some pillar of the community that they'd triumphed.

The lepers immediately set about breaking camp, stamping out their little fire. Amn hoisted a disheveled Bergha back onto her cart. Wicked wheals puckered her skin. She clutched at the moth-eaten priest's neck, dirt-stained and tear-streaked.

Jiminy's anger crackled, undimmed. As Amn strode by, it flashed, grounding itself on the man's moral high ground.

"Why'd you stop me?" he demanded, grabbing an elbow.

Amn turned a tranquil look on him.

"Because," the man said, "those boys didn't deserve to die."

His hand sprang open, letting Amn amble off.

Perhaps, he thought, he'd overestimated how well the yellow hid who he was.

* * *

Hooves thundered. People shrieked. Metal clanged. Horses screamed. Wood splintered, fountaining up-

Marco's breath caught as the mounts flashed past one another.

The unhorsed rider was borne to the ground, hard. The victor held aloft a broken lance, galloping the length of the pitch. The penned spectators' cheering redoubled serenading the winner. More sedate clapping filled the royal pavilion, where Marco stood.

A knightly sport, played from horseback? He shuddered.

This was barbaric. They called it sport? People were being *carried* from the field. One man had had to be cut free of his dented breastplate, just so he could breathe. And a particularly violent clash, that had left riders *and* steeds sprawled, had ended with the horse being put down. A *horse*. Right there on the field.

It was slow murder, being conducted to fanfare.

Hands clasped tightly behind his back, he spared the spectacle only brief glimpses. The pavilion's benches were packed with nobles – the cream of society, supposedly. Having seen one grandmotherly matron *ooh* appreciatively at the blood sport, he reserved judgment. Each bout that caught their collective interest set their feathered fans beating harder. Like a murder of crows.

'Murder' was why he was so on edge. Assassins weren't cheap. Whoever held that pagan practitioner's purse strings, he reasoned, was likely sharing this very pavilion with him…

A loud crash announced another victor. Even Dailill clapped daintily. If not for her sympathetic winces, he'd have written the Renali nation off as unsalvageable – and never mind the summit.

She sat beside her lord father, in the seat vacated – early on – by her interminably ailing baby brother.

The pale little prince had looked peaky, in his royal circlet and bundling furs, even before his nurse had led him off.

Now, Dailill made bright conversation with the king. But that was in stark contrast to her silent and unsmiling sister.

A woman with an uncanny knack for knowing when she was being watched. He quickly turned his head as she glanced his way.

As had become their habit, he let his eyes sashay over their surrounds, seeking shadows. But the sun stood high in the sky and the tent fabric was light. Similar pavilions flanked it, sheltering lesser nobles and dignitaries, such as Keeper Justin.

Satisfied that the princess was in no obvious danger, he returned to observing the nobles. As a 'servant', he was all but invisible to them. So he spied all the meaningful glances, pointed glares, conspiratorial smiles, haughty sniffs and obstinate frowns – even if he had no idea what any of it meant.

From having stood in on the princess's late-night meetings, he knew this pavilion played host to enough family feuds and preserved slights to color any pot black. Seating arrangements had been an organizational nightmare. Thankfully, no one had drawn steel yet, preferring to cut each other with snide remarks. Still...

His eyes coasted carefully back toward the elder princess-

"Jump at any shadows yet?" whispered an unwelcome voice.

He jerked from the unexpected proximity.

Princess Dailill's *other* bodyguard lounged beside him.

"Luvid," he greeted coldly.

Goddess forgive him, how he *loathed* the man. Apart from their first meeting – on the sea-serpent stairs – they'd rarely seen each other. And, since Marco had taken to guarding the princess, Luvid was even less in evidence. He'd have suspected the man of being bitter, if not for the air of scorn that clung harder than those sleek leathers. And that smile – sharp as a naked blade.

He hadn't needed Dennik to tell him to be careful of this man.

'*He picks fights when he's bored. And he maims for fun...*'

Luvid smiled, savoring the sudden wariness in his stance.

"Enjoying the view?"

The man's permanent leer slunk in Dailill's direction.

Marco gritted his teeth.

"Doing my job," he ground out, "as you should be."

He knew it for a mistake the moment he said it. Luvid thrived on confrontation and took great pleasure in making him squirm. Strangely, the man let the comment pass.

"If you insist, squire," the man mock-saluted, turning away.

Many noble ladies' heads turned to track Luvid's progress, fans working a little faster. Men tracked him too, thumbing their dirks.

Luvid slid, unmindfully, through their attention – a pike in the reeds. The bodyguard leaned to whisper in his princess's ear – and smirked at Marco when she touched his arm in acknowledgement.

Dailill exchanged quick words with the king, receiving a nod.

He didn't miss the way her elder sister's head swiveled to follow her, as she rose and made her way over.

"Is she watching?" Dailill asked, gathering him up.

"Oh, yes," he assured, words lost in a tumult of applause.

"Good! Let's go!"

Feeling like a political rebel, he fell into her wake. Knowing that Villet would disapprove of anything Dailill might enjoy, he took a childish pleasure in thwarting the elder princess.

Luvid had disappeared once more. Instead, two royal guards fell into step as they left the pavilion. Preceded by two more, bearing the royal crest on tall halberds, they braved the throng.

"Where are we going?" he laughed, the princess's mood proving infectious. He cautioned himself to be a bit more formal.

"You'll see," she promised, flashing a smile.

She moved with impressive speed, considering her full skirts – a wealth of fabric gathered up into one hand. But, as they made their way through the heart of the festival, the press grew more fierce. The crowd did its best, parting as for the prow of a ship. Waves of bows bobbed in their wake. But their progress slowed.

This was unlike the Solstice Celebrations in Tellar, he reflected. Compared to the brilliant shades of bright silk, and the unifying toll of the parade, this seemed dull and disorganized. But the people appeared happy. Flowers twined in their hair and they danced, to the beat of drums and the outlandish bleating of bladder pipes. Scrumptious scents wafted from the food stalls. A man, twice as tall as the tallest Inith he'd ever seen, stilted by. Another passed, juggling torches. And, unless he missed his guess, he'd just glimpsed a man actually *swallowing* a sword. Craning for a better look, he almost collided with the princess.

"Here we are!"

They'd mostly left the stalls behind. Now, the beat of hammer and anvil drowned the drums. If anything, more people milled here. These seemed to be of a more serious cast than the other merrymakers. Burly working men and brightly dressed servants bustled about.

They were deep in the belly of Marliev.

"Come along," the princess commanded, leading them toward a solid wall of people's backs. Someone spotted the approaching halberds and the spectators respectfully made room. A coral of some sort was revealed – a two tier fence surrounding a patch of churned earth. Even as he wondered at its purpose, two helmed men tramped across it, earnestly trying to kill one another.

Helia's mercy!

Massive swords bit at pitted armor. Metal keened and one behemoth's back struck the barricade, almost on top of Marco. He couldn't help his hurried back-step.

"Match point!" cried a small man, appearing inside the tourney field to stick a staff between the two. "Garron of Underdale wins!"

The crowd cheered, beating fists on the outer fence. To one side, pages rushed to rearrange painted markers on a tall board. In the arena, the victor helped his opponent to his feet and the two tottered off, laughing and punching each other's padded shoulders.

"That's you!" the princess beamed, pointing.

He caught his breath. A page was slotting a stylized shield onto the board. Its paint, glistening wetly, was the Imperial Seal – a golden sun on a field of red. Murmurs ran through the crowd.

He goggled. And not just because the Emperor's flag was being floated as his own personal crest. He'd finally figured out what he was doing here. And it was worse than horse riding.

"At first, I was at a loss," the princess was saying, blind to his panic. "Until I remembered Luvid saying that you have swordsman's callouses. Is this not grand?"

She finally turned to him and, after a moment, her face fell.

"You don't like it?" She snatched her hands to her mouth, eyes wide. "You *don't* like it!"

Helia help him, he couldn't disappoint her. Desperately stuffing his distress out of sight, he pasted on a smile. "I... am thoroughly surprised, highness. I truly don't deserve such kind consideration."

She stared hopefully. "You really like it?"

"I am at a loss for words," he said truthfully.

"Yay!" she clapped her hands. "Here, go with these squires – they'll get you outfitted. And have fun, alright? You deserve it!"

He had just enough presence of mind to drag the orin, sheath and all, from his belt. "Keep this safe for me?"

She gave him an excited wave as he was wrestled away.

The guardsmen were grinning behind their cheek guards.

Bundled into a tent, the squires stuffed him roughly into a rank gambeson, rushing to buckle boiled leather and crude iron atop the underpadding. Mildew, saddle soap and rust assaulted him.

"Does this one suit, sir?"

A length of blunted steel, awkward and overlong, was pressed into his gauntleted hands. His 'blade', he realized. Masha'na and Renali sword styles were both two-handed. But that was where the similarities ended. He grimaced as he hefted the unwieldy thing.

"Good!" the man pronounced, moving on to something else.

"Wait-!" He staggered as he was hit squarely on the pauldron.

"Got's to settle the armor," the second squire apologized.

Grimacing, he squared up to receive another blow.

"Can't I-?" he began, only to have a grill-faced helm muffle his objection. A pale green tabard was added as an afterthought.

"All done!"

He was pushed out of the tent and straight into the corral. He stumbled in the soft sand, feeling like a tortoise. Into his diminished vision stepped the diminutive match caller.

"In the green!" the man cried, staff held high. "For the first time in history! For the Holy Heli Empire – Marco dei Toriam!"

Catcalls and lackluster applause greeted this announcement.

"In the red!" the man continued. "From High Reach! Youngest son of House Norvalis! Former silver winner – Keppin Norvalis!"

The crowd surged, beating at the barricade.

"Contestants," the match caller motioned them close, speaking quickly and by rote. "I want an honorable bout. When I say break, you back off. Three points each for a clean strike to the head or chest; two points for limbs. Lose one point to your opponent for a successful riposte. Disarming wins the bout. A discarded weapon forfeits. Fight to ten points or until I call break. Clear?"

Without waiting for assent, the man stepped back.

"Red, ready?" the match caller pointed with his staff.

For the first time, he looked to his opponent. The figure in the red tabard was half a head taller than he, but lithe as a bullwhip. Not at all brutish. Face hidden, the lord raised a sword in salute.

For an instant, Marco saw a dark rider, mace whirling.

He recoiled, as if from wagons afire. The memory of acrid smoke stung his nostrils and coppery blood coated his lips-

He shook his head. He did not feel that red rage, burning in his belly right now. But his fear of it turned his stomach anyway. He could not succumb to that again. Not ever.

His legs wobbled.

"Green? Green, ready?"

What else could he do? Chest tight, he raised a shaky arm.

"Fight!"

He barely got his unwieldy blade up in time.

Clang! Clang! Clang!

His back plowed into the palisade.

"Break! Three points red!"

His head rang from the blow, magnified inside his helmet. The crowd's approving howls sounded far off.

Helia's mercy!

He'd stayed upright only by dint of desperate footwork. His arms were trembling. And not just from the speed and power of Norvalis's blows. Abruptly, the feel of the foreign hilt in his hands filled him with revulsion. He made to drop it – and an inflectionless voice cut across the crowd's crowing. It bypassed his pounding heart and swept aside his panic.

Focus… leave your mind behind… let your blade lead…

"Breathe," he told himself, tightening his grip on the weapon and his will both. Like it or not, he was competing for the honor of the Empire. With Master Crysopher's voice in his head, the feints and footwork his opponent had just used crystalized. He knew those counters. He'd been drilled in them.

His teacher's imagined scorn brought a peculiar sense of relief.

Righting himself, he stepped up to his line.

"Green, ready?"

He nodded.

"Fight!"

Blows snapped toward his brow and breast. Steel bleated as he turned them. Norvalis dogged him, herding him around the perimeter – while he picked out patterns and familiar forms.

Such terrific speed and strength came at a cost. When Norvalis eventually began to tire and slow, he'd press his advantage-

"Break! Two points, red! One point, green!"

Damn! He'd barely managed a riposte. A lucky cut, to the underside of Norvalis's wrist, had won him a point. But only after he'd suffered a rip to his green tabard. That had *not* been the plan.

The lord didn't seem any happier with the exchange than he was. Stalking back to his line, Norvalis squared up to him stiffly.

Ah, the man suffered from temper…

He hadn't sparred with Jeral Stalia, his nemesis at Clatter Court, for a very long time. But those bitter bouts had shown him how derision could dull an opponent's blade.

"Fight!"

Powerful, precision strikes drove him back. He circled, concentrating on turning each one. Norvalis was clever, leaving subtle gaps in an otherwise sterling defense, trying to entice him.

He made no attempts to reach past that sham guard. Instead, he batted at the lord's sword, again and again. He could feel the mounting frustration behind the ever more forceful disengages.

Finally, fed up, Norvalis flung the toying touch aside with too much fervor – and he leapt into his opening.

"Two points, green! One point, red!"

Goddess's grace! Even caught off guard by his lightning charge, Norvalis had managed a riposte. He would have to rethink-

The blow came out of nowhere, landing full on his face plate.

"Break!" he heard faintly as he rolled in the dust.

This wasn't working, he reflected, blinking the bright blotches from his vision. He wasn't fast enough. He wasn't *focused* enough.

The streaming trance beckoned within him. He could only hold it for a few moments at a time. But, at the speed Norvalis moved, that might be enough. He didn't feel like losing to this lord.

And, besides, Dailill was watching.

Staring through steel slats at a blue sky, he relaxed and allowed the trance to well up. The crowd noise subsided as he sank to a place of peace.

"-can't get up, let go your sword, Green. Green?"

With a thought, the world tilted upright. No longer feeling the encumbrance of the Renali blade or armor, he rolled his shoulders.

"Green, ready?"

He took his stance.

"Fight!"

He met Norvalis's incensed assault head-on. The crowd *ooohed* appreciatively as the two of them traded blow after blow after blow. Not slowing. Until their blades blurred together in a silver cascade that occasionally spat orange sparks-

"Draw!" the match caller belatedly cried. "No points!"

The crowd gaped. Norvalis and he stood in mirrored poses, blades arrested a hair from each other's helms.

A moment of jubilation threatened to collapse the trance.

Not yet, he controlled himself. *Not yet...*

"WATCH IT!"

Erom's mad dash saw him stumbling from yet another collision. He slalomed, almost fell, but struggled on. Why was running so hard? He glanced down for a clue. Wait... these weren't his legs. Some feckless bastard had filched his legs while he was passed out on the alehouse floor. Whoever's legs *these* were, they were obviously drunk off their ass. But they'd have to do...

Fortune flog me, he gibbered, *Master is going to kill- Hic!*

The ground leapt at him, lunging for his face. He battered it away. He thought he'd succeeded but he couldn't *feel* his face. He tried probing at it with his fingers but couldn't feel those either-

A tent peg snagged his borrowed feet, flinging him down.

"Blegh!" he rolled over, spitting sod.

His flailing hands found solid purchase and he pulled himself up. Something about a wooden frame, topped by velvet cushions, communicated itself directly to his skin. Oh, wonderful sleep...

"Hey!"

The owner of the stall he slumped across glared at him.

"No, *you*'se drunk!" he accused the blurry man.

Wait, 'slumped'? He was supposed to be running.

Roaring on principle, he dragged his defective legs along. He was so late! He'd woken up in the gutter, with the sun high overhead. If he missed Master's tourney, he might as well go back to that ditch – and have someone scoop dirt over him. Making a fist, he tried to flog a little more speed from his flagging legs.

He missed.

"Hoomphff-!" The borrowed appendages tried to draw up into his abdomen, after his ascending balls. He tumbled end over end. Only the certainty of impending unemployment – and the dry spell sure to follow – had him crutching upright.

"'m c'ming, masher!" he yelled ahead.

A woman, bearing a tray of savory snacks, stepped into his path. He sent her flying. Spilled sausages smiled from underfoot.

"S'not funny!" he yelled, slipping as he limped on.

All this sword foolishness! If he were a young lord, of money and means, he'd spend his time on fetching young ladies. Not fencing practice. But the master got worked up over the most in*con*... incon*sid*... incon*sec*- Over the *stupidest* stuff!

Erom, where's my baldric?

Erom, why isn't this sword oiled?

Erom, did you pass out in a pigsty?!

Erom, show up drunk again and I'll sell you to a slave galley!

Oh, fortune's fickle fanny! Poor Erom! Pulling oars on a slave ship! With not a drink in sight!

Spurred by the thought, he turned the last corner. *There* stood his master's tent, looking like salvation. He skidded straight in.

"'m here, marster! 'm *hic*-!" he pitched from his feet, plunging in among the dueling gear. He came up with a double armload.

"Quick'y, mazz'r," he rushed, breathless. "No time to looz! I's gots yer ball'prick all shiny an' yer shord all sharp an' yer pad'n prop'r thtinky... Armsh up, masser, armsh up an' we'll... we'll..."

Unnerved by the lack of shouting, he stalled.

"Mash-ter? Mar-shter?"

A faint groan answered him. Blearily, he glanced down.

Keppin Norvalis lay, atop a bleeding squire, trussed and clearly unconscious. A bruise was slowly rearing on the master's face.

"In the red!" the ringmaster's faraway voice intruded. "From High Reach! Son of House Norvalis...!"

Shedding equipment, Erom swiveled toward the sound.

"...former silver winner – Keppin Norvalis!"

The crowd roared its approval.

"But..." Erom objected, mystified, "master, if you's in here-"

A sausage slowly sauced its way down his shirt front.

"-then who'sh that out there?"

HELD IN THE trance, the smile Marco felt didn't rise to his face. His sword edge hovered, level with Norvalis's ear.

Hidden behind their helms, they appraised each other anew.

Abruptly, the lord's sword drooped and Norvalis stepped back. A strange change came over the man's slim frame. All hints of ire winked out. Shoulders relaxed. The blockish set, that underpinned all Renali forms, smoothed away. The man shifted into a completely unfamiliar – somehow insolent – stance.

He eyed it uneasily. He would recognize the Purli shamshir form and the Rasrini rapier form by sight. This was unknown.

The match caller drew breath. "Fi-!"

Norvalis surged, sword seemingly everywhere at once.

Even cushioned inside the trance, shock set Marco back a step. Then another. The swiftness and savagery bearing down on him were so far removed from what he'd faced a moment ago, he might as well be fighting someone else entirely.

He retreated from the onslaught.

Within moments, his arms ached from the effort of warding the whirlwind of blows. Breathing through gritted teeth, he tried to slide sideways, from under the brunt of the attack. A scything cut – that would have snapped his neck, had it landed – prevented him. Through wide eyes, he watched an overhand blow – fit to fell an ox – fall toward him. He turned it at the last moment, his weapon nearly sprung from his grip by the force. And still the steel symphony didn't let up.

Cold realization carved a pit in his stomach. Norvalis had dropped all pretense and was trying to kill him outright. He could sense the intent behind every cut.

His back struck the fence with stunning force, fouling his elbows and his defense both. And still blows hammered down, pounding him into the palisade.

"Break!" the match caller shrilled. "I said break!"

A tasseled staff tried to intrude between them... and was repulsed in pieces. The match caller fell with a yelp.

He had no thought to spare for the man. His arms were leaden with effort, on the verge of seizing. His sword, a ruin of nicks and notches, keened under the pressure. He was no longer turning every blow. Norvalis was slowly battering him unconscious.

His thoughts turned from victory to survival. Surely someone would stop the deranged lord? He needed to stay standing until they did. He needed to still his opponent's movements, if he could. Helia's mercy – he needed to catch his breath!

And he needed to do it *now*.

The melody of tortured metal echoed down the tunnel of his vision, barking like chains.

They hadn't taught dirty fighting in Clatter Court, he'd learned his next move on the road. Sliding a blow along his blade, he stepped all the way into it. Pinning Norvalis's forward foot beneath his heel, he bulled into the man with his shoulder.

Thank you, Bear! He thought, even as something sharp punched into his side. With a crash, those half-heard chains snapped taut, jerking him down and into darkness.

DENNIK STOOD OBLIQUELY across the coral from the princess's party, maintaining a careful distance. He'd just followed them here. With his Royal Guard helm, tucked under one arm, he was simply one more unremarkable face in the sword tourney's crowd.

He'd half suspected the princess was headed for the Marlie-games, where brightly dressed jesters refereed a hodgepodge of hilarious competitions also fit for ladies.

Instead he watched, sidelong, as squires converged.

A poleaxed-looking Marco was hustled away.

So, Princess Dailill meant him to compete? Hah!

The bashful boy would *detest* being the center of attention.

He grinned, anticipating all the teasing the morrow would bring.

The elder princess's instruction rang through his head, startling the moment of levity into flight.

"You've won the scribe's confidence," she'd pronounced.

"As you commanded, highness," he'd said, from one knee.

"Tell me what you've observed."

Swallowing the taste of betrayal, he'd complied. "He is bookish. He speaks of histories with the same ease other men talk of horses and he quotes their holy scriptures by heart. For all of that, he is very young. Gullible, even, and easily unnerved."

"This timid child," the princess had noted dryly, "bested the Royal Guard and scaled the royal tower bare handed."

He'd nodded. "There can be no doubt that he is trained. And that he's capable of great daring. But violence does not seem to be in his nature. If I hadn't seen it myself, I'd not have believed it."

"And my sister," the elder princess had prompted.

He'd stumbled over his suspicion. "I believe he is… quite taken with her, highness. Although I doubt he is himself aware."

The princess had sat, silently observing him. "Tomorrow is Marliev. You've been assigned to my detail, as a pretext. Follow this smitten child. Observe him with my sister. Do not be seen.

"You've done well," she'd added, "befriending this boy."

Except, he now reflected, as he was jostled by the tourney crowd, *I have no idea how to* pretend *at befriending someone.*

"…for the Holy Heli Empire – Marco dei Toriam!"

He dragged himself back to the present – and his bitter task.

Marco, he saw, fairly waddled in the tourney armor. The princess clapped to see him, bouncing on the balls of her feet. Poor boy, he sympathized. These days, he knew all too well the plight of being caught between a princess and a hard place.

"…Keppin Norvalis!"

Joining in the applause, so as not to seem out of place, he leaned across to his neighbor. "Is that the same Norvalis who fought the Raif of Rayborn last year?"

"Oh, aye," the man – a fiery redhead in a farrier's apron – agreed. "An' look at 'im. Grown by a head if he's grown a hair. That empire lad's in for a hidin', ain't he just?"

He secretly hoped not. Keppin was an honorable sort, by all accounts. If the princess had had a hand in picking Marco's opponent, as he assumed, she could have done much worse. House Norvalis' lands lay to the north, where hate of the Empire was less... pronounced. Still, he didn't know the young lord's politics.

One thing was sure – Marco had no supporters in this crowd.

Almost none, he corrected, spying the princess's bright smile.

"Fight!"

Any hope he held out was immediately dashed – as was Marco. He cringed at hearing the crunch of sword on helm. Glancing over, he saw the princess worriedly gnawing a knuckle. It seemed she'd misjudged Norvalis's sentiments too.

"'at's right!" his redheaded neighbor whooped. "Wallop 'im!"

He shook his head in sympathy as Marco squared up once more.

"Fight!"

Norvalis was flawless in both form and footwork. He could see why the young lord was lauded as a prodigy. So he was more than a little surprised when Marco, this time managing an ordered retreat instead of an outright rout, snuck a point in edgewise.

"Two points, red! One point, green!"

Yes! he silently cheered.

But the referee hadn't called break – a fact Marco had missed. A spectacular two handed blow laid the boy out.

Pitying groans underscored the crowd's vicious pleasure.

"'e's had it!" the farrier predicted.

"Green," the referee was insisting, "can you continue? If you wish to yield, relinquish your arms. Green? I said, if you can't get up, let go your sword, boy. Green? Green?"

"I guess even an Imperial is worth somethin'," someone in the crowd quipped, seeing Marco stir, "if you put 'im in Renali steel!"

Amazingly, Marco made it back to his feet without a stumble.

Dennik sighed in relief, relaxing his desperate grip on his helm. This – not knowing who to root for – was exhausting.

"Fight!"

He was not alone in catching his breath as Marco and Norvalis met… and matched each other, move for move. He daren't blink his surprise. Had the scribe been holding back? If so, the boy had been severely underplaying his prowess. The crowd, allegiance momentarily reversed by this rare showing, brayed, loving it.

"Draw! No points!"

A disbelieving guffaw burst from him.

"Fortune balding ball sack!" his neighbor echoed, displeased.

The spell held the combatants still a moment longer.

Then Norvalis fell upon the scribe in earnest.

"Give 'im what for!" the farrier enthused, as the crowd finally took exception to what they saw as an Imperial ruse.

"That's the way!" the unseen wit added.

No, he thought, taking a half step nearer.

That was most certainly *not* the way. He'd just spotted a killing blow, mixed among the attacks. And there! Another! The referee, frowning furiously, followed the battling pair to the barricade.

"Break!" the man commanded urgently. "Break, I said!"

Without so much as glancing aside, Norvalis lashed out. The referee's staff and shirt parted along a neat line, pitching the man from his feet.

Fortune's fetlocks – that blade was sharp along the back end!

This was no match. This was attempted murder.

His helmet dropped from nerveless hands. "Halt!"

Pushing confused people from his path, he hurdled the first barricade and ducked the second, drawing his sword as he ran.

"Stop! In the name of the king!"

Marco made a last ditch attempt to grapple with Norvalis.

From his vantage, Dennik saw what the boy could not – a rondel dagger, its triangular blade tapering to a needle tip. It pierced the boiled leather, slipping between steel plates to punch into organs. Thick blood jetted as it was yanked free for another stab.

"Stop!" he cried, swinging.

Norvalis dragged Marco's armored bulk between them.

Screaming with the effort, Dennik aborted his strike. He plowed dirt, stumbling so his friend's form fell atop him.

Through a haze, he saw the fleeing murderer leap the fence. A nobleman, sword half drawn, moved to intercept. The richly dressed man fell back, a round hilt sticking from one eye.

The crowd recoiled as the killer plunged among them.

"After him!"

Halberds struggled against the tide of panicked spectators.

The princess's escort formed a protective cordon, shouting furiously. She stood in their midst, shoulders drawn around her ears and face hidden behind her hands.

He had no time for them. Fumbling at the straps, he flung Marco's helm aside. Dark eyes, in a deathly pale face, met his.

"Dennik-" the boy tried once, blood flecking his lips.

Oh, fortune's pitiless fulcrum...!

"Help!" he yelled into the milling mass. "Help!"

He wasn't sure anyone heard.

"Keeper Wisenpraal, are you well?"

Justin blinked dumbly at the Purli diplomat.

The oily man in the turban pretended concern. "You just... drifted off there for moment. Mid-word."

"Apologies..." he meant to say, but couldn't. Another flash of fear, on the heels of the first, jolted through him.

And he knew its flavor. He'd felt it once before.

Marco!

He was on his feet and out of the pavilion before he knew it, leaving the desert ambassador to feign affront.

He rarely hurried. He was, in fact, rather famous for it. Today, he hitched his robes to his skinny knees and *ran*.

His secret, self-made sigil – Empath's Echo – coalesced. The fear and panic he felt roared from it, rolling over the crowd and clearing him a path. Merrymakers and musicians fell silent, backing away from the sudden, inexplicable terror.

He had dressed in his feast day best and looked exactly like what he was: a sorcerer priest, from the insatiable Heli Empire.

He would work at stitching up tattered trust tomorrow.

Right now, he needed room to run.

Please, merciful goddess... he prayed, pale calves flashing.

The high arcanist's warning weighed him down.

It's too soon, he railed. *Too soon!*

He smacked into a solid mass of panic and confusion that overwhelmed his influence. He resorted to pushing people aside. A sea of elbows and shoulders battered at him.

A wooden spar, slamming into his waist, brought him up short. Beyond it, in a miraculously clear space, a royal guard knelt.

Justin's eyes went straight to the prone figure before the man.

Oh, Helia's mercy, he begged. *Please, no-*

He floundered to a halt at the guardsman's shoulder.

The sending had stopped. For all of the waves of emotion, breaking around them, this island was dead calm.

Sight of Marco's lifeless face lamed his faculties and his knees both. He fell to the soaked sand beside his ward.

Pragmatism, and years of practice, shunted his loss aside.

"Move," he commanded the guardsmen, feeling for a pulse.

Can't find it! Damn this obstructing armor!

"Where's the wound?" he demanded, his hands hunting for it.

"They were sparring..." the guardsman stammered in shock.

He didn't have time for this. He needed extra hands and this guard was closest. Empath's Echo swept over the man, drowning out hysteria and ringing with stalwart purpose.

"Where?!" he pressed.

"His side," the guardsman rallied, "here."

"Get this off him, quick."

Shearing through straps, they lifted plate and leathers from the boy. Though the guardsman trembled, he was deft enough with his dagger. Tears tracked the young man's face as they worked.

Marco's undershirt was a great crimson stain. Justin tore at it with his hands, exposing a gaping hole in the flesh beneath. Blood flow had ceased along with the boy's heart.

"I need this." He plucked the dagger from the guard's grip.

Wrapping the blade with his fingers, he stilled, calling Fire.

It was the strangest streaming prayer he'd ever offered.

Please, please, please...

He gritted his teeth against the pain. In his hand, the metal pinged, heating to an angry red. Wisps of black curled as he quickly cauterized Marco's wound. The steel spat and sputtered, raising the stink of charred flesh.

Discarding the dagger, he dug his crystal from its pouch with his undamaged hand. The older spell scar, marring Marco's chest, accepted its shape exactly.

Healing dead flesh was tantamount to necromancy. Even so, it was the least of the sins he would commit this day.

Breathing deep, he hummed a note of calibration and manifested Illian's Augur. It revealed a disaster of punctured innards and severed arteries. Swallowing his despair, he set about repairing what he could. The dead flesh was intractable, its memory of life fading. Spending lavishly of his own lifeforce, he streamed Nekar's Knit into the puncture. He strained and cajoled, finally convincing it to seal haphazardly.

Collapse threatened him.

Not yet… not yet…

He gathered up the cooling knife.

"Don't touch him," he cautioned the guardsman. "Or me."

Burnt fingers settling on the crystal, he held the other hand high, stabbing into the belly of the sky.

The alchemist, Mor Iset, had theorized that this was possible. But the man's work had been confiscated before it could be tested.

Justin knew only the basic outline of those purpose-built sigils. The rest, he scrawled in desperately as he went.

Please Helia, let me be strong enough for this…

Digging deep, he flung Perception to the firmament.

The emptiness dragged at him, expanding him, trying to dilute his energy into its own. But he held fast. Fumbling at the motes of force he knew existed there, he rosined them with Scatter, then added Heat to create friction. Painfully, he inverted Grasp.

Colossal resistance threatened to tear him apart. Angry energies bucked at him but he refused to back off.

He had a sense of ponderous motion. Like a vast weight, leaning off its axis. Far overhead, a lazy churn started in the ether. The first warning rumble sounded. Hurriedly, he prepared Fallow.

"What was that?" he heard above the frisson. "Thunder?"

Unseen pressure built above him. Swelling, coiling, coruscating. It cleared its throat with a hollow boom. His skin crawled as his hair strained away from him, trying to escape what was coming.

Now...

He manifested the major sigil of Root.

Blinding light leapt from the blue sky, whipping toward his upthrust dagger. White pain exploded behind his eyes. In a fraction of a blink, he'd funneled the brunt of it into the ground.

The rest ran, through the conduit of his flesh, and down his fingers. His crystal blew apart, shards raking his arm. Beneath it, he felt dead flesh jump. And then he felt no more.

Smoke rising from his singed frame, the priest keeled over atop Marco and was still.

PART III

The final days of the Age of Magic
The day of the Fall
The Battle of Thell

"Take heart!" he bellowed hoarsely, moving behind the besieged shield line. His soldiers stood, gasping for breath in this brief interlude between onslaughts.

'Heart? What can I get for an arm and a leg?'

'Here, I've got a claw!'

'Is it too late to put in for a transfer?'

These witty retorts had died. As had all the reinforcements.

The heavy infantry were exhausted, their ranks depleted. During the course of the day, they'd suffered grave losses and two near breaches. Now, they stood their ground stoically, sagging behind shields that were as beaten and battered as the soldiers themselves.

Close to hand, a bearer collapsed. He moved to put a hand under her elbow. Between him, and her long hafted spear, they levered her back to her feet. She gave him a grim nod.

They'd fallen back as far as they could. Else they'd risk the heaped corpses overtopping their defenses. The promontory at their backs narrowed and had saved their thinning line from being overrun. But they'd now run out of room to retreat. Once the enemy was done, dragging their dead clear, they'd charge again.

He regarded the roiling mishmash of creatures beyond the shield wall, drawn from a hundred conquered worlds. Many were eating the fallen. From either side. Feral, furred forms fought over scraps. Scaled monstrosities slithered about. Jagged shades flitted from place to place. Armored undead stood, still as statues. And the earth quaked to the passage or enormous, lumbering brutes.

His eye – and his shield – caught an arrow, arcing his way.

An emaciated creature, bow held aloft, danced a mad jig.

"Bastard," he swore, regarding the bleached and barbed bodkin – that had punched clean through metal and his forearm. Reaching over the shield rim, he snapped the shaft, then pulled the arrow stub all the way through. Glaring, he tightened his shield straps.

The distant archer, capering at its success, caught flame. Its shrieks seemed to amuse its fellows, whose cackling redoubled.

The whip of fire reeled back toward its master.

"Holy one," he saluted, as the priest approached.

Soot-smeared and blood-pocked, the battle-mage ignored him, looking instead to their massing enemy. Though the man stood tall, his skin was sallow and his eyes jaundiced. Fresh branding ringed his bare arms. He was worn thin by prolonged use of Helia's Gift.

It mattered little. They would none of them survive this day.

"We have failed," the priest observed.

"Together we fall," he said, tightly. "Unity through faith."

"No," the priest surprised him. "*Something* must survive. When the retreat sounds, take yourselves to the shore."

"Retreat?" he stared. "Boarding the transports will take all day. *That*," he pointed to where a new onslaught was assembling, "would be on our backs within two steps. We'd die in the shallows, in droves. No. We'll stay here. And face death on dry feet."

Greater men than he had succumbed, taking such a tone with one of Helia's anointed. But the priest did not so much as blink.

"Have more faith," the holy one instructed, stepping back.

He put the mage from his mind, turning to the matter at hand. They were moments from what would probably be their last stand.

"Ready shields! Stand firm! Check your partners and-"

A distant boom drowned his orders.

The shield wall wavered, like wheat stalks in a breeze.

He looked to the south, where the Eight held another defensive line. Fire lit the dark clouds there, coiling towards the ground.

Another boom sounded to the north, where the Eleventh still held, announcing a similar phenomenon.

"What the-?"

The crash sounded, right on top of him, throwing him from his feet. Flat on his back, he stared up at the frayed priest, carven arms outstretched and eyes blazing with holy light.

Above the man, the sky tore open, spiraling with godly fire.

He scrambled to his feet as the molten maelstrom touched down, marching across the enemy line and sweeping monsters before it like ash.

Mouth agape, he watched the fiery finger draw a line in the sand, joining up with those to the north and south. A curtain of incandescent flame, all along the promontory, separated them from certain death. The sheer scope of it was staggering.

A mournful horn sounded the retreat.

"To the boats!" he yelled, mouth dry. "Double time!"

Shaken and flash-burned, his soldiers began filing past.

He stayed until the end, eyeing the inferno and the silhouettes raging beyond it. Finally, the last able soldier struggled by, dragging a leg. He drew her arm over his shoulder.

His last backward glance showed him the priest, who blazed still, and hadn't moved. It was a harrowing image – the haloed man, surrounded by the dead, holding the dark at bay.

We will *survive*, he vowed, turning for the shore.

CHAPTER 12 – A NEW DIRECTION

Pella Monop, Journal entry #112

The scrolls housed in the elder archives have proven to be as dense and difficult to decipher as I'd feared. And that's discounting the dated script. The old writings follow a peculiar weft. They are formulaic – frustratingly so – yet also oddly poetic. And persistent. Just this morning, I found myself mouthing an outmoded prayer over breakfast. A prayer! Me! I blame exhaustion. But I persevere, despite the 'aid' of my Temple appointed assistant, Cecine. I send her on errands as often as I am able, else she simply stands and stares at me.

"WALK WITH ME?"

Bemused, Jiminy wordlessly followed Amn.

The lepers were camped downriver of a sympathetic town. The novelty of being both sated and safe had them bantering about.

But theirs was a black sense of humor.

"Then," Hersh was saying, "I says to the innkeeper, 'Mistress, if'n ye can't stand the sight o' me, I'll leave.' And she turns around and says, 'My hand to Helia, I's not you what's the problem. I's yer blind friend...'" Hersh rolled his eyes at Old Paroke, who had neither eyes nor teeth. "'...'e keeps dipping 'is bread in yer bac-'"

"So," Amn said loudly, narrowly saving them from the punch line. The riverbank loomed. "You've been adjusting well?"

Peering from between his wraps, Jiminy appraised the man.

He shrugged. "Well enough. Why?"

"A leper's life is hard," Amn mused, looking out over the water. "While the spirit and the stomach starve, sickness carves away at the core of you. It's not the kind of life anyone would *choose*."

At the slight emphasis, Jiminy shot the man a suspicious look.

"By the goddess' grace," the man continued, "we have a clear path of pilgrimage and alms along our way. But we are, at best, tolerated – even by the most holy. So it is very rare to find someone who will risk life and limb in a leper's defense."

So, this was about what had – nearly – happened at Hedrik.

"Wasn't *me* at risk," he scowled, remembering. He would have been fine. His actions, though, would have doomed the lepers.

"Oh, I'm not criticizing," Amn assured. "In fact, I'm humbled."

Humbled?

Obviously, Amn had misunderstood his motivations. He didn't have a soft spot for lepers. He just had a really sharp spot for bullies. But saying that aloud probably wasn't smart.

The failed priest saved him from thinking up a response.

"I look at my old vocation, now, and I look at my current condition – and I see divine providence. I believe my goddess has equipped me, and sent me, to serve my fellows."

Salt and silver, I hope she never sends me *anywhere.*

Diplomatically, he kept the thought to himself.

"Whereas," the man continued, "I suspect you don't have any fellows among us. Not in the sense of sickness, at least."

He shifted subtly. He'd not yet seen the pacifist take that walking stick to anyone. And he'd not like to see it now.

"Is it because I'm not the right shade of yellow?"

What unified the lepers wasn't their skin color but their plight. His harsh comment did not sidetrack Amn, as he'd hoped it would.

"Hah!" the man laughed, facial sores seeping. "No. I saw you wince, when Bergha rolled over your foot the other day."

"She's damned heavy for half a person!"

"I'm aware. But if you are already hiding your face, then your fingers and toes should have little feeling left." To illustrate, the man took the walking stick to his own foot. "See?"

Ah, crap...

He'd hoped to hide in the lepers' shadow until it fell over a goodly sized city. Somewhere he could make a fresh start.

Somewhere with stuff worth stealing.

Amn didn't sound like he was leveling an accusation though.

"D'you want me to leave?" he offered at last.

"I'm hurt you would even ask."

"Then why bring it up at all?"

Amn gave him a searching look. "I can't begin to imagine the kind of trouble that would spur someone to seek our company. Save that it is the kind that can afford pursuit on horseback."

He glowered, remembering the mercenary outside Genla.

"I thought lepers lost their eyesight first. *You* see far too much."

"And I hear even more," the man said, in perfect Purli.

Jiminy missed a step at the sound of his mother tongue.

"Do you know," Amn asked, "what they call a missionary of Helia in the desert cities?"

Despite his wariness, Jiminy grinned. "'Everybody's purse.'"

He'd made several withdrawals himself.

Amn pointedly eyed his head wraps and he realized his mistake.

Damn. He'd have given good odds that no one, on this side of the world, would recognize the pattern his fingers had woven by rote. But variations of this face mask were favored by robbers, burglars and sneak thieves back home.

"Are you hoping to turn me in for a reward?"

He doubted it. He felt no prickling of danger down his back and Amn didn't seem the type. But the man had mouths to feed, all the same, so he would stay wary.

"On the contrary," Amn said, "I'd like to offer you sanctuary."

For a moment, he imagined the unarmed – and also un-legged – lepers, facing off against the dread mage's mercenaries.

"Ha!" he snorted. "You and what army?"

They'd crested a slight ridge. Before them lay a field of what appeared to be beets. Tonsured men in roughspun moved about the rows. A tolling bell drew his attention to a large temple.

Amn motioned expansively. *"This* army…"

* * *

THE CREATURE SLAMMED from a breach in the nascent. The force of its expulsion uprooted several nearby trees, holing the alien jungle's canopy.

The realm-relative oscillation had been judged sufficient to allow something physical to pass.

The judges had been wrong.

The creature had been sheared by the forceful transition and spilled, broken, from the rift. Its bright green blood curdled, gray, around its body.

Gasping, weak, it tried to heal itself. But the rough passage had wrung it dry. Desperately, it reached for the power of the uncooperative greenery, all around. Broad leafed plants drooped, hanging vines let go their grip and dead leaves rained down.

The creature drank deep.

* * *

"'TCHOOOOO!"

Small birds scattered from their boughs along the riverbank. Jiminy wiped gingerly at his raw nose. He'd been sneezing like a fiend for days. Where sunlight speared the green water, he could actually see frissons of plant matter riding the air. Between that and the dust of the barge, his head was thick as a clay brick.

More tubs plied the waterway ahead and behind, piled with trade goods and produce. Poling it toward Sutlam – the merchant hub of the southern rivers – were brawny, sun-browned people.

He marveled at the sight of a caravan on the water.

"You should be staying out of sight," a pinched voice said.

He snuffled loudly, saying nothing. Little rubbed his chaperone, Inrito, the wrong way like being ignored. The aspiring priest's shadow appeared, stooped and beaked as one of the tall river birds.

If the man had his way, Jiminy would spend all of his time hiding. In one of the cramped little cabins.

"The exarch put me in charge of you," the acolyte sniffed.

What the monastery's master had *actually* said was for Inrito to 'accompany' Jiminy as far as the trading post.

When these zealots granted someone sanctuary, they didn't mess about. Sutlam was fast approaching.

"Now! Get out of... sight. Immediately."

The man had plainly almost said '*my* sight'.

Jiminy suspected Inrito's fellows had volunteered him for this errand, so as to safeguard their own vows of non-violence.

The fool was not the only fly in the honey but he was the most obvious. True, Jiminy got to rest his feet and was given three meals a day. But no one went to these lengths out of the kindness of their hearts. Not even a supposedly selfless religious order.

He intended to disappear, long before their bill came due.

"I said move, you pagan *pustule-!*"

It didn't take much to hoist Inrito's temper. It tended to take the acolyte's timbre with it – strangling into a high-pitched honk.

Grinning, Jiminy listened to the mortified man flap off.

He settled back on his crate, kicking his heels.

"Tiffing with the priest again?" Limella laughed, strolling up.

The daughter of the *karwan* – the 'trader captain' – sat down beside him. She smiled sidelong at him, a habit that lent her an air of mystery and also hid her lazy left eye.

"Can't be a tiff if I don't say a word," he argued.

"Ah," she said, sagely, "I've seen my mam use that technique on da. He mostly ends up losing too."

"Nothing to lose if there's no tiff."

"Must be why my parents are so happy," she suggested.

He said nothing. For all that the sedate pace of the river seemed to have soaked into these people, with their slow eyes and speech, they could be boisterous. Their screaming matches, in particular, were impressive. As might be expected of a people who lived their lives in plain sight of one another, privacy was not highly prized.

A couple of barges ahead, a naked child toddled over the side with a splash. Jiminy started up in shock. A moment later, laughter broke the surface as the girl-child churned smoothly along. She latched onto an offered pole and an oarsman popped her from the water and onto the next barge over.

"Not comfortable around the water, are you?"

Only then did he notice Limella's hand, lingering on his thigh, where she'd pressed him back in his seat.

"Can't say I grew up around much of it. Didn't learn to swim until I was old enough to shave."

"Shave what?" she demanded, leaving off his leg to grab his chin. He pulled away, sucking his teeth.

"'Old enough to', I said."

"And how old are you?" she asked, leaning to indicate interest.

He gave her a shrug. "No idea."

"Can't count?" she guessed.

"*I* can. It's just that no one else bothered to."

"Ah," she said, understanding. "Orphan?"

"I'd ask you to cry me a river but..." he gestured around.

"Ha-ha," she said, squinting, and not the least bit sympathetic. "I'd put you around nineteen or twenty. Those crow's feet make you look older, but then, I'm guessing you've seen a lot of sun?"

"Purlia *is* a desert," he shrugged.

She sat back proudly. "I'll be seventeen this month."

"Oh? Well, then, happy birthday."

She preened.

"I wish I'd known," he added. "I'd have gotten you something."

Perhaps he could still steal something of Inrito's.

Stretching lazily, she pulled her arms behind her head. The fabric of her tunic drew tight over two clear invitations.

"There will be a party soon," she promised. "Dance me off my feet and we'll talk about your present again."

Bouncing up, she did a sultry twirl and sashayed off.

A glare sizzled Jiminy's skin like a sunburn. Across the deck, he met the hot gaze of Limella's brother – a bull of a youth, whose shaven scalp bunched with the force of a clenched jaw. The long pole Olu clutched seemed in danger of cracking.

Jiminy gave him a cheery wave… and throttled his natural desire to steal a thing simply because it was guarded.

He still needed the *karwan*'s goodwill for a score more leagues.

* * *

THE SPECTER POURED from the crack in the ether, its transition to the new plane smooth, its protections taxed but intact. It took a moment to steady itself after the tumult of the world corridor.

It stood in an unnatural clearing, the breathless jungle blighted in a roughly circular swathe. Power bled from the center, where a gnarled tree had taken root.

Sharp brambles crowned it and corrosive green sap bled from it. A face, frozen in pain and anger, twisted its bark.

Interesting. The advance agent had been told that the alignments were ripe for passage. It had not known that its true purpose was to provide fodder for the specter who would follow.

That the creature would crudely cling to life had been part of the larger plan. Its puissance was to be preserved.

The method by which it had survived was surprising, though.

No matter. Its new, wooden flesh would serve as well as its old.

But before the specter could begin carving out its ritual, it needed hands. Physical ones.

Scenting the air, it drifted off though the trees in search of prey.

* * *

DUSTING HIS HANDS, Jiminy watched honey cake crumbs flake into the breeze. Far below his perch, the river burbled among the reeds. The sawing of a fiddle sounded from upriver, where the barges had been bridged together for the night. He caught the occasional glow of bright paper lanterns through the leaves.

A sigh overflowed him.

He'd escaped jackals, slavers, pimps, knockers, knife hands, redbacks, blackeyes and princes. Yet here he sat – treed by girl.

Limella had cornered him only once during the celebrations. She'd have made a decent pickpocket, the way she'd had his breeks halfway unbuttoned before he'd even formed a protest.

"Your brother?" he'd managed, in between stifling kisses. His nose was still stuffy and she'd been literally stealing his breath.

"What does it matter? Tomorrow, you'll be gone…"

Fearing she might be right, he'd seized the opportunity – and his sagging pants – at the first interruption. By the time she'd turned back from her ill-timed well-wisher, he'd made tracks.

Her brother was every bit as persistent, set on an unnecessary sabotage campaign. The man, and his covey of musclebound friends, had pecked determinedly through the crowd after him.

The aggravation had nearly stirred him to take up Limella's offer. But that wouldn't have been fair to her. And her amorous feelings were unlikely to survive his cutting up her brother.

All of which was to say, he didn't feel like walking the rest of the way to Sutlam.

The lone highlight had been when Inrito had stormed into sight, hissing about the noise. At sight of the lusty drinking and salacious dancing, the almost-priest had had a fit. Shouted damnations had squawked thin as the man was twirled from his feet, pulled along by shirtless young men and girls with dresses slit to the thigh.

With any luck, they'd force some of their piss-colored liquor between the man's teeth and kill him. That stuff might be better suited to stripping pitch off barge bottoms. And they'd been guzzling it by the barrel full. If any of the revelers regained consciousness before midday next, he'd be very surprised.

Thought of the delay pricked uncomfortably along his spine. Though he told himself his route had been erratic onto obscurity, he couldn't shake the feeling of being pursued-

-something moved in the undergrowth below...

He strained his ears, but the night sounds here were so different from what he was used to. The silent shifting of the dunes, the half-heard flit of a bat and the stuttered chirp of a beetle… They would drown beneath the cacophony of this rushing river, rustling leaves and its menagerie of nocturnal beasts.

"-sure you saw him come this way?"

Limella's brother, Olu.

"Yeah, he snuck off careful-like, but I spotted him."

"I don't see no fire," a third voice offered.

"Idiot, he's hiding. He wouldn't've made no fire."

"So how d'we find 'im? D'we split up?"

"What if he doubles back? I'd double back, if it was me."

Olu should probably be more worried about that *guy.*

"Shut up," Olu spat, "I'm thinking."

Up in his tree, he rolled his eyes. They could be here all night.

"Fine," Olu decided, as it dawned on him, too, that his list of problems might be longer than one prick. "We'll head back."

Undiscovered, Jiminy sighed in relief.

A sigh that stuck in his throat. Eyes widening, he felt the sneeze inflate to fill his head. He pinched his nose, scrabbling for a secure handhold. Even if he didn't launch himself right off this branch, he was still about to give his position away to the buffoons below.

The sneeze seared along his sinuses, pressing behind his eyes. He wasn't going to be able to stop it. He rose to meet it on his feet, balancing on the bough. His head poked into the canopy.

"'Tch-!"

"-hwaa*ooonk-*w*hoonk-whoonk*!!!"

He blew the slumbering bird off its nest in an explosion of feathers and panicked flapping.

"What was that?" Olu asked from below.

Jiminy stood absolute still, dripping snot.

"Blue billed warbler," someone said authoritatively.

He didn't move until sounds of their progress had faded well away. Then he fished out Inrito's handkerchief, mopped his face, and flicked the bedraggled ball away.

He couldn't risk returning to the barges tonight, he realized. Whether he ran into Limella or her brother, he was screwed.

Sighing, he set about finding a more comfortable fork.

Plagued by the wetland noises, and imagining all manner of tree-dwelling monsters, he didn't manage much sleep.

The next morning saw him, raw eyed and dew damp, stumbling up the gang plank. Limella was waiting to scowl at him. At least, he assumed it was at him, but her wandering eye left him unsure.

Mood-sour and limb-sore, he stretched out on a tarp, hoping the sun would soon arrive to thaw him. His fears, concerning a late start, seemed to have been groundless. The barge goers must have cast-iron innards.

Groaning, he hid his gritty eyes under an arm.

A shadow fell over him.

"Piss off, Olu," he growled, not in the mood.

"Ahem."

He peeked with one eye. "Apologies. Piss off, *Inrito*."

The robed man wore a gloat like it had been tailored to fit his face. "The evils of drink are manifold and ruinous-"

"Did none of those half-clothed girls manage to tire you out?" He tilted his head. "Or were you holding out for one of the boys?"

Huffing, the man stomped off, taking his sermon with him.

"No judgment here," he assured, hiding his eyes again.

He dozed fitfully, jerking awake at every passing footfall. He fully expected an oar in the head before they made landfall.

Reaching Sutlam without incident came as a mild surprise.

As afternoon neared, he stood on the docks beside Inrito, yawning. The minor priest was prattling away at the trader captain, apparently oblivious to the man's flat stare.

"-should count yourself fortunate," Inrito was saying. "Coin is small reward compared to aiding the anointed in their holy works-"

As the promised purse was finally produced, the barge captain snatched it, shook it, and promptly sauntered off.

Jiminy laughed openly at Inrito's ire.

"This way?" he guessed, setting off up the muddy main road.

The priest attempted to overtake him, determined to have him follow behind. He stretched his stride to keep abreast of the man, who began puffing before they'd gone two blocks up the incline.

Obviously Inrito was a stranger to exertion. The man's current color must be the closest he ever came to working the beet fields.

"D'you need me to slow down?" he offered innocently.

The man's cheek twitched. "Once I hand you off to the local Temple ... feel free to set your own pace ... straight to perdition!"

"I'll save you a seat," he promised.

The man turned on him, anger adding to his ruddy complexion.

A finger vibrated beneath Jiminy's nose.

"You–!" Inrito squawked, voice shredding through two scales and into illegibility. "I–! Insolent–! Ghaa…!"

He reached out to pat the purpling man's shoulder.

"I know," he said. "I'm going to miss you too…"

Wow. The last time he'd *watched* someone's eyes go bloodshot, he'd been manually strangling them. He shied from the temptation.

Beyond words, Inrito stalked off.

Jiminy followed, smiling.

The town was larger than it had appeared from the river and it had a temple to match. Its head priest was a round, rosy little fellow with a button nose and crinkly eyes.

They all sat, listening to Inrito's impromptu report. It was a litany of Jiminy's severe shortcomings. 'Insolence' was a recurring theme and 'caning' was suggested more than once.

He spent the tirade staring out the window, smothering a smile.

He'd like to see someone try to take a cane to him.

The head priest interceded, once spittle started flying. Pumping away at a slightly wild-eyed Inrito's hand, the man thanked him profusely... all the way to the door.

"Off course, excellency," a wan Inrito agreed, having exhausted himself, "I suppose I could use a lie-down..."

Jiminy turned to stare at the acolyte's back. He'd have to think of a way to thank Inrito himself. He wondered what the fool would look like, without those supercilious eyebrows...

"Ahem."

He blanked his expression, meeting the exarch's shrewd gaze. What was the man's name again? He hadn't been listening.

The monastery master rounded the enormous desk. Clambering into the chair made no discernable difference to the man's height.

"Well," the head priest said in his startlingly deep voice, "you certainly made an impression."

Not yet, he thought, contemplating his knives.

The exarch inspected the scroll of introduction Inrito had brought, breaking the seal with a thumb.

"We don't often get sanctuary seekers," the man mused. "If you'll pardon my saying so, most of them aren't exactly as..."

A wave indicated the entirety of him.

"Tanned?" he offered.

"*Colorful*," the exarch suggested, "as you appear to be..."

They knew they were smuggling him away from something worse than an abusive spouse. But no one had yet asked *how much* worse. He kept carefully mum about mercenaries and dread mages.

Because however influential these priests pretended to be, they'd run for the hills if they knew. He might tell them eventually – when they began extorting *tat* for all the temple *tit* he'd suckled.

But not until he'd milked a few more precious leagues from this sanctuary business.

The holy man's attention returned to the missive.

Jiminy had *borrowed* it from Inrito, during their river journey. Resealing the waxen crest, without a crease, had served to relieve some monotony. However, since he didn't read Heli, he still had no idea what it said. The head priest's face offered no clues either.

It was a short scroll, though.

The man set it aside, in favor of a small silver bell.

Its lilting peals, so out of place in the heavily furnished office, summoned footsteps to the door.

A tonsured young man poked his head in. "Yes, excellency?"

"Joss, where is Neever right now?"

"At choir, I believe, excellency."

"Have him fetched, please."

"Yes, excellency."

The door shut. They turned to a silent study of one another.

"Did you enjoy the river travel?" the man enquired at last.

"Sure," he lied.

He'd have thought Inrito's account had been answer enough.

The priest's glance twinkled pleasantly. "Do any fishing?"

He stared. "I may have caught a cold. Does that count?"

Unperturbed, the head priest returned to smiling silence.

Suspicious, he began to wonder whether keeping barge girls off one's bait-and-tackle was a common problem. He gave the exarch another look. Was the man's expression just a little bit sly…?

A knock sounded. "You sent for me, excellency?"

"Yes, come in, Neever."

He twisted in his seat. He'd been expecting another wet rag, like Inrito. True to form, this soft-spoken newcomer was entirely unassuming. Jug ears jutted from a mop of mouse-brown hair, frizzing to gray down the long sides. Not at all imposing.

Yet he found himself rising casually from his chair, hoping it looked like courtesy. Something, in the way this Neever moved, set off an instinct that had him balancing on the balls of his feet.

"Neever," the monastery's master introduced, "please meet…?"

"Olu." Jiminy spoke the first name that sprang to mind.

"Master Olu," Neever greeted, with an open smile.

He shook the man's hand warily. Callouses – rough as a scouring stone – gripped him as gently as a morning moonbud.

Oh, yes, he thought, forcing a smile. *Definitely dangerous.*

"Brother Neever will be accompanying you on the remainder of your journey," the exarch informed him.

If this was news to Neever, the man gave no sign.

The monastery master winked. "I'm sure the two of you will get along just swimmingly."

He grimaced, hoping that was a hint at more river travel ahead. Not a sly reference to him being in over his head.

The soles of his feet itched, suggesting he make a run for it. He overrode them. He'd wait to see what the priests had up their sleeves, first. He very much suspected they had need of a thief. And, while he couldn't imagine what a bunch of holy men might want stolen, it promised to be sinfully expensive.

"Swimmingly," he agreed, not taking his eyes off Neever.

If *this* man had just come from choir practice, it was a choir he'd not care to meet on a moonless night.

"Master Olu," the exarch said, reaching for the bell again, "why not take this opportunity to rest up? Joss will show you to a room and bring you whatever you need. You can set out at first light."

Ignoring the hairs stirring on his nape, he left them to conspire.

Once a nice, solid door stood between him and Neever, he draped an arm around Joss's shoulders.

"You wouldn't know which room my friend, Inrito, is in?" he drawled. "I'd hate to leave without a proper goodbye…"

SOMETIME LATER, THE exarch watched the door close behind Neever, having finally completed instructing the chorister monk.

Dangerous times, when those of the faith were forced to sneak around, dealing behind closed doors. He levered himself from his seat. Although autumn was still weeks off, a small fire flickered in the hearth, blunting the office's chill. He stirred it to life with the poker, watching the flames and letting his thoughts wander.

This 'Olu' – obviously an alias – was sharp. The youth had pegged Neever as more-than-a-monk immediately and, what's more, hadn't been intimidated. Now, if only the boy's burgling skills were as impressive, he might indeed be the one they needed.

He unfurled the little scroll again. Hidden among the mundane salutations and scribblings concerning sanctuary was a cipher.

Thief candidate. Test.

Neever would take care of that part.

He fed the scroll to the fire, watching until it had crisped away.

This shadow recruitment business went against the grain. Had things always been this bad? Had he just been too naïve to see it, in his youth? Grimacing, he dusted his hands and made for his desk.

Writing implements lay ready and he touched flame to a taper to begin heating wax for a seal. Neever would need a letter of introduction. Setting quill to parchment, he tucked the true message away as he went.

Deliver to Father.

The top drawer of his gargantuan desk was the only one that locked. Leaving its small key around his neck, he popped the bottom drawer instead, twisting at its nob. The face board came off in his hand and, without it, he rammed the drawer a bit deeper into the desk than it should be able to go. A catch released, its click muted by the thick oak. When he drew the drawer out again the flat box, that had detached from the tray above, lay in it.

Inside was a seal, cushioned on a bed of velvet, identical to his official seal in every respect. Save that it sported an imperfection, too small to see unless you were looking – a crosshatch on the milling around the edge. Easily explained by minor damage or miscasting. A clear sign, for any modernist with the sense to see.

Ignoring the way the molten wax spread like blood, he pressed his seal to it. Helia send they were doing the right thing.

"Joss!" the mews master greeted, blinking from behind giant spectacles. The carrier pigeon, cradled between the man's fingerless gloves, craned its head toward Joss as well.

Morning mist couldn't reach them this high up in the Temple, despite the glassless arches. But its bite was fierce nonetheless.

"I brought you tea," Joss said, hefting the steaming pot.

"Goddess bless you, boy. Here, sit, sit!"

The hunched figure flustered about, clearing space among the crates and cages, scattering dust and dry bird droppings.

"Some oatcakes too," Joss added, knowing how the man prized the crumbs for his favored birds.

The provender came from the breakfast table, where Joss had sidled up to the acolyte, Inrito. An odious fellow. But informative. The fool had been fresh from a fruitless meeting with the exarch – complaining of the criminal loss of his eyebrows. Some miscreant had shaved them off while the man slept.

"Wonderful!" the mews master clucked after the oatcakes.

"Quiet morning?" he inquired, looking out the aviary window. On the ground below, two sets of footprints marred the frost – Neever, and the unnamed sanctuary seeker.

"I could wish," the old caretaker scoffed. "The exarch had me sending off a dozen urgent birds before sunrise."

"Oh?" he inquired lightly, pouring tea. "Whereabouts?"

"Ah, all over, as usual. Sutlam, Marvellack Post, Tellar…"

He nodded along, stirring honey into the man's tea for him.

"I suppose," the master said, receiving his cup, "you're here to send your next move to your mystery sidestep partner?"

He nodded. "I think I may actually win a game, for once."

"Huh," the older man narrowed owlish eyes at him. "In my day, if you wanted to woe a woman, you didn't challenge her to a game of sidestep. And if you did, you made damn sure to sit across the board from her. All this move and counter-move by post…"

"It serves to keep temptation at arm's length," he shrugged.

"Pah!" the master scoffed. "You're an acolyte yet, young Joss. You've no vows to break. No one would fault you."

The harmless fool was, of course, wrong in all his assumptions. This was no simple game of sidestep. The ones waiting for this intelligence were bent on much more than romance. And the vows he'd sworn to them superseded all oaths that had come before.

"*I* would fault me," Joss said.

Hearing the honesty in his voice, the mews master sighed.

"Let's have it then…"

He handed over the onion skin scroll, scrawled across with cramped figures. It would, at first glance, appear to be no more than a flowery instruction for the next move in a friendly game.

He glanced again at the tracks below, trailing off into the mist.

Pawns rarely thought any game 'friendly'.

* * *

ONCE, JIMINY SUPPOSED, it may have been a prosperous inn. But the warped floorboards were pulling away from their frames and foul flotsam clogged the corners. Badly smoking lanterns cast feeble light on the faded walls and the whole place stank of failure.

Going by the proprietor's disbelief, when Neever had ordered them each a meal, he doubted travelers normally ate here.

Disgusted, he unearthed a bone from his bowl and chucked it at a passing rat. Far from fleeing, the rodent scurried over and dragged the morsel off into the gloom.

Bile rising in his throat, he pushed his plate away.

"Something the matter?" Neever asked companionably.

"Are you serious?" He stabbed a finger at the bristly meat in his bowl. "I've seen sparser beards on caravan captains."

Smiling indulgently, the monk took another mouthful.

He swallowed back his own hairy repast as it fought to escape.

"I've been served better food in gaol," he griped, glancing about the decrepit common room. "Better accommodation, too."

The soft-spoken monk shrugged. "We'll be glad of full bellies, and a dry floor to sleep on, when the rain arrives tonight."

"So will the fleas," he said, eyeing the rotten rushes beneath their feet and absently scratching at an ankle.

Neever chuckled as though at a joke.

For all that his every instinct screamed at him that the monk was dangerous, he'd yet to see a smidgen of proof. Neever never so much as raised his voice. A statue would be less serene.

Which was, perhaps, why he'd been doing his damnedest to put a crack in the monk's long-suffering mask.

"You seem at home in this hovel," he prodded. "And with these backroads, too. Have you spent time locked up yourself?"

He doubted it. But people were more inclined to rectify wrong assumptions, rather than confirm correct ones.

Apart from turning morose, the monk gave no sign of offense.

"We are all prisoners of our own natures. Some more so than others. You yourself seem so capable, Master Olu, I'm surprised at this admission that you've seen the inside of cell...?"

"None ever held me long," he jumped to defend his reputation. "Besides, getting nabbed doesn't count if it's part of the plan-"

Sand swallow him whole! He'd fallen for it again.

He snapped his jaws shut.

The monk was uncanny – a master at turning probing question back upon the questioner. He'd lost a wealth of information before he'd gotten wise to the trick. Nothing crucial – thank his stars – but he'd yet to learn a single salient detail of Neever's life.

When it became apparent Jiminy wouldn't continue, the monk turned back to his meal without complaint.

Well, poor fare though it was, at least he wasn't paying for it. The roughest roughnecks kowtowed when they saw Neever's robes coming. And Jiminy was getting a guided tour of the empire. Or, at least, of its pockmarked backside.

These two-and-a-half reasons were not *quite* strong enough to keep him stuck to Neever's side. But, for now, he was intrigued.

"What crime were you falsely accused of?" the monk asked.

He recognized his own tactic – the false assumption – being turned back on him and smiled.

Drowning some bastard in a bowl of hairy broth...

"Whereto, tomorrow?" he said instead, ignoring the question.

"Marvellack Post," Neever supplied. "It's a sizable town, with a Temple where we will be welcome."

Good. He'd sleep in the Oaragh sewers again, with blackeyes scouring the streets up top, before he spent another night in such a rat hole as this.

"And after that?" he wheedled.

As yet, their final destination was known only to Neever.

"We'll follow the western road."

"Follow the western road *where*?"

"West, of course."

He gave up. Neever was a vault he hadn't the picks to penetrate.

"Best we turn in," the man mused, as the proprietor went around, dousing lanterns. "We've another early day tomorrow."

"I won't sleep a wink," he predicted dismally, reaching for his blankets and longing for the hammock he'd left on the Isus Spear.

He lay awake until the rain came. The memory of waves eventually lulled him into a doze.

True to his word, Neever roused them at dawn.

Tired and footsore though he was, he was happy to see the back of the horrid hostel. Late morning found them wending along a rutted road, their feet caked in red clay. Midday brought a brief respite of cold sausage and hard bread. They crested the hill, on which sat Marvellack Post, as the sun touched the western horizon.

It was a walled town, built entirely of rust-colored bricks. A few of the newer buildings were plaster and thatch, but most were baked clay, roofed in blackened lead. The gate was a sturdy affair, flanked by uniformed guards lazily nodding travelers through.

Jiminy had left the bulk of his crimes beyond the Barrier Range but sight of the greycapes still put him on edge. There had been that scuffle in Genla, after all. And magistrates were notoriously difficult to convince – on the point of pre-emptive self-defense.

He stayed by Neever's shoulder, trusting in the monk's robe to dash any undue attention. The temptation to tug his hood forward was strong. He resisted. Nothing attracted a guard's gaze like someone trying to hide.

They passed without challenge and he breathed easier once they'd cleared the gatehouse's long shadow.

A distant bell drew his attention. "Is that your temple?"

"It is," Neever assured.

They seemed to be walking in the opposite direction.

"And we're going…?"

"It's the Day of the Meek," the man explained, pointing with his staff. "Nothing but oats for dinner, that way. After last night's disappointment, I thought I'd treat you to a real meal."

Jiminy perked up. "Damn straight!"

"You'll be pleased to know," the monk said, "that the tavern in question is famous throughout the prefecture for its mutton pie."

"Hmm," he murmured happily. "As long as it doesn't look like it crawled into my bowl to die, I'm not fussy."

Neever, apparently, wasn't immune to the prospect of a good meal either. The man seemed unusually chatty, pointing out landmarks and sharing snippets of local history.

Jiminy *ooh*-ed and *aah*-ed in all the right places but otherwise reserved his attention for more important things. The lead roofing, for instance. Would it hold his weight? Was it more or less slick than ceramic? Would the red brick offer decent handholds or, alternatively, would the mortar hold climbing pegs?

This was the first place since Genla that looked worth robbing.

"During the settlement wars," Neever was saying, "the river was diverted to run through the fort. That left the old mill high and dry – quite literally. It's a tavern today but this bridge and that water wheel – see there? – survived."

Beneath its Heli sign, someone had scrawled, 'The Old Mill'.

"And that?" he asked, looking past it.

Neever answered without turning to see where he pointed – a shining manse, built of much grander stone than its surrounds.

"The governor's mansion," the monk supplied. "Marvellack Post hasn't been a border town in ages. Once the generals pushed the front south, the governors moved their households down here."

Shading his eyes, Jiminy cast them toward the distant fort – a red-bricked kiln, squatting atop the hill and slowly shouldering in front of the low sun.

"We haven't seen anything but underbrush all day," he recalled. "Who were you fighting, out here in the middle of nowhere?"

The door to the Old Mill stood open, wafting music, laughter and the merry clunk of crockery. Neever motioned him through.

"The tribes." The monk's smile was sad. "To the east lies the Great Grasslands, traditional hunting grounds of the Neril. This hilltop stronghold was proof against their pony circles."

Once over the threshold, the scent of braised lamb and rich gravy scattered all thoughts of thievery. Neever led them to a table in the corner, where the monk leaned his walking stick out of the way and shrugged out of his heavy pack.

To one side, a zither player was picking out a jaunty tune and brightly smiling barmaids sped between the tables.

"Bitter and bah?" one asked, halting at theirs.

"Times two," Neever said, apparently understanding.

"Excellent!" she commended, caroming off again.

The place was homey and he fought hard not to relax outright.

Drinks arrived with commendable speed.

"Ah, fresh from the Temple brewery," the monk attested, raising the red-glazed pottery pitcher.

"Your temple brews beer?"

It seemed somehow sacrilegious.

"Ale," Neever corrected. "Hereabouts, wheat springs up like weeds, the woods are overgrown with gruit and the river is rotten with isinglass. If *that* is not divine providence, I'm not a monk."

At Neever's urging, he took a tentative sip. Then a surer one.

"It's good," he granted reluctantly. Lucky for him, the bottom of his pitcher blocked out Neever's smug smile.

"What's 'isinglass'?" he belched, setting half his drink down.

"Dried swim bladders," the monk said. "Added for clarity."

He paused in the act of stretching his legs.

"Swim bladders?" he stared. "As in… fish?"

The monk nodded happily.

He peered into his pitcher. "There's fish in this beer?"

Neever nodded again.

"Sear my tattered soul," he marveled at last, taking another sip.

"Bah and bah, by the by," the barmaid announced, depositing two steaming crocks of whole pies.

"Salt and silver!" he said, seeing the size of it.

"Dig in."

He didn't need telling twice. He'd inhaled fully half the scrumptious serving before he came up for air.

"Yours is a strange god, Neever," he said, eyeing the last of his ale. "What was the commandment, here? 'Let there be beer?'"

The deserts didn't have religion, as such. Oh, there were gods aplenty – none of them particularly divine. And fools enough to form cults by the dozen. But, in his experience, a man was better off avoiding the attention of spirits. Even the supposedly sacred ones ended up demanding sacrifice. And he was passing fond of his testicles and pinky toes and whatever else a god might prize.

"Is it so inconceivable," the monk asked earnestly, "that the goddess wants you to be happy? To live a good life, work hard, and enjoy the fruits of your labor?"

"And conquer the odd continent?" he prodded.

Only the Dry Sea had kept the empire out of Purlia. If imperial shipwrights could have figured out how to make warships sail over sand, the deserts would have been colonized long since. Oaragh herself had been razed and rebuilt twice, by the *falahd*'s own hand. 'Scorched earth' suited the desert's defenses down to the ground.

"That," Neever demurred, "might have less to do with Helia's will and more with her followers' fervor."

Jiminy decided he'd pushed the man enough for one night.

"I don't buy the ideology," he said, downing his dregs, "but this fish beer has come closer to converting me than anything before."

Neever gave him a pleased grin.

A whiff of scented oil announced someone at his shoulder.

"May I join you?"

"By all means," Neever said, with characteristic unconcern.

Jiminy watched as the man pulled up a chair, noting the well-cut clothes and shiny boots. If there wasn't a knife, hidden in one of those, he'd eat the man's doffed cap.

"Olu, this is Breese," Neever introduced. "Breese, Olu."

"Charmed," the newcomer said, flashing a cat's grin.

He looked from one to the other.

"A pimp?" he guessed. The man was slick enough. But the barmaid, whom Breese accosted for a beer, didn't recoil. He'd trust a woman's instinct – for sniffing out men who abused women – ahead of his own.

"I'm mortified," Breese mock-clutched at his breast. "If that's the image I project, my tailor is in for a stern talking-to."

His appetite fled, Jiminy pushed back in his seat, crossing his arms – it put his hands that much closer to his hilts. This Breese was obviously from the city's underbelly. That the man was on a first name basis with the mild-as-milk monk gave him pause.

"How do you two know each other, then?"

The two men were forcing a familiar, convivial air on the table. Jiminy wasn't fooled. Glass edges lurked in the soft clay of the conversation. He would feel his way forward carefully. Until he knew whether they were turning a coin pot or a funerary urn.

"Breese is a purveyor, of sorts," Neever said. "He aids the Temple in acquiring goods – when a kind word and a helping hand are not enough to satisfy the seller."

A fence, maybe? He eyed the man skeptically.

"And what type of 'aid' does he provide?"

They held each other's eyes as Breese's beer arrived.

"Less kind words," the man toasted him. "Unhelpful hands."

Ah, not just a smuggler, then, but a clan head of some sort.

He looked to Neever. "Down to business, at last?"

The monk inclined his head.

"'Sanctuary', my ass," he pitched his voice low, sitting forward. "Then let's get this straight. You want me to steal something? Fine. I figured as much. But I don't need your reasons. Keep your secrets, since you'll only end up wanting them back.

"That said," he growled, "you lay out the *whole* job – not a jot less – and *I*'ll decide whether you get my help or not."

A barge ride and a decent beer wasn't worth a prison stint.

He met Breese's eye. "And 'unhelpful hands' be damned."

The clan head winked, eyes flat.

Neever regarded him silently, face unreadable.

For his part, he reviewed the four escape routes he'd singled out before they'd sat down. He could overturn the table on them and be gone in a blink.

"Fair," Neever judged at last, nodding to Breese.

"This inn," the man began without preamble, "backs up to the governor's mansion. There's a cherry tree out back, with a rope and grapnel tucked among the upper branches. That'll get you over the garden wall." Wetting his fingers, the man eked out a floorplan, in ale, on the tabletop. "Guards patrol the grounds and the halls both. You'll want the governor's study, on the second floor, *here*. There's a lockbox behind the desk. That's your target."

"How accurate is your information?" he asked, watching the schematic evaporate and feeling the first hint of a thrill.

"We're fairly confident."

He frowned at 'fairly'. "It seems pretty straight forward."

"Helia forfend," Breese said.

Something scraped across the floorboards. Jiminy looked down.

"I have my own tools," he dismissed the oblong satchel.

"Whatever you have," the man promised, "will be insufficient."

The skin of his back pricked. "Warding magicks?"

"Expensive ones."

"Hang on," he objected, recalling a conversation with the urchin, Gav. "Don't you need a writ or something? I thought the use of magic was strictly controlled in the empire?"

"It is," Neever explained. "But arts that are inherently inert – that do not affect mind, body or spirit – are more readily licensed. There is good money to be made, in the Empire, as a wardsmith."

"On that note…" Breese continued, eyeing them wryly for their interruption. "There's a bell, inside the house, with a clapper that'll swing toward any break in the perimeter. As you may imagine, that makes a noise. The members of the household each wear a scattering crystal. We've provided you one – a small pendant."

The bag beneath the table bumped his foot insistently.

"Fine."

"Then you've got the study door. Only the governor, and the wardsmith who made the lock, have the keys to open it."

He grimaced. Spelled locks were a pain to get around.

"I don't suppose you have the key?" he hoped.

"Then," the man ignored him, "you've got the study itself…"

"Salt and silver, there's more?"

"…a simple sigil, that detects warm breath."

"It triggers another alarm?" he guessed.

"Close. It triggers a killing cold snap."

"Cat scat on a skewer!"

Neever sat forward, frowning at Breese. "You're sure you weren't misled? Even a master streamer would struggle to construct a static working of such power."

"You going to lecture me on killing with crystals, *chorister?*"

Neever rocked as if at a blow, letting Breese continue.

"We're talking entropy – not energy – which is much easier. It simply saps all heat from its surrounds. Including whoever happens to be inside its influence at the time. And, before you ask, it *has* the capacity. The governor paid a fortune for his crystal chandelier. I'm told it clashes horribly with the furnishings."

Jiminy looked from one man to the other. He hadn't understood – or cared – for much beyond 'killing cold snap'.

"Not to worry," Breese grinned. "There's a phial in there – looks like salt. Pour it on your tongue. It'll mask your breath."

I should be gone by now. This chair should be empty…

"And your lockbox?" he pressed.

"Is a different kettle of fish," Breese said sourly. "For all its small size, it weighs several stone, so you'll not be sneaking it out under your arm. Also, the governor opted for, shall we say, 'alternative' safeguards in this respect?"

Neever sat up straight. "Witchery?"

Breese nodded. "If any but the governor try to open it, the contents… I want to say incinerate? It's notoriously difficult to get a straight answer from these pagan practitioners."

Neever's eyes narrowed. "You tracked down the witch?"

Ignoring the monk, Breese turned to Jiminy. "We've given you a small, drawstring bag. Encircle the box, and yourself, with the contents and light it. While it burns, the box will think you're the governor. Relock it before the hair line fizzles out."

"Hair line?"

"Exactly what it sounds like. We paid a wax witch-"

Neever shifted uncomfortably.

"-a very *minor* wax which," Breese soothed, "to prepare it from the governor's own hair. And don't ask me how we got the hair."

The two men settled back, watching him expectantly.

"Oh, I wasn't going to ask *that*," he assured. "I was going to ask, 'What's the punchline?' Because this is obviously a joke. Just when were you planning to kick off this fool's errand?"

He'd half suspected, but their faces confirmed it.

"Tonight?" he scoffed. "This is hilarious…"

"Too hard for you?" Breese baited.

He glared at the man. "Too hard for anyone *but* me. Honestly, how did you dimwits think you were going to find someone to do this? A lesser thief wouldn't have a prayer."

It was true. Even as he said it, he felt the treacherous excitement – of a caper begun – close on him like a vice.

"Prayer has brought us you, Master Olu," Neever said solemnly.

"Well, I will need more than prayer. I'll need paying."

It was a last ditch effort, a way for him to justify walking away, if they refused. Apparently, he wasn't so lucky.

"You're up to it then?" Breese challenged.

He sat back, studying the tabletop, going over everything he'd heard. This was a foolhardy plan, its execution premature, its outfitters unproven. And yet… he was rearing to go. It had been more than a season since he'd heeded his true calling.

Sun bleach my bones, I'm such an easy sell…

"Yes," he answered, scowling severely.

Neever nodded, as though he'd expected nothing less.

"Then you'll need one more thing…" Breese announced.

A short while later, after some intensive haggling and eventual handshakes, he stood under the Old Mill's cherry tree.

In his hand, he held a paper wrapper, a poison lozenge inside.

'*In case you're captured,*' Breese had said.

He flung the thing into a piss-reeking corner of the yard. He didn't care that the governor was an unhinged sadist, or that torture devices hid in the man's basement. He wasn't about to get caught.

He rubbed a thumb over the pendant that would hide him – a little jade teardrop on a leather thong. His ring said it was doing *something*. Slipping it on made him feel no different.

He turned his attention to the tree, eyeing it for handholds.

* * *

SOMETHING, HIDDEN IN the darkened brush, scurried near Inrito.

Squealing, he stepped on the end of his robe and sat down hard. The dust of the road reared up around him, pale in the moonlight.

He was at his nerves' end. His palms were gouged by gravel, his knees scuffed, and his soft shoes worn through by stones. In a fit of temper, he fought to free himself from his flopping hood.

All of this was that desert ruffian's fault!

He'd been living an exemplary life, at his Temple. None could have faulted his strict adherence to scripture, or his diligence in pointing out when his fellows failed to be as holy as he.

And yet, had he received any thanks?

No, he'd had the honor of babysitting that heathen reprobate.

Shooting to his feet, he dusted himself vigorously and tugged his torn robes into some semblance of respectability.

The hostelry he'd passed that morning had flat-out refused to provide him a mount. Even after he'd taken pains to explain to the mulish proprietor that she should be honored to aid one of Helia's anointed. That priests were due certain fundamental... generosities.

It was hard to seem imperious with no eyebrows. And there had been no eastbound wagons to importune into carrying his person.

So, instead, he'd been reduced to sullying his hands with coin.

The donkey he'd hired – at an exorbitant price – had thrown him, halfway between nowhere and not-anywhere-yet.

He'd wasted a good bell or more, chasing after it, back the way he'd come. Every score paces, it would turn to consider him, long ears perked toward his pleas and bribes. Each time, as he shuffled to almost within reach of the reins, it would take off at a stiff-legged trot again. He'd finally snapped and taken to flinging stones and insults at it.

'Equine error in judgment! Dark places take you!'

He'd now been walking since noon.

He sustained himself with thoughts of how his travails would serve to inspire others. Step by wearied step, yes! Footsore but unflagging in his faith. Limping yet unbroken! Like storied Mlachai, trekking barefoot across the spine of the mountains-

-he stubbed a toe.

"Ack! Pox, pestilence and perdition!" he spouted, hobbling.

He was thirsty and weary onto death. The dark landscape hemmed him from all sides. In hindsight, even the barge people and their godless exuberance would have been preferable.

Nothing good came of being outdoors, in his experience. The mysteries of the natural world were kept *inside*, between the covers of books. If those authors had spent their time, traipsing around the wilderness, how would they have gotten any work done?

No, no, no. He needed to wash all this nature off him. Once he got to civilization, he would rouse someone to fill him a tub.

Sweat stung the sunburn where his eyebrows used to be and he probed gingerly at the stubble. He couldn't believe the exarch had refused to have that miscreant fetched back and flogged. No matter that he hadn't actually *seen* who had stolen his celebrated brows – who else but that infidel would dare?

Why, if he'd gotten his hands on the fiend he'd have-

Something skittered through the bushes by his side.

He shrieked, trying to scoop stones as he staggered away. But the missiles were all unhelpfully embedded in the road's surface.

When a dozen haggard breaths had passed with no threat or further noise forthcoming, he hurried on his way.

He walked a little faster now, glancing frequently over his shoulder and praying to see village lights around the next bend. Goddess grant he didn't have to spend the night out here, alone.

The positive point, he soothed himself, was that there were no witnesses to see him fumbling and falling around in the dark-

With a gulp, he stumbled to a halt. He'd been peering behind him and hadn't noticed the person appear ahead of him.

A long, dark cloak and cowl, a little ragged around the edges.

A beggar? A hermit, perhaps. His heart leapt. A villager!

The person stood curiously still, their back to him, the hood tilted up to regard the engorged moon.

Silently, he righted his robes and ran his hands through his hair.

First impressions were important.

"I say," he called, in his best pulpit voice, "are you lost, my child? Might I offer some divine guidance?"

The villager showed no sign of having heard.

He tramped closer. "It is fortunate for you to have met me. The dark is no place for a lay person to be, without Temple protection."

Not so much as a twitch – a deaf mute, maybe?

He laid a hand on the cloaked shoulder. "Sorry to startle you-"

The figure whirled.

Inrito found himself rising from the road, his toes scrabbling at the gravel and his throat caught in a merciless grip.

"'Guidance'?" a sibilant voice hissed. "Yesss…"

"-ng!" Inrito managed, flailing at the arm that held him.

Its sleeve slid back to reveal pale, puckered flesh, blackened in places by blood rot. From beneath that cowl, a smile of sharpened teeth gleamed, gray in the dark.

Witchcraft! Inrito quailed. *Necromancy!*

"We can sssmell it on you," the apparition said. "Where isss it?"

Through clenched teeth, Inrito gibbered a prayer of protection.

"Priest," the smile widened, fissuring dry lips. "You amuse us."

A hand rose, its fingertips discolored and tipped by talons that were ridged and curled like rams' horns. One hooked through the hole in Inrito's circle sign, snapping the sacred pendant free.

"Your meddling goddesss," the thing hissed, "cannot intercede. Her rebel legacy wanesss. She is long passst aiding any of you."

In the apparition's grip, the mark of unity wilted. The wood warped and rotted, flaking to nothing in a pall of noxious fumes.

"Now," it said, raising that deadly nail toward Inrito's face. "You will tell usss. We know it travelsss west. We can feel it-"

Abruptly freed, Inrito sprawled in the road, gasping for breath.

"No!" the apparition seethed above him, its attention directed westward. "It isss being hidden! It ssslips through our sssenses!"

Beyond petrified, his legs unresponsive, Inrito fled on his stomach. Broken benedictions tumbled from him as he went.

He made it maybe six paces before several sharp points pinned him to the ground. The necromantic presence bent over him, breathing putrid words in his ear.

"You will tell usss…" it promised him.

His screams carried long into the night, unheard by any.

* * *

JIMINY PERCHED ATOP the wall, watching the guard pace away into the gloom of the governor's garden. The jade pendant snuggled securely beneath his wraps. Through his mask, he sniffed at his shoulder – the vinegar-and-iris-root stink had washed all the way out, leaving his leper's rags a respectable almost-black.

He recalled Neever's gratified look, when the man had thought he was taking a turn at cooking – and the man's expression when looking into the pot of dye.

Smiling, he slipped soundlessly down among the shrubbery.

The night clung to him, comfortable as an old shirt, while he sailed along the decorative hedges and artful sundials.

The rush of a fresh escapade was upon him and his ribs strained to contain his rollicking heart. The fever elevated him, shunting his thoughts into the grooves of a higher instinct. He drank the dark through his very pores, until he could feel distant footsteps through his soles and see guards hidden in subtle shadows.

The gust of exhilaration carried him, like a windblown leaf, over the veranda railing and into the household proper.

Re-couching his picks, he eased the doors shut at his back.

No sorcerous bell clanged.

An uncontrolled grin overtook him. Oh, how he'd missed this!

The moon was up, the entry hall webbed with shadows. He spun along their filaments, quick feet seeking soft carpet and letting tile and hardwood lie silent.

The floorplan was proving accurate.

He stalled in a small seating area beneath the central stairs. Above him, on a switchback halfway between the first and second floors, a guard rode a spindly chair. The man had an unobstructed view of anyone coming up or down the steps.

Jiminy could easily climb the banister behind the man and choke him out. The nearby sideboard sported a decanter of amber spirits. No one believed a guard – who reeked of booze – when he claimed he'd been knocked out as opposed to passed out.

He dismissed the idea out of hand. That was a tactic for rank burglars and he'd long since graduated to the golden standard of sneak thief. He left behind no broken windows, muddy footprints or tossed drawers. His was a light touch that left little to no trace.

Besides, the guard was a big bastard and might not go quietly.

He swam the shadows behind the free-standing stairs, thinking.

This was what came of not doing one's own reconnaissance. If there were alternate routes to the study, he didn't know them.

As he watched the bored guard balance precariously on the little chair's hind legs, inspiration struck.

Grabbing up a bronze figurine, he flowed up the balustrade. Threading his arm carefully through the spokes, he swung.

The crack of the chair leg, giving way, covered any sound of his descent. The guard cursed, sprawling amid fragments of furniture.

Jiminy held back his hilarity with a hand.

"Hush, idiot!" a voice hissed from the second floor landing. "Are you trying to wake the whole house?"

"S'not my fault!" said an incensed whisper. "Chair broke!"

"Mother's minge – were you riding that thing again?!"

"Was not!"

"Bull squirt! Clean that crap up, and hope to Helia you haven't woken his honor – else you'll have more than docked pay to worry your ass over!"

The upstairs footsteps retreated in a huff.

Gathering up what sounded like kindling, the guard grumbled. "…won't wake for less than a stampede through the solar…"

Grin threatening to burst his cheeks, Jiminy let the man stomp off with his erstwhile seat. Then he leapt the balustrade and sped into the dark hallways of the second floor.

He slipped into the roving guard's wake, following the man on his rounds, ghosting from one pool of deep shadow to the next.

As the study neared, the guard ahead stilled, gasping quietly.

Jiminy disappeared into a doorway, grasping his knives.

Oblivious, the guard stifled the rest of the yawn and padded on.

Heart hammering at his ribs, Jiminy moved too. The far corners of his grin tugged higher beneath his wraps. Who would ever give *this* up for a sailor's life, eating pickles and trawling lines?

He crouched against the study door, easily identifiable by its ornate plate, engraved with mystic symbols. Gold was a lousy material for lock-making. Even more so for keys. But wardsmithing required that the two be smelted from the same ingot. Alloyed for strength, but pure enough to retain a spell.

The lever lock itself was simple to pick. The problem was the ward post, held in a completely isolated pocket of the mechanism, where tools couldn't reach. It would turn only for the matched key, like metal filings toward a lodestone.

There were ways around that. But none as simple as this…

From his own set of tools, he drew a saw, thin as a whisker and only a finger long. He passed the supple blade between the double doors. Teeth, fine as a cricket's legs and hardened by highest alchemy, chirped faintly as they chewed through the golden bolt.

It was one of the crowning jewels in his kit – which was, coincidentally, what it had cost him. But it was worth every whit.

The heat of friction competed with the soft bloom on his ring finger as the mechanism broke down, bleeding magic.

He pushed the study doors open onto a richly furnished room, glossy with padded leather and polished wood. Books lined the walls and a chandelier glittered balefully from the ceiling.

If Breese told it true, the thing dripped with death magic.

Experimentally, he passed his hand along the threshold... and felt a confirming tingle from his ring.

Parting his mask, he drew out the phial of pale crystals. Much as he hated to rely on the preparations of others, he fought off his grin long enough to pour the mixture beneath his tongue.

He choked on the thought of the guard finding a poisoned thief in the hallway. Then he choked in earnest.

On contact with his moisture, the salt crystals dissolved into vapor that blazed along his airways.

Frost puffed past his lips.

Blinking, he watched his breath plume in the balmy air. He blew a streamer into the study, watching the chandelier. Nothing.

Fine then.

The cabinet behind the desk called to him with the same irresistible pull that wheeled the stars in their arcs. But he delayed, rolling the carpet up against the doorjamb where it would block any light that might otherwise slip beneath the portal.

The strongbox was where Breese had said. A square, serious construction. His ring flamed as he trailed a finger over the enameled surface. With a grunt, he carried it to the room's center.

A grimace wrestled with his grin as he drew out the drawstring bag of hair mulch. He sketched a tight circle with it, on the bare boards, around himself and the strongbox. The stubbled powder looked oily and smelled of herbs and raw bone marrow. He made certain not to let it touch his skin.

Taking up the fire tongs, he borrowed an ember from the banked hearth and went to squat inside the circle.

Deep breath...

The hair concoction smoldered sullenly, then caught with a hiss, a coal-red glow racing around him. Holding his breath against the rank smoke, he set to with his picks.

The strongbox sported a mundane, three-pin tumbler lock that surrendered quickly to his ministrations. He whipped the lid open.

Huh...

After all the safeguards and security, he'd expected to discover the *falahdin*'s maidenhood – rendered in gold, studded with jewels, swathed in silk and dusted in cinnamon. But the box's sides were a handspan thick, the shoe-sized compartment stuffed to overflowing... with vellum.

Letters, he marveled.

No wonder Breese and Neever had been unconcerned about him skimming off the top of the trove.

The hair line began to sputter.

Salt and silver! This was no time to be caught staring!

Grabbing up the loot, he saw something glittering beneath – a small, engraved comb. Snatching it, he relocked the lid.

Not a moment too soon.

The spell circle guttered out, leaving scorch marks the rug would cover. The fumes began to clear.

Whew!

He didn't take any time to study his find. He had to right the room and make his escape before the chandelier caught on to him.

Despite everything that still stood between him and escape, he felt uplifted – his soul a banner in the high winds of success.

Shivering sands, when last have I felt so free?

"HOW DID IT GO?" Neever asked, sitting in the small cemetery.

The young thief, Olu, materialized from amid the stone effigies.

"Have you been sitting here in the dark, repeating that to the dead, and hoping to make me think you heard me coming?"

Neever grunted a laugh. He had, in fact, been forewarned of the young man's approach. The Temple steeple, at his back, provided a high vantage. Breese was up there, along with a powerful long-lens, surveilling the governor's mansion.

Up until a moment ago, Neever had been up there too.

'He's out,' Breese had said, peering through the spyglass. *'You'd better go and get ready to meet him.'*

'And?' he'd queried, getting to his feet. *'Is he any good?'*

Breese had answered with rare fervor. *'Thank Helia the boy's a burglar – he'd have been the unholy terror of assassins. Even knowing where to look, I caught only glimpses. He's a ghost.'*

He now turned toward the young thief. "Success, I take it?"

"What d'you want these for, anyway?" the boy scorned, slapping a sheaf of tightly tied letters into his hand.

"Knowledge is power," he said. Nestled in his palm was a trove of privileged communications, describing a vast political network. With this, and a bit of luck, they will have defanged several purist plots. "Power can be stolen, like everything else."

He eyed the boy sternly.

"Speaking of everything else…" He beckoned.

Sighing, the thief produced a decorative hair comb.

He made sure to hide his surprise, turning the tortoiseshell piece over between his fingers. So. Breese had been right.

"Your turn," the thief announced. "Pay up."

He pulled himself from his disturbing thoughts, secreting the prizes in his various pockets. He deliberately met the thief's gaze.

"Your purse is waiting," he promised. "In Tellar."

Olu tensed, eyes hunting among the gravestones for an ambush.

"That," the young man gritted, "was not the deal."

"Hear me out…" He reached into his robes.

Gaze sharpening, the thief rose subtly into a fighting stance.

"Relax," Neever implored, drawing out a scroll. "This is a letter of credit, for a coin house in the capital. It is worth twice what we agreed. All you need to do is go there and collect."

"Why? I've done what you wanted. Why add strings now?"

"Think of tonight," he explained, "as an audition."

Realization lit the thief's eyes. "The real job is in Tellar."

Though it wasn't a question, he nodded anyway.

"So this business with the governor and the poison was all… what? A tall tale? There's no torture chamber in the basement?"

"The man does not even own a riding crop," Neever lied, though it left a sour taste in his mouth. If this Olu was half as good as Breese said, they were in desperate need of his skills.

"You've got some nerve," the boy growled, fists balling.

"So do you," he complimented. "And now, we know that."

Olu eyed the scroll suspiciously. "What's to stop me cutting ties with you and cashing that in my own good time?"

There had been just a slight hesitation before 'ties' where 'your throat' would have fit.

"Nothing," he solemnly promised. "It is yours."

When Olu still made no move to accept the rolled parchment, he set it down on a nearby headstone and backed away.

The boy padded over, panning a hand over the credit letter like it might bite. Snatching it up, the thief turned his back, stalking toward the street.

"But," Neever enticed, careful to keep an even tone, "wouldn't you rather earn *that* ten times over?"

Feet stalled. The thief turned to scowl over a shoulder.

"What could possibly be worth ten times *this*?"

Neever smiled.

Chapter 13 – Out of Sight

Pella Monop, Journal entry #144

Damn these stress headaches! I have been at an impasse for weeks, blindly trying to bridge the clerical gap left in the wake of the Quarin schism. So many works were lost to fire and riot. Surviving records are sparse. The majority are here, at the Mother Temple. Some vandal has scribbled in several of them. I recognize the handwriting – my predecessor, Dayna Bruen. Have I reached the selfsame pitfall that ruined her? I made a morbid joke of this to Cecine, who informed me that my old rival never set foot in the elder archives. A peculiar thing to lie about…

A SEA OF red surrounded Marco. It dripped from the riven ceiling, ran down the cracked walls and pooled on the cavern floor. Despite its vital glow, it illuminated little.

It's just a dream, he desperately told himself.

The knowledge seeped away, leaving him in terror's grip.

A tremor rocked the place, straining tortured stone.

Somewhere below, something was trying to batter its way free.

Without meaning to, he waded among the debris, following the flow of the luminescence down the spiral stairs.

Sounds of savagery clangored up. Animal roars and snarls, rolling amid the bark of chains and the crack of stone.

He stumbled his way down as the unseen struggle shook the staircase. Silence entered the chamber alongside him.

The red slick circled a low platform, itself rearing with massive pillars, its surface hatch-marked and claw-scored. Great chains encircled the uprights, trailing into the murk at their center.

One of the hanging links twitched.

He peered, padding closer.

Coppery orbs turned toward him, pinning him in his tracks.

The force of attention was such, he found himself flattened against the wall, where a door had been but a moment before.

With a drumming growl, those burnished eyes rose, looming up into the dark. Metal slithered, gathering.

His mouth was beyond dry. "I-"

There was a flash of gleaming teeth. A sense of motion. And then chaos snapped taut at the end of its tether, right atop him.

He screamed as fangs snapped madly toward his face-

-and bolted upright in bed, clutching at his cheek.

Pain caught up a moment later, piercing through his middle.

"Agh..." he breathed, folding around it.

"Marco!" a muffled voice exclaimed. Father Justin sagged into a bedside seat, jaw clenched in one hand. His mentor spoke around obvious pain. "Apologies. You were having a nightmare."

Bright details began to coalesce. He recognized the room – the keeper's chambers in Keystone Keep. Blearily, he looked back to Justin. The priest's chin was fast reddening toward a bruise.

His own cheek throbbed. They must have knocked heads when he'd sat up so abruptly.

"Father, I'm sor-"

He caught his breath as agony tried to saw through his middle.

"No, no, no," the keeper cautioned, quickly coming to his side. "Stay still. You've been patched up but it is barely holding together. You're nowhere near well enough to toss about."

Together, Justin's hands supporting his neck and back, they eased his way down among the pillows.

"That must have been some nightmare," the keeper commented, probing at the swath of bandages Marco's belly had become.

Knowledge of the dream skittered from his consciousness.

"I don't remember," he wheezed.

"Just as well. You've been through enough as it is."

Memory of the tourney circle came crashing back.

"Norvalis!"

He started up, only to have Justin press down on his shoulders.

"Stay still, I said," the priest scolded. "And *listen*. You've never met Keppin Norvalis. The young lord was found, unconscious in his tent, before your bout even began."

Confusion gathered. "So who was trying to kill me?"

"The real question is, *why* were they trying to kill you?"

Justin gave him a conciliatory smile. "My high opinion of you notwithstanding, there were higher profile targets to hand. The princess, for one, was just a dozen paces-"

"Dailill!" Justin had to wrestle him flat again. "Is she...?"

"Fine," the priest promised. "Shaken. But fine."

Dread, as at a fatal fall narrowly avoided, stole his breath.

"Was it the same assassin?" he worried.

"You fought him," the keeper deferred. "Quite well, by all accounts. What do you think? Was it the same man?"

Marco lay back, frowning at the ceiling.

His view of the intruder, in the Royal Apartments and then along the darkened roof, had been brief at best. He'd had the impression of someone lithe and limber. This latest encounter had been with someone bulked and blunted by tourney armor.

"I'm not sure," he said. "It *could* have been the same person..."

"Whoever it was," the keeper said seriously, "they knew who you were fighting, as well as when and where to replace them. They had an escape route, laid out in advance. And they didn't so much as try for the princess, despite her proximity."

"She was surrounded by a wall of guards," he protested.

"I'm not faulting you for leaving her side," the keeper spoke to his defensiveness. "I'm saying that this attempt was painstakingly planned and executed. And, unless I miss my guess, it was all bent on you."

He blinked. "Me? Why?"

"Perhaps you're in someone's way. Can you think of anyone whose political plans or pagan magicks you've recently foiled?"

The wry tone fell short of concealing Justin's worry.

"I fear I've let you set yourself squarely in an assassin's sights."

He came to the priest's defense. "I put myself here. Until the danger passes, it's where I intend to stay."

"A moot point, until you can move again." Smiling grimly, Justin rose. "I'll fetch you a cold compress. You're recuperating at a remarkable rate but you're still feverish to the touch. And then I want to change that dressing. I've not had reason to use cautery since the war and I've little doubt you've sprung a leak."

Though his bandages had shown no spotting, he could smell his own blood in the air, so he didn't argue.

Which was not to say that guilt wasn't niggling at him.

"Father Justin, I'm sure one of the palace physicians can see to me. Shouldn't you rather be spending your time at the summit?"

Something, in the set of the priest's shoulders, shifted subtly.

"The king has graciously agreed to absent me from the proceedings. For the time being."

Though Marco was no political savant, there was no mistaking the priest's meaning – he'd been barred from attending.

"Why?" he gaped. "Has something-"

"Keeper Justin Wisenpraal…?" a hesitant voice called.

"In here," the priest directed.

A servant in palace livery entered, clutching a vase of flowers to her chest as though it were a tower shield – and insufficient.

"Another posy from the princess," the woman whispered, edging nervously around the priest with eyes downcast.

"Ah, thank you," Justin said, hands clasped as though blind to the woman's palpable fear. "Please, put them anywhere."

Upon seeing Marco, sitting up in bed and blinking at her, the woman blanched. The smell of her sweat surged above that of the flowers and she made a small noise. The posy was plopped, unceremoniously, on a shelf. The servant made her escape, surreptitiously scrawling a Renali sign to ward off evil in the air.

In the wake of her flight, Marco met his mentor's gaze, seeing sadness and resignation there. And more. For the first time, he noticed the bags under the priest's eyes and noted his bandaged hand. The priest's pallor was sallow, his frame stooped and weary.

"You streamed," he realized, "to save me."

When it came to magic, the Renali were stupid superstitious. When it came to *Heli* magic, they were wholeheartedly terrified. The Temple battle choirs had left them a racial scar a league deep.

Justin shrugged. "I'd do it again in a heartbeat."

"But," he argued, "that's no reason to keep you from the bargaining table! Didn't the king already know, anyway?"

They'd done their best to keep the keeper's empathic abilities under wraps. But most Renali would wager good money on any given Heli priest being a streamer.

"His majesty never asked. Quite purposefully, I think. Now, *everyone* knows. The king must be seen to uphold Renali values – and those are dead set against sorcery."

"It's not sorcery!" Marco gushed, scandalized. "It's streaming!"

"I fear the distinction would be lost on the common man. Now, lie still, before you tear your wound. You'll have an ugly scar as it is – but better that, than a pretty headstone. I'll get that compress."

"Father…" he forestalled, but he didn't know what to say.

The keeper met his agonized gaze with an understanding one.

"Never fear, Marco. Helia will light our path. You'll see."

Distracted, he looked past the keeper, toward the outer passage.

"The ambassador is coming," he blurted, recognizing the tread.

Head cocked in that direction, the priest nodded. "I'll head him off then look in on you later. You try to get some rest, alright?"

Eyes lighting with mischief, Justin waggled bushy brows, undamaged fingers wriggling in mock mysticism.

"Sleep..." the priest enticed in eldritch tones, backing out.

Smiling muzzily, Marco put his head down.

Hah! That's not how empaths work at all...

DEFYING JUSTIN'S BEST estimates, Marco was out of bed and onto crutches in under a week. Streaming had not knit his flesh seamlessly and he still had much mending to do. The keeper's concoctions kept infection at bay but the same could not be said for the pain. At times, he felt as though he'd swallowed a weasel, headfirst, and it was trying to chew its way out.

But he'd have happily clambered up the keep's sheer face again if it meant escaping his sickbed. He'd been cornered in it, by Invigilator Reed and that reptile smile. Justin had stepped in before Marco could confess to stabbing himself.

"It's no joke, Nestor. A man is dead."

"Poor Lord Belmuth," Reed had agreed. "A bungler to the end – couldn't even be bothered to trip the assailant with his corpse..."

Dennik had looked in on him a time or two, whenever the guardsman could be certain the keeper wasn't near.

"He's not some pagan necromancer, Dennik!" Marco had finally given voice to his exasperation.

"So you say," the man had maintained. "But I saw you, lying on that tourney pitch. *I'd* have sworn you were dead."

The Renali mistrust of magic ran bone deep, it seemed, and thick as marrow. Especially among the uneducated.

The princess had come by, hands clenched in contrition, afraid to touch him lest she cause him further injury. He hadn't had the words to convince her that his wounding was not her fault.

"If anything," he'd pressed, "*I* am at fault. My slow recovery has forced her highness to risk herself, with no lookout on duty."

Formality had been forced upon them both by the presence of two ladies-in-waiting – newly armed with elegant daggers.

"Well," Dailill had maintained, "your position – and your weapon – are being kept in my trust. Present yourself, once you are hale, and you may reclaim both… if you remain willing?"

Her gaze had held all the guilt and pleading she hadn't put to words. The two ladies had glared, as though he might refuse.

Even so, he'd preferred their presence to that of Luvid, leaning in the background. The re-instated bodyguard's leer had all but stained the wall.

Some good had also come of his wounding.

For one, he enjoyed spending more time with Justin, and tried not to dwell on why the priest had more time to spend with him.

"Forgiveness is key," the keeper was saying, pace sedate in deference to Marco's crutches. Their theology lesson had trekked a wide circle since leaving their apartments.

"The misconstruing of forgiveness as currency, to be earned or refused, turns faith into just another economic system."

Though he grasped the concepts – by his fingernails – it was often a struggle to uphold his end of the argument.

He clutched at scripture. "Hegemon teaches that grain grows only from the sweat of toil. If forgiveness is given freely, and gotten without effort, then doesn't that effectively devalue it?"

Justin smiled, as though he'd said something clever. "Would it surprise you to learn that Hegemon was a bookkeeper, before heeding Helia's call? His writings often attempt to tally totals and balance bills that need no redress. But even he would be forced to agree – nothing which is dearly sought is ever without worth.

"Besides, your basic tenet is flawed. Forgiveness is not a reward. It is a gift. You cannot *earn* a gift. But you may strive to be *worthy* of it. Often, the mere act of offering solace is enough to set a sinner on a path to betterment.

"Or enough to earn a split lip," Justin concluded, gaze turning inward, at a memory that woke a wry smile.

Mulling this over, Marco noticed for the first time that they'd neared the residential wing, where many nobles made their home during the high court season.

Two guards shifted uncomfortably at their approach. Glancing over his shoulder, he saw the pair that had been sauntering nonchalantly after them peel off.

"I'm sorry," he said, of the surveillance as well as the suspicion the hierarch now suffered because of him. "We should probably turn around..."

"Can't," the keeper said. "I have an appointment."

He didn't miss the way the priest righted his sash, from which hung his satchel, now missing a six-gantry crystal.

He squirmed. The construct had been sacrificed to save him.

"Here?"

Justin took his surprise in stride. "While you were bedridden, the royal physician and I got to talking. It seems a promising chef's assistant had a slipup in the kitchens. The poor girl had cut short her career path – along with every tendon across her palm. She was desperate enough to allow my intervention."

The keeper grinned, pleased. "No one gossips like serving staff. Supplicants have been presenting themselves – discreetly – at the kitchen doors for the past week."

It seemed inconceivable. But if anyone was going to overturn the Renali mistrust of magic, it would be Father Justin.

"And now?" he asked, eyeing the entrance to the residences.

The keeper's good mood turned serious.

"A less happy prospect – or so the royal physician has warned me. In all likelihood I will be called to perform the *novissim'uta*."

Marco's awkward clunking stalled as he drew the circle sign on his breast and mouthed the blessing for the dead.

"Hang on," he interrupted himself, mouth hanging open, "wouldn't than mean that the invalid is an unbeliever?"

The *novissim'uta* was a sacred rite, reserved for the pious. A streamer of Justin's skills could conceivably ease the passing of a confused soul, stubbornly clinging to life. But untethering someone who had no ties to Helia was unheard of.

"Who am I," the keeper said severely, "to stand in judgment of another's life? If Helia finds them lacking, if is for her to refuse them. Not me."

A bandaged hand came to rest on Marco's shoulder.

"You should not have to share in this burden. Can you find your way from here?"

Dismissed, he nodded mutely, watching the keeper walk away.

Not yet ready to return to his sickbed, he decided on a roundabout route. So, he set off, clomping down the corridor.

Despite his many assurances that he was fine, he was panting and sweaty long before he reached their rooms. He'd never been so pathetically grateful to just sit down. Groaning, he imagined a spigot, driven into his side. If he could just figure out how to open its valve, all the pain would come pouring out of him.

He was worse than helpless. If a spell-sword assassin attacked, he'd be *lucky* to trip them up with his corpse.

Through the open door to his adjoining room, he spotted his traveling trunk. It had finally followed him, from his hole-in-the-wall quarters in the Royal Apartments.

Though he longed to be reunited with his orin, he realized grimly that he was not – in fact – weaponless.

Leaving his crutches, he hobbled over.

He had to dig, past books and boots and boxes and spare clothes – all the way to the bottom of the chest.

Lacking a scabbard, the brigand's sword had been wrapped in sacking and bundled with twine. Though he knew revulsion had no scent, the smell of sword oil and soot turned his stomach anyway. Through a memory made hazy by smoke, he saw the screaming horses and felt blood draw tight across his face.

Swallowing, he teased loose the ties, baring the blade.

It had been a long time since he'd handled it. He had, in fact, tried his best to forget he had it. How many of its scars and scratches, he wondered, were due to his…

He realized he wasn't breathing.

Snatching up the sword, he scrutinized it narrowly.

He'd had scant specimens to compare it to, before. But now…

Horrified, he flung the blade down. After a moment's hesitation, he threw the sackcloth over it. When this, too, seemed insufficient, he shoved it back in the trunk and slammed the lid.

I'm mistaken, he thought. *Obviously, I'm mistaken.*

But he had to be sure.

DENNIK SAT, WITHOUT appetite, his stew slowly congealing.

The commissary heaved around him, unheard.

'Straighten up,' the sergeant had snarled at his haggard face this morning, though not a button had been out of place.

He thumbed at his raw eyelids but the memory – of the priest with the blazing eyes – refused to be wiped away. His skin crawled again, as it had in the moment before the man had called lightning.

A deafening clap. A blinding flash. And, as his shaken senses swam back into focus – weak breaths from a dead boy's breast...

He pushed his bowl away.

He should be grateful that the priest had stuck an arm in death's croup, to pry the boy out. It saved him wondering whether Marco's blood stained *his* hands too, however distantly.

The elder princess's plans roamed far afield.

Even so, he could not stop himself picturing her bodyguard, Enderam Lelouch, in tourney armor. He kept his suspicions tightly bottled – lest a sparring accident befall him as well.

No foreign priest would draw *his* soul back against the current.

Regret burned him. The way his discarded dagger had, when he'd stupidly scooped it from the tourney ground. He'd baked the blade in his father's kiln overnight, then tossed the blackened slag in the lake. Good riddance to bad-

"Good morrow, Dennik."

He started guiltily. "Marco. Are you well?"

"Still alive."

Hysteria laced his thin laughter.

While the boy busied himself with crutches and seating, Dennik made an effort to get a tighter rein on his nerves.

"You can't be ready for duty yet," he opined, relieved at how level he sounded. "Did you miss the bad food?"

"I have an odd question," the boy confessed. "If that's alright?"

Panic kicked at the stable door, but he persevered.

"My measure of 'odd' is unreliable these days. Go ahead."

"It's about your sword," the boy said.

He blinked.

This was a safe subject. With equal amounts relief and enthusiasm, he drew his scabbard across his knees.

"What would you like to know?"

The boy looked unsure. "Is it special? Unique in some way?"

"To me, personally? No. You will find a hundred more, in this hall alone, and thousands of near-identical ones throughout the kingdom. It is the quintessential Renali design."

It was a phrase he'd heard his drill instructor use.

Oddly, the boy sagged with relief.

"In fact," he added proudly, "the keep forged blade is the standard after which most other swords are cast."

The boy tensed. "The what-forged-what?"

"This," he illustrated, hefting his own. "See how the six sided pommel matches the quillions?" He bared a handspan of steel. "And how the hollow grind echoes the three-quarter fuller? That's castle craftsmanship, that is."

"How can you be sure?" the boy whispered, eyeing the sword like it might snap at him.

"Easy." He flipped the blade. "The master smith marks all keep forged blades with the Keystone seal. Here, see?"

The boy stared at the little stylized fort, stamped into the metal.

"Here, are you alright? You look a little pale."

"I'm fine," Marco muttered, breathing heavily. "These keep forged blades – only the Royal Guard carries them?"

"Some officers, too. I slaved for years before I earned mine."

Distracted, the boy fished awkwardly after his crutches.

"This master smith. Where do I find him?"

Dennik frowned. "At the Keystone forge. Behind the training grounds, on the river's side." He eyed the swaying boy dubiously. "You're going now? It's a bit of a trek. Are you sure you should-"

"I'll be fine," Marco said, less courteously than was his habit.

Heart sinking, he watched the little Imperial hobble off.

Oh, Marco. You're not cut out for this spy business either.

Rising heavily to his feet, he went to find Enderam Lelouch.

"THE IMPERIAL LAD?" the master smith asked, an eyebrow quirked over the blade he was inspecting.

Its owner nodded. A man of few words, was Enderam Lelouch.

"Aye, he was here. Full of questions, he was, over a sword he'd 'found'. One of mine, it was. I had a mind to take it off the whelp. Only, I been told he's got himself seconded to the Guard…?"

Lelouch didn't gainsay this.

Shrugging, he turned the sword over in his blunt hands, having found no evidence of notches or uneven sharpening. Placing its point on a nearby anvil, and a palm on its flat, he flexed the blade this way and that – pleased by how it sprung back into shape.

"Beat up old thing," he recalled. "Not like this one here."

He hefted the bodyguard's blade, sighting down its length. The flick of a fingernail produced a deeply pleasing note.

"True as the day I made it," he muttered.

"The boy was interested in where the sword came from?"

"Oh, aye," he agreed, testing the blade's edge with a thumb. "Asked me if I was sure it was one of mine. '*Sure.*' Like I don't know every piece that leaves my forge."

He rarely rewarded such lip. But someone, who knew about swords, had recently tried to restore some luster to that battered old blade. It had bought the boy some of his forbearance.

"You told him it was keep forged?"

"That I did," he said, seesawing the sword over a finger. "I even cut the wrap around the hilt for him – showed him the date of manufacture and the apprentice's mark, scratched on the tang."

Come to think of it, why had he gone to the trouble? He should have sent the boy off with a flea in his ear. Except that the child had been so very earnest. And on crutches besides.

He'd looked as ragged as that once – when every smithy in the city had been refusing him an apprenticeship. There'd been no one to stand surety for the by-blow of a backwater farrier. Reduced to a horseshoe helper once more, he'd worked for food – and gotten precious little of it, attached to the army. Pure happenstance had seen him, patching armor for a platoon lost behind Heli lines.

His work had carried them through, safely, and he'd ridden their recommendation straight to the royal forge.

"Could you tell which guardsmen was given the blade?"

Startled from his reverie, he gave the sword in his hand a couple of experimental swings, listening to it cut air. "Not as such. I could tell you when that barrel of blanks was breached and circulated into service, if you like. But that's about all."

Lelouch said nothing, so he let it go. He wasn't in the mood to dig out and dust off his ledgers anyway.

"She's about due for a new wrap," he diagnosed, handing the sword back. "We got some nice silver wire put aside for the captains. I'm sure the king wouldn't begrudge a royal bodyguard?"

Giving him a flat look, Lelouch slammed the sword back in its sheath and turned without a word.

Dusting his hands, the smith went to shout at some apprentices.

※ ※ ※

"Tea?"

Sweat-sheened and sore where his crutches chafed at him, Marco nevertheless swallowed his urgent words.

"How do you always know when I'm upset?" he demanded instead, unwilling to be soothed.

He could tell, by Justin's twinkling eyes and easy smile, that a disarming deflection was coming.

He forestalled it. "And don't say you felt me coming down the corridor. I know that tea. That's your rancid, yak's butter, Marco-is-upset tea. And it takes half a bell to brew."

The priest was understandably taken aback by his harsh tone. Marco himself wasn't sure where the anger was coming from. Only that it was demanding to be released.

"It's no wonder these Renali savages think you're a shaman!"

As soon as the words left his mouth, he tried to snatch them back. But neither gasp nor grasping hand managed it.

Shamans were little better than bonecasters and soothsayers – and both were common classifications of witch.

"Father…" he breathed, horrified, "I'm so sorry… I don't-"

Far from looking offended, the priest spread wry hands.

"Had I known I needed only amend my taste in tea, to improve my public perception, I'd have done it long since."

Shocked silent, Marco swayed.

"As for knowing you were upset, well, we are especially attuned, you and I. Long proximity and repeated healing have left a peculiar… sense. I could point straight to you, anywhere in this keep – provided you were experiencing some strong emotion."

Mortified, he hung his head.

The keeper continued. "Does your sinking opinion of our hosts have anything to do with your sword-shaped parcel?"

Grateful of the change in subject, he limped over to the table, setting the wrapped sword among the silverware.

"Father, I'm not sure what I've found. But I think it's something bad. I think… I think, maybe, we've been betrayed."

The keeper sat, blowing on a thimble sized cup and swirling its sour cream stink about. "How so?"

"This," Marco began, parting the sackcloth, "is the sword from the bandit attack on our caravan. It is keep forged. Crafted here, in Keystone, and carried only by the royal guard."

He met his mentor's eyes.

"The king," he concluded, "tried to kill us."

Unmoving, Justin stared into his tea for a long moment.

"I will grant you," the priest said, "that there are some who wish disaster on our venture. They have already cost us friends and traveling companions. But it is *not* the king. I've been in a room with the man, so I know."

"But-"

"You assume the culprit is a royal. But why not a rogue officer? Or a whole racist unit? Or even a scribe, forging orders?"

"This sword-" he insisted, closing a hand on it.

"Swords," Justin cut across him, "are routinely lost, stolen or sold. Retired soldiers keep theirs. So do deserters. Neither is it impossible to loot one off a slain guardsman. It is more than likely this sword was planted, to birth these exact suspicions."

"The master smith confirmed-"

"Marco," the keeper overrode, not ungently, "there is a good reason why we refer to counterfeits as 'forgeries'. You need not be a master smith to stamp your work with someone else's mark or scribble on it. You need merely be skilled and unscrupulous."

He looked up sharply at that. He'd said nothing of 'scribbles'.

"You already knew about the sword," he realized. Justin did not deny this. "People died! Why haven't you done anything?!"

"Who says I have not?" The priest set down his cup with a sharp clink. "What I patently have *not* done, is play into the hands of our enemy by lobbing baseless accusations at the king.

"Our people died, working to prevent another war. I will not carelessly catapult us into one. Will you?"

Bile bubbled in his throat. He'd done it again.

He'd bumbled into the keeper's business.

"Ow!"

His hand sprang away from strangling the sword's blade.

"Here," his mentor reached over. "Stanch that…"

Bunching the offered handkerchief in his fist, he let the priest bow a head over it. A quick prayer preceded a crawling sensation – done so quickly he had no time to object.

"There," Justin smiled lopsidedly, blotting away the red to show tender pink where a cut had closed. "All better."

He wilted in his seat, head hanging low. After a while, a cup of stinking tea slid in front of him. He was so grateful for the keeper's mild temper, he drank it. The companionable silence stretched.

"Did you perform the *novissim'uta* for the dying noble?"

The keeper accepted the change in topic readily.

"*Not* dying, as it turns out. I was able to divine what the physician could not. Shrapnel, from an old wound, had migrated to rest against the patient's spine. The abscess had been slowly poisoning him for years. He'll walk again, given time."

Marco forced a weak smile. "That is excellent news!"

"Mm. Though I fear I am breeding unrealistic expectations. I am, after all, not a miracle worker. Especially without my crystal-"

The priest swallowed the rest as Marco's guilt surged.

"Ahem. At this rate, the king might even ask me to take a look at the little ailing prince," the keeper smiled.

JUSTIN STOOD IN the doorway, watching his ward crutch away up the corridor, the incriminating weapon clutched under one arm.

He stared at it. When that sword had come to their camp previously, it had come seeking all of their blood.

Shutting the portal on the sight, he pulled the soiled handkerchief from his sleeve, considering.

The way Marco was dangling the evidence in these dangerous waters was cause for concern. There was no telling what might rise to the bait. A responsible mentor would have taken it from him.

He wrung the bloodstained cloth in indecision a moment more.

Deciding, he tore the handkerchief, stained with the same essence that now marked the ill-fated blade. Gritting his teeth, he tore it again, working it into a length of connected strips. Something he could roll into the approximation of a ribbon.

Tonight would see a minor confluence of magical energies, if Cyrus's predictions held true. Enough to charge the yarn charm he was fashioning. Using blood as the connecting medium did not sit well – it skirted too close to witchcraft. But a hook was no good unless you had a line tied to it.

And this way, he reflected, *I don't have to burden poor Marco with knowledge of my schemes. That boy has been through enough.*

* * *

"Phew!" Jiminy huffed, glancing sidelong at his companion.

Unseasonable autumn sun beat down, cooking the road dust and curling the monk's gray sideburns. Neever flapped futilely at his robes, trying to coax a cooler current.

"Might I impose?" the holy man had appealed, some leagues ago, shrugging meaningfully beneath the weight of their supplies.

Jiminy had stretched his stride, preceding the monk by a dozen paces. Then, brandishing a bushel of uprooted grass at the man, he'd clicked his tongue – as one might encourage a flagging mule.

They were wary of one another, since Marvellack Post.

This meant Jiminy's needling pierced closer to the bone. While Neever became even more accommodating, laughing off the jest.

"Tell me what the Tellar job is, and I'll carry it tomorrow."

"I regret, that's not possible, yet."

Accommodating, up to a point.

"I'll carry it the rest of today and the next. Final offer."

"I'm afraid I cannot."

He'd wound some of his dyed rags, green-tinged in the sunlight, into a traditional amori atop his head. Stretching languidly, he now glanced again at the sweat-soaked monk.

"Call this hot? In Oaragh, you can cook a cat on the cobbles."

"That sounds ... desperate," the man said, with no hint of scorn.

He scowled, unsure how to deal with sympathy.

"Better than *raw* cat," he shrugged.

"This is in summer I take it?"

"In Oaragh, it's always summer."

For all of his boasting, this wasn't the heat he was used to. The desert sun baked. This sun boiled. It was like breathing water. It steamed into his nose, lifeless and limp, and escaped from his skin a moment later. He was drowning in air, gasping...

"Water?" the monk offered, misinterpreting his distress.

"Piss off," he wheezed, wiping his lips. "How far still?"

"If Helia wills it, we'll reach Plammic after sundown."

"And will one of your temples offer hospitality in Plammic?"

"Oh, indeed," Neever enthused but did not elaborate.

"Is there something special about this temple?" he guessed, hoping for more fish beer.

The monk's sweating brows beetled. "The distinction would be quite hard to explain to a, um…"

"A pagan?" he guessed, reading the apologetic glance.

The man dissembled. "I was going to say, 'someone unversed in the basic scriptures'."

Jiminy had no fear of being converted. He was by no means an atheist – he'd seen his share of apparitions and avatars. Enough to know that gods didn't give two figs for their followers. What he was, was a punitive non-believer.

Gods. Shivering sands swallow them all.

He spat off to one side. A habit he'd picked up since leaving home. In the great desert, you didn't waste perfectly good spit.

"Well, go ahead," he growled. "Verse me."

"Alright," the monk began. "What do you know of our faith?"

He bit his lip. But the man *had* asked…

"You're a nation of sun-worshipers, whose creed against killing somehow doesn't apply to people sitting on resources you want."

Neever blinked at this blunt summation.

"That's… an oversimplification. But not, all-in-all, incorrect."

The monk cleared his throat. "Helia, whose *symbol* is the sun, commands that all peoples be as one, joined under a single purpose. Our entire belief system is contained in our core precept, our founding commandment – *unity through faith.*

"Unfortunately, the leading faction chooses to spread the scriptures at spearpoint. Effective, I grant you, but lacking a certain… *generosity of spirit* found elsewhere in the scrolls."

Though it was more poignant in Purli, Jiminy translated the old adage. "'We bring peace and prosperity – submit or die.' Hm. You make it sound like you're not all one big, happy family?"

The monk turned a wry eye on him.

"Have you any experience with large family gatherings?"

"Does an orphanage of whores and thieves count?"

"Probably more closely than you'd think," Neever grimaced.

This took him aback. "What? You scrape together some affection but secretly try to screw and swindle one another?"

Jiminy scrutinized his companion's pained expression.

"Alright," he admitted at length, "*now* I'm interested…"

"Understand," the monk began, "that there aren't just two factions. And none but the leading one is outspoken. *Unity*, you understand? But there is a growing movement – the modernists – who are working to… gentle the Temple's methods of expansion.

"But they must work carefully, to avoid notice – and any kind of confrontation – with the purists in power."

"I had wondered," Jiminy admitted, "at your uncharacteristic tolerance of me, Heli holy man. You're a modernist."

Neever's silence spoke volumes.

"Avoiding notice," Jiminy mused over the monk's words, "and confrontation – sneak thief's work, that. And we're headed to Tellar, supposedly the seat of purist power…"

"I can tell you no more," the monk headed him off.

"And how do you intend to conquer the world," he wondered, "once you've beaten your spears into quill nibs?"

"Missionaries," the monk promptly supplied. "We'll build Temples. We'll teach, we'll help, we'll heal, we'll take no-"

"No prisoners?" he seized.

"Ha, no. We'll take no *coin*, for our efforts. We'll show, by example, that a life lived in Helia's glory is worth converting for."

"Sneaky," he approved. "Except that your strategy for supplanting the gods, of generations past, boils down to, 'my dog's better than your dog…'"

Sweat soaked and serious, the monk stilled, turning to face him.

He thought he might finally have gone too far…

"My dog," the man said, slowly and with utter conviction, "*is* better than your dog."

He held himself still. "I damned-near believe you."

Pleased, the monk turned back to the road, trudging ahead.

Phew! he thought again, this time unconnected to the heat.

"So," he pressed, catching up. "This temple we're going to, it's a modernist temple?"

"Not openly, of course," Neever said. "But predominantly, yes. Politics are complicated. Religion, even more so. And priests are sophists by nature. They'll argue whether the Night of Exodus fell on a Merryday or a Turnsday, until they're purple in the face. The exarch of Plammic Temple has made a point of hosting scholars from many minor camps. It makes for very good camouflage."

After that, it became too hot for conversation. They took twice as many rest stops as on any other day.

"Is it just me," Jiminy finally sighed, dragging his headdress down to let dusk's breeze find his damp hair, "or has the sun taken twice as long to trek across the sky today?"

Neever chuckled. "It's the elevation. The Downlands would have offered a more direct route, but is more widely traveled. This way, we get sparser crowds, but full sun."

"I'm *so* grateful for the elevation," he griped, calves aching, as they finally caught sight of Plammic – atop a distant hill, of course.

The small city crawled a slow curve toward them. Pale sandstone buildings, the same color as the cliffs, reflected a brilliant white in the setting sun. A child could hurdle its decorative walls, so different from Marvellack Post's. He said so.

"Of course," Neever confirmed. "Plammic was never a frontier fort. Its closest neighbors were the nomadic Nemil – not to be confused with the Neril – to the south-east. It is all sheep country now. And quite the winter retreat for many rich nobles. The court regulars prefer that their station be reflected in their place of worship. The Plammic Temple is… upscale."

"Also, uphill," he observed bitterly, as they passed into town, with just a blush of orange still clinging to the horizon.

Uniformed men slouched by the gate, ostensibly guarding against a sheep stampede. If all the watchmen here were so lax, Plammic promised to be a worthwhile stop. After all, who would search the companion of a monk for stolen trinkets?

The gambol at the governor's mansion had gotten his blood up and not given it a chance to cool. Which was, perhaps, why his senses were so raw. He'd outlived many of his peers by dint of gall and guile. But, mostly, by instinct. So when the itch between his shoulders started up, he began paying close attention to the darkened side-streets.

"Say, Neever?" he drawled, as they cut through a broad alley. "You know how you said Marvellack Post was my audition?"

Staff clunking on the cobbles, the monk hummed assent.

"We're done with auditions, right?"

"Certainly. Why do you ask?"

"Because if these men aren't with you, I think we're in trouble."

Neever whirled. "What m-?"

Jiminy crooked a thumb over his shoulder. "Those."

Cloaks billowing like vulture's wings, two dark figures stepped into the road, a score paces to their rear. The two separated as they neared, flanking the monk and him between them.

Scuffs on the flagstones ahead announced two more – a large one and a little one – their stride at odds with an evening stroll.

"Were you expecting them?" Jiminy whispered hopefully, his heart sinking as he imagined the dread mage stepping out next.

Neever shook his head.

"Then you'd better get out of that heavy backpack," he advised, loosening his shoulders and feeling the weight of his knives.

The old mix of fear and exhilaration stirred to life in his belly.

With a pained expression Neever shrugged out of the shoulder straps, lowering the pack to the ground.

"Brothers…" the monk began, arms thrown wide.

Inwardly, Jiminy groaned. He'd seen another priest, a leper, perform this part once before. And, although it may have worked on sodden farmhands, it was about to get both of their throats slit. Unthinking, he put his back to the monk's, covering their front.

"This one's a woman," he said over his shoulder.

"…and sister," Neever amended. "There is no need for this. You are welcome to whatever we have. Take it, and go in peace."

He watched a smirk twist the woman's mouth.

"Fat chance," he judged, even as she launched herself at him.

He left his robe behind and sprang to meet her. That smile had given her away and she hadn't expected him to match her, knife for knife. Her flicker of surprise almost killed her.

But he was distracted by a club – as long as his leg and as thick as his thigh – arching overhead. "Shit."

Dodging, he heard the studded collar crack cobbles in his wake.

His killing blow scored a glancing cut along the woman's hip.

Screeching like a scalded cat, she reached for him again as he rolled upright. Her partner, the club-wielding giant, lumbered after.

She was good. Her range, footwork and timing were decently aligned. But she tended to repeat her defensive pattern. And she flinched when cut, he found, as he dragged his edge across her knuckles. His kick put her in the path of the carelessly swung club. Her overeager partner, unable to pull the blow, sent her reeling.

He leapt into the lull.

With the man's thick neck out of reach, he stabbed up under the exposed armpit – and swore, as his blade bit nothing but lard.

Bellowing, the block of a man whirled, the club a beat behind.

It pulled at him, as it blew past, threatening to splatter him across the next three buildings. But it didn't upset his balance.

Changing to a feather grip, he whipped his lead knife down.

Thrown blades were less effective than most people thought. They tended to snag in – or bounce off – bone. Especially around the head or heart, where you'd really like them to go. But a speared thigh, in his experience, was always a winner.

As the giant's jugular stumbled down into reach, he struck out.

Amazingly, the man regained his feet. One hand was daubed bright red, trying to stem a holed throat. The club rose and fell twice more, missing him, before the giant began swaying blearily.

Recovering, the knifewoman raced to her partner's defense. Her hair had come undone and a rictus had replaced her smirk.

He plucked a shorter blade from his brace to meet her.

Three passes and three cuts later, she staggered back, uncertain.

To one side, the giant sat down with a thump. The club clattering from nerveless fingers.

Reassessing her chances, the woman turned to flee.

His hand tangled in her flying hair and she gasped as she was dragged back, his blade angled to find the heart between her ribs.

Chivalry, he'd been taught, was dead – blindsided by a woman it had been too sun-addled to snuff when it had the chance.

Letting her collapse, he turned to help Neever.

But there was no need.

The monk's oaken staff was a blur, slapping at his assailant's swords with dull retorts.

Jiminy had once watched a bright ribbon, caught in the grip of a sandspout, dance. The holy man moved in much the same manner, spinning and twirling, long staff flicking out to pulverize bone.

He stared, as the innocuous length clipped the feet from under one swordsman, the other end rounding to hasten the man's fall.

Dead, Jiminy judged. *Live people don't bounce like that.*

Sidestepping a lunge, a sandaled foot snaked from under monastic robes. The second swordsman staggered, neck meeting the speeding staff, coming the other way. There was a sick crunch. Head sitting askew, the attacker staggered off senseless feet and collapsed, raising dust.

In the wake of their scuffle, the sudden silence was deafening.

Regret plain on his face, the monk grounded his staff, head bowing in prayer. It was quickly done, in short gasps.

"A choirboy, huh?" Jiminy drawled, as the man looked over.

"All my life," Neever confirmed.

He raked a gaze over the dead swordsmen. "Uh-huh."

Keeping an eye on that staff, he backed over to his own would-be-killers. His blade had, indeed, chipped bone where it had buried in the giant's leg. He swore as he saw its broken point. Scooping up the knifewoman's weapons, he found they were well-made but gaudy. Mottled Renali steel, set in birds' head pommels. Eagles or falcons or some such. He could file those down. Blacken them.

"That sound," Neever told him needlessly, as the far-off whistles neared, "is the City Watch. We should leave. Now."

His new scabbards in hand, he rose. "After you…"

He stayed on the monk's heels as they traversed the back alleys, his mind racing even as his feet did. He'd checked the dead but had recognized no faces and found no telltale mercenary armor. Still, if Neever was going to be sticking his neck out, the man deserved to know they might be up against a dread mage. And that the 'key' to true safety was probably somewhere back in Purlia.

"That ... was no ... mugging," he admitted, between huffs.

Only panting breaths answered him.

"Neever? I said-"

"I know," the man admitted over a shoulder, not slowing. "I fear ... the purist faction ... has pre-empted us."

He was glad the monk couldn't see his surprise. "Um..."

"Let us get ... to safety first," the man appealed.

They stumbled on through the night, eventually leaving the whistles behind. Sight of the temple came as a blessed relief. The monk led them around the back, to pound on a little postern door.

A man in roughspun, with a shaven crown, cracked it open. The light of a single candle spilled over them.

"Brother Bariel," Neever sighed in apparent recognition.

Unperturbed by their sudden appearance, Bariel pulled the portal wide, beckoning. They hurried inside.

"I apologize," Neever said, "I know it's late and we must look a fright. How have you been?"

Turning from bolting the entrance, Bariel nodded agreeably.

"Ah, forgive me," Neever continued. "Manners. Bariel, this is Master Olu, a sanctuary seeker. Olu, say hello to Brother Bariel."

He eyed the silent monk askance. "Hey."

He received another beatific smile, and a bob, but nothing else.

"Bariel," Neever interjected, "is the exarch still up?"

Bariel motioned wordlessly upwards, which he took to mean yes, since the man also gestured for them to follow.

They made their way through dimly lit kitchens and prayer halls, finally passing into what he assumed was the temple proper. His travels with Neever aside, he'd never seen one from the inside before. Not like this. 'Upscale' didn't begin to describe it.

Even without any backlight, the soaring, stained glass windows were breathtaking. Golden scones decorated pale pillars and what wasn't sculpted from polished stone was carved in rich wood.

If he could pry loose only the inset stones their lone taper revealed, he'd walk out of here a rich man…

As if reading his thoughts, Bariel glanced back at him.

"Do you ever speak?" he challenged.

Predictably, he got only a smile in reply.

"Brother Bariel has taken a vow of silence," Neever explained.

"I see. Is that something *you* might consider trying?"

Up ahead, Bariel's shoulders shook in silent mirth.

"I pay my penance in other ways," Neever said.

He wondered if he could trick this Bariel into speaking, with a casually asked question or two. "Why a vow of silence?"

"He would have you believe it is to bolster his search for self-knowledge," Neever said. "In truth, he just didn't want to compete with me at canticle anymore."

On the stairs ahead, Bariel raised a warning finger.

"How long is the vow for?" he baited.

Neever answered again. "He hasn't said."

Jiminy pondered a moment before addressing Bariel's back.

"Still got all your testicles and pinky toes?"

Not so much as a stumble. Though Neever looked curious.

"Well," he gave up, "you two obviously deserve each other."

They arrived at a door, no different from any other.

Bariel motioned them to wait and disappeared inside.

I suppose priests don't knock. Or lock.

"Where is he going?"

"To announce us, I imagine," said a straight-faced Neever.

He stared pointedly. "The man can't speak."

"Oh, he *can*. He just chooses not to."

"You'd know all about that," he muttered, leaning back.

The door reopened to lantern light. Bariel ushered them in.

The wood-paneled office smelled strongly of dried herbs, several bushels of which were strung from the rafters. Detailed drawings of plants festooned the walls. A stuffed owl sat on the desk, staring at them with intense startlement.

From a side door, through which he spied a mussed bed, entered the exarch. The monastery's master was sinewy and hard-bitten, sporting a yellow-stained beard. Even blinking in the light, the man may have been imposing – if not for the nightgown and cap.

"Oh, it's you," the man rasped, spotting Neever.

Slippered feet stomped over to the desk, where the man threw himself into the plush chair.

"It figures," the head priest gathered Bariel into his scowl. "First time in years I fall asleep on the first try. Someone *would* shake me awake. Thank you, Brother Bariel. You may go."

Far from being put out, the mute monk motioned helpfully.

Growling, the exarch snatched the cap from his crown and threw it at the door, after Bariel.

"Exarch Pesclior-" Neever began.

"Ah!" the head priest overrode, disappearing below the desk. Papers rifled. A dark bottle plunked onto the desktop, sloshing richly, followed by a single glass. Reappearing, Pesclior bit out the cork with brown-rimmed teeth and poured himself a stiff measure.

"For my heart," the man explained. "Have you any idea how disconcerting it is, to have that noiseless lump latch onto your arm in the dead of night?"

The man tossed his restorative down. "Mother's mercy, I nearly widdled myself…"

Jiminy suppressed a laugh.

"Excellency," Neever tried again, "you look well."

"Ha!" the man sat straighter, refilling his glass. "Don't pander to me, sonny. I look like a sheep's wooly bunghole, and well do I know it!"

Jiminy grinned to see Neever squirm uncomfortably.

"Now," Pesclior's glare dimmed to a glower. "What's all this about? I got a bird, said to expect you. And some other scratchings besides." That glower shifted to Jiminy. "Is this the thief?"

"I've never stolen a thing in my life," he promised, indignant.

Pesclior shared a glance with Neever.

"Well, he's got that part down pat. Sit, would you?"

They did as bid, Pesclior leaning to snatch the scroll Neever offered. A pair of half-moon spectacles were produced, balancing precariously on a porous nose while the priest read.

Something crackled alarmingly as Jiminy lowered himself – a bushel of long dead and withered weeds. At Neever's slight shake, he circumspectly dropped it to the rug and swept it under his chair.

Angrily rerolling the scroll, Pesclior plucked off his glasses.

"Introduce us, why don't you?"

"Exarch Pesclior," Neever complied, "this is Master Olu. A sanctuary seeker and, all evidence to the contrary, a good soul."

The remark almost startled him from his staring contest with the head priest. He didn't like the man's weighing look.

"What?" he challenged. "Have I got something on my face?"

A cough hid Neever's amusement.

"This couldn't have waited until morning?" Pesclior grumped, hands absently crumpling and wringing at the scroll.

"Circumstances may be more dire than anticipated," Neever explained. "We were set upon, by an armed and organized group, no more than ten blocks from here."

The old man's bushy brows humped higher. "Footpads?"

"No. I believe they were expecting us, specifically."

"I don't suppose they were friends of yours?" Pesclior directed at Jiminy, more hopeful than suspicious.

"I have no friends here," he said, in all honesty.

"*Humph*," Pesclior sat back. "Any survivors?"

"No," Neever assured, with obvious regret.

"That may buy us time," said the bearded man. "But they'll know you came here. Which means we are now being watched."

Pesclior's tangled brows fought for control of the wrinkled forehead. Deep in thought, the exarch reached toward the startled owl. The section of branch Jiminy had assumed to be a perch proved itself to be a pipe. Pesclior put it between saffron teeth.

"What are you thinking?" Neever asked, as the man thumbed the bowl full.

All the dried herbs were beginning to make sense.

"If they knew to expect you here, your direction of travel is exposed," Pesclior reasoned. "You are likely to have similar encounters, all the way to Tellar."

The exarch reached for the strangled scroll, reduced to a twist of paper. Peaceful contemplation sat oddly on Pesclior's face, which seemed sculpted for maximum scowl. But under that gaze, the end of the ruined parchment caught fire.

Jiminy pressed back in his chair, trying to look unconcerned.

Salt and silver! Another sand spawned sorcerer!

Somehow, he'd convinced himself these priests didn't hold with magic, when history said they were some of the meanest magickers ever to wade into war.

The exarch spoke through a wreath of blue smoke.

"Our leak, then, is likely within the Temple. We must needs look outside of it, for help, if you hope to continue your journey."

A bronze mortar stood ready to receive the burning scroll.

Neever nodded. "What do you suggest?"

Jiminy looked from one man to the other. It was their *own* people, trying to kill them? So much for priests being sophists at heart – the heated discussion between the purists and modernists had just drawn blood tonight.

He'd found himself in the middle of a gang war. And on the side of the underdog at that – worst luck. Grimacing, he tried to tally up whether the gold on offer was worth making such enemies.

"I have an idea," Pesclior said. "But it will take some careful… negotiation. I'll have an answer for you by midday tomorrow."

The exarch pointed them toward the door with the stem of his pipe, signaling that their short meeting was at an end.

Dismissed, they rose.

"Boy," the head priest stopped him as he was about to exit.

His flat regard made no dent in Pesclior's amber grin.

"Blue? Or green?"

He blinked at the unexpected question. "What?"

Rather than answer, the exarch laughed, waving him off.

CHAPTER 14 – BLUE OR GREEN

Pella Monop, Journal entry #167

Complete immersion and lack of sleep have yielded a brittle boon. As if the barriers of my overtaxed mind have thinned. I have gained near-native fluency with the old dialect and speak it, in my unmindful moments – it costs concentration simply to pen these contemporary words. I am possessed of renewed insight, making impossible leaps of intuition. I find myself musing aloud to Bruen, as though we are active co-authors. Some of her referenced sources are no longer shelved. I came across Cecine, rifling through my notes in my office. She claims she came to drop off some materials and became engrossed. I have stopped sending her after any but the most mundane texts.

JIMINY STARED. "YOU'RE not fucking serious?"

A strangled smile spoiled Neever's apology.

It was the next day and they were back in Pesclior's quarters. Two dresses – complete with supporting underwire, manifold petticoats and puffy shoulders – were draped across the bed.

One was blue. The other was green.

Bariel, who stood in attendance, was scrunched up with mirth.

"Keep laughing, you bashful bastard. This time, I won't stop sawing until I find what ails you."

The mute monk had, that morning again, neglected to knock. For his trouble, Jiminy's new knife had tasted his stubble.

The thief crossed his arms obstinately at Neever. "No way."

"It is a sound strategy," the man chided.

The pipe-addled priest, Pesclior, had appealed to a noble acquaintance. The lady had agreed to smuggle them to Tellar, in her carriage – provided he pose as her niece.

"How about *I* be the driver and *you* wear the dress?" he tried.

"I fear livery will make you no less noticeable. A blind man could see you are desert born. Besides," the monk's serious front slipped, "I don't have the shoulders to pull this off…"

Jiminy's face, apparently, was the issue. Going hooded was too conspicuous. Fortuitously, the dresses had veils. It was what the veil *signified*, as much as the dress itself, that set him balking.

"I will pretend to be a leper again," he emphasized, "before I pretend to be a virgin."

Growing up a runty orphan had cost him dearly. Being slim and slight, he'd been steered toward the prostitution track. Only his skills as a sneak thief had saved him. And he'd be damned if he'd backslide now.

"Come now-" Neever wheedled.

"No! This is a monumentally stupid idea, taken straight from 'Star Eyes and the Moon Princess'!"

"Star- What?"

"A *children's* story, Neever! A fairytale farce! Just like this!"

With a long-suffering sigh, the monk seemed to deflate.

"It is the best plan we have."

"That doesn't make it a good one!" he pointed out.

Neever said nothing, which was a lot harder to argue with.

"Crap," he sighed at last. "Help me with the buttons…"

"And I swear," he added, as the monk approach, "one snigger, one snort, and I'll make you eat this dress."

"Of course," the man promised, the very picture of piety.

Sometime later, he marched into the office, mortified.

"You look stunning," Pesclior said.

Tearing the veil off, he glared. "Screw you."

Feeling strangely vulnerable, despite all the extra knife-space, he realized he would have to hike up his skirts to get at his hilts.

This is going to be even harder than I thought.

"Now, now," said a woman's voice from the seating area, "that is not fit language for a young lady."

Older, and immaculately dressed, the speaker rose. An austere eyebrow took him in, a dainty pipe curling the same blue smoke as Pesclior's. Jeweled combs held her hair back in a severe bun. But it was her eyes – a piercing slate hue – that held his attention.

She circled him with the unhurried gait of a true predator.

"He cleans up nice," Pesclior offered.

"*This* is nice?" she queried skeptically. "He must have been a catastrophe before…"

He fought the urge to lean away from her close inspection.

"His posture is dreadful but he's about the right size," she said.

He scowled at her.

Ignoring him, she glanced woefully at Pesclior. "He looks like a dock rat tangled in a silk net. But it'll do. For now."

Her nose wrinkled. "You could, at least, have scrubbed him down. This dress is Downlands silk… *Was* Downlands silk.

Sighing, she reached into her sleeve.

"Here," she commanded around her pipe stem. "Spit."

He stared at the lace handkerchief she held beneath his nose.

He gave her a flat stare. She returned him one even flatter.

"Either you spit," she said in steely tones, "or I do."

Scoffing, he opened his mouth to say something off-hand.

The noise, as she hawked up phlegm, was not at all ladylike.

He caught her wrist before the cloth could make it to her lips. At her raised eyebrow, he spat obediently onto the kerchief.

"There," she smiled thinly, wiping imagined smudges from his face. He bore it, staring balefully at the ceiling. She stuffed the soiled wipe away up his sleeve.

"We only have time to do the eyes," she said, half to herself, as she clicked open a clam-sized case. "Where the veil is thinnest."

He was distracted. He'd rarely worn sleeves before and had never considered their usefulness in hiding-

"Wait, what do you mean, 'do the eyes'?"

He tried to retreat but she was standing on the hem of his dress. A sharp little brush threatened his sight.

"Don't move," she commanded.

It was a tone he knew well, though it was usually paired with a knifepoint in the back, or a blade's edge at the jugular.

Survival instincts kicking in, he froze while she painted his face, responding to her instructions meek as a lamb.

It was good she asked him to close his eyes. Anyone he saw laughing at him right now, he'd have to kill.

She kept up an easy conversation with Pesclior while she worked. Despite being her canvas, he felt thoroughly ignored.

"Does it truly take such dire circumstance before you'll call on me, Messin? Had I known, I'd have arranged a coup long since."

Messin? These Imperials had strange names.

"A coup?" the head priest chuckled. "Nothing so grand. But, had I known you held aspirations to the Holy Seat, I'd have rather become a cobbler."

She had a much younger woman's laugh.

"Because you were always so good at nailing things?"

"*Ahem.* Now, now. There are ladies present."

"Hardly," she scoffed, stepping back to appraise her handiwork.

"Is it too much to hope," she directed at him, veil in hand, "that you may *legitimately* wear this?"

He gave her what he hoped was an innocently blank look.

"I didn't think so," she said, sounding both wry and resigned. The film of material was affixed across his face. In anything but direct sunlight, it should soften his features to a mere suggestion.

Not so much different from a thief's mask, he consoled himself.

The lady, whom he'd gathered went by 'Lassleider', clasped the old fossil's hands fondly. "Don't wait so long to call on me again."

"Always a pleasure, Hemmy," Pesclior said, heart in his eyes.

Neever arrived, right on cue, dressed in a driver's uniform. With his sideburns shaved and his hair slicked back, the monk looked a different man. Save for the stubborn ears.

"All set, milady."

With a parting pat for Pesclior, the lady swept toward the door.

"Come, Valda," she motioned, waiting at the exit.

Bristling at the command, he stalked past her.

In retrospect, he should have expected the pinch to his bottom. But, as it was, he grabbed up a handful of the stupid dress and scurried ahead, hounded by her laughter.

I should have taken my chances with the dread mage!

Jiminy found the Lassleider carriage to be an expensive affair, lacquered green and blue and drawn by four showy horses. An ingenious suspension system insulated passengers from bumps, which were few and far between on the Imperial highway.

He'd have preferred to share the driver's box with Neever, even if it meant his dress would flap around his ears.

The carriage's interior was luxurious, all buttoned leather, dyed a decadent vermillion. Velvet drapes kept out road dust while filigree vents sieved the air. Drawers and cabinets, beneath the seats, held various luxuries. They had provided the lady's drink, which she held expertly against the rocking of the carriage.

Very snazzy. He could have fenced the whole thing for a fat purse. More, if he sold the horses off separately.

To be fair, he had more experience with palanquins. But he'd only ever been inside one. On invitation. And the owner had set her guards on him, afterwards. Granted, she'd had to, to save face. But she'd been good enough to give him a head start.

"If I'm any judge of men – and I am – then memory of some tryst put that smile on your face."

Perhaps he should have left the veil on.

"Maybe," he scowled, not liking how easily she read him.

Even her chuckle sounded rich.

She was a mystery. A perfect lady, insofar as he understood the imperial concept – until you paid closer attention to the things she did and said. She reminded him, strangely, of some woman clan leaders he'd known – brass knuckles, gloved in silken courtesy.

And why not? He thought. She was a matron of power, in her own way. And though he had no love of domineering women, he usually got on with them quite well. They tickled his inborn urge – to piss people off – more lightly than most.

"Speaking of," he tried. "You and Father Smokestack, huh?"

"Messin?" she feigned surprise at the question. "We were close once, growing up. He, the fourth son of a minor house, was fostered at my family's estate."

Staring into the past, her rueful smile turned malicious.

"Oh, how we *despised* each other!"

"Despised?"

"At a certain age, any strong emotion can pass for attraction.

"But," she sighed, "by the time I buried the rich husband my father had chosen for me, Messin belonged to the Temple."

"I'm sorry," he said at length.

"Don't be," she laughed. "If Messin and I had wed, I'd have buried *him* a whole lot sooner. Besides, there is a bitter-sweetness to be savored – reminiscing on the road not taken."

She toyed with her glass. "Will they make a priest of you too?"

"They can try," he growled, making her laugh.

"I doubt there's enough prayer in the whole Tellar prefecture."

He accepted that for the back-handed compliment it was.

"My own methods," she continued, "are more hands-on. I intend to educate you on the finer points of etiquette, so as to ensure you don't embarrass me. My niece, Valda, has received schooling in these techniques all her life. *We* have mere bells to turn you into a reasonable facsimile."

He tried changing the subject. "Where *is* your real niece?"

"She embarrassed me."

He sat back as she leaned into him with a steely look.

"I will make you the same promise I made her," the woman whispered. "'You will be the perfect lady, in every way, even if I have to get out needle and thread and sew your knees together.'"

He swallowed hard.

"That veil," she continued, "is a sacred rite, not much observed anymore. Save by traditional houses like my own. Bringing you on this sham of a pilgrimage deprives Valda of the opportunity. And, though she might thank you for it – I will not."

She wasted no more time, beginning his instruction immediately. They maintained the same stiff pace all day, stopping only to have food brought out to the carriage. By evening, his head was bursting with useless trivia for 'unattached young ladies of marriageable age'.

What did it matter which hand he used to accept something from a stranger? Or where to rest his eyes in a crowded room?

Blegh!

She'd caught him drifting only once.

"Help you find something?" he'd asked, aware that the prattling had paused while she raked through the carriage cabinets.

"My sewing kit…" she'd murmured.

He'd paid strict attention after that. By the time they pulled into the coach in, he was sitting primly, hands clasped and ankles crossed, staring demurely at the floor.

"Give it a moment more," she instructed, as he made to rise. "Darkness is our friend and dusk is almost done. The fewer people who catch a clear glimpse of you, the better."

He suffered her pinning the veil on him and righting his pleats while they waited for Neever to arrange their stay.

"Is her ladyship ready to disembark?" the monk called through the thick curtains.

"It is about time," Lady Lassleider huffed, all but kicking the carriage door down – she planned to draw and hold as much attention on herself as possible.

She peremptorily accepted Neever's hand down. Her voluminous skirts hid her 'niece' from the innkeeper, who had come out to greet them himself. Not that the man would have seen much, bowed as though beneath the whip.

"Ladyship," the man began unctuously, "welcome-"

"Baths, Master Innkeeper," she interrupted, to the sound of the man's jaw clicking shut. "And a private dining room and…"

The train of demands swept ahead, bearing the poor table master along. The man looked a hunchback, bobbing at every step.

All but invisible, Jiminy trailed them, shortening his stride. He even managed to save his hem from dragging in the dust.

"My very best rooms, milady," the innkeeper was promising, looking hunted. "Will her ladyship be staying long?"

The veil hid his smile at the man's obvious apprehension.

In short order, they were settled in their quarters. The proprietor's shouts marched through the establishment, readying all as the lady had ordered. The scrambling of harried staff could be heard. More than one crash sounded from downstairs.

Lady Lassleider stood behind their closed door, grimacing.

"Poor man. He didn't deserve that."

Jiminy, who'd never had someone scarper so hard who wasn't trying to apprehend him, had enjoyed it all immensely.

"I'd like to try that, sometime," he opined.

"One word from you and our little ruse will be over. Leave it," she added, as he reached for the veil. "We're not done yet."

"It's wearing my nose to a nub," he complained but didn't fuss.

On cue, a knock came at the door.

She silently motioned him to sit with his back to it.

"Enter!"

In the mirror, he watched a serving girl stick her head in, as though afraid of having it bitten off. "Your luggage, lady."

"Put it there."

Word traveled fast. Using Neever as a shield, two stable hands manhandled the trunks inside. Then beat a hasty retreat.

"If her ladyship would care to follow me," the girl squeaked, "a table has been laid in the silver room."

Gathering him up with a glance, Lassleider headed for the door.

The 'silver' room proved elegant, but disappointingly bare of precious metal. A fresh vase of flowers, and a cozy fire, did little to alleviate the gray drapes and table cloth.

The table master seated them himself.

Folding his pleats properly, Jiminy nevertheless caused upset when he tried to pull in his own chair. Thinking Lady Lassleider's glare was for him, the innkeeper fell over himself apologizing.

No less than three serving girls were ushered in, bearing trays.

"May we serve you, lady?" asked the oldest – the only servant so far who'd retained some starch.

At Lassleider's nod, the girls quickly decorated two plates with choice cuts of meat, vegetables and sweet-smelling steamed fruit.

A mouse could starve on the amount they dished for him. Perhaps this was why young noblewomen were always said to be swooning – the poor things were malnourished.

"Lady?" the staunch server offered up a bottle of wine.

He shouldn't have gotten his hopes up. His heart sank as he watched them dilute his small taste with a torrent of water. But he waited until they were alone before speaking up.

"If ever there was a day that called for a drink-"

"You're too young."

"Am not," he objected.

"That's what Valda said. Now she's sitting in a convent, as far from court as I can manage – and I can manage a whole lot."

He didn't know what a 'convent' was, but guessed it was bad.

Feeling rebellious, he ripped off the veil and rose to heap more meat on his plate. His chair squealed loudly.

Unimpressed, she relentlessly corrected his table manners, making it sound like he'd never fed himself in his life. Each morsel to reach his mouth was a small triumph.

Back straight. Elbows in. Each tidbit chewed three dozen times!

He'd heard that a person could drown in a saucer of water. He felt he might starve with a honking plate of food in front of him.

The main meal tired him so, he hadn't the energy to tackle the small pudding placed at his elbow.

He looked up, ears perked.

"Better put that veil back on," the lady concurred.

A diffident knock sounded. "Your baths are ready, lady."

"Excellent timing."

He trailed her down the stairs, traversed the length of the inn and ended in a steam-filled room. Slatted wood saved bathers' feet from the cold stone. Spied vaguely through the vapor were twin copper tubs. The privacy screen between them looked flimsy.

"May I help the lady undress?" said the girl by his side.
Now, wouldn't that be a novel experience for both of us...
Lassleider answered for him. "No, that will be all."

Abruptly alone with the sharp tongued matron, he eyed the baths, grateful for the veil that hid his flush.

She must have read the speculative horror in his posture, because she smiled darkly, closing with hands upraised.

"Let's see to those buttons…"

It was true. He couldn't reach the dastardly things himself. Squeezing his eyes shut, he gave her his back.

"Good," she said, after an interminable while. "Now me."

His eyes sprang open.

"Don't worry," she reassured, flashing teeth. "I won't bite."

He was no stranger to women, night sky knew. And his list of conquests did, per force, comprise almost exclusively *older* women. But never quite so old as this.

Fingers that could pick a seven-pin spring-lever lock – in less than a score heartbeats – fumbled horribly at the little closures.

As the last one gave way, he all-but dove behind his screen. He tried his best not to listen, as the lady divested herself of the rest of her garb, but it was impossible to ignore her pleasure as she sighed into the tub. He hurriedly followed suit. Water sloshed over his bath's brim. Lightly scalded, he spent long moments fighting the urge to jump straight back out. Eventually, he relaxed.

Back home, whole-body baths were the exclusive purview of princes. Which was why he'd once stolen into one of the mosaicked monstrosities. This was much better.

Despite himself, he'd begun to drift off by the time something plonked into his bathwater, splashing him. He fished the half-brick of rough soap from its depths.

"Don't just lie there," came the command from across the divider, "scrub. Everywhere. Your hair too. Twice, or I'll know. I'm not ruining another perfectly good dress on you."

Muttering angrily, he did as bid. Did she think him flea-ridden or something? His argument flopped as the water rapidly grayed.

She kept up a litany of helpful instructions, reminding him to wash behind his ears and between his toes.

By the time he surfaced from his second rinse, she stood over him in a thick bathrobe, staring in dismay.

He sank deeper beneath the murk. "What?"

"I think you may have scrubbed off your tan."

Shaking her head, she held out his robe for him.

Though she ostensibly didn't look, he wasted no time shrugging into it. Chuckling, she towed him by the elbow.

Her own tub was so pristine as to seem unused. Pressing him down on a stool beside it, she forced his head back and proceeded to wash his hair a third time. He hissed his protest at the appearance of scented oils, earning a slap on the forehead.

"Shush."

By the time she let him up, all the stiffness the heat had cured was back. She deftly wrapped his head in a towel, leaving a flap free to veil his face. With a push, she steered him from the baths.

The divider in their room was of sturdier design. She stuffed his hands with frilly cloth and banished him behind it.

Steeling himself, he shook out the dusty rose nightgown.

"You can come out now," she called eventually.

"I think I'll just stay here."

He could wait until she doused the lamp, then sneak into bed unseen. She dashed that hope. And the divider.

"Don't you look lovely," she exclaimed.

The dockside curse that sprang to mind ran headlong into the afternoon's etiquette lessons.

I'm being tamed... he realized.

Beyond resisting, he let the silver-backed brushes have their way with his mane.

"The texture is not bad," Lassleider praised. "Fine and straight. Strong. I'd have preferred it longer – for fashion's sake. But we'll make do. Perhaps you'll start a trend, hmm?"

The first snip came as a shock.

"What are you doing?!"

"Salvaging what I can," she informed him, a stern hand holding him in place. "No self-respecting lady would stand for such a misshapen mop. Whoever cut this last was a butcher."

He habitually hacked his own hair. He didn't care to let anyone else so close with a razor.

Correctly identifying the source of his discomfort, she sawed the scissors for effect. "Best sit still. I've little enough to work with and your last barber apparently already sheared away some ear."

Feeling set upon, watching tufts of his hair float to the floor, he wondered how he'd ever let any of this happen.

"Are you an enchantress?" he breathed his suspicion.

His ring said no, but he'd believe the evidence of his eyes.

She laughed. "Only inasmuch as I *am* a woman."

He grunted noncommittally and resolved to keep an eye on her.

"There," she allowed at last, letting him bound from the chair.

"Go on," she encouraged. "Shake it out. Toss your head."

Smiling wickedly at his glare, she turned to stow her tools.

The floor was strewn with shorn follicles. Frowning, he bent to gather them up. He had too much experience, with deep desert shamans and sundry curse-mongers, to leave such things lying about. He didn't care to be spitting up his own lungs.

Besides, sight of Lady Lassleider's face – when the stink of charring hair hit the hearth – was the perfect revenge.

THE NEXT DAY brought challenges of its own. The inn's serving girls thought that 'Lady Valda' should want a team of shipwrights to oversee her wardrobe and face paint.

Lassleider refused them all, seeing to him herself.

Today's veil was more complicated, its rigging running through his hair. There were braids. And ribbons. Payback, possibly, for burning his cut-offs in the grate last night.

An adherent of the hit-back-harder school of thought, the lady picked him a lavender dress, with gloves to match. There was, she promised, a manicure awaiting him. When he opened his mouth to protest, she sprayed him with a foul pomade.

Though it had nothing to recommend its taste, he thought it didn't smell terrible. He'd just rather that smell wasn't *him*.

She caught him, circumspectly sniffing his shoulder. "Here..."

"I'm already wearing stockings," he objected.

She looked pointedly at his chest. "They're not for your feet."

Valda, it seemed, was blessed in the bodice department. Socks could never stand in for real breasts. But his corset didn't care.

To the table master's quickly concealed relief, they took breakfast in their rooms and were on the road before sunup.

He resisted absorbing more etiquette, citing their closeness to the capital – their room had been hung with a tapestried map.

The lady would have none of it. "Our ruse requires that we follow the pilgrim's route, from here onward. We must detour to Sybaline Springs, which will add days to our journey."

He learned more etiquette.

Why should one not twirl one's parasol? What did it mean, to fold one's fan beneath one's chin?

By the midday meal, one was ready to abandon one's companions and run the dirt road on one's bare feet, dress or no.

Groaning, he turned crosswise in his seat. Perhaps he could fall asleep, before she started up again…

A folded fan whacked him across the nose.

"And that one," she informed him sweetly, "means 'sit up before one wrinkles one's dress…'"

His murderous glare was wasted on her.

Evening brought a release from tedium, if nothing else. Though the town was nowhere near as large as Plammic, it sported several inns. Neever chose the only one that suited the lady's station. Its stable was near capacity with tall, tempestuous horses.

"Have you many guests at present, Master Innkeeper?"

"A contingent of Green Dragoons, milady," the portly man beamed, blind to Lassleider's displeasure.

"Who leads them?" she enquired.

"That would be Lord Brigadier Wramlinn, lady."

She looked over sharply. "Serric Wramlinn? Of Everlinn?"

"The very same, milady."

From her hesitation, Jiminy gathered this was not good news. He doubted the innkeeper spotted anything amiss. The man prattled aimlessly, leading them to their rooms.

"Someone you know?" he asked, once they were installed.

"Serric," she said. "Son of a noble lord of some influence. They're a militant family with very… straightforward views."

"Not friends of the modernist movement?" he guessed.

"To say the least."

"And?" he probed, not believing something so simple would rub her the wrong way. "Has he met the real Valda or something?"

"No," she said, with peculiar vehemence, as though she'd worked hard to make it so. "But people who refuse that family tend

419

to regret it. There are rumors of servants disappearing and I myself have seen them ruin rivals at court. Circumspectly, of course."

"Is that why you're worried?"

"I'm *worried*, because Serric and Valda are an excellent match – from both a peerage and a political standpoint. He is going to want to introduce himself. Especially since…"

"What?"

She ruefully indicated his veil. "Wramlinn is also a traditional house. The Daughter's Pilgrimage is a sign that a young lady has reached marriageable age and is open to being wooed."

Jiminy sat down hard. "Fuck me…"

For a change, she didn't call him out on his language.

"He may try to," she said instead, sounding determined.

A knock on their door had him shooting to his feet. Neever hurried in, the driver's persona falling from the monk's face.

"This is my blunder, lady. I can have the horses hitched again in less than a quarter bell…"

"We don't dare," Lassleider said, waving the apology away. "Serric is every bit as domineering as his sire. No doubt a dinner invitation is already on its way. If we are seen to run, he'll give chase. We have no hope of outdistancing Imperial cavalry."

Jiminy blinked at this. "He would ride us down?"

"In a very decorous way, I'm sure," the lady said, looking grim. "No. We must stay and decline any contact – courtesy be damned."

As though she'd summoned it, someone knocked on their door.

"A message for you, lady," said the innkeeper's muffled voice.

Meeting his eyes, Lassleider pointed imperiously at the bed.

"Look ill," she mouthed.

Obediently, he leapt on the covers, an elbow over his eyes.

The latch sounded.

"Master Innkeeper," he heard Lassleider enthuse. "Have you, by any chance, fresh ginger or willow bark to hand? I fear today's travel has upset my niece's delicate constitution."

"Of course, lady," the man said, not missing a beat. "Shall I have the apothecary roused for some feverfew or butterbur?"

"Thank you, no. What she needs now is silence and rest. If you would be so kind, I will mix her a tisane and sit with her."

"Right away, lady. I take it you shall be turning down Lord Wramlinn request to share supper?"

"Please convey my sincere apologies to his lordship."

Jiminy raised his head, once the door had shut. "What now?"

"Now? We wait out the night, slip away before first light, and hope that doesn't pique the lord brigadier's curiosity."

Despite the danger, excitement soon faded. The evening crawled by.

"Do you play?" the lady asked eventually, following his gaze to the game board in the corner.

"*Ta m'asa mukharat,*" he scoffed. At her raised eyebrow, he translated. "'*I wipe my own ass.*' Means I'm not a prince."

"Everyone should know how to play sidestep," she informed him, bringing the six-sided board over, "prince or not."

She spent some time explaining how all the pieces moved.

"What are 'dragoons'," he mused after a while, experimentally moving a seneschal to flank one of his hounds. He was playing Heart – the red pieces. The lady moved one of her white pieces – Hand – to head off his escape.

"Horses are ruinously expensive on the mainland," she explained. "Too much so to be risked in battle. Dragoons are mounted mobile infantry. Or, at least, they used to be. Purchased commissions have taken over the color brigades."

"Huh?"

She gave him a sharp look.

"I mean," he corrected, "'pardon?'"

She nodded. "Wealthy nobles can purchase military office for their children. It's a bit of a prestige thing. And, also, a favored pastime. The young aristocrats run their companies like little boys' blanket forts. Their parents' influence keeps them deployed here, at home, patrolling for non-existent bandits…

"*Cinkako*," she announced. "Surrounded."

He looked at the new placement of her hero piece.

"I think I'll stick to tossing knuckles for sickles," he mourned.

"Nonsense. Sidestep promotes logic and strategic thinking."

"Plus," he commended, "cheating doesn't spark a knife fight."

She arched an eyebrow at him. "How much would you wager?"

He judged she was at least half-way joking.

They played several more rounds before she banished him to bed. He stared at the ceiling, little marble figures crowding his mind's eye. One piece, in particular, was called the 'mage'.

Unlike the others, with their strict patterns of movement, the mage could appear unexpectedly almost anywhere on the board.

That thought made it much harder to fall asleep.

JIMINY FELT LIKE he'd only just closed his eyes. Then Neever was shaking him awake. The dark of night still held sway outside. But the lady was determined to be gone before the dragoons awoke.

The monk oversaw the silent loading of their carriage and had it pulled around by the time they were ready to board.

Jiminy breathed easier once the wheels began to turn.

Stupid lord, he thought.

As the coachyard's gates neared, the monk reined up.

"Driver, why have we stopped?" Lassleider demanded.

The answer presented itself outside their window, hailing them in an unfamiliar voice. "Good morning, lady."

Jiminy's hackles rose in response to the haughty tone.

Shooting him a warning glance, she twitched the drapes aside, endeavoring to hide him with her shoulders and skirts.

Past her, he spied a rich green uniform. A possessive hand settled on their door sash, as if to prevent four horses pulling away.

"Ah," the matron trilled, to all outward appearances pleased, "Lord Wramlinn. I had feared we would miss you this morning."

"Then I am pleased to have caught you," the man said. "And it is 'brigadier', please, lady. I am in my company colors."

"Of course, Lord Brigadier. Pray tell, what errand has you riding for the Uplands at this time of year?"

"Orders, milady. More than that, I may not say. I could wish it were otherwise, so I might offer you proper escort. But, on the subject of errands, your own seems apparent…"

The man leaned, so as to pierce the gloom of the carriage.

Jiminy got his first good look – at a calm face, ruined by a predatory nose. Long hair was slicked back from a tall forehead.

"Lady Valda," the man acknowledged, turning his fingers up, as though expecting a little bird to settle on them.

It seemed a snare.

At Lassleider's surreptitious motion, he moved to place his hand in it, keeping his eyes demurely downcast.

"Please, do forgive my niece's reticence, Lord Brigadier. She is a fragile thing and the dust of the long road has stolen her voice."

Clued in, Jiminy put a delicate hand to his throat.

"A good omen, perhaps, for your pilgrimage," Wramlinn said, "if it portends a marriage free of dissidence."

Hopefully, his veiled anger would pass for embarrassment.

Unseen, the dragoon caressed the underside of 'Valda's' palm.

Skin crawling, Jiminy risked a glance under his lashes.

The man's mild expression, he saw, was a veneer. A jackal nosed from beneath it, lazily eyeing prey. And it was both surprised – and pleased – at being spotted in turn.

Oh, he most definitely didn't want this man anywhere near him.

Especially not while wearing a dress.

"You mean free of 'diffidence' I trust, Lord Brigadier?"

He didn't think the lady had to work hard at her prissy tone.

Distracted, the lord stepped back.

"Of course, lady. I take it you travel next to the shrine at Sybaline Springs and, hence, to the culmination in Tellar?"

Lassleider spoke with the steely disapproval of an elderly matron, making it seem the man's comment had put her back up.

"Kind thanks for reminding me, lord. Else I'd dawdle all day. Driver, let us not waste any more of the lord brigadier's time."

"Then," the officer said, over the sound of the traces' rattling, "you are late from the shrine at Allerius Outlook?"

"Indeed, lord. Please, excuse our rude leave-taking, lest our early rising be for naught. Helia smile on your day's undertaking."

"On you as well, lady."

Not seeming too put-out at their curt exchange, the man cast eyes into the carriage again. "Lady Valda. Your arrival at court is richly anticipated. I *will* be first in line, for formal introductions."

The man was so unsubtle, in staking his claim, he might as well have pissed on 'Valda's' skirt hem.

The slight jerk as the carriage pulled away came as a relief.

Jiminy didn't need to lean out the window to know the lord brigadier's attention clung to them. It was a sensation that would linger, he suspected. Unconsciously, he scrubbed the hand Wramlinn had molested on his dress, grateful for the glove.

He didn't speak until they had cleared the town limits.

"Do you think we got away with it?"

The lady pursed her lips. "I had intended my snub to set him on his heels. But he is a great one for remembering slights. If I inadvertently set him on our scent, he may sniff after our back trail… which does *not* lead from Allerius Outlook."

Geography had not featured in his lessons.

"What would that mean for us?" he wondered aloud.

The lady frowned into the middle distance.

"Nothing," she judged at last. "Even should my fib be discovered eventually, simple distance should save us."

He would have found that more reassuring if she had not then immediately called on Neever for more speed.

"He looked a bit like you," Jiminy said at last, bringing Lassleider from her reverie. "The nose, the curls...

"Shared blood," she supplied distractedly. "The position of 'Emperor' is ancestral. Family branches that wander too far from the root become ineligible for their spot in the sun.

"That is one of the reasons why Serric wants Valda. Their combined bloodlines would put their issue in the top tier of candidates, should something befall the Imperial family."

Remembering the look in Wramlinn's eye, he thought the lady might be mistaken. Men like that didn't need reasons to want things, other than being told they couldn't have them.

Despite the persistent itch between his shoulders, the day passed in a clop of hooves and a clatter of wheels.

Proving that Wramlinn was also on her mind, the lady schooled him in the accepted practices for dissuading persistent suitors.

"Why can't I just slit open his ball purse?"

His own question brought him up short. He was a famously dirty fighter. But going for the crotch should give any man pause.

Was wearing a dress messing with his head?

"Put that away," the lady bid, eyeing the knife he was absently twirling. "We are not the Renali, whose answer to everything is steel. Our women need not rely on the 'maiden's prick' for safety."

Feeling sheepish, he let the blade disappear and she pressed a paper fan on him instead.

"Besides," she continued, "more often than not, Imperial ladies have had martial training. But you don't see us pelting boys with our fists or feet. We have social protocols that hit harder."

Protocols he endeavored to learn.

"How much longer?" he heaved at last, his head hurting.

"If we commit to Sybaline Springs, and a brisk pace, we'll see the capital before the week is out."

Which told him little enough.

"What then?" he threw in, out of habit.

Neever had taught him to expect no easy answers.

The lady did not disappoint. "I'm afraid I don't quite know."

Whether due to the upsetting encounter with the lord brigadier, or being cooped up in the carriage, Jiminy was feeling prickly.

He let the irritation leak into his voice. "I understand blind obedience from these temple types. But you seem more sensible. We left bodies in Plammic. You expect me to believe you jumped in, with both feet, without knowing what waited at the bottom?"

She crooked an icy eyebrow at him. "Boy, don't go punching holes in the boat you are in. It's a long swim to shore."

"Never had much use for boats," he growled. "My feet have always steered me right. And, right now, they're thinking this whole 'sanctuary' business is just another sinkhole. So, the longer you lot stay quiet, the more certain my feet get."

"Then why are you still here?" she challenged.

Why? he thought, taken aback. *Because your purists apparently know my face, whereas I need you to pick one priest from the next.*

Because temple coin is carrying me clear across a continent faster and in more luxury than I could have managed myself.

Because every moment I spend with you teaches me more about your empire – and how to rob it blind.

Because, mayhap, the safest place against a dread mage is among priests who don't hold with heathen magicks.

Most damningly, because I can't seem to curb my own curiosity.

And because – maybe – you've got a challenge for me.

If he was going to be the best sneak thief alive, there were worse places to try his hand than Tellar.

"Would you believe it's because I enjoy the company?"

The lady became a cold, warning presence.

"Look," he appealed, wishing the veil would let him rub his tired face, "see it through my eyes, alright? You're asking me to tiptoe to your tune, blindfolded, with pitfalls all around. And when I ask where we're headed, you haul on me all the harder.

"Don't *I* get to know what I'm risking my life for?"

He kept a sincere tone. He knew *exactly* what he'd be risking his life for, *if* he decided to risk it – a prince's ransom.

The lady's eyes lit on his fan, unconsciously held in the configuration meaning 'contrite'. A small sigh softened her shoulders and Jiminy's plea bore fruit.

"I tell you true," she warned, "I know no specifics of what awaits you in Tellar. All I can give you are my own convictions."

He slid slightly forward on his seat.

"There has been," she grimaced sourly, "a *schism*."

The carriage trundled on while she awaited his reaction.

"A what?"

Surprise flitted across her features.

"Sometimes," she confessed, "I forget you are a foreigner. It means there is a power struggle, dividing the Mother Temple."

"You're talking about the purists and the modernists, kicking each other's ankles over a sweetroll."

Her mouth corner quirked up. "I fear it is more grievous than that. You see, sophistry – and policy – is the purview of priests and aristocrats. Rarely does some change result from their scuffles. The dust settles and the political scenery looks a little different – but the bones of the land remain unbroken.

"Right now, both sides are taking pains to hide the breadth of the chasm from the populace. Our history has shown that, once the masses pick sides – and they will – peaceful debate over.

"Nothing I say to you can describe the horror of a schism, spilling onto the streets. Lifelong neighbor turning on neighbor, with a religious fervor only a society like ours can breed.

"The Empire would rip itself apart at the seams. The continent would catch fire overnight. The Emperor would step in.

"It is in all of our best interests," she concluded, "to keep our activities as clandestine as possible."

He thought of the footpads, doubtless paid in purist coin, who'd jumped him and Neever in Plammic's side streets.

"How," he demanded, "do the purists know what we're up to, when even you and I don't?"

"They may not," she determined. "Not specifically, at any rate."

"You mean they would snuff me, and Neever, just to make double certain we're not coming to kick them in the shins?"

That *really* made him want to kick them in the shins.

"They'd have done better trying to bribe me…"

Seeing her narrowed gaze, he made up a hurried explanation.

"It seems risky, I mean – likely to kick off your civil war."

"It certainly marks a new high tideline in the conflict," she agreed. "I'm not averse to a well-placed assassination in principle.

It can be the very thing to grease the wheels of progress. But the attack on you was ill-thought and badly orchestrated."

The fact that he might have died didn't seem to bother her.

"I've lived through a couple of civil wars," he offered.

With the princes, forever at odds over turf and prestige, conflict in the streets was a common occurrence back home.

"Not like this," she said vehemently. "The last Heli upheaval predates your birth by centuries. And, not having been a colony, Purlia was insulated against the worst of the repercussions.

"Central government's ties to its vassals snapped. The offshore prefectures revolted. Dozens of petty governors and warlords rose overnight, promising reunification under their rule.

"A repeat would see organized trade and production grind to a halt. You think you left bodies in Plammic?" she threw his earlier indignation in his face. "The infighting will kill millions. The resulting famine will kill tens of millions more-"

"Alright, alright!" he surrendered, palms upraised.

She took a calming breath, her nostrils flaring white.

"As for me," she continued in clipped tones, "I will do all I can to ensure this stays a *quiet* war – with minimum Imperial casualties on *both* sides."

He thought back on his first Heli experience – the Genla serving girl who had so studiously disapproved of him. "No one will miss an infidel, is that it? *That*'s the shine that made them pick me up?"

"In a way," she smiled thinly. "Being a fresh face, with no affiliation and with loyalty only to coin, is an attractive quality."

He sat back. So. He was in the middle of a hidden holy war.

His feet itched.

She eyed him askance, somehow plumbing his mood even past the veil and petticoats. "What's funny?"

For a change, he told the absolute truth, "Not a damned thing."

"And I thought I was in the wetlands *before*," Jiminy muttered.

For the past two days, the view out the window had shown him nothing but ankle-deep paddies and tiered fields, haunted by plodding oxen and muck-footed farmers.

"The 'Downlands'," the lady absently corrected. "Close the curtain. We're entering Sybaline Springs."

"It's a town on stilts," he objected, staring at the timbered buildings' discolored supports.

"Dry foundations are in short supply here. Those who cannot afford to live on the hill must contend with frequent flooding."

Shaking his head in disbelief, he reluctantly drew the drapes.

Cobbles gave way to tightly fitted boards, their hollow clunking overloud in the cabin, until the wheels cut into solid slope again.

"Here we are," Neever announced at last.

Sighing, he readied himself to play 'Valda' once more.

"Chin up," Lassleider said.

"Thanks."

"No, I mean, get your chin up. Your posture is terrible."

Pique lent some stiffness to his spine.

"That's better."

The opening door robbed him of a reply.

Smiling, Neever offered him a hand down. "Lady?"

"Bastard," he breathed his response.

"None of that," Lassleider cautioned. "Kender-style buildings have famously thin walls. While here, we must guard our tongues."

She wasn't kidding, he saw. This night's inn was of a peculiar construction. It emulated the surrounding hills with its stacked terraces. Brightly enameled beams curled at the roof corners. Sliding doors and walls of opaque paper hid the lit interior.

For all that it looked like a feast day lantern, the boards sounded sturdy beneath his feet as they ascended the stairs.

Following the lady's lead, he sat on a fancifully sawed bench while silent servants accosted his feet. In short order, he'd been unslippered and stuffed into a pair of fluffy over-socks.

That, he reflected as he wiggled his toes, was one way to keep the floor planks polished and mud-free.

The interior wrapped around a garden. The ground floor was all mossy boulders and miniature trees, ringed by overlooking balconies. The far side looked like it might be a taproom or common room, but it was hard to tell, given the outlandish design.

Apart from the table master – a stick of a man swaddled in bright silk – the bobbing employees spoke not a word.

"That was eerie," he whispered, once the innkeeper's short steps had retreated from their room. "Why is it so quiet here?"

"This is a traditional Kender hot springs inn – a place of serene contemplation and renewal. It is the next-to-last stop on the Daughter's Pilgrimage and is supposed to be a spiritual experience.

"Alas, the baths are communal, and so, won't be seeing us."

He sighed in relief.

"But we must maintain our ruse. In the morning we will visit the local Temple and obtain a pilgrim's token. By rights, we should already have four. Let us hope the priest tending the shrine does not insist on seeing them."

They had dinner in their rooms again.

"Comfortable?" the lady grinned, kneeling easily opposite him. A Kender 'feast' sat on the knee high table between them.

He eyed her archly. "It may surprise you to know that this is not the first meal I've eaten off the floor."

"That does not surprise me in the least. How is your catfish?"

He glowered at it.

"I've *had* cat. And I've had fish. This," he raised the offending morsel, "tastes like neither. Whoops…"

He fumbled the foreign chopsticks for the hundredth time.

"How is it," he growled, "that people who live on rice and broth don't hold with spoons?"

"Proficiency is considered a mark of refinement," she mourned, watching him chase the harried mouthful around a bowl.

"Speaking of which – tonight, I will tweeze your leg hairs."

The pale fish went scything into the sauce.

"Whatever for?!"

"They could have given us away while you were being shod."

"They didn't!"

"They still might…"

His arguments fell on deaf ears. She chased him around the room, like a bite of catfish in a bowl, until she finally had her way.

He went to bed angry. No other commission had ever seen him caught long enough to experience such torture.

Peaceful contemplation and renewal at last lulled him to sleep-

-and rough survival senses raised his head from the pillow.

Something was off about the night's silence.

This wasn't the quiet of an inn asleep.

The hush of stilled feet and bated breath hung right outside their room.

In silence, he rolled from his blankets, knife in hand.

Presumably their spy was socked. Bare feet would offer Jiminy more traction in a pursuit but make sneaking more difficult. Reveling in the challenge, he padded across the boards.

Discovery, when it came, was due to no fault of his.

Beyond the paper walls clouds parted, moonlight propelled his shadow before him. For a moment, his silhouette stood, starkly outlined against the screen of the hallway.

Sand spawned parchment building!

He leapt for the door, even as heavy footfalls raced away.

He snapped the portal aside and slid onto the indoor balcony. Ahead, the tail-end of a robe rounded the corner by the stairs.

Without thinking, he leapt for the balcony rail. He would swing straight to the balustrade below and cut off the spy's escape-

A hand clamped on his elbow.

"Your face!" Lady Lassleider hissed. "Get back inside!"

Reluctantly, he let himself be towed back into their room. The sound of far-off feet fled into silence.

"You let them get away!" he hissed, safely inside.

"Quiet down. We'll have servants up here soon enough as it is."

She was right. Already the light of a lone lantern was bobbing curiously along the garden below.

Lassleider eased their door panel shut.

"D'you think it was Wramlinn? Or more purist sellswords?"

Or a mercenary scout, in the employ of a dread mage...?

"Hush. It could have been a nosy servant for all we know. Whoever it was, it is good they escaped. Had they glimpsed your face, our painstaking deceit would be undone. As it is, all they heard was two ladies snoring – Helia send there was no accomplice observing from another balcony."

She turned on him in earnest. "And what, pray tell, were you planning on doing once you caught them?"

"Um..." He hid his knife behind his back.

"I thought as much. Men! Never thinking further than the shortest thing to hand. Return to bed. Leave the thinking to me."

He thought to argue further, but concerned footsteps were rounding the stairs. Huffing, he turned toward his blankets.

"Nosy servants..." he scoffed, punching his pillow.

However he tried, though, sleep refused to return.

* * *

THE SPECTER RETURNED to the blighted clearing, wearing one of the locals – a man in bright paint and brighter feathers.

The twisted tree had grown. It now hulked twice as tall. The face upon its bark gritted its teeth in a grimace or a smile.

Even with the specter's senses clogged by flesh, it could feel the revenant leaching life from the local vegetation. It stood, mired amid gray earth and blackened boughs. Only the plants on the periphery showed any green: the weeping puss of corruption.

This was good. There was plenty of residue to power a ritual.

Drawing the local's flint knife, the specter set to carving. Bright, emerald blood welled where it dug into the wooden corpse.

Unseen, roots wormed free of the earth. Branches bent low.

They struck, burrowing into the specter's borrowed body.

In a panic, it tried to flee its physical form, only to find that snaking roots of force had somehow tangled them together.

Meeting its captor's wooden grin, feeling the vitality drain from it, it howled with its human lungs.

* * *

THEIR DEPARTURE FROM Sybaline Springs passed in a blur. Jiminy vaguely remembered being marched into the local temple and pretending to pray before some altar. They had left in a rush.

Despite maintaining that nothing was amiss, the lady's tension showed in the terseness of their lessons over the next few days.

Mid-morning had brought a discernable change, from cobbles to flagstones. He'd risked Lassleider's ire to peek out the window.

Gone were the endless fields and wooded hills. The curtain hid town upon town, with barely a break in between.

They were nearing the capital.

Their inn for the evening proved to be a mansion in miniature.

By now practiced at playing 'Valda', he daintily discarded the cooling, citrus scented cloth he'd just used to dab at his wrists. Their rooms commanded an impressive view. Barely visible on the horizon – and all the more impressive for that, at this distance – the fabled spire of Tellar rose against a sullen sunset.

"I don't understand why we couldn't just push on. We could cover that distance by midnight."

"As the crow flies," Lassleider agreed, setting out tools for some new feminine torture. "If, however, the crow must take a carriage along the capital's grand concourse, it will take a sight longer. And traveling by night invites its own kind of attention. I'd rather avoid being accosted by the Watch, wouldn't you?"

He grunted noncommittally, not about to see sense when he was salivating after the nearby city. It dwarfed Oaragh for size and splendor. He would have no trouble, disappearing there.

"Whatever. I'm anxious to learn more of this temple commission. When is that conversation due?"

"'Commission?' Do you fancy yourself some master artisan?"

He turned.

Being too good at what he did had tripped him up before. It was hard, building a reputation, when people couldn't agree on whether or not you existed in the first place. Infamy – without incarceration – was a tight rope that did not stretch to Tellar.

"You'd be surprised."

Seeing something in his stance, the lady's scorn subsided.

"We will arrive at my family holdings tomorrow," she assured, "and meet your handlers at sunset. That is as much as I know."

He opened his mouth to say something ill-considered.

An urgent knock interrupted him.

"Lady," Neever hissed, "we have a problem."

"That's turning into his catchphrase," Jiminy grumped.

Once inside, the monk in driver's livery peered both ways down the passage before barring the door behind him.

"I've just come from the farrier's down the block," the man whispered. "There's an Imperial destrier there, being reshod. Lady, it's still wet from a hard ride and bears a brigade brand."

"A dragoon's horse? Here? That cannot be a coincidence…"

"Can't it?" Jiminy wondered. "I'd put money on finding a horse at a horseshoe monger's..." They stared at him. "What?"

"You don't grasp the rarity of horseflesh. The Emperor's stables are sacrosanct. A military man would not lightly allow a civilian to hammer at those hooves. And a dragoon would carry his destrier into battle, rather than risk one that has thrown a shoe.

"No, he followed us here," the lady concluded.

Jiminy's throat tightened. "Wramlinn?"

"Not himself," Neever sounded certain. "Else the hostlers would have said. But it is assuredly one of the lord's retainers."

"Our unseen listener, from Sybaline Springs."

Lassleider agreed, "It seems 'Valda' made an impression."

He scowled. He knew exactly the kind of impression he'd like to leave on the lord. And it was near the neck.

"What do we do now?"

"We do nothing," the lady commanded. "We trust in our ruse and continue as before. Neever, see if you can sniff out this dragoon. I'd like to have a look at him in turn."

Jiminy returned to his vigil. This would be the perfect time to disappear. Few on this continent knew his face and none knew his name. Likely he'd ditched the dread mage on the opposite coast. He had gold aplenty – even if it was presently parchment.

Whatever their intentions, the priests had delivered sanctuary.

So why was he still standing here?

"A game of sidestep?" the lady offered.

Outside, the cityscape beckoned. He nodded thoughtfully.

Three games later, Neever returned.

"He is in the common room downstairs, lady."

"Well, then," Lassleider stood, "I could use a drink."

Jiminy all but leapt to his feet. "I thought you'd never ask."

The term 'common' room was misleading. The tables shone, their cloths pristine. Heli crystal stood in flutes and not a single rush marred the floor. Silvered glass ran the length of the bar.

The table master came our personally to seat them. The man was so pale his tracery of veins lent him a decidedly blue tint – yet another patch in the crazed, Imperial quilt of peoples.

"What is your pleasure this evening, Lady Lassleider?"

Jiminy's hopes fell as she ordered, "A pot of Mjalakat tea."

The innkeeper seemed equally put out, teal cheeks turning purple. "Alas, lady. Our stores of Mjalakat have dried up, as has trade with the domain beyond the dunes. Might I offer a Skordian medley instead? Compliments of the house, of course."

"That would be most kind."

The man bowed deeply before taking his leave.

"Don't fidget."

He set aside the spindly crystal, carelessly left to adorn their table. In Oaragh, he could have lived like a prince for a week, just on what he'd get for these two glasses.

"'The domain beyond the dunes'?" he wondered at length, careful to keep his voice close.

"To the far north, beyond your desert cities."

"You mean Traljador?"

She left off righting her silverware. "Is that what you call it?"

"*We* call it '*alsu albarb*'," he offered.

Her brow crinkled in concentration. "'Brutal field'?"

And she had led him to believe she didn't speak Purli.

"Close. Closer would be 'the barbarian plains'."

"There are people even the Purli consider barbarians?"

"You mean *besides* the Heli?"

She let that slide. "Where does 'Traljador' come in, then?"

He gave some thought to his answer.

"The far north is dangerous – which is why your tea is so damn expensive. Only the most daring of the caravanserai risk it. And even they can never know who they will meet there. Among those savages, turf changes face with the speed of back-alley dice.

"Some seasons, the traders find no one. And each group calls their homeland by a different name. 'Traljador' is simply the first one I ever heard and it stuck with me."

"That sounds… needlessly complex."

"Barbarians," he shrugged.

Their tea arrived.

"May I pour for you, ladies?"

"No, thank you, Master Innkeeper." Lassleider pulled the pot toward her, whispering. "So. Have you spotted our dragoon yet?"

"Mm," he agreed, cutting his eyes toward the bar. Three tables back, in a corner by himself, sat a man with muck colored eyes and a glistening cowlick. Among all the rich silks and velvets, the man's woolens stuck out like a sore thumb.

"Doesn't quite look a soldier, does he?"

For all the man's broad shoulders and cropped hair, the mirror had shown him slouched over a pronounced paunch.

"Military issue boots," the lady disputed. "Not being ahorse or in uniform, getting a table here must have cost him a lot of coin."

"At least he has beer," Jiminy mourned, maneuvering his cup beneath his veil. "So, you've seen him. What now? Want me to follow him home and tuck him in?"

He pointedly eyed the unused dinner knife at her elbow.

She frowned her disapproval. "No. Wramlinn was raised on intrigue. If his spy disappears, his suspicions will soar. He'll know that ours is a secret worth killing over."

"Then how about I visit the farrier instead?"

She controlled her shock well. Anyone watching would merely think her companion had said something contrary.

"Absolutely not," she said. "If anything befell that horse, the farrier's whole family could lose their lives or livelihood."

"So we're going to let this lump trail us all the way to Tellar?"

"And why not?" the lady surprised him. "As long as we do nothing untoward, he'll discover nothing untoward."

Grimacing, he ducked his head in agreement.

"Now, finish your tea. All this talk of needless bloodshed has left a sour taste in my mouth."

He subsided, thoughts swirling.

"What vexes you?" the lady asked at last, noticing.

He grunted. "You talk of horses like they're treasure troves. Yet you've got a matching set of four to pull your showy carriage."

"True. Your question?"

"Exactly how well-to-do are you?"

She took a slow sip of tea, her silence speaking volumes.

Hmm. And they would reach her family holdings tomorrow...

She gave him a shrewd look. "I also own several very fine hunting hounds. Are you a dog person?"

He suppressed a shiver. "I prefer to keep my own company."

Despite having only half a day of travel left, Jiminy found himself dumped out of bed at the customary crack of dawn.

The lady was unapologetic. "No doubt our friend has reasoned out our destination. Still, if there is even a slight chance we might slip away whilst his steed is indisposed, we should seize it."

And so, Jiminy and his companions – including the now near constant itch between his shoulders – set off.

It was a measure of the lady's nerves that she neglected their lessons. She sat, contemplatively tapping at her chin.

Jiminy stayed perfectly still – lest a stray movement remind her of his presence. Through a finger-thin gap in the curtains, he watched the Imperial capital swell. The carriage slid under the weight of a massive wall and their progress slowed further, stymied by thick drifts of foot traffic.

"Not hungry?" he asked, as they overshot the midday mark.

"There will be time enough to eat," the lady said tersely.

They reached Lassleider manor while the sun still stood high in the sky. At first, he thought it an even grander, more expansive inn. Until a servant, in livery to match Neever's, rushed to open the iron gates. The coachyard turned out to be a compound garden. A pebbled concourse wound up to a magnificent mansion.

"Yours?" he breathed.

The lady inclined her head.

Not an enchantress or a clan leader, then, he marveled. *I've seen princes' palaces that were more modest.*

"Now remember," the lady roused herself, "our charade is not up yet. Some of the servants here knew Valda and will know if aught is amiss. *They* will not believe demureness or shyness from you. So, keep your head up but meet no one's eye. Feign a fit of pique, if you can. Helia knows that won't be out of character."

"You fear your servants may betray you?"

He was impressed that any had the nerve.

"No. But one woman's gossip is another's deadly scheme. Let us not give my poor servants anything to prattle about, shall we?"

A double file of liveried men and women flanked the short walk from the carriage to the mansion's main doors.

A flurry of bows followed them up its steps.

"Welcome back, milady," said a waiting servant – a middle-aged man with stiff whiskers and a stiffer bearing. The man's clothes were a richer cut than the rest, strained by a low gut.

"Thank you, Tuori. You remember my niece, Valda Lividica?"

The man's gaze gave nothing away.

"Indeed. Welcome once more to Hemlin Hall, Lady Lividica."

Jiminy nodded minimally.

"No time for pleasantries, Tuori," the lady commanded, holding out an arm. "Catch me up. You've received my messages?"

"Your birds arrived safely, lady. All has been prepared-"

The two fell into step, leaving him to catch up.

He let his eyes rove. When he'd been a child, picking pockets and lifting purses, he'd dreamed of stealing his way into waist deep treasure. The reality, of course, was orderly safes and strongboxes, neatly piled and catalogued. Or so he'd thought. The carelessly scattered wealth, all around him, was making him re-evaluate.

I'd need a week, and a hundred camels, to clear this place out...

When they reached Lassleider's personal apartments, he nearly gave the game away in a fit of hilarity. The lady had clearly had no hand in the lace frills that dripped from every upright. And, just as clearly, she didn't care enough to have the rooms redecorated.

Or burned down.

A string of servants crowded in behind them, bearing steaming towels, tea and biscuits. Mindful of the lady's advice, he stood stiffly by the window, his back to the room.

"What news from the interior, Tuori?" the matron prompted.

"Little that is good, lady. Then again, little that is news. The Falia and Winneria factions' feud has deadlocked the Chapters' Chamber again. This leaves the Temple's proposed tax hike unopposed. The palace passages are clogged with mercers and house representatives, bringing petitions before the Emperor.

"The Delvers Chapter are shunting miners' contracts offshore, supporting rumors that the northern lodes are running dry.

"The Tamorian governor's son was stabbed in a Tellar tavern brawl. The governor is struggling to quell the colony's outrage while entreating Temple healers…"

On and on went the report.

"Have there been any reports of deaths or disappearances among the clergy? Any wrongheaded muggings gone awry?"

Tuori blinked. "None that have reached my ears, lady. But I can make enquiries."

"Do," she mused. "Quietly please, Tuori."

"You may rely on my discretion, milady."

"And please see to having the carriage readied after supper. Lady Valda shall be accompanying me to Temple, to complete her Daughter's Pilgrimage."

"Of course, milady," the man bowed himself out.

"So," Lassleider said to his back, once they were alone, "soon you shall be rid of me and 'Valda' both. Are you relieved?"

In truth, he felt a pang of regret. Night sky knew, he wouldn't miss the dresses. And the lady was an unapologetic manipulator. But, in her own way, she had been kind to him.

"I'm looking forward to some straight answers," he said instead.

And may the priests' greedy goddess help them if they refused.

GOING TO PRAYERS required Jiminy to squeeze into his most elaborate dress yet. Even with just him and Lassleider in the carriage, the skirts and lace nearly overflowed the windows.

"So," he asked, to distract himself from the traitorous thought that he must look a treat, "are we headed for the central spire?"

"Oh, dear, no," she laughed, "the Mother Temple is quite inaccessible, except on holy days. No, we are halfway to the *oldest* Temple in the capital. Or, at least, the site where it once stood. The actual building has been rebuilt and remodeled many times as the noble quarter grew. Since most aristocrats maintain their own chapels, it should be quite deserted on a weeknight."

She leaned forward, causing a tidal wave of skirts. "It is said that the ancient catacombs, beneath it, crisscross the city."

He shivered. Bones did not bother him, provided they stayed put. But his people had good reason to practice cremation. The dead of the dunes were wont to wander on moonless nights.

As Neever helped him from the carriage, he resisted the urge to crane his neck. Clearly, the steeple was modelled after Tellar's spire. You'd have to be a fit man, with time to spare, if you intended to ascend the narrow—

As if insulted by his regard, the tower tolled disapprovingly. Other bells, from across the city, took up the dirge. For a dozen breaths, the entire peninsula cried out in a discordant voice.

"Come along," the lady spurred, gathering him up.

He followed, trying hard not to think about being in a building of nobles, each with an eye as discerning as Lady Lassleider's.

A clergyman, in a richly embroidered cassock, bowed them in.

Jiminy eyed the vaulted marble and thick tapestries. The setting sun softened the stained glass to a gentle luster. Impressive.

A handful of people were already seated in the pews.

Not as many as he'd feared.

Right up front sat a family of four, decked in drab silks and sedate jewels. The strained stillness, of the two small boys, suggested that at least one of the parents was an absolute tyrant.

A pair of elderly ladies sat, chatting disruptively, just off the aisle. Feathered plumes bobbed as the old biddies turned to regard the newcomers. Seeing Lassleider, they waved and made to shimmy over. But a priest in resplendent robes cleared his throat from the pulpit. With anticipatory grins, the grannies subsided.

Jiminy sank gratefully into the pew the lady pointed out.

"Posture," she murmured and he jerked up straight.

She'll have me rolling over or playing dead next, he grimaced.

It took all of two sentences for him to lose interest in the service. The Heli being spoken was stilted and difficult to follow.

Also, the pulpit was shaped like a risen sun, lamps lighting the priest with a personal halo. Jiminy was trying to figure whether the design was polished brass, plated gold or simply gold.

I wonder if they lock this place at night...?

At some unseen signal, the congregation rose. He copied them, head bowed over clasped hands. The preacher's rambling turned even more obscure. All Jiminy heard were hard consonants and sudden stops. The parishioners spoke form replies into some of these pauses and he was glad the veil hid his lips. As the priest released them to their seats, he joined the congregation in tracing a circle on his chest.

Then the sermon started up in earnest.

He found some relief, watching the grim boys in the front pew. They fought a silently escalating war of elbows. There was an illegal pinch, followed by a barely noticeable twitch. Their mother glanced their way and Jiminy's entertainment ended.

At long last the priest pulled them to their feet for more prayer.

You could feel the end of the service as a change in the air.

"Brace yourself," her ladyship warned.

He peered around her shoulder. The two old biddies were closing at a speedy shuffle. He fussed nervously with his skirts.

"Hemlin, dear!" the foremost crowed, plumed head whipping up toward her companion. "See? I told you it was her."

The taller one conceded. "Your eyes are better than mine."

Lassleider halted so her skirts effective walled Jiminy into the pew behind her. "Farisa. Lomia. You are looking well."

"Ah, bless you for saying so!" the hen-like one clucked, snatching one of the lady's hands. The other, taller one stooped over her companion's shoulder like a magpie.

Twin smiles beamed.

"We've missed you, you know. Why, just the other day I was saying how much we miss you. Did I not say, just the other day, how much we miss her, Lomia?"

"She did," the magpie bobbed. "She did say we miss you-"

"I thought for sure we'd only see you again next court season," the hen gushed, concern painted over curiosity. "Is aught amiss? Have you decided to winter in the capital this year?"

"Do stay." The magpie's beady eyes flashed toward her companion. "The winters are *so* tiresome-"

"Dreadfully dull," the hen said, gaze sashaying.

"Little would please me more," Lassleider said, "than good company and compelling conversation."

"Marvelous!" the hen exclaimed, pulling on the lady's wrists as though she were a runaway horse.

The magpie fluttered in anticipation.

"There is much to tell," the hen whispered. "Such things-"

"Dastardly, despicable things!"

"-as would make your toenails curl. You know the Tamorian lad, who was stabbed? Guess where he was found?"

"-the Buttered Stair, is where!" the magpie interjected.

"And High House Stalia's brat, the one at Clatter Court?"

"-being brought up on disciplinary charges!"

"And Olingar's failing tea importers?"

"-wait till you hear how he has stayed afloat!"

Behind his veil, he grinned. Lassleider hadn't said *they* were good company. And, watching the two gossips, he could see why.

He must have moved because their gazes slid to him. Abruptly, he felt like he was dangling off a building again, with a crossbow bolt flying at him.

"Ah, but is this not your blessed niece, Hemlin?"

"Indeed." Outwardly, Lassleider appeared pleased.

"Lady Haviena," she introduced. "Lady Massien. This is Valda Lavidica. Valda, meet Farisa and Lomia, two dear old friends."

Not, he dimly noted, necessarily friends of *hers*…

Mindful of his lessons, he made quarter curtsy.

"Dear child!" Farisa gushed. "You could not be in better hands. Why, between Hemmy and Lomia and I, there is not a thing about males or marriage we can't tell you, you'll see."

His stomach contracted in denial.

"Ahem," Lassleider interrupted. "Though she would be grateful for your hard-won wisdom, ladies, she must finish her pilgrimage first. Ah, I see the priest beckoning. Farisa. Lomia. Until later…"

With a deftness that would have put a career card cheat to shame, the lady slipped her hand from Farisa's clutch.

The hen gave him a salacious wink. "Indeed! We look forward to seeing you without your veil, eh? Eh?"

The magpie waggled wispy eyebrows at him.

He let Lassleider lead him down the aisle, the silence a balm to his ear. A heartfelt sigh billowed his veil.

"Don't relax yet," she cautioned.

Delicately squaring his shoulders, he followed her through a recessed door and into the temple's service passages.

More marble, more mirrored lamps.

Stairs led past stone sarcophagi and down to a dank cellar.

A lone candle illuminated Neever's roughspun robes.

"This way…"

They descended still further, until the fitted stone of wall and ceiling seemed uncomfortably close.

"Here." The monk led them into a cramped store room.

A priestess – going by her garb, if not her youthful appearance – waited behind a table, looking out of place.

Jiminy slowed as he spied the second person in the room.

A sword hilt parted the soldier's saffron robes, the cut and color somehow echoing the priestess's clothes. Armored scales glistened in the gloom and watchful eyes sought Jiminy out.

"This is Yoriana," he half-heard.

The priestess bounced to her feet as Neever named her.

"She will be taking over as 'Lady Valda'. I've already relinquished my livery to your new coachman, who is waiting to drive you home." The monk bowed low. "Lady, words cannot express the depth of our gratitude."

"Oh, tosh," Lassleider dismissed, "let us make haste."

"Of course."

Warily eyeing the nameless soldier, Jiminy nearly missed the bundle Neever lobbed at him. A pair of breeches unfurled.

Relief dimmed as he realized there were no room dividers here.

The lady met his scowl with a raised eyebrow.

"Now is no time to be modest," she said, stepping close.

The priestess made to rise as well but his glare had her sinking back in her seat, blushing.

As Lassleider peeled away his layers and petticoats, he made sure to meet no one's eyes. He kept his hands clear, though, in case he had to work fast. He cursed every moment he was stuck in a sleeve or cuff.

Wasn't going to get far in this getup anyway…

The lady gathered up the priestess with a glance and together they took the double armful of frilly frippery next door.

Unstrapping the brace of knives from his thigh, hands hovering near sharp steel, Jiminy felt the soldier's attention redouble.

"See anything you like?" he grinned.

But the man was smart enough not to look away.

He dragged on the breeches and shirt, pleased to see his hip jacket. A pair of soft-soled turnshoes rounded out the ensemble.

"Can someone," he said, "finally tell me what's going on?"

"In a moment," the monk stalled.

"You've run out of moments, Neever."

The soldier shifted slightly in warning. Jiminy didn't care. The itch between his shoulders was clawing up his neck. Somehow, he'd deluded himself into thinking that Neever's ilk were all carrot and no stick. Now, here stood the stick, fingering its sword hilt.

Few things could upset him so much as his own stupidity.

Then, Neever produced a strip of cloth from a sleeve. He watched the blindfold writhe, like the adder it was.

"Not on your life," he declared.

Neever ducked an apology. "And you'll have to disarm, too."

He rocked back on his heels, subtly shifting his feet so as to meet an attack, from either man. The soldier mirrored him.

"So that's how it is?" he accused.

"I'm afraid so," Neever mourned.

This wasn't a brothel. He didn't come here to get screwed.

"Well," he told them, "that makes this easy, then."

He backed toward the door, hands held out peaceably.

"Thanks for the memories. Good luck with your holy war-"

Steel rasped on leather as the soldier stepped forward...

...and stilled, with only a handspan of sword drawn.

Whether at Neever's outflung arm, or at the sight of Jiminy's knives – one poised to throw, the other to stab – was unclear.

"Wait!" the monk begged both of them.

"Don't move, Neever," he warned. "Thanks for the job offer. But I think I'm going to go in a different direction..."

He sidled toward the open door, keeping his eyes on the soldier.

Neever was dangerous too. But that innocuous staff was nowhere to be seen. And, while his knives were not the equal of a sword, that only mattered if he let the thing clear its scabbard.

"Peace," the monk placated. "Please, hear me out-"

"You had your chance to talk. You wanted to play silly buggers instead. Well, now we play *my* game. Hide and seek."

He'd reached the door, the cool air of the passage on his neck.

"Put on the blindfold, monk," he smiled, "and count to-"

The keen edge of a blade parted the hair of his nape.

A second soldier stood ready in the corridor, sword leveled.

"Crap."

For a moment, no one moved.

"Ugh!" Lassleider gushed, marching up. "Men!"

Her disapproval drove the armed soldier from her path and she shoved Jiminy back into the store room, reaching out to flick his ear. Reflexively, he tried to hide his knives and was only slightly assuaged to see the soldier attempt the same.

"Honestly," the lady disapproved, breezing in. "One would expect better of the masha'na."

Neever flinched as she turned on him. "Chorister, do you swear – on your everlasting soul and its ascension into Grace – that you shall suffer no harm to come to this young man, and that he shall be free to leave by the next sunrise?"

The monk visibly blanched but steeled himself to nod.

Flabbergasted, Jiminy let the lady pluck one of the knives from his grip. She shoved its hilt at the holy man.

"Then swear."

Neever flinched. "Lady, it is forbidden to make a blood-"

"Swear it!"

Sweat sheening his upper lip, the monk accepted the dagger. It neatly parted the skin of his thumb. With freshly beading blood, the man drew a small circle on his breast.

"I shall allow no harm to befall this young man. At sunrise, he shall be free to go. I so swear, by my everlasting soul and on my hope of ascension into Grace."

Neever slumped, breathing hard, as though he'd run a race.

"Witnessed," the lady pronounced.

She turned to him, smiling as though she'd solved something.

"Oh, I should trust him now? Because he pinky-promised?"

"Do you trust *me*?" she demanded.

He would never admit it, if he did.

"Then believe that Neever would *die* before he broke that vow."

He glanced at the monk, who still seemed stricken.

"If you're wrong," he growled, "he'll die immediately after."

"That's the spirit," she responded, turning him by the shoulder. In the passage stood the priestess, hands clutched to her veiled face. She looked quite fetching, in all that ruff and lace. He could almost forgive Lord Wramlinn. Almost.

"Young man," Lassleider said, "it has been a pleasure."

He awkwardly took the hand she offered. She'd never taught him how to act the part of the gentleman.

"Likewise, lady." He surprised himself by meaning it.

She stepped closer, turning serious. "Take a care, yes?"

"And everything else I can carry," he agreed, grinning.

Chuckling, she mock-slapped his cheek and turned to go, the priestess bounding at her heels.

In the ladies' sudden absence, the four who remained avoided looking each other in the eye.

Men! Jiminy echoed the thought, somewhat unexpectedly.

He reached for the blindfold. "Let's get this over with…"

Some moments later, sightless and bladeless, he listened to shelves being moved. A key turned in a lock. The smell of damp stone intensified. A hand settled on his shoulder.

"I will guide you," Neever promised, steering him toward what had, a moment ago, seemed a solid wall.

The air in the secret passage felt close and stale.

"Mind your head…"

He listened to the scuff of soles and the shift of armor echo, describing the main and branching corridors to his ears. A larger space loomed, smelling of mildew and bone meal.

The old catacombs… he thought, suppressing a shiver.

Somewhere ahead, keys jangled. Tired hinges squealed.

"Five stairs ahead," Neever warned.

He climbed. There was a moment of increased closeness, as he passed beneath a lintel. Flat echoes sketched a larger room, walls softened by wood or tapestry, both of which he could smell. A faint guttering suggested torches or braziers.

Neever guided his hand to a chair back and stood away.

"Welcome," said a man's voice, wheezy with age or infirmity.

"Please," it invited, "sit."

They hadn't tied his hands. He could rip the blindfold off if he had to. But he wasn't about to be hasty.

Smiling at the pageantry, he sprawled sideways in the offered seat, kicking a leg over the armrest. It was an incredibly arrogant move but he had few enough moves to make. If Neever's vow wasn't going to protect him from a cuff about the ear – or, by extension, anything else – now was the time to find out.

"Master Mystery Voice," he scorned. "I hope *you* know why I'm here? No one else seems to… "

He smelled something alchemical. Turpentine? Oils?

"Do you need me to pose for a portrait?" he prodded.

"Now you've got me considering where to hang you."

He ignored the threat, venturing an educated guess. "How will I steal art for you, if you spike me to the wall?"

"So, *now* you are the picture of cooperation? I'm told that, just a short while ago, you were unwilling to even hear my proposal?"

He grimaced. "Your proposal is badly presented. I don't know how you're used to doing things, but commissioning a master thief is not like hiring a whore off the corner. *You* have to work at convincing *me*, not the other way around. And, so far, all I've had from you is scraps of paper, string-alongs and *this*."

He pointed irritably at his blindfold.

"Indeed. My apologies. Somebody pour our guest some wine."

Wine, yes!

He listened to the happy plug of a cork and the rich glug that followed. A smooth glass was placed in his outstretched hand.

After weeks in the tea-totaling lady's company, he found the scent heady. Poison was not a concern. At least, not until after he'd told them 'no'. He smacked his lips after an appreciative sip.

"The blindfold," he tried next, "is also a bit over zealous."

"Well," the voice apologized, "we *are* zealots. Please put up with it a while longer, until we've concluded our negotiations."

Negotiations. Right.

"Neever mentioned that, for this caper, I'd earn ten times again as much as I did at Marvellack Post?"

"Correct."

"Thing is, without knowing the details of the job, I can't judge whether that is enough. And we've yet to establish whether or not your payment is worth more than the parchment it's scribbled on. I've seen neither hide nor hair of any hard coin."

He wet his throat with some wine before continuing.

"You went to extraordinary lengths to get me here, so you recognize the level of my skill. Finding somebody else, half as good, is going to be a fool's errand. And I gather there's some urgency here. So, let's not pretend your strong-arms are anything but ornaments. Harm to me only harms your chances of success."

His host said nothing. Good. He'd give them an earful.

"I have no lovers or relations on this continent for you to ransom. I have no blackmail-worthy secrets. Even if you found some way to force my hand, what's to stop me abandoning your cause – or absconding with your prize – the moment I'm out from under your thumb?

"In short," he concluded, "you have no leverage. Your only allure is coin. So let's stop talking paper, start talking price, and you explain *exactly* what it is you want me to steal."

Toasting his unseen host, he tossed back the last of his wine.

A slow chuckle sounded from the opposite end of the room.

"You're saying you lack incentive. What of the antidote?"

Unease drew his throat tight.

"Antidote?"

"For the poison you just drank…"

The bottom dropped from his stomach. He'd assumed the alchemical smells were related to art. Were they actually alchemy supplies? As his host's laughter filled the room, he ran his fingers around the inside of his cup but could detect no residue. He brought it to his nose and smelled nothing but wine.

The laughing turned into hacking, then into desperate coughing.

He felt Neever move from his side. What sounded like the same bottle glugged. Someone slurped determinedly from a cup. The convulsions slowly calmed.

"I've heard enough," rasped the raw voice. "Take off his blindfold."

"But, Father...?" Neever argued.

"He speaks true. If we are to continue, we must do so in trust."

Still, the monk hesitated.

"Now, if you please, Brother Neever."

The silk was gently unknotted from his head. He blinked in the light of the torches and saw why they hadn't been too worried he'd snatch it off himself. Mystery Voice sat across a long table from him, cast completely in shadow. As he watched, the old man turned a lantern up. Officious robes glittered under a dull brown cloak. A wispy fringe clung to a liver-spotted pate. But the man's watery eyes held deep wells of willpower.

"Fear not," the priest said. "There was no poison in your cup."

"I figured," he said, eyeing the lone bottle between them.

"Introductions. I am Sitter Cyrus, hierarch of the Holy Temple."

The man waited.

For a moment, he considered maintaining his alias. There was power in names, and not just what they lent to writs of arrest and execution. But the old holy man's challenging gaze dissuaded him.

"Jiminy," he said, cursing himself for a fool.

"Jiminy," the wizened priest pronounced, "I want you to rob the repository at Seven Deep."

They shared a beat of silence.

"The what?"

The man raised a gnarled finger. "I want you to steal the bloom off the Lily – from the top of Tellar's spire, the heart of Heli faith."

Into the stunned silence, Neever bent to whisper in his ear.

"By the way, you're still wearing your makeup..."

* * *

FLASS SAVORED THE sudden silence as he strode, spurs clinking, into the common room. The sight of his brigade colors, coupled with the saddlebags over his shoulder, garnered instant respect.

As he did when astride his magnificent mare, he pretended not to notice the attention as he made his way to an empty table.

The last few weeks had been torture. Traveling in plain clothes and suffering the interrogation of mere gate guards. He'd been forced to show his Imperial writ half a dozen times.

"What can I get you, dragoon?" asked a barmaid, before he'd so much as sat down.

Neither shaving twice a day, nor copious amounts of hair oil, could save him from his commoner's face, he knew. But his rank made him the most handsome man in the alehouse.

He could tell by the serving girl's smile.

"A plate, a pitcher and a place to rest my head," he said.

"I'm afraid all our beds are taken," she apologized.

He looked her up and down. She was plump, plain and sweet as a plum pudding. Not at all like the fragile waifs his lord preferred.

"I'll sleep in yours," he promised.

Giggling, she went to fetch his order.

She could laugh if she liked. They, none of them, laughed at him by the end. And if she had a father or husband or brother who took issue with her bruises, well, he knew how to handle them too.

His special skillset was the reason Lord Serric Wramlinn had kept him close – first as a manservant, now as a dogrobber. After all, the aristocracy could hardly be expected to get their own paws dirty, digging shallow graves.

Some of the young lord's well-bred friends, who'd had nothing but sneers for a calloused servant, were also in the brigade. He took great pleasure in seeing them line up, in military file, so he could harangue them. He'd yet to pay back every single scathing word and snub. But he was a patient climber.

His order arrived and he ignored the barmaid in favor of more immediate appetites, digging in with his fingers. As he ate and drank, he practiced the report he would make to his master.

You were right, milord. Something is awry with the noble pair. When the niece returned from claiming her final token, she was still veiled. Why so, I asked myself, if not to hide her face?

Though he'd seen no signs of illness, he'd also not heard the little sparrow speak, even once. He had hoped to overhear them, scheming in their beds, at the hot springs inn. But they had been cautious. Overly cautious, one might say… What kind of lady rushed to confront a midnight creeper anyhow?

Grimacing, he reached for his pitcher, only to find it empty.

As if summoned by the thought, a full one appeared.

"From the man at the end of the bar," the wench explained.

He looked over. His benefactor was a fit, graying man. A well-worn gambeson showed shiny patches, scuffed by armor straps.

A house guard, perhaps, or even an off-duty watchman. A veteran for sure. One with the proper respect for a dragoon. More importantly, it seemed, one who did not take Flass's silent toast as an invitation to come regale him with the exploits of yore.

He set about finishing his meal, feeling properly mellowed by the ale. He scrubbed his tongue over his teeth. Was there a hint of brandy as well? If so, it was subtle. And welcome

The barmaid came to collect his plate, bringing yet another full pitcher with her. "From your friend again…"

Chuckling, he made a grab for her, meaning to pull her down in his lap. But, for a big girl, she was light on her feet.

Gathering up his drink, he drifted toward the dice game in the corner instead. He saw no sign of the veteran. Good. That saved him the trouble of thanking the man in person.

He drank, gambled… and waited to catch the serving girl alone.

"Ugh…" he belched, putting his empty tankard aside. "Where's the pisser?"

Following the indistinct directions, he stumbled out the back of the alehouse, toward the waiting trough. He fumbled his breech ties open, groaning as he loosed a streak across the wood.

He was mid-stream when the bag descended over his head, drawstrings pulling tight. Someone stepped on the back of his knee. The distant retort of a fist, striking his temple, pitched him onto his side. His first thought was for his ruined uniform, now piss-stained and mud-smeared.

The world spun. He bit back a mouthful of bile and felt himself falling… falling…

He hit the cold water, face first.

Sputtering, he jerked awake, lashed to chair in a dusty basement. A man in mercenary armor stood back, bucket in hand.

"Sober yet?"

He blinked against the faint lantern light. The veteran from the bar, now in mail to match the mercenary's, leaned against the wall.

"Idiots..." he growled. Even mussed as he was, bluster rose to his call. "Do you know what you've done? You've assaulted an officer of the Green Dragoons. Lord Brigadier Wramlinn will have your heads! He will flay you alive, break your legs and make you crawl through salt to escape-"

Another bucketful of water hit him full in the face, flooding up his nose and dousing his rant. He coughed desperately.

"I do not care," the mild veteran told him, "for you, or whoever you call master. You have spent time around the desert-born boy. The slight lad, with the maligned ear. I would know where he is."

"Who?" Flass said, deciphering the odd accent. "What are you-"

The bucket-wielder cracked him sharply across the face.

Reeling, he spat blood at the man.

"Denial won't aid you. It will only drag this out."

Somewhere above, a door squealed open. Lantern light spilled down the stairs. Flass threw his head back.

"Help! I'm tied in the basement! The basement!"

Grimacing at the noise, another mercenary made his way down. The newcomer locked eyes with the veteran. Something unspoken passed between them, before the man installed himself against the wall. A change came over Flass's questioner then. The man drew a dagger and came to kneel by him, gripping his tied forearm.

"Listen to me. Tell me where to find the bearer, now, and I give you my word – soldier to soldier – I will end you swift and *clean*."

He gaped at the man.

Up above them, the door creaked once more.

"Quickly now," the man whispered.

He was still framing his own, confused question when a strange snuffling sounded from the stairs.

Fear flashed in the veteran's eyes before they went carefully blank. Standing, the man sheathed his knife. "I'm sorry."

The honest regret, more than the threat of death, scared Flass.

"Yesss…" came the whisper from the stairs.

His hair stood on end. Unable to look away, he watched a long robe drift down the steps. The mercenaries shifted uncomfortably as the dark disgorged a hooded figure, taloned hands reaching.

"…thisss one."

Flass screamed, long before those claws came to cradle his face.

CHAPTER 15 – UNMASKED

Pella Monop, Diary entry #182

Conspiracy! Bruen and I have retraced her steps to her last referenced source. It proved a hastily gutted cover, hiding Bruen's own journal. She narrated it for me as we hid from Cecine among the shelves. Like me, my predecessor had puzzled over the missing period in history. What she uncovered was a shakily written summary, left by a scribe. He had stumbled on an incorrectly shelved scroll – an alternate account of the schism. Both vanished soon after. But not before the prescient scribe hid his epitaph among the books. Bruen, scholar that she was, righty expected history to repeat itself. Hence, her journal, left in hopes that another would happen upon the secret. I shall disappear next, should my newfound knowledge come to light:

There was no schism. There was a purge.

"WHERE'S THE RABBIT...? Find the rabbit... Rabbit, rabbit..."

The odd chant circled the cell's scored walls, dragging its lone occupant behind it. "See the rabbit... catch the rabbit..."

If Mop could only remember about the rabbit, everything would be well. But the memory had gone haring off, as hares were wont to do. He shuffled on, bare feet wearing deeper the groove of years. Five steps, turn. Four steps, turn. Five steps...

His foot-bottoms were permanently blackened. He'd noticed one night, while taking a wee.

At the time, he'd been clinging to the window bars by his teeth, feet splayed on the wall and aiming between the uprights by sheer force of will. Alas, abject relief ran counter to a firm grip. He'd fallen and, whilst lying prone and widdling in his own ear, he'd had a taste of his own black sole.

Come to it, he'd gone deaf in that ear for most of a season.

Or had it been a year? It was so hard to tell, in here...

Itching, he scraped the harness – that held his arms motionless against his midriff – against the wall. The misshapen buckles grated mortar, holding on by dint of long familiarity alone.

Mop's hands might be tied, but the fleas were free to roam, the ungrateful bloodsuckers. Still, he didn't scratch too hard – there was nothing quite as torturous to endure as irate roommates.

A cockroach crossed his path.

"Dammit!"

He reversed direction. Four steps, turn. Five steps...

"Need to mind the rabbit... where, oh, where's the rabbit..."

There was a distant clang – this wing's door, yawning open on rusted hinges. The malaise from the nearby cells took an upswing.

"Here it comes!" someone gibbered "Here it comes!"

Mop gave up pacing, pelting manically from wall to wall. A progression of clunks, cackles and screams made its halting way down the corridor. The lunch trolley trundled closer, carried on the backs of four squeaking mice. Their excitement was infectious.

"Oh," he moaned. "Almost here, almost here!"

Today was the day. And he still hadn't solved the rabbit.

"Down the... um... over... Log! Rhythm! Logarithm! To the base of the... tree! Knot! Square... square root! Of... pie? With four-and-twenty black... hares? Cannot hit a tortoise with a... Duck! Does not echo! Echo... echo... echo...

"Quack!" he concluded, as his door finally swung open.

"No, no physician today, Mop," the orderly laughed, keys jangling. "Just me. I've brought lunch. And a special treat..."

The guard, though obviously mad, was well meaning. Rooting around in a burlap sack, the man produced a bright red apple.

"Oh, boy!" Mop enthused, dancing from foot to foot. "Gimme!"

Laughing at his folly, the orderly lobbed him the fruit.

Mop tried to snap if from the air. It bounced off his cheek.

"Again!" he demanded.

"Now, Mop, everyone only gets the one-"

"Again! Again!" Mop insisted, chasing a tail he didn't have.

"Oh, alright. Here…"

Surprising both of them, Mop caught the apple. In his hand. The sleeves of his restraining jacket dangled to his knees.

"Dammit, Mop, have you wriggled out of that thing again?"

Rather than answer, he snatched the other apple from the floor, making the two orbit each other in a tight ellipse.

"Another!" he enthused, capering around the cell.

"I didn't know you could juggle, Mop…" the guard said, faint amusement warring with flat-out disapproval.

"Another!"

The man hesitated. An apple bounced off Mop's hip, pretended to fall, then propelled itself up off an ankle again.

"Oh, fine then," the orderly fought a grin. "Here…"

The third fruit blended seamlessly into the tumult, balancing on Mop's chin, then rolling across his shoulders.

"Yay…" the orderly clapped twice. "Alright, enough. Well done. Now, let's get you strapped back into that jacket. Just- Hey!"

A bushel of keys, jingling glee, joined in the fruits' chase.

Mop shared a horrified look with the guard.

"That's not supposed to happen!" he admitted.

"Mop! Dammit, give me those!"

The orderly lunged for his keyring. But, being young apples and obviously misinterpreting this as a game, the cheeky bunch dragged Mop out of reach. A helpless bystander, he hung on as the fruit spun and twirled him around the cell, the guard in hot pursuit.

"It's a revolution!" he realized as the keys whizzed around.

"Mop, so help me! If you don't hand those over right now-"

"Ack!" Mop complained, roughly towed along.

A door slammed.

"No!" the guard's pounding, from inside the cell, sounded muffled. "Mop! Open this door! Let me out! Mop? Mooooop!"

"Look what you've done!" he accused the flushed fruit.

Far from contrite, the corrupted globes careened up the corridor, Mop their unwilling accomplice. Patients howled from their viewing grates to see him pass. The frenzy did not go unnoticed.

An orderly came bursting into the wing, just as Mop arrived.

"What in blazes is going on in here? Quiet down you crazy-!"

"Eek!"

It would be nice to say that he finally put his foot down. But it was the sight of the guard's ready baton that rooted them in place.

Surprised by the sudden stop, the apples winged ahead.

The orderly did well, stepping and swinging blindly through the barrage. If the man's boot had not come down on a skidding bushel of keys, he'd probably have been fine.

"It was them!" Mop appealed to the downed guard, pointing. "They made me do it!" Hearing him snitch, the apples turned their crimson regard on him. At which point, he realized he was wearing most of one of their comrade – the orderly had gotten a hit in.

"I'll just… Yeah, I think I'm gonna… Oh, is that the time…?"

He made a run for it.

This was wrong. This was all wrong! If only he could remember about the rabbit, everything would be alright.

"Find the rabbit… Get the rabbit… Where's the rabbit…?"

He surprised a guard at the top of the stairs.

"D'you know the rabbit!?"

"Whoa-!" the wide-eyed man reeled back, lost his footing and went tumbling end over end down the steps.

Mop followed at a frantic jog. "Sorry! Sorry! Sorry!"

He only caught up at the bottom, where the orderly lay in a disordered heap. Gingerly, he patted the man's upthrust bum.

"I'm sure that'll buff right out."

He headed on, into the guards' deserted dressing rooms.

A short while later, his rags and harness exchanged for a uniform, he bent to his most crucial task.

Sweat beaded his quivering lip, a shoelace held in either hand. This was it. The crux, the lynchpin, the pivotal moment. Swallowing hard, he brought his trembling hands together.

"The rabbit jumps over the log…" he recited.

The guard on duty at the sanitarium's main gate was new. He hadn't had time to learn all his fellows' faces yet. He'd have tried harder to memorize this one, too, if not for the diverting tangle that was the man's bootlaces.

* * *

KEEPING A DUTIFUL eye on the dark alleys and side streets, Jossram ghosted along in the keeper's wake. Back home, priestly robes offered greater protection than even his masha'na armor.

But these Renali had not yet seen the light, hence this escort.

Father Justin made it easy enough to guard him, which Jossram and his troupe appreciated. And he didn't give them grief about piety, celibacy, propriety or other unpleasant things ending in 'ee'. That the priest had spent time on the front lines showed. It had earned him a respect approaching that of a chaplain.

Not expecting to see any action, Jossram let his mind wander.

As it usually did, it detoured toward his stomach.

What in Helia's name was 'squab', anyway?

The Renali harbored very clear notions of what constituted so-called 'commoner food', as opposed to what their betters ate.

The masha'na compound's cook had seemed insulted when he'd asked for chicken and fearful when he'd mentioned mutton.

He truly felt for the Kingdom's shepherds, who probably went their entire lives without tasting the prime cuts they raised.

Whereas the masha'na were stuck in some gastronomic niche where the platters were populated, exclusively, by game birds.

Squab, grouse, quail, pheasant, partridge, duck...

Helia preserve us, is there anything more disgusting than duck?

When the cook – with profuse apologies and a heavy heart – had served fish, he'd rejoiced. Initially. But these weren't the crisp, salt-scoured fish of Tellar. He'd sworn he could taste duck shit. The bottom-feeding fish obviously subsisted on the stuff.

The cook had fled, in tears.

A good thing, too. Else he might have stoppered the man's gob with an apple and popped him in his own oven.

He adjusted his following distance as the priest ahead slowed, casting about. He re-evaluated the likelihood of trouble. They were in the Narrows. A poor, rough neighborhood on the outskirts of the city. As far from the keep and its peacekeepers as you could get.

Up ahead, the keeper halted, having found the right hovel. Its rickety door, bucking beneath light knocks, opened immediately. Lantern light smeared the keeper's shadow across the street.

Trusting the empath to root out any malicious intent that might lurk within, Jossram took up station under a likely awning.

Squab, he thought. *Even the name sounds unappetizing...*

While he waited for the priest to reemerge, it began to drizzle.

Sounds he'd been tracking for a while resolved themselves into three neighborhood youths, swaggering aimlessly up the road. He recognized the type. Helia forfend, he'd *been* the type, before the masha'na had raised him from the muck. These ones were up to nothing and no-good, whichever proved least constructive.

Two were deep in overloud conversation. The third's eyes swept past where Jossram lounged... and jerked back, an involuntary arm halting the others. Clumping, they sized him up.

One stepped forward, displaying the beginnings of a grin.

With a sigh, he parted his cloak, giving them a peek at his scabbard and sleek armor.

Language barrier my ass- he thought, as they scurried off.

A chance squelch, from behind, was the only warning he got. The point of a blade bit through his robes, scoring the hardened plates beneath. He whirled, sword hissing in an angry arc.

Steel clattered to the cobbles, amid the softer bounce of severed fingers. Figures crowded the alley behind him. The foremost, maimed, stumbled away to foul the steps of the one behind.

Adopting a close-quarter form, Jossram followed, lunging past.

His edge found jaw instead of jugular but the panicked pair went down nonetheless. He stabbed at their tangle of limbs, point punching between ribs. Which was when the third attacker stepped into view, squinting from behind a drawn shortbow.

A heartfelt curse can be a warrior's fondest prayer.

He swung, nearly losing his grip to the impact. A sliver of wood peeled from the passing arrow, the rest ricocheted off the walls.

I can't believe that worked...

The archer gaped, fumbling for another shaft.

An *orin* isn't meant for throwing. But he ripped the shortsword from its sheath anyway and sent it wheeling away.

Having just seen him cut a shaft from the air, the archer – understandably – jumped as the steel came flying at him.

By the time the man realized he was unharmed, Jossram had covered the distance between them. His first cut sheared bowstring and hamstring both. The second sank into stomach and he sawed it smoothly out below the ribs.

In less than a dozen beats, two lay dead. The last whimpered, blinded by his own blood and trying to claw out from beneath his fingerless compatriot's corpse.

"Now. Let's you and I have a little chat, yes? Who hired-"

Unaccountably lightheaded, Jossram caught himself against the wall... and saw the tasseled dart, sticking from his shoulder.

"Aww, f-"

The world tilted. The steadying wall slid from beneath him. He fell, staring muzzily up into the drizzle.

Helia, please don't let my last meal have been squab...

STOWING HER BLOWPIPE up her sleeve, Anochria stepped from the shadows to survey the carnage. She had warned them that three guardsmen could not hope to kill a Heli holy warrior. They'd thought her boastful. Now, here lay the proof, all cut to pieces...

"It seems you were right," her Renali contact said, coming to stand at her back.

Staring ahead, she let that comment sit in its own stupidity.

"The priest?" she prodded.

"Being collected as we speak."

The Renali had laughed off her cautions concerning the masha'na. But their bred-in-the-bone fear of all things magical had made them overcautious of the keeper. A good thing, too, since it was terribly difficult to catch an empath off guard.

"And this one?" she wondered, waving at the mewling man who was missing most of his face.

"Such a scar will make him memorable. Useless to me." There was the sound of a dagger being drawn. "Best he not leave here..."

Making as if to brush by her, the Renali agent went for her eye.

People never expected either speed or agility from her plump form. But her round legs and middle hid thick slabs of muscle. And she was low-slung as a cat, albeit a fat one.

She caught his wrist in the crook of her pick blade, guiding his strike past her. Her return flick cored the apple from his throat.

She observed with dispassion as the gurgling man collapsed.

He had been one of Mattanuy's agents. What had presaged this betrayal? Was the inquisitor so sore, at having *her* oversee things, that he'd have her killed? He'd initially wanted the keeper smuggled back to Tellar, to pry loose the modernist's secrets himself. Her master had put paid to that idea. Or so they'd thought.

Alternatively, was this a Kingdom double-cross? The agent was Renali-born. If the heathens were mad enough to precipitate war with the Empire, what else might they think was a good idea?

In any event, it was clear she had no allies here. That suited her just fine. Enemies, after all, were less complicated.

The defaced, pinned man was feigning death but began to struggle again as she neared.

She claimed her third kill of the night. A good start.

Flinging blood from her sickle-shaped blade, she snapped the weapon closed. It disappeared back up her sleeve. The cruelly beaked baton had once been an agricultural implement, meant for shearing rice stalks level with the soil.

Stooping for her poisoned dart, she waddled into the shadows.

She would shear them *all* level with the soil…

PASSING, JUSTIN NODDED a greeting to the gate guards. With the keep at his back, the pressure of many more minds loomed from the dusk-lit city below. But this stretch of road was bare.

He settled his satchel more securely over his shoulder.

He'd have preferred to heed these summonses during the light of day. But he understood that there was stigma attached to having a Heli priest seen at one's home. And he wanted to help people, not have them cast out by their neighbors.

With his masha'na minder a comforting presence at his back, he strolled purposefully down the dim streets. His thoughts turned – as they so frequently did – to the dilemma of Marco.

No matter his precautions, he seemed unable to ward the boy from disaster. If he were Renali, he might have believed that luck or fate or some such, had scrawled a dark mark against the child.

Though Justin lived in constant fear of the memory dam's failure, he refused to believe it would spell the end of the boy's life. They had both worked too hard for that. And, if the child had proven anything at all, it was that he was resilient to a fault.

But, also, too forthright for his own good.

It had been a struggle – when his ward had arrived, keep forged sword in hand – to safeguard his suspicions. Marco bore his heart on his sleeve. A dangerous trait, in a game of subterfuge.

And while he told himself he simply did not wish to weigh his ward down with his own paranoid musings, the truth was that Marco's mind was not a safe repository of secrets. When the dam burst, there could be no telling what would flood to the fore.

Unconsciously, he ran a hand over his pocket, where the yarn charm bulged. He had suspected that someone might come to recover the incriminating blade, after Marco so blithely paraded it around. His tracking charm had proven barely sufficient but he'd been able to trail the sword and glimpse the culprits.

He had not yet decided what to do, concerning his discovery. He chewed over the problem while he walked.

The sun had fully set by the time he'd finished following the terse directions. Even by Narrows standards, the abode before him was poor. Gaps in its warped walls were wind-proofed with clay and scraps of cloth. These did little to plug the sickness he sensed, seeping from within.

Taking a moment to make sure his escort, Jossram, would wait outside, he rapped at the lashed boards.

The face of the old man who opened the door betrayed none of the surprise – nor the quickly quashed hope – Justin sensed.

"You came. I didn't think… Please, come in."

Bowing, he ducked beneath the low lintel. A wreathe of garlic, and a pungent fish oil lamp, did their best to combat the stink of illness and lean living. A swaybacked cot took up the whole rear wall and still barely had space for the shrunken woman on it.

The old man most likely slept on the floor.

The woman's breaths wheezed, like a punctured bellows, and she was deep in the throes of fever.

He knelt by her side.

"What's this?" he mused, gently cradling one of her arms. Her hands were mottled in odd colors, up past the elbow.

"Leather dye," the man explained. "She plied the vats and I the racks at the tannery. But when her cough got so she couldn't work, we hadn't the coin to keep our house. I save my wages but…"

But. The healers willing to work for coppers were butchers at best and charlatans at worst. Wondering which of the two the old man thought him to be, Justin nodded.

"Do you mind if I pray?" he asked, pushing up his sleeves.

He ignored the deepening discomfort that came with assent.

"Holy Helia, guardian mother," he entreated, in Renali, "turn your eye upon your hardworking daughter in her time of need…"

Mustering his will, he manifested Illian's Augur. The sigil settled on the old woman as a skein, slowly sinking inward.

The discoloration proved only skin deep, sitting atop wasted muscle. His perception sped as it was swept along the blood's pathways, stuttering to the old woman's heartbeat. Reaching the wreckage of her lungs, he struggled not to recoil.

"Do they use lime at the tannery?" he wondered in a whisper.

"Betimes, yeah. Is that what did her in?" the old man sounded skeptical. "Lime?"

"On its own? No. But the excrement used in the tanning process attracts ill humors. Breathing the lime lamed her god-given resistance long enough for the disease to take hold."

Allowing his scrying efforts to lapse, he faced the old man.

"It is the wasting wet." He used the local name for ring cough.

His host's shoulders rounded, as though a great weight were settling. A crack speared across the man's neutral exterior and Justin could sense the defeat it held in check.

"Thanks anyway," the old man muttered. "For coming."

He looked again at the dying woman's sunken face.

Habit had him reaching for an absent streaming crystal. With it, he could have layered Jessin's Stays on top of Fever's Crucible to protect the patient, isolate the illness and burn it down to its component parts – to be safely absorbed back into the body.

Without the crystal, he could think of no single sigil that would accomplish all three goals.

This is a terribly ill-considered idea...

"Let's not give up hope just yet," he said, all the same.

Mentally steeling himself, he manifested the minor sigil of Grasp – subordinate of Root, in the Life aspect. Through it, he reached for the old woman's lungs.

Immediately, the disease latched onto him.

It was not a physical touch. They were separated by his construct. But, true to its nature, it was trying to spread. He could feel it, infecting his spirit and birthing its simulacra in his own flesh. Grimly, he tightened his grip, expending more and more energy to ensure he had a firm Grasp on it. The effort dragged on.

"Bring that bowl over and sit her up," he instructed the old man.

When he felt he held the entire mass by the root, he pulled.

Coughing wrenched the woman awake. Wet, hacking rasps that spewed black bile into the cup being held to her lips. Appalled, the old man rubbed comforting circles on her back.

Doing it this way had demanded a great deal of power.

But it was still only half the battle. The entire exercise was for naught if the old woman's body could not defend against the disease when it inevitably re-sprouted.

Letting Grasp lapse, Justin manifested, Recovery. It was a greedy sigil that always took more than it gave. And his patient was in her twilight years, her body too worn down to metabolize the energy efficiently. This only spurred him to give her more.

Finally, shaking, he caught himself on the cot's edge. Coughing overtook him as his spirit pitted itself against the ghost disease. Its symptoms would persist until he could convince his body it wasn't real. As an empath, that should be soon. But, for the moment, he was stream-sick with the wasting wet.

The old man was rocking the woman in his embrace. Both their faces were tear-streaked. Their shared wonder was a balm.

Worth it, Justin thought, as he wheezed for a breath.

He managed to right himself as he was being introduced.

The old woman's disbelieving eyes found him, playing over his robes. Her gratitude stumbled to a halt as she registered his sallow skin, his cracked lips and his sunken gaze.

His breath rattled audibly, in a way that would be familiar to both of them. The old man's dismay was obvious.

He made to reassure them. "Do not fear for me-"

Jossram's death – a sudden absence – was like missing a step on the stairs. He might have fallen, save that he already knelt. Across his raw senses, spikes of malicious intent dragged closer.

In a flash, he understood.

He staggered to his feet, shrugging off the couple's concern. Their fish oil lantern burnt his fingers as he pinched it out, plunging them into darkness.

"Make no noise," he commanded, pausing in the doorway. "And, no matter what you hear, do not come outside."

His head was spinning and his knees unsteady, but he marched himself to the center of the street. If they found him in plain view, perhaps his ambushers would overlook the old couple.

It was a tenuous hope, but he clutched at it.

His options were near non-existent. If the ones coming had been sent to cut him down, he would die here, in the middle of the road. But, if they meant to take him, he might still play the long game.

Gravel crunched and a man stepped into the sour moonlight.

The out-of-uniform guardsman was big and hale and would easily run down an ailing old man in long robes.

Despite this, the rest of them malingered out of sight, wary.

The urge to clear his scratchy throat was powerful.

"Your information is correct, sirs," he called out, stealing the initiative. "My magic is, indeed, spent. I shall not resist."

Their trepidation surged. To their minds, this was exactly what a mage would say, if he had a deadly spell tucked up his sleeve.

Docile as a lamb, Justin offered his wrists to be tied – and noted which ones flinched at the motion.

Incensed, at being seen to hesitate, their leader strutted up.

Justin continued in a calm voice, "I assure you, I can-"

He stumbled, as the man shoved him roughly in the shoulder.

No fireballs flared. No lightning bolts cracked.

Over the sound of Justin's uncontrolled hacking, the officer glanced back at his companions and shrugged.

The priest struggled to straighten. "As- as I was saying-"

A blow he hadn't sensed was coming knocked his head askew.

As he fell, he lamented that some men could do swift and sudden violence, without so much as a shift in mood.

✱ ✱ ✱

Despite the tension in his back, Jiminy resisted the urge to sweep the stupid charts and schematics off the table.

"Explain it to me again," he insisted, his jaw stiff.

Half his irritation came from being cooped up, in this labyrinth, with no one but Neever for company. The monk's metaphorical nail-biting wore on his nerves.

The other half was the weight of Tellar's tower, somewhere overhead, pressing down. Waiting for him to move.

"I don't know how else to explain it," the monk said, in a tone approaching terseness. Tempers were wearing thin, all around.

Jiminy tackled the problem again.

"You know the entrance to the repository is *here*." On the schematic, he pinned the tower's summit with a finger. "You know your prize is seven levels down, hence 'Seven Deep'."

He measured seven stabs of his finger.

"So why," he railed, "must I go *up* to come back *down*? Why can't we just knock through a wall *here* or *here*-"

"-through a wall?!" Neever sputtered. "This is *the* Holy Temple! Sacred stone, shaped by a saint's hands-"

"Then pull up a floor! Or saw through a ceiling!"

"There *are* no adjoining walls, floors or ceilings to be found."

They both started. Neither had heard Cyrus come in. Clearly, they weren't being as quiet as it behooved of burglars.

The monk avoided his senior's stare.

Jiminy crossed his arms. "Cat scat."

"You think so?" The old priest took his time, divesting himself of staff and satchel. "These walls you want to demolish... you're certain that they, specifically, are hiding Seven Deep?"

He frowned uncertainly. He'd gone over every architectural drawing with a fine toothed comb – and had come away cross-eyed. *If* Seven Deep wasn't a myth, then at least half the tower's interior must be mislabeled.

"Do you imagine," the priest continued, "that the repository is a narrow stair? Cramped by shelves? No.

"It is a vast archive. A sprawling library. It is a museum of cultures crushed by the Empire's millennia-long march."

The old man's vehemence was impressive.

"Wow. I've got goosebumps. You're saying your forebears squeezed a museum into a space the size of a privy closet?" He scoffed. "Magic like that does not exist."

"No longer, perhaps," Cyrus agreed. "But the Lily is the oldest structure on the continent. Sorcery was young and strong when the Prime, Coramoor, raised her. And she is rife with secrets.

"Just as you could dredge my old body for blood and bone but find not a drop of faith, so too do the vaults and sweeps of the spire hide an unseen heart. Does that answer your question?"

"Salt and silver, I've nearly *forgotten* my question. Perhaps try answering again, without the flowery words."

The elder slid the schematic sharply from beneath Jiminy's fingers. "How about this? You take my pay – you do it *my* way."

Unappeased, he shook his head. "All this? For a musty book?"

"Not just a *book*!" the old priest objected. "The lost... lost scripture of Juris... Juris Arbiter-"

As the coughing fit worsened, Neever guided the elder to a seat.

Jiminy watched the monk pour some water, worried that his new patron would not live long enough to make payment.

"Juris Arbiter," Neever took over the explanation, "is a Prime – one of our four founders. Scripture by his hand could shift the cornerstones of the Empire."

"Mm," the somewhat recovered Cyrus rasped, peering into his half-empty cup. "The way things stand, the Temple is a tinder stack. Every time our factions knock heads, sparks fly. Arbiter's gospel is the pail of water we need to douse dissent."

Blankly, Jiminy looked from one man to the other.

"Sounds like a real page turner."

"That is the hope," Cyrus toasted him, tossing back his dregs.

Something in the turn of phrase struck him as odd.

"Wait," he realized. "You haven't read it?"

Neever shrugged. "No one has. Not since the first dynasty."

"Skewer me!" he swore, putting the pieces together. "You're just *guessing*! Borris Backbiter might not have *been* a modernist-!"

"Juris Arbiter!"

"Him. He might have been a complete lunatic. There could be good reason why his scribbles are under lock and key."

Neever shook his head. "Juris Arbiter was the *Mediator*. In the same way Coramoor was the *Mason*, Sybaline the *Sister* and Allerius the *Soldier*. If modernism is to have help, it will be by his hand. *That* is why the warmongers wish to hide the text."

Cyrus spoke, voice stern, despite the obvious effort.

"I have spent decades stalking this scripture, through obscure mentions and margin notes. I'll be damned – quite literally – if I let it gather dust for even one more lifetime."

Looking at the wan priest, Jiminy couldn't help thinking that it would be a near thing…

"At least tell me," he sighed, "you know what it *looks* like…"

***

He heaved himself over the roof's lip and sprawled, bleeding across the leads. Overhead, stars swam in Keystone's smog.

Damn that diminutive woman and her accursed blowpipe!

With a trembling hand, he hunted along his shoulder for the poisoned dart. Plucking it free, he stropped it across his tongue.

Graveworm!

He spat the poison's bitter taste out.

Fingers rapidly numbing, he dug a phial from beneath his baldric. Biting out the waxed cork, he let the grainy contents slough down his gullet. The antidote took his throat lining with it.

He writhed beneath the scudding clouds as the two elixirs wrestled over his life. Waves of heat and nausea washed over him.

He lost a little time and jerked awake, weak and groggy, face-down in a pool of bloody vomit. His every muscle trembled with the memory of spasms. He'd shit himself.

But he was still alive. And the night yet held.

Emion Hallet's big-boned terrier had probably left off his scent in pursuit of larger game – the Royal Guard. The duplicitous bastards must have bolted with the prize by now.

They were supposed to keep the meddling woman at a dagger's length from Keeper Wisenpraal. Preferably, with a few shovels of dirt added in between. Inquisitor Mattanuy had questions for the wayward hierarch and did not intend for them to be overheard.

But they, all of them, had severely underestimated the round little priestess. He had watched her mow down a handful of his cohort – spewing death, hooking stomachs and ankles.

He wobbled determinedly to his feet.

If Anochria had taken even one of his fellows alive – as seemed likely – she would know the supposed secondary location was a lie. She could be on her way to kill the priest right now.

Much as he hated to admit it, none of them were her match. How then, was he to protect his master's interests?

Hmm…

Right now, all the keeper knew was that he had been kidnapped by the Renali, who themselves had never heard a whisper of any Inquisitor Mattanuy. If the keeper were recovered, the kingdom would bear the blame. And the knowledge his master sought would be preserved, inside the preacher's head, for a later date.

He turned toward the quarter where, he knew, the masha'na were barracked. A carefully dropped word or two, and the holy warriors should do all the hard work for them.

And if they happened to cross paths with the belligerent priestess, before he did, all the better.

Marco's dreams were getting worse.

The palace physician, who had declared him physically fit, was at a loss to explain his lingering exhaustion.

The man knew nothing of Marco's desperate, rearguard action against sleep. Staying awake had become a war in its own right.

It was still preferable to the nightmares that stalked him in mounting frenzy. In his dreams, he relived the bandit raid and reveled in the slaughter he dealt. Only once he stood upon a cairn of corpses did he recognize the faces of the dead.

The baker and his seamstress wife. Kryskin. Justin. Himself.

He dreamt of a butcher's abode, close and fetid, filled with heaving flies. They buzzed laughter as they swarmed, choking his ears, his nose, his mouth. The gore-slick floor denied him all traction, no matter how he scrambled.

And he dreamed of a freckled little girl, her shock of rust-hued hair flying. He felt, again and again, the nauseating *crack* of her head, hitting an alley wall. And, when she rested atop her grave of garbage, she would turn death-dulled eyes on him and ask why he had murdered her.

Still worse were the ones he couldn't remember. The ones that hounded him awake and seemed to permeate his very skin, promising – with absolute certainty – that *something* was in the room with him.

Last night, one such had chased him from bed and into a corner, knees drawn about his ears. Like a child. He'd sobbed, partly in shame but also in abject relief at being awake.

Shivering in the nightmare's aftermath, he'd finally worried that he'd woken the keeper. It would not be the first time the empath was shaken from sleep by Marco's terror. But no sound or telltale light had come from the keeper's quarters.

Now, dreading a return to slumber, Marco leapt as a knock sounded on the outer door. It was unusual, to say the least, to have callers in the dead of night.

Rubbing his eyes, he stumbled into the seating area and found why Justin had not come to look in on him. The portal to the priest's room yawned, the bed empty and unslept in.

A more insistent knock pried him away from the mystery.

A sour faced guardsman confronted him from the threshold.

"Yes?" he ventured.

"You've got a visitor. At the front gate."

"The keeper isn't here," he stammered.

"Didn't say it was for the priest, did I? Said it was for *you*."

"Me?"

Exasperated, the guard turned. "Come on, if you're coming."

Grabbing up his boots from beside the door, he hopped after the man, managing to shoe himself despite his long nightshirt. He drew level with the guard's purposeful stride.

"Who is it that wants me?"

Apparently as bitter at being awake as he was at the prospect of sleep, the man didn't deign to answer. Marco was getting better at ignoring the royal guards' general rudeness but it still stung.

The palace passages were deserted, but for the occasional servant, spotted in the distance. The dark of the spiral stairs parted reluctantly for the guard's lantern. As they traversed the narrow space, the man's breath wafted back to him. Rot lay heavy on it.

"A bud of clove, wadded in cotton and soaked in brandy, will relieve the pain of that bad tooth. But you should have it out, before the abscess makes you ill."

Ahead, the light seesawed crazily as the man missed a step. Marco caught a flash of wide eyes in the gloom.

"Sorry," he muttered, allowing the man a little more space. He'd not meant to cause any embarrassment.

They reached the keep's central courtyard, lit by braziers.

"Bear?" he marveled, forgetting all about the guard, as the main gate came into view. The masha'na's form was unmistakable, hulking beyond the portcullis.

The Temple warrior was menacing in his full armor and helm, gauntleted grip resting casually on sword hilt.

Keep guards squirmed nearby, holding tight to their pikes.

"What's wrong?" Marco asked, racing up to the grate.

"Not here," the masha'na said, in Heli. Beckoning him to follow, the holy warrior strode off into the dark.

The guards quickly unlocked the wicket gate for Marco.

Regretting his nightshirt, he caught up to the masha'na within a score paces. "Bear? What's going on?"

"Is the keeper within?" the man nodded back at the castle.

"What? No. I mean, I don't think so. At least, I haven't seen him since supper and his bed hasn't been slept in."

"Jossram's dead."

Not understanding, Marco grinned stupidly.

"He- What?"

"Jossram was minding the priest this night, on one of those missionary errands. A little while ago, we got word at the compound of a Heli soldier, slain in the Narrows.

"Jossram's dead," the man repeated. "And the keeper's gone."

Forgetting what they were about, his feet stalled.

"What do you mean *gone*?" he breathed. "The keeper can't-"

A great hand closed on the back of his head, not ungently.

"Don't stop moving. We haven't much time..."

Feeling like he'd taken a seirin to the gut, Marco was forced forward. Bear's voice came from far off, competing with the ringing in his ears.

"-closer to him than any of us ... see something we missed-"

Ahead, the road ran on through the dark. Bleak and abandoned.

The keeper? Gone?! It was impossible. He would have felt the bottom dropping out of his world. Were they not 'especially attuned'? The tectonic shock should have shaken him from sleep-

Oh, no... he thought, thinking of his nightmare.

He forced himself into a half-run.

Bear merely stretched his stride.

Gradually, cobbles gave way to dirt, houses to hovels. They left braziers behind to venture into the night, working their way deeper into the disreputable quarter known as the Narrows.

His stomach turned at the familiar iron tang in the air.

He found he'd pressed between several armored figures, made haggard by torchlight. The alley before him lay littered with corpses, the dirt clotted and dark.

"...scavengers made off with swords and gear..."

"...damned Renali... probably pawn..."

"...keeper... first concern. Over by..."

"...not got much time before the guard..."

No, Marco thought, backing away.

This was wrong. He didn't want this. Where was the keeper? Where...?

He stumbled on, up the street, to the stove-in door of a shack. Staggering against the doorjamb, he could force himself to go no further. Blood glistened, thick as molasses, on the hard packed floor. It dripped from the brittle planks, soaking the blankets of the collapsed cot. And the two decrepit figures, pinned atop it.

A watchful masha'na swiveled toward him, lips moving.

"...old man...put up a fight...bless...brave soul..."

The scent of sickness and slaughter snatched Marco back, across a span of years, to a butcher's abode and the horror within.

"...don't look so good... going to be sick?"

His next swallow stuck sideways. Eyes and nose tearing desperately, he stumbled from the shack, clawing as though through cobwebs. He fell to his knees in the street outside.

"...Marco...you alright?"

Uncontrolled words tumbled from him in his panic. "The keeper. Came outside. Confronted them. They hurt him. Here..."

Reflexive torchlight panned over where he pointed. Against the gravel was a scattering of darker drops.

"They took him." Marco panted. "That way..."

The silence heaped heavily around him. He turned to find himself the focus of a semi-circle of motionless masha'na. Wavering light carved harsh lines in their expressions.

Kryskin came to crouch by him, putting them at a level.

"How do you know?" the man asked intently.

"I-"

Marco's mouth snapped shut as he heard the words, waiting to be spoken. But the scent was undeniable – sandalwood, crisp ink, cured vellum and curdled butter. *Justin*.

"I can smell him," he whispered thinly.

"Say again?"

"I can smell him," he admitted, to himself and his audience.

Disbelieving scoffs and scowls ran among the warriors.

"Could be true."

All eyes turned to the speaker.

"Bear?"

"On the way from the keep, the lad seemed to sense where we were headed. He's an empath's apprentice, so I hung back and let him lead. It's the whole reason we fetched him here, isn't it?" Massive shoulders shrugged. "Here we are."

Marco started. He didn't remember doing any such thing.

Ryhorn stepped forward, mace-kissed mouth turning the words sideways, "More likely he was part of the kidnapping plot."

Kryskin made a gesture, silencing further discussion.

Marco squirmed beneath the leonine masha'na regard.

"Can you follow the trail?" the man demanded at last.

He gaped. "I... don't know. Maybe?"

The masha'na captain pulled him up by the shoulders, turning him in the direction he'd pointed.

"Try," the man commanded in his ear, stepping away.

Heart thumping, he closed his eyes.

Oh, holy Helia, he thought, *what am I doing?*

What if it turned out he *could* do this? It would make Father Justin's faith in him a lie. It would prove he was no anointed of Helia's. That he had not seen through that assassin because he was beloved of the light. Rather, that he'd sniffed it out because he was tainted by the dark. That he was base. Beastly. Beneath upliftment.

A scarier thought occurred.

What if it turned out he *couldn't* do this?

Oh, Helia's mercy. Justin...

Stilling, he inhaled the scents of the street.

The acrid taste of iron, the bitter resin of sword oil, the sweet stink of sweat... and many more, made an impenetrable mélange.

He breathed out through his mouth, letting the disparate notes linger on his tongue, searching among them...

Pickled fish and brined eggs, lingering beneath someone's nails.

Chewed mint, hiding brandy on someone's breath.

A razor's nick, slathered under lye soap.

And amid the cacophonous confusion... Justin.

He took a step. Then another.

Justin smelled like home. He was going home.

A hand on his shoulder steered him away from a collision with a stationary cart. He realized he'd broken into a lope with his eyes closed. Ahead, the trail wended, crisp and clear. A muted jangle of armor brought up the rear. He set to, following the scent in earnest.

He led them on a back-alley route through the Narrows, to where the city petered out. Muddy reeds stood ankle deep in pond scum, low hillocks indistinct in the distant dark. He slowed.

Rawhide. Saddle soap. Tallow wax. Animal sweat. Dung.

"They had horses waiting," he realized. "That way."

Kryskin caught ahold of his robes. "Hang on. If they're mounted, we won't catch them on foot. They've got several bells' head-start. We'll assemble the troupe and mount a proper pursuit."

"Pursuit of what?" Someone else objected. "The boy don't look to me like he's got a tail that wags. We got only his word..."

He shut out the argument as the keeper's scent strengthened. He padded in among the reeds, combing through the tall grasses, hunting for the source.

"...got horse tracks here. They milled around, like they were waiting...at least one carried double... way the lad said-"

"Marco, what is that you've found?" Kryskin cut Finch short.

He turned to the masha'na captain, mutely offering the bit of linen. The kerchief had been expertly rolled and worked into a yarn charm. Bedraggled and damp though it was, it smelled strongly of the keeper and, more faintly, of Marco himself.

Yarn charms were not a Renali tradition. He doubted there was another like it in the entire city. He could see the same conclusion settle in Kryskin's eyes, as the man turned the token over and over between his fingers. Finally, he offered it over a shoulder. Ryhorn stepped up to take it, frowning.

For a moment, Kryskin's eyes lingered on Bear. But when he spoke, he was addressing the little woodsman.

"Finch, can you follow those horse tracks?"

"Easily," the masha'na said. "But they headed south west. That's marsh country out there. Even I can't follow tracks through knee-deep soup."

"Could a bloodhound?"

Finch's gaze shifted to Marco. "Yeah, maybe."

For a moment more, Kryskin hesitated.

"Alright, listen up. Double time, back to the barracks. Gear up and mount up. We set out by dawn. Our kidnappers were kind enough to leave us a trail and we're getting our keeper back."

If any of the masha'na had further reservations, they kept it to themselves.

Marco found himself jogging beside Kryskin, rough boot leather gnawing at his unsocked heels.

"You," the captain was telling him, "need to take word of what has happened to the keep. Don't try to see the king, or anyone else who might bog you down with questions. Time is of the essence. Outfit yourself and get back to the rally point. Got it?"

Huffing, he nodded an affirmative, barely listening as Kryskin dished out orders to other members of his squad.

He felt somehow adrift. As though, without the becalming presence of the priest, his world was reduced to little more than the reflection on a soap bubble – bright but easily banished.

In a daze, he left the masha'na at an intersection, receiving a brusque shove to set him on the path up towards the keep.

The same gate guards were still on duty and glared suspiciously as they let him in. He ignored them, taking the stairs two at a time.

Slamming the apartment doors shut at his back, he stood a moment, gasping. The empty rooms seemed an affront. Pulling himself up, he went to kick the trunk from beneath his cot. He had no armor. But he had sturdy riding clothes and – by Helia's grace – thick stockings to assuage his budding blisters. And a sword.

He hefted the burlap-wrapped bandit blade, sparing a thought for its erstwhile owner. Was the dead murderer's master with the keeper right now? What strings had they pulled to-

He narrowed his eyes at the knots, tying the sackcloth closed. He'd been in a state, and none too neat, when he'd tied them last. Yet now they cinched the burlap with military precision.

Not my handiwork, he realized.

Feverish in his haste, he undid them.

He stared at the six sided pommel and cross-guard. He ran a finger down the three-quarter fuller and felt the hollow grind.

It was the quintessential Renali sword.

But it was *not* the sword he'd set inside these roughspuns. Nor was it, he was sure, a keep forged blade.

Someone had been in here. Someone had switched them out.

Had it been this? Was *this* the reason Justin had been taken? Could he have spared the keeper, if only he hadn't poked his nose in their unknown enemy's business?

Nose?

Experimentally, he held the sackcloth to his face and inhaled. He had little idea how to use his newfound sense. But a scent definitely lingered. He'd been able, in his head, to draw together the distinct odors that added up to Justin. These ones, however, remained a mystery. He would recognize this person though, he was sure, if he smelled them again.

Standing, he slipped the naked blade through his belt and still felt ill prepared. It felt wrong to be relying on it.

Well, he had promised Kryskin he would carry word to the keep. There was one person here he trusted. And they had a holy weapon that would make up for any shortcoming of his.

The guard outside Princess Dailill's door gave the sword on his hip a shrewd glance. "Finally got a promotion, eh, scribe?"

He recognized the man as one of the few friendly faces among the Royal Guard. But he was too shaken to recall the man's name or return his smile.

"Nothing so grand," he said stiffly. "Does the princess sleep?"

As if in answer, the door opened, allowing a lady's maid to bow herself out. Dailill herself spied him over the woman's shoulder.

"Sir Marco!" she enthused. "Please, won't you come in?"

Frowning disapproval, the guardsman was forced to step aside.

"I'm pleased to see you standing under your own power," the princess said, resplendent in courtly dress despite the early bell. "Does this mean you are healed and ready to resume your duties?"

As the door closed behind him, she turned toward her corner library, patting at her myriad hairpins. He followed at her back.

He was not eager to say his piece. But he would have to, before his nerve gave out. He hadn't much time.

A reading lectern stood beside the high window, catching the first hint of a graying sky through the mullioned glass.

"Why, Marco, you look positively grim. Is aught amiss?"

Pressing ahead, he fell back on the formality she hated so much.

"Something has happened, highness. My mentor, Keeper Wisenpraal, was taken during the night. By abductors unknown."

"Fate's favor!" she snatched a hand to her mouth. A moment later her brow drew down decisively. "The Royal Guard shall scour the city. Where was the priest last seen?"

"Highness, he appears to have been taken beyond the city limits. Our Temple warriors are, at this very moment, mounting a pursuit. They await only me.

"Our countries' provisional accord prevents us from acting." He bowed low. "I would ask that you allow us to proceed. And, also, that you delay in assembling your own response. We do not wish any misunderstandings, highness, and we must move quickly."

She cast a skeptical eye over him. She knew it was a sham. Short of drawn swords, the masha'na weren't about to stand down for anyone. But if a Renali royal claimed foreknowledge, it would go a long way toward preserving the peace.

"Knowing what I do of my father's... *court*, I shall not ask why you've come to *me*." She bit her lip. "But why should *you* go?

Eleven masha'na are an army. Not to belittle your skills, but would you not do better to remain here and plead your case to the king?"

He shook his head. "The masha'na need my help, highness."

Her lips went flat with some suppressed emotion. "We have a saying. 'Pride is the provender of fools.'"

"It is not simple pride, highness," he grimaced, struggling.

He had no wish to admit his deformity before this perfect girl.

Unworthy, a voice whispered in the back of his mind. *Unclean.*

But she had the power to stop him, to prevent him. Then, Justin's kidnappers would escape. No, he had to convince her.

Without inciting her disbelief.

Or her disgust.

Even the thought of a lie tasted bitter. He would speak the truth and let her come to her own, wrong, conclusions.

"My mentor is a powerful empath, highness," he admitted.

Justin had suspected that the king knew. So, apparently, did the daughter. She showed no sign of surprise.

Marco steeled himself. "And I have the means to find him."

She could not know he referred to his nose, as opposed to some mystic connection.

She was educated and had grown up with a high arcanist on call. If contemplating the Heli arts unsettled her, she hid it well.

"You are certain?" was all she said.

He nodded.

Visibly coming to a decision, she drew herself up. "Then I shall help however I can. Your temple warriors carry both longsword and shortsword into battle, not so?"

She motioned him towards the reading lectern.

The lacquered box that sat atop it was the size of a large scroll. Or, conversely, the size of a short sword.

All but huffing in relief, he rushed over.

The moment his touch fell on the lid, pain flared throughout his frame. He recoiled. Or tried to. His muscles set like quenched lead, holding him immobile. Heat nettled across his skin.

A cry stuck in his throat and he strained away from the ensorcelled case, heavy as an anchor against his fingertips.

He couldn't twitch. He couldn't talk. He could barely breathe.

Behind him, Dailill continued, oblivious.

"...shall speak to Father. A diplomat's abduction..."

Desperately, he rolled his eyes in her direction, they responded with incremental slowness.

Cold dread offset his burning skin.

This was the work of the assassin.

They had found a way to hide their pagan magicks from Marco's sight – inside this innocuous box. He had triggered a trap, meant for the princess. The assassin must have managed to-

"Good," Dailill breathed, lips brushing his ear and scattering his thoughts. "I had worried that you would win free of this too."

She sounded so unlike herself, he tried step away in shock, but the agony held him in place.

"I must thank you," she continued, in the same bedroom voice. She pressed up against him, soft curves flattened to his stiff back, hands snaking around his chest. "You really *did* save my life, that night." She chortled huskily. "Sort of. More fool me – believing a contract killer when they claimed to work alone. Now, I have to contend with a vengeful sidekick? How tedious..."

He struggled to parse her words, his rigid sides preventing him from gathering a full breath. She sighed.

"I would have preferred to keep you. With your priest gone, I suspect you would have been pathetically grateful for guidance-" her hand slipped down his stomach, "-and you are *so* easily led..."

She cupped his crotch.

Again, he struggled against the spell but it held him fast.

"Alas," she mourned, "it appears this is a night for betrayals. "Your countrymen are out there, killing each other, instead of keeping up their end. I'll not hand over the priest now. Not after their lackluster attempt to incriminate my dear sister. With Villet removed, and Father soon off to war, I'd have been regent to my thumb-sucking brother within the year."

Her displeasure bore down on the handful of him she held.

"Villet has never taken to me. And she's the *one* person who has never been taken in by me. Not even when we were children. Cold, calculating bitch that she is. *She* convinced Father to hang you around my neck – well-meaning millstone that you are."

Grip relenting, she patted at the front of his breeches.

"Not to worry. We can still salvage this."

She moved into view, languidly drawing the bandit blade from his belt as she went. Her bright eyes were shaded with malice and her sweet smile had turned sharp and contemplative. She propped an elbow on her hip, sword held casually as a parasol.

"This might work out well for me," she judged, "though Luvid is sure to pout, poor man. Ever since he failed to kill you in the tourney, my loyal bodyguard has fumed without surcease."

He watched in shock as she raised the sword, her voice thickening with pain as she dragged its edge along her forearm.

"In a moment or two," she explained, "I'm going to scream."

Her pearly sleeve bloomed crimson.

"The guards will burst in," she gritted, repeating the process with the other arm, "but be too late to help."

Gasping, she surrendered the sword to the now red-spotted rug.

"You see, the plucky little princess will have slain her Heli accoster, all on her own."

From the writing desk, she hefted a silver letter opener, its blade a delicate needle, its handle an elegant swan.

"I will have my war," she promised him, stepping close to caress the back of his neck. "And I will have my throne."

The silver stiletto drew back. Paused.

"Isn't it funny?" she smiled. "If you had died in my mountain raid, that assassin would likely have reached me. I must be favored by fate, after all…"

Eyes frozen open, thoughts arrested in fear, Marco saw the window at her back darken as a shadow spread across the dawn.

Perhaps she spied something in his stricken expression. Perhaps she was warned by the waning light. Either way, by the time the casement exploded inward, she was already dodging aside.

A dark shape swooped through the shower of glass – the assassin, face hidden but intent bared. The heel of a cloven slipper hammered the lectern. It spun away, fouling the princess's escape.

The box atop it was ripped from beneath Marco's fingers.

Muscles, cast in lead, liquefied. He was borne to the floor under the molten weight, head thunking into the carpet. Gulping air, he struggled to raise his head from among his puddled limbs.

Chaos raged around him. The princess's scream finally pealed out. He caught sight of her as she darted from the cover of a fainting couch, its upholstery studded with throwing stars. A snarl marred her pretty face as Dailill upended a decorative suit of armor at the assassin. Steel plates bounced along the stone, drowning out the doors as they banged open. The princess ran for the corridor.

The onrushing guard yelled, "Highness! Down!"

The assassin slipped casually past the hurled halberd but it cost a crucial moment of pursuit.

Dailill tumbled in among a growing cordon of guards.

For an instant, Marco lost sight of the assassin.

Then he was being hoisted from the carpet by his hair, a blade alighting alongside his neck.

Seeing a hostage levered up, the royal guard slowed.

The assassin towed Marco toward the shattered window.

"They're in league!" rang Dailill's voice. "Kill them both!"

Hesitation vanished. Halberds rushed in.

The assassin hooked an elbow around Marco's throat.

He flung his hands out blindly but missed catching the window frame. The world tilted. Sky replaced ceiling. Cold wind burned his cheeks as the royal tower raced away above him.

He couldn't help himself. He screamed.

All the way to the bottom.

KRYSKIN TUGGED HIS steel backed gauntlets tighter and ran a palm along his ready sword hilt. He'd spent little time here – in his office at the Heli compound.

Feeling more himself in his armor, he marched down the stairs.

His mounted troupe milled in the courtyard, a collection of hard eyes and set jaws.

Chapter Master Bulgaron's militia, and Ambassador Malconte's military escort, eyed them uneasily. Strike-Captain Iolus watched from a second story balcony, back rigid with disapproval but powerless to intervene. In the keeper's absence, only the ambassador had the authority to countermand them. And they planned to be long gone before the man returned from the day's peace talks.

Better if the politician could claim ignorance in any event.

Kryskin vaulted into the saddle, frowning over a headcount. "Marco?"

Finch grimaced in answer. The boy had not yet arrived.

Perdition!

The sun was well and truly up. If the young scribe wasn't here, he'd most likely been bogged down by the bureaucracy. If so, a contingent of royal guards might be galloping this way right now.

They could wait no longer. The priest was their priority. They would just have to rely on Finch's woodcraft – and their faith.

"All right," he bellowed, digging in his heels, "move out!"

"Hold!"

His sawed his reins in surprise, his steed kicking up dust.

A double file of mounted Guard, the white stork rampant on their surcoats, filled the compound's arched entryway. Displaying superb horsemanship, the newcomers wheeled into the courtyard, encircling the masha'na within moments.

He glared at their casually couched lances, picking out their commander by the man's plumed helm and the fur-trimmed greatcloak trailing across his destrier's croup. The officer cantered up last, horse slewing, as if to singlehandedly block their escape.

"By what right do you detain us?" Kryskin demanded, anger thickening his accent.

The Renali smirked, upsetting a viciously oiled and pointed moustache. Kryskin thought the man's ornate plate hid a paunch.

A functionary, then. Not a fighting man.

"We," Kryskin continued, "are envoys of the Heli-"

"*You*," the man loudly overrode, "are agents of the Heli temple. Less than a notch ago, another agent of the Heli temple made an attempt on the life of her royal highness, Princess Dailill."

Shock ran around the courtyard. Even those who spoke little Renali shifted at the sudden change.

"And now," the officer condemned, lidded eyes laughing beneath a helm's brim, "here *you* are, attempting to flee."

Marco... Kryskin thought, tasting bile.

"Per royal decree," the officer continued, "you are *all* to disarm and desist. Until Justin Wisenpraal and Marco dei Toriam are found and brought before the throne, none will leave here..."

...*alive.*

He saw the truth of that in the man's mad little eyes.

A charged silence descended. The kind only achieved by very dangerous men being very still.

Though their eyes remained on the encircling Renali, he felt his troupe's attention on him. The slightest spur, the smallest signal, and they would carve their bloody way free.

The foolish fop seemed eager for it.

Kryskin considered the Guard's numbers and the confined space. He could lose a lot of good men here. And the pursuit, sure to follow, might force the survivors off the priest's trail.

His knuckles cracked audibly where he clutched his scabbard.

The wind had shifted against them.

If they managed to win free, now, they would no longer be an unsanctioned rescue party. They would be an invading force on Renali soil. One that had done murder to outrun arrest.

He took in his fellows – the Imperial Elite and the chapter mercenaries. This would force a difficult decision on them too.

He had no doubt as to what course of action the keeper would counsel, were he here.

Too bad he isn't *here.*

Settling back in his saddle, he let the fighting focus suffuse him, meeting the fop's glittering gaze.

Careful pressure popped his blade's collar free of its scabbard mouth. Such a small, distinctive sound. It echoed all around him.

Too bad for you...

With parade precision, the fools lowered their lances – in these close quarters – to threaten the Temple warriors.

Their audience swore, looking to their own officers and reaching for weapons.

He saw Bear slip boots from stirrups, heard the rustle of Finch thumbing a shaft. He shifted his weight to draw-

"A moment, gentlemen, if you please!"

Into their tense moment galloped an older man on a leggy roan. Richly robed and armed with nothing but a rolled scroll, the man's authority was apparent by the way lances shied from him. Horses sidestepped nervously.

"Invigilator," the arrogant officer blanched, moustaches stiff. "Your presence is appreciated, sir. But, as you can no doubt see, I have matters well in hand-"

"What you have," the older man grinned, "is your arm – up to the elbow – in a wasp's nest, sheriff. Now, kindly be quiet while I save your life."

"Sir!" the officer sputtered, "I must protest–"

"Oh, if you *must*, then please do so quietly," the invigilator dismissed, turning to him. "Captain Kryskin, I believe?"

Ignoring the sound of the sheriff's teeth gnashing, he eyed the scroll the newcomer extended. It seemed hastily scrawled, on scrap paper, its seal smudged by the sender's hurry.

He'd felt more at ease with the lance pointed at him.

"Instructions from your ambassador," the invigilator said, showing yellowed teeth. "Shall I tell you what it says?"

Already knowing what it said, Kryskin unbuckled his blade.

"Masha'na," he seethed, "stand down."

As he and his men dismounted, he grimly considered what he'd heard. Both the keeper *and* his scribe were missing?

Helia, he prayed, *let the boy be alive. Let him be ahead of his pursuers. And let him be hot on the priest's trail...*

* * *

Ribi cantered down the length of the cattle train, aware that all the envious glances were going to his pony, and that the wry amusement was reserved for him. He couldn't help sitting so tall. His nameday gift – a spotted horse – was a rare convergence of bloodlines. One of only a handful foaled in his lifetime.

Other Mali tribesmen would now approach him to barter stud fees and he would begin to build his own household. Attract a wife. Maybe gift his own sons such steeds, when they came of age.

Spotted horses had been sacred even before they'd carried his people ahead of the empire's hungry expansion, generations before. The tribe's eldest often complained of their new home, in the Renali foothills, cursing the cold and the wet and the green. Longing for prairies and golden grasslands they had never seen.

Which, somehow, never stopped them singing its praises.

Ribi preferred tales of the great cities, with their soaring towers of stone and their man-made marvels. Half his nerves were because of their destination. The cattle market at Keystone, capital of the kingdom, was finally within sight. Unable to contain his excitement, he sought out the one man he knew who had actually been within the walls and would speak of the wonders there.

"Ho, Darom," he greeted, reining his pony around to walk abreast of the godless priest.

His people had no love of missionaries and had very nearly gifted the stranger's bones to the earth when he'd first arrived among them. But the fresh faced foreigner had claimed to be something other than a godmonger and had espoused no interest in converting anyone. After long debate, the elders had decreed that the druid – as he called himself – possessed a reverence for the land that rivaled the Mali's own.

Even that might have been insufficient to spare him. But Darom's knowledge extended beyond the soil and the things that grew in it or grazed upon it. His clever advice had curtailed the Renali lords' taxes by a third and opened the way to the Keystone market. This year, the Mali would reap its rewards directly.

"Come see what you think of this, Ribi," Darom invited.

Curious, he swung from his saddle and joined the druid afoot, beside the manure wain. What could be so interesting?

The man drew the tarp aside, allowing the pungent stink to stagger Ribi. Swatting away a handful of flies, he peered inside. A neat divot had been excavated in the dung, all along the sideboard.

"Someone snuck past the sentries and stole sackfuls of shit?"

Ten score' head of cattle left a lot of excrement on their trail, and it was valuable as both field fertilizer and fire fuel.

The druid's eyes twinkled. "You think someone brash enough to slip past the Mali's slings would be satisfied, stealing poop?"

Ribi raked an eye around the wooded hills, wary of rustlers.

It was true. Taking the cowpat – when you could have the cow – was stupid. For starters, cattle didn't need carrying. And while the Mali were careful of killing the lords' serfs, the clay clods they used for projectiles did sometimes prove fatal.

"What, then?"

The druid's grin grew sympathetic, if a little strained.

"I suspect this was someone's safe haven. A hiding place."

It took him a moment – because his mind rebelled at the idea – but then he saw how a man might worm his way beneath the manure, breathing through the cracks between boards. Hidden.

"Ugh!" As if it would rid him of the image, he spat. "Why?!"

"Perhaps they needed a ride?" the druid shrugged.

"We would have obliged them!"

"Before or after you robbed them?"

"*Traded* with them," he corrected severely.

Darom just laughed.

Still, he thought, eyeing the reeking burrow. *What nerve...?*

He wondered, idly, where their brash guest had gotten to.

PHELAMY MOP HAD no trouble wading through the throng of petitioners, waiting to enter Keystone. Merchants, purveyors, farmers, entertainers and sightseers... all retreated instantly from the sight of him. Or rather, from the reek of him.

His passage could be tracked by the cursing, coughing ripples in the crowd. Until he came, skittering, toward the raised portcullis.

"You there!" cried one of the gate guards. "No more beggars!"

"Eh? Buggers? Bears, you say? If I see any, I'll let them know!"

A long pike was lowered across his path.

"I mean you, you daft bear! I mean, bugger! Get you gone!"

"Me? I'm no bear! I'm a pear. A pearl! No! Earl! I'm an earl!"

"Earl?" the guard scoffed. "You got flies circling your head."

Affronted, Mop straightened his coat, causing a minor cloud of insects to take to wing.

"My attendants," he explained. "As befits any earl. Did I say earl? I meant the other thing. What's the word?" He appealed to the guard. "'s got to do with numbers. An integer. An even. Odd?"

"Well, you're certainly that," the guard's companion added.

"Count!" Mop crowed triumphantly, snapping his fingers. "That's it! I'm a count. And a good one, too. I'm at least a seven."

He reached up to smooth his hair, managing something that was – for lack of a better word – a cow*lick*.

"Seven and a half, when I try," he said modestly.

A nasty grin slowly overtook the guard.

The foremost among the petitioners crowded closer, the better to witness the queue-jumper's comeuppance. With their long pikes, the guards could beat the beggar bloody, without laying hands on him. Hopefully, there wouldn't be too much splatter.

"A count, are ya?" the guard winked at his companion.

"Nope," Mop corrected, "I tell a lie. I meant the other thing. The singing one. Soprano. No! Tenor? That's not it, either. Baritone. Baron. Baron? Yes, baron!"

"You've got your horse hitched wrong way around, friend," the guard advised, sidling closer. "A baron ain't higher than a count."

"Ah," Mop realized, understanding. "You counted too high? That's called *altitude* sickness. Very bad for you."

He squinted at the guard.

"Yes, I can see the signs now. Shoulders slouched by fatigue, expression pinched by headache, and you're even short of breath."

"Because you reek, you filthy-!"

"Alas," Mop overrode, "no visible evidence of loss of appetite."

He stared pointedly at the guard's protruding gut.

Someone in the crowd guffawed. The guard's companion turned away, shoulders shaking.

"How long," Mop pursued, watching the man's cheeks flush, "have you had that peripheral edema?"

"Purr- What?"

"That fat face," Mop clarified.

What had been suppressed snorts and giggles, scattered among the crowd, turned into open laughter. This was going to be *good*.

"Why you little...!"

There was undeniable evidence of redness and swelling in the guard's face, now. Polearm forgotten, the man grabbed a fistful of Mop's soiled shirt. "I'll *kill* you, you stinking arseho- *Och!*"

Overwhelmed by the stench, the guard stumbled back.

One of Mop's flying entourage idly trailed after him. Caught in a desperate, indrawn breath, the fly fought pitifully. And, buzzing, disappeared. Down the guard's gullet.

The man hiccupped his surprise.

The crowd caught their collective breath. Even those who hadn't witnessed the fly's fate felt the stunned disbelief.

Frozen, the guard frowned furiously. An eye twitched. A tentative throat-clearing sounded. Followed by a high-pitched cough and a huge, wet-sounding swallow.

A moment longer the laden stillness held.

Then the guard flew into panicked motion, eyes bulging as he clawed at a constricting throat. Pike clattering to the cobbles, the stricken man stumbled about, thumping at his own chest.

The guard's comrade took an uncertain step forward.

"He's choking!" Mop dismayed, dancing from foot to foot.

The crowd swelled, clamoring at cross purposes.

"Do something!" Mop shot at the second guard.

Another pike clattered as the man rushed over, pounding on his friend's back, fit to buckle the poor man's knees.

"Not like that," Mop wailed. "You have to releviate him! Hug him from behind and bear up on his panorama! Like this…"

Taking one look at his rapidly bluing partner, the guard did as bid, hauling his friend up.

"Again!" Mop keened, yanking at his own hair. "Harder!"

The cross-eyed man fought feebly against the manhandling.

"Harder!"

The crowd added their own screamed support and advice.

Hold him upside down!

Get him some water!

He has to hold his breath!

He's doing that…

Scare him! You have to scare him!
That's for hiccups, you idiot.
You're an idiot!
"Harder!" Mop howled.

Straining, screaming, the guard heaved his companion right off his feet and the two of them slowly toppled.

The impact proved sufficient.

A single, bedraggled fly shot into the air.

Transfixed, the foremost in the audience *ew*-ed.

A great, life-affirming breath filled the gatehouse.

The crowd cheered.

The dazed fly, discombobulated by its experience, tried to right itself. It trekked a drunken path into the city proper.

No one noted its absence. Or, indeed, that of its ride.

Now, Mop thought, hurtling among the alleys, *to find a hat...*

Chapter 16 – Deep

Pella Monop, Diary entry #201

Willful obfuscation of history! Callous reinvention of past events! I had faith in facts and am now experiencing a crisis of faith. Scripture says Helia descended to do battle beside her legions, turning the tide of perdition. In victory, Helia led the legions to a promised land of plenty, there to thrive and sow her glory.

Lies! The legions failed. Helia fell, pulled down by their inadequacy! Perdition's gullet is plugged with her holy corpse. The Heli arrived on this continent a routed, godless army. All else is artifice. The 'schism' was the Temple – destroying history's dissenting versions. The religion is a lie.

The goddess is dead. She's been dead all along.

HOLDING THE PRIESTLY robe at arm's length, Jiminy grimaced.

"Still trying to convert me, huh?"

"It's just a disguise," Neever assured. "And look, it has a *hood*."

Appealing to the thief in him.

When he looked no happier, the monk turned consoling.

"At least it's not a dress, right?"

Well, there was that. He perked up.

"And I'll have plenty of room for my knives," he added.

He ignored the holy man's disapproval, unwilling to revisit their argument. Neever and Cyrus had wanted him to go in, unarmed, so he wouldn't be tempted to kill any sentries. But since they couldn't tell him what *else* might be guarding Seven Deep, he'd prevailed.

"You would be safer *without* weapons," the monk tried anyway.

"It's that kind of crazy talk that makes right-thinking people leery of religion," he observed, donning his disguise.

The monk stepped up to help him with some of the more elaborate knots. "Do you want to go over the plan again?"

"Nope."

He'd supplied most of the plan anyway. Scholars though they were, the priests' original scheme had been a superbly choreographed disaster. Also, as the familiar fever – of an escapade begun – built, he had less and less patience for words.

"What's funny?" the monk wondered, smiling.

He only half-heard, bouncing on the balls of his feet. "Eh?"

His skin was tingling.

A deep, brass note tolled the midnight bell.

"It's time."

He shrugged on the green sash. No temple healer's satchel had ever bulged with such an assortment as *this* one.

Hand on the door latch, the monk hesitated. "I hope you will not take it amiss, Master Jiminy, if I said a quick prayer for you?"

He pulled his hood up over his scowl. "Don't jinx it."

The monk swallowed. "Then, I'll just wish you good luck."

The hateful waiting was done. Jiminy squeezed past the monk. A heavy droning filled his ears and his skin prickled all over.

Each step down the deserted passage was like turning a peg. His jangling nerves tautened toward crisp notes. His surroundings crystalized into keen edges. His pace and pulse smoothed.

Long, confident strides carried him toward the infirmary.

Robed figures drifted between the neat rows of curtained cots. No threat to him, they were little more than silhouettes in the flow of the hall. He joined their current, blending effortlessly. Amid the soft snores, labored breaths and dull groans, he went unremarked. Just another pair of slippered feet in the sprawl.

He found the stairwell on his left, where it should be. Hoisting a handful of robes, he flashed up it.

General living quarters on all sides now. He strolled along, his attention a sinkhole for every sight, sound and scent.

He sensed the truth of Neever's assertion. Thousands lived here. Even so, a Purli face would stand out.

Head held low, his feet followed the map of memory.

First, right... Then left at the fork...

A priestess paced down the corridor toward him. Soft shoes, and the sound-drinking carpet, had masked her presence. Also, it was a *long* corridor. She plodded with the obliviousness of an insomniac, eyes downcast. She hadn't seen him. Yet.

A nearby door beckoned. He placed a palm against it and knew there was no one was awake within. Also, it was unlocked.

Silently, he swiveled inside and out of sight.

Back pressed to the portal, he listened to the faint snores coming from the coils of blanket in the corner.

He struggled to keep his lips drawn over his bright smile, so his teeth wouldn't reflect in the gloom.

Outside, he heard the priestess pass.

Three more stairwells, he thought.

He steadily wormed his way deeper into the building, his way barred only once, by a workman's door – a maintenance access.

The home of the Heli goddess was a city unto itself. Six overlapping courts – or petals – surrounded a central steeple. From on high, it would resemble the Lily Spire's namesake. In nature, the flower's innermost filaments did not twine together to form a tower. But then, a bloom didn't have to house-

'A what?' he'd asked.

'An elevator,' Cyrus had explained.

'What does it elevate?'

He had no view of the cage, which the healer had assured him resembled a simple, round room. Instead, he stared up at the massive mechanism, which ratchetted said cage to the tower's top.

He'd never seen the like.

Toothed cogs and wheels loomed, silent, like the innards of some Rasrini safe. Chains, thick as his thigh, wrapped massive pulleys, encrusted with black grease. Gargantuan counterweights sat, stubborn and seemingly immovable, stinking of clammy iron. A floor grate rumbled with the sound of rushing water.

A chain twitched fitfully, echoing up the endless chimney.

Somewhere far above him, Cyrus was in place, ready to ride the elevator down.

Jiminy shed his priest's garb. His thief's wraps would do a better job of hiding him from here on out. Cinching his tool belt, he hefted the pale healer's satchel, now empty.

Its supple leather fit snugly through the counterweight's fastenings. He slung its sturdy silk securely about his wrists. When the chains shivered to life and the ballast went groaning upwards, he went with it. He watched the ground dwindle between his feet, soon drowned out by the encroaching black.

He'd expected it to be high. He'd expected it to be loud. He'd even expected it to be cold. He hadn't expected it to be *quick*.

Behind his mask, his grin stretched wide. While the stone shaft sped by, he wrestled with the wild laughter filling his chest.

The cage plummeted past, plucking at his wraps. The light of a glow globe seeped from its seams.

How was it that a glass marble, filled with light, was magic? But a room that crawled about a building like a spider was not?

Shaking his head, he felt the ascent slow.

Far below, the massive mechanism's guts rumbled to a halt.

That was it for Cyrus. Now, he was on his own.

Pivoting, he pinched the counterweight between his knees, pulling his hands free. For a half-dozen beats, he dangled upside-down over the abyss, held by nothing but his own daring.

Then, he leapt into the void.

The metal rungs of a ladder slapped against his fingers.

The doors leading from the shaft were finely filigreed metal. Clinging outside the nearest one, he toed its release latch.

He could have easily climbed further up, but the higher apertures all spilled light into the shaft and were under watch.

Something all guards had in common, he reflected, as he slipped into the sleeping billet – they somehow thought that trespassers would take great pains to skirt their center of operations.

The converse would be rather like a hop mouse, barging into an adder's burrow. And, since snakes slept with their eyes open…

Steering wide of the faint snores and hushed voices, Jiminy swept up the stairs, quietly as any desert critter.

Harsh, magical light marked the upper hallways, leaving not a shadow for him to hide in.

A peek down the passage showed one of the temple soldiers, stationed to keep both the elevator and the stairs in view.

Impossible to slip past unseen.

From his belt, he drew a hollow reed, popping the corks from either end. The thought of Neever, stumbling around the temple gardens after this item, made pursing his lips difficult. He blew.

A little puff of grass seed, its fine hairs all but invisible, shot out. Slowing, it twirled in lazy spirals towards the masha'na – and was caught by a downdraft. It skimmed the carpet and lay still.

Damn.

He reached for his second cylinder. And stopped, as the fallen grass seed scrabbled in a circle. In fits and starts, it wobbled almost to the ceiling… and looped across the guard's field of vision, carrying the man's attention away up the corridor.

In a blur, Jiminy shot from the stairwell and out of sight.

He found the right apartment and brought out his picks.

It was a visceral relief to step from the light and back into the dark. He stood a moment, senses extended toward the interior of the suite while his eyes became reacquainted with the gloom.

An antechamber slowly took shape.

Soft breathing came from the bedroom.

He picked his way across the rug to a towering bookcase. Dust caked beneath his fingernails as he quested along the join…

Click.

The entire panel swung smoothly open.

'Secret passages?' he'd scoffed, when Cyrus had started chalking them in atop the tower's schematics.

'Even the corridors of power require the occasional back alley deal,' the priest had explained. *'For that, you need back alleys.'*

Feeling more sullied than he had when navigating Oaragh's sewers, Jiminy slithered into the gizzards of the spire.

Narrow, he thought, straining around a corner.

Unable to turn, he shimmied himself into a tight spot, with the exit flush against his back. He would have to pay more attention to which way around he entered these passages, he thought, straining his shoulder to reach the little latch behind him… *There!*

He might have sat down hard if not for some fleet footwork. He deftly caught the panel before it could slam shut and wake the world, easing it closed. It was a full body portrait of some stern patriarch. He grinned to see the man's disapproval.

Satisfied that the air in the apartment tasted of sleep, he slipped towards the main door.

Sadly, the network of passages provided no direct routes. The aisles shifted to mirror political alliances being built up, torn down or bricked over. Where Cyrus's knowledge of the landscape failed, Jiminy would have to risk the lit passages.

He crouched, ear to the wood, attentive to its whispers. Boots passed in the corridor beyond and he breezed out behind them.

He padded at the guard's back to the next door.

Its lock was easily seduced.

He spent a hundred heartbeats, sifting the new apartment's currents, before venturing deeper. This next passage branched from the bedroom and he had no wish to disturb a dozing priest.

He needn't have worried. The fat, naked holy man slept in an exhausted heap. However, the nubile young woman, unconsciously clawing away from that clammy embrace, raised her head.

Jiminy let the shadows gather him in, smoothing his outline. He unfocussed and the background swallowed him. Peering through his lashes, so not even the whites of his eyes showed, he waited.

The tousled curls panned past him twice before sinking back to the covers, street-bred survival instincts appeased.

Properly warned, he held still until her breathing had deepened once more. Only then did he pad over to the curtained water closet.

Its drape hung from brass rings that would gnash noisily if he drew them altogether. Individual attention kept them quiet.

Flipping the lid down on the musty piss pot, he stepped up toward the back panel, levering at it with his fingernails. The thin plank came loose and he folded himself into the exposed gap, drawing the board back into place behind him.

Recently disturbed dust showed where his and the mistress's paths diverged. Ha! What would she make of *his* footprints?

Grinning at the thought, he came to a dead end.

The egress had been sealed shut, rusty nails curling from the wood on this side. The occupant must not abide midnight visitors.

Jiminy backtracked, revising the chalked lines and annotations in his head. A detour, then, adding two apartments and a risky dash across the open.

No matter. A master thief developed a *feel* for the building being burgled. Whether it was abandoned or bustling or fraught. And this one *wanted* him to succeed.

Which, he reflected, as he fed oil to some rusty hinges from his dropper, *is not to say it doesn't also want to be wooed.*

He alighted in a plush bedroom. An elderly priestess, thankfully clothed, lay a-snore with her mouth wide.

Her cat perched on the coverlet, one leg akimbo while it licked itself. It paused, topaz orbs tracking his progress.

He shrugged at it. *At least it's not a yappy dog.*

Easing open the main door, he peered about. It nestled in the armpit of a junction, visible down three very long passages. Only one of which he could safely surveil. He would have to gamble-

Something snatched at his shin.

Stifling a scream, he watched the cat wind between his ankles and go trotting off up the passage. He swore silently.

Sand-spawned, flea ridden, wind worried, stillbirth of a-!

"Hey, you."

He froze.

So did the cat, to stare up at the unseen speaker.

Armor scales rattled as the guard bent to rub the feline's ears.

The animal ducked, sweeping haughtily down the passage.

"Fine," the guard grumbled after it. "Be that way."

Chainmail rustled, growing faint as the woman moved off.

Blessings on that cat... Jiminy corrected, skimming across the corridor like fat on a griddle, to spill into the next apartment.

Almost there...

A progression of swiveling cabinets, cobwebbed spaces and curving stairs brought him closer and closer to his goal.

When the next apartment proved to be a penthouse, thick with carvings and encrusted with gilt, he knew he'd reached the rooms of the Emperor's advisor – the second most powerful priest in this circus. The splendor showed a layer of disuse.

Cyrus was right. The man spent barely any time here.

Luckily, that meant the seating room's man-high hearth was bare and cold.

With a slippered toe, he depressed the ornamental dragon guarding the grate. There was a muted clunk and a slow ratchet of gears. Marveling at the workmanship, he watched the fireplace – grate, hearthstone, rear wall and all – turn crossways inside the flu.

Smiling, he headed up the spiral staircase so revealed.

The top of the steps held the mirror of the mechanism below. But the heat, coming off its metal pedal, indicated a recent fire. He trod on it, gingerly, and the solid wall turned sideways to show him a bed of banked coals.

A circle of chairs faced the fire – all mercifully vacant.

He stepped out.

The hush of sleep was thick here.

Good.

This floor was given over entirely to the head of the hierocracy. The chambers were expansive, replete with riches and handy nooks to hide in. He flitted from one to the next, hunting for the bedroom.

Ah.

Doors, that would have shamed a border fortress, stood open.

Just as well. I have no picks that could reach those tumblers.

Within, he spied what looked like a ship under full sail – the high archon's four-masted bed, festooned with silk and gauze. It could sleep a modest harem – and clothe a hundred more – but held just one, wizened old man. Gnarled feet poked above the waves and uneven breathing sounded from near the center.

The robes of office stood, imperious upon their stand, begging to be pawed through. Jiminy drifted over. Snorting, he put the paper thin 'bronze' headdress aside. Quick fingers rifled through pockets and nearby drawers and boxes.

Damn. He must sleep with it on...

A grin cutting deep furrows in his face, he turned toward the four-posted monstrosity.

Permission to come aboard...?

His experience on the Isus Spear coming in handy, he swung into the rigging and soon found himself hanging by his feet. Face to face with, arguably, the most influential man in the world.

Who might wake up at any moment to go take a piss.

Sobered by the thought, Jiminy spotted a glint of gold. A fine chain snaked off beneath a frilly nightshirt.

First things first...

'Now be careful,' he recalled Cyrus's warning. *'Haraveera is extremely potent. Two taps only.'*

He handled the little muslin bag, containing a thimble of powder, with the utmost care. Fine, pink particles sifted forth as he tapped it. Twice. The high priest's next breath drew it in.

'Will more kill him?'

'No. But he's an old man. He doesn't need the nightmares.'

Jiminy held his breath until he'd stowed the parcel safely away.

'How long should I wait?'

'For haraveera this fine?' Cyrus had scoffed. *'Don't wait.'*

If what the healer claimed was true, he could now hoist the high priest by his neck and swing him around, without fear of his waking. But there were things a sneak thief simply did not do.

He fished the medallion from its tangle of gray chest hairs and drew it over the fossil's bald pate, turning it over for examination.

A small, many rayed sun, rendered in gold.

So much for the easy part...

He swung down to the carpet, prize in hand, and headed for the high archon's private chapel.

It took pride of place, in what he suspected was the centermost room of the tower. There were no riches here, unless you counted the single cushion, worn to dimples by skinny knees. Or the exquisitely frescoed walls – a riot of color on snowy stone.

The mural ran around the entire circumference of the room, a succession of images in the typical Heli style. So bright was the veneer, so sharp the gloss, it was hard to remember he wasn't looking at a sunlit window in one of their houses of worship.

Banishing the thought, he began to examine the design.

There! Four figures ahorse, side by side...

He reached for the stylized sun above their heads.

Even with Cyrus's assurances, feeling the switch *give* a hair's breadth beneath his fingers came as a surprise.

He stepped closer, inspecting it, but could spy no joins or borders. It sat flush with the wall, its level of artistry superb.

He went in search of the next image...

A battle scene, between an army of light and a dark, faceless horde. A hero stood atop a hill, defiance blazing in his hands.

The hero's sword sunk slightly under his touch.

Next, a carriage, drawn across the stars by fiery birds.

Then, a smith's hammer, ringing down on a glowing ingot.

Lastly, a veiled woman, offering a pearl in her cupped hands.

He stood back expectantly.

But no telltale click sounded. No hidden gears whirred to life.

No panel swung wide and no alcove popped open.

He scratched his head.

Sun, he recited, *sword, carriage, hammer, pearl.*

He'd gotten them all. And in the right order too.

Perhaps he should try agai-

A suggestion of motion had him whirling, knives out. He glared around. But he was plainly alone. So what had…?

In horror, he watched the figures of the mural *move*.

They flowed like ink, bleeding through water.

Mouth lolling open, he watched horses stamp into life beneath their riders and thunder into the next story panel, only to dissolve.

He danced back several paces as the armies there writhed, the hilltop general leading the humans in a rout – and into dissolution.

Colors swirled in frenzy, figures rioted around him, acting out their parts before the white stone shunted them aside.

The mural was receding.

The flaming birds towed their charge beyond night and into nothingness. Where the smith's hammer struck, white sparks blighted the scene.

Color siphoned from the sheer stone, concentrating on the center image, where stood the veiled woman.

Slowly, serene features were revealed. Her eyes remained shut as she sank into the white, as though into a still pond.

Only the pearl remained, the focus of a whirlpool of color, swelling as the very stone remolded itself. It settled into the shape of a many rayed sun – the reverse of the medallion he'd stolen.

It took a while before he could swallow, let alone move.

Keeping a firm grip on one knife, he shuffled nearer, to press the pendant into what was – obviously – a keyhole.

The emblem clung there of its own accord.

He shook his head, thinking sweat had gotten in his eye. He blinked furiously to clear his vision. Then he realized the wall *was* actually moving. Like interlaced fingers – or interlocked teeth – sliding apart, massive spars of stone receded into the floor and ceiling. Tons of rock, moving in absolute silence.

He stared down the pale throat before him – a gentle ramp that spilled sepulchral air, smelling of dry rot and incense.

His heart slowed toward a mere sprint.

He glared an accusation at his ring – cold as a corpse throughout the chapel's transformation.

I'm definitely asking for more money, he mused, setting off into the brilliant unknown of Seven Deep.

PART IV

The final days of the Age of Magic
The day of the Fall
Continent of Thell

HIS SWORD SAWED at the air, like a bird snapping to wing.

The creature lunging at him – all fangs and madness – parted through the middle. Pieces tumbled down the corpse-strewn hill.

Breath misting in the furnace of battle, pink bones crunching beneath his feet, he came to the crest of the carnage. Buried under him somewhere were his honor guard. A handpicked elite. They'd fought to the last man.

But their foes had been anything but men.

Downslope, a *krinjala* squatted, maw buried in a fallen soldier's ribcage. Its eyes tracked him, even as it fed, seeming unconcerned.

That was neither animal indifference nor human arrogance. Oh, it had cunning enough to pass for sentience, and it had fury to spare. But what held it immobile was simple fearlessness.

With his free hand, he hefted a severed head from the pile – he didn't wait to see whose – and launched it.

His aim was true. The alpha, however, was lightning. It flashed beneath the missile and flew for his throat.

Talons scored his pauldron as he turned into its charge.

Canines cracked beneath the impact of his fist.

His blade punched through the alpha's heart as it sprawled and slowly went limp. There was little chance that it would recover from that. But he stomped its head flat anyway.

The stillness of death came, at last, to the cairn of flesh.

Once, the charnel bouquet would have filled him with fierce energy. Now, its fetid breath left him supremely fatigued. Whipping blood from his blade, he cast off his melancholy as well.

Straightening, he took stock of his surroundings.

Pitched battle had plowed the earth from horizon to horizon.

The continent of Thell had not known rain in an age. Now, it sported a vast morass of crimson mud. Burned and blackened banks glowed bright magenta where wild sorceries had flowed.

His kind were not known for being attuned to nature. But even he could sense that the soil he stood upon was desecrated – dead – by what had been unleashed here. Nothing good would take root in it ever again, and even its most resilient scavengers would die of despair before long.

He felt a moment of pity for this young world, marred by such an ugly scar. Still, it was the least of the sacrifices this day would demand.

The Heli army was broken. Routed. Pillars of smoke, on the far horizon, signaled their retreat.

They, and he, had failed.

He could feel the truth of that – could feel the rent, somewhere out there, among the foothills. He could feel the power of it, bleeding all too familiar avarice – and armies – onto this plane.

No. They had to deny the enemy this foothold, this beachhead between realms. The suppurating sore needed to be seared shut. And they were going to scorch more than earth to do it.

The unfamiliar feel of failure woke cold rage in him, and he wanted nothing more than to join the rest of the rearguard in slaughter. But there was a different pull he had to answer first.

He jammed his sword home, unmindful of the ichor that wept down his scabbard. Picking his way with care, he crossed the colossal graveyard the prairie had become. Had he cared to, he could have put names to the slain creatures, drawn from other places and distant worlds.

But he had attention only for her, waiting up ahead.

She stared out over the plain, her back to him. Spotless robes billowed to a breeze that did not touch the surrounding hills.

He joined her in her far-flung examination, avoiding her gaze.

Her influence, extending to envelop him in, was a welcome reprieve. Before his eyes the leagues of battlefield darkened, replaced by a vision of depthless space, speckled by bright stars.

Orphans of lost worlds tumbled through the void, silently dragging the debris of memory, and unfamiliar suns smiled down on alien realms.

He took a moment to breathe in the relative calm.

"So peaceful," she said at long last. "Yet filled with the potential for appalling violence."

He briefly considered whether she meant the expanse, or him, but decided it didn't matter.

"Such is life," he shrugged.

He could imagine the exasperated smile she turned on him, then. But he couldn't bear to look at it, lest it undo him.

"I hope to one day cure that immortal cynicism of yours."

He heard the affection – and the goodbye – in her voice.

It rocked him as no blow could.

"I pray that, someday, you may succeed," he managed, before words failed.

"I know you do," she agreed. "I hear your prayers, after all."

She did him the courtesy of letting him wrestle his sadness in silence, her presence a simple but profound gift.

At long last, she gestured, drawing his attention to the void.

"My chariot."

Only then did he notice the stars darken to the passage of something colossal. A heart of jagged stone hove into view, virtually on top of them. Its sheer mass was staggering, its face riven with mountainous ravines and cratered by ancient impacts.

He could sense the behemoth's pull.

"Your tomb," he corrected angrily.

She imitated his shrug. "Such is life."

Desperation was alien to him, still...

"We can find another way to close the rift. You don't have to-"

"Yes," she interrupted. "I do."

What could he say to that? This was her world. Her people.

His own kind had outstripped gods, long, long ago. He'd slain his share, finding them petty and pathetic, once their power was spent. He had never thought to meet a god, ready to sacrifice for her followers – rather than the other way around.

He'd expected to fall for that god even less.

For his race, love was both uncharacteristic and criminal.

It would be folly to think they'd followed him here, solely out of spite. They were conquerors. It was simply their nature.

He glanced at her. He retained sufficient power to force her from here. Away from this course of action. Against her will.

There were other worlds. Other worshippers.

But she would never forgive him.

And he was too selfish, still, to live with that.

The cant of her head said she had caught the train of his thoughts and wasn't worried. Her faith in him beggared his own.

The eclipse slowly lifted as the colossus passed.

"My moment comes," she declared, stretching up on tiptoes to kiss his stained cheek. He held himself still, certain that if he moved, he would break.

"Go now, brave one," she bid. "Be good."

Turning, he staggered down the slope, feeling the weight of millennia on his shoulders. And wishing, for the first time, that his kind were capable of tears.

Goodbye, my Helia, he prayed, knowing she would hear him.

Sorrow occluded all else. He had no hope of rising above it. But he could rail at it, for a time…

His sword leapt eagerly to his hand. He set out to undo as many of his kin's doomed creatures as he could.

And save as many of Helia's beloved humans as possible.

And he *would* save them.

Because it was one thing, to be given a god's love.

It was quite another, to know one had faith in you.

CHAPTER 17 – UNBOUND

Pella Monop, Diary entry #203

It's been days. I can halt neither my racing thoughts nor my thumping heart. I have barricaded myself in my quarters, claiming ailment. Cecine forced her way inside this morning. Convinced she had come to kill me, I promptly collapsed from fear and vomited over her shoes. This allayed her suspicions, somewhat, but I have little time. If I am not to end up like Bruen and her nameless scribe, I must master my trembling fingers and faculties. A difficult feat for I am, in truth, fevered. I fear I am coming unhinged. Bruen agrees.

MARCO HAD FOUND abject terror physically unsustainable. So, he'd spent the last couple of bells oscillating between desperate struggle and breathless panic. Leather ties held his wrists and ankles in the small of his back, so he couldn't even sit up. As night fell, the damp of the disused warehouse floor slowly seeped up through his robes, making him shiver.

A cluster of candles gave the only light, casting monstrous shadows whenever the assassin moved about.

His mind shied from remembering the fall, out the princess's window. The sickening weightlessness. The howling wind. The heart-stopping anticipation of impact.

Instead, his stomach had lurched toward his feet as *something* fought to arrest his fall. He'd glimpsed gossamer strands, sawing discordantly – a thousand crickets, playing out of tune.

He'd hit his head. Or been hit. He remembered the dankness of sewers and a sharp knee in his back as his hands were tied.

A knifepoint, pressed to his spine, had prodded him through the gloom. He vaguely recalled passing through a grate, the rusty bars bright with recent cuts. There had been a culvert, its bottom littered with crumbling brick and stone rubble. A trap door. Then this.

An abandoned brickworks, perhaps, or even a quarry dump.

Upon cresting the ladder, his legs had been unceremoniously swept from beneath him. Winded and trussed, he'd been dragged to this corner and, basically, ignored.

He was a limpet, stuck in a low tide pool, waiting for a sharp stick that had not yet arrived.

Fearful thoughts had crashed, over and over, on the breakwater of his exhaustion and he'd finally lost a few bells to fitful sleep.

For him, slumber offered no escape from terror.

He slammed awake, a scream in his throat. His bindings bit his raw skin as he sought escape. Escape from what, he did not know.

Slowly, the dark corners and dirty surfaces resolved into the now familiar warehouse, echoing with his frantic wheezes.

He got a faint whiff of blood. His rude awakening had done what a death defying fall, and rough handling, had not. It had torn the near-healed wound in his side.

The assassin watched him.

His own fear obscured the scents of rock dust and wood mold. A tickle of musty fur and dry droppings said rats nested nearby. He could hear them, small claws clicking in the rafters. He recognized the bitter scents of weapon oil and the beeswax-sweetness of supple leather. There were some fungal spores and mercurial stains he couldn't place. An overlay of sewer-stink. And, beneath it-

"You're a girl!" he blurted his revelation.

The hooded head cocked and she propped one hand on her hip. Something in her bearing changed. The difference was subtle, but significant, making his observation seem stupidly obvious.

He didn't know how he hadn't noticed before. The slight build, the fleet footwork, the consummate grace... No wonder she never spoke – it would doubtless ruin her disguise.

Perhaps she'll speak now? Perhaps I can reason with her...

"Could I get a drink of water?"

Losing interest, she turned from him.

"Please?"

Nothing.

"You know, I'm going to have to pee at some point!"

He instantly regretted his insistence as she spun about.

With overdone deliberation, she gathered up a waterskin and came sashaying up. She loom over him, cold menace pouring down, joined a moment later by lukewarm water. It soaked his hair and ran down his face. Trying not to drown, he turned his head so he could manage a few second-hand swallows.

"Thank you," he sputtered. But the deluged didn't let up.

She let the skin run dry, drenching him.

Coughing miserably, he glared through his sopping fringe. Her eyes were dark, flat and dispassionate as river stones.

The analogy made his bladder hurt all the more.

Finally, she moved off, tossing the empty skin aside.

"About that visit to the privy...?" he pressed.

He didn't see the throwing star arrive, only heard it thunk into the boards above his head. She was there the instant after, plucking it free and pulling him roughly up by the chin. He grunted as his neck took most of his weight. The flat of the throwing star was pressed to his lips in a shushing motion.

Her eyes, so cold a moment before, sizzled. They drove her point home more eloquently than the steel mashing his mouth.

Strung like a bow, he struck his jaw as she released him.

He tasted slurry.

Desperation lent him courage.

"In case you hadn't noticed," he shouted at her retreating back, "she ordered her guards to murder *me* too!"

The shrouded figure paused, hooded head askew.

"Why?"

Her voice was rough. With an accent he couldn't place.

"Why," she repeated, "was the royal trying to kill you?"

He'd had a day to think on it – to agonize over Dailill's words.

He'd examined them from every angle. But, however he pulled them apart and pieced them back together, they spelled betrayal.

Even so, it was chokingly painful to speak it out loud.

"She-" He winced. "I think she means to start a war."

The assassin scoffed. "And killing *you* would accomplish this?"

He met her disbelieving gaze with a level one.

"Killing my *master* would accomplish it. Accusing me of her attempted murder would make doubly sure."

She regarded him in silence for a long moment.

Then, "Who are you?"

He couldn't stifle his surprise. "You don't know?"

She crossed her arms. "You obviously think yourself very important."

"It's not that," he stammered. "It's just... You don't recognize me? From the royal apartments? The chase across the rooftops-"

He choked off as he was hoisted, bodily, by his collar.

"You're the Heli bodyguard?!" she realized. "*You?*"

Perhaps it was the lack of air, but he thought he saw tendrils of angry smoke coil from her shoulders. A crackle, like dead leaves, clawed at his ears.

"*You* saw through my shroud?" she sneered. "You're a child!"

She threw him to the ground. Hard.

A kick woke agony in his side.

"How? Is it a talisman?" She kicked him again. "A charm?"

"I don't-" he squawked between blows. "No!"

She left him gasping for breath and was back a moment later, brandishing a candle that she stuck upright, out or arm's reach.

She hauled him up by his hair. Steel glinted. For a moment, he was sure she meant to slice his throat.

"For your sake," she said, "I hope it's not embedded in you."

There was the purl of parting cloth. Cold air, and colder steel, rosined his bare skin. The timbre of his panic changed then. Half-held memories of a night sky, glimpsed between buildings, crashed down on him. The feel of calloused hands, pawing at him…

He couldn't help struggling, or the small sounds he made.

"Hold still," the assassin growled above him.

She examined his naked flesh, top to bottom, her touch cold and impersonal. She was thorough, combing through his scalp and checking between his toes. She even thumbed up his eyelids.

"Keep them open," she growled. "Or I'll slice them off and hold them to up to the light…"

Her fingers lingered over the old burn scar on his chest.

"Stick out your tongue," she commanded at last, peering at the insides of his cheeks and the underside of his palate.

Frustrated, she stood away. "Which of the dark disciplines do you follow? *Trahmet*? *Urtsyde*?"

Working up enough spit to speak was a struggle.

"I don't know what those are," he whispered.

This time, he watched it happen. Writhing shadows, such as a bare tree might cast on a bedroom wall, shivered away from her. With a sound like skittering leaves, they swept up to envelop her.

"Can you still see me?" she asked, her voice thin and far away.

Any cunning had departed along with his dignity. He nodded.

The dark mass swirled across the room, merged with a patch of shadow and reappeared to sway along the rafters. Too late Marco realized he was tracking it with his eyes.

With a rustle, the concealment spell scattered. The assassin dropped, catfooted, in front of him.

"How? How are you doing this?"

"I don't know."

"Can anyone else do this?"

"My master says it is Helia's blessing," he insisted.

He quailed to think what else it might be.

She swatted the notion away. "I've stalked Heli before. Mm... Never a priest, though. Not yet."

She was silent for several beats, then her eyes narrowed on him.

"Your master... He is the mage who plies the poor quarter? Mending the maimed, raising the dead and taking no money?"

"The keeper is no necromancer!"

Bound, and surrounded by the scraps of his clothes, he sounded nowhere near as staunch as he'd intended.

She appeared not to hear him, speaking to herself.

"The little Renali prince is said to be in near permanent poor health. And now the second runner-up is plotting war? Why? Her sister would still stand between her and the throne."

Abruptly, the assassin stiffened. Whatever realization she'd come to, it eluded him. But this talk of succession...

"Did Dailill's sister hire you?" he voiced his secret suspicion.

Tossing him a scowl, she strode off.

He called after her, "Can *I* hire you?"

"I don't work for coppers, boy," she sneered, not slowing, "and I don't take coin to let people live."

"Please, I have gold."

Snorting, she indicated his heap of ruined robes.

"Not on me," he corrected.

"Obviously."

"But the keeper brought a sizable stipend from Tellar."

How much, he didn't know. But, since it was intended to purchase a building large enough serve as the new Temple mission, it had to be substantial.

"Good for him," she said. "Too bad for you."

"I don't mean me."

That brought her up short. "What?"

He swallowed. "I'm not bargaining for *my* life. I want to hire you to rescue the keeper."

For the space of a single breath, she stood stunned. Then she threw back her head and laughed. One quick, callous burst.

"Seriously? I'm an assassin. I *kill* people. I don't save them."

"You saved me," he argued. If she hadn't broken that box's curse, and hauled him out the window, he'd be a corpse right now.

"You were a human shield, entirely expendable."

"Yet," he pressed, "I'm still alive. Why is that?"

She puzzled at him a moment. Then her demeanor changed. The line of her shoulders evened and her feet splayed.

He was reminded of a cat, coiling to spring.

"Good question," she admitted.

Blackened steel came to her hand, his death clear in her eyes.

"No! Wait!"

She straddled him, pressing his head back to get at his neck.

"I'm still alive," he rushed breathlessly, "because no one is paying you to kill me." She'd avoided naming Dailill. But he'd seen her eyes flash when *he* had done so. He made a desperate leap, "And I don't think anyone is paying you to kill *her*, either."

Yes, that was it. That's what he'd seen. Pure, burning hatred. Whatever was between them, it had nothing to do with coin.

"*This*," he gritted out, "me dying – my mentor dying – this is *her* plan." She nearly crushed the word 'mentor' from him. "It may be your knife, but it'll be her hand, all the same. Are you really alright with being her instrument? Her accomplice?"

The razor vibrated at his jugular.

"No."

He collapsed onto his face as she released him.

Panting, he rolled over as far as he was able, craning his neck to meet her eyes. Their blaze had been banked, swept over by cold calculation.

"What," she asked, "do you propose?"

He spent the next several breaths telling her, making it up as he went along.

"My fee for such an undertaking would be… extravagant."

"How much?"

"One thousand and one Renali crowns."

He had no idea how much money that was.

"Done."

She searched his eyes. Whether or not she found what she was looking for was unclear. Either way, she gave a tight nod.

"I must be out of my mind," she muttered, parting his bonds with one sure pass of her knife.

Covering his nakedness as best he could, he scrambled to his feet, ignoring the rampant pins and needles.

"Marco," he introduced himself with a bow.

She narrowed her eyes at him. "Nin."

"Pleased to meet you. Do you think I could have some pants-?"

He trailed off.

He hadn't realized how attuned his ears had become to the quiet of the warehouse, where the only city sounds arrived on intermittent gusts of wind. Now, a new noise had joined the hush. Boots, crunching across the gravel.

"-most of the male clothes are disguises-" Nin was saying.

"Someone's outside..." The realization dropped from his lips.

"No," she assured, busily rummaging in a barrel. "I spun wards every dozen paces. No one is getting close without me-"

She straightened abruptly, head snapping around to focus beyond the flaking walls. For half a dozen heartbeats, she stood frozen. Then stepped up and roughly shoved him to the floor.

"Stay there and stay still..." she instructed in clipped tones.

She dragged a musty tarp from a beam and dumped it over him.

Dust assaulted his sinuses, worse than Purlian pepper. Coughing, he fought his way clear, gasping for clean air.

Through stinging tears, he watched shadows wreathe Nin. The ebon mass crawled up the wall and the assassin reappeared, balanced on the lintel above the main door. Clutching wicked-looking daggers, she shooed angrily at him.

She'd pinched out the candles. Yet, he could see her perfectly, even in the pitch black. And she could, apparently, see him.

His shiver had nothing to do with her glare, or even the cold, as he drew the stiff canvas around himself again, breathing shallowly.

Eyes wide, motionless in the gloom, Marco waited.

ENDERAM LELOUCH, SWORDSMAN extraordinaire and bodyguard to the elder princess Villet, was rattled.

It was a novel experience for him.

He found it not to his liking.

It had been years since anyone had tried laying hands on him. And years more, since anyone had succeeded. Now, in the space of two days, there had been as many attempts.

The most recent of which, shockingly, had succeeded.

He had dismissed the first. The previous night's accosters might have been mere unlucky footpads. At least, until their bodies had turned up ropes and a leather hood, presumably meant for him. One of them had sported a Heli circle sign, tattooed on his chest.

Lelouch knew better than to think any of it was directed at him. Whoever's scheme this was, it would be aimed at his mistress.

He'd applied his prodigious mind to the problem but had been unable to puzzle it out with so few pieces.

As a child, he'd quickly seen that he was smarter than his lowborn peers and neighbors. He'd also seen that being smart was a bad thing to be. And not just because it attracted bullies.

"Brains in a commoner are as useless as balls on a mule," he'd once heard a nobleman say. The other nobles at table had laughed. But the person who had enraged little Lelouch the most had been his servant father, unobtrusively refilling that noble's goblet.

His father – a leader in the community, someone to whom others brought their dilemmas and disputes – had said nothing.

Lelouch had made his decision then. If his intellect could not buy the nobles' respect, he would spend it purchasing their fear. It was the only way to be safe. It was the only way to be *him*. And it was one of the few roads by which the common man might rise.

So, he'd taken up the sword.

He had lacked physical co-ordination and innate talent both.

It turned out that intellect, and unflinching focus, could cure a host of shortcomings. His parents had objected, of course. They'd depended on the coin he'd earned, working in the keep's kitchens.

His refusal had earned him a number of beatings. But he would sell his labor only to those capable of teaching him the sword.

He'd been a season short of coming of age, as yet unbearded, when he'd finally reasoned that he was ready.

There were two ways one might become a master swordsman.

One was to have a quorum of three swordmasters bestow the title, after a series of skill tests and duels. But such a gathering of swordmasters was rare. Especially since the only three swordmasters in the kingdom ran their own combat schools and jealously guarded their patrons. They would not willingly create competition for themselves.

He'd presented himself at Swordmaster Quon's. The old man had mocked his commoner's garb and his second-hand sword.

By the time he was done demonstrating his mastery of the cardinal cuts, Quon had no longer been laughing.

No doubt thinking to put the brash, base-born brat in his place, Quon had set the school's best pupils on him.

He'd bested them all, and had then called out their teacher.

Because the *second* way to become a swordmaster was to slay another master in single combat.

The threat had worked. The sweating master had sent out urgent missives and they'd waited, for the other masters to arrive.

They had been every bit as blustering and belligerent as expected. And they'd insisted on putting him through his paces, again. Their best students had been tasked with crippling or killing him, if they could.

He'd won through, though he'd taken a bad cut to his forearm. One that would limit his reach and threaten his grip.

Confident that they had defanged the threat, the masters had passed judgment, declaring him unfit. With careful words, they'd goaded him into challenging one of them.

He hadn't disappointed them.

Smiling once more, Master Quon had sauntered up.

He'd shifted his sword then, from his injured right hand, to his dominant left.

Quon's smile had died, and the master had followed, soon after.

The remaining masters, reassured that he did not intend to start his own school, had left well-enough alone.

Lelouch had joined the Royal Guard, to live in relative luxury. But the station – and fear – he'd found there had been... unsatisfying. He'd spent his days standing guard, or beating his fellows at either swordplay or sidestep – neither of which served to hone his skills.

He'd fallen into a kind of bored detachment.

It hadn't been until his third consecutive loss that he'd looked across the game board to find his opponent to be a little girl.

She'd been quiet, earnest and royal. In that moment, he'd recognized a kindred spirit – one whose innate drive and natural abilities would amount to nothing, because of her birth.

Because of her gender.

And – he'd been able to tell – she'd recognized him, in turn.

Ever since then, he'd acted as an audience of one to her brilliance. One of the few capable of seeing it.

Together, over a span of years, the two of them had carved a place at court for a princess whose worth was not reckoned purely by her ability to breed. One whose highest praise would not be won by dint of her embroidery, but by her political acumen.

They'd beaten a path the younger princess had exploited.

The light of day had fallen on a few more puzzle pieces.

"My little sister seems set to ruin Father's work," Villet had said. "If we are to save face and save the summit both, we must exonerate the Heli, preferably without exposing Dailill's schemes.

"Go," she'd commanded. "Find the priest. Failing that, find the scribe – if he yet lives. If they are smart – and serious about pursuing peace – they will do the expedient thing and aid us."

She had not needed to say what was to happen if the Imperials were *not* set on pursuing peace.

Early morning had turned into early evening, while he fruitlessly ran down every clue he could dig up and every lead he could conjure. He'd left a city of nervous den masters and sweating kingpins in his wake, with little to show for his efforts.

Lelouch knew the Heli priest had been taken by force, in much the same manner someone had meant to take him. The timing made it likely that the incidents were connected. The culprits may have been Imperials... but a contingent of guardsmen, loyal to Dailill, had mysteriously gone out 'on maneuvers' the day before. Put that together with the keep forged blade the Heli boy was not supposed to have and a pattern began to form. He knew the scribe had not tried to assassinate the younger princess. He'd seen the boy fight, at the tourney, from afar.

If the lad had wanted Dailill's head, he'd have it.

Lelouch had been no closer to turning up either priest or scribe.

Also, he'd become too accustomed to people scurrying from his path. Especially when he wore a scowl. Bumping into a person on the street had come as a surprise.

Assuming there had *been* a person under that possessed hat.

It had been a haberdasher's nightmare – a crooked chimney of riotous colors, stuck with plumes and brooches and fanciful odds and ends. The ridiculously expansive brim had drooped nearly to the wearer's shoulders, hiding their face.

The hatted head had said, "Oof!"

Fresh from an abduction attempt, he'd had to control the urge to take off the apparition's hat and head both. Murdering a jester, in the middle of the road, was unlikely to help. Even if it would make him feel better. Then, to his shock, hands – hidden somewhere beneath that brim – had patted at him.

"Humblest apologies, dear sir!" the manic voice had said. "We have walked straight into you! Oh, we hope you are not injured?"

He'd stepped away from the unwelcome touch, and the equally unwelcome odor of cow dung, trying to peer beneath the hat's brim. But the frippery had followed doggedly.

"Who are you?" he'd demanded.

"Introductions! Yes! *You* are the royal ornithologist! *I*, myself, am hunting a black tufted duck." The feathered hat had leaned, precariously close, to whisper, "Have you seen one?"

That particular bird was the source of a *private* joke between himself and his princess. She frequently threatened him with a knighthood, when displeased, and said she'd foist the black tufted duck on him as his sigil. The drab bird was remarkable only for its daring, defending even an empty nest from large predators.

Alarmed, he'd made a grab for the unseen wearer and missed.

Jostled, the hat had dragged a plume between his bared teeth.

He'd staggered back, sputtering. By that time, he'd been convinced – the hatman was dangerous. The mere fact it had taken him so long to realize it was a measure of *how* dangerous.

He'd reached for his sword.

Only to find it gone.

"Ahah!" the threat had followed, "I knew you for a fellow birdwatcher from the moment I hat capped... *had clapped* eyes on you!" A blinding array of color, as the wearer spun in place. Lelouch had braced himself for a blow but none came. "What are you on the prowl for? The mantled raven, perhaps?"

His fists, poised to deliver deadly blows, had paused.

The mantled raven, also called the 'little executioner', roosted up high and was well known for carrying off so-called prayer mice.

If Lelouch was the black tufted duck, would the mantled raven be the assassin who had absconded with the Heli scribe?

"I knew it!" the hat had crowed, flouncing as its wearer capered.

Dangerous, he'd thought, but also weirdly well informed. He'd needed answers more than he'd needed another dead enemy.

"Where can I find the raven?" he'd asked between gritted teeth.

"She nests up the old white oak!"

Before he could voice another question, the wearer had begun to sing, hat bobbing along to a nursery rhyme.

"Wheatlips! Daisies! Sickle and twine!"

"You," Lelouch had finally observed, "are mad."

Not ceasing its sway, the hat had responded.

"Merely slightly miffed, I assure you! Fourteen silvers for this hat? Now, that's mad! Daylight robbery! And I should know – I stole it! Hahaha!"

Whirling after its wearer, the hat had fled into the crowd, the same children's song staining the air.

"Greencorn! Vainleaf! Say you'll be mine!"

Transfixed, he'd plunged in pursuit, but too late. A superbly hatted man, once divested of said hat, became invisible in a crowd.

His sword, at least, had not been stolen as he'd feared. It had somehow been moved along his belt, to hang on his opposite hip.

Mightily miffed himself, he'd scowled into the crowd, thinking.

Mad or not, the jester's clue was the only one he'd had.

He'd headed for the city quarter called White Oak – the old mason's district. The slagheaps had soured the well water there, claiming dozens of lives. It had been abandoned and boarded up, by royal decree, years ago.

The barriers and padlocks he broke, to get inside, were old. There was evidence that scattered vagrants had tried to home here, at some point, but had since given up.

Now, seen in the dregs of dusk, the lifeless quarter was sinister.

Alright, hat-man. Let's see if I'm mad too, for being here...

Feeling foolish, he recited the harvest song to himself.

Wheatlips, daisies, sickle and twine.

A dilapidated alehouse, its only patrons now rats and pigeons, boasted a faded sign. It read, 'Daisy's'.

He set off in that direction.

A little further down the road, he found the ruin of a shop that had once specialized in whetstones. Used for sharpening *sickles* and all manner of agricultural implements.

Greencorn, he thought, *vainleaf, say you'll be mine.*

Greencorn was a traditional component of funeral wreathes.

There was a gravestone carver's within sight. He headed for it.

Vainleaf was a climbing vine. Also called stoneskirt. It was often used to strategically cover those pieces of statuary that were too immodest for modern sensibilities.

In a sculptor's courtyard lay a crumbling piece, only half-way freed from its block. A broken arm pointed him up the road.

Ahead was a dead end and a decrepit stone dresser's workshop.

Mother will smile, Father will frown,
Crops will all lie down and drown.

The chains on the door were crusted thick with rust. A good kick sent them careening inwards, sweeping dust and debris before them. While a hint of light still lingered outside, night had already claimed the interior.

It, and the last verse of the rhyme, gave him pause.

But you I will love,
'Till death from above.

Like most children's chants, it predicted catastrophe. Specifically, famine, in the face of a harvest destroyed by hail.

And the mantled raven also favored striking from on high.

He glanced up.

Fine dust sifted from the beam overhead.

He peered into the gloom. Small footprints marred the grime. A barrel spilled a pair of woman dresses, evincing social stations too dissimilar to be anything but disguises. And hatman *had* said the raven was a 'she'.

"Won't you come down, lady?" he called into the gloom.

"WON'T YOU COME down, lady?" a male voice enquired.

Beneath his muffling tarp, Marco flinched at its timbre.

There was a moment of silence before Nin spoke, her voice fraying eerily under her concealment spell's effect.

"I do not normally answer my door after dark. I doubt you saw the friendly lights burning, so – how did you find this place?"

Sounding slightly strained, the man said, "It was child's play."

"Ooh, I'll play. Shall we play *drowsy deer*? Do you know it?"

Marco did. He used to play it at Temple, with the other novices. Basically, the wolves rushed the deer while it wasn't looking.

Their intruder seemed to consider.

"That would not go well for you."

"O-ho. You know this for a fact?"

"From experience," the man assured. "You would not be the first assassin I'd felled. Merely the first I'd been forewarned of."

"Not a lot of incentive for me to come down, then."

There was a rustle. Marco heard something arch through the air. It landed with the recognizable clink and spill of coins.

"What's this?" Nin demanded.

"Incentive."

"For?"

"For starters, you have Master Dei Toriam under that sheet. I would like to see him."

Surprise jerked Marco to his feet in a cloud of biting dust. Too late did he consider that the man might be bluffing. Almost, he let his stiff canvas slide to the floor. He snatched it back in time to cover his nakedness, squinting towards the doorway.

"Enderam Lelouch?" he recognized, lilting in surprise.

The bodyguard glanced at – and then dismissed – him.

Nin's voice moved among the rafters. "As you can see, he is in no fit state to entertain. So, if there is nothing else…?"

"My mistress," Lelouch continued, "offers a commission."

Nin's disembodied chuckle was ominous. "Discreet enquiries said your mistress was not in the market for my… *services*."

"She does not seek her sister's death. She seeks only stability."

Marco found that, even with his newly sharpened sense of hearing, he could not pin down Nin's progress among the beams.

Her voice drifted down. "So what has changed?"

The tilt of the bodyguard's chin invited a guess.

The rafters ceased their creaking as Nin considered.

"Stability… You want the kidnapped diplomat returned."

In Marco's breast, hope reared up like a siege engine.

"We will need the masha'na…!" he blurted, before the bodyguard's flat stare quelled him.

"They have been moved to the Third Regiment's barrack, in the Brewer's Quarter. Our agent will be ready by the rear gate at moonrise. Horses will be waiting at the hostelry on the corner."

Marco boggled at the bodyguard.

Visible once more, Nin dropped between them, commanding the man's gaze. She toed idly at the bag of gold.

"Kill no one at the barrack," Lelouch instructed her.

"Or what?"

The air turned thick with impending violence. The bodyguard turned a careful degree at the waist. Nin slid subtly to meet him.

Marco caught his breath, smelling their sweat, hearing their thundering heartbeats, feeling their mounting readiness-

Lelouch shrugged. "Or you'll void the remainder of your fee."
The moment passed.
With that, the bodyguard turned, heading for the broken doors.
Nin let him go.
Belatedly, Marco pieced together what his nose was trying to tell him. This scent had been on the burlap wraps. "Wait!"
Pausing, the bodyguard peered over a shoulder at him.
"It was you," Marco whispered. "You took the sword – the keep forged blade – from my trunk."
"Stability," the man said at last, "is not the same as justice."
The bodyguard walked off into the night.

* * *

"I DEMAND THAT-!"
Kryskin forced himself to stop and take a deep breath. His patience was at its breaking point.
"Colonel, sir," he continued, in what he hoped was a more reasonable tone, "I must insist that I be allowed to see the ambassador immediately."
He and his fellow masha'na were currently 'guests' of the Third Regiment and had been for the entire day. It was nearing midnight and their host had only now agreed to an audience.
If you could call it an audience.
The colonel – the noble knight in charge of the regiment – sat at a desk, staring stonily into the middle distance. The man had yet to say a word, leaving all the talking to his aide, Lieutenant Heiss.
Who remained infuriatingly reasonable and utterly unhelpful.

"As I'm sure you can appreciate," the man maintained, "your ambassador has already retired for the evening and cannot be reached. However, I understand you were given standing orders?"

Sitting-on-our-hands orders, more like... Kryskin seethed.

"I was," he admitted. "But-"

"Well, there you are, then," Heiss concluded.

They weren't going to let him plead his case to Malconte. Which might, or might not, be at the man's behest. A stink currently clung to the masha'na. Malconte, consummate politician that he was, would be trying to distance himself from it.

Kryskin bit back his frustration. "I need to make a priority report. The ambassador does not have all the facts-"

"You may make your report to me, if you wish, or commit it to paper," Heiss offered. "I will ensure it gets to the right recipient."

Kryskin doubted the 'right recipient' included the ambassador.

Giving up, he gave the aide his full attention. He knew the type – who took pleasure in abusing their paltry power.

He eyed the man pointedly, letting his true opinion leak.

"Lieutenant, I could no more give my report to a suit of armor stuffed with straw. It would violate my chain of command."

Heiss bristled.

Proving that he'd been listening, the colonel waved a dismissal.

Kryskin's 'diplomatic escort' opened the door at his back, remembering themselves in time to stop from seizing his elbows.

He was marched back to the bunkroom where his troupe had been installed. A draft preceded him through the door but could not cool his temper. As the lock turned behind him, his masha'na rose.

"No luck," Finch inferred, looking at his face.

He shook his head.

"What a fine mess this is," Ryhorn scorned, slumping back onto a stripped Renali bunk.

Nods rounded the room.

What a mess indeed....

One of their own was dead. Their chaplain was taken. A child in their charge was wanted for regicide, or near enough. And their sainted ambassador seemed to have washed his hands of them.

The summit was a blazing hay wain, on a downhill slope.

And here sat the masha'na, like misbehaved dogs, told to *stay*.

He swallowed his despair. Morale had suffered enough.

"Join me in prayer," he commanded.

Gathering in a ragged circle around him, the masha'na knelt.

"Holy Helia, guardian mother, we find ourselves becalmed in blackness and beset on all sides by foes. Look upon us, your chosen. We remain, stout of heart of and sure of purpose. Gift us your guiding light, Helia. Illume our hearts, so we may carry your glory into the dark.

"Unity through faith."

"Unity through faith," his troupe answered.

Into the somber silence, Finch wished aloud, "Goddess grant that Marco is hot on the keeper's trail."

There was spate of doubtful nods and hopeful grunts.

"He'd better not be," a woman's voice said. "I told him to wait at the hostelry."

Chaos, as masha'na shot to their feet, heads whipping around in search of the intruder. Kryskin clutched at an absent sword.

"Who speaks?" he challenged.

"You must be Kryskin," the voice continued, ignoring him.

He whirled toward it but caught only a whisper of movement.

The voice came again, from a different quarter.

"He described you well."

Scowling, his unarmed masha'na backed toward one another.

"Though, I'd imagined you taller," the intruder said.

"Reveal yourself, denizen!" he demanded.

Up near the ceiling, the corner he faced seemed to crawl. As he watched, shadows peeled like burning paper. A figure, impossibly upside down, unfolded lightly to the floor.

"Marco said you'd call me that," the masked assassin laughed.

FUMING, HE MADE an effort to stand straighter at his post. He was a royal guardsman, for fortune's sake! He was meant to watch over kings. Not play swineherd to Imperial pigs. It was doubtful the sty stink would ever scrub out of the bunkroom at his back.

Best to burn it all, preferably with the zealots still inside.

Nursing a hangover, he tried to ignore the steady pour of words from his partner. Just his luck, to be paired with the-thing-that-won't-shut-up. Half the guard suspected the man was slow. But since the simpleton was a savant with a pike, and could stand at attention for whole tapers at a time, he was tolerated. Barely.

The dolt was recounting his morning shift – starting with getting out of bed – like it was a bard's epic. Some petty thievery, involving a hat-maker, and the artisan's lifelong practice piece.

Cursing his lot, he leaned surreptitiously against the doorframe.

He blamed the Imperials, of course. Personally, he didn't see why the king should bother making peace. It was obvious the empire was wary of them. Why else would they invade lands across the vast ocean but give their closest neighbor a wide berth?

Of course, you couldn't expect them to act rationally. Their minds were moth-eaten by prayer and stained by centuries of magic. Instead of coins, their goddess demanded countries. Women fought in their wars. And, rumor said-

He jumped, as the lock turned loudly behind him.

Swearing, he and the simpleton swung about, giving themselves space to lower their spears. His cry of alarm stalled as an angry horde failed to boil forth. He was not about to embarrass himself by panicking.

Especially not if some Imperial was simply testing the latch.

To his horror, he saw the door open a crack... and shut again.

Spear vibrating in his hands, throat dry, he gathered a shout.

"Funny-looking candle..." his companion commented.

"Wha?" He glanced down.

The little ceramic sphere looked nothing like a candle. Except that it had a wick, fizzling away-

There was a muted thump. The air turned thick with stinging smoke. Coughing, staggering, he heard the simpleton go down. He didn't see whatever it was that slammed into the side of his head.

CAUTIOUSLY ENTERING THE passage, Kryskin waved away a few clinging coils of smoke. The assassin crouched over two prone guards. Her tight cowl and contoured mask left only her eyes bare.

It seemed she was serious about not taking any lives.

"I thought you said it would be best if no one saw you?"

"They did not see me," she assured him, rising. She was tall enough to look him in the eye. What he saw there gave him pause.

"You're her, aren't you? The one who went after the princess?"

"Twice," she agreed. Reading the hesitation in his stance, she twirled a brass key. "Would you rather I locked you back in?"

He shook his head, unsure how much of her information he could take at face value. This could all be a clever ploy to lead him and his masha'na to slaughter. But she claimed that Marco had hired her. And when he'd asked for proof, she'd handed him a yarn charm, cut from some old canvas.

'He said you'd know what it means...'

"Alright," he said again, as his men filed out behind him. "Secure these two. Finch and I'll spearhead. Bear, you're rearguard. Everyone, on your tiptoes. I'd prefer not to have to fight the whole regiment on our way out of here."

"Ain't fighting no one without no weapons," Longjaw objected.

"We cannot leave without our swords," he told the assassin.

Her leather mask was black and intractable, and it matched her eyes in every respect. Only the hitch in her shoulders showed any emotion. "Yeah, he said you wouldn't. Fine. Follow me…"

Beckoning them, she raced away, her cloven slippers silent on the boards. Shadows embraced her and she disappeared. Literally.

A low whistle announced Finch, by his shoulder.

"We sure about this?" the man whispered worriedly.

"I'm sure we're not doing the keeper any good, stuck in here."

In comparison to the cowled woman, the masha'na clomped along like cattle. She reappeared at intervals and intersections, signaling them to hurry on or stay hidden. Crouching beneath a shadowed stair, he flinched as she suddenly coalesced beside him.

"The armory is on the upper level," she explained. "Much more light, many more eyes. A dozen men won't pass unseen."

She pointed. "This corridor joins a storage area. It is unlit and the cellar doors open not far from the postern. The rest of you wait there. You, pick one other man and follow me."

Not waiting for a reply, she shot up the stairs.

He nodded to Finch. "Take the troupe. If I'm not back by your third hundred-count, get out and go after the keeper."

Gathering up Bear with a glance, he leapt up the steps.

"You had to pick the biggest one," the assassin complained. "This way…"

She sped ahead of them and, at her third step, vanished.

Gritting his teeth, he kept on toward the junction.

He almost trod on her, as she blinked into existence directly in his path. She casually slapped down the fist he'd raised by instinct. A shushing finger across her mask, she herded him and Bear flush up against the wall. Only then did he hear footsteps approach.

He counted at least six pairs.

Gesturing them to stillness, the assassin reached for their faces. Though it went against his every instinct, he allowed her to hold his eyes shut. Abruptly, his stomach lurched sideways and his sinuses closed to a sudden shift in pressure. The air around him shivered, like he'd pressed a seashell to his ear. No – to his soul.

Holy-! He bit off his prayer, lest it dispel her heathen magic.

Long moments passed while his muscles strained.

"They're gone," she whispered at last, letting the world snap back into focus. It felt like coming up for air.

"I don't appreciate being blind," he said coldly.

"You'd have enjoyed being able to see even less," she promised, sounding hoarse. She had broken into a light sweat.

She looked the slightly green Bear up and down.

"Think you can break down that door, big man?"

Moving up beside her, the masha'na leaned around the corner, to see where she pointed.

"With a run-up," Bear rumbled dubiously. "Maybe."

"Try. I'll stick in your shadow. Once you're in, stay down."

He didn't like her ordering his men around. But her tactical knowledge outstripped his. And, Bear was already squaring up.

With a deep breath, the big masha'na rounded the corner, lumbering toward a sprint. The assassin loped behind.

He hared off after the pair and blanched as he saw the door.

Slabs of solid oak, banded in iron.

Too late to turn around, they thundered down the corridor.

A spyhole slid open an instant before Bear arrived. The pair of suspicious eyes, peering out, widened in shock.

A concussive crack, then Bear disappeared into the armory, door and all. The assassin raced in, right over top of him. Kryskin would have followed, had the lamps inside not sputtered to the touch of a sudden, sorcerous darkness.

Eyes wide, he skidded to a stop, watching the storm of grainy ash rage. Its gray currents roiled from rushes to rafters.

One long, horrified breath – and it was over. Light resurged.

He peered inside. The assassin was lowering a limp guard to the ground. The man's helm had been knocked clean off.

Kryskin did a headcount.

"Four?"

"Five," she pointed.

He hurried to drag Bear off the unhinged door and the unconscious guard squashed beneath it.

"Whazif...?" the dazed masha'na asked.

"Slowly, Bear, slowly. Can you stand?"

As he coaxed the masha'na up, he took in the sprawled guards.

"Why weren't they screaming their heads off?" he wondered.

Helia knows I would have been...

"They were," she assured him. "I hate inverting the shroud like that. It strokes my fur the wrong way."

He started, and even Bear turned a bleary eye on her.

She stiffened. "I'm kidding. Obviously, I don't have fur."

"Right," he drawled.

"Look," Bear slurred. While everything else was neatly arranged, the masha'na arms had been left in an artless pile.

"Alright," he spurred. "Let's move."

He propped the door up against its splintered frame. From a distance, it might fool the eye into thinking it was still secure.

Someone was bound to come investigate that crash, sooner rather than later, and this might buy a few precious moments.

Burdened by their steel, Bear tottered behind him as he trailed the assassin down to the cellar, mercifully unseen.

"Made it by a hair's breadth," Finch greeted, gratefully snatching his bow. Weirins and orins were quickly parceled out and stuffed through sashes. The change in the atmosphere was palpable. The Temple warriors had teeth once more. And they were aching to give someone a bad nip.

"Lead the way," Kryskin growled at the assassin.

She eased the cellar doors open and popped her head out. A moment later, the rest of her followed.

He and his troupe trotted after, crossing open courtyard and staying as low as they could. The moon seemed awfully bright.

Ahead, the postern gate loomed, strangely unmanned.

At only a few paces away, the portal swung wide.

Kryskin glimpsed Royal Guard colors.

His sword leapt from its sheath like a salmon, laying its silvery belly alongside the guardsman's throat.

The man's eyes rolled white at the blade's touch.

The assassin sniggered, slipping unconcernedly past them.

Oh, he thought. Only now did he notice that the sword the guard carried was swathed in sackcloth.

"And you are?" he asked, easing back.

"Dennik. A friend of Marco's. At least, I'm trying to be."

IT WAS LATE – or early – and Old Farool found his mind wandering. He turned his squinty eye on the young Imperial, watching the lad squirm.

His lopsided eyelids had proven an asset, in his accidental profession. They put people off balance and allowed him to press his luck. It's how he'd gained his hostelry – in a card game, with a friend who should have known better than to try and outstare him.

Former friend, seeing as the man's wife had chosen to stay with the enterprise, rather than her spouse. At the time, Old Farool had counted it a coup. Of course, he hadn't been *Old* Farool, then. Recently, he'd begun to wonder whether his wife's first husband hadn't had the right idea – weighing himself down with a bag of horseshoes and a belly of rum and going for a swim.

She hadn't shed a tear, then. And, not long ago, he'd caught her eyeing the fat baker with the booming business across the street.

His stomach rumbled, reminding him that a lukewarm meal waited at home. His cold-hearted wife was surely asleep by now.

He cleared his throat loudly, making the Heli boy jump.

"Son, I don't think your masters are coming, and I'm for bed."

Who'd ever heard of a moonlit ride, anyway? It was a good way for a horse to step in a hole and break a leg. He had, of course, added a commensurate surcharge. But that wasn't the point.

"Just another quarter bell- I mean, another notch, please-"

"No, no, no, no," he sternly drowned the boy's objections. Ride roughshod over them, that was the key. Less certain, he added, "Your astro- astro… astro*gophers* will have to view the stars some other night."

Surprising him, the boy showed some spine. "Money has changed hands, sir. Surely, you don't intend to renege?"

He didn't know what 'renege' meant, but he didn't care for the sound of it. Scowling, he squared up to the brat.

"Your payment will be returned." Inwardly, he cringed. "Minus your deposit and sundry fees." There. That sounded better.

This could actually work out to be quite lucrative, he reflected.

Dusting his hands, to signal that this was his last word, he stood.

"Up, you louts," he shouted, rousing his slumbering hostlers and, not incidentally, overriding the boy's polite objections. "Let's get those mounts unsaddled and put away. Quickly now! We haven't got all night!"

Secretly satisfied, he struggled into his overcoat.

"I'm sorry," he said, for the sake of occupying the air and allowing the boy none. "But my employees have homes to get to."

Not true, since he insisted they all sleep here, in the hay of his stables. It provided extra security for his horses.

"It is not fair to deprive them of their home lives like this."

"But-" the boy panicked, no doubt fearing a beating at the hands of these astrobadgers. The lad looked rough enough as it was.

Pity pockets no coin, as his wife was wont to say.

"I wish it could be otherwise," he lied. "My hands are tied-"

But the boy, ear cocked toward the street, wasn't listening.

"They're here!" the youth yammered, bolting outside.

Caught mid-word, Old Farool scowled.

"Fortune shit on my luck," he said sourly, turning to the stables.

He plastered on a professional smile for the astrobeavers.

The words of welcome dried in his throat as a drove of Heli warriors strode into his stables, looking outlandish in their orange robes and brown lacquered armor.

Beaming, the boy approached, shoulder gripped by a honey-haired man with hard eyes. Others followed, faces equally fierce.

"I'll take this one," a feminine voice enthused.

He spun. A woman, dressed head to toe in dark leathers, stood stroking the nose of a black mare. When had she slipped past him?

"Now, hang on just a moment-" Old Farool harrumphed.

"Goodmaster," the blond one interrupted, accent and odd form of address strangely unnerving, "thank you for your diligence. Helia's blessing on your efforts."

All around them, men with businesslike manners were mounting up.

Abruptly, Old Farool worried that he'd never see any of these horses ever again.

"I think there must be some misunderstanding," he intervened. "These mounts have been reserved for a group of astron-otters."

Vaulting into the saddle, the spokesman frowned at him.

"Are you implying my friend doesn't look like an astronomer?"

Old Farool felt a shadow eclipse him. Shrinking, he met the intense regard of a massive man, towering over him. He made a quick recalculation, factoring in retention of limbs.

He swallowed hard. "You're welcome to them, of course…"

The giant lumbered off. Horses began trotting outside.

"There-" he wet his lips, "-is still the matter of late fees…"

The blond one, with the worrisome eyes, reigned up beside him.

"You may forward any outstanding bill to the Holy Temple in Tellar. The masha'na quartermaster will see it settled."

"Hurry up!" the woman called from outside, her horse prancing.

And then they were gone. The sound of galloping hooves faded slowly, like a bad dream. Fearfully, one of the grooms approached.

"Sir, should we…?"

"Yes, yes," he nodded. "Close it all up and lock it – quickly now!" He hadn't slept on a hay bale in years. But he certainly wasn't braving the road home. Not with *them* out there.

"And," he stayed the groom, with a desperate grip on the man's shoulder, "not a word of this to my wife, understand?"

His squinty eye twitched uncontrollably.

✱ ✱ ✱

BEHIND HIS WRAPS, Jiminy's grin had become a rictus and the usual tingle of excitement had devolved into an unhealthy crawling of his skin. At first, as he'd descended, he'd tried to fit the spiral passage into the schematic of the tower he had in his head. He'd quickly realized it was too spacious and too consistent to coexist with what he'd seen of the spire's innards.

Despite everything, he'd half expected Cyrus to be full of shit.

But the smooth alabaster was, without a doubt, magic-made.

It produced a luminescence so evenhanded it robbed him of a shadow. Unrelieved white blended the ceiling, walls and floor into a single plane that wound around in a blind curve.

Which, possibly, went on forever.

It certainly felt like he'd been walking for turn after turn of the glass. His feet were sore and his nerves thrumming. Even with the wide, gentle slope, he should have reached bottom long since.

The thought spurred him into an uneasy lope, which became more and more difficult to maintain with each circuit. Finally, throat afire and knees shaking, he stumbled to a halt.

And still, the unmitigated white stretched on.

Cat scat on a skewer! There's no end to this.

Gasping, he dragged his wraps down about his neck, though there was no breeze to touch his damp hair. He would have to turn back, he realized, or risk being stranded down here, come sunrise.

Huffing, he braced his hands on his knees. Disconsolate sweat stung his eyes and dripped from his nose. The luminous stone swam, making it appear the bead of moisture ran uphill.

He blinked his vision clear but still the illusion held.

Wait, what?

Dropping to his heels, he stared intently.

A fingertip, placed in the droplet's path, caused it to pool normally. He examined it, rubbed at it, smelled it. Tasted it.

It was sweat.

He squeezed his eyes shut against a moment of vertigo. Had he somehow gotten turned around? True, the ramp's incline was so fine as to appear nearly flat. But was it possible he'd been battling uphill without noticing? Or was his sweat simply more turned around than he?

He glared at his ring, which sat quiescent, at room temperature. If *it* was being fooled, no doubt *he* was too. The head priest, slumbering upstairs, had been a fossil. No way that decrepit wreck trekked down here at midnight and made it back in time for morning prayers.

He'd missed something. Something important.

A horrible suspicion took shape.

Dragging free his face wraps, he abandoned them on the floor.

I hope I'm wrong, he thought, breaking into a run once more.

It didn't take long until he spied a speck of black in the corridor ahead. Disbelieving, he approached his discarded mask. Concerned that it was somehow counterfeit, he kicked at it.

It unfurled as he would expect.

Cursing, he reversed direction, putting it at his back once more. A short while later found him glaring down at the cloth again.

Searing sands! he thought, snatching it up. He was stuck in an endless loop, unable even to distinguish upslope from downslope.

But the drop of sweat hadn't been fooled…

Digging in a belt pouch, he came up with a handful of hard beads. In a pinch, these could foul a pursuer's footing. He guessed this qualified as more than a mere pinch.

He flung out his arm, scattering them wide. The small spheres swarmed the pale stone like locusts, bouncing and careening.

At first.

Reaching consensus, they all began to course in the same direction. He trailed them as they gained speed, gradually crowding together in the crease where the outer wall met the floor.

Just as he began to worry that they would outpace him, winded as he was, their momentum fled and they milled uncertainly.

Confused, he skidded to a stop. Was it his imagination, or were there fewer beads? He frowned at those that remained as they continued on for several paces, slowing – then reversed direction.

Like seawater seeking a scupper hole, they drained out of sight.

Well, skewer me sideways... he thought, stretching out to touch.

His hand failed to find the expected wall.

He stumbled, physically and mentally, at the sudden shift in perspective.

White on unrelieved white hid a broad doorway, stretching from floor to ceiling. The same steady light that stole his shadow softened the branching corridor's edges and smudged its corners until it was virtually invisible.

Curious, he took a step back and immediately lost sight of it.

Clever... he admitted, his admiration spiced with relief.

He carefully skirted the thought that he'd failed to find the entrance – or, more importantly, the exit – on his endless round.

He pressed on, one hand held out before him, to ward against any other unseen walls that might flatten his nose.

As if to mock his efforts up to that point, he descended a bare dozen paces into an everyday antechamber.

Twin statues guarded the lone passage that led ahead, shaped from the same pearly stone. The figures were lithe and ludicrously lifelike, except for being three times life-sized. In fact, so detailed was their musculature, Jiminy had no problem believing they could actually complete their arrested sword swings.

Swings angled to cut anyone who dared passed between them.

Gulping, he glanced at the weapons in question. They glimmered with an edge he associated with steel, not stone.

"We're not going to hurt each other, are we, fellas?"

Though they returned his smile, he was discomfited to see that the sculptor had given them each double rows of sharp teeth.

Muttering curses, he began scouring the antechamber for more hidden passages. The statues' eyes seemed to follow him as he moved about.

Sands swallow this place and its uncanny, livened stone! he swore, as he was finally forced to give up.

"Fine then," he told his audience. "Screw this. I'm leaving..."

He took several steps back the way he'd come.

Enough for a run-up.

He whirled, accelerating to his top speed within a bare handful of paces.

He had no idea if one could startle a statue.

But surprise *was* his middle name.

Slamming onto his forward foot, he sprang into a dive, turning it into a flat spin. His trajectory should take him between the two stone swords – provided the sentinels couldn't adjust their swings-

He stumbled as he landed, pawing at himself to check he was in one piece. The statues, of course, stood unmoving and immovable.

Heart beating its way out of his breast, he recognized the brilliance. After seeing a mountain's worth of stone move at the entrance, anyone might conclude that the rest of the rock could too.

Clever bastards, he griped.

For the first time, he turned to see where his daring had led.

As above, a sprawling ramp spiraled downward. The lintel above the door held the Heli numeral for 'one'.

He'd reached the first level of Seven Deep.

Taking a steadying breath, he stepped through.

It was not what he'd expected. To either side, the slope sported broad, cut-away pieces – flat surfaces for stacking... junk.

Shelves upon shelves held nothing but moldy scrolls, half-burnt books and sheaves of musty parchment.

The second round, past the numeral 'two', looked the same.

Feeling decidedly let down, he picked up the pace.

By the third level, small items began appearing amid the ruined texts. A shell necklace here. A miniature portrait there. Some painted figurines or whittled toys.

Not a library then, but a flea market. And not the fun kind.

Level four was chock full of broken urns and cracked crockery.

Five was festooned with collections of bones, strapped together and glued in manners that mimicked life.

Six had the most variety yet and his thief's curiosity had him examining several items closely. How serious had Cyrus been when he'd said to take noting, save the text?

Lowering what he'd thought was a string of desiccated mushrooms, he scrubbed his hand vigorously against his wraps.

Perhaps he should take the hierarch's caution to heart.

After that, he controlled himself, despite several items snagging his attention. There were carven masks that somehow captured a sense of savage nobility. Sculptures of wood, stone and other materials he had trouble identifying, called to him. These, he realized, were smashed icons. Once objects of worship, they had fallen before the Heli advance.

So warned, he averted his gaze. He didn't need any broken gods or mad spirits clamoring for his aid. He could all but feel their pull.

Approaching the lintel marked 'seven', he hesitated.

Beyond it, the stone's light deepened into a rich, golden glow.

He was reminded of honey or hot molasses – something thick enough to snare and snuff hapless insects.

Drawing a knife, he drove it through the divide. It met no resistance and, when pulled out, was neither sticky nor warm.

He tried his beringed hand next, with the same result.

If this were a ward of some sort, his jade pendant would hopefully shield him from notice, as it had at the governor's mansion. No one had asked for it back, so he'd kept it. Patting at the little teardrop, hidden under his wraps, he stepped through.

He drew his first breath shallowly, in case the air was somehow poisoned. It smelled stale and was dryer than a spoonful of raw oats. But it seemed serviceable.

The sunlit glare was harsh but not, it seemed, harmful.

This level *sounded* different too, pressing close to his ears, as though it were a much smaller space than it appeared.

Shaking off his discomfort, he forged ahead.

The largest pieces – and the most disturbing – languished here. There were broken columns of pink quartz and a scattering of chalcedony menhirs. Other monoliths lay forlorn, gathering dust. The icon of a slender woman reared from a pedestal, arms hacked off and eyes, mouth and ears hammered shut with bands of silver.

A rattle, as of reeds, brought him around. A hunchbacked puppet swung from tangled strings, head malformed by huge teeth.

It swayed gently to the breeze of his passage.

He kept a wary eye on it, until the curve of the ramp hid it.

Something brushed the back of his neck.

Biting back a foul oath, his knives flashed.

The suit of armor didn't follow, though it wobbled on the stand he'd jostled. Its design was vaguely Imperial, but he could not name the source of the overlapping scales or pebbled hide that constituted it. The helm was fronted by a monstrous faceplate.

Weird.

Wiping his slick brow, he made to sheathe his knives.

A still figure crouched among the detritus. Squat and impossibly broad, it seemed ready to spring from the shelves.

Its eyes glinted in the yellow haze.

Jiminy's blades fanned between fingers, ready to throw.

Tense moments passed as the two of them appraised each other.

"You alive?" he demanded, feeling foolish, but aware that he'd already been spooked by a puppet and a propped-up suit of armor.

He forced himself to pad closer for a clearer view.

Sighing in relief, he put his weapons away.

Some taxidermist had given borrowed flesh to this nightmare. He doubted its like existed in nature. Any predator would give its eye-teeth for such a collection of fangs. In fact, several likely had.

He turned away from the creature's glassy gaze.

But he kept an ear out for slinking footsteps anyway.

A six-armed serpent-lady stood twice his height, rendered in gold. He lingered over the gloss of her bare chest, calculating its value in coin. Even given the fangs and the threat of constriction, he figured he'd bedded more dangerous women.

Finally, he came to the bottom of the well.

The small, circular space was gilded, carved and carpeted about – giving the impression of a scholar's private study. In its center stood a six-sided bookcase. The sun emblem, rising from its dome, gave a clue as to the kinds of texts assembled therein.

Finally, Jiminy thought, rubbing his hands together.

Cyrus had made him memorize the relevant Heli scribbles. And, as he pulled out the first title his hand fell on, he recognized them.

On the first try? He frowned. *No way I'm that lucky...*

He pulled out another, at random, and saw the same characters.

In horror, he viewed the bookshelf – broad as an ancient oak and about as heavy. Did the gospel run across so many volumes? He couldn't carry a tenth of these out of here! He-

No, he strangled his panic. *The old coot was very clear.*

It was supposed to be *one* text. One.

The others must be decoys, screening the true copy.

His heart sank.

If that were true, it would take a scholar to sort through them all. He was barely literate in his own language, never mind Heli.

There's some trick to this, he hoped. *This place keeps trying to trip me up and, each time, it turns out to be something simple I've overlooked.*

He glanced around. "What am I not seeing?"

It would be something obvious, provided you brought the right mindset to bear...

Slowly, his gaze shifted to the golden crest, crowning the bookshelf. The noonday sun beats directly downward.

Scattering books, he climbed the shelves, until the medal was within reach. He didn't even have to twist it. It lifted straight out, revealing itself to be a scroll cap. Thickly rolled velum followed.

He handled it with care, mindful of its age.

He didn't need to unroll it know he held the real thing.

For starters, no one went to this much trouble to hide a fake.

And, for another, he recognized cured human hide when he saw it – courtesy of many a raider's carcass, encountered on the caravan trail. The script had been inked in truth – by tattoo. He pitied the poor bastards who'd given the skin off their backs to preserve these words.

Casting an eye over the mess he'd made, he sighed.

Sneak thieves leave no traces.

Popping off the scroll cap, he jammed it back atop its cubby hole, so the scroll's absence would not be immediately apparent. The gospel itself, he wrapped in a sling across his shoulder.

Then he set about restoring order.

The moment he stepped from the little library, the desire to be gone became overwhelming. It wasn't simply the angry glare or the abrasive breath of Seven Deep, spurring him. This was the most critical part of any caper – and the leg where most would-be cat burglars fell short.

The clean getaway.

His return to the sixth level let him literally breathe easier. He couldn't afford to relax. There was still a whole tower to traverse-

"So close."

He skidded to a stop, daggers in both hands.

"Ssso close," the voice said again.

This time, he pinpointed it. A dozen paces distant, a shadow moved behind a line of shelves – the silhouette of a hooded priest.

It stepped out from the concealing clutter to bar his path.

His blood ran cold at the sight of the tattered, black robes.

The dread mage – who had hounded him from his home and nearly cornered him in Genla – looked solid this time around.

"I've waited long to meet you," the apparition said, wicked claws reaching to lower its cowl. "In the flesh, asss it were."

Jiminy staggered back in shock and revulsion.

No, not a priest at all. Not, in fact, even a person.

The peeling lips and mottled skin belonged to a month old corpse. One cheek had completely crumbled and the chin had split to the bone, running thick with pus. A swollen ear fed an infected tracery across its scalp. Pearled eyes, such as an asp might leave behind in its molt skin, pinned him.

"Surprisssse," the apparition said, savoring his street name.

Cursed dead of the dunes... Not a 'dread' mage. A 'dead' one.

"How did you get in here?" he sputtered in his shock.

He had a sudden vision of bodies, carpeting the corridors above.

He began to back away and the thing trailed him leisurely.

"You thought I could not follow? Into thisss monument of futility? Ha! Your kind's daysss of barring our way are long over."

Still holding his knives, Jiminy spread his fingers peaceably. "Easy now. Why don't we-"

"When you did not ssset sssail for Thell, I should have known you would come here next. Inssstead, I wasssted monthsss, chasssing you. Then your clericsss hid you with their bauble."

A talon pointed to the jade pendant that had escaped his wraps.

"I was sure the augursss had anssswered you, then. But your trail continued here. *That* isss when I realized-" it gurgled as it laughed, "-you don't know what you have. And neither do they. Oh, the sssweet irony…"

Heart pounding, he backpedaled faster.

"Look whatever I took-"

"I am curiousss, though," it rasped. "Why aid thessse adherentsss of a lossst caussse? Hasss your plane not sssuffered enough? Ssslumbered long enough? Do you not yearn to retake your place among the woken worldsss? Your retreat wasss an overreaction. After all thisss time, sssurely you can sssee that?"

Despite its supplicating tone, it continued to stalk.

"What," he managed, despite his dry throat, "are you on about?"

The dead mage paused, but the false pity that pulled at its face made it look only more hideous.

"I weep for you mortalsss and your short lived memoriesss. You carry a map but know not where it leadsss. You hold a key but have forgotten what lock it fitsss. I expect ssssome ancient *prophecy-*," it spat the word, "-told you to pursssue this quesssst, eh? Chosen of Helia? No matter. You have helpfully retrieved the map and sssstill bear the key. I shall have both. *Now.*"

A clawed hand cupped in his direction.

He did not have to fake his confusion. "What map? What key?"

Its hand clenched angrily, its voice turning dangerously soft. "The map in your bag. And the key on your dragging knuckle!"

The silver band, lackluster beneath its veneer, warmed.

He clutched his daggers tighter. "This? This is a ring."

"I am not fooled," the thing assured, grimacing through blackened and broken teeth. "And if you force me to trail you one ssstep further, I shall take your entire arm, before I take your life."

Then, why haven't you, yet? he wondered, halting nonetheless.

Where were the dread magicks? The sandstorms and plagues?

For the first time, he tried looking past the fact that the approaching body was dead and looked for body language instead.

He snorted. "You're bluff-"

It was on him in a blink, striking with clawed hands.

Nan had always said he was the fastest she'd ever seen. Even so, he managed to duck only the first blow, scything for his head. The second ploughed through his guard and threw him from his feet. Dry shelves smashed around him, raising droves of dust.

Stunned, he coughed and gasped. He'd only been hit so hard once before – by the ground, after a three story fall.

"I am quite ssskilled at desssecration," the dead mage said, beyond the gray veil. "I shall leave a messsage, here, for the misssguided clergy. To show that they have lossst. You will not mind lending me a hand – and ssseveral other partsss – will you?"

Sensing the grab before it closed in his hair, Jiminy rolled to his feet – struck – and put several pained skips between them. The dead mage straightened unconcernedly, a knife studding its ribs.

Despairing, he watched it pull the tar streaked blade free and toss it away. It showed no discomfort whatsoever.

If he could not kill it, perhaps he could outrun it? He carefully did not eye the ramp, leading upwards. Quick as the creature was, he was sure he could get past it, given a distraction.

In fact, it seemed to be leaving the avenue open for him.

That alone was reason to hesitate.

Even so, he could not stay here. How was he supposed to fight something that shrugged off a lung-puncture and felt no pain?

"You are going to die here," it solemnly promised him.

Jiminy suffered a knee-jerk reaction. "Make me, handsome."

"Asss you wish."

Even with the moment's warning, its next swing nearly took his face off. He narrowly avoided the second, which would have gored him through the kidneys. The dead mage fought without caution, shrugging off every stab and slice he landed. The air between them reeked of rotten blood and putrefaction.

He could afford neither to block nor parry. It was too strong and its claws spread too wide. But he also could not keep evading. The shelves he'd crashed through had been riddled with dry rot but he'd still taken a hefty hit. He was breathing with difficulty, whereas his opponent didn't have to breathe at all.

Once he tired too much to slip its blows, it would cut him to ribbons. As though to affirm this thought, he stumbled as the ridged claws – spearing toward his face – turned from their feint.

Lines of liquid heat sloughed across his hip.

His scream was cut short as a kick audibly cracked his sternum.

He tumbled down the ramp and sprawled on his face.

Ears ringing, he pushed to his knees, not nearly fast enough.

Fire dug a trench across his back. The yell that tore from him took his strength with it and he collapsed.

"There now, you sssee?" Bony fingers closed about his nape, drawing him up and up, to dangle from his scruff like a kitten.

"Helplesss."

Turning, it flung him.

Tumbling end over end, he crashed through another series of shelves. Their contents and scattered parchments spilled atop him.

"Hopelesss," the dead mage said, coming to stand over him, watching him try and fail to catch a breath.

"To think," it gloated, hands clasped behind its back, "your weak-minded kind – and your paltry godsss – once thought to ssstand against my masterss' will. Look at you now…"

With nerveless hands, Jiminy fumbled through the flotsam for his lost knives. A sharp stick. A heavy book. Anything remotely weapon-ish.

"You are troglodytesss," the dead mage declared, "gathering what little light you have left under thisss upturned bucket and itsss oppressive ssseal." It grimaced around at the stone, teeth showing through its cheeks. "At leassst you'll have a fitting cairn…"

Ridged nails reached for him, just as his hand fell upon a hilt.

Flesh sizzled loudly.

The dead mage stumbled back, screeching. A line burned across its palm, flesh shriveling and shedding embers. It danced its pain, wails echoing up the well.

His vision dim, Jiminy pushed to his knees. The silver dagger nestled in his fist, rotten blood evaporating from its edge.

Well, alright then, he thought, wobbling to his feet.

Clutching its maimed hand, the mage watched its thumb crumble away. Its baleful gaze panned toward him.

Unless you want to go home with that… Jiminy thought at the silver dagger *…stick around, alright?*

He padded toward the glaring corpse.

The dead man closed with him much more cautiously, flinching from his feints and aborting attacks rather than brave his blade. Through gritted teeth, it echoed every hiss of silver searing its flesh. But it did not let up, swinging at him with both its hale and its clubbed claws.

Jiminy herded it downslope, maintaining the high ground, but the truth was he was a hair's breadth from passing out. His ears rang insistently, it hurt to breathe, and a burning numbness was spreading steadily from his hip and back, where it had raked him.

As the dead man leaned away from a looping cut, its elbow passed beneath the lintel of Seven Deep's lowest level. The golden air spat and crackled angrily.

Yowling, the corpse snatched its singed limb to safety.

Grimly, Jiminy grinned, his suspicion confirmed.

Why had it waited in ambush on level six instead of pursuing into seven? Why had it threatened him into halting his downward retreat? And why had it left him an upwards escape route?

"You talk too much," he told it. "I got no clue what a 'troglodyte' is. But I understood 'oppressive seal' just fine."

It was this place. Something about the spire had hobbled its power.

He took a tighter grip on the silver dagger.

"You tripped up on the last leg of the caper."

Screaming temper, it rushed him.

Marshalling every shred of his speed, he sprang to meet it, slicing and slashing – his blade a ribbon that trailed smoke.

The dead mage misjudged its retreat. Only by a smidgen, but that was enough. Its back brushed the barrier, which kicked into violent life. The howling corpse staggered forward and he met it, quenching his knife to the hilt.

It gaped in disbelief as he shouldered it toward the sunlit glare.

The golden wall woke at the contact, blazing and enraged.

Jiminy would have loved to cover his ears. Or his nose. But he held the dead mage's frame flush against the barrier, fighting the paroxysms and the outpouring of putrid smoke. Adding his screams to its screeches, he wedged an elbow under its chin.

Finally, the heat forced him back.

Withdrawing his blade spilled cinders down the dead mage's front, its chest collapsing in a charcoal ruin.

Only once the corpse had blackened beyond recognition did the barrier subside, though the air still sizzled and steamed.

The burnt-out husk tumbled forward, forcing him to step back further. His longtime pursuer didn't so much collapse as dissolve against the floor. Fine ash washed up against Jiminy's feet.

His legs knew it was over before he did and they sprawled spectacularly. His breath did what his legs couldn't and fled. Shivering, he hugged himself.

Still alive.

Though he'd forbidden Neever from doing so, he said a quick prayer to the goddess whose house he was robbing:

"You make a mean grill, lady."

Then he turned his glare on the sterling dagger in his grip.

'Key' my ass. So, you are what all the fuss was about?

He hadn't considered it. Mostly because the ring was one of the few things he had *not* stolen but had *bought*. With *actual* money. If he'd known, he might have traded it for his safety – since it wasn't very reliable. If only it wasn't so stubbornly attached to him.

As usual, its magic had dawdled until he was damn near dead.

"You want to help?" he told it. "Go and fetch me a healer…"

With his last bit of strength, he lobbed it over his shoulder.

There was no clatter or clunk of its landing and, a moment later, a metallic chill snaked around his finger. He felt the band re-solidify as the silver motes drew together.

He sighed. He wanted nothing more than to sit here a moment, just a moment… His head dipped and his heart's lullaby slowed.

Angrily, he shook himself and pain flared all over.

He clutched at his shredded hip. The blood there was liver-dark, the gouges burning like wasps' sting. His back felt even worse. One of those claws had sheared through his shoulder strap and he spotted the scroll bag, half-buried in broken bookshelves.

Wincing, he eyed the widespread destruction.

So much for leaving no trace.

Then, thinking of the endless trek back up, he winced again.

If those priests are still alive up there, I'm *going to kill them...*

NEEVER SAT, NERVOUSLY twiddling his thumbs.

The steady passage of bells had worn his nerves to nubs.

Too restless to sit for long, he sprang up once more, to pace.

What can possibly be keeping Master Jiminy?

There was less than half a bell left before the Temple woke.

Around him, the great vats reared, turgid and cold, smelling of suds and lye. But soon, the washer women would arrive to work, and he'd have a tough time explaining why he was in their laundry.

The wind moaned disconsolately from one of the stone chutes.

He started every time it did that, imagining the drawn out wail of someone descending at speed.

So far, it had only issued more loads of dirty linens.

Unable to help himself, he added more soft sheets and pillowcases to the cart, positioned beneath the aperture. It was already piled high. Thinking better of it, he removed them once more. He didn't need Master Jiminy bouncing off when he finally came pelting from the chimney's spout.

Using the chutes as an easy escape route had been the young thief's idea. Their definition of 'easy' differed greatly.

Neever maintained the drop was a death sentence. To his mind, it was merely one of a litany of things that might go wrong.

He tried to tell himself that the lack of alarms was a good sign. But, if someone were caught in Seven Deep, no doubt the archons would bury the fact, along with the trespasser.

The Lily was, and would remain, inviolable.

If worse came to worst, he would understand if Master Jiminy's heathen ghost came to haunt him. For however long he had left, before the Inquisitori came to kick his own door down.

He held no illusions. He knew how these things worked.

A witness would 'remember' seeing him on the road, near his home Temple – which he would never reach.

Poor Cyrus would take ill and be placed in secluded care. And, once bled of all the modernists' secrets, would tragically succumb.

He'd lain all this out for Jiminy, with a fresh suicide lozenge.

'But I didn't get you anything,' the thief had protested.

He'd prevailed, in the end. And now hated himself for it.

Faintly heard, the day's first bell tolled.

It rang with the knell of failure.

He bit his lip.

He was supposed to leave, now, to go about an ordinary day.

But he wouldn't. Not while there was the slightest chance-

Without even a whisper of warning, the laundry cart exploded.

He whirled and met a wall of linens head-on.

The wave towed him under. Everything went white.

"Master Jiminy?" he sputtered, muffled beneath the mound.

A low groan answered him.

He flailed his way free. "Oh, thank Helia-"

Then he saw the blood.

The boy was a dark splotch on the pristine sheets, his clothes shredded and his face sheened with fever sweat.

"Helia have mercy!"

The thief's eyelids fluttered

"Neever... dead mage... poison..."

He felt the urchin's forehead and snatched his hand back.

"You're delirious. We need to get you to help."

With something to do, his hands finally steadied.

He hurriedly gathered the soiled sheets together. The boy would make an awkward bundle. But it would be less conspicuous than carrying a body down the corridor.

"Come on," he grunted. "Sitter Cyrus is going to fix you up."

And, he added to himself, *if the old healer balks, the Inquisitori is going to be the least of his worries...*

Chapter 18 – Rescue

Pella Monop, Diary entry #208

I can all but feel the garrote, closing about me. I am making some effort to go about my usual routine but the façade is fragile. There are eyes on me. My rooms are never exactly as I leave them. Feigning concern, Cecine has refused to leave my side. My every scribble is inspected. I've taken to wearing this journal next to my skin. I suddenly grasp the significance of being ordained: should a Temple tribunal charge me, neither the Institute nor even the Emperor could intercede. I am in the stronghold of my enemy. There is but a single course left. I must flee. It shall have to be sudden. None must suspect, until I am gone. Not even Bruen.

MARCO LAY IN the wet brush, black loam and leaf mulch intense beneath his nose. Icy condensation fell from the forest canopy, soaking his borrowed clothes and sending rivulets down his spine.

He could hear himself blink, his eyelids gummy and grating.

Kryskin and Finch lay on his flanks, also watching the wooded bowl below, where the ruins of a Heli-style monastery reared.

Any other time, he would have welcomed a discussion on how such a thing came to be in Renali territory.

But, right now, he had eyes only for the roving guards.

His attention was feverish – his surroundings reduced to smudges and smears – but the enemy stood out starkly.

It felt like forever since he'd slept. They'd ridden through the night and into the morning, maintaining a reckless pace that petered only when they lost the trail. They were deep into the mountains now. So close he could scent the snowcaps.

"Patrols, pickets, sentries… these are soldiers."

It took him a moment to decipher Finch's whisper.

"Royal Guard," he corrected, earning sharp glances.

"We don't know that."

"Makes sense, though," Finch opined. "If the princess really-"

"No," Kryskin overrode. "We don't *know* that. I see no colors, no crests, no insignias. As far as we *know*, these are mercenaries."

Finch nodded, understanding. "Serves 'em right."

"The keeper has got to be in there…" Marco muttered, his hot gaze on the main hall. It was the only structure still semi-standing.

"Along with who-knows how many reinforcements?"

They didn't speculate. The answer would not sway them.

Staying under cover, they worked their way back over the hill. Giant ferns curled up from the carpet of red needles and the soaring, black-barked pines bristled with spring growth.

Masha'na appeared from the underbrush as they approached, the warriors' ochre and umber colors suited the terrain well.

The spent horses, they'd left in the next dell over, where a chance whinny wouldn't announce their presence.

"Alright," Kryskin said, "gather around…"

He found it hard to concentrate while the masha'na commander laid out their plan of attack, scratching lines in the forest floor.

He felt fragile. Exhaustion and nerves soured his stomach and set his hands shaking. Holding on to his thoughts cost inordinate effort. And, when he sought to be still, images from his nightmares seeped through… Bodies and spraying blood and unspooling guts-

"Better ease up, before you break that." Nin nudged him.

Startled, he relaxed his stranglehold on the bandit blade.

He had been poleaxed when Kryskin had produced the weapon.

'From a friend of yours, named Dennik. He said to tell you, he wouldn't presume to apologize. But he thought you deserved a keep forged blade. He said you would know what that means.'

He shook his head. He didn't have the time or capacity right now to reason out Dennik's betrayal.

"I can do that," Nin offered casually, responding to something Kryskin had said.

The masha'na commander cocked his head. "Are you sure? You're under no obligation to help us. Or the keeper."

"On the contrary," the assassin said, amused eyes on Marco. "I'm under contract for a thousand and one Renali crowns. Just don't look to me to lead any charges. I do my best work unseen."

Into the shocked silence, Kryskin said, "Understood."

The briefing wrapped up and, nodding, everyone dispersed.

Marco dogged Ryhorn and Longjaw's heels, dropping into a nearby ditch alongside them. Their small group would wade in the knee deep water, working their way as close to the main doors as they could. Their objective, when the assault began, would be to cut their way to the keeper's side with all possible speed.

They were then to protect the priest, until the rest of the masha'na could either come to their aid or clear an escape path.

This crucial role should rightly have gone to a more seasoned warrior. But they would have had to fight Marco for it.

The masha'na were outnumbered by two-to-one or more. Further skewing the odds, the enemy would be rested and provisioned, whereas the Temple force was overtired and underequipped. Surprise would be a key factor in their success.

Marco's trio proceeded by increments. Ryhorn's permanent grimace made the threat of discovery feel even closer.

Finally, they could go no further under cover. They crouched at the ready. Silt slowly worked its way between Marco's toes.

Birdcalls sounded as, somewhere up above, Finch and Leffley coordinated their attacks. None of the Renali seemed alarmed at this evidence of an invasive avian species and only Marco heard the fletchings fly.

The sentries' blood, on the breeze, turned his stomach in a way that was at once sickening and scintillating.

Coppery saliva flooded his mouth.

Nin flitted from cover to cover, her shroud dragging its feet in the morning light. The specter was a manifestation of moon-shadow, coaxed from a graveyard willow – at great personal cost. It was the single most versatile asset in her assassin's arsenal.

It also had a terrible tendency to sulk, whilst the sun held sway.

She sympathized, up to a point. She was a creature of the dark as well. But her own discomfort had little to do with committing murder by broad daylight.

She worried over the imagined dismay of her late mistress.

Sure, two clients were paying her to do the same work.

But, as her mistress's heir, coin wouldn't become Nin's worry for a long while yet.

Also, letting the promisor tag along on a job was a good way to get her payday killed.

Plus, she wasn't particularly optimistic about collecting from the royal coffers.

So she might end up getting no remuneration at all.

Citing vengeance would have impressed her mistress even less. Killing was a cold profession. It was one of the first tenets Nin had been taught. Her murderous rage would have earned her an object lesson and a corrective assignment.

But her mistress *wasn't* here, to stop her. That was the problem.

Dailill, the traitorous patron, had robbed Nin of the one person who had meant something. Who had meant everything.

And all for what? Some haired yams?

Gritting her teeth, she coasted along the monastery wall. A sentry – features indistinct through the shroud – chanced to turn toward her. She stilled, straining to draw the specter's limbs more tightly about herself. Sweat wicked her neck…

The guardsman gave up his study, turning back to the woods.

Controlling her breath, she padded on.

The Heli boy was odd, no doubt about that. The bare fact he could perceive her shroud should have earned him a swift death. And sniffing after a scent trail? She still wasn't sure she believed that. Except, here she was, sneaking up on the evidence.

He could become a problem for her, in the near future.

But the boy's appeal, on behalf of his teacher, had played unexpectedly on her heartstrings – even out of tune as they were.

Sentiment…

She shuddered to think what her mistress would have said.

Dark thoughts wound, unerringly, back to the princess. She had imagined killing the royal a thousand different ways. She would settle for ruining whatever scheme of Dailill's *this* was. For now.

She slipped behind the Renali patrols and into the lee of the building. The semi-shade bolstered the shroud somewhat, but not enough to help root her to the stone. She suffered scaling the wall by strength alone. The specter's gift of perception was a greater loss. Peering through its ghostly brambles, she could have counted the number of hearts inside the ruin, even through the brick.

The shroud wilted as she topped the sundrenched roof.

No matter.

Picking her way among the mossy tiles, she soon toed the eave above the main entrance. With quick motions, she uncoiled several loops of cord from around her forearm. Below her lounged two Renali soldiers. They would need to be silenced simultaneously.

The *hangman's lament* coiled in her grip. Woven from the hair of the condemned, it was far more substantial than moon-shadow.

Banishing her shroud, so as to bring her full weight to bear, she whipped her arm down.

To her ears alone, the lament raised a chorus of wretched wails as it struck, snapping around the left-most guard's throat.

She stepped off the roof, the cord cutting across the swaybacked eave. The sentry was plucked skyward.

The right-most guard turned toward the noise. She alighted behind him. At her silent command, ghost knots slithered around his neck, cutting of his gasp. And then he, too, was being snatched off his feet.

With a thought, she directed the lament to snag wrists and elbows too. Within moments the choking and kicking had stilled.

Job done, she retreated into the shroud once more.

EASING HIS SWORD from its loop, Marco watched the black mass stalk across the roof, its human shape just barely discernible.

"Get ready," he said, for the benefit of Ryhorn and Longjaw, who couldn't see it.

"Helia's mercy," Ryhorn swore, as the sentries were strung up.

"Come on!" Marco spurred.

He vaulted from concealment, his legs waterlogged and cold. Covering the distance from ditch to door took forever. He charged straight at it, optimistically meaning to kick it off its hinges.

Longjaw caught his collar and Ryhorn slipped in front of him.

Something was lopsided about their features – each held one eye closed. It took him too long to realize they were pre-empting their transition from bright daylight into unknown darkness.

They hadn't told him to do that! He seethed.

Ryhorn raised a fist and knocked an offhand tattoo.

In the tense silence, he imagined he could hear Finch and Leffley drawing back bowstrings and Kryskin and the rest of the masha'na readying to charge.

Inside, a bar was lifted from its bracket.

"Your shift ain't over yet, you lazy…"

Ryhorn shouldered the door into the lax guard's face.

Marco bulled his way inside after the two masha'na.

High, thin windows failed to light the interior. Fallen stone and neatly arranged blankets littered the floor. Makeshift trestles held scattered plates and upset tankards.

A dozen men turned in alarm.

Marco took it all in at a glance.

The nearest guardsman rushed them with a greasy eating knife.

Marco moved first. His form was blockish. His movements crude. His sword's edge was too straight and its blade too springy.

But he clove the attacker from collarbone to crotch all the same.

The man's dying scream shook the high ceiling.

Men boiled from their seats and bedrolls.

Marco only paid them any mind because they hampered his view – he'd spotted Justin. The priest was bound and blindfolded, slumped against the old, cracked altar stone. His keeper's robes were in disarray and bloody spittle hung from slack and split lips.

"Father!"

As battle cries went, it was unremarkable. But it overflowed with fear and pain and the desperate desire to share both.

He raced ahead of the masha'na, murdering the sword form called 'catching the kite string', spinning and springing sloppily.

Bloodied guardsman staggered away from him.

They had hurt Justin.

They had hurt Justin and there could be no forgiveness.

A blade whistled past and he sawed into the shoulder behind it. Red misted his vision and he blinked irritably at its film.

"Father!"

The form called 'threshing the rice stalks' turned unrecognizable in his hands. Steel spat sparks, casting his opponents' faces in stark light.

Venting his frustration, he abandoned all finesse, chopping away as though clearing brush. Lifeblood fountained and maimed men flailed. He hewed them from his path, howling all the way.

A fearful stop-thrust slid past him and he stove in the attacker's throat with his fist. The crumple of cartilage was fiercely satisfying.

His blade crunched through a skull, bursting an eye and sticking in the bone. The impulse to abandon it – to set about with his bare hands – was strong. But he wrenched himself, and his sword, free.

"Father!"

Whether by effort or happenstance, a path had cleared.

Paying the raging fight no mind, he leapt for the platform that held altar, pulpit and priest. Justin looked even worse up close, his right jaw mottled black and outlined with red.

Gently, he reached for his mentor's blindfold... and froze.

Marco's own hand was unrecognizable to him. It was slathered in blood and caked in gore, like it had stirred a bucket of chum.

Unclean. Unworthy. Unloved.

Justin could not see him like this. Bloodlust drained away in an instant, leaving him lightheaded and lost.

In a small voice, he appealed, "...father?"

The kick came from out of nowhere. On his haunches, with his sword held clear, he was hardly in a position to counter.

Such was the force of the blow, Marco spun from the platform.

He landed badly, bowling over several bodies.

It was worse than the time he'd mistimed his dive from the peach tree to the lily pond and landed full on his belly.

Stunned, squinting through black spots, he thought he saw a familiar sneer before unconsciousness claimed him-

-something snarled in his ear and he sat bolt upright.

He had lost time but not much.

The fight still raged but its timbre had changed.

Dazed, he peered around at all the dead Renali.

"We can't break through!"

He tracked drunkenly toward Bear's voice. The big masha'na held a masonry chunk, sweating over a battered trap door.

The furious exchange of steel slowed.

"It must exit close by." Kryskin's tone held the flat, inflectionless calm of the fighting focus.

Marco twisted toward it.

The man's curls were dark with sweat, sword leveled at Luvid.

The younger princess's bodyguard seemed amused, his heavy falchion held in a recklessly relaxed grip.

"Take the troupe," Kryskin continued, "and scour the woods. They can't have gotten far. Not while carrying the keeper."

Oh, sweet goddess, the keeper...

His swung his gaze back to the barren stage.

Bear rumbled uneasily, "What about you-?"

"*Now*, Bear."

Growling, the masha'na lumbered out the door.

Contemptuous green eyes watched the big man go.

"Tsk," Luvid sneered. "At least when there were two of you-"

Kryskin gave the braggart no time to finish.

The masha'na was lighting, his every cut clean and clinical.

In comparison, Luvid seemed to conduct a slapdash defense, swinging his one-handed sword haphazardly.

And yet, where Kryskin's brow was puckered in concentration, Luvid seemed on the cusp of laughter. Without missing a stroke, the bodyguard gave Marco a merry wink.

This was bad.

Trying to move sent sharp pains throughout his frame. His sword, he saw, had landed nearby. Biting off a whimper, he groped toward it and used it to push to his feet.

By increments, the symphony of metal slowed as Kryskin's assault wound down.

Not even breathing hard, the bodyguard stepped forward.

A backhanded blow sent the holy warrior reeling. Grinning, Luvid followed. Calculated, overpowered swings swatted the masha'na this way and that, threatening his footing. Kryskin tried to turn the attacks but was clearly being overwhelmed.

Lips arching hungrily, Luvid leered over at Marco.

His sword hilt was sweaty. His knees trembled.

If he cracked his teeth to call for Bear, or Ryhorn – he'd vomit.

He took a tottering step and then another, slipping on the slick stone. Fear had doused his moment of foaming rage. He stood a better chance of threading a needle in the dark than of achieving the streaming trance in his state.

But Kryskin was about to die, right in front of him.

Cobbling together a rough focus, he leapt into the fight.

Instead of the bodyguard's back, his blade bit stone floor.

Sword couched in apparent unconcern, Luvid grinned from just beyond striking distance. The man had still made no move to draw the long-knife – almost a twin to the falchion – at his belt.

"Knew you had it in you, scribe," the bodyguard cheered, readying his sword. "Now, let's have a closer look at it."

Panting, Kryskin stepped up beside Marco.

Even if he'd accomplished nothing else, he'd bought the masha'na some breathing room. It was a measure of how overmatched the commander was that he didn't tell Marco to run.

Luvid's emerald eyes lit with pleasure as they came at him. The man set about turning their attacks single-handedly.

In disbelief, Marco redoubled his efforts, straining...

And then Luvid did laugh, head thrown back and roaring at the ceiling – keeping them at bay without even looking.

Shocked, he and Kryskin skidded back.

"Oh," the bodyguard beamed, wiping an imaginary tear, "you have been a balm to my boring existence. But, unless you can do a whole lot better, I'm about done with you."

Fear froze Marco in place. An instant later, Kryskin flew past.

The masha'na delivered the opening strokes to the gambit called 'knocking the roof nail'. It was the first tandem fighting form Clatter Court taught. It was also half-jokingly called 'knocking the *coffin* nail', because it was a sacrificial stratagem.

Only his training dragged Marco forward to deliver his part.

He traded off with Kryskin, lulling Luvid into a pattern. Gentle taps, to settle the nail in place. Like the waltzes Dailill had described. One, two, three. One, two, three. One, two-

Reverse!

Luvid took the bait. Marco leapt into the opening.

The sword edge, suddenly slewing towards his face, had already been slowed by raking through Kryskin's ribcage. Seeing it, he faltered and slipped. Even so, it would have taken the top off his head if two throwing stars hadn't flashed by.

The bodyguard staggered in surprise as the projectiles found his shoulder blade. The falchion's flat landed alongside Marco's head.

The ring of steel was drowned by the ringing in his skull. The floor lay down beside him and time seesawed sickeningly...

"Come on! Come on!"

Someone was flicking his face, none too gently. He jerked away and wished he hadn't when pain hit him, coming the other way.

"Nin? What happened?" Panic sparked. "Where's Luvid?"

"Ran off," the assassin griped, ripping the hems off dead men's jerkins to bind his head. "Your masha'na are still out looking."

Masha'na?

"Kryskin!" His vision swam as he strained upwards.

"You should stay still."

"Help me stand," he wheezed, tasting bile.

With an uncaring grip, she dragged him up by the arm.

The leonine commander lay prone, pink foam flecking his lips as he gasped shallowly. A hasty compress wrapped his chest. Lamellar plates, from his riven armor, were strewn about.

Meeting his eye, the masha'na commander pawed feebly at the air, fighting for breath. "Find… Find… keeper…"

"Punctured lung," Nin observed. "Nothing we can do for him."

That wasn't true.

"The keeper can fix him," Marco declared.

"Like I said," the assassin nodded. "Nothing we can do."

His sword's point dragged as he gathered it to him.

Nin watched him stumble off. "Are all Imperials this stubborn-stupid? You're like a damned dog with a bone. Were you even watching that bastard? That wasn't swordplay. That was a dark discipline. The kind you only get to see, up close, once. Let it go."

Pagan arts, yes. That made sense.

"Can't," he slurred. He could not leave the keeper in the clutches of such a creature, even if it meant his end. His own soul might be beyond saving, but if he could spend it to secure the keeper's survival, he would die a wealthy man.

The surrounding ruins were deserted, not counting the dead.

The masha'na were off, searching for the keeper.

Nin sighed. "Fine. You go that way. Shout if you see anything."

He gave her a surprised look.

"What?" She shrugged. "They absconded with my bounty."

Without a backward glance, she set off into the trees.

He took stock. He was feverish, concussed and fatigued. His flesh was a mass of shallow cuts and bone-deep bruises and the old wound in his side bled freely.

Even so, what really hurt was the thought of failing Justin.

He *had* to use every weapon at his disposal, even if it meant damnation. He would be a dog, with or without a bone.

Purposely sniffing the air, he angled off to his left.

With every step, he tried to shed a little more emotion, sidling his way closer and closer to the streaming trance-

Pressure spiked behind his eyes and nausea broke over him.

Leaning against a bole, he threw up, ignoring the clots of blood.

-the trance wobbled as he wrestled with his uneven breathing.

A prayer mantra would help and he reached for one, only to find that the rote words were gone from his memory.

He pushed away from his pool of sick and found Justin's scent again, carried on the breeze. That helped. His breathing found a rhythm and, for a time, there was only the next tree and the next.

Gradually, another noise intruded.

A low, rumbling drone.

Almost, he stumbled blindly through the scrub brush and over the gorge's edge. A torrential river raged far below.

Vertigo joined the queue of maladies making his head spin. From this height, through the crystalline mist, the water looked to be immobile. Only the roar of the rapids, crashing up the canyon walls, gave it the lie.

The opposite bank seemed as distant as a different country. But that's where the smell was coming from. Turning into the wind, he trailed it downstream, trudging through the gorse.

With his concentration bent on quieting his mind, he might have mistaken the overgrown path for a game trail. But Luvid's resinous stink clung to it, nearly spoiling his control. He blundered after it.

The small clearing was right on the bluff. Absurdly green grass sprouted little white blooms. A gap-toothed bridge spanned the gorge, little more than a rope ladder. Its cords, once as thick around as his wrist, wafted frayed beards in the breeze. Bright pulp bristled where wet rot had burst the boards.

Movement, on the far side – two figures, dragging a third.

"You surprise me again, scribe," Luvid said.

The bodyguard barred access to the bridge.

"No one else, in this backwater, has managed as much. That was the second time I was sure I'd killed you. After the tourney, I had hoped that the Heli had found themselves a new champion. But you and I know the truth, don't we scribe…?"

Letting the nonsensical words wash over him, he hefted his weapon.

"You've come to pen your epitaph," the man observed.

Out of the quiet echoed Master Crysopher's voice.

'When it is kill-or-be-killed, it is often the less skilled but more focused who leaves the battle alive…'

The streaming trance coalesced, welling up. He sunk gratefully into it, drowning his fear, his pain and his doubt.

He flowed toward the bodyguard.

"Third time's the charm," Luvid encouraged.

They clashed in the middle of the clearing. Metal sang.

Even with throwing stars, standing starkly from his shoulder, the man's blows landed like a sledge.

Inside the trance, partially shielded from the shock, the sword form called 'breeze in the river reeds' rose unbidden.

Luvid's smile widened as his first strike was turned. Then the second. And the third. The man chortled delightedly and the attacks fell even harder, too fast too tally.

By some miracle, Marco matched the man, stroke for stroke.

'Spume over seawall' softened the bodyguard's strikes.

Slowly, Luvid's smile soured.

The man lost composure.

Now.

Surpassing his own limits by a league, he drove Luvid back a step, then another, flitting from one form to another.

Cursing, the bodyguard leapt clear of a looping cut.

At the man's back, the gorge yawned.

Metal screeched as their blades bit at one another in frenzy. The bodyguard's back heel scattering pebbles into the abyss.

The trance was straining thin. Marco's body was at its limit.

Roaring, he threw reserves he didn't know he had into a last rush. Luvid's guard was battered aside.

'The full lunge overextends you,' Master Crysopher's voice warned. *'Use it only if your opponent has lost footing-'*

He lunged, straight for Luvid's hateful sneer.

It was over. He'd won-

Clang!

The hunting knife hooked his sword aside, snaring it between itself and the falchion. He stared in disbelief at its empty sheath.

"Well fought, scribe."

The two single-edged weapons scissored outward. There was a *snick* as they sheared through Marco's keep forged sword.

A slight pressure, as they passed through his chest.

Staring stupidly, he toppled. The thump of his landing was faint, heralded by blue sky. Misting blood colored the nearest blooms pink. The trance dashed itself apart.

He convulsed as pain flooded into its absence.

The bodyguard stepped into view above him.

The harsh light of Marco's shock set the man's green eyes aglow, erasing the whites. Double vision made it appear that dual pupils swam in each. They held a putrid, pearlescent sheen.

The apparition swore and the alien word held power that slapped at Marco's staggering soul.

"Now, look what you've done," it rumbled, voice echoing oddly. "This shell is ripped."

An arm, extending past its cuff, craned over the bodyguard's shoulder. The limb bent impossibly, allowing Luvid to pluck a throwing star from his own back and hold it up for inspection. Incandescent, emerald ichor corroded the weapon as they watched.

"Ruined," the thing judged, tossing the star aside. Then it glared down at him. "I've changed my mind. I hope you survive a third time – to see your world, ground out beneath our heel."

And then Marco was alone. Just him and the rush of the river.

Joke's on you, denizen, he thought.

Because it had been too much. He'd forced himself too far. He'd broken something inside of himself he had no name for. He could feel death – and dissolution – filtering through the fractures.

Keeper, forgive me my failure, I could do no more.

Above him, the heavens began to blur.

Holy Helia, guardian mother-

✷ ✷ ✷

LEAGUES AWAY, IN a Keystone tower, sudden silence echoed in place of a sorcerous note. Distracted, the Royal Arcanist fumbled his tiny shears and an entire limb tumbled from his toana tree.

Stricken, the old man sat down on a plush stool.

So, the Heli boy's song has faded from the choir...

With gnarled fingers he knuckled his tired eyes.

It had been a long time, since the lives of others had held more than academic interest. He'd quite forgotten the poignancy of loss.

"My lord arcanist?" asked a hesitant voice. "Are you alright?"

His spotty apprentice stood in the doorway, spindly arms heaped high with scrolls.

Briefly, he considered telling the boy to take the day off. To forget about those musty texts. To dine with his family, drink with his friends and to dance with a pretty girl.

The moist rag would probably do it, if ordered – and do it badly.

"Youth is wasted on the young," he deplored. Then his razor wit cut inward. "And wisdom is wasted on the old."

He thought of poor Marco. "And that's if you're lucky."

His apprentice goggled at his sudden melancholy. "Milord?"

"Leave me!" he hissed, lashing out in his borrowed grief.

Shedding scrolls in his haste, the gangly youth fled.

Alone, Peril wondered whether old tears would be wasted on a youthful passing.

CHAPTER 19 – AN END TO DREAMING

Pella Monop, Diary entry #212

I have made a terrible mistake. I should have walked off into the night, taking only myself. Instead, I absconded with all of my research, a false name and a fast ship. An Imperial trireme was sighted in our wake at dusk and has signaled us to furl sail. I can hear them boarding now. My life's work is going to see me dead. I should have burned it all. Perhaps I still can…

[Inquisitor's note]: Seditious materials, under Inquisitori seal and censure. Recovered from wreckage of Rasrini merchant ship, Sobolone, set ablaze and scuttled five leagues off the Renali coast. Cause of fire, apparent arson. Suspect, presumed lost at sea with seven other souls. Investigation closed.

MARCO STOOD WITHIN the nightmare.

The weeping rock had finally failed, drowning the dream in red. Only the central chamber remained. And it, too, was flooding.

The creature at its heart thrashed in its bonds, seeking escape.

He looked down at himself.

His torn flesh bled, adding steadily to the rising tide.

The unrelenting clatter of chains drew him and he turned toward it, unafraid. Terror was for the living.

And yet… the dream held something. Some slim chance…

He stepped between the columns and into the beast's demesne.

Immediate silence as unseen eyes seized on him.

For a moment, there was only the gush of the invading torrent.

"Well?" he demanded.

It stalked from the black, burnished orbs holding him captive. An impression of bulk, its fur snarled and soaked. Wicked claws padded into the half-light, pushing its rancid musk before it. And then it rose, on limber hind legs, drawing his gaze up and further up. Black lips peeled soundlessly. A maw, filled with fangs, hove close. Its rotten breath rolled over him.

In its ancient, amber-flecked eyes, he saw his death reflected.

Then the beast stilled, sensing his intent.

"Just this once…" he told it, and reached up.

Hidden in its matted mane, his fist closed on a collar of iron.

The metal shattered like struck ice.

Animal glee filled the creature's eyes and it arched its back and roared. A sound of such bloody anticipation, he felt himself blown away by it, buoyed by it.

It reverberated through his bones and burst from his own breast.

Small, blood-speckled blooms bent from the force of it.

The world righted itself and he stood on a bluff, its rope bridge hanging in tatters, its distant supports undone.

The opposite bank drew his gaze and, an instant later, the rest of him. Water roiled, far below, as he arced over the chasm. He hit the far side at a dead sprint, clawing his way among the trees.

The molten blood of the beast demanded a hunt. And, somewhere ahead, was their quarry.

He threw back his head and *howled*.

LUVID JOGGED BACK through the trees.

Ahead, he could hear the half-dozen soldiers he'd sent across the gorge. It sounded like the fools were taking a rest.

He trotted into their midst, a tongue lashing at the ready.

"Up! Up, you lazy sons of bitches! Up! Those Imperials will be on us again in two shakes."

Not true, of course. He'd destroyed the only bridge within a dozen leagues. But he needed this lot distracted. Despite his best efforts, his essence was seeping – a symptom of overexertion. Soon, his human skin would start to unravel at the seams.

They had to be far away from here before that happened. He was in no fit mood to be carrying an enemy priest down the mountain. And he'd have to, once he'd murdered these witnesses.

Damn that boy!

"Move, you layabouts!"

The guard closest to him gaped.

Gentling his tone, he averted his eyes – the most difficult bit to suppress – and strode to the front of the formation.

"Pick up that priest! This isn't a picnic! Come on!"

Their fearful grumbles followed him into the forest.

It galled, having an agent of the suicidal goddess at his back. He'd rather see all the architects of the insurrection on a mass pyre. But his assignment was to sow dissent among this realm's forces. And his princess's insipid schemes certainly did that.

Not that the Heli of this age were the same magnitude of threat their forebears were. All that power – all that fire and fury – sacrificed on the altar of their own foolish pride.

And, the best part was, they didn't even *remember*.

He grit his teeth at the joke. When this world woke once more, it would offer no resistance. Not through any effort of his, nor that of any other advance agents, but simply because the fields of foreknowledge had lain fallow and untilled for too long.

Idly, he wondered whether he would be allowed to keep his 'lady princess' as a pet. She was sufficiently devious to entertain-

A ululating cry rose above the trees, halting him in his tracks.

By chance, they'd found themselves in a clearing, hemmed by forest on three sides and the fourth dropping into the gulch.

A guard swore, "Fortune's hairy fetlocks! What was that?"

"A wolf, maybe?"

"Ain't like no wolf I ever heard…" someone said nervously.

"No," he muttered, disbelieving. "Not a wolf."

He drew his sword. Uncertainly, his soldiers followed suit.

Cursing his frail shell, he felt his second heart stir to life in response to the threat. He was past suppressing his nature now.

"...don't normally attack men. And a group this large-"

The authority on wolves swallowed his tongue as something massive burst from the underbrush.

The creature slowed in the full sunlight, allowing them to look their fill. Its mad stare made no bones as to its intentions.

"Oh, fortune flog me..."

"*Krinjala*," Luvid identified.

It shot toward them, drawing screams from the Guard.

Jaws flensed. Claws scythed.

The nearest soldier disintegrated in a spray of guts and gore.

The man's neighbor, too close – or too scared – to flee, swung wildly into the mess. And stumbled back, staring at the stumps of his arms. The stricken man looked up in time to see the slavering jaws that closed around his face, crushing his head.

Showing some sense, the next nearest guard turned tail. And made it half a step, before sharp claws hooked his ankles and he was dragged, shrilling, back into carnage's embrace.

The soldiers bearing the priest shrugged off their burden and stepped forward to meet the threat.

At least, one of them did. The other dropped his sword and ran.

Finding himself suddenly alone, the stalwart guardsman stared after his compatriot with wide eyes. A paw snapped the man's head the rest of the way around and he sat down limply.

The coward who had run puffed hard toward the tree line, fumbling at his armor straps. He didn't see death speed after him.

The beast bore him to the ground and began ripping. The terrible sounds and screams pealed into the woods.

Only once silence descended did the krinjala rise, a strip of flesh dangling from its teeth.

It shook out its fur, painting everything within reach a rusty red.

Head low, it loped back toward him.

The lone remaining guardsman backed up, sword aquiver.

The stitching of Luvid's leather cuirass split loudly. Reaching out, he grabbed the last survivor by the head and tossed the man into terror's teeth, where he went to pieces.

"You're not supposed to be here!" Luvid raged. "You're supposed to be extinct!"

Unblinking, utterly ferocious eyes bored into his.

Meeting its challenge, he bared his own teeth and all his power.

Tough leathers tore like a tarp in a gale, exposing olive green skin. Bones cracked and reknit to accommodate a double spine. His tripling mass drove his soles into the turf and he towered, even over the krinjala.

Hefting his puny, human weapons, he snorted around his tusks.

"Come, then! I shall wear you for a loincloth!"

In an instant, it had pounced past his guard and landed on his chest. He staggered at the impact, feeling its claws dig deep.

Letting go both sword and dagger, he hugged it to him, trapping its jaws before they could take any more than skin from his neck.

Even for his prodigious muscle, its thrashing proved hard to hold. His efforts to dig at it with his tusks snagged only tough pelt.

He tightened his grip, meaning to squeeze the life from it.

Muffled, it snarled thunderously, hind claws scrabbling at his belly. One scored though his thick hide.

It would succeed in disemboweling him before he smothered it.

Cursing, he flung it away.

It twisted agilely as it landed, circling him on all fours, its topaz eyes ablaze with promise.

His flesh crawled as his wounds began to close.

It charged him again and he lashed out with a foot.

The kick could have cracked a menhir. It certainly sounded like it had. The krinjala dug furrows in the loam as it skidded back. It faltered for all of two paces, then coughed, righting broken bone.

"Come closer," he growled, "I'll beat you like a drum."

It leapt – a feint, he realized too late. His blow missed the banking mirage and a gobbet of flesh disappeared from his underarm. Swearing, he lost track of it for the space of a blink.

It announced itself, clawing up his back, clinging obstinately as he tried to buck it off.

Razor jaws closed about his nape in a vice.

"Aaagh!"

His triple-jointed arms let him reach for it. But its coat was greased and gory and allowed no firm grip. He gasped as those jaws started sawing back and forth, working steadily through his stout flesh. Frantic, he tore out bloody clumps of fur.

Its growled response reverberated down his backbone, its jaws bunching anew with his every effort.

Finally, he got ahold of two handfuls of hide. He strained.

Curved talons anchored themselves deeper among his ribs.

With a savage shake, it forced him to his knees.

He was struggling to breathe.

His arms fell limp as some connection was severed.

No! This was impossible!

The snap of vertebrae was a dull shock to his ears. His vision pivoted as the last tissues parted. He pitched to the ground, rolling strangely. Something heavy landed beside him – his corpse.

Green ichor spurted. Huge hands twitched spasmodically. Dead flesh began graying and sloughed off to the earth.

Suddenly seeing the hilarity of the situation, he smiled – and would have laughed out loud, had his lungs not been *over there*.

GAGGING AT THE foul taste, the beast rose.
Its roar of victory bounced from the distant peaks.
But it wasn't done killing – it would *never* be done killing.
"Marco... Where...?"
Its dripping muzzle swung toward the sound.
An old one, this. Blind. Lame. The weakest of the pack.
It would snuff this easy prey and go hunting hardier game.
Licking its chops, it padded over.
"Marco...?"

MARCO WAS A prisoner inside a monster's skin.
Unwilling, he shared its every salivating impulse. He felt the pounding of its paws against the earth, shared in the bellows of its breath. And – as it found prey – he had the sick thrill of slaughter thrust upon him.
Flesh parted, intestines unspooled and bones cracked.
Powerless to halt the torrent, Marco screamed, tasting marrow on his tongue. On *its* tongue.
As though he might wrest his way from a nightmare, he scrabbled to assert his will. But he had become damned – held fast in the Dark Places. The denizen took no notice of him.
From out of the carnage rose a new creature, to contest their claim to the spoils – the moss-colored monster towered over them, its eyes blazing alchemically.
Gibbering, Marco sought to flee.
The denizen that held him attacked instead.
He wailed his terror as the two titans beat at and savaged one another.

Bitter resin stung his gums as his captor clamped down on the giant's nape. The grate of bone translated through to the roots of his teeth. The crack of monstrous vertebrae shook him.

In pieces, the challenger sprawled.

His denizen's exultation echoed through the Dark Places.

It turned to its next victim – to Marco's next torture.

"Marco…?"

His mentor's voice rasped across his raw senses.

He went cold.

The scriptures were right – the Dark Places plumbed the depths of your personal dread, raising just punishment for your sins.

It had reduced the normally impressive priest to a pitiful figure, crawling and casting about blindly.

His captor started forward, drooling.

No!

He fought the familiar paralysis of sleep, lashing out with limbs he could not see. At a whisper, as of fur beneath his fingers, he lunged. He hugged something, large and rank and rock-hard, to him. It bucked, battering him. Furious snarls snapped at his ears.

He held the denizen all the tighter, terror lending him strength.

Justin, he sobbed, unheard. *Justin, run!*

JUSTIN'S HEAD WAS splitting.

His last clear memory was of a rickety shack in the Narrows-

No, that wasn't right. There had been men…

Recalling Jossram's death hit him like another blow to the jaw.

Vague impressions followed – a hard saddle beneath his belly, the chafe of hemp at his wrists and ankles. He couldn't see.

'He's coming around.'

Pain, as something hard had struck his pate-

The mutter of dull voices had pulled him from senselessness.

Echoes, as of an enclosed space, damp and redolent with wood smoke. There had been the chill of stone at his back.

'Where am I...?'

Rough hands had seized his chin, forcing a spigot between his teeth. His feeble resistance hadn't amounted to much. He'd choked on a concoction of bile and poppy and bryony and hemlock and...

The soporific had stolen his will to fight, to think.

Sometime later, his muddled thoughts began to resurface.

Groggy, confused, he struggled to parse the commotion.

Yelling. Screaming. The ring of steel. A battle.

No, it can't be. The front line was decades behind him. Who would bring a blind old man to war? But there could be no mistaking this sound. Or this smell.

He quailed.

Amid the slaughter, a child cried out for its father.

It wasn't right. Children had no place in war. Neither did the decrepit. When they came to fetch him away, he thought it proper.

Young men carried him. Soldiers.

"Leave me," he tried to tell them. "Save the children."

But they didn't. He tried his best to walk, to not be a burden.

As his old heart hammered, the poison in his veins began to thin, his thoughts clearing.

Why was he blindfolded?

Someone slapped irritably at his questing fingers.

Beneath him, the world wobbled alarmingly. A bridge. Cold gusts plucked at his robes and, far below, he heard water churn.

Shadows overhead now, smelling of spruce and pine.

Harsh panting, as they set him down.

"The old coot is heavier than he looks."

Renali! His fugue lifted further.

"Be grateful we're out of that scrap. Did you see those Imperials? Fortune's balding balls! Swordmasters, every last one."

These were his abductors, then, running from his rescuers.

"You're talking out of your bunghole! I, for one, would have loved to cross blades with one of them bastards."

"Ha! If you had, *your* bunghole would've pursed and spit."

"Screw you, coward! I saw you, shaking in your boots-"

Turning a deaf ear, Justin concentrated on his extra sense. He could just about feel the six closest to him. But the dregs of dwale, still in his system, made a muddle of the rest.

He wouldn't be able to stream a lick if his life depended on it.

Your life might *depend on it, old man. So you'd better-*

"Up! Up, you lazy sons-of-bitches, up!"

A seventh presence joined them. An officer, he guessed. There was something odd about this one. His feelings fit together strangely. Toxically, even.

Justin could tell he was not the only one to notice – unfocussed fear made the men's movements jittery as they hauled him up.

He missed the rest of the discussion as hard fingers dug into his arms and they dragged him along.

He kept his focus on their leader. Someone, so steeped in malice and scorn, should be foaming at the mouth. Not sound calm and-

-shocked!

The surprise spread quickly. The soldiers staggered to a halt.

"What was that?"

They'd heard something. Something the thick cloth had hidden from his ears. A rescue party, perhaps? Ignoring their speculation, he strained his senses along their back trail...

There. Something sped toward them. Something... ravenous.

"Oh, fortune flog me..." one soldier gasped.

Dread pushed up, all around, like poisonous toadstools.

Someone screamed.

With Justin's mental guard in tatters, even the death of a stranger cut keenly. Gasping, he dropped from their grasp.

Another connection was snipped short. The backlash whipped wetly across his face and he sprawled.

Death lashed him several times more, leaving him dazed.

In the chaos, someone strained and swore – actual curses that clawed at his soul, the words mercifully devoid of meaning.

Teeth snapped. Bones broke.

A malodorous rot – akin to the discharge of the tree-burrowing stink-beetle – rolled over him and he choked on it.

The sounds of struggle died down.

Justin gathered the scraps of his shredded consciousness to him – and felt a familiar presence brush by. He strove to sit up.

"Marco… Where…?"

The sense was strange – bodily nearby, yet incredibly remote.

Finally remembering, he fumbled the blindfold from his eyes.

"Marco…?"

Blinking against the glare, he got the impression of a clearing on the edge of a crevasse. Then the blinding light coalesced into a creature, straight off the pages of an illuminated manuscript – a depiction of the Dark Places and the denizens that dwelled there.

All fangs and fur and madness, the creature clambered over the corpse of an even larger monster.

"Helia, have mercy," Justin muttered, scooting back.

The denizen was daubed in blood and ichor. Welts showed in bald patches of its pelt. Ropes of mucus swung from its beard.

As it padded over, its searing attention pinned him in place.

Goddess, grant this monster does not find Marco.

Reflexively, he reached for the connection he shared with his ward, reassuring himself the boy was not in harm's way…

The link recoiled, giving his mental grasp rope burn.

Marco!

Shocked at what he'd sensed – even in that brief moment – he seized the tether in a vice, trailing it to its source.

The denizen froze, the unreasoning fire in its eyes ebbing.

The sense of Marco's presence surged.

Something wrenched the creature away from Justin.

It stumbled onto its hind legs, clawed hands clutching at its head. It bugled, a hybrid sound of bestial wrath and human sorrow.

Justin's tenuous connection to Marco strengthened.

Pushed by something unseen, the creature pitched from its feet.

It caught itself, digging long talons into the turf. Over its shoulder, it peered balefully at Justin.

His ward's presence petered.

But he'd found the boy.

"Fight it, Marco!" he encouraged, tottering to his feet.

There were no detailed manuals on denizen possession. At least, none that had escaped the Inquisitori's keeping.

Were he a normal hierarch, he would have to muddle through on prayer and purifying elixirs.

But he had more to draw on.

Ignoring his pounding head and splintered senses, he maligned Empath's Echo into form. The sigil was tremulous, barely holding together. But it would not have to reach far. He breathed his faith and encouragement into his connection with Marco.

The creature had rekindled its rage and gathered a leap-

"You can do it, son! Hold on!"

-it faltered awkwardly, plowing into the clearing's floor.

It snarled at him, angrily shaking out its fur.

"That's it, Marco!" he told its dimming eyes. "Come back!"

Though his connection swelled with confidence, his vision swam. He was contending with injury, intoxication, fatigue – and was streaming despite them all. If he didn't drain himself unconscious, and soon, the strain would kill him.

But he would not abandon the boy. Not now. Not ever. Not to anyone. Most definitely, not to a denizen.

What were priests for, if not exactly this?

He let his belief in the boy resound through their bond.

"You can beat it! Cast it out!"

For an instant, the embers of the beast's eyes banked. They showed an all too human expression, echoed through the tether.

Sorrow. And apology.

It jerked once more, tumbling toward the cliff's edge.

Only then did he grasp his ward's plan. "No! Marco, don't!"

Thrashing, the monster was dragged another grudging step toward the abyss, leaning as if against a gale.

THE SHAPE OF Marco's soul had become clear to him, in his struggle against the denizen. It had mirrored his physical form, at first. Now, its substance was riven. Its seams undone and its stuffing swept away, like a ruined Solstice puppet.

There was still one last thing he had to do.

Growling, fit to compete with the beast, he tightened his hold.

From the corner of its eye, he gauged their distance to the chasm. With its ears, he heard the crashing water, far below.

Once he faltered, Justin would fall.

Unless the denizen fell first.

At the start, it had resisted him with scorn. Now, it fought with fierce determination. And there seemed no end to its energy.

Marshalling what little substance remained to him, he shoved.

The denizen stumbled toward the edge – and their shared doom.

Bracing himself, he heaved once more and they rolled closer.

The cool breath of the gorge ruffled the monster's mane.

Its fury howled at him, peeling at his being.

One more. Just one more...

Sensing him flag, the beast abandoned its frenzy and strained forward with all its might.

Marco felt his grip slipping, felt himself thinning into nothing. His phantom shoulders tore from their sockets and muscles stretched apart like taffy. He had nothing left for the final push.

The beast was pulling away, strand by strand.

Ghostly tears swirled away on the current.

Oh, Helia. Justin, I'm so sorry-

FINCH'S SEARCH BROKE through the scree.

Seeing him, Leffley straightened from studying the ground.

This bluff had seen fighting. Grass had been scuffed up in swathes and little pink flowers leaned brokenly.

"Any word yet on Kryskin?"

He shook his head.

Leffley swore. "Looks like this is a day for losses, then. Because our quarry definitely high-tailed it over this here bridge."

"What bridge?"

"Exactly."

He eyed the unstrung supports. "Ah. Any other way across?"

"Not that I've seen."

"Yes."

They both turned.

The assassin woman, inscrutable in her supple leathers and mask, stared at them.

"This way," she added, disappearing back into the scrub.

Returning Leffley's shrug, the two of them set off after her.

She led them upriver a ways, finally pointing out a lip of rock. "Down there."

Dubiously, he approached the drop-off... and leaned over.

Centuries of snowmelt had undercut the canyon walls. A spar of rock, as tall as a redoubt, had broken loose. Instead of tumbling to the water, it had stuck crossways, spanning the gorge. Its distant end was couched in stone, a dozen hands from the ridge top.

On *this* side however...

Beside him, Leffley whistled.

"That's a killer climb if I ever saw one."

He silently agreed. "Can we find some rope and rappel down?"

"Dunno. We could drag up that ruined bridge and dangle it-"

Neither of them had paid any more attention to the assassin. In retrospect, this seemed an oversight.

On silent feet, she slammed into them.

"Ssshhhiiii-!" he screamed, as they all three went over.

"-aaaggghhh!" Leffley screeched in his ear.

The assassin clutched their collars, eyes narrowed in concentration. The canted rock rushed up from below.

His stomach continued on, past his boots, as they snapped out of freefall. Only the woman's uncanny grip kept him from splattering.

Whatever held them snapped.

They fell no further than a man's height. But his legs were scared stiff and folded beneath him. That didn't stop him scurrying away from the assassin, who had landed smoothly.

He leveled a shaking finger at her.

"Don't! *Ever!* Do that again!"

"Please," Leffley added, in a small voice, from flat on his back.

He could not be certain. But he thought she smiled. "Alright."

Wide-eyed, he looked to the cliff top, easily a hundred paces above. Semi-translucent strands of... *something* frayed in the mist.

"Is that spider's web?" Hysteria heightened his voice.

"Sort of," she allowed. "I wasn't even sure it would hold us all."

As she sashayed past, she clapped her hands, like she was herding goats. "Don't dally. I'm getting soaked."

She ignored Leffley's outstretched arm, so it fell to Finch to help him up.

"You look terrible."

"Really? That's funny. Because I feel amazing."

His shivering had almost subsided by the time they'd scrambled their way up the embankment. He unlimbered his horn bow – blessedly undamaged – and Leffley did the same. They skirted the cliff's edge until they reached the demolished bridge.

The tracks told it true. Their quarry had passed this way.

A distant shout caught his attention. He could make out Bear and Parish on the opposite bank. Bear cupped hands to his mouth.

"-they go that way?!"

The words were distorted by distance, but distinguishable.

He signaled an affirmative.

A moment while the next question wafted to them.

"-there another way across?!"

Nervously eyeing the assassin, he signaled an emphatic 'no'.

"-move downriver! -meet you there!"

He waved that he understood.

"-luck!"

This arrived a beat after the others had turned from the ledge.

"Alright then," he announced. "On me…"

He led the way into the forest proper, following the trail.

They hadn't gone far when Leffley almost tripped over him. Crouching, he wondered aloud, "What in Helia's name?"

The other masha'na peered over his shoulder. "A wolf print?"

"What wolf you ever seen's got five toes? And look at the size of its stride. Thing's huge. And it passed by recently."

Leffley eyed the trees sidelong. "Let's get the keeper and go."

"As quickly as possible," he agreed.

Up ahead, sunlight slanted through the trunks.

"I hear something," the assassin said.

He stilled, listening. "That sounds like the priest!"

They broke into a run, pulling up beside the last line of boles.

The clearing ahead was a scene of slaughter. Bodies, and bits of bodies, were strewn about. What might have been a compost heap – or possibly not – lay, smoking gently in the sun.

His eyes tracked toward the hubbub… "Guardian mother!"

The keeper confronted what could only be described as a denizen. He could not hear the chaplain's commands, but it must be powerful prayer indeed, to be holding such a beast at bay.

But the preacher was clearly on his last legs.

"Take its heart," he ordered Leffley. "I have the head…"

Their bows creaked with tension. He kissed the fletching–

"No! Wait!" the assassin hissed.

Two strings thrummed. He didn't need to watch to know the shot winged true. He turned to the tense woman.

"What?"

But she didn't answer. Above her mask, her eyes were pained and she dug into the tree beside her with blunt nails.

"What?!" he asked again.

As though his desperate prayer had conjured them, Marco saw holy warriors appear. Helia would not leave one such as the keeper to the Dark Places. Not without sending a sortie after him.

The denizen had not yet noticed.

And, quick as it was, it could not be allowed to.

Despairing of his useless limbs, Marco set to with his teeth.

He bit down on something that flooded his mouth and mind with hot rage and roiling hate.

He reared back, dragging the surprised denizen with him.

Divine intervention arrived.

Two armor-piercing bodkins, gifted by the goddess's boundless mercy, bored into the beast. He shared its flesh – and its pain – as a shaft punched into one side of its throat and out the other. A second arrow stove in its ribs.

He felt his captor lose its equilibrium and, for a moment, he stood alone in its frame.

He met his mentor's eyes.

Justin… I did it…!

The denizen's weight dragged him down and into darkness.

JUSTIN WAS HOARSE from pleading. Sharp pinches plagued his joints. A late warning sign of excessive streaming. Even so, he allowed his adept mind to hold only one thought – saving Marco.

"That's it, son! Just a little bit more!"

The denizen's amber eyes rolled, showing their onyx undersides. Deadly claws flexed, shaking with strain.

"You can do it, have faith-"

Blood slapped his face. An instant later, another arrow struck, puncturing the creature's chest. It staggered.

Stunned, he watched the fire gutter from its eyes.

"No…" he muttered in disbelief.

By increments, the denizen keeled over.

"Nooo!"

Rushing, reaching out, he threw himself down on the ridge top. Far below, he caught a last glimpse of a tumbling body. Then the foaming river swallowed it.

"Marcoooooooo!"

* * *

JIMINY CAME AWAKE with a jerk.

He'd been falling through a nightmare, a moment from impact. As pain made itself felt – seemingly all-over – he considered that the dream might have been grounded, as it were, in fact.

"You're awake."

He tried to turn his head. "Neever?"

The monk looked haggard. "We worried you wouldn't make it."

Their staging area, he saw, had been converted into a sickroom.

"This," he observed, surprised by how wan his voice sounded, "is either a pretty nice prison, or a seriously shitty afterlife."

"It is neither," Neever promised. "You succeeded."

He blinked at that. "Really? Yay. Though I don't expect failing could have hurt worse. Is it possible for a person's hair to ache?"

"You are feeling the after-effects of poison."

"Poison?" Disjointed images sleeted past his mind's eye.

"The dead mage…" he breathed, remembering.

Neever's gaze sharpened. "You said something like that before, while in the grips of fever. Will you tell me what happened up there? You looked like you'd been mauled by a bulkbear."

He wasn't about to own up to anything. Not until he'd had a good think, to get his story straight. He'd never told Neever's lot what their sanctuary had saved him from. And now it looked like the magicker had been *their* enemy, rather than his, all along. He hadn't understood a lot of what it had said, but he'd gotten the distinct impression Arbiter's gospel was more than simple schism glue. And that his ring was somehow connected to it.

Considering the suicidal lengths the priests – and the dead mage – had gone to, to get the one, he wasn't about to admit the other wouldn't leave his finger.

Besides, he really didn't know what a 'bulkbear' was.

"Don't change the subject. Poison? Am I dying or what?"

"You're lucky," Neever said. "Sitter Cyrus is our foremost healer. Anything less and you would likely not be here. The venom was unlike anything he'd ever seen. I won't pretend to understand. The point is, he nearly killed you, driving the ill humor out."

"Ill humor? Am I now no longer funny?"

"Believe me, Master Jiminy," Cyrus entered, looking dour, "you are *exactly* as amusing as you were before."

"Ha ha."

The healer busied himself with the assembled beakers and bottles on the side table. "I fear I had not the strength to also knit your wounds. Brother Neever performed admirably in my stead."

"I apologize for my clumsy needlework," the monk said solemnly, "and for the scarring you shall suffer as a result."

A shrug pulled uncomfortably at the skin of his hip and back.

"Glad I was out cold for that, then."

"Speaking of..." Cyrus thrust a squat cup at him. "Here. This tastes of feet but it will ease your discomfort and help you sleep."

He thought to argue – he'd just woken. But he sensed a jagged mess of pain, stumbling to catch up to him. And he'd rather be unconscious by the time it arrived.

"Alright, help me sit up. And slide over that chamber pot..."

He was disgusted by how weak he was. But, more so, by the potion being pressed to his lips. "Bottoms up!"

Cyrus duly held him as he sputtered.

"You may go, Brother Neever," the man allowed. "You have been here all night. I shall sit with our young thief awhile."

The monk bowed deeply, though it was unclear to whom.

"Hey, Neever?"

The man looked back from the doorway.

"Next time you talk to your goddess, tell her 'thanks' for me."

The monk smiled slightly. "You might tell her yourself."

Shaking his head, he slurred around a thickening tongue.

"Not my style…"

AS THE MONK left, and the thief's breathing slowed toward sleep, Cyrus relaxed his rigid control. Immediately, sweat sprung from his bald pate and violent tremors overtook him. He clasped his shaking hands to still them, raising his eyes to the ceiling.

But he did not pray.

Several floors above his head, the scripture of Juris Arbiter sat like a headsman's axe.

He'd rushed through his translation and may have gotten a couple of the details wrong – but the gist had been clear.

Bitterly, he wrenched at his wispy hair.

Gifted pragmatist that he was, he thought he'd long since made his peace with death. He'd even come to appreciate the irony – that the Temple's foremost healer was unable to save himself.

Now, he was being asked to save… *everyone.*

To fight a battle so big, he couldn't even begin to comprehend its scope. To confront enemies gods had not been able to best.

And, what's more, he was being told he had to do it alone.

No, he didn't pray. Not now he *knew* no one was listening.

How could we not have known? How was this *ever hidden?*

The faith within him was failing, assailed by knowledge. He was not a priest at a Temple. He was the minder of a mausoleum. And, worse, he and his predecessors had done a piss-poor job of seeing to the interred's last testament. They'd squandered millennia in petty pursuits and, now, it was nearly too late.

The heightened ambient magic in the world was a sign. A sign that the stay of execution Helia's sacrifice had won for them – and the world – was played out.

Gone, while they'd sat arguing doctrine.

Control yourself. He wiped his face. *Before Justin sees…*

He laughed. The world about to end, and he worried that his friend – on the other side of the continent – might find him being less than resolute. The thought helped steady him.

That's right – I'm not alone, am I?

"We'll just see about this 'end of the world' business…"

* * *

MOTHER ANOCHRIA, SPY-MISTRESS and personal assassin to Emion Hallet, trekked through the muddy Renali mountains. She'd failed to silence Mattanuy's traitorous cell of agents, back in Keystone. But that had worked out in her favor. The survivors had somehow set the masha'na on the keeper's spoor. And those blunt instruments had left behind a trail a blind boar could follow.

She was getting close. Already, her mind had turned to how she would break the empath, once she had recovered him. Of course, she would have to kill the Renali who held him. Now that Mattanuy had fumbled his part of the deal, it was unavoidable.

She hadn't been involved in that part, but she'd heard that one of the royals had *nearly* lost their lives to a Heli assassin. Sloppy.

She was less sanguine about murdering masha'na. But, one way or another, she would complete her errand.

She'd stolen a mount but had since set the beast loose in a field. A woman rider was just too conspicuous, to her mind. And, no matter how the hooves were socked or the harness wrapped, it was impossible to sneak up on someone while ahorse.

As illustrated by her unseen – but not unheard – ambushers.

Survivors of the traitorous cell, she would wager.

At least they were tenacious, if not talented.

As if to underscore her thought, a figure barreled from the bushes, daggers bared in an obvious feint. She took in the angle of his approach, sighted along the lines of fire afforded by the trees and deduced the position of his friend with the crossbow. At the sound of the spool, snapping from the sear, she stepped smartly.

The shooter cursed as the bolt passed in her wake.

At least the knife-man, whom she now rushed, did not flinch.

Her pick-blade snagged his jugular and she pulled his body around to shield her own, her blowpipe already rising.

To his credit, the crossbowman ignored the dart – suddenly studding his neck – to concentrate on reloading. His struggle with the goat's foot lever grew ever more fumble fingered. Shouldering the stock, he spent bleary moments trying to reason out which one of her to fire at. He'd not yet to decide when he collapsed.

She let the corpse she held do the same.

Stillness returned, the forest indifferent to the slaughter.

Thumbing a fresh projectile into her blowpipe, she took stock. She would collect their horses, she decided. To better transport the keeper – or flee – should that become necessary-

She whirled.

She'd have staked her life on the fact that there were only two. Now, it seemed she had done exactly that. A lithe figure, in soft leathers, regarded her quizzically. Masked in the Rasrini style.

Anochria's dart was in the air before she'd stopped to think.

In the face of this threat, the latecomer... vanished.

A pagan practitioner!

What was Mattanuy playing at?

Her pick's beak glinting in one hand, a skinning crescent appearing in the other, she turned slowly.

She watched the seabed of needles for signs of movement, senses straining for a hint of her oppo-

A miniscule shift in the air told all. She lashed out.

The moment of closeness receded. The storm of leaves, kicked up around her, slowly resettled. She smiled.

These charlatans often relied on a single parlor trick – when it failed, they invariably panicked.

Her assailant reappeared, feigning calm, at a safe distance.

Ha! She would-

Wetness ran down the inside of her thigh.

Started, she glanced down...

...and spotted two daggers, driven to the hilt.

Nin watched the strange, round little woman frown.

Graceful as swans, her arms – and their odd weapons – drooped. The stumpy assassin keeled over, legs kicking high.

Bemused, Nin shook her head.

When she'd left the rescued clergyman in his soldiers' care, she certainly had not expected any more undertakings today.

Undergods! Just how many killers are wandering these woods?

And she'd thought the Kingdom of Lakes would be boring.

It had been a strange day, all-round. Rescues and reversals, politics and priests... The business with Marco – and that creature – had unnerved her. She'd needed space, to clear her head.

Obviously, it wasn't working.

Somewhere close by, a horse whuffed.

Shrugging, she went to see if it wanted to give her a ride.

MATTANUY STALKED DOWN the night darkened corridor.

An inquisitor of his station, one might suspect, suffered sleepless nights as a matter of course. In truth, insomnia and he were strangers. He was content to leave the wringing of hands and biting of nails to simpler minds. Even now, his malady did not circle some moral qualm.

He'd yet to hear word of his Keystone sect's success – the kidnapping of the keeper and the killing of that intractable eyesore, Anochria.

He reminded himself, again, that the distance between the two capitals would delay news for some days yet. Even so, something about this heavy silence smacked of failure.

He had contingencies in place, of course. But even he could not foresee every eventuality. And agents, no matter how effective, were prone to err.

He loathed relying on other people. A necessary evil-

Motion. In the passage ahead.

A shadowy figure, straightening from a moonlight vigil.

Recognizing the fox fur stole only set his heart pounding harder. He'd have preferred meeting an assassin over facing the Imperial Advisor this night. Not that they were mutually exclusive.

Eyeing the shadows, he kept to a steady pace.

"Archon Hallet," he greeted quietly. "I fear I've yet to receive any report-"

The Emperor's council cut him off, the gesture tight with tension. "Whatever has come of your foreign schemes will have to wait."

Ah. "A problem closer to home, then?"

Scowling, Hallet spoke reluctantly, through gritted teeth, "I am in need of a witch."

Had he allowed them to move, Mattanuy's brows might have bisected his scalp.

"A peculiar request, to make of an *inquisitor*..." he mused.

"Oh, spare me the sanctimonious scruples!" Hallet spat, mood flashing to anger. "Your chapter is swimming in declined writs. And we both know how you ply those shallows. Hook me a little fish. One you've allowed to slip free so far. Surely, you can manage that much?"

He considered. Having the Emperor's advisor in his debt was preferable to relying on the man's good graces. And prying loose some blackmail-worthy secrets was better still. Especially if the Keystone gambit had failed, as he suspected. Or, Helia forfend, if Anochria had somehow survived.

"In these waters," he rebuked mildly, "even reeling in a little fish is no small effort. What is this *modest* catch intended for?"

"That is not your concern."

"Ah, but I would hate to deliver something that does not pair well with your purposes..."

He left that hanging. Knowing the type of practitioner the man needed would tell him much.

Hallet glared but had to bow to the inquisitor's superior knowledge of the pagan arts.

"There has been a theft," the man admitted, the words dragged from him. "I need a minnow that can navigate the muddy waters left in the burglar's wake."

"I'll see what I can do," Mattanuy promised.

And then he took great pleasure in continuing on, past the archon, without having been dismissed. He let his careful mien melt into a fierce grin.

Epilogue

A sun, newly risen. A pastoral scene. A lone figure, trudging in the distance. A perfect picture – or so Phelamy Mop surmised.

He felt strongly that it needed a jaunty whistled tune.

Yet all his efforts produced only more off-key raspberries.

Frustrated, he recited the steps again. There were only two.

"Lips pursed! And blow!"

He did, with all his might, turning red with the effort.

Another rude, farting noise.

The blowing wasn't the problem. It had to be the pursing. He prodded at his mouth to make sure he was doing it right-

"Gah! Phut! Phew! What a horrendous flavor!"

He inspected his black rimed and chipped nails. Experimentally, he sniffed one. And recoiled.

"This smells like somebody wiped their ass with it!" He spun. "Who has been wiping their rear on my finger?!"

A covey of birds took flight at his shout. Glaring imperiously at the surrounding trees, Mop suffered a flash of intuition.

"You! *You* know! Tell me!"

The pine, so addressed, adopted a wooden expression.

"Don't feel like talking, eh?"

He hefted his felling axe. Fortuitously, he'd found it in a chopping block, outside a farmhouse with a billowing chimney. It had obviously languished, forgotten, for a long time.

"I have something here that will loosen your tongue! I mean *trunk*." He considered. "Any limb at all, in fact. Teehee!"

Sharing his axe's bright smile, the two of them menaced the petrified bole, only to be brought up short.

Half-held memories of pre-pubescent mischief were resurfacing at speed. He felt the ghostly sting of a switch.

Straightening with a snap, he almost brained himself.

"Who me? Nothing!"

The cleaver and he fled, scampering off into the woods.

"That was a close one-"

His foot snagged on a root.

It was a magnificent summersault. He ended it by plowing a furrow in the loam. With his face. His legs attempted a further tumble, hung abashedly above his head... and fell flat.

Pine needles sticking to his cheeks, he spat dirt.

The axe came down sharply a moment later. The shiny blade stuck in the earth a hand's breadth from his face. His eyes shot wide as he stared at the reflective steel.

"Nose hairs!"

Curling closer to the mirrored surface, he maligned his nose this way and that, plucking the offending follicles free.

That kept him busy for some time.

When he rose, he did so with one bald nostril. He felt significantly emboldened. He was on an important errand, after all.

"I'm gonna whittle me a whistle!"

Settling his whittling axe across a shoulder – almost losing an ear in the process – he set off.

Late morning light and birdsong played among the branches. He felt strongly that the scene needing something. Skipping, perhaps?

If children could do it, it couldn't be that difficult, surely?

He gave it a try, eventually managing it with both feet at once.

How do rabbits do this all day?

"Jumped up little bastards," he gushed between gasps.

He bounced himself to the brink of collapse. But he'd arrived.

Sweating and near swooning, he dragged his feet. The axe dragged its head. They left a snail's trail toward the sound of rushing water.

The river was rabid – foaming at the mouth.

"It does look choppy," he agreed with the axe's assessment.

His mismatched nostrils flared. "Best get on with it, eh?"

He flexed his knees and swung his arms, bending at the waist.

"Limbering up. Very important."

Feeling eyes on him, he turned. Recognition dawned.

"You!" he spat with venom.

It was the same tree. He was sure of it. It had followed him.

Hefting the axe high, he charged, trailing a wordless battle cry.

Stopping abruptly, he snatched the weapon down, frowning at it with a worried expression.

"No," he muttered. "That's scissors. Don't run with *scissors*."

He resumed. "Aaagh!"

He buried the hatchet, squarely in the bole. Splinters sprayed. One stung his cheek and he staggered back.

"You barked at me," he said in surprise. His dabbing fingers came away red. "You bit me!"

He attacked in earnest. "Bad log! Bad log!"

The sapling began to skew. He was supposed to shout something. What was it, again? Oh, yes…

"Four!"

"Oh, alright," he amended, as the timber landed mostly in the river, "four point five. Next time, stick the landing."

He moved on to the next tree, wetting a finger to test the wind

Gah! Phut! Blegh! What is that?!

This was going to be some whistle! Or perhaps a canoe. Or clogs! He'd always wanted clogs. No, a dam, like beavers built.

Caught up in the moment, he made up a woodchuck's chanty.

"Blood in the white water! Chop, chop, chop!
"Black fur on the breeze! Chop, chop, chop!
"Bloody dam in the river! Chop, chop, chop!"

As he began to whistle, the sound wended its way around the roaring bends and tight turns. Where, far upriver, something furred and bedraggled slipped over the first set of falls.

– END OF BOOK I –

About the Author

André van Wyck is a South African-born writer and law school graduate. Although the necessary evils of a day job and the inconsiderate programming of AMC keep him fairly busy, he finds time to do the occasional spot of writing.

"Just to fill in the lulls while I'm waiting for my own favorite authors to publish their new works."

Since *A Clatter of Chains*, he has also published the second book in the series, called *A Fray of Furies*. *Stumbling Stoned*, a dark urban fantasy, heads a different series: *The Patchwork Prince*.

He lives in Luxembourg with his wife and imaginary pet rock.

visit:
---www.andrevanwyck.com---

Printed in Great Britain
by Amazon